Seeking REDEMPTION

EDEN SUMMERS

Seeking VENGEANCE

EDEN SUMMERS

1

LAYLA

I PLACE A SWEATY HAND ON THE RESTAURANT DOOR, MY FINGERS HOLDING THE SLIGHTEST tremble of anticipation as skin meets glass.

I've waited two years for this.

No. It took two years to know I *needed* this.

The retaliation.

The validation of revenge.

Two years where I forced myself to believe I was a bigger person, when in reality I'm nothing but a carbon copy of the monsters I'm now determined to end.

I shift my fake glasses farther along my nose and push my way inside, the aroma of fresh basil sinking deep into my lungs.

I discovered Perfezione on my last excursion to Denver, my novice detective work leading me to this Italian masterpiece with immaculately polished china, pristine tablecloths, and sparkling chandeliers.

A last-minute no-show was the only reason I gained a reservation when I previously walked through these doors. And an insanely generous tip secured a seat for tonight.

This place doesn't do walk-ins. It does millionaires and prestige. High-class and pomposity.

I give my fake name to the maître d' and keep my expression impassive as a young, slim waitress escorts me to my table—the two-seater I requested in the far back corner, right next to the window.

She pulls out the chair closest to the wall, but that's not where I want to be. I decline the offer with a polite smile and reach for the opposite seat, descending into the padded cushion with my back to the room.

There's a beat of confusion in her expression. The slightest pause where she looks at me in judgment for picking this position instead of hers. "Is someone else joining you, Ms. Javernick?"

I give a subtle shake of my head, the strands of my fake blonde wig skimming my cheeks. "Not tonight. It's just me."

There's another pause. Another perplexed glimpse asking why I wouldn't want to stare at the restaurant's opulence instead of the plain cream wallpaper. Then she nods and increases the wattage of her beaming smile. "Can I get you something to drink?" She hands over a leather-bound menu and grabs my cloth napkin to delicately place it on my lap.

"White wine, please. Pinot Grigio if possible."

She inclines her head. "Of course."

I'm left alone, the hum of conversation brushing my ears and adrenaline warming my veins. But it's the intoxicating promise of vengeance that consumes my thoughts.

The past few months have been filled with one idea after the next, each potential strike against my enemy joining a long list of possibilities.

I've contemplated financial ruin, family destruction. I've even humored the idea of loss of life. Nothing is off-limits. Nothing can be if I want to sleep peacefully in the future. Because this isn't just revenge. It's also vindication. I need to earn back the respect of those I love.

My wine arrives while I scan the menu, my eyes reading the words despite my wild mind not letting them sink in. I'm too eager, my nervous energy ratcheting my pulse and feeding my vicious hunger.

I still have many questions to answer before I strike.

I haven't decided if I'll outsource the attack—physical or otherwise.

Mercenaries are an option, however trusting a stranger is an issue. I have the stomach to do it on my own, though. Murder won't haunt my conscience. I already have a vial of cyanide in my purse posing as cocaine, the poisonous powder awaiting an unwilling victim. It's the panic over a lengthy jail sentence that gives me pause.

Either way, I won't reignite a war in the middle of a five-star restaurant. Tonight is merely reconnaissance.

I'm two sips into my alcoholic relief when a skitter of awareness shimmies down my spine, awakening my nerves.

They're here.

I can't see them. Can't even hear them yet. But I know the Costa family has arrived.

I fight against the discomfort of having my back to the room and take another sip, making sure my shoulders appear relaxed as my waitress escorts them to the table behind me, just as I anticipated.

Goose bumps whisper along my arms, all the way to my nape. I feel naked, my little black dress suddenly nothing but a slip of material as the gentle breeze of the air conditioner kisses my exposed skin.

I'm hidden, though, unrecognizable beneath the colored contacts, fake glasses, and long-flowing blonde wig. Even if we do come face-to-face, I doubt they will recognize me.

I hold the wine glass to my lips and tilt my gaze to the window, discreetly watching them in the reflection as they sit at the round table, all of them exuding an air of snobbery.

There's Emmanuel Costa. His wife, Adena. The younger men I know to be his sons—Salvatore and Remy. Then closest to me is Abri, his viper of a daughter, whose back is parallel to mine.

"We will have to make this a quick meal," Salvatore mutters. "I have plans tonight."

"Plans with who?" his mother asks. "A woman? Have you met someone?"

I listen intently, hoping for the details of his rendezvous, my heart beating heavy against my ribs. Lovers provide vulnerabilities. I learned that lesson the hard way.

The waitress approaches in my periphery, her increased proximity dragging my attention from precious seconds of information. "Are you ready to order, ma'am?"

"Can I have a little more time?" I keep my voice low, hoping she'll allow me to drag out my stay for as long as possible. "If you could give me five more minutes that would be appreciated."

She nods, her smile forced as she saunters away.

I spare a second to properly read the menu, picking a few items before I return my attention to the window, my ear cocked toward Emmanuel's table as I drink in their secrets with each sip of wine.

"We need to tighten our distribution channels," Emmanuel advises in accented English. "We have weak links that will cost us greatly if they're not handled."

"They'll be handled," Remy replies. "They're always handled."

"Not always. There was the issue with border security two years ago—"

"And you've never let us forget it. Since then, everything has been tight. We take care of any cracks that surface."

It's clear they're not talking about distribution for items in their designer fashion label. When our worlds collided years ago, it had been because Emmanuel wanted to diversify from their clothing empire and force my brother into a partnership revolving around my family's drug trade.

I guess they paved their own way. Or found a sucker to swindle to show them the ropes.

"How about you, Abri?" Emmanuel asks. "Have you done what was asked of you?"

"If you mean, have I sowed the seed for you to blackmail your latest target, then the answer is no." Her voice is a velvety purr, the confident drawl holding the faintest undertone of resentment. "He's proving to be a hard man to deceive."

"Well, try harder. You don't have the luxury of—"

"Can we *please* leave the topic of business for later?" Adena asks. "I want to hear about more important things like when my children will bless me with grandbabies."

Someone sighs. There's a groan, too.

"I'm happy to be artificially inseminated, mother," Abri snips. "But it will become increasingly harder for me to extort and manipulate men if I have a child on my hip. And then what value would I have to you?"

"Don't start," Emmanuel mutters under his breath. "Your lack of gratitude is beginning to grate my last nerve."

"And being constantly leashed by my father has long since grated away all of mine."

Silence follows. Tense, palpable silence for several heartbeats.

I don't need to search for Abri's lethal glare through the reflection in the glass. I feel it.

Pretty little bitch can't cut the parental ties. What a shame.

"Control yourself." Salvatore snarls the warning. "You're starting to make a scene and—"

"Have you decided what you'd like to order?"

Shit. I clasp a hand to my throat, startled by the waitress's return. "I'm sorry." I swivel to meet her waiting gaze from the corner of my eye. "I'll have the beef carpaccio to start and then the corzetti. Thank you."

"My pleasure. How about more wine?"

I swallow over my increased pulse and glance at the puddle of liquid in my glass. "That sounds perfect."

"Great. I'll return right away." She beams.

I throw back the remaining alcohol as she walks away, needing the wine to smother the chastising voices in my head.

I'm slipping.

Faltering.

I'm better than this. Underhanded tactics are practically a birthright. I was born to scheme. To be devious and manipulative. The ability to drag the Costa family to its knees is in my genes and I plan to lean into those intrinsic skills to get this job done right.

Focus, Layla. Don't get distracted.

I've worked too hard to mess this up now. I've tracked their fashion label on the stock market since February. I have online notifications set up for each property in their portfolio. I have files on all their legitimate employees. I've done background checks and rummaged around many skeleton-filled closets.

They *will* get what they deserve.

And I *will* be the one to dish out their punishment.

"…Well, I just don't understand how the gardener can't keep on top of the bug infestation that's destroying the roses at the back of the property," Adena whines. "What are we paying him for if the blooms are constantly ruined?"

I sag into my seat as the discussion diverts into menial topics that are of no use. The five of them discuss the weather, of all things. Then cryptocurrency.

I grow impatient as my first meal arrives and their conversation moves to Salvatore's next car purchase—an Aston Martin that I hope he wraps around a pole.

When my main is served, they're murmuring about an upcoming vacation, the parents requesting the company of their adult kids while Salvatore, Remy, and Abri decline with varying lackluster excuses.

Salvatore will be at their fashion label's flagship warehouse, meeting with management. Remy can't join the sun, surf, and sand because contractors are scheduled to paint his bedroom. And Abri gives no more than an "I'm busy" as she continues to sulk.

I finish my meal without another morsel of insight into their illegal dealings. No names to investigate. No meetings or locations to stake out.

I order another drink and force down a plate of tiramisu to justify my extended time at the highly sought-after table. But it isn't long before the waitress brings my bill, subtly announcing her desire for me to leave.

Goddammit.

I've outstayed my welcome and I can't risk not gaining another reservation in the future. I have no choice but to tip big and make my way to the bar for another glass of wine.

I refuse to walk away until the Costas do. It doesn't matter that I'm now out of listening range. I can still watch through the mirror behind the wall lined with liquor bottles, hating every breath they dare to breathe.

I try to read their body language. Their straight shoulders and tight jaws. I attempt to decipher the reason behind the occasional scowls from the three siblings, but the distance between us slaughters the deeper levels of observation.

When they pay their check and stand, I gulp my last mouthful of wine and pull my purse strap over my shoulder as I slide from the stool.

They walk for the door, one after the other, Abri in the lead, Salvatore and Emmanuel at the back like the protecting wolves of the pack.

I wait until the old man is at the entry before I follow, my footsteps immediately halting when a bulky suit-clad man pushes back from the bar to block my path.

"Excuse me." I attempt to walk around him only to have him pivot into me, countering my move, his hulking body deliberately obstructing my escape.

Hard blue eyes meet mine as his lips thin. "Take a seat."

The bitter taste of panic soaks my tongue. "I'm sorry, I think you've mistaken me for someone else. I don't know you."

I do, however, recognize his vibe. The ruffled dark-blond hair and perfectly smooth skin do nothing to assuage the distinct edge of malice I've been surrounded by since birth.

"Sit," he growls.

Shit. Shit. *Shit.*

"I'm confused. Are you a member of staff?" I raise a brow, feigning ignorance. "Did I not leave a big enough tip?"

He steps closer, his upper lip curling as he leans threateningly close. "Sit before you make your intentions more obvious, and tell me exactly what you have planned."

2

———

LAYLA

Two years ago

I pace the carpet of the Sacramento hotel penthouse, every limb trembling, every thought brittle and panicked.

They took my daughter.

Abducted my baby girl as she slept.

Right from my brother's home.

I can't stop shaking, can't cease the bile-inducing mania that hisses through my mind on a loop of building desperation.

The things they could be doing to her… The things they could've already done.

I fight against the bile clogging my throat and shove my hands through my hair, tug, tug, tugging, wishing the burn of the pulled strands could distract from the madness. It only adds to my onslaught.

"It's going to be okay." My sister, Keira, approaches with caution. "They're following the kids. Nobody will let them out of their sight."

They — my husband, Benji, his brother, Luca, our enforcer, Hunter, and his woman, Sarah. Then there's the Fed, Anissa, who seems to have worked her way under my brother's skin to steal a heart I never knew existed.

"Is that meant to make me feel better?" I glare. "Have you spared a thought as to what could've already been done to them? They were sedated, Keira. Their babysitter murdered."

My baby girl and my half brother, Tobias, who I've only just met.

Keira winces, stopping a few feet away as if scared to get within striking distance. "Maybe a sedative will help—"

"Fuck you and your sedatives."

8

They forced enough of those pills down my throat yesterday, giving me no choice but to sleep through my daughter's suffering. But I won't take any more, not even when the allure of escaping this nightmare calls my name.

"They've found Cole."

My head snaps to Decker on the sofa, my sister's partner raising his cell in front of him.

"Where?" I ask. "Are they still following the children?"

I rush toward him and snatch the phone.

Found Cole. We're out of town. Will keep you posted.

"Out of town where?" My hands ache from trembling. "I want to go. We should follow."

"I know as much as you do." Decker grabs the cell from me and slumps back into the sofa. "We're not going anywhere. Just try to relax and let them handle this."

Relax?

I fuse my molars. Clench my fists. Swallow.

I want to scream. To wail and sob and scratch the torturous emotions right out from beneath my ribs with my fingernails. They have no idea what this is like. They don't understand how torturous your own imagination can be when your nine-year-old daughter is in the hands of monsters.

I return to my pacing, walking back and forth while my legs grow heavy and my mind paints blood-filled images narrated by little girls' screams.

What if they've touched her? Raped her?

I shove a fist to my lips, demanding the howl clogging my throat to remain inside.

Emmanuel Costa has my daughter. A man who had ties to my now-deceased father.

Most people would grow comforted by the family history. But most people aren't spawned from the devil himself.

Luther Torian was a despicable man and the worst part was his ability to hide it for most of my life.

Minutes pass. Hours, too. Silence blankets the luxurious penthouse even though my ears continue to ring with haunted screams.

I can't handle this. I *can't.*

I need to do something. Anything.

I shake my hands at my sides and breathe deep, the oxygen only stirring the bile pooling at the back of my throat.

It's been too long. My little girl has been taken for almost forty-eight hours. More than enough time to emotionally scar her forever.

"Can you quit the pacing?" Decker mutters. "You're giving me a headache."

I pause, about to let out the torture congealing in my chest when the hotel door swings open and Penny rushes in, relief written all over her pretty face.

"What is it?" I run to her, gripping her upper arms before she can get a word out. "What happened?"

"Luca called. They're coming back." She smiles, the perfection reaching her dazzling eyes. "There was some sort of confrontation with the Costas, but we've got the kids."

Time stops.

My breathing, too.

My hands drop to my sides as I retreat a step, and for a moment, there's silence. Pure, euphoria-filled peace as I stare at her, anticipating the weight of my daughter returning to the security of my arms.

"And Cole?" Decker pushes from the sofa and limps forward.

"Him, too." Penny's expression infuses with more brilliance when she meets my gaze. Her cheeks are high. Her eyes are beaming. "It's over. Stella and Tobias are both okay. The Costas have fled. Our guys are making their way to the cars to drive here right now."

All the air leaves my lungs on a heave of relief but the shaking increases. My arms and legs tremble beyond my control as my pulse grows fractured and rampant.

She's coming back.

My little girl is coming home.

"Oh, God." Tears burn my eyes. Emotion sears my throat. "They got them back."

I don't care how it happened.

I'm sure I'll relive it with Stella as many times as she needs to put the tragic events behind her. I'll do whatever it takes to give her back a childhood that I've always endeavored to make normal even though she was born into a family of crime.

Keira walks to my side. Her arm wraps around my waist, a kiss presses to my cheek. "Everything is going to be okay." She leads me to the sofa and helps me to sit. "I'm going to get you a drink. Something to take the edge off. The more grounded you are when the kids return, the safer they'll feel."

I nod, placing my hands between my knees, rocking back and forth while she walks to the liquor trolley on the far side of the room.

My daughter is coming back to me.

All those who were taken are coming back—Stella, Tobias, Cole.

I never thought my loved ones would return. The relief doesn't seem real through the layers of certainty I'd piled upon their death. I'd been convinced karma had arrived, seeking payment for my mistakes. My many, *many* misdeeds.

"Here." Keira kneels before me, placing a scotch glass in my hands with what I assume is a finger of vodka. "Sip slowly and tell me if you want more."

"I just want to get out of here as soon as possible." There's a tremble in my voice. "I need to get Stella home."

"We will." Decker gives me a fleeting look, one that speaks of judgment despite his deep-seated relief at the good news. "If they're coming here it means we've got time to spare. Otherwise, they'd want to meet us at the airport to make a quick exit."

I ignore the silent guilty verdict he places on my shoulders and down the vodka, then push to my feet in search of more. I drink and pace, drink and pace until the penthouse door opens again, the tiny squeak of hinges and whoosh of displaced air assailing me with temperamental anticipation.

Anissa walks in first, the Fed's face a picture of exhaustion, followed closely by Hunter. I stand rooted to the floor as those placed in charge of my child's rescue pile into the room, Tobias shoving past Sarah's hip to make a mad dash for Penny.

My heart squeezes painfully at the sight of him. His red-rimmed eyes. His dirt-stained clothes.

They embrace in a mass of clinging hands and relieved gasps while I remain still, my relief fracturing as my brother enters the room with my daughter limp in his arms.

"*Oh, my God.*" I rush for them, my arms outstretched.

She's covered in blood. Her clothes. Hands. Arms. There are even marks on the normally smooth skin of her cheeks.

"She hasn't been hurt." Cole's tone lacks inflection, his face devoid of emotion. "It's not her blood."

"Then what hap—"

"She was upset. I needed to sedate her."

I hold his gaze, trying to siphon the information he's keeping from me as sorrow plants its seed in my belly, the roots burrowing deep.

He hands Stella to me, her slim body pliant in my arms, her face so incredibly pure despite the blood stains. Everything else ceases to exist except her. The friends and family fade from my consciousness. The whispered words and mumbled conversation don't breach my ears.

I sink to the plush carpet, unable to stop myself from squeezing Stella tight. I nuzzle my nose against her neck. Breathe the faint scent of her kiddie shampoo. She's at home in my arms, her face peaceful with sleep, her head seeming to instinctively nestle into me as the slightest whimper leaves her lips.

The aftermath of tears is evident on her face, her skin red and puffy around her eyes. She survived a war. She was thrown into one of the deepest, darkest pits of this world and made it out.

God, I'm grateful.

I rock her in my arms, just like I did when she was a newborn—forward, back, forward, back—while the room grows quiet.

I don't want to face our audience. Not yet. I need this moment with her. I need a lifetime of me and my daughter and nothing else. If only I didn't have so many gnawing, clawing questions that demand answers.

"What did they do to her?" I raise my gaze to Cole.

His cold eyes are already fixed on my face. "We can discuss it once the children are settled elsewhere."

"Why?" I frown, glancing from my brother, to Anissa, then Sarah and Hunter. All the people before me stare back without emotion. There's no jubilation. No celebration. Not even anger over what must have happened to claim victory. "What did they do to her?"

I drag my gaze farther to little Tobias who now stands at Penny's side, his arms around her hips, his tortured gaze on me.

There's no relief in his expression. Not even a glimpse of happiness at being returned to his family.

Something is wrong.

Something is very, *very* wrong.

"What the hell did they do?" I demand.

"Let me take her for a while." Penny steps forward.

"No." I cling tighter to the precious gift in my lap.

"Do it, Layla," Cole mutters. "Penny can take Tobias and Stella into my room." He jerks his head to the open door a few yards behind him. "This won't take long."

"*This*?" I haul myself to my feet, carrying my daughter with me.

"Just do it, for fuck's sake," Cole snaps. "*Now.*"

I balk at his viciousness, but I'm not surprised. I'd wondered how long it would take for his pity to wear off. I'd mistakenly thought I'd have more time. That maybe I could find my feet not just in this room, but in life, before he fed me the animosity I deserve.

I close my eyes, continuing to rock as I place a kiss to Stella's forehead. I can't let her go. I *never* want to let her go ever again.

"It's okay." Penny reaches for her, Tobias still at her side. "She's safe. I promise."

A garbled cry clogs my throat as I admit defeat and hand my daughter over. Releasing her soft body after everything she's been through is akin to being gutted. Neck to pelvis. Hip to hip.

Nausea comes back with a vengeance as Penny cradles Stella's limp form in her arms, carrying her to the bedroom with a subdued Tobias following close behind.

I watch every step. Every movement.

When the bedroom door closes behind them, I struggle against the impulse to collapse into a fit of hysterical tears. I don't have that luxury though. I never have. Torians don't show weakness. We're not allowed to falter.

"Tell me." I straighten my shoulders and suck in a measured breath as I turn to face everyone. Flakes of dry blood cover my top, the gore threatening to break me. "What the hell did those monsters do to her, Cole?"

My brother's expression wavers, the animosity fracturing to expose something that holds a hint of sympathy.

Oh, God.

I scan the faces of those by his sides. Anissa lowers her gaze to the carpet. Luca's eyes are bloodshot and glistening with unshed tears. Keira's are, too. She knows something I don't. Something that must have been shared while I was lost in the reunion with my precious baby girl.

"Tell me." I glance from one person to the next—Sarah, Hunter, Decker—seeking out my husband. I reach the end of the semi-circle of friends and family without catching sight of his dark eyes.

"Benji?" I trek my attention back the other way—Decker, Hunter, Sarah, Keira, Luca, Anissa, and finally, Cole. "Where is he?"

Cole's chin hitches as if he's stealing himself for an upcoming onslaught.

"Where is my husband?" Icy dread slithers down my spine, catching on every nerve.

He has to be parking the car. Packing our things. Checking out at reception.

Keira whimpers, decimating my wishful thinking.

"Where's Benji?" My voice fractures, emotion tightening my vocal cords. "Why isn't he here?"

"He's gone, Lay."

Cole's calm words steal the air from my chest in a massive upheaval, the oxygen stripping itself from my lungs with jagged claws.

"No." I shake my head.

My husband and I were guilty of horrible things. Of traitorous, treacherous acts. But he wouldn't have fled from his punishment. He wouldn't have left me and Stella behind.

"You forced him to run?" It's hard to get the question out. Even harder to understand him leaving without saying goodbye. "Where did he go?"

Luca lowers his attention to the carpet and sniffs with a hard swipe of his hand over his nose. His fingers are stained with remnants of blood. More faint splotches mark his dark shirt.

I shake my head again, fighting the whispers in my mind telling me that a hardened man like Luca wouldn't cry over his brother skipping town.

"No." I suck in gasps. One after another without relief. I'm suffocating. Drowning in the karma I knew would come my way.

"He's dead." Cole steps forward, his face bleak as he opens his arms and envelops me in his hold.

"No." I batter his chest. "You're lying. You're doing this to punish me."

How had I not noticed Benji didn't return? I hadn't spared him a thought. My focus had been on Stella. On our baby girl he went to rescue.

"They shot him. He couldn't be saved," Cole whispers the horror in my ear. "I'm sorry for your loss."

A sob escapes, my eyes searing with a firestorm of tears.

I heave for breath, for understanding, pummeling and scratching at my brother's suit-covered chest as my legs threaten to give out.

"Don't cry." He continues to hold me, but those words are nothing more than a formality. No warmth exudes from him—only sterility. "Don't cry, Layla," he whispers. "We both know tears are a privilege for those who lack guilt."

3

LAYLA

Present day

I cross my hands on the bar and stare at the gloss scratched from the wood, wishing the crevices held the insight to get me out of here.

"All I want is answers," the man mutters from the stool beside me.

"And I gave them to you. I like sitting near the window. Most people do."

"*Most* people don't eavesdrop on neighboring conversations the entire time. *Most* people would sit with their back to the wall, not the room. And *most* people wouldn't hang around until the exact moment the patrons behind them left."

My cheeks heat. No matter how hard I concentrate on measuring my breathing and remaining calm, my skin doesn't stop burning, potentially exposing my guilt.

"You'd want to start talking, sunshine." His endearment is far from kind. "Why are you here? Who do you work for?"

So much for being discreet. Turns out my presence held the blinding discretion of tractor beams. But still, I've done nothing wrong. I overheard a conversation. I haven't broken any laws.

"I have no idea what you're talking about." I slide from the stool. "And I'm done pandering to your paranoia. Like I told you, I have somewhere else I need to be."

The man follows, his shoulders broadening, yet again blocking my escape route. He doesn't look at me, though. He stares over my shoulder, those icy eyes focusing on something behind me.

"I can take it from here, Bishop." A voice etched with smooth superiority and graveled confidence brushes the back of my neck.

I swallow, my pulse thunderous.

There's no threat in the newcomer's tone. It's far less abrasive than his colleague's. Maybe it even holds a hint of humor. But since my father's schemes ruined my life, I'm not easily fooled by cadence and timbre.

Bishop glances from me to the unseen guy at my back, pausing a moment before inclining his head and swinging around to walk away. Just like that, the threatening ogre takes his leave, meaning whoever stands behind me is far more powerful.

"You can take what from here?" I turn, my pulse catching at the mischievous chocolate eyes that capture mine.

The handsome stranger grins, his smile subtle and exuding just the right amount of friendly flirtation. He wants me to feel at ease, and for the slightest second, I do, gently coaxed into his web of sex appeal.

Then intuition kicks in.

"You can take what from here?" I repeat.

His grin deepens, the slight flash of wicked intent catching me off guard. This guy is good. Manipulative. Everything about him is perfect. *Too* perfect. From the expensive designer suit, to the devilish graze of stubble along his chiseled jaw, all the way to his finger-tousled dark hair.

Charming yet destructive.

Attractive yet lethal.

"Join me for a drink." He doesn't wait for my response before he raises a finger to attract the attention of the bartender, ordering another Pinot Grigio and a scotch.

He's been watching me. Closely enough to know what I've been drinking.

"You look concerned, but there's no need to be," he adds. "I only asked Bishop to keep you inside until the Costas were well and truly gone."

Fuck. I've definitely been caught. The only question now is—by who?

"Did you also ask him to pepper me with accusations?" I raise my brows. "You didn't want to do it yourself?"

"Maybe I was too busy spying on our shared target."

I frown, in part due to how I can't stop staring at him, but mainly because of his explanation. He's admitting to spying on Emmanuel? To me? A stranger? "What is it with you two and this Costa family? I honestly have no idea what you're talking about."

"And I honestly know you're full of shit." His gaze holds mine, those playful dark eyes keeping me captive. "I never forget a beautiful woman. You were here a few weeks ago. In a flowing navy dress that plunged at the neckline and exposed an impressive amount of leg." He leans closer and adds with a conspiratorial whisper, "A word to the wise—maybe wear something that doesn't make you look like a goddess if you don't want to draw attention."

My throat tightens. I have to drag a hand to my neck to ease the building tension.

Not only is the blatant seduction entirely foreign after years of celibacy, but this man is right about the navy dress, meaning I wasn't caught tonight.

I failed weeks ago.

I drag my gaze from his knowing smirk and focus on the bartender. "Thank you, but I won't be needing another drink. I'm leaving."

"Tell me I'm wrong." The cocky stranger casually glides onto the stool in front of him. "You had your hair out, the same as it is tonight, the blonde strands hanging over your shoulders. And you wore the sexiest pair of two-inch pumps. They were white, if I'm not mistaken."

Cream, actually.

"I don't know what you're talking about." I keep my expression in check and return my attention to his.

Christ. That was a mistake.

His potent stare intensifies, his gaze starting a leisurely trek down my body. I feel his attention like a caress as he visually devours me, from my breasts to my hips all the way to my toes.

"I distinctly remember the shoes." His voice reclaims the hint of a low whisper. "Because I imagined what they would look like crossed behind the back of my neck."

I choke on thin air. "You're quite forward aren't you, Mr…?"

"Call me Matthew." He reaches for the scotch the bartender slides toward him and jerks his chin in thanks. "Don't forget that glass of wine."

My eyes widen. "No. Don't." I fix the young bartender with a scowl. "I'm not going to—"

"She'll drink it," Matthew answers with an unhinged level of superiority.

To any other woman, this boldness from an excessively attractive man might be endearing. Unfortunately, I've been down this cocky, charismatic road before.

He thinks he's catnip to my animalistic senses when in reality he's merely a ticking time bomb in a cover model package. I should know—I married someone exactly like him.

"Are you always this arrogant, Matthew?" I need to get out of here. I should storm for the door without a backward glance. What's this guy going to do? Tackle me to the floor in the middle of a busy restaurant?

"What's the difference between arrogance and confidence?"

"Excuse me?"

"Why do you call me arrogant and not confident?" His brows furrow as if he's truly perplexed and one hundred percent invested in my response while he takes another sip of scotch. "Because confidence is the self-assurance that comes from appreciating one's abilities and qualities. While arrogance is an exaggerated sense of one's importance and abilities. In which way have I been arrogant?"

That goddamn grin, for starters. The curve of those perfect lips wordlessly boasts how he could devour me in one sitting when that will never happen.

"For God knows what reason, you're flirting with me," I state flatly. "Not only that, you're giving me the distinct impression you think you could easily seduce me. Which, my friend, is an exaggerated sense of your abilities, which, in return, is your definition of arrogance."

His player smile doesn't waver as he drawls, "Are you sure it's not confidence?"

My pulse stutters. It's not so much the question, but the smooth way he asks. The superbly adept way he seasons his masculine tone with the tiniest glimpse of a dimple in his left cheek.

"Yes." I snatch the fresh glass of wine the bartender places on the counter and take a gulp. "I'm leaving. Good night."

His smooth chuckle haunts me. "But I don't even know your name. What am I going to write on our marriage license?"

Yet again, I'm caught off guard, all the pulse hammering and skin tingling colliding in a mass of hysteria that sends a shocked laugh bursting from my lips.

I can't remember ever being hit on like this. Being the wife to a notorious criminal, within an already infamous crime family, tends to keep men distanced. Even if I was experienced, I'm sure this guy would still leave me unsettled.

He's too damn good at this game.

"That right there." I point a finger at his chest. "Pure arrogance."

He takes another leisurely sip of scotch. "Is it, though? Really?"

I release another spontaneous chuckle, take a final gulp of wine before returning it to the bar, and then step back. "It was nice meeting you." It's an exaggeration, although, honestly, not a lie. I haven't enjoyed a heartfelt laugh in years. "It's too bad I'm not the woman you think I am."

I swivel on my toes and make for the door, my neck awakening with goose bumps as soon as I turn my back on his charm.

"Come on, *amore mio*," he calls after me, the Italian words spoken with a pristine accent. "We could help each other."

I don't stop.

"With the spying," he adds, louder, drawing the attention of four nearby women who hush their table conversation to stare at us with curiosity.

I halt, my feet rooted in place, not only because he's outing me in front of staff and strangers alike, but because he's potentially offering me something I want. Something I desperately need—a way forward with my Costa plans now that I've been discovered.

Footsteps approach behind me and I suck in a ragged breath when his warm hand comes to rest on the small of my back, his woodsy aftershave teasing my senses. "I have a room at the Lydell Hotel two doors down. They've got a great bar. Let's go there and talk."

4

LAYLA

Two years ago

THE SILENCE IS STIFLING AS MY HUSBAND'S CASKET IS LOWERED INTO THE GROUND, THE descent of the shining steel box seeming to steal the gossip from the mouths of those in attendance.

Stella nestles closer against my side, my daughter's tears soaking into the black material covering my hip, her lone sniffle sinking deep into my heart to stab at my composure.

I breathe it in. Her agony. Her suffering.

I take all the misery she releases into the world and make it my own because it's what I deserve.

Then, all too soon, the service is over.

Benji is buried. Gone. His all-encompassing life was summed up in a few paragraphs.

Tissues are shared, words of condolence are given out like cheap candy, and the whispered rumors that follow once the guests walk away brush against the outer edges of my hearing, poisoning me further.

The entire scene plays before me as if through a stranger's eyes, the depth of my grief barely felt over the strangling claws of guilt at my throat.

I killed my husband.

I may not have pulled the trigger, but I caused the lethal blow.

I stole happiness from those I love, replacing it with sorrow. And I'm not sure I can redeem myself to them, let alone forgive myself for the mistakes.

After the mourners leave the cemetery, Stella and I follow where my brother leads, Cole's hand guiding me from the crook of my arm until we're in his sports car.

Nobody speaks. We barely breathe, the air around us now tainted by my callous decisions.

Once we reach his house I'm left to stand alone before the glass doors leading to the manicured gardens, a head full of unrelenting nightmares and a heart carved from jagged glass.

Stella and Tobias sit at the dining table, playing a subdued board game. Their similar ages have made them inseparable, which is nice. They're thankfully both young enough to be easily fed lies to cover up the truth of Benji's murder, but unfortunately, they're old enough to be scarred by my actions regardless of the cover story they were told.

The people I call family are on nearby sofas, discussing mundane things I can't fathom while my world collapses around me. I don't deserve to be a part of their lives anymore. . . At least, that's the way they've made me feel.

I don't belong here even though I'd beg until my last breath to stay.

I've never been so lost. So alone. Without support. Lacking grounding. I'm loathed by everyone, despite how they hide their contempt behind sympathetic glances and sad smiles.

I'm no longer trusted or appreciated. Well, except by my daughter, who knows nothing of my loathsome betrayal.

My perfect little girl will be forever haunted by my actions but, God willing, she will never learn I sold out my own brother to a father who based his moral code on the devil himself, which caused a chain reaction resulting in my husband's death.

A death that will forever weigh upon my shoulders.

Footsteps approach behind me and I stiffen, my lungs painfully tightening at the thought of company.

There's only one person it could be. The heavy steps. The willingness to reach out. My suspicions are confirmed when I see Cole in the reflection of the glass door, the faint touch of my brother's palm coming to rest on the back of my neck.

He doesn't speak. He doesn't have to. We both know words won't change what I did. Nothing will.

There's little comfort to provide a woman as pitiful and vile as me.

"Thank you for arranging the beautiful service. I think Benji would've been surprised at how many people attended." I pretend as if most of those who came to mourn didn't arrive merely to snoop. I'm well aware the majority only wanted to learn how a healthy, middle-aged man passed from a supposed heart attack.

"He was your husband," he states flatly. "He received a family burial."

"Even though you think he didn't deserve it," I whisper.

I can hear it in his voice. The thinly veiled resentment. The biting betrayal that still lingers.

"We both know he didn't. But this lifestyle is nothing if not a masquerade to the masses. We all do what needs to be done."

I wince, not only at the games that have to be played, but the ones I don't want to participate in.

I turn to face him, my pride in my throat, my heart on my sleeve. "I need to ask you for something." I have no right to request anything. I don't even deserve to maintain my place in this family. But... "No, not just ask." I shake my head. "I'm begging, Cole."

He straightens as his hand falls from my neck. "What is it?"

The request scorches my throat leaving scars in its wake. "Nobody here deserves to be put through any more destruction. Our father and I have already caused enough damage. We need to think of Tobias and Stella's future."

His brows pinch, as if he's waiting for me to inflict a verbal blow.

"I don't want you to chase revenge over what happened to Benji." I suck in a breath, strengthening myself against the increased judgment in his stare. "At least not now, while our wounds are still raw. I need you to promise there'll be no more bloodshed. That the danger surrounding the children won't intensify. Let the kids grow a little older first. Let them have some peace."

Those brows dig deeper, his silent opposition settling between us.

"I'm pleading for you and Luca to let this go." I clasp my hands in prayer, knowing Cole's the only one able to persuade my brother-in-law to put this tragedy behind us. Temporarily or not. "We all know I'm to blame for what happened. Nobody else. There's no reason to start a war."

His jaw ticks, his nostrils slightly flaring. "You're asking too much."

"*Please.*" I glance at Stella, needing him to agree for her sake. For the safety of everyone under this roof. If he retaliates toward the people who shot my husband, more of us could die. And I'll be responsible for those deaths, too. I won't be able to live with the increase in blame. I can barely breathe as it is. "Don't risk those we love because of my mistakes."

His eyes harden, the pity vanishing. "That's not how things work. We need to make it known that we don't accept—"

"*Please*, Cole." I grab his wrist. "I'm begging you. My daughter was already stolen from me once. I can't spend each day thinking it could happen again."

He keeps that hard stare on me, his judgment building.

"I'll do anything," I plead. "Whatever you ask, I'll do it. Just don't break this family more than it already is. Don't risk their lives like I did. *Please.* I'll never ask anything of you again."

His lip curls in a snarl as he switches his attention to the backyard.

For long moments there's silence between us, the murmur of conversation in the background becoming static when pitted against the punishing heartbeats in my ears.

"I don't want to put those kids at risk any more than you do." He addresses the glass, not meeting my gaze. "But if I don't retaliate I'll be seen as weak. We all will."

"By who?" I step closer. "Nobody knows what happened."

Spiteful eyes find mine, the palpable hostility daunting me. "*They* know."

They—the family who pulled the trigger. The people who held my daughter and Tobias hostage.

"And they got away with murder." I lower my voice, making sure the children don't overhear. "They'll never make it public knowledge. We all know they made a mistake in targeting us. They learned their lesson. If you let this go, at least temporarily, nobody will find out what truly happened. Our enemies won't know how easy it was to bring us to our knees."

"And nobody would need to learn how much of a snake you've been," he hisses.

I snap rigid, every muscle pulled so tight the slightest touch could sever me in half. "That's not what this is about."

He scoffs. "It's just a bonus, right? If I sweep this under the rug, nobody will learn the part you played."

I crinkle my nose, willing the threat of tears away. I can't deny that hiding my crimes is also part of my plea. If Stella finds out about my actions I'll lose her, too.

I'll lose everything.

"I'm begging you." The words push their way through the bile rising at the back of my throat. "*Please.*" The first tear falls, burning a trail down my cheek.

Cole follows the path of moisture with his gaze, the muscles in his jaw flexing as he clenches his teeth. "If I do this, you'll owe me. I'm not talking about a family-friendly debt either, Layla. You'll owe me like everyone else. And when it comes time to pay, you'll hate the price."

Fear trickles its way into my chest, adding to the hollow beat of my heart.

It's what I deserve. My penance.

I nod. "I understand."

His eyes narrow in scorn. "Well, then, sister, I'll think on it. But I'm not making any promises."

5

———

LAYLA

Present Day

I ATTEMPT TO CONVINCE MYSELF I'M NOT MAKING A MISTAKE AS WE WALK SIDE BY SIDE along the footpath toward the hotel. It isn't easy when his buddy follows behind us in the distance like an imminent threat.

"Ignore Bishop. Deep down, he's a puppy."

"He didn't act like a puppy when he interrogated me." He resembles the exact opposite actually. Broad and menacing. "Is he a bodyguard?"

"Of sorts."

That means Matthew is someone important. Or a target. I can't tell which.

I slow as we reach the hotel, my stomach filling with butterflies as the bellhop pulls open the towering glass door for us to proceed. "Who are you exactly?"

"We'll discuss that inside." Matthew returns his hand to the small of my back, adding slight pressure. "Don't worry. You'll be in public view at all times and can leave whenever you like. You've got nothing to fear from me."

I'm not stupid enough to believe him. I am, however, intrigued enough to continue inside, remaining close to him and his intoxicating aftershave as he escorts me to the bar and pulls out a seat near the window.

"This is your favorite type of place to sit, right?" he drawls. "Near the window with your back to the room."

I glare and sink into the cushioned leather. "Your thug already critiqued my choice of seating. I don't understand why it's such a big deal."

He shrugs and claims the chair across the table. "Most people feel more comfortable with their back to the wall. It's instinct. And when you add the way you stared into the glass reflection the entire time you were at the restaurant, your neck slightly craned, it made your intentions obvious to anyone watching close enough."

My face heats with the failure.

"Are you a scorned lover?" His question is almost a purr.

I ignore him. I battle to ignore the building butterflies in my stomach, too, their fluttering wings now born from something other than curiosity.

"Or maybe you're a reporter." He rests back in his seat, seeming to shelve the playboy charm for a more serious, business-type approach.

"No." I scan the room, looking from one couple to the next until my gaze lands on Bishop seated at the bar.

"Cop? Fed? DEA?" Matthew asks.

"DEA?" I raise a brow and return my attention to his, appreciating the first piece of validation he's given me. "I thought the Costas ran a reputable fashion label," I hedge, despite knowing the truth. "Why would the Drug Enforcement Agency be sniffing around?"

"I'm merely guessing." He shrugs. "You're not giving me a lot of feedback."

A waitress saunters toward us to place a tray on our table. "Excuse me for interrupting. The gentleman at the bar ordered these for you." She places a glass of scotch before my handsome companion and a wine within my reach. "Enjoy."

"Thank you." Matthew claims his drink, inclining it in toast to the waitress before she walks away.

I'm not as eager to grab my gift. The warm kiss of intoxication is already gently caressing my senses, and although it's becoming clear I'm not the master spy I'd hoped for, I'm not careless enough to be unaware of a potential threat hidden in the liquid.

"There's no obligation to drink the wine." Matthew stares at me over the rim of his glass. "But I assure you it isn't drugged."

His promise doesn't provide comfort. All it does is bring me closer to the edge of unease.

Normal, everyday people wouldn't accuse others of spying. They wouldn't contemplate spiking a drink or assume that others in their employ could be accused of doing the same.

So, either this man is like me—living within sinister circles—or he's badge-wearing scum. Neither option will have me spilling my secrets.

"Who are you, Matthew?" I cross my legs, attempting to appear in control. "Are *you* a cop? A Fed? DEA?"

That could explain Bishop. The burly guy might not be a bodyguard, but instead, a partner. Then again, cops don't have the income for the expensive threads these men wear. So maybe something higher up the food chain.

"I'm a businessman." He takes a sip of scotch, his gaze never leaving mine. "With a vested interest in what the Costas are up to."

He's a force to be reckoned with as well. An enigma. He's got me intrigued. Cautious yet captivated. I want to learn everything there is to know about this man. And I have a sense he feels the same about me.

"You're in the fashion industry?" I could buy that. He's certainly dressed well enough. "You're obviously not local if you're staying in a hotel."

"I live in D.C. But no, I'm not on the fashion scene. I'm more on the hospitality side of things."

It's my turn to grin. "You're being very vague, Matthew."

"Me?" He snickers, smooth and deep. "I've told you where I live, the industry I work in, and what hotel I'm staying at. Yet all I've learned in return is your ability to bewitch me with that stunning dress."

My heart kicks, thumping and throbbing. His player game is on point, and I'm loath to admit it's chipping away at my defenses. It's been too long since I had a man's attention.

Since I had *any* attention.

I reach for the wine, throwing caution to the wind as the liquid coats my tongue, the taste far more exquisite than what I'd been served at the fancy restaurant.

"Don't worry, I'm a patient man." His gaze dips to my mouth and I can't stop my tongue from swiping out to moisten my lower lip. "I don't give up easily."

The thumping and throbbing increases, pounding in my ears.

"I'm going to settle on my first assumption." His smirk returns. "You're a scorned lover out for revenge. Or, better yet, you're an opportunist, trying to secure a wealthy future by winning over one of the Costa heirs."

He's goading me and that's okay. He's not the only one who can play games.

"Maybe." I cross my legs and the split in my dress parts, exposing skin all the way to the bottom of my hip. "Do you think I'd have much success?"

His attention lowers to my thigh, his nostrils flaring. "*Amore mio,* you could take down an entire empire with your beauty."

I press my lips together, unsure how to respond.

I'm thrumming. Buzzing. Brought to life.

Benji never looked at me this way. At least, not once we found out I was pregnant after what was meant to be a one-night stand. He'd been sentenced to a future of parenthood and criminal activity due to an unplanned conception, but not once did I blame him for the resentment he spent years trying to hide.

"Did I say something wrong?" Matthew asks.

I glance away to regain my composure.

My late husband deserves more from me than this. Even though our marriage was forced, we still grew to love each other. We might have even grown into one of those all-consuming romances if we weren't so much alike—both ignorant and stubborn in all the wrong places.

"No." I keep my gaze averted as I take another sip of wine. "You didn't say anything wrong."

"I've upset you, which only brings me back to the belief you're a scorned lover."

I sigh. "What makes you think that?"

"Your eyes. I can see the emotional toll of whatever they put you through. The pain runs deep."

I don't correct him. It's better if he thinks I'm brokenhearted over one of Emmanuel's sons than to dive into the sticky depths of the truth.

"How did they not recognize you?" There's genuine curiosity in his voice. "You do realize they had their own security duo watching from both sides of the room, right?"

No, I hadn't known.

Goddamnit.

"That's why I had Bishop intervene when you stood to leave," he adds. "Although the family were on their way out the door, one of their guards still watched the room."

My failure continues to compile, the pressure growing heavier.

"How did they not recognize you?" he repeats. "Surely no man could forget a body like yours."

I smile despite knowing he's buttering me up for information. "I had a slight disguise." I remove the glasses, placing them on the table between us, then the colored contacts, and finally start to unfasten my wig, letting my dark hair tumble free.

I ruffle the long strands between my fingers and spy my reflection in the window, making sure I'm somewhat respectable.

When Matthew doesn't comment, I return my attention to his, curious at what brought on his silence.

He stares, his attention intense. "I wouldn't have thought it possible, but I find this version even more stunning."

The rampant flutters in my belly rise to my chest. My throat. I swallow, hard, struggling to fight his seduction as I dump the wig on the table.

"You're gorgeous." He studies me.

My hair.

My eyes.

My mouth.

Wherever his attention strays, heat follows, scorching me from the inside out.

He scoots his chair to the side so the table no longer stands between us and leans forward, his elbows falling to his knees, his dark focus unwavering. "Spend the night with me."

He asks with such surprising simplicity.

No, it's a subtle demand, the underlying conviction holding a curious hint of what sounds like awe.

Declining is the only option. Yet, I still find myself pausing to daydream about what a different future could hold. The two of us forging a bond through a common goal of destruction. Him protecting me from my enemies. His hands on my body. His words even more evocative behind closed doors.

I shiver from the possibilities, the thrill touching every nerve.

"Say yes," he whispers. "And I promise to make those men a fading memory."

6

———

MATTHEW

She grins, the curve of lips the prelude to a rejection. "You don't even know my
name."

"I don't need to."

I'll find out everything soon enough. Her name. Her intent.

"I could be anyone," she continues. "That doesn't concern you?"

That's exactly why I want to crawl on top of her, where I'm at my best. I'll learn her secrets through her body, and we'll both enjoy every second of it.

"I already know enough."

She's cunning. Determined. She may not be the best undercover agent, but she has potential. She's also holding out on me. I'm hungry to know what information is hidden behind those mesmerizing eyes.

"And would your friend join us?" she asks.

She's messing with me now. Playing.

I grin, appreciating her sass. "I'm sure he wouldn't decline the proposition."

She laughs, the sadness I glimpsed moments earlier disappearing with the flash of a perfect smile. "You're too much."

"Just wait until I start seducing you."

"You mean that's not what you've been trying to do since we met?"

"This has merely been conversation. If I were intent on seduction, you'd know about it."

Her laughter fades, but that smile settles in place, almost blinding in its humble simplicity. "I'm not so sure about that. I've never met a man who oozes seduction more than you do. I can't imagine how you could increase the severity."

Challenge accepted, amore mio.

I shove the table to the side and lunge forward, grabbing her chair legs around the outside of her calves. She squeals as I drag the furniture toward me, not stopping the progression until our knees bump.

26

"Holy hell." She clasps a hand to her throat while the other clings to the armrest, her eyes wide as she glances to the couple seated nearby who watch our exchange with interest. "You're making a scene."

I nudge my knee between hers, the material of her dress slipping farther apart to expose more of her legs, bare inches away from what I assume is tempting designer underwear.

I want to taste what's hidden beneath. To devour and sate us both. Even if what she's hiding is poison.

"Okay. I get it." She keeps frantically glancing at the nearby couple. "You can stop the performance now."

"Look at me." I splay my hands on her thighs, trailing my calloused palms higher and higher. "Don't worry about who's watching."

She squares her shoulders, gaining composure, but I can tell she's a skittish lamb. Hungry wolves can sense that type of thing and I'm goddamn starving.

"Look at me," I repeat, squeezing my fingers.

Slowly, she complies, her wild eyes meeting mine as she hisses, "What the hell are you doing?"

"Showing you the difference between conversation and seduction." I want to know which brother broke her—Salvatore or Remy. Then I want to crush every memory she holds of the son of a bitch. "Aren't you having fun?"

Her lips part, and I swear she's about to give an adamant denial until she snaps her mouth shut.

She wants me.

Wants *this*.

I could almost laugh at the absurdity. The serendipity. Who would've thought I'd find someone else at the same restaurant, spying on the same motherfuckers, on the very same night I was? *Twice*.

"You can't deny you're attracted to me." I lean closer, inhaling her sweet perfume. Jasmine and vanilla. "And there's no way I can do the same."

I slide my hand beneath her covered thigh.

She sucks in a breath. "We're in the middle of a bar filled with people. Do you have no shame?"

"Do you have no sense of adventure?" I counter with a grin. "Surely a woman of your beauty has done far more scandalous things than be admired in public."

The way she stiffens is a clear indicator she hasn't. *Fuck*. She isn't used to being wanted. Craved.

"This isn't admiration." She clears her throat, her shoulders remaining stiff. "This is a man attempting to get information."

"Can't it be both?"

For a second, she holds my gaze, tense and unyielding. I don't breathe. Don't move. It isn't until she huffs a derisive laugh, her mouth yet again forming that fucking tempting smile, that my pulse kicks back in again.

"Matthew, I apologize for misleading you, but I have no information to give. I wish I did, but I don't."

I don't believe her, and right now, I don't care. She's pretty when she lies. Pretty, tempting, and an increasingly more enjoyable challenge.

"Follow me to my room and let me show you a glimpse of your worth." I rub my thumbs in circles, trailing my touch higher along her inner thighs. "Let me treat you the way you deserve."

Her tongue snakes out to moisten her lower lip, her dazed eyes fixated on mine.

She's going to succumb.

Any second now, she'll announce her submission and let me claim victory.

"No, thank you." She blinks away the bewildered look and violently snaps her knees shut. "We're done here." She shoves back in her seat and stands, forcing my hands to fall into thin air. "Follow me and I call the cops."

With a snatch of her belongings from the table and a flick of her dark hair, she storms for the entry, passing Bishop at the bar who slides from his stool to stalk toward me.

"We're letting her go?" He glowers over his shoulder, watching her stride through the reception area, his focus predatory.

I should leave her alone. No matter what her connection is to the Costa family, she's nothing but a pawn in a vicious game. But I'm too fascinated to end this here. Too fucking intrigued. I have to learn her secrets.

"Follow her." I casually clap him on the back, downplaying the adrenaline-filled interest coursing through my veins. "I want her name and any other information you can dig up before sunrise. Don't let me down."

7

———————

MATTHEW

The fucker let me down.

Bishop allowed the woman to slip through his fingers.

He didn't get her name. Or her number. He didn't even catch the direction she went in because apparently she disappeared into thin air. Now all I have are lingering memories of ocean-blue eyes and hair dark as night to go with the semi hard-on I've had since our chance encounter.

I return to D.C. the following morning, unable to get her out of my head. I keep replaying our conversation on a loop, telling myself I need to search for hidden clues to her agenda only I get caught up on other things. Like the way her sass increased my pulse, or the ingenuity that made me determined to get to know her, or those damn inviting rebuffs to my advances that made this more about winning her over than gaining information.

I want to know what she's up to. And I want to know why. But most of all, I want to know how long it will take to get her beneath me. On *top* of me.

When evening comes, I make my way to my latest club acquisition to check on the staff who don't seem to appreciate the way their new boss runs things.

They're scared of me, too, which doesn't help.

The dark crevices of my reputation aren't well-known around here, but someone must've broken the silence.

"I've stocked all the bars." A short-skirted, slim-waisted, cleavage-bearing waitress stops beside me, her hopeful smile doused in deep red lipstick as she eyes the dancing crowd before us. "And noted all the liquor levels like you asked."

She's a brown-noser. There's always one. Even in a crowd of staff filled with animosity over my overbearing ways. They're the reason this club had been run into the ground. Them *and* the previous owner, who was too busy living the highlife in the Caribbean. But their failings are my gain.

I'll flip this club within a year and make a mint, all because they'd plummeted its value to begin with, allowing me to buy it for pennies.

"Your hard work is appreciated." I raise my voice above the loud music. "Are any of the staff continuing to have problems with the way I do things?"

Her wide blue eyes glance away and she shrugs. "Not really."

"Tell me who?"

She nibbles her lower lip. "Maybe Reece. I think because he managed this place for so long before you took over the transition is harder for him."

Then I guess Bishop and I need to have a chat with Reece.

"Thanks for the information." I walk away, skirting the dancing crowd three steps below, the thoughts of my Denver woman assailing me as soon as I'm left alone.

I haven't been able to concentrate since our chance encounter. Can't think straight, either.

If she's an ex-lover looking for payback for Remy or Salvatore, she may not know what her actions will instigate. The Costas aren't the type of people anyone should taunt. Not only are they vicious, but they're fucking stupid. It's a lethal combination.

I stop at the railing separating me from the bopping, booze-infested club-goers and grip the cold metal in both hands. It's not them I see, though. It's still her. The dark hair. The unfathomably deep blue eyes.

I need to find her. To touch more of her velvet-soft skin.

The brush of her thighs was enough to haunt my dreams. The jasmine and vanilla scent of her hair will live with me forever. All of her will. Never has a woman been so intriguing. Strong yet scared. Confident yet unsure.

A commotion starts on the dance floor before me. One man shoves another before my bouncers push from nearby walls to silently threaten their involvement. But it's not the shoving or the hired thugs that attract my attention.

It's the woman swaying her hips to the beat a few feet in front of me, her arms raised high, her dark hair cascading down her back.

For a second, I think it's her—*Denver*.

The figure matches. The lush hips, the slender waist.

It isn't until she turns that my fantasies take a nose-dive. Everything else about her is wrong. The lips uneven, the lower far bigger than the top, not precisely symmetrical. The face is round, too, not oval with high cheekbones and mysterious eyes.

My body doesn't care though. My blood pumps faster at the diluted comparison. My cock hardens, wanting relief from the obsession.

I watch her, pretending the swaying woman is mine, not taking my gaze off her as the flashing lights blink over her body.

Need pulses in my throat by the time our eyes meet. It's a simple travelling glance at first. A brief scan of her surroundings. Until she notices me staring. Then her intent snaps back to mine, her smile quick to form.

That's wrong, too.

The curve of lips doesn't dazzle or intrigue.

It's fucking disappointing. Almost deflating. But my cock doesn't get the memo because it's still in full-blown Denver mode.

My libido thinks she's here. *She's* the one dancing before me, her wild eyes intoxicating, her delicious body coaxing.

The woman continues to hold my gaze, her hips rolling, her arms moving above her head. I cling tighter to the banister, my knuckles aching, my throat drying.

I'm going to succumb.

After twenty-four hours obsessing about a mystery woman—living and breathing the questions that continuously slam my mind—I need relief.

I fucking deserve it.

I crook a finger at the dancer. Her mouth flattens for a shock-filled moment before she lowers her arms to her sides and saunters toward me.

The closer she gets, the paler the comparison, but I'm too far gone to divert this train wreck.

She stops on the lower level before me and calls out, "Did you want me?"

No, I want Denver.

"Yes." I rake my gaze over her, my pulse lessening with the new misgivings now apparent up close. The irises that are brown not blue. The bump on the bridge of her nose. "Care to join me in the VIP room?"

Her eyes widen, then she swings around, glancing toward her friends in the crowd. She waves them farewell without a thought to her safety and returns her focus to me with a grin. "Let's go." She hustles along the outside of the dance floor, up the three steps, then straight to my side.

Self-loathing is a constant companion as I lead her to the upper level filled with more dancing drinkers, then through the guarded doors to the quieter, exclusive part of the club.

But it's early on a Thursday night, so nobody with a glowing reputation has arrived yet.

It's just us, the bartender, and two couples who would've shed a couple hundred bucks for a once-in-a-lifetime experience that reeks of egotistical exclusivity.

I buy my companion a drink, pretend to listen to her life story, and flash my winning grin whenever I feel it's necessary. But I can't hold her gaze. She's nothing in comparison to Denver. Not with her over-the-top bubbly personality or her constant need to flick her hair as if she's involved in some fucking pathetic mating ritual.

Problem is, my dick won't cooperate. He's still all in, demanding something to numb the infatuation I hold for someone else.

"Have we met before?" The woman asks in a garbled rush. "Do we know each other? Because I'm sure I've seen you around. Your face is familiar. Handsome, too. You're like this quiet, mysterious type. It's so chill." She pauses for a breath and a sip of her cocktail, then giggles to herself. "This is surreal… But damn, I really need to pee."

She's fucking high—the frantic speech, the glazed eyes.

I'm fully aware I'm scraping the bottom of the barrel, and I still can't stop.

When she stands from our booth to go to the bathroom, I escort her, always a fucking gentleman. Then I wait in the hall, my shoulder leaned against the wall, my arms crossed.

These minutes alone, with the bass thumping beneath my feet from downstairs, and my hunger building for a stranger, only increase my impatience. My fucking addiction.

I have to find Denver.

The restaurant staff told me her reservation was made under the name Adley Javernick. A ghost. Someone who doesn't exist in Colorado or any of the surrounding states. Not even online.

She covered her tracks, which only reinforces my belief that she was spying for underhanded reasons.

I'll make Bishop return to Perfezione tomorrow. He can obtain the security videos from my friends in management. If I'm lucky, she may have fled our hotel rendezvous toward the restaurant, maybe caught a cab and been lax enough to use a credit card as payment.

"You waited for me?" The brunette saunters over from the bathroom, her lipstick reapplied.

"I did." I push from the wall, hating how much she's a poor substitute. Hating myself even more for moving forward regardless. "I thought we could use a little privacy."

I grab her hand and drag her into me. She giggles like a child and I slam my mouth to hers to shut her up. But this isn't Denver. The kiss is awkward, her lips taking too damn long to match my rhythm.

What I picture with my fantasy girl is far more brilliant.

Fated and perfect.

The only reason I keep my mouth fused to hers is the knowledge that I need something more than my own hand to gain relief from my suffering. Five fingers and a sweaty palm won't dislodge the woman commanding my thoughts. I'm not sure anything will.

I keep our lips meshed and drag her hips into me, settling her against my cock. She moans, the vibrations filtering along my tongue, into my chest.

I picture the most brilliant blue eyes. The lushest thighs. The sexiest coy smile.

With rough hands I spin her, making her face the wall. I guide her flush against the cool plaster, her long hair cascading over her back, the sight a hundred times easier to manipulate in my mind.

This is what I want. What I fantasized about on the jet home. The slim waist. Beautiful hair. Athletic legs. I close in against her, my mouth on her neck, my hard dick pressing against her ass.

"You've made me crazy," I growl into her ear. "Fucking mindless."

She giggles, the sound stifling the illusion. It goddamn slingshots me from fantasy to sickening reality, the hardness of my cock taking the brunt of the downfall.

"Shh." I clasp a hand over her mouth. "You don't want anyone walking around here to see us, do you?"

She whimpers in agreement and wiggles her ass against me.

"Good girl." I close my eyes, willing myself to see *her* again. To picture Denver. "From the moment I saw you, I knew I had to have you." I graze my teeth along her neck, delighting in her shiver. "So confident, yet so pure."

She whimpers again and this time the sound is masked by my palm.

"I'll make sure you never forget me." I hitch her skin-tight dress higher with my free hand, dragging the material over her thighs to her waist, then yank at the flimsy string of underwear until it breaks. "You're mine."

"Oh, wow. You're so dominant." She tilts her head away from my hold on her mouth, glancing at me over her shoulder. "When did you first notice me? Was it tonight or has this been going on for a while?"

"Quiet." I speak through clenched teeth. Through pure frustration. "Don't talk."

"But I need to know. I want to understand." Her words continue to run a mile a minute. "How long have you been obsessed with me?"

I squeeze my eyes shut. Clench my teeth. *Shit.*

My cock falls limp like a turncoat little bitch.

After dealing with a day-long half-mast dick, the fucker decides no flags will be flying tonight.

Fucking great.

"This was a mistake." I step back, my jaw tight with tension, my palms slick with sweat. I should've fought this shit out instead of trying to fuck it.

"No, it's not." She turns, her mound on display. "I want this. I *really* want this."

She's nothing like Denver. I don't know how I convinced myself otherwise. Her makeup is overstated. Her clothing cheap and tawdry. And that face. *Jesus.* What the hell was I thinking?

"Cover yourself and return to your friends." I right my jacket. "This isn't happening."

"But I want it to." She grabs my lapels, attempting to drag me into her. "I'm so horny."

I snatch her wrists. Tight. Her mouth gapes with the impact, her eyes wide. "I said, this isn't fucking happening." I shove her arms away. "So lower your goddamn dress and go find your friends."

She blinks. Slow. Stupid.

"Fucking walk," I growl.

She snaps rigid, her chin hitching a notch. "Fuck you." She glares as she scrambles to lower the hem of her dress. "You're crazy."

No argument there.

"You're a piece of shit, too." She raises her voice, no doubt attempting to bait me into an argument. "Fucking weirdo."

The bartender comes into view at the end of the hall, his eyes on me. "Everything all right, boss?"

"We need security." I start toward him.

"You wanted *me*, motherfucker," the woman rails. "*You wanted me.*"

No, I wanted Denver.

This piece of fluff is nothing in comparison.

The bartender jerks his chin at me in understanding, then focuses on the woman as I continue walking away. "I think you need some fresh air."

"I don't need anything, you son of a bitch."

I don't listen to the rest of her plight. I get the fuck out of the VIP area, opening the door to the consuming noise of the lower level, then don't stop until I'm in my car.

THE DAYS PASS. The obsession doesn't.

I can't quit going over my time with her, rerunning our conversation, trying to work out her angle. If she's a scorned lover, why eavesdrop in a packed restaurant? Why risk being recognized?

I don't bother attempting to sate myself in another woman. Instead, I shuffle my tight schedule and fly back across the country.

I return to the Italian restaurant where the Costas have a weekly standing reservation and make my way through the staff entrance at the back. Emmanuel may have claimed his favorite seat in the house, but I'm the one who pays to watch every minute of his meals.

"You're back sooner than usual." The head chef shoots me a glance as he flips something in a sizzling frying pan. "I might be able to retire early if you keep this up."

"Maybe." I slip a folded stack of cash into his pocket as I pass and continue to the swinging doors leading to the dining area with Bishop at my back.

Usually, I don't have to make my presence known. I can sit in my rental from the street out front and eavesdrop on their conversation via earpiece thanks to the listening device under their table. But this time, I'm not here for them.

It's her I'm after. The woman who doesn't fucking show.

I'm forced to walk out of there like a chump while Bishop wordlessly questions my motives, his judgmental stare increasing my annoyance.

I repeat the trip the following Wednesday, my impatience building when dreams of blue eyes haunt me on the daily. It's not normal. Denver triggered something and I'm not sure how to shut that shit off. But again, she doesn't show.

By the third week, I'm agitated as fuck.

It's not often I lose, at least not since my teenage years, yet here I am. I lost Denver. Without a trace. She slipped through my fingers and I can't figure out why the hell it matters.

Was it the challenge of bedding her? The thrill of a common enemy?

"How many times are we going to do this?" Bishop asks from the driver's seat as we sit in the rental parked on the other side of the road from Perfezione's entry. "I fucking hate Denver."

"We both fucking hate Denver, but we'll do this as many times as necessary." Until I get answers. Closure. "If you have a problem with the working conditions, feel free to fuck off."

He huffs a low chuckle. "You know this is messed up, right? It can only lead to drama."

I don't respond, partly because I don't answer to him, but mostly because I'm robbed of speech as a familiar figure saunters along the sidewalk to push through the front doors of the restaurant, her beauty captivating as she speaks to the maître d'.

She wears an auburn wig this time. A white dress. The glasses remain perched on her nose while she draws my attention to her perfect mouth etched in more subtle lipstick.

She's pure temptation.

Still way too beautiful to blend.

"She's here." I meet Bishop's stare and push open my door. "This time, you better not lose sight of her if she runs."

8

MATTHEW

I stalk my way across the room, not giving a shit who sees me as I pull out the chair opposite hers and sit. "It's been a while, but finally, we meet again."

Her face pales as our eyes meet, those gorgeous blue depths widening. "Are you crazy?" She frantically glances over her shoulder at the bustling restaurant. "What the hell are you doing?"

My pulse quickens at her panic. It fucking vibrates with euphoria. I can't help a grin. "Costa's not coming."

She frowns. "What do you mean?"

"He's in Italy. There won't be a family dinner tonight."

She blinks, her shoulders losing their rigidity, her expression falling. "Well, there goes a wasted flight."

I disagree. I think her trip here is the best money she's ever spent.

I've already discovered she lives far enough away to have to fly here.

It's astounding, but seeing her again, after all those days fantasizing about her, it's hard to believe she's more alluring than my memories allowed. Her eyes more mesmerizing. Her lips more inviting.

She clears her throat and rests back into her chair, regaining confidence and composure. "If you knew they weren't coming, why are you here?"

"Isn't that obvious?" I rake my gaze along the parts of her I've missed during her absence—every single visible inch above the table. "I'm here for you."

Her brows rise. The color in her cheeks does, too, as a timid smile curves her mouth. "That's smooth. But I don't buy it."

"No?" I rest my elbows on the table and lean closer. "Do you mean to tell me this obsession isn't mutual?"

She laughs and my dick takes notice of the hypnotic sound.

So pretty.

So real.

I know she's here for underhanded reasons, that's always been clear, but there's a gentle innocence about her, too. A fucking purity that's so subtle it makes me ache.

"Nice try," she drawls. "Why are you really here?"

A waitress sidles up beside her, placing a glass of wine on the table. "Would you like a drink, sir?"

"Scotch. Thanks."

The young woman nods and leaves us to our wicked games.

I swear the entire world ceases to exist for a few moments as Denver and I stare at each other with equal amounts of superiority and suspense. The air between us vibrates. The sexual tension crackles.

I narrow my attention to her mouth, her lower lip now slightly pulled between her teeth. *Jesus.* She's a tease. "I apologize for scaring you when we first met."

"You didn't scare me." She reaches for her wine with casual confidence, and I'm sure it's to prove her point.

"Well, whatever I did to make you run, I apologize."

She sips from her glass, eying me over the rim. There are no words between us for long moments, only a heated stare that bubbles my blood.

I don't know who the fuck this woman is but she's beyond temptation.

"Do you have a new lover since Remy or Salvatore? Is that why you took off?" I want the truth. Every last detail. If there's another man in the picture, I need to know who to get rid of.

"No." She takes another sip, her gaze still linked to mine. On the surface she appears unfazed and calm. It's her thumb rubbing over her wedding finger that's a tell.

I focus on her hand. On the lone digit.

There was no ring weeks ago. I made sure of it. I don't usually waste time on taken women. Yet for her, I'd make all the exceptions in the world. I'll break every one of my rules just for a taste.

She places the glass on the table and lowers her hands to her lap, deliberately out of sight.

"I have a husband." Her murmured admission packs a punch.

Fuck. I don't ruin marriages. Yet here I am, already planning the downfall of the relationship this woman has with her spouse.

"I thought you were a scorned lover?" I keep my disappointment in check. "So is it safe to assume you cheated on your husband with Remy? Or is Salvatore more your type?"

The heat building in my veins demands I find out who she was with—the younger, more emotional prick or the older, more conniving asshole. But I can't push her either. My impatience won't withstand another one of her disappearing acts.

The slightest narrowing of her eyes is her only response.

"Does he know you don't wear your wedding ring? Or is that integral to your disguise?"

Her lips part, only to have the waitress return with my scotch. We're silent through the interruption. Neither of us move or speak until Denver reaches for her wine to take another sip.

I don't glance at her hand this time. I don't dare to take my gaze from hers. I want to read every hint she gives. To see all the facets she doesn't know are on display.

Once we're left alone she tilts her chin as if preparing to announce war, but instead, she says, "My husband died two years ago."

I straighten.

That explains a few things. Especially the subtle glimpses of pain I've witnessed a time or two.

I palm my glass. "I'm sorry to hear that."

"No, you're not." She gives a derisive laugh. "You've been trying to sleep with me from the moment we met. I bet the death of my husband is welcomed news."

I frown and clutch dramatically at my chest, pretending she's not entirely on the mark. "You don't think very highly of me, do you?"

"I haven't thought enough about you to bother making an assessment."

"Now who's lying?" I smirk and clasp my scotch. "At least I'm honest enough to admit my infatuation. When you did the Cinderella routine weeks ago, I went crazy trying to find you. There wasn't even a ruby slipper left behind for me to trace back to you. Not even a name."

Her lips twitch. "First of all, the ruby slipper was in *The Wizard of Oz*, and second, I vaguely recall you mentioning you didn't need my name."

Touché.

"I assure you I paid a hefty price for that mistake. I almost lost my mind not knowing how to find you."

Her lips kick even farther. Not quite a smile, yet enough to raise her cheeks and brighten her eyes.

"Well, don't hold out on me, *amore mio*. Tell me your name."

She contemplates me for a moment, probably wondering whether to lie while she takes another sip of alcohol.

"Layla," she gently murmurs.

Victory consumes me, rushing hot and fast through my veins.

She's telling the truth.

I'm not sure how I know, but I do.

"Do you have a surname, Layla?"

"Yes." She answers simply, without elaboration.

Fuck me, she's phenomenal. All sass and charm.

I can't help but snicker, and it's beyond rewarding when she follows suit, chuckling along with me.

"Okay, Layla. I don't need anything more than your given name."

She raises a taunting brow. "Good for you."

"Don't get me wrong, *amore mio*. I'm happy to delay the exchange of information, but you're going to eventually give me a few more details. I need to know the history of the future mother to my children."

More laughter tumbles from her lips. Whimsical, entrancing laughter. "You need to stop before I choke on your massive ego."

I'd love to give her something else to choke on. I can already picture it. *Feel* it. But I need to be cautious of her boundaries. I won't risk losing her again.

"Take off the wig." I gentle the demand. "Let me look at who you really are."

Her mirth tapers under seriousness. "Not here."

"Then we'll leave. I'll take you somewhere more subdued."

She pauses. Hesitates. "I haven't had dinner."

It's not a rejection. If anything, it's an open door of opportunity.

I pull my wallet from the inside pocket of my suit jacket and place some bills on the table. "Come on." I push from my seat and hold out a hand. "I'll find us somewhere more appropriate to eat."

9

———

LAYLA

Matthew leads me from the restaurant and into the chilled fall air, the sound of Denver's nighttime traffic bustling around us.

I shouldn't be doing this again. It's stupid.

Problem is, this sizzling chemistry is potent enough to deafen the thoughts of caution.

"Your friend isn't joining us tonight?" I shoot him a sideways glance as I take off my glasses and place them in my purse, my heart thudding harder when he looks my way.

"Bishop?" He returns his attention to the path ahead. "He's always around."

"He's here?" I spin, scanning the sidewalk behind us as we continue walking.

The ogre isn't visible. Not hiding in the entries to closed shopfronts. Not lingering in alleys.

"He has eyes on us from somewhere."

Apprehension tickles my neck as I pivot back around, Matthew slowing until I catch up to his side.

"Want me to tell him to take the night off, *amore mio*?"

Yes, is my instinctual response. But I don't want him too aware of my concern. He's playing me for information and I need to do the same, even though my usually hibernating libido is under the impression I'm here for different reasons.

I'd been shocked at the first sight of him tonight. Panicked. Yet there'd been something more adamant that soon took over my emotions. Something that had nothing to do with fear and everything to do with the way his sinful gaze devoured me.

"I'll call him." He stops and pulls out his cell.

"No, wait." I reach for him, only to have him lock devilish eyes with me.

"It's okay. He doesn't need to hang around." He tilts his head away, connects a call, and raises the cell to his ear. "Take the night off. I'll see you in the morning."

I don't hear Bishop's reply.

"Yes. Don't let me find you tailing us." He lowers the cell and disconnects. Simple as that. No farewell. No apology for the dismissal.

He's smooth, his excessive level of charisma continuing to slip under my skin.

"You didn't have to do that." As long as we stay in public, I don't have anything to worry about. I can hold my own, maybe not in strength, but definitely with the defensive goodies in my bag. And tonight isn't going anywhere private. Racing pulse or not.

"Of course I did." He pockets the device and grabs my hand. "If you're uncomfortable, I'll always be obliged to do something about it."

My breathing hitches as he drags me into his side and continues our trek along the path. But it's not just his vow of obligation that leaves me shook. It's the possessive, comforting grip of his fingers. Both tag team to leave me speechless.

I've been deprived of male touch since Benji's death. And before that, hand holding wasn't a part of my life. Displays of affection didn't exist. In public *or* private.

Now, I can barely think through the warmth of a stranger's hold.

"It's through here." Matthew leads me to the mouth of an alley, the path subtly lit by a dubious string of twinkling lights attached between the towering buildings above.

I stop, my heels planted.

He continues forward, not noticing my hesitation until his arm is outstretched and I pull my hand away.

"What's wrong?" He turns to ask. "You don't trust me?"

I raise a brow, glancing from him to the darkened alley and back again. "Not in the slightest."

"Beautiful and smart. How the hell did I get so lucky?" He steps forward, once, twice, his casual approach not stopping until we're toe-to-toe, those deep dark eyes staring down at me as his palms take liberties by sliding over my hips. "What if I promise to remain respectful at all times? I'll only bite if you want me to."

"What if I tell you I have a gun in my purse," I lie, "and I'm willing to use it?"

He grins. "That works, too. But let's settle on going somewhere else. You decide the location."

He keeps saying all the right things. Making all the smooth moves to bring me one step closer to his honeytrap. But it's those eyes. The shades of rich earth and chocolate that make me contemplate stupid things... like following anywhere he leads.

"What's down there?" I jerk my chin at the alley that's far cleaner than any I've seen before. No garbage litters the asphalt. No graffiti. It's all looming bricks with no windows in sight.

"An Indonesian food truck. It's somewhat of a hidden treasure." His fingers begin to move, kneading the flesh of my hips. "They've got an online presence. You can search them on the map. I promise I don't plan to drag you into the shadows to have my wicked way with you." His grin increases, a tiny dimple peeking out beneath the rich stubble. "That comes later, once I've gained permission."

I shouldn't be endeared. I shouldn't be goddamn turned on either. And I definitely shouldn't want to press my lips to his to assuage my curiosity over his taste.

But I do want.

I want and need and crave more than I can ever remember feeling with Benji. The thought is enough to leave me cold with guilt.

I step back, dragging my attention from penetrating eyes to the alley. Four people walk toward us. Smiling, laughing, the noise echoing off the walls. There's nothing nefarious about them or their mood.

"Let's keep moving." Matthew reclaims my hand and continues along the sidewalk.

"No." I tug him, making demands of my own. I want to see this hidden treasure. "Take me to the Indonesian food."

"Are you sure?"

Nope. Not one little bit. But the hazardous impulse flowing through my veins makes me nod. "Yep."

"Whatever you wish, *amore mio.*"

God, he kills me each time he uses the endearment. Even though it's glib, it still affects me—how easily he can confess love when I've been denied those words my entire life.

My father rarely professed the sentiment. My brother never will. And although I assumed it from my husband, I rarely heard the admission from him. It came maybe three times in the nine years of marriage.

Matthew is similar to the men I'm used to in a lot of ways—his confidence, his authority. It's the aspects that are shockingly unfamiliar that leave me hungered and achy.

He has soft undertones. A gentlemanly nature that lives in parallel with the sharp edge of wicked intent.

If only I wasn't questioning whether every single part of him was some well-constructed act.

"You're quiet." He strolls beside me under the twinkling lights, taking me further into isolation. "Everything okay?"

"You're guiding me down a darkened alley, without your bodyguard, while dressed in a designer suit. I think it's normal to fall quiet from contemplating how many times we're going to be mugged."

"It's safe. I'd never knowingly put you in danger. I promise. And while we're back on the topic of Bishop, he isn't a bodyguard. He's more of a business partner. At times, he's my driver. My confidant. My eyes and ears. He watches my back. But I also watch his."

His words trigger subdued alarm bells. They should be louder. Deafening. But the fact that he sounds like my brother washes off my back without leaving residue.

"Your job sounds hazardous for someone who works in hospitality." I shoot him a sideward glance.

"You've obviously never been on the receiving end of an influencer's tirade when their dirty martini isn't quite as dirty as they would've liked. Some of my staff expect danger money when certain people walk through the club doors."

I smile and return my attention to the foursome who continue to laugh and chat as they pass. "So you own a club?"

He shrugs. "A couple."

Yep. He's sounding more and more like Cole. The only difference is restaurants to clubs.

The reasons to turn on my heels and escape are compounding, yet these shoes won't pivot. My body refuses to walk anywhere apart from straight ahead.

"We're almost there." His thumb rubs gently over mine. "It's just around this corner."

I keep my hand in his, my palm tingling as we reach the end of the building.

"Here." He tugs me around the corner into the open space where I'm sure a building once stood. Now the area is claimed by a food truck draped in white twinkling lights with park benches scattered on top of bright green fake grass.

Office skyscrapers loom around the oasis, with more strings of lights crisscrossing overhead. It's humble. A hidden haven, just like he promised. With at least twenty people eating and drinking.

"What do you think?" Matthew stops to look at me, those confident eyes scrutinizing. "I found this place years ago. I swear nobody cooks quite like Reza."

"What I think is that you're doing a great job of keeping me on my toes. I never would've expected you to escort me from a Michelin-starred restaurant to a food truck. I'm not sure if I should be impressed or confused."

He smirks, dropping my hand to slide his palms around my waist. "If you want to be impressed, you should've taken the invitation to my hotel room. It's not too late to head there now."

I burn. White hot. His touch sears me.

I'm almost tempted to sell my soul for a few minutes of suit-clad privacy. But I can't. I won't.

I don't know this man, and even if I did—even if this was a regular date between people who didn't have deceitful similarities—my baggage is full.

I have a daughter, a dead husband, and a family who don't welcome outsiders. Ever.

"You're dreaming if you think I'll follow you to your room." I chuckle to dissuade the lust.

"Let's call it forecasting."

"I won't go back to your hotel, Matthew." I attempt to hold his gaze, yet the draw of his mouth steals my attention. "Not tonight."

"How could I change your mind?" He leans closer, the intoxicating scent of his smooth aftershave consuming my fractured breaths.

"You can't," I lie. "I barely know you."

His stubbled jaw grazes my cheek as he inches closer to my ear. "That's what I'm trying to resolve." His attention lowers. His lips brush my neck with a torturous glide of connection. "I want to know everything about you, Layla."

I shudder, my eyes closing of their own volition, my entire body enraptured by the rough resonance of his tone. "I don't enjoy one-night stands."

"One night would never be enough."

Oh, God. I want to succumb.

With everything I am, I itch to grasp these stomach-tingling feelings and ride them for as long as possible. Just one taste of happiness even if it isn't deserved.

"You live in D.C.," I whisper.

"Yes." He nuzzles the sensitive skin below my ear. "And you live where?"

"Somewhere farther away from you than Denver." Much, much farther. So unbelievably far that this questionable attraction isn't worth humoring. I pull back, stricken with unwanted reality, and retreat a step. "I don't have casual sex. You're wasting your time if that's what you're after."

"Stop thinking so little of me." He counters my withdrawal with a forward stride, his hand sliding behind my neck, the other tightening around my waist to haul me closer. "This might be about fucking, but that's not all it's about."

I want to believe him. The rapidly building wildfire rushing through my veins makes it impossible not to.

His mouth descends on mine, the softness contrasting with the possessive grip around my neck.

For a second I'm dumbstruck, my purse strap precariously hanging on the edge of my shoulder as he consumes me.

I haven't kissed in… forever. I also haven't been held with such possession. And I've never, ever been so alive with choking jitters.

His lips move, coaxing mine to do the same. I can't deny him. I'm enslaved to give him what he wants, conceding with the softest whimper. Our mouths dance as I claim his chest with my hands, my fingers tangling in the material of his silk shirt.

He parts my lips with a firm glide of his tongue and a low growl of appreciation, and I'm done for. My nerves awaken in response. Every pound of my pulse is deafening.

Then, all too soon, he breaks the connection, gradually leaning back to stare at me with hungry eyes.

"Waiting until you're ready will kill me," he murmurs. "But the torment will be worthwhile."

He turns, reclaiming my hand to lead my mindless ass toward the food truck, acting as if he didn't just sweep me off my feet with a decimating kiss. He seats me at an empty park bench and says something about ordering food. Then he's gone, leaving me to stare at his fine form from a few yards away.

I honestly don't know how I got here. How I could possibly have traveled halfway across the country with intentions of destruction that guided me to romance?

Minutes later, he slides a heaped plate of marinated chicken sticks into the middle of the bench and takes a seat opposite me. "I hope you like satay chicken. They may not be the least messy option, but they're the best thing on the menu."

"It looks delicious." My gaze remains riveted on him as I suck my lower lip.

The subtle tweak to his mouth makes it obvious he knows I'm talking about him. *God.* I have to look away to curb the lust. I'm out of my element here. Entirely ensnared.

"Hey." He slides his hand across the table and claims mine. "I feel the same way, okay?"

No, he doesn't. He couldn't. I'm caught up in feelings I've never felt. For a man I barely know. In a situation that is rife with danger and subterfuge.

"I don't chase women," he adds. "And I definitely don't beg for their attention. I assure you, I'm equally caught off guard."

I don't look at him. His reciprocated emotions only make this seem all the more surreal. I'm in Denver for revenge. For destruction. Not indulgence.

"How about we change the subject?" His touch retreats. "Tell me why you're watching Costa."

I chill at the whiplash in conversation. Here I'd been stuck in visions of heated flesh and sweaty skin while he's had Emmanuel at the forefront of his mind the entire time. "Why are *you*?"

He grins. "I'm sensing trust issues."

What he's sensing is annoyance. I shouldn't have been stupid enough to let down my guard. Instead of exposing my emotions, I grab a chicken stick and force myself to eat.

"I still think one of them broke your heart," he continues. "What I can't figure out is if it was recent. Maybe this is a childhood grievance. That would explain why you were so close to them without fear of being recognized."

"You're partially correct," I concede, hoping the slight forward momentum will be enough to tide him over. It isn't a lie, either. I didn't need to be in soul-deep love with Benji to have my heart shattered when the Costas stole him from me. He wasn't merely a husband. He was a father to our gorgeous daughter. And a good father at that.

"Which one?" He wipes the back of his hand over his mouth. "Which brother is to blame?"

"Does it matter?"

He eyes me for a long moment. Staring. Scrutinizing. "I guess not."

"It's your turn now." I finish the chicken stick and reach for another. "Why do you spy on them?"

"They've screwed me over more than once, and I don't plan to let it happen again."

The hair on the back of my neck rises. "Business or personal?"

"Does it matter?" He mimics my previous reply.

Yes, it does.

He said he works in hospitality. He owns clubs. In the eyes of the naive world, Emmanuel Costa is nowhere near that line of work. But I know better. I'm well aware the ties likely to bind them are drugs.

"I've said something to scare you." He discards his bamboo skewer on the side of the plate and frowns. "What is it?"

"I'm *not* scared." I take another bite of chicken, acting casual even though the risks are rising. "Why do you keep asking that? Are people usually frightened of you? Is that why you assume I'm the same?"

He eyes me, his gaze never wavering.

I'm right.

He's feared.

Why?

The thought should be enough for me to join the tally of those who are fearful. It *should*. However, the tingle running down my spine is far from fear-based.

"You're not going to answer me?" I taunt. "Why is that, Matthew?"

His jaw ticks as he breathes deep, letting the air out slowly. "You're right. I guess it is a default."

"Are you going to tell me why?"

His stare narrows. It isn't in anger. The intensity is something else. Shame, maybe. "Designer suits and fancy restaurants haven't always been a baseline, *amore mio*. I've had hardships, and those dark times had me doing anything to claw my way to the light. But that's where I am now—in better days."

His honesty is unnerving. Invigorating. I'm not used to people being open with me. Not when the men who usually surround me hoard their secrets as if their lives depend on the truth remaining buried.

This conversation is a gift. An offering.

"Were those hardships caused by the Costas?" I ask.

He continues to stare, long heartbeats ticking by as his chocolate gaze builds bridges between us. "Some. Yes."

Another thrill skitters down my back, the tingles hitting every nerve, spreading through every muscle. He's giving me so much. Information. Insight. Maybe my trip here wasn't a waste after all.

"Now it's your turn." He rests his elbows on the bench, unshakable. "Tell me what knowledge you're seeking about them. Tell me what you already know. Better yet, tell me about *you*, and put those assholes to the back of your mind."

Guilt stabs between my ribs. Sharp and fast.

This business of secret spilling was always going to be one-sided. He can't know about me. Not the *real* me.

"I've learned a few things about them that isn't common knowledge." I dilute my admission, hoping to appease him with tidbits. "And not all of it makes sense. I'm aware Costa has four children, but he only acknowledges three of them. Their oldest son, Dane, is in hiding, for reasons unknown."

"It's Dante," he corrects. "And he's estranged, not in hiding."

My heart kicks with the insight. "You know about him?"

"Of course I do." There's the slightest edge of superiority to his tone. Or maybe it's disappointment that I haven't done thorough research. "They attempted to bury evidence of his existence years ago. But there are still clues if you look deep enough."

"I also know Emmanuel's wife comes from a long line of Italian mafia," I add, hoping to redeem myself.

I don't.

He doesn't react to the meatier morsel of information either, making me question if he's a master of schooling his expression, or if he knows all there is to know about my enemies.

"Were you aware of that, too?" I raise a brow.

"I was, but not many people are. They go to a lot of effort to keep that information from going public."

"They should've tried harder."

I'm boasting for no reason. Cole was the one who obtained the knowledge. Not me. I only had the good fortune of overhearing him relay the news to Hunter.

"You're quite the sleuth, aren't you?" His compliment is slight, even a touch sardonic, and yet my heart warms. My stomach tenses.

This isn't good.

I'm succumbing to him. It's ridiculous and uncalled for. Dangerous and entirely stupid. My siblings would despise the choices I'm making. The risks I'm taking. And they already hate me enough.

"I'm sorry, Matthew, but this was a mistake." I hitch my purse strap onto my shoulder and brace my palms on the table. "I should go."

"What? Why?" His brow snaps tight, concern taking over his entire face all the way to the thinning line of his tempting lips. "We just sat down."

"I know, but..." The squeeze in my stomach increases, the war between want and obligation waging inside me. I came here for revenge. For redemption. *Not* for a romantic rendezvous.

"But you don't want to share any more of your secrets," he finishes for me. "You've decided you've got what you want and now it's time to leave."

Yes... No... Maybe.

I can't tell him what he wants to know. I refuse to divulge who I am or why I'm really here.

He wouldn't look at me the same way if I did, and I want his devouring attention to stay with me forever.

"I have a lot more information to give, Layla."

My insides twist. Not only due to the potential intelligence I'm giving up, but because he wants me to stay. Nobody has ever wanted me to stay before.

"I know." I swallow and push to my feet. "Regardless, it's best if I leave."

"Why?" The question is growled with delicious determination. "At least give me the respect of telling me an honest answer."

Honesty is tough. It always has been. From my childhood years, when I had to lie to myself about how my family made money, to my adulthood, when those lies had to be fed to everyone else.

"I could lose myself in you, Matthew," I murmur with a sad smile. "I barely know you, yet I'm well aware I could fall head over heels and never recover. And that's not what we're here for."

"Says who?"

My heart flutters. "I need to go." I walk around the bench only to be stopped by his hand grasping my wrist.

"At least take my number."

I want to take more than that. So much more it kills me to deny us both.

"I'm no threat to you, Layla. I have to go back to D.C. tomorrow morning." He pushes to his feet to stand before me, not letting go of my wrist. "I don't even know your full name. I don't know where you live. But if I give you my number you can at least reach out if you change your mind."

I hesitate. Having a lifeline to him isn't something I need. It will only act as an opportunity to succumb in the future.

"It's just a number." He steps closer and reaches for my purse.

I don't stop him from retrieving my burner phone. I even reluctantly enter the pin code when he holds the device in front of me.

He messes about with the screen. Tapping. Swiping.

When he hands it back, I notice he's sent a text message, the sneaky bastard, not merely giving me his number, but taking mine in return.

"I want to see you again." He reclaims the possessive grip around my neck. "And I know you want to see me, too."

I do.

God, how I do.

I want to touch, and taste, and breathe in more of his phenomenal aftershave. To strip him naked and kiss every inch of his perfect skin. To learn all about him—who he is, where he's from, what he stands for.

Unfortunately, I have a job to do and there's no place for distractions.

"Goodbye, Matthew." I place a kiss to his cheek.

"For now," he growls, his hand falling to his side. "We'll meet again, Layla."

10

———

LAYLA

He messages me before I leave the alley—*I'm in suite 1309 of the Delcato if you change your mind.*

Fate is such a tempting bitch.

Of all the hotels in all of Denver, we have to share the same one. But I'm not going to give in. Instead, I catch the closest cab and make quick work of hiding in my hotel room before there's another chance of us crossing paths.

I send sweet messages to Stella to distract myself. When that isn't enough, I call my brother. I make up a lame story about enjoying an out-of-town shopping spree to keep him off my trail. Then I shower and spend the rest of the night staring at my suite door, trying to fight the instinct to go in search of a stranger's bed.

I toss and turn for hours. I even reach for my phone twice, debating whether or not to cave.

Thankfully, I pass out before I can succumb. The sun peeking through the curtains announces I made it through the torture to the other side. Waking up alone doesn't feel like a victory, though.

I order room service for breakfast, not willing to see Matthew in the restaurant before his flight. Then I head out to shop my blues away, knowing he would already be on his way home to D.C.

I purchase dress after dress. Shoes. Makeup. Books.

Thoughts of him follow me the entire time. I even fantasize that he watches me from a distance. Stalks. I imagine his attention fixated on my body, and my skin shivers everywhere his make-believe gaze strays.

But he isn't here. I make sure of it by glancing over my shoulder like a paranoid bitch every few minutes.

When my cell vibrates with a call after lunch, so does my pulse, because his name is the one displayed on my screen.

"You messaged me straight away," I say in greeting. "Then call me the next day. I thought men weren't meant to show interest for weeks."

He laughs, and I close my eyes briefly to enjoy the sound. "If so, I've severely messed up because I ditched my meeting this morning and stayed in Denver, hoping you might change your mind about spending time with me."

My stomach free falls, giddy greed consuming me.

"Where are you?" he asks.

Anticipation swirls beneath my sternum, my heart thundering like a drum.

"Layla?" His voice drops to a purr. "Don't deny you spent all night thinking about me, because you already know I did the same damn thing."

The reciprocation kills me. It eats away at my caution and makes me want to run to him. Just for a taste. Just one more kiss.

"I'm shopping. The mall is about a ten-minute drive from the hotel." My pulse thrums with the admission.

"Mine or yours?"

"Ours. We stayed at the same place."

There's a beat of silence. I swear, I feel his disappointment roll through the connection. It hits me right in the throat, stilting my breath.

"Tell me where you are," he says. "I'll come find you."

If I give him my location I'm done for. There will be no more restraint. No more talking myself out of this. I'll give in to temptation despite the risks.

But this could be my last taste of happiness. The one quick gulp before I return to judgment and resentment.

"I'm at the Cherry Creek Shopping Center." My blood surges. My pulse, too.

"Give me an hour."

He disconnects, leaving me to second guess if this is the most stupid decision of my life. And I've made some pretty wretched ones in the past.

I have to force myself to continue shopping as a distraction, but all I do is walk aimlessly from store to store, not taking note of the clothes or shoes or sales because all I can think about is him. He's all I see.

Within ten minutes, I'm outside, needing fresh air to dilute the suffocating apprehension. The traffic makes things worse. All the hustle and bustle increases the noise inside my head.

This can't be a thing—me and him.

Catching up is only to feed my curiosity. To answer the myriad of unspoken questions.

I pass unseen people and shopfronts, trekking in circles, getting lost. It isn't until I'm standing at the mouth of an alley that I stop, my shopping bags limp at my sides as the looming walls remind me of the night before. How Matthew had shown me a slice of Denver I never knew existed. How his kiss made my soul ache.

This alley isn't the same, though. Garbage bags are piled against the building walls. There are no hanging lights or laughing friends to lull me further into daydreams. The contrast to last night's environment only acts as an added warning that maybe things won't be as sparkling and shiny with Matthew in the light of day. That maybe catching up with him again is a mistake.

I continue into the isolation, seeking clarity, and the farther I trek, the more conflicted I become.

Matthew is an indulgence I'm not allowed.

Not after I spied on Cole for my father. Not when I contributed to Benji's downfall and Stella's abduction. And especially not with all the things I did in an attempt to keep my transgressions secret.

Happiness isn't a part of my all-inclusive life package. Mine revolves around heartache, guilt, and regret. There are some bonus pride-filled moments that revolve around my daughter, but I don't get to upgrade until I make amends.

I stop halfway to the street ahead and rest my shoulder against the brickwork, placing my shopping bags on the ground at my feet. The emotional drain of two years weighs me down. No, it's been longer than that. The heaviness has been a growing constant since the day my father asked me to spy on Cole.

Now the pressure is unbearable.

Each breath is etched in pain. Each step is more grueling with all that piles on top of me.

I retrieve my cell from my purse, my heart hurting as I acknowledge the rendezvous with Matthew has to be cancelled.

If I see him again, I'll kiss him. And if I kiss him, I'll sleep with him. And if I sleep with him, I'll never be able to get him out of my system.

Would the hours of bliss be worth the future filled with torment?

I have less than thirty minutes to decide.

"Give me your purse."

I stiffen at the male demand coming from directly behind me.

"*Now*. Hurry the fuck up." Hard metal nudges the back of my skull. A gun.

I slowly raise my hands, my fingers trembling, my mind on Stella and if I'll ever see her again. "Take whatever you—"

He snatches at my purse strap, the aggressive yank tearing at my shoulder.

I scream, the noise adding to the deafening rush of my pulse in my ears. He yanks again, harder, pulling, wrenching my arm as the gun grates into my head.

"Stupid bitch." He shoves me toward the wall, the side of my face hitting brick.

My muscles slacken with the impact. My arms fall to my sides. I become fluid, slithering to the ground as he claims his prize and snatches at some of the shopping bags on the ground.

I'm too stunned to move. In too much pain to think.

He runs for the far end of the alley, the clap of his footsteps a dull clip over the noise in my head, his black cap shielding his face before he disappears around the corner.

I crumple onto the remaining shopping bags, my left cheek throbbing, the bone beneath having taken the brunt of the impact with the wall. My shoulder burns from the assault from the purse strap, too. But what flames hotter is my blood, the rage flowing through my veins turning volcanic at my stupidity.

Not only did I daydream myself down a secluded alley with my arms filled with brand-name shopping bags, but I didn't notice I'd become a target until that asshole had been right on top of me.

I can't even figure out if it was luck or idiocy that I didn't have my gun.

If my weapon had been stolen, I'd have to report this to the police, then Cole would find out and the reasons for my out-of-town trips would be unraveled.

I hadn't even attempted to protect myself.

I didn't have the instinct to fight. I'd stood there, statuesque. Still and fucking pathetic.

Cole would be ashamed of me. Yet again.

I press my head back against the cold brick and whimper. How am I going to get out of this without him finding out? I'll have to cancel my credit cards. And my cell… What the hell happened to it?

The device had been in my hand. Now it's gone. When did it go missing?

Oh, shit. The cyanide.

Bile creeps into the back of my mouth, threatening to spill onto my dirty blouse and scuffed jeans.

"Jesus fucking Christ." I rest against the wall, my cheek tight from swelling, my pulse pounding through the tender flesh.

Why do I keep failing like this? My life has become a compiling stack of misgivings. One stupid move after another. Over and over again.

I'm not worthy of my family's notoriety. I bring nothing but shame to our name.

My throat tightens with emotion.

All I ever wanted was to make them proud. To help build our empire. And instead, my every decision has worked against that goal. I'm a liability. The most despised part of what has always been a vicious environment.

"I'm worthless." I cover my face with my hands, my nails digging into my forehead. I want to scream. To claw and scratch until the internal voices subside. But they never will. It never does.

The bags beside me rustle, the rhythmic vibration coming from my cell.

I straighten, riffling through the purchases worth far more than anything in my purse, and find my phone, the pink casing now cracked in the top corner, the screen alight with Matthew's name.

I shouldn't answer. Of all the things I should be doing right now, speaking to him isn't one of them. Not when I have to figure out how to cancel my credit cards without Cole knowing, which is going to be goddamn hard when he's the main account holder.

But my fingers work of their own accord, numbly swiping the screen. I answer without a greeting and sniff to dislodge the tingle in my nose.

"Hello? Layla?" He pauses. "Are you there?"

It's sickening how those few words wash me in comfort. How a stranger can ease my suffering without even knowing it.

"Yeah." I clear the fragility from my voice. "I'm sorry, I'm going to need to cancel catching up with you."

"What's wrong?"

I squeeze my eyes shut. He cares. The passionate concern in his tone takes hold of me and grips tight.

I don't know why it matters. Why it affects me even in the slightest. Having my purse stolen is nothing in comparison to what life has dealt me. A throbbing face and sore shoulder aren't in the same league as the threats I've endured as the sister to a drug boss. Or the heartache of the lonely nights spent in a forced marriage.

It doesn't even hold a candle to the disgust that brought me to my knees when I found out my father was a sex trafficker.

This is nothing.

No-thing.

And still, frailty threatens to drag me under.

"Layla, talk to me," Matthew demands. "What's going on? What's wrong?"

"Nothing." I scowl, willing the inner voices to quieten. "I'm fine. I just… My bag was stolen and I'm flustered. I need a minute to think—"

"Where are you?" he repeats.

"It doesn't matter—"

"*It matters*," he growls. "Tell me where you are."

I'm used to protection. I've been shielded from hideous threats all my life. But never before has someone's need to care for me hit this hard. Someone who barely knows me.

"Layla," he implores. "I'm on my way to you. Just tell me your exact location."

The disgust in my veins increases. The tightness in my throat, too. "Outside the mall. In an alley nearby."

"Give me a name, *amore mio*. Do you know what alley?"

I look for the street sign and find nothing. "I don't know. I can't see—"

"As soon as I hang up you need to text me a pin on your location. Can you do that?"

I nod through the frantic emotions.

"Can you do that for me, Layla?"

"Yes." My voice cracks.

"Okay… Good. Stay where you are. I'm on my way."

11

———

LAYLA

I'm slumped against the wall, my heart and thoughts in Chicago with Stella, when a black Lincoln Navigator pulls into the alley, the glossy vehicle stopping in front of me.

Matthew flings open the passenger door, and despite not wanting it to, my heart squeezes in relief. He jogs forward in another stylish suit, falls to his knees before me, and cups my face.

"Fucking hell." His eyes harden as they focus on my injured cheek. "They hit you?"

"No. I was shoved into the wall. I should've put my hands up to stop the impact but..." I shake my head within his gentle hold. "I guess I didn't have time. I don't know... I wasn't thinking straight."

"It's okay." His attention softens. "You're going to be fine."

I'm not so sure. Not with my sinister intentions now out in the world in the form of a tiny cyanide vial. But it's nice to hear the assurance, to have such a confident and compelling man almost demand my recovery.

"What did they take?" His thumb strokes my uninjured cheek as Bishop climbs from the driver's seat. "Did you call the police?"

"It was just my purse and a few things I purchased. The cops don't need to be involved." They can't be. I wouldn't even know how to start explaining my reasons for carrying poison if my bag was found. Although not illegal, cyanide is a controlled chemical and I have no reason to have it, especially not on my person and concealed in a drug vial. "It's only a few credit cards and some cash."

"You sure?" His gaze narrows. "This is serious."

He has no idea.

I can't explain how I obtained the murderous powder. The name of my contact would only raise more red flags. Could I go to prison? Or worse, if the Costas find out I'm here, and why, will they then target my family again in retaliation?

54

The blood drains from my face in a rapid vacuum.

"Layla, it's going to be okay. Just talk to me. You look like you're about to faint."

What if someone were to think the vial of white powder was cocaine? What if they snorted it?

"I…" I fight against the overwhelming need to blurt my fears. "I had something in my bag."

Matthew's shoulders straighten, but his confident attention doesn't waver. "Something illegal?"

I nod.

"A weapon?" The question lacks condemnation. He holds no surprise. Not even disappointment.

"Of sorts… If it got into the wrong hands—" My stomach lurches.

"It's okay." He leans closer, demanding I believe him with his close proximity. "I'll take care of it."

"How? What could you possibly do?"

"I've got contacts. If the bag is found, nothing is going to be tied back to you." He releases my face and glances over his shoulder, sharing a silent communication with Bishop who stands a few feet away before returning his attention to me. "You're a single woman alone in a foreign city. You're entitled to have protection, whether it's illegal or not. And if someone is harmed…" He pauses, his tone gaining conviction before he finally says, "I'll take care of it, Layla. I promise you."

I believe him. Even though he assumes I had a gun. Even though the aftermath of mistakenly snorting cyanide could be far worse than a gunshot, my traitorous insides relax a little at his assurance.

"Let's get you out of here." He helps me to my feet, then sweeps me into his arms.

"I can walk." My protest is faint at best.

"I know you can. But this is the first opportunity I've had to prove myself to you, so let me take it."

I look away, not wanting him to witness the effect of his words.

If this had happened at home, and my friends or family had rescued me, I'd be dealing with chastisements and judgment. The fear from my loved ones wouldn't come through in kindness. Only criticism.

This is such a sweet balm to my nauseating idiocy.

Bishop opens the back door to the Lincoln and I'm bundled inside, gently slid into the middle seat before Matthew takes his place at my side.

I don't get a chance to pull on my seatbelt before he's lifting me again, dragging me onto his lap.

"What are you doing?" I whisper.

"Holding you." He wraps his arms around my waist, bundling me against his pristine suit. "You're shaking."

I am. I can't help it. Even my heart trembles.

This shouldn't be such a big deal. I've been through worse. But the shaking doesn't stop. Not when Bishop climbs back into the car with my bags. And not once we start moving, with me still on Matthew's lap, his tight hold acting as my seatbelt.

"Tell me you're okay," he murmurs.

My throat burns with adoration. With appreciation. I lean into him, my head against his shoulder, my heart yearning for more. "I am. It's only shock."

"You sure?"

I nod. "Positive."

We fall silent, the low hum of the radio filtering through the speakers, the luxury of his hold cocooning me. I should be strengthening my emotional walls against him, against all the weakness, but for just this once, I decide to let someone else take the lead. To quit pretending I'm a force to be reckoned with and simply succumb to Matthew's rescue.

We reach the hotel without another word, then the underground parking lot. Once the car stops near the elevator, my savior opens the door, then slides out from beneath me to haul me from the vehicle and back into his arms.

"This isn't necessary." I press a hand to his chest in another feeble objection.

"I know." He nuzzles his nose near my ear, his breath tickling my neck. "I'm still taking advantage until the shock wears off. God knows once you're strong enough you'll return to being the independent woman who doesn't want a piece of me."

I huff a faint laugh despite his false assumption.

I *do* want a piece. I want all the pieces.

"What about her room key?" Bishop asks through his lowered car window. "Should I get a new one from reception?"

"Mine should still be in my pocket." I double-check to make sure, finding the plastic card in my stained jeans.

"Regardless, she'll be staying in my room," Matthew adds. "Park the car and we'll meet you upstairs."

I don't argue. I'm smart enough to acknowledge I need company right now. I don't want to be out of these strong arms. I'd love to stay here forever, constantly protected by someone who doesn't despise me.

I keep those thoughts to myself as I'm carried to the elevator, the confined space taking us to one of the top floors, then escorted to a freshly made suite far bigger than mine. We bypass a compact kitchen. A spotless living room. Then continue down a hall.

"Where are you taking me?" My question becomes redundant as we enter a bedroom, Matthew's stride not faltering until I'm gently placed on a king-size bed.

"You can rest here." He presses a kiss to my forehead and backs toward the door, a dedicated knight in shining armor. "I'm going to get you a stiff drink to settle the adrenaline. I'll arrange an ice pack, too, and run you a bath. Want anything else?"

I'm lost for words. Speechless.

"Food? Water? A fresh change of clothes?" His gaze falls to one of the large dirt stains on the side of my jeans. "I could go to your room—"

"No. I don't need anything else." Only company. I don't want him to leave. I swing my legs off the bed, preparing to follow him, needing his proximity. "Apart from a dose of the shakes, honestly, I'm fine."

"Stay." His voice drops in a gentle warning as he pauses at the threshold. "You need to rest. Let me look after you. I'll be back soon."

I fight another protest, the isolation hitting hard as soon as he's gone. The minutes spent alone only give me time to relive what happened. The demand for my purse. The harsh shove. The painful collision with the wall. Then the panicked aftermath.

I kick off my shoes and wither into the pillows, trying to think what Cole would do in my situation.

The cyanide is a big deal.

I could easily say it was planted in my bag, but that's not what I'm worried about. My panic revolves around the potential of an innocent victim. Then again, in my brother's case, I'm sure he wouldn't spare a stranger's death a second thought.

He wouldn't care.

If only I were that heartless.

I roll to my side, pull out my cell, and do a mental catalogue of the personal items I lost. My identification was definitely in there—photo ID for the airport who sometimes need more than the digital license stored on my phone. Then maybe one bank card. An AMEX. The rest were loaded to my cell months ago.

Realistically, I could get away with putting a hold on one account. But Cole would still find out.

I groan and navigate to my bank's website, connecting a call to the correct department before I can talk myself out of it.

After providing every speck of personal detail known to man, I cancel the card and disconnect. The reordering of my license will have to wait for a time when I don't feel as though I've run a marathon.

Even the allure of nearby running bathwater doesn't ease my pulse. I'm still shaking, my limbs heavy.

I stare at the ceiling, fighting against the inner voices telling me how much trouble I'm going to face once I get home.

"You doing okay?" Matthew appears in the doorway, a scotch glass in his hand.

I am now. The mere sight of him brings overwhelming relief.

It has to be his commanding presence. The strong way he holds his shoulders. The chiseled angle of his jaw. And those eyes. *My God*. The intense way he looks at me makes me shiver.

"Layla?" He raises a brow.

He has to know the effect he has on me. It's obvious. He walks into a room and the chemical shift is unsettling.

He's always lured me in with the tease of escapism. And for once, I want to grasp the offering in both hands and leave the darkness of my world behind. If only for a few hours.

"I'm good." I drop my cell to the mattress and push from the bed. "Thanks for taking care of me." I walk toward him, my heartbeat excited although I'm still filled with hesitance.

He watches my approach with hungry eyes, the drink hanging limp in his hand, his arms strong and sure at his sides. "The bath is ready. It'll help calm the nerves."

"My nerves are calm." I don't stop until my toes brush the leather of his shoes.

I need to get lost in him. To lose sight not only of my failures but of myself. I don't want to be this person anymore. I want to be free.

"If anything, this morning's events have made me emboldened." I lean up on the pads of my feet, place my palms on his hard chest, and inch toward his mouth.

My tongue tingles as I get within a mere breath of his lips only to have him turn his cheek, rejecting my advance.

"Layla," he warns. "This is the adrenaline."

I stiffen in horror, mortified.

All the air leaves my lungs on a rapid vacuum of humiliation, the scent of his exquisitely perfect aftershave only increasing my suffering when I have to draw in my next breath.

I drop back to the soles of my feet and retreat with heated cheeks.

"Wait." He wraps an arm around my waist, holding me captive. "Don't get the wrong idea. I—"

"You brought me into your room." I push at his arm, attempting to break free. "You placed me on your bed."

"Because I want you to be comfortable. I need you to feel safe." He frowns and leans closer until we're almost nose to nose. "But don't get me wrong and think I'm not interested in you. I've made my feelings crystal clear. I want to fuck you within an inch of your life, *amore mio*. What I won't do, though, is cross the line when you're making decisions based on shock."

I blink rapidly at his explicit detail. At the completely sordid image that inspires wildfire in my belly.

His arm tightens around me. "You've barely returned any of my interest. You only came to me now because you're scared and need comfort. And I can give that to you. I just won't do it in a way that will fill you with regret later."

All his aggressive compassion only endeavors to increase my attraction.

"Are you listening, Layla?" He stares into my eyes, waiting. "My need for you defies sanity. But I won't have you unless your appetite for me will hang around after the adrenaline wears off."

"It will," I whisper. "It will hang around."

He keeps staring at me. Reading me. Then, with the flare of his nostrils and a barely audible growl, his mouth is on mine, setting me aflame.

I close my eyes, descending into a different type of darkness, this one born of passion and possession.

He devours me with harsh lips and a controlling hold. I can't get close enough. Not even when my nails are digging into his shirt and my tongue is tangled with his.

It's bliss and euphoria.

Compulsion and addiction.

I struggle to catch my breath, not wanting to pull away, not wanting this to end. I need everything from him. More than lips and hands.

Matthew leans back abruptly, as if it takes all the power in the world to separate us. He pants, his chest rising and falling, while I do the same.

"Drink." He raises the glass in front of me, his eyes glazed with lust, and retreats a step, shoving his free hand through his hair. "It will dull the insanity."

I hesitate, my engrained caution toward the alcohol holding me immobile for a split-second. Just long enough for him to frown.

He gives a breath of a scoff and lowers the offering back to his side. "So you want to share your body, but still don't trust I'll give you a drink that isn't spiked?" He sighs. "Take a bath. You'll feel better afterward."

"That's not it." Well, it is, but…

He retreats again and again, understanding and disappointment staring back at me. "It's okay. I get it. You barely know me."

"No, you don't get it. And how could you when you barely know me in return?" I accuse. "I've had excessive caution drummed into me all my life. I couldn't even accept drinks at my friends' birthday parties when I was a child." I follow after him. "Caution isn't just a tale my parents told me to encourage good behavior. Vigilance has always been something that kept me alive against the harshest threats."

He stills in the middle of the hall, his eyes narrowing. "What threats? Who are you, Layla?"

"I'm someone with a target on my back." I raise my chin with confidence. "And that's all I'm going to say about it."

His gaze remains narrowed, digging under my skin from the few feet of distance between us until finally he nods. "I've got enemies of my own. Enough to know you're worth the risk of more."

My traitorous heart squeezes.

He raises the glass to his lips, takes a gulp, swallows, then steps forward to hand it over again. "It's safe, okay?" He raises a brow, wordlessly asking if his display is enough to gain my trust.

"Thank you." I take the offering and bring it to my lips. The smooth scotch awakens a slight burn all the way down my throat. I don't stop drinking until I've consumed every last drop.

"You're welcome. Now, how about that bath?" He takes my hand, gently placing it in his. "You're still trembling."

"Did you ever think that maybe I tremble because of you?" I entwine our fingers and squeeze to mask my vulnerability. "You unsettle me."

The pad of his thumb sweeps across my wrist, back and forth, gently exquisite. "You unsettle me, too. Beyond anything I've ever experienced. Why do you think that is?"

I wish I knew.

It's clear this pull has something to do with the thrill of the unknown, only the more I learn, the more my attraction grows.

"Maybe there doesn't need to be a reason." I inch forward, reaching for him, tangling my fingers in his shirt, feeling the hard muscle beneath. "Maybe this is just a phase that hit us both at the same place at the same time."

"You're no phase, *amore mio*. I can guarantee that."

When he says those things—the endearing luscious words—I fall for them every time. My skin becomes awash with goose bumps. My breathing falters. Now is no different.

"What if that's all I can offer?" I tug him into me. "What if right now is all there is?"

"You said you don't do one-night stands."

"It's still daylight outside." I grin, undoing the buttons on my blouse, exposing the lace bra beneath.

"I already told you, once will never be enough. I meant it, Lay." He presses his forehead to mine, ignoring the skin I've put on display. "You need to go take that bath."

"Why?"

"So I'm forced to leave you alone."

I close my eyes, drowning in the closeness. In the pure affection that's entirely new to me. "And if I don't want to be left alone?"

A gentle groan rumbles in his throat. "Take the bath, Layla."

I nuzzle my nose against his. "I don't want to."

The groan builds, the sound increasing my thrill.

I slide my mouth over his, the connection featherlight. In an instant, he's all over me, stalking into me until I'm backed into the wall, the glass taken from my hand to be dropped to the carpeted floor with a heavy thud.

He steals my mouth. My decency.

I claw at him, yanking at his shirt, forcing him closer. He responds with a harsh grip of my ass, his fingers digging into my flesh, his groan changing to a growl.

"I need you," I murmur against his lips. "Now."

He ignores me, kissing, clutching, parting my knees with his own. I'm so ready for this. *Too* ready. It's almost embarrassing.

"Take the bath." He snakes his tongue over mine. "Walk away because I'm too weak to make the decision for you."

I can't. I wish I could. This isn't in the best interest of either of us. I know this. I know it with every fiber of my being. And still I can't move.

"Take it, Layla," he begs. "You're not ready to sleep with me yet."

"I'm not?"

His chuckle is faint. "No, *amore mio*. You're not."

My blood runs hot, my pulse pounding at the apex of my thighs. But I believe him. The warning slips through the lust haze to give me a good shake.

"Okay." I plaster a hand to his chest and force myself to retreat. "I'll take the bath."

"Good." He turns and stalks away, disappearing into what I assume is the bathroom.

I pause a second to regain my composure before I follow, entering the gleaming white room a few steps behind.

He stands in the middle of the tiled floor, staring at the tub already towered with bubbles, the fluffy clouds piled above the rim, a towel folded and waiting on the vanity along the back wall.

"You didn't need to do this for me." I move farther inside. "I could've run the water myself."

"I'm sure you could, but I like having someone to indulge." He shoots me a lack-luster smirk, his attention skating over my cleavage to my stomach. "It's been years."

"A romantic? Don't worry, your secret is safe with me."

It was meant as a joke, but the seconds that follow become far deeper than that. Tense. I've fractured the lust by bringing us back to the real world.

We both have information we could use against each other. Ammunition. The repercussions potentially run deep.

"And yours with me," he promises and makes his way toward the hall. "I left a robe hanging on the back of the door. Take your time. Relax. Call out if you need anything."

"And if what I need is you?"

"Then maybe hold off for a while." He meets my gaze for a beat before returning his attention to the hall. "When we're finally together, it won't be fast. I assure you, Layla, you're going to want energy in reserve."

12

———————

LAYLA

HE PULLS THE DOOR CLOSED IN HIS WAKE, LEAVING ME TO PICTURE EXACTLY HOW LONG fucking him might take as I remove my clothes.

My shoulder protests the movement and once I'm naked, the angry red lines marking my body explain why. The purse strap had a free-for-all with my skin.

A quick glance in the mirror doesn't come without a pained breath, either. My left cheek is viciously swollen along the bone, the puffiness almost reaching my eye.

I force myself to turn away, shoving my concern about Cole finding out to the furthest reaches of my mind, and climb into the bath.

The warm water is quick to soothe me, the heat coating my exposed skin in a sheen of sweat as the bubbles cuddle my chest all the way to my neck.

It doesn't take long for the scotch to go to my head, numbing me perfectly, making the shaking stop. The silence will be my downfall, though.

The long stretch of quiet gives me too much time to picture this energetic sex Matthew alluded to. My imagination runs rampant with wild scenarios that aren't entirely my forte.

It's been a decade since I experienced passion. Even longer since I felt adored.

Benji and I made things work because of Stella and the family business. And we played our roles well. But below the surface, we were far from wedded bliss. We flat-lined before our daughter was born. No romance. No energy. Little lust.

It wasn't long until I discovered my husband was cheating on me, and I was okay with that. I always thought he was owed a mistress or two for what he was forced to give up. Especially when I would quit sleeping with him for months on end.

I kept the knowledge to myself, too. I never betrayed him to Cole due to fear of the punishment that would follow. Or worse—the death sentence.

Maybe it was wrong to pretend I didn't know. Maybe Benji would've stopped if I asked. But I kept quiet for my own sake, too. Not just to keep my daughter's father alive, but because it was a relief to rely on strangers to fulfill a duty that was meant to be mine.

Not once did I feel gnawingly hungry for sex like I do now.

Not once in more than nine years of marriage.

"How are you doing in there?" Matthew asks from behind the closed door.

"I'm good." My chest fills with butterflies as I picture him in the darkened hall. "Do you want to come in?"

"You didn't lock the door?"

I bite my lower lip. No, I didn't. I thought about it, though. "Would the flimsy lock have stopped you from breaking in if you wanted to?"

If Matthew's intent was to hurt me, he could've done it many times already. He could've whisked me out of the city while I was disorientated from the incident in the alley. He could've kidnapped me that night at the food truck. He could've forced me to do anything from his sheer masculine power alone.

The knob turns, the door gradually inching open to expose the man I've been daydreaming about for these unending minutes. *No*, for the last three weeks.

He leans against the doorframe, his gaze taking me in with hunger. "I made you another drink." Another glass of scotch rests against his hip as those dark eyes devour me.

"Thank you." I tilt my head to the side when he remains in place. "Do I have to wait until I get out for you to give it to me?"

"That's probably for the best." His attention lowers to the bubbles. "It's not a good idea for me to get any closer."

I press my lips tight, holding in a smile.

God, I love the predatory lust in his gaze.

"Where's Bishop?" I raise my arm from beneath the water, slicing open a path of bubbles to guide a stray strand of hair behind my ear.

"Out."

"Out?" I hold in my delight at his gruff response.

"He's busy rescheduling my flights. *Again.*"

My heart pangs at the reminder of our limited time. "When do you leave?"

"Tonight."

I play with the bubbles, raking my fingers through them, spreading them one way, then back the other, attempting to tease him with the possibility of exposing what the thick cloud hides.

"That doesn't give us a lot of time." I keep swirling, decimating the foam further and further with each swipe.

"No," he murmurs. "It doesn't."

When he falls quiet, refusing to continue the conversation, my thoughts become more daring, my curiosity growing wings.

I raise my leg onto the side of the tub and shiver when his nostrils flare.

"Are you deliberately torturing me?" he growls.

My heart kicks. Wild and unrhythmic. "Torture you?"

He raises the scotch, downing the contents in one fell swoop before returning the glass to his side. "You know exactly what I'm talking about."

There's a warning in his voice. A delicious subtle threat.

My throat tightens. My chest, too. Everything is so painfully, invigoratingly restricted that I have to fight hard to maintain level breathing.

I raise my other leg, crossing both at the ankles against the rim of the tub. I shouldn't be doing this. Warning bells ring in the farthest recesses of my mind. If only they were loud enough to put a stop to the craziness. "Join me."

His jaw ticks. That's his only response. No movement. No words.

"Matthew?"

His features tighten, almost setting in a glower as he grates, "Be sure about this, Layla."

"I think I am," I lie. I'm not even partially certain. I'm running on instinct alone. No, not instinct—infatuation.

"Then I'm staying where I am." He crosses his arms over his chest, the glass moving to rest in the crook of his arm.

"Why is this—"

"I'm on the precipice here. I can only pretend to be a stand-up guy for so long, then I'm going to start pushing my own agenda. So don't play with me, *amore mio.*"

My cheeks blaze as I retract my legs from the rim of the tub to sit up straight. "I wasn't…" I shake my head. "I'm not…" I don't know what to say.

"What?" he asks. "You're not what?"

"I wasn't playing. I like being held by you. I just never assumed the offer had to come with a predetermined conclusion."

"It does and it doesn't." He raises his chin as if stricken. "If at any time I did something you didn't appreciate, you'd only have to say the word and I'd stop. But that's where your problem is going to be. I'll make sure you appreciate everything I do. I'll make you want me, Layla. I'll push you further than you anticipate and I won't regret it."

I shiver. Head to toe. Every inch of skin sizzles with goose bumps.

I don't doubt him. He's already pushed my boundaries. I've accepted numerous open drinks. I climbed into the car of a stranger. I've left myself vulnerable to him.

These are all cardinal sins set out by my family since birth. Yet, I don't regret breaking them.

I want more.

"Join me," I whisper.

He leans over in a swoop, placing his glass on the tile before he deftly shucks his suit jacket to the floor. Then, with one button after another, he exposes me to a torso of carved muscles, his hard work ethic and determination etched into the peaks and curves of his chest.

"Something wrong?" He raises a brow as he drops his shirt to the floor.

"My imagination didn't do you justice."

He smirks, his strong hands latching onto his belt. He holds my gaze as he pulls the leather from the clasp, but I can't keep the connection—not when my cheeks flame hot.

I tilt my face away, stupidly bashful, the heat in my cheeks seeping down my neck.

My heart thunders at the continued clink of the belt buckle. In my periphery, I see him discard his suit pants to pile them on top of his shirt.

He snickers, the faint sound making me shiver. "What's wrong, Lay?"

I pull my legs to my chest and focus on the bubbles as he continues to undress, removing his socks, then his underwear.

"Don't tell me you're shy." He approaches, stopping directly over my shoulder, almost out of sight. "Another bashful flutter of those lashes and I'm done for."

I focus on levelling my breathing as I hug my thighs. "Not shy. Just respectful. It's rude to stare."

There's another muted snicker. "Let me make this clear—the things I've pictured us doing are far from respectful. Now scoot forward. Let me sit behind you."

I do as instructed, shuffling farther along the tub.

Every one of my nerves tingles as he climbs in, raising the water level along with the horizon of bubbles. The moment his legs slide around me, I tense, my nipples beading painfully. It's such a strange sensation, this hyper anticipation coated in brutal nervousness.

"Relax." His hands find my forearms under the water. "Lean back against me."

I don't know how. I'm frozen. All the overflowing confidence I had moments earlier has vanished, the traitorous bitch leaving me to fend for myself.

"It's okay." His voice is soft as he guides me to recline against him, his hands adding tender pressure on my shoulders. Then he falls quiet, not saying a word as I settle into him. There's only the gentle ebb and flow of his breathing and the thrilling hardness of his dick against my back.

"You're still shivering." He glides his fingers over my arms, gently teasing me below the surface. "The adrenaline is taking its time to wear off."

"It's not the adrenaline." I clear the discomfort from my throat while his touch climbs higher to my biceps, then farther.

He massages my shoulders, lightly kneading. "You've got no idea how much I appreciate knowing I have an effect on you." He nuzzles my neck, awakening the sensitive spot below my ear. "You're a hard nut to crack, Layla."

I tremble, the vibration skittering along my chest. "You poor thing. Did my restraint batter your excessive ego?"

"Like you wouldn't believe." The words hum against my skin before his lips follow with a brief kiss. "But don't worry. I'll turn the tables."

I hold in a smile, fully aware the tables have always been turned. Soon they may even be flipped.

"How's your cheek?" He scrapes his teeth over my shoulder, his hands continuing their gentle onslaught down and around my waist.

"Throbbing."

"Room service shouldn't take long to bring a bucket of ice. And the concierge is arranging a cooling pack."

"Thank you. But I shouldn't need all that. The swelling will go down soon." If it doesn't, Cole is going to be on the warpath.

"I ordered a bottle of champagne, too."

"Now *that* I would accept with open arms." I need to reclaim the confidence I had when he was standing in the doorway. I want the upper hand, not these flimsy, flaky responses.

His fingers move to my belly and I stiffen with the intimacy before I can stop myself. The low hum of his laughter only increases my tension. He's so incredibly sure of himself. So deliciously confident.

"Relax, Layla." He kisses my shoulder. "You're safe."

Safety isn't my concern. What I fear is disappointing him. Our connection felt different when he was struggling for restraint at the door. Now he's in his element, having already won this game of seduction, and I didn't even leave the starting blocks.

"Easier said than done." I struggle to loosen my muscles.

"Why?" His touch trails lower, along my abdomen, inching farther and farther toward the apex of my thighs, where I already feel his effects the most.

"You know exactly why." I'm unsettled. It's clear he has me tied in knots.

"How would I know? You've been successful in exposing very little about yourself." He places another kiss to my neck, the kindness followed by a rough scrape of teeth. "Am I moving too fast? Too slow?"

I don't know.

Nothing is certain anymore. There's only sensation, and it's taking me over like a drug.

"Maybe," I croak.

"Maybe too fast?" His touch continues to descend, gliding over the slim patch of curls at my pubic bone. "Or maybe too slow?"

I suck in a ragged breath, my pussy clenching as his fingertips divert farther down along the path where leg meets crotch. I shake my head, unable to answer, no longer even sure of the question.

"Too fast or too slow, Layla?" he murmurs.

I whimper, the blanket of bubbles doing nothing to stop my mind from visualizing what's happening below the surface. His strong hands consume my vision. The image of his lips on my skin makes me throb.

He adds pressure to my legs, parting them, exposing me beneath the water. "Want to know what I think?"

I breathe harder, clenching my eyes shut.

"I think your fragile little whimpers mean you're hungry for more but don't know how to ask for what you want," he rumbles under his breath. "I think you're throbbing, your body begging to be sated. I even think you might finally be realizing all the pleasure that could've been yours the first night we met if only you'd allowed it. How we could've been like this weeks ago."

He continues to speak against my skin, punishing me with wave upon wave of goose bumps as his fingers continue to sweep back and forth along the apex of my inner thighs.

"And just think, *amore mio*—I'm barely getting started."

I clench my molars. I'm going to moan. I feel the release build in my throat, determined to escape. There's so much tension. Too much. My body craves. My heart pounds.

"Tell me you want more," he teases against my neck.

"I want more." I respond too quickly. So damn fast my answer should be humiliating. But the embarrassment will have to wait until the aftermath. Right now, craving is all I know. Hunger entirely consumes me.

His fingers continue to creep, swiping closer and closer to my core. "How much more?"

Everything.

The moan escapes, my head falling back to rest against his shoulder.

"You can't say it?" he asks.

No. I've never asked for sexual favors before. Never even voiced my need.

"Please, Matthew," is all I can admit.

"It's okay. I won't make you say it. Not today." He sweeps those fingers closer. "But soon."

The threat shivers down my spine. The warning that I will one day have to admit my desires fills me with unstable excitement. I'm high. Euphoric. Entirely mindless with lust. I never knew this heightened state of hunger existed. This clawing, savage need.

"I enjoy seeing you like this." He continues the external sweep of his touch. "Worked up. Greedy. This is how I've felt since we met. My cock hard as stone, my thoughts always on you."

I shake my head. "You barely know me."

"That's the crazy part. I don't know a damn thing about you, and still, I'm infatuated."

Those fingers skirt the edge of my pussy. Back and forth. Up and down. Constantly teasing. I grasp his wrist, clinging tight. He has such inspiring control, such unwavering confidence.

I wiggle my hips, eager for this torture to end.

"Don't worry, I'm impatient, too." He kisses my jaw, my neck. "So fucking impatient, *amore mio*. But this is merely the beginning."

I'm about to force his hand where I need it the most when a knock sounds on the furthest reaches of my consciousness.

I freeze, blinking back to reality.

Matthew growls in frustration.

"What is it? What's wrong?" I brace to sit up, but he holds me down with those strong hands clamped around my crotch.

"It's only room service." He tilts his face away, calling a loud, *"Come in,"* toward the hall.

I tense further, ready to fling his hand off me so I can scramble for a towel.

"Stay." He keeps me held tight. "They'll be gone in a minute."

My pulse thunders as the suite door creaks open, the unmistakable rattle of a trolley quickly following.

"Sir?" a man calls. "Would you like me to leave your order in the living room?"

Matthew steels his hold, his legs tightening around me. "No, bring it to the bathroom."

13
____

MATTHEW

"Jesus Christ." She scrambles, wiggling and slushing water over the edge of the tub in an attempt to get out.

"It's okay," I purr in her ear. "Your modesty remains intact. You're completely covered by the bubbles."

"Matthew, please." Her hands snatch at my wrists.

"Breathe." I kiss her shoulder, the back of her neck. "*Relax.*"

We're barely getting started. And to be fair, I warned her. I told her she wasn't ready.

The rattle of the trolley continues down the hall, making her nails dig into my skin.

"I've got you," I whisper. "You can trust me."

The door is pushed wider by a kid barely in his twenties, his eyes bugging at the sight of us before quickly lowering to the tiled floor. "Umm. Where would you like your order, sir?"

Layla remains stiff against my chest, her fractured breathing brushing my ears.

"You can bring it over here." I relax my legs around her and loosen my hold on her thighs, gently running my fingertips in circles a bare inch from her pussy.

She flinches, her spine snapping rigid.

I grin into her hair, loving her unease, as the trolley is wheeled closer.

"Here?" The kid stops a foot away from the tub, his gaze cautiously flicking from me to Layla then back to the floor.

"Yeah, that's perfect." I trail my touch closer to her heat, over the smooth softness of flesh leading to her pussy, as I murmur against Layla's neck, "Would you like him to open the champagne?"

She moans and shakes her head. Fast. Fucking rigid.

It's a chore not to laugh.

I kiss her shoulder and tilt my hips, nudging my cock against her ass. "You sure? It will only take a second."

She remains quiet, her chest rising and falling in a rolling wave.

"Just open it." I meet the guy's gaze. "It'll save me having to get out of the water."

The kid nods and reaches for the bottle seated in a metal bucket, the slush of ice filling the energetic silence.

Layla's breathing quickens, the rapid cadence shifting to a gasp when my touch skims her pussy lips.

Her virginal jitters are a drug. The tension. The sharp nails piercing my skin. I close my eyes and press my face into her hair, focusing on those breaths, letting them fuel me as I trail a teasing swipe right down the middle of her sex.

She shifts against my cock, and I could groan from the exquisite friction.

I could fucking come.

I've imagined this for weeks. Pictured every scenario. Daydreamed a bucket list of sordid ideas. But they didn't live up to this. They weren't even close.

The *pop* of the champagne startles us both, the bath bubbles slushing against the upper curve of her breasts.

"Matthew," she whispers, her legs clenching.

"Mmm?" I inhale the floral scent of her shampoo. The sweetness. The purity.

She doesn't respond, not with words, only fractured inhales as she remains statuesque, not portraying the depravity going on below the surface.

"Would you like the bottle down there?" the kid asks. "Glasses, too?"

I tease a fingertip around Layla's opening, circling wider and wider. "What do you think, *amore mio*?" I edge deeper, gliding slowly inside her, that delicious pussy clamping down around me in an instant. "Do we need glasses?"

"No." The response is nothing more than a rushed breath while she shakes her head. "Nothing. We don't need anything."

"It sounds like we're all good here." I jerk my head at our guest. "If you check the pockets of my pants on the floor you'll find a tip." I sink my digit all the way inside her, making her shudder as I smirk into her hair.

"Ahh… Sure thing." He backtracks toward my clothes, chancing a glimpse at the beauty in my arms, before snapping his attention away. He rummages through my pants while I slowly twist my finger inside her. Teasing. Dragging out her pleasure.

Her fingers claw at me. Her core clenches. And those hips I love so much, they fucking jolt oh so slightly. Not once does she protest my advances. Her digging fingers are a pleading sign for more.

"Want me to get him to hang around?" I whisper in her ear.

She whimpers as the guy straightens from bending over to pull the clip of cash from my pants pocket, his attention returning to the bath.

"Excuse me, sir, how much would you like me to take?" He stares at Layla, his Adam's apple bobbing with an arduous swallow.

He envies what I have. And so he should. The woman in my arms is beyond compare. Not only in appearance. In class, too. In seduction, and sensuality, and above all else, the trust she's placed in me.

"That depends." I slide another finger inside the most perfect pussy, and her body rolls in the subtlest of waves, her back arching, her chest stretching. "What's the going price for discretion?"

His lips part, his skin turning a paler shade. "There is no price, sir. I would never—"

"Then take it all, my friend. Enjoy yourself."

"All of it?" He gapes. "Are you sure?"

I slide another finger inside her. "Positive. I'm always happy to reward loyalty."

The guy pauses a moment, watching as Layla's head rests back against my shoulder, her teeth buried in her lower lip as she nuzzles shyly into my neck.

I slowly pulse my digits, enjoying how he watches her. How he *wants* her.

She needs to bear witness to that. To how she's desired. Adored. This gorgeous woman may be confident in battle, but right here, gloriously naked and wanton, she seems far from empowered.

"Like what you see?" I ask.

The kid nods.

"She's beautiful, isn't she?" I want him to say it. To tell her how perfect she is. How revered.

"She's gorgeous," he murmurs.

Layla moans, the sound seeming born from pained modesty and heightened pleasure while she hides her face deeper against my neck.

I need her to know she's hungered for. Treasured.

"Matthew," she whispers against my skin. "Please ask him to leave."

My lungs restrict at her polite plea. The delicate cadence. The charm of her voice. "Of course. Anything for you." I nuzzle her hair, working my thumb over her clit as I meet the guy's gaze. "You can leave now."

He blinks. Once. Twice. "Yes, sir. Thank you, sir." He backtracks, stumbling to the hall, disappearing into the shadows, his footsteps retreating until the suite door squeaks closed in the distance.

"You okay?" I keep gliding my fingers inside her. Punishingly gradual. Torturing us both.

She doesn't respond. Not in words. She keeps those claws embedded in my wrist, her pussy clenching with each new slide of penetration.

"He wanted you," I utter against her ear. "Anyone who could see you like this would want you. You're so fucking beautiful."

She pants. Mewls. Scratches.

"You're breathtaking, Layla." I increase the pulse of my fingers. "So fucking breathtaking."

"Don't... stop." Her core clenches, her nails breaking through skin to bring the most gratifying burst of pain. "*Please.*"

I plunge deeper inside her. Press harder against her clit. With my free hand, I grab a fistful of her hair, guiding her neck to the side so I can devour her throat.

"Matthew," she wheezes.

I kiss.

Lick.

Suck.

"This is just the beginning, *amore mio*." I feast on the flesh below her ear as she shudders in my arms. "Wait until I fuck you. Wait until my cock is buried so goddamn deep you can't remember what life was like before I was inside you."

Air leaves her lips on a rapid rush. Her pussy flutters around my fingers. She comes undone, grinding into my touch, one hand reaching behind my neck to tear at my hair.

She cries out in orgasm, riding me, fucking killing me in the best possible way as her back arches, her breasts breaching the surface to give me the perfect view of her ruby pebbled nipples.

She whimpers. Whispers my name.

Then finally, she collapses against my chest, the arm around my neck slithering back to her side.

I slide my digits from her core, but don't stop touching her. I trail my fingertips around her pussy lips, straight up her center, and over her clit, the leisurely path lasting long minutes as she regains level breathing.

"I can't believe that just happened." She retracts her claws and slumps farther against me, sinking lower until the water is at her neck.

"Did you enjoy that little bit of fun?"

"Little bit of fun?" She glances over her shoulder, eyes wide. "I've never done anything like that before… In front of someone, I mean… It was…"

I'm about to grin at her purity when she turns back away, the faintest glimpse of shame flashing in her gaze before her face is no longer in view.

"Hey." I grab her jaw in gentle fingers and guide her stricken expression to look at me again. "You didn't enjoy yourself?"

"I did." She swallows and licks her lips. "But I'm…" She shakes her head. "I don't know who that woman was. All I know is it wasn't me."

Shit.

I release her jaw and inch back, extricating my softening dick from her tailbone.

I told her I'd push.

I warned her this would happen. I warned us both. I thought that had been enough to prepare her.

"Forgive me." My apology is unwittingly growled, my tone laced in self-loathing.

"No." She turns her entire body toward me, a wave of water escaping the lip of the tub to patter to the tiles. She's trembling again, the swelling on her cheek now darker and beginning to bruise. "I didn't want you to stop. I just…"

Just what? I want to beg her to continue but she's skittish. One wrong push and she'll run. I can see it in her eyes.

"You don't need to explain. I'll give you privacy to get out on your own." I lean forward, poised to stand when her hands clamp down on mine

"No. Don't go." She gives a bashful smile as she lowers her attention to my chest. "I'm sorry… I'm just shocked. That was the most thrilling thing I've ever done."

Her expression undoes me. The modesty that stands meekly in the shadows of a woman who seemed fearless last night.

"Tell me which part was thrilling, Layla." I settle back against the tub, relief pumping through my veins. "I want to know every little detail."

"All of it." Her teeth rake her lower lip, her attention still on my chest. "I'm making a fool of myself, aren't I?" She glances up through dark lashes. "I feel like a virginal teenager."

I reach out, gliding a stray strand of hair behind her ear, then gently brush my thumb over her damaged cheek. The bruising is deep, almost as deep as my anger toward the person who inflicted that pain.

"You're far from foolish." I guide my touch to her lower lip, grazing the soft flesh as I grin. "And don't worry. I like my women confident on the streets, and easily scandalized between the sheets."

Her laughter is instantaneous. Melodic.

Something about her finds a home inside me. Something that meshes without flaw.

I don't know how she came to be so perfect. But she is. Her courage and determination out in the real world is remarkable. Then the contrasting meekness once she's naked and vulnerable is enough to have me entirely hooked.

I envisaged her being a tigress in bed. Sure and poised and bold.

This modest kitten is far more detrimental to my composure.

"You're the devil." She holds my gaze, the bubbles licking over the tops of her breasts. "But do you know what?"

"What?"

Her face flushes as she whispers, "I'm starting to think I might really like you."

I snicker and push to my feet. Water and bubbles rush down my abdomen and thighs as she quickly glances away from my exposed dick. "Well, welcome to the party, *amore mio*. You arrived late, but I guess it's better than nothing."

14

———

LAYLA

I keep my gaze averted as he dries himself, my hands clinging to the rim of the tub, my heart wildly fluttering.

He likes me.

He actually likes me.

It's pathetic, but after a childhood when I was constantly watched by overbearing males who didn't allow boys near, then being forced to spend years with a man who found it hard to love me, all while being the daughter to a monster who used me for his devious games, the confounding exhilaration of someone actually liking me—*me*, Layla Hart—is such an incredible relief.

"You okay?" Matthew pulls on his suit pants in my periphery, then yanks at the zipper.

"I'm better than okay." I meet his gaze and the collision has his face falling.

"No, you're not." He frowns. "Something has upset you."

I shake my head and smile. It's a forced expression, but only due to the over-whelming whirlwind of sensation taking over my insides. "I'm perfect."

I really am.

For the first time in more than a decade something other than my daughter has brought joy to my life, and it's come in the form of a muscle-etched, stubble-ridden, gorgeous human whose eyes are currently scrutinizing mine.

"I'm going to give you space to clear your head." He snatches his shirt from the floor and slides his arms into the light material. "Have a glass of champagne. Call out if you need me."

"You don't want to stay?"

His grin returns. "I don't want to leave, but you need a moment to breathe. I'll come check on you soon."

He grabs his jacket and belt from the tile, and walks toward me, grabbing the ice bucket to place it closer. "Are you hungry? Is there anything else I can get for you?"

Just you.

Only you.

"Are you sure you don't want to stay?" The sound of my own fragility tightens my throat. I'm not going to be this woman—this needy, pathetic excuse for a full-blooded Torian. "Ignore me." I cringe. "I'll be out soon."

He leans down and kisses the top of my head, his fingers trailing along my shoulder in the briefest tease of contact. "I'll be waiting in the living room whenever you're ready."

He straightens and I feel the loss immediately. His steps toward the hall are torture. The isolation once he closes the door behind him is hell.

It takes all my self-control not to chase after him and finish what we started.

He didn't get a release.

He didn't ask for one, either.

Benji would never have let that happen. He didn't do selfless acts. Not in the bedroom. And—*shit*. I need to stop this. I have to quit comparing Matthew to my late husband because it always ends in guilt.

I'm not doing it anymore.

Benji is gone. And Matthew is only temporary.

I need to start enjoying this for what it is and leave the comparisons behind.

What I need is champagne.

I grab the bottle, pour myself a glass, and sip what has to be excessively expensive alcohol. And all the while, Matthew's touch haunts me like a ghost.

The memory of his lips on my neck.

The tingle from where his firm hands spread my thighs.

The more I drink, the more he fills my head. Not only sexually, but how he rescued me, too. The way he cradled me in the back of his car. The cadence in his words as he promised to look after me.

I push to my feet, wobble with the sudden shot vertical, then place my glass on the floor and grab a towel.

In less than two minutes I'm cocooned in a plush hotel robe, the champagne bottle in my hand along with the glasses as I pad to the end of the hall and find Matthew on the sofa.

He's hunched forward, elbows on knees, his back to me as he talks on his cell in snarled tones. "Tell him this is unacceptable. We had an agreement."

I wait there, not wanting to interrupt, not willing to get in the way of his work.

"I don't give a fuck," he snaps. "I think you know me well enough to understand I'm livid right now."

I stiffen at his vehemence, never having heard it before, and the glasses clink in my hand.

"I've gotta go." He straightens. "Layla is out of the bath."

I wince, wishing I'd been more discreet even though I refuse to be a snoop.

"She's doing well." Matthew glances at me over his shoulder, his annoyance nowhere in sight as he takes me in with appreciation. "The swelling is getting worse on her cheek, and there are marks on her arm, too. But she's strong."

My stomach warms with the compliment. With resurging lust and need, too.

I approach, placing the bottle and glasses on the table in front of him, remaining a foot away. I take him in while he leans back, relaxing into the sofa like a king atop his throne, one arm stretching along the headrest, an ankle crossing over his knee.

"Handle the situation, Bishop. Thoroughly." He rakes his gaze down the length of me, his eyes hungry. "I'll be ready to fly out at five." He disconnects the call and places the device on the far cushion. "You're flushed."

"It's the champagne," I lie.

It's definitely him. All him.

He leans forward, reaching out to grab the front of my robe to pull me closer. "I promised myself I'd give you space." He drags me down onto his lap, his hands fisting my lapels. "You're turning me into a liar."

I grin at our similarities and settle against his thighs, my palms finding his silk-covered pecs. "I don't want space."

"No, but you need it." His lips brush mine, once, twice, the kisses commanding but oh, so gentle. "Yesterday, you wanted nothing to do with me." He lowers his hands to seize my hips and guides me to move onto the cushion beside him.

"That's not true. I've wanted more from you since the moment we met. It's the complications that kept me away."

"And have those secretive complications changed since you were mugged?" He stands and stalks to the kitchen to grab a drinking glass from a cupboard, then fills it with water from the fridge. "I think I can answer for you in saying they haven't. The only difference from last night to today is a chemical imbalance brought on by shock." He returns, holding the chilled water out to me. "Drink. You can't live on alcohol alone."

Goddamnit, he's charming.

Big and broad and conniving. Yet sweet enough to cause cavities.

"Thank you." I stare up at him as I take his offering.

Maybe he's right. Maybe the fixation gnawing at my insides is only due to the scare I received. But even if it is, what does it matter? There's no future between us. There's only now, and I want to take advantage of our limited time.

"In answer to your question, no, the issues keeping me from being able to see you again haven't changed." I take a sip from the glass, not realizing how much I needed water until my throat throbs with the cool relief. "This is all we have. And I'm willing to take advantage of every minute if you are."

He moves to the armchair opposite me—the farthest seat in the living room—and sinks into the cream leather. "Minutes aren't what I'm after. A seized night every other Wednesday whenever I'm lucky to catch you at Perfezione won't be enough. I want more from you. Everything else is merely a provocation that won't satisfy."

I school my expression, not having anticipated the rejection. "Does that mean you want me to go back to my own room?"

"No." He scowls. "What I'm saying is that touching you—tasting you—only works as a taunt when I know I can't have everything. And I'm too old to torment myself that way."

Everything he says is a compliment.

I'm not sure if he's even aware of what he's doing. But his words act as a confidence booster. He tells me all the things I've dreamed of hearing. One after another, each perfectly constructed sentence making me crave him all the more.

"How old are you?" I ask, fighting the need to bite the inside of my mouth.

"Thirty-three. Old enough to no longer be satisfied with casual sex." He kicks his ankle back over his knee. Suave. Sophisticated. "What I want is a wife, *amore mio*. And children. Both of which I can easily picture with you."

"Excuse me?" I sputter, needing another sip of water to stop myself from choking.

"You heard me." He grins. "But my point is that fucking you isn't my only aim. Getting to know you is."

I swallow. Clear my throat. Swallow again.

Even if this didn't have to be temporary, I can't give him what he wants.

Dragging him into my world isn't an option. I already forced one man into the darkness that consumes my family. I refuse to do it again.

"Come back to D.C. with me tonight." He remains composed through the gentle demand. "Let us get to know one another. You'll have access to my jet to return home whenever you like. You'll be safe at all times."

My pulse increases as a lifetime of emotions batter down on me.

I can't withstand the yearning. The hope. There's happiness, and excitement, too. But they're all washed away with the tidal wave of guilt, heartache, and longing.

I'm not meant for happy things.

"I'm sorry, I can't." I place my water on the table, using the movement as an excuse to drag my gaze from his.

"Why?"

It's a simple question. If only the answer wasn't entirely complex and multi-layered.

There's my family. My lifestyle. The dangers and threats. Not to mention why I'm in Denver in the first place. But I can't tell him any of that. He can't know who I am.

"Why, Layla? Can't you give me that much? Is it your job? Do you have responsibilities to get back to?"

I wince, not wanting to lie to him. "It's a lot of things I can't explain."

"Can't or won't?" He sits forward, returning to his elbows-on-knees position, his attention bearing down on me. "I already know you're spying on the Costas. What else do you need to hide?"

If the question is a provocation to get me to look at him, it works. I meet his gaze, my pulse hammering in my throat, my heart squeezing with each rampant beat.

I want him to know me. *Truly* know me. But the knowledge wouldn't work in my favor.

"Talk to me," he demands. "You don't get to share your body then simply walk away."

If I don't simply walk away, you wind up dead.

I don't tell him that, though. I don't give him the truth that would stop this inquisition in its tracks.

Instead, I resign myself to giving him a different glimpse into my life. A slightly less confronting admission to get him to back off. "I have a daughter."

For a second, I don't think the news bothers him.

His confidence and sophistication remain in place. Then, gradually, as if being siphoned by the smallest filter, his forthright stare turns weak. Those dark eyes lose their intensity. His lips part.

The change is incremental. Entirely punishing in its lethargy. But it's there, the disappointment blinking back at me under midnight lashes.

"See? This is why I didn't want to say anything. *This—*" I indicate the disturbance and turmoil now surrounding us with a wave of my hand, "—is exactly why I wanted to remain anonymous."

And to think the existence of Stella is merely the tip of my complicated iceberg. He has no idea who he's trying to get involved with.

"I guess it's best if we part ways now." I push to my feet. "I appreciate everything you've done for me. I'll see myself out."

"No, you won't." He follows suit, bridging the distance around the coffee table in three determined steps to grab my robe-covered wrist. "You can't blame me for being caught off guard. I didn't expect you to be a mother. Not when there are no scars on your body. No stretch marks. Not even the barest hint of imperfection to indicate you carried and mothered a child. But that's all this is, Layla. Shock." He leans his face into mine, demanding I meet his pleading gaze. "Having a kid isn't a deal breaker for me."

Christ.

Who is this man? And what is he doing with my previously cemented conceptions of the opposite sex?

"Well, it is for me." I square my shoulders, steeling myself against his charm. "Nothing is more important to me than my daughter. Nothing ever will be." I twist my arm from his grip. "I still think it's best if I leave."

I hate the hesitance in my voice. I want him to stop me and I need him not to in the same breath. Before I can fall victim to my own weakness, I trek to the hall and into the bathroom to reclaim my clothes, wishing things didn't have to be this way.

My shoulder doesn't ache nearly as much when I pull on my stained blouse and jeans. It's my chest that takes the brunt of my pain.

The emotional toll of this romantic rendezvous gets to me, sinking deeper and deeper until I raise my gaze and find him standing in the bathroom doorway.

"Is she—" His question falls short, his brows pinched as he drags a rough hand over his mouth. "Is one of those assholes her father? Is that why you've got eyes on Remy and Salvatore? Did they turn you away once they found out?"

"*No.*" I glare, despising the thought of those men fathering any child, let alone mine. "My *husband* is Stella's father. She's almost eleven."

Matthew's features relax.

That's what he was worried about?

That's what caused the change in his demeanor?

I guess I can't blame him for thinking my enemy was my baby daddy when I've played along with his scorned lover assumption.

"My daughter has nothing to do with me being in Denver." I ignore the regret that accompanies the lie. I can't allow her to become more involved in this. "But she's one of the reasons we can't go beyond today. I'm a mother who lives on the opposite side of the country to you."

"Portland isn't more than a plane flight."

Panic descends in a blinding rush, stealing the breath from my lungs before I can rein it in. I stare at him, aghast, partially livid, entirely caught off guard. "I never told you where I was from."

I should've held my cards closer to my chest. Should've played along, pretending I hadn't noticed the insight I never gave. But out of all the time we've spent together, right here, right now is the only instance where I hadn't expected him to surprise me with deception.

Everything he's done for me today lulled me into lowering my guard.

"I overheard the tail end of your conversation with the bank." He raises his hands, offering surrender. "I was checking on you, and when I heard private information being shared I didn't hang around."

I want to believe him. The added squeeze of discomfort in my chest makes it obvious this isn't just personal, it's emotional. I've already been swept off my feet.

"What else did you hear?"

"Nothing." His hands fall to his sides. "You still have your anonymity for now."

I hold his gaze, trying to see any hidden deceit.

All that blinks back at me is sincerity. A cloying, agonizing seriousness that makes me want to blurt everything to him—my secrets, my failures. I need him to know the ins and outs of my life so he can find me lacking, because having him stare at me with adoration is a gift I don't deserve.

He moves forward, approaching with slow caution.

"Don't." I backtrack, needing more time to catalogue the seriousness of his newfound knowledge. "Give me space."

His jaw hitches as if I've struck him. "Why? Am I the enemy now?"

No, he's the exact opposite. He's the blessing I'm not entitled to. The warmth and happiness I haven't earned. At least, not yet.

"Why, Layla? Tell me."

I shake my head, attempting to fight how he's already come to mean something to me even though we remain strangers.

"Tell me." He continues up to me, his palms gently gliding over my biceps. "If you want me gone, I'm gone. I'm only staying in town for you." He leans his hips against mine, suffusing me with warmth. "Tell me what you want from me."

"I don't know," I whisper, backtracking farther, only endeavoring to drag him along with me.

"Then tell me what you don't want." He follows until I'm caged against the vanity.

"I don't want to do something I'll regret." I've already endured too much of that. I can't take any more.

"Like getting caught up with me?"

I close my eyes. Even behind clamped lids I see him. His intent. His hunger. "Like missing an opportunity to be with someone like you," I admit.

His grip tightens on my arms. "Then don't." He leans closer, the brush of his breath skating over my lips. "We'll find a way to make this work."

"It's not that simple."

"Make it simple." His voice becomes a growl. "Forget the complications."

"I have a daughter," I repeat into the darkened void.

"And where is she now?"

My heart squeezes. "At boarding school." Far from where I want her to be— under my roof, in my arms. I'd had no choice in her leaving at the start of the first semester a month ago.

Cole had made plans to send Tobias to the illustrious school in Chicago a year prior. What I didn't anticipate was my crippling eruption of grief when Stella begged to go with him.

"She doesn't live with me," I whisper.

I'd tried to talk her out of leaving for months. I'd pleaded, bribed, and coerced to the best of my abilities. But nothing I did persuaded her to change her mind, and I couldn't bring myself to make the decision for her. I'd already stripped enough from her life.

I also refused to take my concerns to Cole.

He granted my wish the day my husband was buried. He went against his usually unbreakable beliefs on retaliation and let those who pulled the trigger on Benji walk away scot-free.

I had no right to ask for more favors.

"That's why you can travel to Denver whenever you like?" Matthew asks.

I nod. My daughter's absence is why I'm here. For more reasons than one.

Within days of her leaving, I'd realized the innumerable sporting and craft distractions I'd scheduled to fill her time since her father's death were actually a benefit I'd also grown reliant upon.

I'd needed those long drives to baseball and the homework sessions to keep *me* occupied. To divert *my* thoughts. Because with her gone, my idle mind became a vicious mistress who demanded action.

"I'm here for a reason." I open my eyes, my inhale hitching at the deep brown that stares back at me. "I can't afford to be distracted."

It's clear in the tight set of his lips that he understands what I'm referencing.

I've spent every spare minute stalking my enemies since Stella moved away. Learning exactly how wonderful the Costas' world became since they murdered Benji.

I don't regret begging Cole not to retaliate. The years of peace were necessary to get my daughter and I back on our feet. But my spying made it clear it was now time to set things straight.

I need redemption, and they deserve to suffer.

"I don't want to be a distraction." Matthew lowers his hands to my waist, gripping me tight to raise me onto the counter. "The Costas aren't a family to be messed with, Layla. Snooping around isn't safe. I can fuck with them enough for us both. Just tell me which one of them to target and what you want done."

And with those admissions, I'd be handing over insight I'm not willing to give.

He'd know I wasn't a scorned lover focused on a single family member. He'd be fully aware my thirst for revenge runs far deeper, my intentions more vicious than spying due to lover's heartbreak.

"Let me think on it," I lie.

I can't.

I won't.

I have to do this without him.

I spread my thighs, welcoming him between my legs, succumbing to the allure of his strength just for a moment. He has no clue *my* family are far more insidious than the Costas.

Dark folktales have been created about my brother. Worse were made with my father in mind.

It's a given in the criminal world. Ghost stories are brought to life from a slither of reality. Like the Butcher Boys of Baltimore.

The Dark Death in Dallas.

Freddy Fingers from Arizona.

My brother's enforcer—Hunter—has his own moniker, too, one I'm sure was built on fact.

But Emmanuel Costa is different. He isn't a blip on the underworld radar. And he sure as hell doesn't scare me.

"Think as long as you like." Matthew leans closer, brushing the tips of our noses, the intimate contact making me yearn for things I can't have. "There's no rush as long as I know you're mine."

His possessive words coil around me, strong and delicious. I eat them up despite knowing they're not meant for me. Not *made* for the type of person I am.

He wouldn't even think them if he knew who I was.

"You don't under—"

He cuts me off with a kiss, punishing and hard, before retreating. "I can make this work, Layla. Just tell me it's what you want."

It is.

God, how it is.

I want him and us and this.

I want fun and happiness and lust.

I crave all the things he's shown me and all those that wait in the wings. But—

"Stop thinking yourself out of this and tell me what I want to hear," he whispers against my lips. "I want you, *amore mio*. And I know you want me, too. Chemistry doesn't lie."

No, it doesn't. I'd never even known the power of attraction until we met. The strength of it. The delicate suffocation of sense and control.

I stare into those demanding eyes, hating how easy it would be to lead him on just for a few more moments of bliss.

He teases his mouth over mine, his tongue grazing my lips. "Tell me."

I whimper, too weak to withstand temptation. "I'm yours," I whisper.

For now.

Until the moment he leaves for D.C.

15

———————

LAYLA

After unending kisses upon the vanity counter that send my blood racing, Matthew swoops me into his arms and returns me to the sofa.

He ignores my panted breaths, and the lust I know glistens in my eyes with every docile blink, and places distance between us like a devout gentleman, making sure I hold a cooling pack to my cheek for hours.

We talk. Laugh. And even though I don't want to, I fall, not just hard, but whole-heartedly, for a man I barely know.

He orders room service. We eat oysters and drink more champagne. He asks question after conversational question and listens to the answers with a level of interest most don't pay me. And he isn't intrusive.

He asks about my happiness.

He wants to know all the intricate details of my soul. From my favorite sounds, to the places in the world I love most, and every trivial piece of information in between.

He takes in the tidbits I share with unwavering focus, devouring the insight like I'm an anticipated book he's finally able to read. Not merely listening, but learning. Studying. He seems to take note of the cadence in my voice, and holds my gaze longer when I attempt to guard myself, waiting for me to expose the truth.

And I do. For the most part.

Everything I tell him is real. It just isn't deep.

I skate on the shallowest depths of my being, never truly letting him in even though I want to.

And although we don't kiss or claw at each other's clothes again, he has me in a constant state of thrumming tingles with his attention, his gaze raking over me with slow deliberation.

By late afternoon, I have a full belly and a body that has succumbed to adrenaline detox. Yawns come every other minute until Matthew demands I rest my head on a cushion he places on his lap.

81

We continue learning surface-level details about each other, neither of us asking the finer questions because we both know everything else is off-limits.

And our time together is still perfect.

I don't need to know his surname and he isn't getting mine. I don't ask about the darkness from his past, but I learn of his love for Switzerland and his hatred of hot weather.

He finger-combs my hair, his touch perfectly gentle for such a strong man, as I lay cuddled around his waist.

He makes sure I still have access to money to get home. That I have ID stored in my cell to be able to board a flight. He treats me like a treasure as my heart becomes full and my eyes grow heavy.

Sleep is inevitable. The adrenaline and alcohol knock my feet out from beneath me, and all I want is a nap. I just expected him to still be here when I woke.

Instead, the only thing left behind is a note on the coffee table in a now empty suite.

AMORE MIO,

I couldn't wake you for two reasons:

1. It seemed sacrilegious when you sleep like an angel.

2. I didn't want to give you closure by saying goodbye.

This isn't the end for us, even though I assume you've told yourself it would be. We will see each other again. I'll make sure of it.

M.

I'M SUCKER PUNCHED by the intense level of desperation and heartache that overwhelm me once I realize he's gone.

His presence lingers in the bedroom. His delicious scent clings to the sheets. And even after I leave his suite, I can't release myself from the hold he has on me.

I cancel the last remaining night on my reservation and return home to a place that doesn't feel the same as it had when I left.

I'm not the same.

The tingle in my chest inspired by Matthew's existence stays with me. I can still smell him. Can still feel the brush of his lips against mine.

But when Stella and Tobias come home Friday night, I put the infatuation to the back of my mind and dedicate the time to my daughter.

I thrive in our moments alone, because thanks to my brother, I only get to see her one weekend a month.

We watch movies and talk about boys. We eat popcorn, give each other mani-pedis, and make up for the distance usually placed between us.

As much as I hate her living in Chicago, it has become clear she's flourishing with the independence.

Maybe I am, too.

She didn't even notice the swelling on my cheek, the bruising now hidden beneath numerous compacted layers of foundation.

We spend two wonderful days together, made all the better by the sordid text messages Matthew sends me on the regular. He's become my dirty little secret. A treasure for me and me alone.

Each silenced vibration of my cell chips away at my resolve to keep things casual. I grow empowered by his determination, loving the way my confidence builds with his attention.

Our monthly family lunch on Sunday at Cole's house feels different, too. Usually I have a sense of underlying heartache whenever I'm surrounded by the perfect pigeon pairs. Everyone has a partner to rely on. Cole has Anissa. Then there's Hunt and Sarah, Keira and Decker, as well as Luca and Penny.

This time, there's no pain or jealousy.

I can't even wipe the subtle smile from my face as we all hug in greeting.

It feels like Matthew is here with me. Or maybe could be in the future.

I spend the meal daydreaming about what my perfect world would look like. How Matthew would take the seat by my side at upcoming dinners. How he'd understand who I was and where I came from without judgment or anger.

I deliberately skip past the introduction phase in my mind, knowing the first few months would be filled with paranoia and interrogation from Cole. But what came afterward would be bliss.

We'd cuddle on the sofa, unashamed of any public display of affection. We'd have each other's backs. And for once, I'd be the one to make everyone jealous because my relationship was enviable, not fake and devoid of emotion.

It isn't until Stella and Tobias leave the dinner table to escape into the backyard that my daydreaming stops.

Everyone else's hype and excitement over having the kids home disappears as if it were a facade. Keira, Penny, Sarah, and Anissa fall quiet. Cole, Hunter, Decker, and Luca's conversation becomes stilted, their responses turning sharp and gruff.

I missed the cause of the transition while in my imaginary state.

Something that must have been important.

I glance at each of them as I nibble on a bread stick, the hair on the back of my neck standing on end when more than one of them meet my gaze before quickly glancing away.

This is about me.

The tension seeping into the air is somehow my doing.

I discard the half-eaten bread stick onto my plate and pat the corner of my mouth with a cloth napkin. "I'll pack the dishwasher."

I push to my feet, preparing to cut and run. Nothing good can come from this vibe.

"Sit," Cole grates. "We've got things to discuss."

My stomach grows heavy. "Like what?" I reach for my sister's cutlery to my right, pretending I'm immune to the tension.

Anissa pastes on a friendly smile. "How have you been handling life without Stella?"

"I'm doing well." I fight a frown. It's no secret my brother's wife and I have had our share of trials over the years. We don't do feelings, which is why it's strange for her to ask. "Obviously, it's tough. But I'm handling it."

"You're glowing," Penny adds. "Have you met someone?"

My hand pauses in the middle of reaching for the dirty serving spoons. I'm caught at what to say and know it seems entirely forced when I chuckle a few seconds later. "I guess my new skincare regime is working. I have late-night online tutorials to thank for that."

"It's definitely working," she adds. "I've never seen you like this."

My heart pangs. Guilt follows.

She's never seen me like this because I've never felt like this. Not even while married.

"Is this new skincare regime the reason you cancelled your credit card?" Cole raises a taunting brow. "Have you been making purchases from a disreputable company? Were you scammed?"

He's playing with me. Mocking. The worst part is, nobody attempts to save me from his underlying recrimination. They all sit and stare, waiting for answers.

"I lost my purse." I hold my brother's gaze. "It's not a big deal."

"When you were out of town?" Keira asks.

"Yes," I grate. "While I was out of town."

I keep staring at Cole as his eyes narrow, the authority in his gaze raising my apprehension. I know this look. I know what comes along with it, too.

"You've met someone." Keira pushes from her chair and grabs my dirtied plate topped with cutlery. "That much is obvious. You walked in here with a bounce in your step and this subtle giddy smile." She starts for the kitchen. "I don't know what I've done to be blocked from the happiness in your life, Lay, but it hurts that you didn't share this with me."

I don't deny her observation.

I keep staring at my brother as crockery clutters into the sink. He's angry, but not like my sister. The tightening in his jaw lets me know he's positively fuming.

"What, Cole?" I sigh. "You told me months ago that it was time to move on. Are you retracting your approval now that you've seen me happy for once?"

"So it's true?" He leans back in his chair, crossing his arms over his suit-clad chest. "You've met a man?"

I raise my chin, unwilling to voice a response.

Despite daydreaming about romance, I didn't let myself truly believe there was a possibility of a relationship until now. Until the moment when my brother could destroy it for me.

"Is he the one who hit you?" he seethes.

All eyes remain on me, the weight of their scrutiny making me nauseous.

"No." I square my shoulders, raise my chin, and bite back an emotional response. I can't win this battle unless I focus. "He didn't hit me."

"Then who did?"

"I fell." I use all the conviction I have to continue holding his stare. "I tripped on the sidewalk and stumbled into a brick wall. It's no big deal."

Cole shoves aggressively from the table, the legs of his chair screeching across the tile. "Don't fucking lie to me." He leans forward, placing clenched fists on either side of his dinner plate.

I don't react. Don't move. One badly timed blink and he'll dig in his heels, demanding to know everything. Not only about Matthew, but about where we met, and why I was there.

He can't learn about Denver. If he finds out he'll put a stop to my plans, then I'll never be able to make amends or prove my loyalty to him.

"Cole," Anissa warns. "Calm down."

His nostrils flare as he glares. "Who is he? Tell me his name."

My heart lodges in my throat. "It wasn't him."

"*Bullshit.*"

I swallow, caught between wanting to scream and needing to crumple. "You think I'd be walking around with the giddy smile Keira mentioned if the man I was interested in hit me?"

"I don't know, Lay. Especially not when you married a man you didn't love and watched him fuck around on you for years."

My face drains of warmth, all the blood seeping from my cheeks.

He knew.

Of course he did. It was stupid to assume otherwise.

I guess it was even more idiotic to assume my brother would care enough to do something about my husband's indiscretions. But it's the humiliation that stings. They won't understand why I ignored the existence of Benji's mistresses. They'll assume I have no self-respect.

"Careful," Luca warns. "Benji isn't here to defend himself."

"This isn't about your brother," Cole snarls.

My pulse increases, pounding in my throat.

Usually I can understand Cole's protective nature. I don't always like it, but there has always been an understanding of why he is the way he is.

Now is different, though. This isn't merely protection. There's resentment in the mix. Disgust, too. Both byproducts that stem from the bad decisions I made in the past. Decisions he refuses to stop holding against me.

"Fine." I speak through clenched teeth. "I was mugged. That's why I needed to cancel the credit card. My purse was stolen and I got shoved into a wall. I'm not being abused. I haven't made any more bad choices. I was just in the wrong place at the wrong time."

Silence descends before the most out-of-place chuckle carries from outside as the kids remain oblivious to our argument.

"Why didn't you say something?" Hunter mutters. "If you're in a position where you're getting mugged, you need to—"

"*What?*" I fix my brother's enforcer with a scowl. "I need to do what, Hunter? Quit leaving the house? Lock myself inside? Go back to living a non-existent life just so you think I'm perfectly managed?"

"Watch your mouth," Cole warns.

"No. I won't." I glare. "I didn't tell you—I *couldn't* tell you—because I knew how you'd react. You always fly off the handle. You've spied on me like I'm a goddamn traitor since Benji died."

"You can't deny your track record of making smart decisions is lacking."

His verbal strike hacks at my confidence. "You're never going to let me forget my mistakes, are you?"

I never should've given my father information on Cole. I'd naively thought I'd been looking out for my family because, back then, my brother was a hothead who enjoyed spilling the blood of anyone who glanced sideways at him.

There were whispers he'd start a drug war for frivolous reasons.

For pride. Or spite. Or even arrogance.

So I kept my father updated on his son. I gave him insight when he couldn't seek it for himself because he'd fled the country. And I convinced Benji to do the same.

It was for the family's safety.

For our future.

Back then, I hadn't known who my father was. *What* he was. I would've killed him myself if I'd known about the sex trafficking.

To me, he was the same man who'd always denied me attention.

Affection.

Love.

His request created the only bond I'd ever had with him. The one connection between us. So when he offered financial compensation for the information I'd already been giving freely, I didn't see it as a bribe. It was merely a strengthening of our building relationship.

At least, that was what I told myself until he proved otherwise.

The thickening tension builds.

The men at the table judge me with annoyance and disappointment. The women do the same with shame and embarrassment.

Every second, every blink, every sigh or noise of displeasure scampers under my skin, the toxicity finding a home inside me.

"I think we need to end this conversation before it gets out of hand." Sarah pushes from her chair and grabs the salad bowl. "I vote that the women clear the table and the men stack the dishwasher."

This is far from over.

Cole will keep hounding me. Will keep holding everything against me until I finally stand up to him.

"I'm not done." My eyes burn as I stare my brother down. "I've apologized over and over again. I've tried my best to make amends. I let you bug my house when you said you couldn't trust me. I allowed your guards to follow me—to invade my home and my privacy—because that's what you wanted, even though I despised having strange men in my home when Stella and I were at the height of our grief."

"And?"

I bite my tongue, caught between crying and screaming. "And I didn't protest when you deliberately sent Tobias to boarding school because you knew Stella would follow. She was all I had, Cole. The only thing to bring me happiness, and I let her go.

All for you. I've done everything you've asked of me. But I won't allow you to dictate my life anymore."

"You won't allow me?" He raises a brow, his livid rage crackling below the surface.

Someone curses under their breath. Hunter or Decker. I'm not sure because I don't drag my gaze from the severity in my brother's eyes.

"Yes. I won't allow you." I stand my ground. "Everyone at this table has made mistakes. Every single one of them. Yet, two years later, their sins are forgiven and mine seem brand new. Why is that?"

"They're not blood," he snarls.

"They're not *blood*?" My voice rises without my consent, the tone filling with feminine emotion I despise as I swing an arm toward my sister in the kitchen. "Keira made mistakes, too. And don't get me started on your wife."

He flashes his teeth in a snarl. "Choose your words wisely, sister."

"I have. For *years*. I've done everything wisely, with extreme caution, always keeping everyone here at the forefront of my mind because I want to make up for what I did. For how I allowed my own father to manipulate me. But that's what it was, Cole—manipulation. Our father tricked me. *Used* me. Just like he used so many others. And yes, I know it's still my fault. And yes, I profited from it and have to live with my decisions for the rest of my life. But what I won't live with is you throwing it back in my face whenever the whim takes you." I sniff to kill the tingle in my nose. "I won't take the overbearing protectiveness anymore. I won't play along with you thinking you can decide where I go and what I do. Or that you need to know why I cancelled my credit card or how I got a goddamn bruise on my face. What I do now is my business."

Cole raises his chin, slow and deliberate, the anger receding as smug superiority takes its place. Then he inclines his head as if in agreement.

"That's it?" I frown. "You're not going to say anything?"

He gives a faint shrug. "You're doing me a favor."

That hurts.

Really hurts.

I want to hunch from the pain he slices through me, his rejection tearing open old wounds as my eyes burn like wildfire.

"Cole," Anissa pleads. "Don't say something you'll regret."

"I won't regret it, little fox." He keeps his gaze on me as he speaks to his wife. "As far as I see it, this is perfect timing. Layla no longer wants me to know her business, and I'm more than happy for her not to know mine."

There's an ominous ring in his tone. Something that alludes to a deeper meaning.

"You see, sister, I've wanted nothing more than to claim retribution against those who murdered my niece's father for years. But I held back because you begged. You fucking pleaded in the most pathetic display of weakness I've ever seen. So I gave you what you wanted. What *you* needed to move on, because I couldn't risk you jumping further off the rails. But with this new outlook on our relationship, I guess I'm no longer burdened by your wants and needs. I can take what I'm owed. What we're *all* owed."

I stiffen, my lungs tightening.

He's going to claim the retribution I've been trying so hard to achieve. He's going to take the only chance I have to right my wrongs.

I panic, wanting to backtrack but not knowing how. "What are you going to do?"

"I'm sure you'd love to know." He looks at me with self-righteous indignation. "Unfortunately, though, it's now clear we don't share that kind of information."

16

LAYLA

"You're not going to tell me?" My limbs quake with fury.

"You tell me yours. I'll tell you mine." Cole smirks, the curve of his lips sickening in its arrogance.

"Fuck you, you manipulative piece of shit." I shove at my place mat, the heavy material scooting forward to topple the salt and pepper shakers. "You're just like our father."

His eyes flare. I don't stick around to take more of his toxicity. I storm for the sofa, snatching the old purse I'd found at home to tug the strap over my shoulder.

"Layla, wait." Keira hustles toward me from the kitchen. "Don't go."

"I'm not staying." I continue to the sliding glass doors leading outside and yank them apart, plastering on a fake smile as the gentle breeze brushes my face. "Stella, it's time to leave, sweetheart."

She raises her gaze from her cell screen and snaps a glance toward Tobias sitting on the lounger beside her. "I'll see you at the airport?"

"Yeah." He jerks his chin and gives me a quick finger wave. "See you next time."

I should hug him goodbye. I should at least walk out there to speak to him properly, but I'm the shortest step away from my breaking point. One inch in the wrong direction and I'll drop this temperamental bag of emotions and cause a scene.

A *far* bigger one.

I keep my sham of a smile in place for Stella's sake and wait patiently at the front door for her to say her farewells, my animosity bubbling below the surface.

Cole and I always disagree. We fight. It hurts. This isn't a first.

What derails me, though, is how I'd become used to the idea of me being the Costas' downfall. That I'd be the one to gain vengeance for my daughter being abducted and my husband's murder.

I wanted that accountability.

The atonement.

I need it.

I battle the panic of approaching failure as I escort Stella to my car parked out front and drive us both home. I don't allow her to see how my world is crumbling. How I've let her down again.

While she's busy packing for her return to school, I do the same, grabbing clothing and toiletries. I also arrange store-bought debit cards and stockpile cash for a longer-than-usual escape. And when it comes time to drop Stella at the airport, she has no idea a suitcase of my own is stashed in the trunk.

I kiss her goodbye in one heartbeat and stride my ass to a check-in counter to book a flight to D.C. in the next.

I don't spare more than a thought at not knowing Matthew's surname, or where he lives, or even works for that matter.

I fly across the country on impulse, arriving after nine at night with absolutely no clue where to go once I climb into a cab.

Layla: Tell me about these clubs of yours. What are their names?

My text to Matthew spits in the face of the anonymity we've tried to maintain. Our contact since Denver has been mostly seductive or complimentary, and my stomach twists with the possibility of him ignoring me entirely.

Matthew: Why, amore mio? Searching for skeletons?

I should be. By now, an extensive background check would've been done if Cole was involved. But I haven't snooped. Instead, I've fallen deeper, and allowed trust to blossom where skepticism should.

Layla: One day I might make a surprise visit. But I can't do that if I don't know where you work.

His reply is instantaneous—*Don't tease, woman.*

Layla: Me, tease? Never. Just tell me where you're likely to be if I arrive in D.C. unannounced.

He doesn't respond. Not for several long minutes that turn my stomach into a bile pit.

I glance out the cab window, my teeth gnawing my lower lip as I watch the illuminated skyline pass by.

This can't be a mistake. I won't let it be.

If I misjudged Matthew's interest I won't allow the rejection to sting. He may have wanted me here days ago, but those were his terms. His timeline. Now could be different. There may be another woman on his arm. And God knows we're far from claiming exclusivity.

If things don't work out, I'll take this as an endeavor to gain breathing room from my family. I'll indulge in spa treatments. Get my hair done. Dine in fancy restaurants.

Three dots appear in the text chat, the anticipation of his response forcing me to hold my breath.

Matthew: Mon-Tues, I'm usually on the coast. Wed-Thur, in Richmond. Fri-Sun, I'm in DC at Trend or The Mill.

I exhale in relief.

In appreciation.

He's opening up to me. *Trusting* me. And he's also in town.

Layla: You know what they say—all work and no play makes Matthew…

The dots appear again. This time, the reply comes quicker. *It makes Matthew preoccupied with work so he doesn't fall victim to thoughts of the woman he's obsessing over.*

I smile, big and bright enough for the lingering swelling in my injured cheek to make itself known.

Layla: Does this woman know about us?

I bite my lip, hoping for a flirtatious response.

Nothing comes.

I'm driven further and further into the heart of D.C. Closer and closer to the hotel I booked last minute, yet those three dots never reappear.

It's hard not to take it as a sign. Maybe he does have another woman. Maybe I'm the mistress this time.

I refuse to dwell once I'm delivered to the front doors of my accommodation and check into my room.

I change clothes, pulling on a tight black dress that leaves little to the imagination, before perfecting my makeup. The bruising on my face is now easily hidden, but that's no longer all I'm striving for. I don't merely want to cover up.

I want to slay.

When I'm as flawless as I'm going to get, I grab my purse and make my way toward the first club he mentioned—*Trend*.

I don't tell him I'm coming. I don't even message once I arrive at the front of the building to find an illuminated white script sign of the club's name elegantly placed above an entirely black brick wall, the lone door framed by two hulking bouncers.

This needs to be a surprise. Not only so I can judge if he's excited to see me. It's to cast aside any lingering concerns. I don't want him to have time to prepare or hide those skeletons.

If he has secrets, I need to know now, while I can still walk away with my head high.

"You can drop me off here." I unclasp my belt and pay the cab driver in cash before getting out.

I join the end of the small line of people waiting to get inside, show the ID stored on my cell when it's my turn, and then walk into the darkened entry, the carpet beneath me barely visible as loud music thunders from the dance floor up ahead.

I reach the main area without drama and stop at the railing that sets me apart from the dance floor a few steps below.

For a Sunday night, the interior is swarming with people bopping and drinking along to the techno beats.

The place is massive. A two-level rave fest with a glowing purple bar in the center of the ground floor with more along the side walls, and a glass-encased room upstairs.

I can't help being impressed. But it's not the hyped crowd or glistening bars that steal my attention. It's Matthew, who stands on the middle landing of the metal staircase leading to the upper level, both hands gripping the banister as he scrutinizes the crowd, the flash of lights making him look hardened and devilish.

My heart flutters.

He's wearing another stylish suit, his stubble now thick along his chiseled jaw. His hair falls around his eyes, framing the perfection, while his lips are pulled thin.

God, he's attractive.

My body reacts as if he were made for me. Born to the exact requirements that stoke my libido to its highest peak.

I don't know how it's possible to be this captivated. This magnetized. But I am.

All the way down to my curling toes.

He remains a statue of confidence before the crowd as a woman climbs the stairs toward him, her long, dark hair plaited over one shoulder, her attention intent as she sways her hips in a skirt that has to be giving those on the dance floor an indecent view.

My throat dries the closer she gets, my heart taking on a panicked rhythm.

She stops at his side, placing a hand on his arm, the touch seeming sexually familiar even from this distance.

Shit.

I step back, wanting to shrink into the shadows.

Matthew stands there without reaction, still eyeing the crowd as she inches into him, her breasts brushing his bicep as she speaks close to his ear.

They're together.

They have to be. A woman wouldn't approach a man with his current icy demeanor unless she had carnal confidence.

I retreat another step, apologizing as I bump into someone behind me. But I can't take my eyes off him. I can't quit staring at the approaching car wreck that will knock my feet out from beneath me.

I can already feel it. The impact of heartache. The collision of fantasy and reality.

I fell too hard, too fast.

I'm stupid for thinking our tryst had depth when even our conversations didn't.

I shake my head, attempting to dislodge the self-loathing as he continues to eye the crowd, the woman now leaning in to press her mouth to his neck.

I'm such an idiot. We've only spent one goddamn weekend together and a handful of texts, and here I am, shattered.

Matthew jerks back from the dark-haired woman and turns on her, a flash of overhead light illuminating a face filled with anger. He says something, his words unkind if the way she straightens and balks is any indication, while my pathetic ass clings to hope.

They're arguing.

Fighting.

He remains cold as he speaks, his confident posture unwavering until she raises a hand to slap his face.

I jostle with the impact more than he does, and blink in shock as she storms back down where she came from. I don't realize I'm panting until she disappears into the dancing crowd.

All the while, Matthew remains unfazed, pivoting back to grasp the railing like nothing happened.

I'm more stunned than he is, and I don't know whether I should leave or stay. The flighty flutter of my heart has no intention of letting me escape without answers. The brutal twist of my stomach makes me question if I want to learn the truth.

I'd thought of him as a gentleman. A sly, devious gentleman, but a gentleman all the same.

Now I'm not so sure.

And still, I crave.

Even after witnessing that drama, I can't stop wanting him. Can't stop making excuses for what just happened.

The woman obviously couldn't take no for an answer.

His body language had been clear. Hell, I could see his lack of interest and I'm ten yards away.

What unsettles me, though, is the difficulty in aligning this severely frosty man with the flirting and smoothness of the one I'm accustomed to. This side of Matthew doesn't fit the person I've been fantasizing about.

This guy is different.

I'm about to turn on my heel to rethink my options at the hotel when someone else climbs the stairs. A hulk of a man this time—Bishop.

The temperamental offsider leans in to say something to his friend and this time, there's an immediate reaction.

Matthew stiffens, his face pinching as his attention glides in a straight line right to where I stand. Those eyes take me in, holding me immobile while his harshness evaporates with a sly grin.

Goddamn. Gorgeous.

I swallow over the desert claiming my throat and curse my fluttering pulse.

He maneuvers around Bishop and descends the stairs to the ground floor. I can't see his face as he parts the dancing crowd like a warrior destined to decimate.

His eyes don't meet mine again until he's a breath from the few steps in front of me, his confident stride jumping them in one fell swoop to stop before me.

There are no words. No niceties.

He wraps a hand around my neck and hauls me in to steal my mouth with his.

I gasp against his lips. My doubts vanish. Self-control disappears.

I'm breathless, my mind spinning as he awakens my body with his kiss. Then, just as fast, he pulls away and instructs me to follow him.

He grabs my hand, leading me back to where he came from. Through the crowd, up the metal stairs, to the glass-encased room.

My palm is at home in his. The tight hold. The possession consuming.

He escorts me inside the soundproof area, the noise still loud but from chatting people this time, and takes me to the bar, the counter illuminated by a dark blue glow. Then he kisses me again, one hand clutching mine, the other tangling in the hair at my nape.

I lose myself in him. The concerns disappear, too.

Despite the crowd around us, it's only me and him. The two of us in our own little world.

"This is a nice surprise," he murmurs against my lips.

"Not as much of a surprise as I wanted." I keep my eyes closed, our noses touching. "Did Bishop see me arrive?"

"You're hard to miss. Especially in that phenomenal dress. How the hell do you keep knocking me off my feet?"

I meet his hungry gaze and fight a needy whimper.

He evokes so much animalistic ferocity it's agonizing. I'd give anything to be alone with him. One-on-one. Naked.

"You have the same effect," I admit, raising my hand to trail my fingers over the red mark on his left cheek. "Who was that woman?"

His expression doesn't falter. I don't catch the slightest glimpse of guilt. "Do you really want to know?"

Yes. *No.*

I sigh. "Unfortunately, I can't unsee what happened and my imagination isn't kind."

He straightens his shoulders. "Let me get you a drink first."

Shit. Is it that bad?

"Wine?" He raises a brow and steps away to walk around the bar. "Vodka? Maybe a cocktail?"

"Surprise me."

He smiles as if appreciating my trust, and begins making my concoction, swirling bottles, deftly adding shots while the bartenders ignore his liberties.

He needs to quit impressing me, otherwise I'll never return home.

Never ever.

He snatches a bottle of gin and pours the liquid into a tall glass, his gaze downcast. His confidence bolsters mine. I don't get it. In a new city, in an unknown club, I should be cautious and concerned. Instead, his presence empowers me, turning me into a wildcat, my claws barely hidden below the surface.

The only thing decreasing my self-assurance is that other woman. I'm not sure I want to hold his gaze while he tells me about her. I'll be a slave to my emotions. How I feel will be written all over my face. Then he'll know exactly how much power he has over me.

"Who was she?" I take the opportunity to have the unwanted discussion while he's occupied.

He grabs for the vodka, adding a nip of alcohol to the glass. "Obviously someone who doesn't appreciate my charm."

I swallow the dryness building in my throat. "Is that all you're going to give me?"

He looks up at me, stray strands of hair shading one eye. "She's someone I almost slept with." He holds my gaze for a beat, then returns his attention to the drink, adding juice, before stirring with a plastic swizzle.

I don't want to ask. It makes me nauseous thinking about it, but the question slips free. "Almost?"

"Yeah." He pours himself a scotch, then rounds the bar, placing my drink in front of me before raising his own to his lips. He holds my attention over the rim, his focus intense in its honesty. "Things got heated. But I didn't follow through."

Jealousy eats me from the inside out, the sharp teeth burrowing deep. "When?"

"A few weeks ago," he admits.

A few weeks?

After we'd met, but before we'd kissed.

"What else do you want to know?" His question isn't angered, or a taunt. He's offering genuine transparency and I'm no longer sure I want it.

"Do you like her?"

His mouth kicks up as he takes another sip. "Did it look like I like her?"

"It looked like she liked you up until the second before her hand slapped across your face."

He shrugs. "She wanted to finish what we started. I didn't."

His candor grates me. Will I be the next woman who wants more when he doesn't? Is my heart his next victim?

"You're judging me again," he drawls. "I thought we were past this."

I thought so, too. I really did. Now I'm not sure.

"Fine." He sighs, his brows pinching. "I guess you want the full story?"

I don't know. Part of me needs to understand how he could be unabashedly cruel. The other doesn't want any more knowledge of him with another woman.

He leans in, dominating my personal space and grazing the stubble of his cheek along my jaw, his lips near my ear. "The truth is, I got back to Washington after meeting you for the first time and I couldn't get your fucking phenomenal body out of my goddamn head."

I shudder. Hold my breath.

"I couldn't sleep," he continues in a seductive murmur. "Couldn't think straight. So I found someone to replace you. A woman with the same hair. A similar figure. A pretty face."

My skin erupts in goose bumps, my nipples beading for reasons unknown.

His nose nuzzles the sensitive skin below my ear as he says, "I wanted to fuck her while pretending it was you. But no fantasy could live up to the hype."

I shiver, every inch of me tingling.

"Less than an hour spent with you, Layla, and I was obsessed." His lips brush my neck, the graze of his stubble providing the most deliciously contrasting friction. "Seeing you again only heightened the infatuation."

My breathing labors. My core tightens. "But you didn't sleep with her?"

"No." His response is instant.

"Have you slept with anyone else since we met?" The need for answers is pathetic. I can't help it.

"No." He tastes my skin with a minuscule slide of his tongue. "And I won't."

I believe him.

I believe his words. His vibe. The hunger in his mouth as it delicately devours my neck.

Lust bubbles in my belly, seeping out through every nerve.

I don't understand this yearning. This desire. It's all-consuming. Mind-numbing.

I slide a hand around his neck, grazing my nails along his scalp to hold him close. "How long until we can get out of here?"

He snickers, the sound devilish enough to make my pussy clench. "As soon as you'd like."

17

LAYLA

He leads me back downstairs, my hand in his, then through a staff door, along a shadowed hall, and out into a gated parking lot.

Matthew directs me to a black Roadster nestled between a line of sedans and compact vehicles, and opens the passenger-side door.

We're on the road within silent minutes, the blood pounding from my building libido the only sound.

"Are you having second thoughts?" He flashes me a look of concern.

It makes me want him more. "I'm right where I want to be."

His lips tweak in the slightest curve of approval before he concentrates on traffic. We head into the heart of the capital, not far from my hotel, and stop inside another parking lot, this one below a towering apartment complex.

He entwines our fingers as we walk to the elevator, my tongue tingling, my chest throbbing. I wait for him to maul me inside the enclosed space, but there's no voracious kissing session. He maintains his air of calm, not showing a hint of this obsession he spoke of, and takes me to the top level.

The penthouse.

I'd envisaged we would've been all over each other by now. Fingers clawing. Legs tangled.

It's the opposite. He's suave with his sickening patience, opening his front door wide to allow me to take the first step into his perfectly appointed space.

I'm not sure what I expected—maybe a bachelor pad with sleazy art or clothes strewn on the floor? But that isn't what I stand in front of. This place is beautiful, the kitchen before me entirely spotless from the marble counters to the stainless-steel appliances, and all the way down the floor-to-ceiling wine fridge.

"Want another drink?" He closes the door behind me, then strides ahead.

"I'd love one." I'd love anything that might taper the rabid beat in my chest.

"Do you have a preference?" He opens a cupboard and pauses, waiting for my response.

"I'm easy. You decide."

He reaches inside for a glass and grins to himself, as if he can't wait to test just how easy I am with a million X-rated surprises.

I place my cell on the kitchen counter and turn in a slow circle, taking in the home that suits him without flaw. The furniture is commanding and elegant. All polished woods with white coverings, from the lounge setting in the adjoining room to the dining table a yard to my left.

Everything is immaculate. No clutter. Not even dust.

Eclectic art lines the walls. From abstract to surrealism and pop. The different pieces draw attention to what must be expensive taste.

"Your home is beautiful." I turn back to face him as he makes our drinks.

"*Our* home," he corrects without missing a beat.

I chuckle, and slowly sidestep toward the mail farther along the counter. "Are you like this with all your women?"

"*All* my women?" He pulls out a drawer, the clink of liquor bottles following the movement. "You say that as if I'm not obsessively picky with who gets to share my time."

"So I should be flattered?"

"Don't go twisting my words, *amore mio*. You're special. I think you know that."

Arrhythmia takes over, the fractured heartbeats overwhelming me. I focus on the three letters on the bench as he pours alcohol into the glasses, and read the name on the top line of the address.

Matthew Langston.

I let the syllables roll around in my head with slow lethargy and fight the compulsion to say *Layla Langston* out loud just to hear how it would sound.

I may not have slept with him yet, but this is moving fast.

I'm picturing my life here, in this penthouse, in his world. Away from the drama of my family and the complications that always follow them.

"Here." He rounds the island counter to hand me what looks like a glass of juice. "A screwdriver."

"Perfect." I take a sip and watch him do the same with his scotch.

For a few seconds we simply eye each other between subtle swallows of alcohol. No words. Only blazing attraction.

"I'm going to preface this next question by telling you I've never ended a work night on a better note," he murmurs. "But why are you here, Layla?" He places his glass on the counter and cocks his hip against the marble, his full attention remaining on me.

My throat tightens, not only with the way he reads me, but in contemplation of the truth.

He's opened the door to his life, allowing me free rein, and I'm still hesitant to unlock mine. Even just a little.

"You owe me a goodbye." I shrug.

He steps closer, the tips of his shoes nudging mine. "Well, you're going to be disappointed." He cages me against the counter, one hand on either side of my waist. "There are no more goodbyes for us."

I hold in a smirk. "Ever?"

"Ever." He leans in, but doesn't touch. I'm almost certain it's a strategy. To make me want what he holds back. "Is there anything else I can compensate you with?" The question is purred with the most sinister seduction.

He wants me to voice my desires. To ask for sex. "I'm sure we could find a suitable compromise."

His lips kick with a grin as he glides a gentle hand through my hair. "You captivate me. You're bold and fearless enough to fly across the country to see me. Yet hesitant and almost unsure when it comes to voicing how much you want to fuck me."

I suck in a shallow breath.

"You're a puzzle I need to solve." He slides his hands over my hips and lifts me onto the counter, just like he did in the hotel bathroom in Denver.

"And once you have me figured out?" I raise a brow. "What then?"

"I don't think that will happen. This is a rest-of-my-life type of task."

I laugh, my humor quickly smothered by his mouth swooping down on mine.

He kisses me with severity. With strength and conviction and lust. His lips are so damn commanding. His hands a steel-like grip at my waist.

When he pulls back, I'm panting, struggling to catch my breath… my thoughts.

"You think I'm kidding, *amore mio*," he whispers. "But this isn't a game. You mean something. *We're* meant to mean something."

"What if you're wrong?" My insecurities voice themselves before I can rein them in. "What then?"

He narrows his eyes, staring at me with fascination. "Then you can walk away without any animosity between us… But that's a future that isn't in the cards."

He makes everything seem so easy. So dreamy. And maybe that's what our world could be like—all rainbows and unicorns—if I were another person.

"We're adults, Layla," he continues. "I'll make sure you don't regret your time with me."

I want him to be right. *God,* how I want it.

I want to be protected. Not by an overbearing brother, but by an adoring, passionate lover. I want more of this giddy feeling in my stomach. I want freedom and happiness and a fresh slate.

"I think you might be right." I lock my legs around his, encouraging him to decimate the space between us, the hem of my dress rising to my crotch. "I want this."

He lowers his hold from the adamant force at my waist to the most delicious hold on my upper thighs. He keeps his hands there, his thumbs mere inches from where my body demands attention as he stares down at me, waiting.

"Do you want me to beg?" I ask.

"No. You never need to beg for anything." He digs his fingers into my flesh. "My hunger isn't a charitable donation you ever need to plead for. But I do want more of an assurance that this is what you want, because every other time I've had my hands on you it's felt like shock or intimidation has played a role."

I nod, even though the devil on my shoulder whispers I'm only here because I've fled my family and he was the only one I had to turn to. The only person I know who doesn't owe my brother favors.

"I'm here for you." It's still the truth. "All the other times I was, too. Even under duress I can make clear choices."

"Be sure, Layla. I'm playing for keeps."

"Are you trying to talk me out of this?"

"Never." His eyes glaze with lust, his nostrils flaring slightly before his mouth steals mine again.

It's a frenzy of lips and tongues and teeth. A wild dance of my snatching fingers at his collared shirt and his strong hands on my heated skin.

"It feels like a fucking lifetime since I had you naked." He reaches around the back of my dress, finding my zipper to drag it down. "I'm going to burn all your clothes."

He grabs the heaped material at my thighs and helps to pull the dress over my stomach, my shoulders, my head. "On second thought…" He leans back to take in my fire-red lingerie, a lone finger reaching out to trail along the tiny strap of silk circling my waist that holds up the even tinier V of lace at my crotch. "You can keep these… at least temporarily."

"You like?"

"That's a fucking understatement," he growls. "They look brand new. Tell me you bought them for me."

"I bought them for you," I whisper.

"*Jesus*." The oath is groaned. "You're so goddamn obedient. Such a fucking treasure." He pushes farther between my legs, the hardness behind his zipper a mere inch from where I want it to be. "After all the things I've fantasized about doing to you, you'd think I'd know where to start." His fingers creep higher and higher until they're at the crotch of my panties.

I jolt at the briefest swipe of his thumb over my pussy as his lips approach mine.

"You missed me." He holds my gaze, staring deep into my eyes. "You're already soaked."

I bite my lip. Nod.

"What did you miss most?" He strokes his thumbs back and forth along the lace V, sending a mass of tingles through my clit.

I close my eyes and nuzzle his nose, working my fingers down his buttons, popping them one by one. "I missed the empowerment I feel when I'm around you. You increase my confidence."

"And you feel confident now?" he asks against my lips.

"Yeah. I do."

He kisses me, soft and gentle. Teasing and slow. "Okay then, *amore mio*. Show me."

18

MATTHEW

She isn't startled by my request, yet something lingers on the edges of her expression, spitting in the face of the confidence she claims to have.

I step back, readjusting the stiffness in my pants. "Strip for me."

Her chin lifts, as if in defense, but she holds my gaze and snakes her arms around her back, unclasping the see-through bra in silence. The straps loosen at her shoulders as she cups her breasts, guiding the material into her hands, then dropping it to the tile floor.

"Slow and steady doesn't always win the race, *amore mio*." I'm not sure she's aware of how much she's teasing me. But I'm dying here. The anticipation of sinking home between her thighs is fucking killing me.

"Do you use that endearment with everyone?" she purrs. "It means *my love* in Italian, right?"

"Right." I fight against the need to claim those perfect tits with my hands, my mouth, my cock. I want to cover them with my seed. Mark her like a fucking beast. "Would you prefer *tesoro mio*?" *My treasure.* "Or *bella mia*?" *My beauty.*

Her lips curve. "I'd prefer an honest endearment. One without the player charm."

"Then hear this, *sei tutto per me*." *You are my everything.*

She blinks back at me, lost for a moment, her hands gripping the edge of the marble counter.

"Want me to translate?" I lick my lower lip, itching to taste her, to plant my head between those thighs.

"No." Her response is breathy as she grabs my jacket and yanks me forward. "It's best if you keep quiet. You undo me in both languages, and I need to keep my wits about me."

I snicker as she drags me in for a kiss, one arm curling around my neck, the other working on her underwear as she jostles from side to side.

I help her, yanking the string of material down her smooth legs, letting it fall to my feet. She's exposed, her thighs spread, yet she holds me close, not allowing me the freedom to look my fill.

This attraction has a life of its own.

I was consumed by it from the first night we met when I'd been watching her from the restaurant kitchen, her expression filled with determination and strength as she spied on the Costa family dinner. Then, in a split-second, Bishop scared the confidence from her features, and the frail panic triggered regrets from my past.

She needed saving. And unlike those I failed in my youth, I refused to let her suffer.

"*Ho un debole per te.*" *I'm weak for you.*

Completely powerless.

I would fall to my knees for her. In lust. In protection. For no other reason than this maddening chemistry between us.

"Shh." She presses her mouth harder to mine, demanding silence as our chests brush.

I snicker, dragging my palm to the apex of her thighs, sliding my fingers over her mound as our tongues tangle. I'm worked up. Hard as stone. Determined as hell. "*Nessuno potrà mai competere con te.*"

She gasps. "Stop it. You're killing me."

"And not being inside you is killing me."

She whimpers and holds me tighter to her lips.

I glide my fingertips to her slit, finding her wet, making her hips roll. The growl of gratitude that vibrates in my throat is uncontainable.

I'd hoped she'd be like this—utterly perfect—and prayed she wouldn't be in the same breath. There's no withstanding her. Not now. Maybe never.

I sink my fingers inside her, the walls of her pussy clamping down on me while she shudders.

"Matthew." Her voice is nothing more than a breathy plea. "You make me crazy."

She grinds into the curl of my fingers, kissing me harder, gripping tighter on my neck.

I need a fucking drink.

A time-out.

Something… anything to keep this from ending too fast. One blink and it will all be over.

"You have the same effect on me." I reluctantly remove my fingers from her heat, needing to savor this, and clench my fist as I pull back. Her juices dampen my palm, the exquisite texture tempting me to lick my own damn skin.

She stiffens with my retreat, panting, her brow furrowed. "What's wrong?"

Everything.

I don't just want to fuck her—I want to watch her. *See* her. *Know* her.

I raise my knuckles to the underside of her chin, tilting her face flush with mine. The scent of her sex lingers between us, the heady perfume filling my lungs.

Does it drug her the way it does me?

Is she drowning in lust, barely functional due to her need?

Those deep blue depths staring my way keep me grounded.

"Nei tuoi occhi c'è il cielo." *Heaven is in your eyes.*

She licks her lower lip, her gaze lust drunk as her hands circle my wrist, guiding my knuckles higher. With a gentle touch, she unfolds my fist, and tilts her face to align my fingertips with her lips.

I hold my breath. Captivated.

Then she plunges fantasy into reality, gliding her mouth over my digits to suck them against the warmth of her tongue.

Fuck.

I feel the suction all the way to my dick. I picture it, too—her lips along my shaft, her tongue teasing the slit.

"You're destroying me," I grate, "in the best possible way."

She chuckles and pulls my fingers from her mouth with a pop. "Do you have protection?" She reaches for my belt, undoing the buckle.

I tense, already close enough to end this with one damn stroke. "In the bedroom."

"How far away is it?"

"Too far," I growl, smashing my lips to hers.

She begins to stroke me through the material of my pants, gentle and slow. "Are you clean?"

Sweet Jesus.

"I've never fucked without a condom." I clench my teeth to fight the pleasure, the delicious drag along my shaft driving me to madness.

She increases the pace. The severity. "Are you willing for me to be your first?"

"Amore mio, I'm willing for you to be my last."

She pulls back to meet my gaze, her eyes glistening in that sexually timid way of hers even though her palm circles my dick. "Don't say things you don't mean. It makes me hopeful."

"Are you asking for a commitment, Layla? Because I'll give it to you."

Her brows pull tight and she shakes her head. "I just want you. Just for tonight."

Tonight is only the start.

I lower my zipper, pull out my cock, and align it with the sweetest pussy known to man as she makes quick work of my jacket and shirt, shoving them off my shoulders to fall to the tile.

I grip her hip in one hand, digging my fingers deep, and guide the head of my dick to her slit, dragging it back and forth through her heat.

She closes her eyes, releasing a moan as she leans one hand against the counter, thrusting those breasts toward me.

Fuck, she's flawless.

Malleable. Eager. Yet with the slightest hint of innocence.

I increase the pace, rubbing back and forth, each graze of my cock making her back arch, her hips tilt.

So fucking incredible.

I lean forward, no longer able to resist those gorgeous tits, and suck a stiffened nipple into my mouth.

She moans, the feminine sound filling my ears, her fingers finding my hair. She pulls tight, causing pain to lash my scalp. The harder I suck, the stronger she pulls, until the burn running through my head is the best fucking thrill I've ever had.

I suck until she writhes. Until I can't concentrate on grinding her against my dick because I'm too fucking wound up from her whimpers and moans.

"You ready?" I growl.

She nods and shuffles closer to the edge of the marble, positioning herself right where she needs to be. I don't tease us a moment longer. I thrust home, sinking my shaft to the hilt as I palm her hips.

Those gorgeous eyes roll. Her head lolls back. She keeps those breasts in my face, and I latch on, sucking, grazing, as I pound a hard rhythm inside her.

"Oh, God." She tightens her legs around me. "This is going to be shamelessly quick… I've never…" Her pussy clamps tight around me. "Matthew…"

She scours my skull with her nails, but I don't stop the suction on her nipple. I ride out her orgasm, her pleasure filling my ears, sinking into my memories.

It takes all my restraint not to follow after her, not to spill my seed and make her mine. I wait her out, tensing every goddamn muscle until she's done riding the high.

"Good?" I ask.

"So good." She wraps her arms around my shoulders, nestling close. Chest to chest. Skin to skin. "I've never come so quick," she whispers in my ear. "Not even by myself."

Fuck.

The image of her touching herself is punishment of the most exquisite kind. Cruel and divine in one carnal visual.

"Lay down," I grate. "I want to see you stretched out before me."

She pauses a moment, then pulls away with a shy grin to rest against the marble, her hair splayed, her nipples hard.

I continue riding her, forcing myself not to blow as those tits bounce from my thrusts. *"Potrei guardarti tutto il giorno." I could look at you all day.*

It's no lie.

I could keep her like this forever. My masterpiece.

She groans, her hands reaching above her head for the other side of the counter.

I run a palm from her hip over the smooth planes of her waist, then between her breasts, learning all her curves. Committing them to memory. My other hand glides along her abdomen, my thumb finding her clit.

"Come sei bagnata." I groan. "So fucking wet…"

She gasps. Moans. Squeezes her core around me. "For the love of God…" She groans. "Stop talking."

"Non ti lascerò mai andare." I tweak a nipple, grazing a thumb over the pebbled peak as I place pressure on her clit. *"Vieni di nuovo per me.* Come for me again."

She shakes her head, her brows pinched as if in concern.

"You okay?" I slow even though it's torture, even though heaven is right there waiting to be conquered. "Talk to me."

"Nothing's wrong. I just…" She keeps shaking her head. "I've never come twice… and I'm… I can't believe I'm so close."

I despise her fucking husband, and whoever else she's slept with. But those assholes did me a favor. They made it easy for me to win her over. She'll never dare to walk away when I continue to treat her like a queen.

"Then come, *amore mio*. Let me watch you."

She blinks, dazed with lust. "I'm not used to being watched either."

"Well, get used to it. I'm going to witness you doing some filthy fucking things, Layla. And you'll enjoy every minute of it."

"Is that a promise?"

"It's a vow." I lean forward, replacing the hand at her breast with my lips. "Soon you won't recognize yourself."

"I already don't." There's a tremor in her voice as her fingers reclaim my hair. "You've changed me."

"You've changed me, too." I thrust harder, stoking us higher. The harder I suck her nipple, the more frantic her pace builds beneath me, the roll of her hips becoming fearless.

I groan against the flesh in my mouth and close my eyes to the bliss.

I'm beyond ready. A brief step from the finish line.

"Matthew…" Her breathing fluctuates, her chest rising and falling beneath me.

I beat back the need for relief, vowing not to come until she does, promising to reach the end together. "*Mi far stare bene.*"

I fuck her savagely. Faster. Harder.

She tenses, her legs a vise around me. "I'm…"

I open my eyes and she's gaping, her lips trembling as she shudders.

I'm powerless to stop myself from following her this time. I come undone, spilling inside her, losing myself to the climax and promising myself this will be the first of many.

19

———

LAYLA

I LAY STREWN ACROSS HIS COUNTER, MY SKIN COATED IN A SHEEN OF SWEAT, MY HEART fluttering like a sail in a hurricane.

"I'll get you a cloth." He moves out from between my legs and grabs my hand to pull me into a sitting position. Then he walks around the counter to claim something from a drawer. The faucet turns on seconds later. In the next blink he's back in front of me, handing me a clean damp dish towel.

There's nothing smug in his expression. No egotistical victory. He gives me the offering with respect in his eyes and steps away, allowing me a modicum of privacy to clean up the sinful mess between my thighs as he rights his pants.

"Do you want to take a shower?" He shoots me a sideways glance and picks up his shirt and jacket from the floor. "Or would you like something to eat? There's a takeout place nearby that stays open late."

"I'd love a shower… if you don't mind."

He winces. "I want you to feel comfortable here. In my city. My home. My bed. Take whatever you need."

My stomach swells, doing a somersault of appreciation. So far, two out of three can't be bad.

I'm entirely comfortable in D.C., in his penthouse. And we may not have used his bed, but I think I took quite a few liberties to make myself feel at home on his kitchen counter.

My problem is the exact opposite of what he wants. I should be feeling cautious. Skeptical. Cole would want me to be entirely vigilant.

I've been none of those things.

Neither has Matthew.

"You barely know me." I scoot to my feet, ignoring the bite of self-consciousness now that he's righted his clothes and I'm wearing nothing but shiny red heels.

"Aren't you worried I could be a gold-digger? Isn't that what you thought I might have been with Remy and Salvatore?"

"You're no gold-digger. And even though I might not know you as much as I'd like, I'm learning." He grins. "And thoroughly enjoying the lesson."

That swoopy, somersaulty thing takes over my belly again, then quickly fades into guilt. He has to be more wary. The thought of disappointing him when he learns the real me is punishing.

"There might come a time when you don't like what you learn." I give him a pointed look, trying to be his voice of reason. "Don't put me on a pedestal. I won't live up to the hype."

He inclines his head and gives a subtle nod. "Okay. Point taken. Neither of us are pillars of the community. But there's something in our chemistry, Layla. You feel it, too."

I do, and it's maddening in its potency. I don't think I could escape the clutches of this attraction even if I wanted to.

"Umm…" I tilt my head toward the hall on the right of the open living area, then do the same toward the darker one to the left. "Which way to the shower?" I point my ass to the counter and bend to unclasp the straps of my heels, leaving them on the tiles.

"Use my personal bathroom. To the left. Last door on the right. Want me to show you?"

"No. It's okay." I start walking, needing a few minutes of breathing space to regain my equilibrium. "I won't be long."

I pad onto the carpet of the hall, glancing into rooms as I pass, appreciating how every space is neat and tidy. Without flaw.

I stop at the threshold of his bedroom and flick on the light, taking a moment to let the sight sink in. It's another perfectly appointed room. Dark wooden furniture. Even darker bed coverings. Not one piece of strewn clothing or speck of dust in sight.

It doesn't take long for my stare to move beyond appraisal and into daydream territory. I picture us both on the king-size mattress, his body atop mine, his movements hard and rhythmic.

Then he has me bent over the chest of drawers. Or my naked breasts pressed to the glass doors leading to the balcony as he takes me from behind.

I need help.

I sidestep past the walk-in closet and move into the bathroom where I use the facilities and shower quickly. I should get back to my hotel. For anonymity's sake. To make sure I don't push the already fragile boundaries of my stupidity.

I dry myself with fast strokes of a clean, plush towel, discovering that some parts of me are already deliciously sore from his attention. Then I shuffle from the bathroom with the thick material wrapped around my chest.

Matthew sits waiting for me on the side of the bed, his feet on the floor, his elbows on knees. He glances up from under dark lashes, his chocolate eyes meeting mine with an expression I can't quite read.

"Feel like you've been catfished?" I ask, suddenly aware that this is the first time he's seen me without a mask of makeup.

He reaches out a hand, wordlessly beckoning me forward. My feet comply without my consent, bringing me right before him.

"You floor me with every new layer you expose." His fingers glide around my wrist, leading me between his open knees. "I'm not worthy of your attention."

I wither inside, my strategy for space disintegrating. I want to climb onto him and cuddle in his lap. To be his very own purring little kitten.

"Your cheek is still swollen." He reaches for my face, gently cupping my jaw, his thumb sweeping over the healing skin. "Does it hurt?"

What hurts is the destruction it caused.

The drama.

Then again, I wouldn't be here if I hadn't been mugged. I would've walked away from Matthew, possibly never seeing him again.

"I don't notice it most of the time." *Especially not when your hands are on me.*

He nods, continuing to stroke the bruising, stoking my sensuality with each pass. He drugs me with his touch, building an addiction that will require a multi-step program to achieve recovery.

"Tell me why you're really here," he murmurs.

I tense before I can stop myself.

"Don't lie to me, *amore mio.*"

I step back, fearful of his scrutiny while something inside me yearns for transparency.

His touch falls away with my retreat, but those eyes slay me with their questioning.

"You didn't come all this way to sleep with me," he continues. "Do you need information on the Costas? Did you decide to take my help?"

I wince for so many reasons.

For starters, he's wrong. I *did* come all this way to sleep with him, no matter how desperate and dysfunctional that sounds. It's deeper than that, though. Painfully deeper.

"No." I swallow and straighten my shoulders. "I didn't come here for information. This has nothing to do with them."

"Then why?" The question barely breaches my ears, the gentleness painfully coaxing.

Because I'm alone.

Because I had nobody else.

Because my family hate to love me, and love to hate me in equal measure.

I turn away, starting for the door. "I need to get my clothes."

"Your clothes are gone, Layla."

I swing back to face him, panicked. "Gone where?"

"I put them in a dry-cleaning bag and sent them down the laundry shoot." He reaches for something beside him, claiming a handful of dark material that almost matches the covers. "You can wear one of my robes."

He's trapped me. Not behind bars, but with nudity.

"You're judging me again," he warns.

"Because you're effectively holding me here until I can get my dress back."

His placid face hardens as he hunches over, elbows back on knees. "I have a room full of clothes if you're in a hurry to run. Take a sweatshirt. Take my whole fucking wardrobe. I'll have your clothes sent to your hotel first thing in the morning." He shoves to his feet. "Forgive me for thinking I was doing you a favor."

He stalks to the door, shoving the silk robe into my hand as he passes, then escapes into the hall.

Damn it.

I'm not used to this.

I have no familiarity with someone doing things for me out of kindness instead of strategy. The compliments are all new. The affection foreign.

My walls may be down where attraction is concerned, but I guess snap judgment is still my default defense mechanism.

I return the towel to the bathroom while feeling like a complete bitch, then shove my arms into the billowing robe, tying the sash around my waist.

I'm pushing away the best thing that's happened to me since Stella's birth and I don't know how to stop.

Vulnerability isn't an enjoyable sensation. It's caustic and cruel, its sharp teeth nipping at my heels. But denying the exposure means giving up on this connection. This passion. Even if it's temporary.

I pad back along the hall, finding him in the kitchen, one hand on the counter, the other on his scotch glass.

"Want me to arrange a driver?" He peers at me over the rim of his drink before taking a gulp. "You wouldn't have to wait long."

Do I go or stay?

He takes another mouthful, leaving the glass dry, then drops it down to the counter with a heavy thud. "You're not my fucking hostage," he mutters. "I'm not keeping you here."

"I know."

He frowns. "Do you?"

"Yes." I wince. "And I'm sorry. You caught me off guard."

He remains quiet as he watches me, unappeased.

"I felt stupid when you said I didn't travel all this way just to sleep with you, because the truth is I kinda did." My wince deepens. "But it's even more pathetic than that."

"What do you mean?" His expression softens.

My throat tightens with the resurfacing rage I harbor toward my brother. "I had a fight with my family and needed to get away. It's hard to admit I had nowhere else to go."

The confession hurts. Soul deep.

There's nobody else in my life. All I have is Stella, my innocent daughter, who I'll never burden with my troubles.

Matthew releases a long breath and wipes a rough hand down his face. He's tired of me already. Bored of my bullshit within an hour.

He doesn't say anything as he walks toward me, probably preparing to reintroduce me to the front door. I bite my lip as he approaches, each step leaving me more vulnerable in an already isolated world, until he stops before me.

His gaze rakes my face, a subtle frown pinching his brows as he conducts the appraisal. "Are you okay?"

I release a tight breath.

He's concerned about me? After I accused him of having bad intentions, he's still acting protective?

I blink through the sharp burn in my eyes and step back, needing to distance myself from the weakening effects of his patience and concern.

"Hey." He reaches out, grasping my fingers to drag me into his chest. "Tell me you're okay."

I hold in a whimper, the fragile sound built from overwhelming gratitude. I wither against him, lowering my head to his shoulder, wrapping my arms around his waist.

In his embrace, I'm good.

I'm sheltered.

I'm whole.

"I don't need you, Matthew," I whisper against his skin. "I'm not someone who can't take care of herself. I just…" I squeeze my eyes shut. "I'm not used to having someone care for me. Not like this."

"I understand." He kisses the top of my head. "I don't have anyone either."

I lean back, needing to see the truth in his expression. "What about your family?"

"I have a mentor. But apart from him, Bishop is all I have. All I trust."

He has it worse than I do, and now that I know of his isolation, I can see it. Loneliness is hidden beneath the confidence in his eyes.

"I have a feeling we're similar in a lot of ways," he continues. "Maybe that's why I'm drawn to you."

"And here I was thinking I'd captivated you with my body," I tease.

"That, too." He doesn't laugh—there's only the slightest upward curve to his mouth as he gives me a subdued kiss. When he pulls away, the humor is gone. "I want you to trust me."

"I'm trying."

"It doesn't come easily for me either." He kisses my rose. My forehead. The sweetest brushes of gentle lips. "We have to give it time."

I sigh, nestling back into his shoulder. "It sounds like your life is as messed up as mine."

"It was. But not anymore. I left it behind. You can, too."

I close my eyes, picturing this dream world of his. One without notoriety etched into my family name. A place where tables aren't turned on the daily and I don't have to constantly watch my back. A utopia where Stella would always be safe.

"Want to tell me about the fight?" he asks into my hair.

"It was about you."

The muscles of his chest stiffen. "You told your family about me?"

"No. But they guessed I'd met someone. Apparently, my face has a tell when I've received my first non-self-administered orgasm in years."

He snickers, deep and sinful in my ear. "If I'd known it'd been that long—"

"*Nope.*" My face heats as I snap a finger to his lips, silencing him. "We are *not* talking about my abstinence."

His grin presses into my fingertip, the glimpse of a dimple teasing me from his left cheek. "But understanding why you're confident in one moment and shy in the next is fucking cute."

"Stop it." My eyes flare. "There's nothing cute about being daunted by someone else's prowess."

He's right though.

So fucking right.

I guess I grew up being self-assured by my family's power. Of how to conquer and rule. But when it came to sexuality, my teachings came from a man who would've preferred never to have met me.

"You're daunted by me?" he teases.

I shove at his chest. "You know I am."

He sobers, the flirtatious vibe seeping away as silence builds.

"I don't want you to be daunted by me, *amore mio.*" He grabs my hand, raising my knuckles to his lips. "You told me before that I made you feel empowered. That I gave you confidence."

"You do that, too." I shake my head. "I wish I could explain…"

I can't find the words. *No*, I can't find the honesty. The truth about how Benji made me question my desirability isn't something I'm willing to discuss.

"A man gave you these insecurities," he answers for me.

I glance away, unsettled by his insight.

"It's okay." He kisses my knuckles again. "I'll fix that for you. It won't take long and you'll realize the power you have over me with your body alone. I'd start a war for you."

The blush creeps down my neck, heating my breasts.

A war is what it would take for my brother to let me be with an outsider.

"Tell me the problems with your family," he adds. "Maybe I can fix that, too."

"*You* are the problem… Well, the assumption you're responsible for the bruising on my face, anyway. They think I'm shacking up with an abuser."

His face falls. "Why would they think that?"

"My past preferences, for a start."

"With one of the Costas? Did Remy or Salvatore hit you?"

I want to correct him. To set him straight once and for all and confirm that I had no sexual relationship with my enemies. But I can't expose that much of myself.

"It's a long story," I hedge. "Suffice to say I didn't appreciate their judgment, and they didn't welcome my anger. So when I delivered Stella to the airport, I caught the first flight to the only place I wanted to be."

"It'll blow over." He tugs me back into his chest, pressing his lips to my forehead, holding me close for long, silent moments. "I'm sure they'll be crawling back before you know it."

"Apologies aren't their strong suit." They can't even accept ones they're offered. "But you're right. It will blow over." Eventually.

I place my palms on his waist, running my fingers over his smooth skin. The quiet stretches, yet the emptiness is filled with comfort.

I lean into the ease of simply being with him. I breathe him in and close my eyes to enjoy his warmth. It isn't until a yawn takes over that his arms slowly fall to his sides.

"Do you want me to arrange a driver?" he murmurs into my hair. "I won't hold it against you if you leave."

The struggle of right against wrong and should against shouldn't whispers in my ears. But what I *want* is this. More moments like here and now. More me and him in our own little world, even if it's temporary.

I forced myself to stop feeling guilty about my life with Benji. Why can't I stop questioning every forward step with Matthew, too? Just for a little while. Only until he grows tired of my anonymity and starts searching for more. Then I could leave.

Why not dive deep until then?

"Lay?" His lips press to my temple. "Are you staying or going?"

I suck in a deep breath, hearing Cole's warnings in my head, battling against a life where I've been force-fed the line that I shouldn't get close to strangers.

I wrap my arms around him, sinking in to what feels right. What feels whole. "I'd like to stay."

20

LAYLA

"You sure?" The devil enters his voice. "You'll get more sleep at a hotel."

I graze my nails along his flesh, awakening goose bumps. "Sleep can be overrated."

He palms my chin. "It definitely will be tonight." He kisses me, soft and sweet and slow. Then incrementally, the connection changes. Soft builds into firm. Sweet shifts to wicked. Slow transforms to rabid.

We're back to being all hands and lips and gasps, and it feels like my decision to stay is paving a brighter future, not inching toward impending doom.

We're together all night, our bodies either entwined in passion, or collapsed in exhaustion. And in each moment, he treasures me. With his words. His touch. His gaze.

I can't take one breath without it catching in my chest, the air latching onto feelings that morph and build beyond my control.

When morning comes, I wake to his lips on my shoulder, his whispered words greeting me to a new day. But I drift back to sleep, cocooned in bliss between his sheets.

I don't know what time it is when I finally wake, the subtle noise in the living area keeping me conscious this time. I left my cell silenced in the kitchen knowing Cole would blow up my inbox as soon as he realized I fled Portland, and there's no bedside clock in this room.

Matthew is no longer beside me. I can't see him or smell his intoxicating aftershave. The only thing kissing the air is the faint hint of coffee, which is enough to drag me to my feet.

I contemplate walking out to him in my birthday suit, hips swaying, seductive smile in place. But I'm not that woman yet. After the obsessive adoration paid to my body last night, I'm a few steps closer to sexual confidence. I can sense it within reach —I'm just not quite there.

I grab the black robe strewn on the floor and cover myself as I pad from the room, already eager to place my mouth on Matthew's.

Too bad Matthew isn't the one sitting at the dining table. It's Bishop's scowling blue gaze that peers over the cell in his hands to look me up and down.

"Morning," he mutters.

"Morning." I cinch the gaping lapels higher around my chest as I glance over the open living area, searching for my life preserver.

"He's not here." Bishop slaps his cell on the table. "He had to go to the coast for business and didn't want to wake you."

"And he asked you to stay with me?"

"Apparently, I'm here to make up for my bad first impression by offering my services. I don't think he anticipated you sleeping away my entire day, though."

I focus on the microwave in the kitchen, squinting at the tiny numbers.

"It's almost twelve." There's a bitter growl to his tone. "And I've got more than your shit to take care of, so I'm going to need to know the name of your hotel."

My gaze snaps back to his. "Why?"

"To retrieve your things. You're staying here from now on, aren't you?"

"Yes," I whisper, raking a hand through my tangled hair. How the hell did I sleep until noon? "But you don't need to get my things." The contents of my suitcase are strewn across my suite—lingerie, toiletries. There's also a whole heap of cash in the safe. "Could you give me a ride instead?"

He holds my gaze, those severe eyes doing absolutely nothing to retract his first impression. "As long as you're not going to take up the other half of my day. Like I said, I've got shit to do." He pushes from his chair with a jerk of his chin toward a garment bag on the end of the table. "He said that was for you."

"My clothes." *Thank God.*

"Can you be ready in ten?" He stalks for the kitchen, entirely intimidating with his bulky frame beneath his suit. "I'll make you a coffee while I wait."

"Yeah. Okay. Thanks." I hustle for the table to grab the garment bag, then rush for Matthew's bedroom to get changed.

I pull on my now clean underwear, then shimmy into the dress, ignoring how I'm about to do the walk of shame into a five-star hotel, with a bruised face and tangled hair. Not to mention all the fresh marks now clinging to my body from Matthew's rough kisses and enticing, ruthless hold.

When I walk back into the kitchen, my heels clapping on the clean tiles, Bishop greets me with a huff and a travel mug in his outstretched hand.

"Ready?" He starts for the door before I answer.

"Let me get my phone." I hustle to snatch my cell from the counter and follow him, taking a sip of steamy heaven once I step over the threshold to the elevator.

The preview on the locked screen triggers my guilt—*eight messages and five missed calls.*

Cole will be responsible for most.

"Something wrong?" Bishop leans against the back wall, his legs crossed at the ankles.

"No. I'm fine." I unlock the screen and open the messages, skimming over the mass of capital letters and exclamation points from my brother without reading them, and focus on the text from Matthew.

Morning, amore mio. *I had an important meeting I couldn't postpone. But I've changed my plans to be home in time to take you to dinner. Be ready by 7. Don't miss me too much. I'll make up for my absence when I return.*

I grin, juggling the coffee in one hand with my cell in the other as I reply—*After-noon. I don't think Bishop appreciated me sleeping in. What should I wear tonight?*

I lock the screen, ignoring the messages from my brother, and jostle when the elevator reaches the parking lot.

"You going to tell me the hotel?" Bishop strides into the cement jungle filled with six-figure cars, maintaining his glower of annoyance.

"Avarden Towers."

He shoves a hand into his pocket and the indicators of a nearby Lincoln Navigator flash to life. "Get in."

I bite my tongue against the deliberate dictatorship and climb into the passenger seat, biding my time until I can get my belongings and place distance between us. The ride is silent—nothing but city traffic and the barely heard hum of the radio.

It isn't until we're at the hotel and he follows me into my suite that his look of disdain gets to me.

"You don't like me very much, do you?" I grab my scattered underwear from the bed and place them in my suitcase, the silence stretching the air thin. "No comment?" I shoot him a look.

"Of course I like you," he drawls, heavy with sarcasm. "I love complications. They make my life more colorful."

"I have no intention of being a complication."

"Right… And what about your plans with the Costas?"

I pause, my hands filled with lingerie, my paranoia finally waking after the night of bliss. "I'm not here because of that. I don't want my time with Matthew to have anything to do with them."

He scoffs. "Does he know that?"

The superior undertones in his voice bug me. "Yes, he does."

"Then you're already well aware he won't stand to be left out of any plans you have. There's no way you can keep him in the dark."

Watch me.

I clamp my mouth shut, keeping my thoughts to myself.

"Look, Layla. I don't know you. But the fact you're in the same circles as the Costas is a sign you're bad news. I don't need more proof than that."

"You don't think that's hypocritical?" I storm for the bathroom and make quick work of snatching my makeup and toothbrush to shove into my toiletry bag.

"Regardless of if it is or isn't," he calls from the other room, "I think you know you're trouble. And Matthew's worked too hard to distance himself from that shit, changing every part of his life to keep his nose clean, to have you drag him back in."

His words hit home, squeezing at the parts of me already filled with remorse over the tryst I can't walk away from.

I hang my head and grip the counter, hating that he's right. Hating how he can sense the pandemonium that shadows me like a vengeful ghost. Hating even more that Matthew has slain unknown demons to correct his life and I'm threatening to revive them.

But I promised myself I'd lean into happiness despite the obstacles. That I'd take what I could while I could, until the first glimpses of drama surfaced. And this self-righteous asshole won't talk me out of it.

"I thought you were meant to be making up for a bad first impression." I clutch my toiletry bag under my elbow and force a smile as I saunter back into the main room.

"Yeah…" He shrugs. "Doesn't really seem like my thing, does it?"

I laugh. "I actually think you nailed your first impression. In hindsight you were authentic. You came across as a bully, and it's now clear that's exactly what you are."

"I'm no bully, sweetheart. I'm a loyal friend. There's a difference."

I continue to the bed, shove my toiletry bag into the suitcase, and swing around to face him, his attitude scraping against the nerves already made raw by my brother. "I'm here in D.C. for no other reason than to spend time with Matthew. What I do in Denver is my business. I don't want his help. Or yours, for that matter."

"You were never getting mine."

I fight a wince at how easily he loathes me without even knowing me. "Thanks for clearing that up."

"You're welcome." He drops his arms to his sides and pushes from the cabinet to stand tall. "You ready to leave?"

"I need to get a few things from the safe. Can you give me a minute?"

He gifts me with another appraising look, still finding me lacking. "I'll meet you at the car."

I FOLLOW A FEW MINUTES BEHIND, catching up to him in the parking lot.

We don't speak again. Not on the short drive back to Matthew's penthouse building. Not even when we ride the elevator. He keeps quiet, swinging open the penthouse door and holding it wide for me to proceed, then slamming it closed with him on the other side.

"Great," I mutter.

Without a key, I'm effectively caged in. Again. But I'm not going to go chasing Bishop about it.

I busy myself for the rest of the afternoon by getting changed, then familiarizing myself with the many rooms in Matthew's home. I open every door, careful not to snoop, but eager to learn more about him.

I admire the expensive artwork decorating the walls and the books on the shelves. I use the jacuzzi in his main bathroom and research his clubs online. I drink coffee on the balcony and text Stella to send her my love. And all the while, I fight against rerunning my conversation with Bishop this morning on a continuous loop.

Even here, away from my family and the mistakes of my past, I'm still the bad guy.

Bishop knows it.

I know it.

But as soon as Matthew returns that night, his grin subtle despite the unfiltered appreciation in his eyes, all my worries fade.

"Fuck, I missed you." He drags me into his chest, his mouth roughly claiming mine. "You look stunning."

I *feel* stunning.

I'm wearing white tailored pants and a mauve halter-neck top, yet he makes it seem like I'm dressed for a red-carpet event instead of dinner.

"I need to freshen up." He speaks against my lips between hungry kisses and scrapes of teeth. "Help me get undressed?"

I smile, my eyes closed, my heart in heaven.

He didn't just need help undressing. He wanted assistance bathing, too. He dragged me into the shower with him, his focus on learning more of my body instead of freshening up his own.

But this time it didn't feel like sex.

It was something different. Something that started off voracious and passionate, then petered into a slower connection that was far more intense. He lavished me in slow kisses, one hand cradling my chin, the other between my thighs. He murmured his dreamy Italian promises between strokes of tongue and grinds of hips.

He made love to me, and it made me realize I'd been a virgin to the experience up until this point.

By the time I dried, dressed, then redid my makeup, it was after eight.

He held my hand as we walked into the rooftop restaurant, letting everyone know I was his and he was mine. The waitstaff greeted him by name, with smiles and enthusiasm, before escorting us to a table in the corner with an unfettered view of the Washington Monument alight in the clear night sky. And the whole time, I couldn't wipe the smile off my face.

"Is that happiness ebbing from you, *amore mio*?" He eyes me with contentment across the table. "You seem in good spirits."

I sip my wine, willing my rampant heartbeat under control. "I am, despite being locked in your penthouse all day."

He frowns. "Why? Didn't Bishop tell you about the spare key?"

To hell with Bishop.

"No." I return my gaze out the window. "That must have slipped his mind."

That asshole deliberately kept me caged. He wanted to have the last word, and it came in the form of my isolation.

I continue to feel Matthew's stare from my periphery, the slight gleam of white announcing a building grin.

"What?" I ask. "Do you like knowing I was trapped in your penthouse like a damsel in distress?"

"No, but I'm beginning to understand why you were so excited to see me when I returned home." The grin lessens, the subtle lift falling flat. "Bishop told me the two of you had an intense conversation this afternoon."

"Intense is one word for it."

His brows knit with curiosity. "How would you describe it?"

An ambush.

An assault.

I shrug. "I guess intense is accurate enough. I'm surprised he told you, though."

"It's the bonus that comes from working with someone who always thinks they're right. They never have anything to hide." He relaxes into his chair. "But just to be clear, I didn't appreciate what he said."

I take another sip of wine, biting back how much I didn't appreciate it either.

"Why didn't you call me to tell me what he'd done?" he asks. "Or tell me once I got home?"

"For the exact reason I argued with him in the first place. I'm not here to cause trouble."

"Bishop being a prick isn't you causing trouble."

I hold his gaze, wanting him to understand my sincerity as I say, "He's one of the few people you have in your life, so even if he's an absolute asshole—which he most definitely is—" I smirk. "—I'm not going to bring that up with you. I can understand him being protective."

Matthew raises a brow and inclines his head, his mouth set in an understated smile as he falls silent.

It's unnerving. The way he admires me with quiet fascination. It's energizing, too.

"What?" My cheeks heat the longer he looks at me.

"I'm just adding more attributes to the list of what I find entirely endearing about you." His voice is a murmur of underlying seduction. "Along with picturing how many times, and in what positions, I can have you once we finish dinner."

My cheeks flame hotter, the inferno creeping down my neck.

I've been picturing that, too.

I can't stop.

His touch haunts my skin, the possessive grip of desire keeping me chained to memory. Problem is, it's also distracting me from the other important motivation for flying across the country.

"We should really discuss the Costas before we become sidetracked again." I lick the dryness from my lips. "I'm not going to lie. Our common interest in them is another reason why I'm here."

"I figured as much." He leans back in his chair, the confident seduction leaving his expression. "But they're not going anywhere. Why not enjoy getting to know each other first?"

Why not? Because I don't deserve the pleasure.

Because I need to focus on my mistakes.

His lips curve, the wickedness returning to his eyes. "Let's make a deal—once you think the chemistry between us is fading, we can divert our focus to scheming."

"Once I think…? What about you?"

He grins, sly and handsome. "It won't fade for me."

That has to be a lie.

Before I can question him on it, a muffled beep sounds from his suit jacket.

He drags in a long breath and retrieves his cell. "I need to take this call." His brows pinch in apology. "I won't be long."

I nod and grab for my own device on the table, reluctantly turning it over to read the screen as Matthew walks away.

Five missed calls.

Two texts.

My chest tightens. Every notification will be from my family. More regrettably, my brother.

I open my inbox, the preview of the most recent message hitting my eyes.

Answer your fucking…

I shouldn't open it. The time away from them has been a wonder drug of positivity. Unfortunately, curiosity gets the better of me.

Answer your fucking phone and help sort this out like a fucking adult. The least you can do is let us know you're all right. Your sister is worried sick.

My sister… but not him.

Do you think this is a joke, Layla? We still have enemies. You still need to tell me where the fuck you are so I can make sure you're safe.

He doesn't care about my safety. His concerns lie with the chess pieces that will topple if anyone successfully targets me. It would make him look bad. Weak.

But he's right about Keira. I don't want her to worry.

I dial my sister's number, my ribs tightening with the dial tone, my breath halting when she answers.

"Layla?" There's panic in her voice. "Are you okay?"

"I'm fine. I just need some space."

"Where are you? Hunter found your car at the airport."

Of course he did.

"It doesn't matter." I reach for my wine, needing the alcoholic calm. "I'm safe. That's all you need to know."

"Lay, please, you're freaking me out. Why are you acting this way? I know it's been hard on you since Stella moved away, but it doesn't mean you're alone. I'm here for—"

"Don't say you're here for me, Keira." I cut her off. "We both know that's not true."

"W-what do you mean? You're my sister. I'm always here if you need me."

I shake my head, pained by the lies. "I haven't been your sister since the night Benji died and you know it."

She gasps. "Is that how you really feel?"

"It's two years later and you can barely look at me after what I did."

"No," she pleads. "I'm sorry if you think I haven't forgiven you—"

"You haven't. None of you have."

"That's not the case, Layla. It's just different now. Things changed. *Everything* changed. There was my relationship with Sebastian, then the news of what our father had been doing. Then what happened to Richard. It was an avalanche of adjustment even before Dad died. Then Tobias entered our lives and everything became chaos. And Benji…" She sighs. "I guess in the aftermath, I inched away from everyone and hid in the comfortable world I'd built with Sebastian because it was easier."

She might like to believe that story, but it's a lie.

She pulled away from me. From what I did. Just like Cole, Sarah, Hunter, Decker, and even Luca, too. They made me a pariah. And although it was initially deserved, I didn't earn a lifetime of this suffering.

"I haven't held it against you," she whispers. "I want you to be happy."

"You want me to be happy—you just have such a low opinion of me that you think I'm weak enough to be with a man who would hit me."

"Jesus Christ. You can't blame us for making assumptions when you're deliberately being secretive. You keep escaping out of town without letting anyone know and not using your credit cards to make yourself untraceable. Even now, you took off after withdrawing a whole heap of cash. What are we supposed to think?"

I glance out the window, heartbroken and needing to diffuse the conversation, while being angry and itching to blow it up at the same time. "Forgive me for not wanting to be stalked like a fugitive. Two years ago, my husband was taken from me. Now my daughter has been shipped away. I had to find something to distract myself from a house that has become hauntingly quiet. It's goddamn lonely, Keira."

"But why hide where you're going?" she asks softly. "You had to know your actions would spark Cole's paranoia."

"Maybe I want to be free from our family for a little while... Maybe I want to pretend I'm someone else." Someone who doesn't have skeletons to hide and mistakes to resolve.

"I can understand that. I've thought the same thing many times. It's the—"

"I don't want to talk about this anymore," I interrupt as Matthew returns to the table, his raised brow questioning whether I'm okay. "I only called to check in and now I've gotta go. Tell our brother to stop contacting me. I want to be left alone."

"Layla—"

I disconnect, not waiting for her response, and place the cell face down on the table.

Matthew takes his seat, his jaw tight. "What happened?"

"It's nothing. Just family drama." I grab my cloth napkin and place it over my lap, unable to maintain eye contact.

"Want to talk about it?"

I can't share those parts of my life with him, no matter how much I want to. "Honestly, it's nothing."

"Honestly, *amore mio*, I can tell that's not true." He reaches over the table, sliding his hand out for me to take.

I stare at the offering. The lifeline.

I want nothing more than to take it. To latch on. Cling tight.

"That was my sister on the phone." I raise my gaze and paste on a fake smile. "My family don't appreciate me disappearing to places unknown. Apparently, they can't stop me from making careless mistakes if they don't know where I am."

"Are you prone to making mistakes?"

"Yes," I admit. "I've made a few. I've trusted people I shouldn't and paid the price."

He appraises me for a moment, his weighty consideration stripping me bare. "Trust is a favorable quality to most. Would we be here together without it?"

No. But my husband would be alive and my daughter would live without nightmares if I'd been more hesitant when offering my faith.

"My family is different." I slide my hand to meet his, our fingertips kissing on top of the table. "We usually function in our own little utopia, so it's hard when things go wrong."

"I'm sure they'll forgive you."

I scoff a laugh. "It's been two years."

"Damn." His eyes narrow. "Well, I'm glad you're here with me instead. Did you tell them where you are?"

"No. And I've been using cash so they can't track my whereabouts through the bank, but my brother will find another way eventually."

He pulls his arm back, sitting straighter. "He's trying to track you?"

Shit. I've said too much. "It's not that extreme."

His chin raises, his posture growing tense. "I should speak to him."

"*No.*" God, no. I press my lips tight to suppress a delirious laugh. Cole would kill him on sight. "It's not as bad as it seems. We have joint accounts. Any purchase I made through a credit card would announce my location."

"You don't need to worry about money while you're here. I'll take care of it."

This time I'm the one to reach farther across the table, my fingers seeking his. "I appreciate the offer, but I withdrew enough before I left to tide me over until I return home. I can look after myself."

"Believe me, you've demonstrated that without fault." His hand finds mine again, the calloused palm skating over my knuckles. "The thought of taking care of you brings me pleasure."

I blush, my mind sliding into the gutter. "You're doing that just fine without any financial contribution."

He laughs, the utterly brilliant sound tickling every sensitive part of me. "Why don't we get our dinner to go and take this conversation back to the penthouse?"

My pulse increases, the fluttering wings of arrhythmia swooping through my limbs. "Will we be merely conversing, Mr. Langston?"

He grins, smooth and flawlessly seductive. "No, *amore mio*, but a lot of my plans involve what I can do with my mouth."

21

——————

LAYLA

ONE NIGHT SWOONS INTO ANOTHER, EACH ROMANTIC EVENING MEAL DISTRACTING ME from the reason why we met.

Sometimes Matthew is gone when I wake. At other times he remains in bed, his arm wrapped possessively around my waist like I'm a priceless treasure. And no matter how much he's at work, he always makes me his priority.

His out-of-town trips never last overnight. We either spend hours together in the morning or the evening, and it's never enough. Not with the way he listens intently whenever I speak, or how he continues to offer exaggerated, outlandish promises for our future that make me ponder if they could actually become reality.

Could we forge a life together even though we're still yet to talk about the common goal that made our paths cross in the first place?

The days have passed with the Costas not being more than a passing word. Neither of us seem ready to fizzle the sparks between us by bringing up the elephant in the room, even though it needs to be discussed sooner rather than later.

We've kept our truce in place regarding personal information. He gives me space when I call Stella. He doesn't ask questions. Doesn't demand insight I'm not willing to give. But every day my walls grow fragile, tiny fissures forming to allow slips of my life to spill free.

"Get dressed, *amore mio.*" Matthew walks into the bedroom from his private bathroom, a towel wrapped around his waist, his muscles glistening from the shower. "You're coming to work with me today."

I sit taller in his bed, the tray loaded with my empty breakfast plate rattling on my lap. "I am?"

"Yes. My commitments won't take long." He discards the towel and pulls on a fresh pair of boxer briefs from the chest of drawers. "Then we can do whatever you like afterward. I'll arrange a hotel room for the night. You just need to pack a change of clothes and your toothbrush."

I pull back the covers and glide to my feet, not showing a hint of curiosity at learning more about his life while trying to hide my fear of what he wants from me in return. "When are we leaving?"

"As soon as you're dressed."

"I guess that's my cue to hustle."

I shower quickly, brush my teeth, and paint on a subtle layer of makeup in record time. Then I shimmy into a long ruby sundress and fill the remaining space in the small suitcase Matthew left open for me on the bed.

"Ready?" He stands at the bedroom door, one shoulder cocked against the frame, a subtle smirk of appreciation tweaking his lips as he takes in the loose material dancing over my legs and the low neckline that cradles my breasts.

"Ready." My heart beats a dull throb, my eyes eagerly eating up my view of him dressed head to toe in black—suit, shirt, tie.

He's a dark prince, the stubble covering his jaw making him appear all the more devilish.

He pushes from the doorframe and prowls toward me, slow and sleek.

My body melts like it always does. My nerves flutter. I stand still, wondering if his predatory approach means we're about to delay our departure.

He stops beside me, the grin continuing to linger as he leans around me to zip the suitcase closed and drag it to the carpet. "We don't have time, *amore mio*."

"Time for what?" I purr.

"For that look in your eye."

He kisses my temple and takes my hand, leading me from the room, from the penthouse, then into the elevator, our mini suitcase trailing along at his side. When we reach the underground parking lot, Bishop is there to steal my buzz. He waits in his idling Lincoln, the window lowered, his arm resting on the frame.

"Morning." He scowls at me.

"Morning." I hold his gaze, refusing to cower under the intimidation.

"Get in." Matthew releases my hand. "I'll put the suitcase in the back."

I nod, bathing in Bishop's death glower with every step toward the rear door, then slide inside. I've been lucky not to have seen him since our confrontation almost a week ago. He hasn't been to the penthouse. There's been no talk of him at all.

Too bad it didn't last.

"It's so lovely to see you again," I drawl. "What have you been up to?"

"Just the same ol' same ol'—preparing for when my buddy's latest conquest is going to blow shit up and make my life a living hell."

I glare at him through the rearview mirror as Matthew opens the cargo space to store our suitcase. I wait until the trunk door is closed moments later before I say, "Well, if you're the cleanup crew, I guess I should make sure it's a worthwhile explosion."

Matthew climbs in the opposite side of the Lincoln, and I'm not sure whether it's his presence or my spite that keeps Bishop quiet. But that's how things remain as the car exits the parking lot into the midmorning sunshine.

We drive through the city traffic, Matthew's hand gliding over mine on the middle seat as we pass block after block, then head onto a freeway to take us toward the suburbs. I relax, expecting a long journey ahead when twenty minutes later, Bishop slows into the turn to send us to Dulles Airport.

We bypass the parking area, driving away from the main buildings and alongside the boundary fence, then come to a temporary stop before metal gates that are opened for us by a young man. Bishop inches the car into the airport yard, slowly passing one metal hangar, then another.

"What are we doing?" I ask.

"It's time for a change of transport." Matthew caresses my fingers as Bishop breaks and shifts the car to park.

A whisper of something unwanted slips through me, the lifelong teaching of a paranoid and overly protective brother ringing in my ears.

You're being careless. You're putting us all in danger.

No. I know Matthew.

I might not have intimate knowledge of the events that make up his life, but I know *him*. I know his unwavering commitment. His building affection.

That's why I didn't ask how far we were travelling. Or who was coming with us.

I've learned to trust him—with my body, and now, also, my safety.

"I'll get the luggage." Bishop climbs from the driver's seat, the engine idling as he lobs the fob at the young man who opened the gates.

All I can do is watch in silence while I force Cole's voice from my mind.

"You're nervous." Matthew's hand slides from mine. "Are you questioning my intentions again? You don't have to accompany me, Layla. I can have you taken back to the penthouse."

"I'm not questioning you." My heart hurts at the disappointment in his features.

"You're apprehensive."

I could claim a fear of flying. Hell, it wouldn't be difficult to make up any number of reasons to explain the devil on my shoulder.

Instead, I give him what he deserves. "I've told you my brother doesn't appreciate my current secrecy. If he was aware I was about to jet set to places unknown with someone he's unfamiliar with, he'd judge me harshly."

Matthew's jaw ticks. "It sounds like he judges you harshly regardless."

I don't deny it. I want him to understand that part of me. The part that may affect him the most. "He does."

"He's controlling," he adds.

I don't deny that either.

The trunk door opens and Bishop steals my focus as he removes not one but two suitcases from the cargo area. Of course the asshole is still coming with us.

"Do you want me to arrange a driver?" Matthew asks as the trunk door closes. "The last thing I want to do is—"

"No, I'm excited to go with you. I promise. I just hadn't anticipated your meeting to be far enough away to require a plane." I unclasp my belt and smile. "You're not taking me to Paris, are you?"

He huffs a breath of lifeless laughter. "No. We'll have to do that trip another day. And we're not taking a plane either."

I'm about to ask for clarification when he swings his door wide and escapes the car to round the hood.

I follow, climbing from the back seat as a loud mechanical whir fills the rustling fall breeze, the sound coming from the other side of the hangar to my left.

"We're taking a helicopter?" I meet Matthew at the hood of the car but fall quiet, not wanting to interrupt the younger man who's relaying departure and arrival details as the unmistakable *whoop, whoop* floods my ears, the rush of energy growing around us.

I bite my lip, struggling from the whiplash of flipping from apprehension to exhilaration.

"I hope you're not scared of heights." Matthew steps away from the chatter to wrap an arm around my waist.

"I'm not. But how far are we going?"

"Virginia Beach. Is that a problem?"

I wince, wishing I hadn't shown my temporary slip of confidence in the car, the hesitation now gone as if it never existed. "I'm sorry." My voice barely carries over the air chopping around us. "I..."

I'm not sure what to say. I can't tell him I was brought up in a family who doesn't believe in trust. Or relay the justifiable reasons for them being that way. He'd never understand and I wouldn't want him to.

"You don't have to explain." He leads me toward the hangar, the wind growing more fierce the closer we get to the corner of the building.

Once we reach the edge, elation takes hold, sending blood rushing through my veins.

A sleek black metal bird sits yards away, the glossy paint gleaming in the sunlight. It's beautiful. All polished curves and extravagant masculinity with the pilot under the propellers, standing in wait.

I'm breathless.

Speechless.

"It's not too late to change your mind." Matthew tightens his arm around me.

"I won't. I want this more than anything."

I do.

I want the new memories with him.

I want a new life.

He leans in, kissing my temple like he has so many times before. "Then let's do this."

He holds me close as we approach the helicopter, and exchanges shouted greetings with the pilot. Matthew guides me inside, the back cabin lusciously appointed with leather seats and pristine carpet. He encourages me to take the far window seat before he climbs in after me to hand over a headset from a hook on the wall adjoining the cockpit, guiding the restrictive weight over my loose hair to settle against my ears.

The deafening sound gentles but the rush in my veins doesn't slow. Matthew leans against me, his arm tight around my waist as I stare out the window, preparing for my fascination to increase. I'm rabid with rapture, my limbs thrumming, my pulse a giddy staccato.

My heart flutters with excitement while Bishop and the pilot settle into the cockpit. They talk, their mouths moving without the words filtering through the headphones.

"We can hear each other. They can't hear us." Matthew's voice glides into my ears. "It shouldn't take long for us to be off the ground."

He's right. Within moments, the gleaming monstrosity is wobbling off the tarmac, hovering for a second before it glides forward, taking my breath with it.

I'm not new to luxury travel. My family have been boarding jets without a thought to cost or environmental damage since I was a toddler. But this is a first for me.

I've never traveled with a man's arms wrapped possessively around me, the potent devotion sending my head into the clouds.

Lightness overwhelms me the farther we ascend. Buildings become tiny blocks. Cars turn into ants gliding along black curving trails that stretch as far as the eye can see. A cluster of suburban homes transform into an ocean of green trees and sunburned fields, all while Matthew guides me to rest against his chest, the side of my head nestling into his neck.

I'm Cinderella. Once, I was dirty and corrupted by my family's choices. Now, I'm swept off my feet by a devilish prince who only seeks to earn more of my trust.

"Stella would love this." I picture the surprise in her beautiful eyes. Her smile. The awe. "She'll be entirely jealous."

"We can bring her along whenever you like." His hand splays on my hip, no hint of hesitation in his actions or words.

My child doesn't daunt him. Not like she did Benji.

I know it's different. One was a paternal parent conscripted into fatherhood. The other is an outsider who can easily walk away. But Matthew has no fear. No doubt.

He's all in on this insane fairy tale, eager and enthusiastic to keep me from the darkness I'm meant to return to.

"You're such a good guy." I keep my attention on the patchwork fields. The tiny puffs of trees.

His mouth brushes just below the base of my neck, planting the softest, sweetest kiss. "You wouldn't say that if you knew what I was thinking."

My chest blazes with heat, the naked skin on my back prickling with goose bumps.

That's all it takes. A few words. A strategically placed glide of lips.

I fight against the need to glance over my shoulder to see the expression that matches the wicked words, but I visualize it in my mind, all sinful and sly.

His touch teases my shoulder, his fingers straying to the thin spaghetti strap. "Have I told you how gorgeous you are in this dress?"

"You don't need to," I whisper. "I always feel beautiful when you look at me."

A rumble in his throat is his only response as his mouth continues to lead me astray, the sweet kisses turning into erotic flicks of tongue and rugged scrapes of teeth.

I bite my lip against the tingles in my breasts, the hitch of my pulse. I succumb to the need to see him and turn, my gaze finding his, his mischievous grin sending the flames inside me far lower.

I stare for several punctuated heartbeats, each thump an exclamation of need.

He's such a phenomenally handsome man. Sensuous eyes dark as night. A jawline chiseled from stone and covered in masculine stubble. Then the smoothest lips a woman would sell her soul to kiss.

God, do I want to kiss them.

But not now. Not when a taste of him will make me want to devour.

"You're missing the view." His arm around my waist descends, his hand on my hip falling to the top of my thigh.

I look back to the window, attempting to break the trance, and freeze when his fingers slowly hitch the material of my sundress, creeping higher and higher.

"Matthew…" His name is a barely heard entreaty.

"Mmm?" He keeps hitching, not stopping until the hem is raised to my crotch, the gentle breeze of filtered air sweeping against my panties. He nudges closer to me, his body turning into mine, shielding me. "Keep admiring the view, *amore mio*, and I'll keep doing the same with mine."

I shudder, unable to control my body's reaction, helpless against the moisture dampening my sex.

"Let me play." His fingers skim the waistband of my underwear, his entire hand sneaking beneath to cover my mound.

"*Matthew.*" This time it's a plea. A gasped warning.

I shoot a frantic glance toward the cockpit. One glimpse over Bishop's shoulder and he'd see. Everything.

"He won't look," the devil taunts through my headphones. "It's just the two of us."

His touch slides lower, grazing my clit, parting my folds.

Nerves tingle. Limbs throb.

An inner voice is aghast at what I'm doing. How tawdry I've become. Yet, my blood boils for more. My pulse thunders to an erotic rhythm.

"We can't do this here." I grasp his wrist, the hold lackluster at best.

"Why not? We did it in a hotel bathtub with a stranger present. This time nobody is watching." A finger teases my entrance, the digit effortlessly sliding through my slickness. "I'm the only one to admire your beauty. It seems like such a waste."

"Bishop is *right* there." I shake my head accidentally bumping our headphones. "Do you like being watched?"

"I like *you* being watched. Being *wanted*." He leans tighter against my side, his fingers plunging deep.

I hold in a gasp, the air tightening my lungs.

"I enjoy the look men get when they see you," he murmurs against my neck, slaying me. "When they admire how fucking gorgeous you are. How perfect. How compliant."

I wish I could argue otherwise. That I'm not quick to obey or easily malleable. But in his arms, I'm all those things and more.

A puppet.

A servant.

A slave.

He curls his digits inside me, his entire body pressed to mine, his other hand sliding into my panties to find my clit. "Fuck my fingers, *amore mio.*"

I'm helpless to deny him.

I want to do this. For him. For me. For happiness that is usually stretched thin and far between.

I close my eyes, grinding into his touch, becoming one with pleasure.

I can't breathe.

There's too much… everything.

Bliss. Lust. Lies.

I want him to strip me bare. Not merely of clothes and underwear, but of secrecy and deception. I want him to know me. The real me. The person my family don't see. The woman my husband never noticed.

"I'm so fucking hard for you, Layla," he murmurs into my headphones. "I promise you'll be sore and sated before the day is through."

I don't doubt it.

Not for a second.

"I want to taste you," he growls. "To plant my face between your thighs until you're lost for breath."

I picture him doing exactly that. On his knees. My dress raised. My hands in his hair with Bishop a few feet away, able to catch us at any moment.

Oh, God.

My core flutters with an approaching orgasm. "I'm so close."

"And so sensual." His touch becomes more firm against my clit, wiggling back and forth, faster and faster. "So tempting. So fucking perfect."

I pant. Gasp. Wheeze.

"Non ne avrò mai un altra."

His softly murmured Italian is my undoing. I latch tight to his wrist with my nails, holding him deep inside me as I grind and thrust and shatter.

My pussy convulses, the spasms building and morphing.

"See?" His appreciative growl hums in my ears, the viciousness tattooing my soul. "Perfect."

I whimper, climbing the crest, riding the wave.

I want to scream for him. Cry. Vow.

I could give him everything in this moment. My promises for the future. My commitment to togetherness even though I told myself this would be temporary.

How can I ever walk away from this? I never want to be without him.

I come down from the peak with clawed fingers and heaving breaths. "You have too much power over me."

"You have it all wrong, *amore mio.*" His voice grows somber, his lips once again finding my shoulder for a gentle brush of affection. *"Sei quella con tutto il potere."*

22

LAYLA

We land at a heliport far from the city buildings, my hair scattering from the *whoop* of the helicopter blades as Matthew leads us to an awaiting town car.

Our driver doesn't say a word as we glide toward the coast, the sea breeze filling my lungs from Bishop's open front-seat window, before we pull into a beachside hotel.

"I'll get us checked in." Bishop shoves open his door. "I'll meet you in the restaurant."

Matthew follows, holding out a hand to assist me in sliding along the back seat to step into the warm sun as a young male bellhop rushes toward us.

"Mr. Langston, it's a pleasure to see you again." The boy beams. "Do you have any bags I can help you with?"

"The trunk." Matthew jerks his chin toward the rear of the vehicle and discreetly slips the man a tip. "Has Lorenzo arrived?"

"Yes, sir. He's waiting inside."

It doesn't surprise me that Matthew is recognized on sight, or that the man he's meeting is familiar to staff. What concerns me is the slight hint of tension that enters Matthew's shoulders as he turns to face me, his dark eyes tight with hesitation.

"What's wrong?" I scrutinize his expression, trying to understand the change in him.

"Come with me." He grabs both my hands, entwining our fingers. "Come to my meeting."

I hold my surprise in check, unsure if I should be concerned or appreciative.

This is a far bigger step than I anticipated. A massive switch from the information injunction we've had in place. And as much as I want to learn everything there is about him, I know I'm not ready to reciprocate at this level. Not yet.

"Who is it with?"

"An old friend. He's a mentor of sorts. At least, he used to be."

"You want me to meet your mentor?" That's big. *Huge.*

"I'd be honored, and so would he." He raises one of our joined hands and kisses my knuckles. "And if you haven't figured me out by now, the request was a courtesy, but your attendance is compulsory." He grins and tugs me toward the hotel doors. "You'll be joining us, Layla. You've got two minutes to prepare."

Two minutes? To prepare to meet his mentor?

"Are you kidding?" I scope my disheveled appearance in the glass windows as we approach. "I look a treat."

"You better fucking believe it." He shoves past the doors and leads the way into the reception area. "You always look edible."

I ignore the heat rushing to my cheeks. The tingle in my belly.

I'm not succumbing to lust right now. Nope. Not again.

"Can we just stop for a minute." I plant my feet and squeeze his hand, forcing him to comply. "Please."

He turns to me with a frown. "What's wrong?"

"What's wrong?" I huff a laugh. "This is a big moment for me. And I think it is for you, too."

The frown deepens, but he doesn't deny my statement.

"This man is important to you." It's not a question. The evidence was his tightening posture when he realized Lorenzo was already here. That he was about to dictate for me to meet someone he cared about. "I don't want to make a bad first impression."

He steps forward, wrapping a rough arm around my shoulders to drag me into him, his face finding my hair, his aftershave filling my lungs. "I thought giving you no notice would be easier." There's forgiveness in his tone. "He will adore you, Layla. Just as much as I do."

"And if he doesn't?" I close my eyes, relaxing into him for the briefest respite.

"Then he's out of my life," he murmurs into my hair. "Gone. Done. I won't spare him another thought."

"I'd never let you do that." No woman of worth would. "If you were considering getting rid of Bishop, on the other hand…"

"That's different." He snickers, pulling away to guide my hair back behind my ear. "What you get from him isn't personal. It's personality."

"Well, his personality sucks."

"I don't disagree." His fingers trail my jaw, my chin. "You'll like Lorenzo."

I have to trust him. Trust that this meeting will go well. That these new steps toward full disclosure are the right ones to make.

"The two of you will get along fine." He places a kiss to my hairline, then reclaims my hand and continues toward the entry of the restaurant, the maître d' watching us approaches with familiarity in her gaze.

"Welcome, Mr. Langston. I think you'll find Mr.—"

"It's okay, Sophie." He interrupts her speech and guides me to stride past her. "I can already see him."

I scope the open dining area, seeing couples and families, none of them sparking interest until I reach the three men standing together at the bar. Two are younger, bulky and tall. The other is older, grey-haired with a shorter build. All of them wear dark suits, stylish and formal.

I'm underdressed.

The older man catches sight of us as he places his scotch glass before him on the polished wood, his grin quick to form. He strides toward us, spreading his arms, his light blue eyes beaming with pride. "*Figlio mio.*"

"Lorenzo." Matthew squeezes my fingers before releasing my hand and accepting the offered hug. "It's good to see you."

They embrace with strong arms and claps on the back, all masculine in their affection as the two other men turn to witness the show from a few feet behind.

Matthew's mentor isn't what I expected. He's far older, maybe in his sixties, with sun-kissed skin gentled by a myriad of deeply etched laugh lines. The only thing I anticipated correctly is his air of success. He oozes triumph, exactly like his mentee, the confidence in his expression bordering on arrogance.

"It's been too long." Lorenzo retreats to look him up and down. "You seem different. Overly carefree and alive."

"I'm not sure I'm carefree, but I definitely feel alive." Matthew returns to my side, placing a protective palm on the curve of my back. "This is Layla, the cause of my new lease on life and *quella che possiede il mio cuore.*"

I tense at the words spoken in a foreign language, slightly unnerved at being kept from part of the conversation.

"The one who owns your heart?" Lorenzo's brows rise as he steps forward to grab my hands in his. "I can see why. It's such a pleasure to meet someone whose beauty is profound enough to ensnare my Matthew. I've heard so much about you."

I glance to the man by my side. What the hell has he said about me? And why the hell has he said it? Is he really entrenched in this connection enough to have already told his mentor about me?

The slight raise of his chin, as if steeling himself against my response, makes me wonder even more.

"I assure you her beauty is merely part of the allure." Matthew winks. "She's captured me on every level."

I can't respond.

Not in words.

Instead, I blush. Cheeks to neck. Inside and out.

Compliments from strangers aren't new. People who want to get close to my brother often attempt to get there through me or Keira first, with most using kind lies and false admiration. But this is different.

I'm not a potential asset.

I'm of no use to these men because they have no idea who I am.

"I see you both have the same remarkable skills of flattery." I smile at the older man, his grandfatherly face seeming oddly familiar with its warmth and kindness. "Is that something you taught Matthew?"

His laughter rumbles like rolling thunder. "I wish I could take the credit, but he's always had his own ways when it comes to women. After all these years, you're the first I've had the pleasure of meeting."

"And if I have anything to do with it, she'll be the last." Matthew shakes the hands of the men looming in Lorenzo's shadow, then walks farther into the restaurant. "I need coffee. Are we sitting inside or out?"

"Out. We can't remain inside when we have the ocean to stare at." Lorenzo links his arm with mine, leading me after Matthew who directs us toward the glass doors to the al fresco dining area, the two other men following behind. "I reserved the best table just for us."

I walk on numb feet as a crowd of emotions seeks attention inside my chest.

Jubilation dances with twists and dips of hope and possibility. The kindness I've been welcomed with by these men is a blessing. I'm overwhelmed with gratitude to be so freely accepted. But the bitter edge of my shady upbringing still itches from the scars it's left behind.

How darkly tainted is my life that this is the first time I've felt free from judgment?

With each passing minute, I want to settle more into Matthew's world. To plant roots in soil that wasn't made for me. But could it be?

Could I change who I am to remain with him?

Maybe I could be accepted for who I want to be if I'm willing to sever ties with my brother. With my entire family. With the crime and danger and lies.

Could I do that though?

Could I start over with Stella, placing her boarding school days in the rearview to live like a normal person?

"Tell me about yourself, Layla?" Lorenzo pats my hand as we step outside, the rush of waves crashing in the distance. "How did you meet my Matthew?"

I open my mouth, then pause, cautious at what to offer that won't incriminate me. "We met in Denver."

Lorenzo's fingers twitch on my arm. "Matthew has been to Denver?"

"Stop plying her for information, *zio*." Matthew continues to stride ahead, passing dining customers to enter a private cordoned off part of the seated area, making himself at home amongst the empty tables. "If you have questions for me, you know who to ask."

"He's always been touchy," Lorenzo murmurs near my ear, his accent thick. "I don't know how you put up with him."

I grin as we reach a table in the far corner next to a waist-high hedge blocking us from the public bike track that's busy with people exercising.

"Are more people joining us?" I take in the sea of emptiness around us, all the nearby tables bearing reserved signs just like ours.

"No, *bella*." Lorenzo jerks his chin at the two men who came with him, sending a silent message that has them taking sentry positions at the farthest corners of the cordoned area.

Not business partners. Bodyguards.

"It's for privacy," the older man continues. "I can't have everyone learning my secrets."

Even though his comment is tongue-in-cheek, I'm tempted to ask what type of secrets could warrant reserving such a large area of the restaurant.

"Vecchio mio," Bishop calls behind us, his stride long as he approaches to engulf Lorenzo in a hug with clapped backs and foreign greetings.

The two of them reunite like father and son, and for the first time, the man I've grown to despise doesn't seem entirely feral thanks to a generous smile and sincere affection.

"Sit." Lorenzo breaks the embrace and waves a hand toward the table. "Take the chair opposite me, Bella. Bishop and Matthew can protect us from the prying eyes of the world by sitting on the outside."

I'm certain he's more intent on keeping his prying eyes on me, but I comply, happy to have his attention.

"The room isn't ready." Bishop slides a plastic suite card across the table. "They said to give them half an hour."

Matthew pockets the offering and we all take our allotted seats, Bishop and Matthew against the hedge, while I settle in front of Lorenzo, who clicks his finger in the air, gaining the attention of a waitress who hustles over.

Coffee is ordered. Cake and bagels and croissants, too.

Once the waitress is gone, Lorenzo sits back in his chair, his warm eyes fixed on me. "Tell me about yourself, *cara mia.* Spare no details. I want to know everything."

"Lorenzo," Matthew warns. "Don't push."

"I'm not pushing. Merely getting to know the woman of your heart, *figlio.*"

"It's okay," I lie, wishing I knew how to defuse this conversation respectfully. I don't want to offend Lorenzo by staying silent. I also don't want Matthew to think I'm willing to open up to a stranger when I've spent the duration of our relationship hiding. "I guess the thing that defines me most is that I'm a single mother." I pause, hoping the usually disparaged label will end my time in the spotlight. "My daughter is eleven going on twenty-three."

The older man laughs. "They're all the same at that age."

"You have children?" I latch on to the information, hoping to divert the conversation from me.

"Many. Some by birth. Others by fate." He glances to Matthew and Bishop.

"You must be very proud."

"I am. Now tell me more." He flares his eyes with exaggerated excitement. "I want to know everything. I'm in awe of the way you've ensnared such a stubborn bachelor."

"*Zio,*" Matthew growls. "You're making her uncomfortable."

"*Se la metto a disagio, sicuramente me lo può dire.*" Lorenzo frowns. "Isn't that right, Layla?"

I balk, his words going completely over my head.

"I'm sorry." He reaches across the table to touch my hand. "Do you not speak Italian?"

"No." I wince, physically pained at the thought of disappointing him—a stranger—someone I shouldn't care about. And yet, I do. I want his approval more than anything. "I enjoy listening to your beautiful language, though, so please don't stop on my account."

"Matthew will have to teach you."

I glance to the man in question, my heart warming with the ease of the smile staring back at me.

"I agree." There's a teasing hum to his tone. "All I need is for her to commit to the long process."

He's not talking about a commitment to a language. His intent is on a pledge of another kind, and right now, I'm mindless to think of one reason to deny him.

"We can talk about this later." I force my attention back to Lorenzo. "Is it my turn to learn more about you? Matthew told me you're his mentor."

"He did, did he?"

"You know it's true," Matthew mutters. "Stop fishing for compliments, old man."

Lorenzo laughs, carefree and bold. "Okay, okay. I know it's true. I taught Matthew everything I know about business."

"And arrogance. You taught him that, too." Bishop shoots me a glower, as if pissed I'm taking over the conversation.

"I assume you were there for that lesson, too." I quirk a brow at him.

Matthew snickers. "Without a doubt."

"So you're in the club business?" I ask Lorenzo.

There's an awkward pause as the fatherly figure holds his smile, his focus moving to Matthew. Nobody speaks. Or acknowledges the question as the two stare at each other.

I've said something wrong.

Bishop shifts in his seat, placing his arm against the hedge to watch the bike riders as they pass.

My question has made things awkward. And with the necessity for guards and a private seating area, I should've been less forthright in asking for information.

"I'm sorry… I didn't mean to be—"

"Don't apologize." Lorenzo returns his gaze to mine. "Yes, *bella*, I own clubs. Many clubs. I only hesitate to discuss the topic because it's become somewhat of a point of contention lately. Especially with Matthew."

The awkwardness continues, prickling my skin.

Bishop glowers at the passing bike riders while the gorgeous man beside me turns impassive, his expression not giving a hint of emotion.

Footsteps approach behind me as the quiet stretches, the chatter from pedestrians filling the awkward void.

"Who ordered the latte?" The waitress stops beside our table with a tray filled with food and drinks, her smile beaming into the discomfort.

"That would be me." I focus on the cream tablecloth, wishing I hadn't siphoned the enthusiasm from our heartwarming arrival.

"Don't worry." Matthew leans into me, whispering in my hair. "We've been destined to have this unwanted conversation for a while." He inches away to refocus on Lorenzo. "I guess it's time we discussed your retirement."

"It's been time for months." Lorenzo juts his chin. "Have either of you considered my offer?"

Matthew doesn't move. Not even a flinch.

Bishop continues to stare at the bike track, or maybe even farther to the street traffic.

"Your offer is something that should be reserved for your sons. Your *real* sons." Matthew reaches for his piccolo, calm and controlled as he takes a sip.

"You already know they've received the same offer. You're also well aware that hard work never suited them."

"It's not the hard work they're opposed to," Bishop mutters. "They're already successful in their own right, and so are we."

"*Il tuo successo non è niente in confronto alle profondità dell'impero familiare.*" An edge creeps into Lorenzo's tone. "*Saresti uno sciocco a rifiutare l'offerta.*"

"Then call me a fool." Bishop returns his attention to the conversation. "As tempting as the offer is, I have no plans to return here."

"*Questo è un insulto alla famiglia.*" Lorenzo glares. "You both know this."

"It's not meant as an insult." Matthew sighs. "Don't take your frustration out on us. It's your sons you should be speaking to."

"*Fanculo i miei figli.*" Lorenzo slaps a hand down on the table, startling me. "They don't deserve to be part of this."

"*Calmati,*" Matthew says, a warning in his tone. "If I'd known you were going to push the issue, I wouldn't have brought Layla here to sit awkwardly through the exchange."

I press my lips tight at his protection. Appreciating it. Loving it.

I've always hated when my brother did the same.

Lorenzo's shoulders loosen, his face losing the harsh lines of irritation. "My apologies." He drags in a long breath, regaining composure. "Forgive me, *bella*. As you can see I've grown frustrated at my children for turning their back on the family business. I didn't raise them to be ungrateful."

"Families are tough. I know that better than most." I pull my cell from my dress pocket. "But please don't censor the conversation on my account. I've got messages and emails to return. Pretend I'm not here."

He holds my gaze, admiring me in silence for long moments before he says, "*Non lasciarla andare. È una da tenere stretta.*"

"*Lo so.*" Matthew shifts his chair closer to mine, sliding his arm over the back of my seat, the heat from his suit jacket sinking into my shoulders, the strength of his body settling in against me.

I glance at him, hoping for a translation. Our eyes lock, and without words, I understand the silent message he conveys.

Lorenzo approves.

I'm considered worthy.

The realization is enough to make my stupid throat dry.

He leans in, placing a kiss to my temple, a whisper to my ear. "You're amazing."

I flush, so much more than cheeks and chest. I feel the heat everywhere. Arms. Legs. Stomach. No place more potent than my heart.

"Enough of the PDA bullshit," Bishop mutters. "I'm not here to watch soft porn."

"If whispering in my ear is considered soft porn, I truly feel sorry for your lovers." I give him a smug smile.

"Who says I'm talking about a whisper?" He gives me the same look in return. "Maybe I meant the helicopter flight."

I stiffen, my temper flaring.

"Watch it," Matthew threatens him while he squeezes my shoulder.

"It's jealousy, *bella*." Lorenzo claps my nemesis on the chest, a gesture that's harshly shoved away. "I doubt poor Bishop has experienced love."

Love?

I ignore the implication. "Nonetheless, I think I'm becoming a distraction. I should go for a walk on the beach—"

"No, stay." Matthew's hand remains firm on my shoulder. "Eat. Enjoy your coffee. Our conversation won't take long."

Bishop keeps his feral stare on me as I concede with a nod, clinging to the cell in my hand.

They continue talking without me, the Italian more heavily spoken than words of English. I sit there and stare at my locked screen as the sea breeze dances in my hair and Matthew's accent plays havoc with my libido.

What if this is love?

We barely know each other… yet what I feel for Matthew holds a romanticism and tightly woven affection far more potent than anything I've experienced.

I yearn for him. All the time.

Even with him by my side, his arm around me, his voice in my ears, it's not enough.

I want more.

Birds chirp, people ride past, waitresses clean tables, and all I can do is simmer in infatuation, my life shifting to revolve around the man beside me as if nothing else exists.

He's becoming my world.

I swallow, attempting to alleviate my parched throat, and unlock my cell to swipe through numerous unread messages from my siblings. I make sure to keep the screen tilted from view as I scan Cole's condemning texts, and those from Keira that are equally accusatory but cleverly intoned with concern.

Would either of them care that I'm at peace here?

Would they deny me this happiness?

I reach for my latte and take a sip, wishing I had someone to talk to, but my sister is the only confidant I've ever had.

I haven't risked the luxury of friends since childhood. My family's reputation has kiboshed the ability to trust anyone outside our inner circle.

There's only Keira. A sibling who usually forgives but never forgets.

Matthew's fingers brush reassuring strokes against my shoulder as I contemplate reaching out to her. I breathe deeper of his scent, sink further into the confidence in his tone. I become bolder in his embrace. Stronger.

My pulse pounds as I hover my fingers above a new text, Keira's cell number the recipient.

If I tell her, there's no going back.

I won't be able to pretend this is a temporary fling. Our relationship will be real.

Undeniable. I'll have to commit to telling him who I am in the future and face the possibility of him walking away.

My heart plunges. My stomach, too.

I tilt my face to look at him, watching intently as he speaks flawless Italian, trying to hide my lust when he shoots me a knowing smirk before returning his attention to Lorenzo.

He leans in again, his heated breath tickling my neck as he murmurs, "Don't look at me like that or I'll be forced to fuck you on this table."

I sit taller. Clear my throat. Pretend my sex isn't already preparing for the actions of his threat, and start typing—*Keira, I think I'm in love.*

23

LAYLA

HER RESPONSE COMES THICK AND FAST.

What?!

Where are you?

Who is he?

How long have you known him?

I could've maintained my elation if it weren't for the last text.

Goddamnit, Layla, don't do anything stupid.

Those six words hit hard, her judgment threatening to convince me I'm not worthy of happiness.

I fight against the potential downfall. Glare at the screen. Cling to the last vestiges of my pride until my self-respect slowly returns.

I'm tempted to reply. To tell her exactly how I feel about my despised position in the family with far more clarity than I did in our last conversation. I'm even inclined to answer the call she puts through seconds later just so she can hear the renewed confidence in my voice as I tell her about the possibility of me never returning to Portland.

But the allure isn't worth instigating another fight. Or disrupting Matthew's conversation.

I'm in love, not a masochist.

"You okay?" he whispers in my ear. "What happened?"

I lock my cell and shake my head. "Nothing."

"It's something."

Lorenzo and Bishop continue their conversation as Matthew leans closer. "Is it your family again?"

I hate how he hits the bull's-eye easily. I'm grateful for it, too.

My family has always been my destruction.

I never would've been painted a traitor if it weren't for my despicable father using me in the first place. I wouldn't have had the chance to drag my husband through the mud with me if we weren't forced to marry. And I wouldn't be here, ignoring the vibration of my sister's continued calls, if my siblings didn't make me feel like a leper.

But I guess that's the silver lining.

Him.

Matthew.

They may be my ruin, but he'll be my rise.

I won't retreat from what we have because of Keira. I won't continue to be conditioned to believe I'm unworthy of even a second of the heaven I feel when I'm with him.

"Talk to me, Layla. Tell me what's going on."

I turn into him, our lips a breath apart when I whisper, "You're special to me."

He inches back, his brows furrowing.

I've shocked him, and I guess it's to be expected.

He's spent all our shared time calling me *amore mio*, promising me his devotion, showing me his commitment. And this is the first I've given it in return.

"You're going to do this to me *now*?" He places a hand on my upper thigh, his palm possessively sliding higher. "Here?"

Hunger ebbs off him, the fire beaming in his eyes.

I blush, my cheeks undoubtedly stained crimson as I turn away. "We'll talk about this later."

His fingers pause at the crotch of my panties. "We're going to do a hell of a lot more than talk."

"Stop it." I shoot him a playful glare. "Pay attention to the conversation." I jerk my chin at Lorenzo who talks to Bishop, the older man giving me a brief smile before asking Matthew something in Italian.

The three of them continue chatting while I ignore another call from Keira then turn off my cell. I won't speak to her again. Not until I'm stronger. More immune.

Instead, I focus on the foreign debate around me, attempting to decipher the topic. "*Ricchezza*" and "*Cruciale*" are spoken numerous times. Matthew repeats "*la mia risposta è no,*" more than once.

Sometimes they converse in English, the sentences holding just as much insight as those spoken in Italian when there's no prior context.

And through it all, Matthew's hand remains on my thigh, no longer a sexual taunt, but a companionable reminder that I'm not alone.

I sip my coffee between their laughter and hostility. The ups and downs come thick and fast until Lorenzo heaves a heavy sigh to focus on me with fatherly kindness.

"Alas, *bella*, I fear my boys aren't to be convinced." He clucks his tongue. "Who raised such stubborn fools?"

I grin. "I could make a wry comment about all men and their stereotypical stubbornness, but now probably isn't the time."

He chuckles. "I think we would all appreciate your restraint."

Matthew squeezes my thigh again and I take the gesture as encouragement. His appreciation settles in the air between us, our building bond tightening around me.

"You've barely eaten." Lorenzo frowns at all the untouched food spread across the table. "None of us have."

"It doesn't help when you're trying to tear us a new one." Bishop reaches for a pastry and takes a bite. "I'm fucking starving."

Matthew grabs a croissant. "Me, too."

I admire his strong hands, eager to find out how they'll be put to use later as the roar of a motorbike rumbles in the nearby intersection behind me, loud enough to momentarily deafen.

I wince, sipping the last of my latte, but hesitate in placing it back on the table.

Bishop sits taller, his attention cutting toward the sound. He stiffens as the thunder continues, the roaring muffler coming closer.

"What is it?" Matthew places the croissant on his plate and turns to look.

There's no response. Nothing other than a poised hardening of Bishop's stare.

I glance over my shoulder to the traffic lights, my gaze catching on the red that turns to green, but it's the motorcycle cutting away from the street to mount the bicycle lane that raises my hackles.

"We've got trouble." Bishop shoves to his feet.

Matthew's quick to do the same.

I'm unsure whether I should follow, the latte glass now frozen in my hand.

I glance between the men surrounding me, all of them on edge. All now standing, including the two bodyguards at the farthest corners of our secluded area. Both of them rush forward as the leather-covered biker howls toward us, face unseen below the darkened visor.

"What's going on?" I brace to stand, only to be stopped by Matthew's steely grip clasping my shoulder to hold me in place.

"Stay down," he barks.

I scramble to figure out what's going on, glancing from one man to the next, then back to the biker who reaches around his back to swing an automatic weapon toward the hotel.

Screams ring out. Chairs scrape and scatter.

"Get down." Matthew slams into me seconds before the *ratta-tat-tat* of gunfire rings out.

I topple backward to the cement. My elbow takes the brunt of the fall. The latte glass shatters on impact, splintering around me.

I cry out as he smothers his body over mine, covering me head to toe. But the reverberation in my throat doesn't make a dent on the nearby sounds seeking supremacy.

Women scream. Footsteps scramble. Glass smashes. More gunfire blasts the air. Closer. Louder. More threatening. Someone is returning fire.

Lorenzo is taken to the ground by his men. Shouts ping-pong around me.

"Lay flat," Matthew demands. "Straight against the ground."

I don't comply. I can't. I cling to him instead, wrapping my arms around his neck, burrowing my head against his shoulder as splinters of glass dig into me from all angles.

The bike grows louder. So close I feel the vibrations in every nerve.

I'm going to die.

I'm going to be shot while plastered to the cement, and my daughter doesn't even know where I am. I'll never get to speak to her again.

"I've got you." Matthew keeps me pinned, every inch of him holding me in place as the gunfire recedes, the hacking rumble of the engine speeding into the distance.

Then silence.

There's only the rasp of my fractured inhales against the ringing in my ears.

"Are you okay?" Matthew inches off me, his gaze frenzied as he scans my face.

"Yeah… I think so."

"I'm getting you out of here." He raises to his haunches. "Don't get up until I tell you."

I nod, but nothing fully penetrates the shock.

Men snarl and snap above me, the Italian words attacking with none of the beauty they held before.

I turn onto my side and hiss from the broken glass poking through my dress to my ribs, quickly discarding the hazard only for it to be replaced by ten more. I brush my arms, the shouts and screams from strangers rising above the bell tolling in my ears.

Diners slowly drag themselves to their feet in the distance. Others peer over the waist-high hedge from the bike track to take in the destruction. There are offers for help. Calls for the police.

Matthew. Is he okay?

I rake my gaze over him as he snaps words in Italian, scrutinizing the way he stands, how he holds himself, the way he moves his arms, needing to make sure he's uninjured. Then I focus on Bishop who clutches a gun at his side, and Lorenzo's guards who do the same, their weapons at home in their grasp as they shield their employer.

The show of defense brings another wave of apprehension.

I assumed they were armed. It's their job to protect.

But the air of calm under pressure is far too familiar, enough to inspire déjà vu. This snapshot is like so many others in my life. The shattered glass. The screaming women. The men with guns poised to retaliate on an unseen enemy.

"Were you shot?" Matthew demands of his mentor.

My attention snaps to the parting guards who expose Lorenzo sitting on the ground behind them, his hands clutching at his chest.

"No," he wheezes. "I'm good."

I push onto shaky hands and knees, needing to see for myself.

"Stay down." Matthew steps closer, towering over me as he plasters his phone to his ear then barks foreign garble.

"I'm fine, *bella*." Lorenzo gives an unconvincing smile, his face starkly pale. "It's nothing more than the temperamental heart of an old man."

"We need to leave." Bishop shoves chairs aside to squat before Lorenzo, helping to pull him to his feet. "That fucker could come back."

"Who was that?" Questions slam into me. "Who were they targeting?" I look to Matthew, the man who previously told me he had enemies.

He glances away, shoving a hand through his hair as he sneers more Italian into his phone.

My scrambled thoughts turn inward, the need for answers overwhelming.

What if I was the target?

I choke on an inhale, struggling to breathe.

Emmanuel has to know my family don't forget an injustice.

What if he found out I'd been in Denver? What if news got back to him that a stolen purse had been discovered with my ID and a vial of cyanide that all but had his name on it?

"Who the fuck knows? This could be anything from terrorism, to attempted assassination, to sabotage against the hotel chain." Bishop jerks his chin toward the restaurant. "But from the look of those bullet holes, it was either a warning or the person taking aim reads braille."

I follow the direction of his chin to see the shattered windows and the pockmarked facia above the frames. All the holes are well above head level. Too high to be life-threatening.

"Get Lorenzo out of here." Matthew pockets his cell and leans down to glide his fingers over the back of my arm, gently coaxing me to my feet.

"No," the old man growls. "I'm not leaving until I have answers."

"Don't be a stubborn fool." Matthew keeps me close at his side as he narrows his eyes on Bishop. "Go with him. Take him home to see his doctor. Make sure he's okay."

One of Lorenzo's guards holsters his weapon beneath his jacket. "Or at least wait inside."

"You'll take him home," Matthew demands, his face contorting with aggression. "*Now.*"

He's barely recognizable. The sophistication is gone, replaced with lethal authority. Feral fury. I don't know this man.

"I dare you to defy me," he warns. "You may gain his anger for dragging him out of here, but I'll kill you if he gets hurt."

I stiffen.

He walks into me, hustling us from the outdoor dining area by the crook of my arm, not allowing them a rebuttal or me a chance to think.

I'm hurried through the restaurant and into the hotel reception, my feet numb, my ears still ringing, my panic making thoughts unclear.

"Where are we going?" I struggle to keep up as he increases our pace, dragging me past staff who run in the opposite direction, their blurring faces rushing toward those yelling for help from the restaurant. "Matthew?"

"It's best if we get to our room. You'll be safe there."

I stop, needing the stillness to settle my foggy mind.

If the attack was targeting me, I'd be more safe at home. With my family. Where security is part of our genes.

With siblings already sick of your complications.

What's more important is that I need to get to Stella. To make sure she's all right. To ensure I haven't put her in harm's way.

"Layla, we need to keep moving." He pulls me toward the bank of elevators.

"No. Wait." I tug my arm from his grip. "I can't stay here. I have to get to my daughter."

"Your daughter is fine. *You're* fine." He leans close, his beseeching eyes demanding me to understand. "Once we get to the room, the quiet will help."

The confidence he exudes makes it easy to believe him. To at least trust mindlessly while my thoughts remain scrabbled.

He reclaims my hand and drags me to the elevators, my fear making me pliable. I blink in a daze as he presses the call button. I breathe shallow while more shouts reverberate off the walls and the blare of sirens approach.

We just walked out of there. A crime scene. A possible attempt on my life. Or was it his? Or Lorenzo's? Maybe the target was the hotel and its owners.

So why does it feel like it was all me?

My mistakes.

My problems.

My life on the line.

The metal doors open and Matthew closes in behind me, guiding me forward with heavy hands on my hips.

The air around us grows thicker in the confined space. My chest tightens. I can't get enough oxygen. I can't fill my lungs.

"You're okay." Matthew presses a button to close the doors, then moves in front of me. Foot to foot. Eye to eye. "It's over. You don't need to worry."

He has no clue.

This profoundly protective man has no idea I might have been the cause of this. That I would bring more untold danger into his life if we remained together.

"You're in shock." He presses a kiss to my forehead, the caress barely felt through my turmoil.

His affection is sweet… and caring… and something I'm entirely unworthy of.

I put him in harm's way. If not today, then with my actions in Denver.

The elevator jolts as it starts to ascend, the whir of movement increasing my turmoil. "I don't want to go to the room, Matthew. I want to go home. I need you to take me back to the helicopter."

"It's over, *amore mio.*"

I shake my head. "You don't understand."

Even though I've been careful—covering my tracks, using cash for every payment—Emmanuel still could've found me.

He may have got his hands on airport passenger lists… or tracked my phone somehow… or… *Fuck.* Could the Costas be watching Matthew like he's been watching them?

"Breathe." He cups my cheeks, his hard eyes demanding compliance. "I understand just fine. Trust me. I looked after you in Denver, right? And I've given you no reason to doubt me ever since. I'll take care of you, Layla. I promise."

His assurance crumples me. Sickens.

This is the exact drama I promised not to bring into his life. It has to be far worse than Bishop could've anticipated. My existence could ruin them both.

The elevator bumps to a stop, the doors open, and nausea overwhelms me when Matthew strides for the hall.

I can't follow.

"I need to go home." I inch toward the button panel. "I'll find my own way to the airport."

I don't care about my belongings. They're replaceable.

What I can't handle is another death on my hands.

"I won't let you leave on your own." His voice is barely contained frustration.

"I'll call my brother."

I'll tell him everything—my plans to take down the Costas, my stolen purse, the vial of cyanide. I'll beg for understanding…

And then what?

I'll become a bigger burden. A more despised part of the family.

A sob clogs my throat. "I have to go."

"I said no." Matthew storms into the elevator, hauls me off my feet, and lobs me over his shoulder. "I swore to protect you, and if that means from your own bad decisions, then so be it."

"Put me down." I wiggle with his booming steps, only resulting in him tightening his hold around my waist. "Matthew, I'm serious. Put me down."

"And *I'm* fucking serious," he growls. "You're not leaving. I need you with me."

I need you.

I. Need. You.

Each word slices at my skin, the unfamiliar sentiment tearing a sob from my scorched throat.

Nobody ever needs me. Not my family. Not my husband. Not even my daughter, who left for boarding school without a backward glance. The only person who ever claimed to need anything from me was my father, who used those words against me.

Matthew doesn't stop his vicious pace until we reach an open suite door. I push against his back, moving high enough to see around his waist to the housekeeping trolley standing idle a few feet inside the darkened hall.

"Is someone in our room?" His question is a commanding boom.

"Oh," a female replies, a scuffle of noise following. "Yes, sir. It's housekeeping." A petite brunette pokes her head around the corner, her face in flickering shadow. "I'm sorry, I haven't finished preparing what was request—"

"We need privacy." He storms forward, carrying me like a sack of potatoes.

I should fight. Run. Leave him to a life that would be less dramatic without me, but… *I need you.*

That declaration. That honesty.

God, I need him, too.

I need the assurance. The protection. The authority that quietens the screaming within.

"Please put me down." I soften against him. "Please, Matthew."

He trudges ahead, the scent of candle wax hitting my nose sweet seconds before we reach the open living area where he places me on my feet next to the sofa.

I pause in confusion, the sight not computing.

The housekeeper stands before the kitchenette, a silver wine bucket on the counter, a lighter in her hand. The room is emblazoned with dozens of flickering tea lights. The beauty steals my breath, the glow emanating from every horizontal surface.

Rose petals are scattered over the carpet, the sofa, the television stand.

Matthew requested this?

"It will only take me a moment to finish." The woman's gaze shifts between us. "The bathroom just needs—"

"Leave." Matthew shoves a hand through his hair.

The woman winces, nods in apology, then rushes to a dark corner of the kitchen to retrieve a box of rattling candles. "The food you requested is already in the fridge. Again, I apologize." She scampers for her trolley in the hall, the rattle of shampoo bottles and cleaning supplies filling the room before she pulls the door shut behind her.

Then, more silence.

Thick, painful quiet which contrasts with the beauty of the dancing flames around me. Hell consumes my thoughts, yet heaven fills my vision. The opposites add to my instability.

I need something to make sense.

Anything.

"Do you want a glass of water?" Matthew begins to pace, both hands raking into his hair, his fingers clawing against his scalp. "Maybe wine is best. Or food? Do you need something to eat?"

His questions are fast and emotionless. Spoken without thought or follow-through.

I watch him, noting the sweat beading his brow, the rapid rise and fall of his chest. He's spiraling. Descending into shock as he trudges back and forth along the carpet.

"Matthew…" Guilt consumes me. "I need to leave." It's harder to say this time. Harder to admit the truth in the face of his torment. "This has to end."

He stops abruptly, his hands falling to his sides as he scowls. "What did you say?"

I cringe against the surprise in his eyes. The rejection.

But I made a promise. I said I wouldn't cause drama.

"I never should have come here." My heart squeezes with the admission. With the lies and secrecy and unending mistakes. "I think I caused this."

He straightens. "Why would you think that?"

I don't want to tell him specifics. To ruin the fairy tale. To witness his opinion of me disintegrate like so many others have before.

"Layla, why would you think that?" His eyes narrow in confusion.

"I'm not who or what you think I am…" I backtrack toward the door, each syllable pulled from me like a deeply rooted tooth. "I'm not a good person."

"Hey." He prowls toward me, eating up the space, reclaiming my cheeks in his palms. "Stop it. This wasn't about you."

"You don't know that." The truth sits like bile at the back of my throat, needing to be expelled. "I've put you in danger with what I've done with the Costas."

His eyes scan me. Scrutinize. "Tell me everything."

"I can't." I'm too ashamed.

"Layla." His voice drops in warning. "Emmanuel has nothing to do with this. Neither do you. So whatever it is you're worried about, don't."

He's in denial. About me. About Emmanuel. I step back, needing to leave. To end this before I drown in him any further. But he holds me captive with his palms, matching my retreat with a bigger advance. He keeps us toe-to-toe, hip to hip, almost heart to heart, weakening me with his savior complex.

"The purse that was stolen from me in Denver had cyanide in it," I blurt, needing him to let me go. "If it got into the wrong hands, along with my ID, and the Costas caught wind of it…" I cringe, hating the shocked scowl peering back at me. "They'd know they were my target. They'd want to strike first."

He doesn't speak. Doesn't move.

It's only harsh eyes and harsher energy bearing down on me.

"Now will you let me go?"

"No," he repeats with steadfast conviction. "Downstairs had nothing to do with you. Lorenzo was the target. He's *always* the target. So if anyone is to blame, it's me for placing you in danger."

24

MATTHEW

This moment has been destined. It's only ever been a matter of time. And even though I've known it's been approaching since the moment we met, I'm far less prepared than I was the night she walked into my life all confident and magnificently mysterious.

"How do you know?" She blinks back at me, confused.

"He's a powerful man." I release her cheeks and retreat, needing a break from her scrutiny.

"How powerful?"

I wipe a rough hand down my face, becoming less ready for what's to come with each passing second.

I don't want her to deal with this now. I was meant to tell her in my own time. In my own way.

I huff a deep breath. "Powerful enough to—"

A pounding knock sounds at the door. She startles, gasping at the noise, exposing just how fragile my decisions have made her.

"Who is it?" I bark.

"Bishop," comes the mumbled reply. "Open the fucking door."

I stalk for the entry only to be stopped by Layla scrambling in front of me, her eyes stark with determination.

"Tell me." She splays her hands on my chest, her heavy palms feeble at best against my strength. "Who is he?"

I stiffen against the pent-up air in my lungs, the pressure of a lifetime's worth of bad decisions caging me behind tightening ribs. "Let me get rid of Bishop first."

Stall. Stall. Stall.

That's all I've fucking done with her.

Delayed the truth.

Delayed her disgust.

Delayed the end of us.

I step around her and stalk for the hall, checking the peephole to find Bishop's scowl before I yank the door open. "You're meant to be taking Lorenzo home to see his doctor. Why—"

"The old prick is still downstairs. He told me to take a hike. I'm not going to baby him."

I clench my teeth, battling against rage. They're both as prideful as each other. Both pains in my fucking ass. "He needs a doctor."

"He needs a lot of things, but mothering ain't my strong suit." Bishop juts his chin toward the inside of my suite and lowers his voice. "Nice mood lighting. It's almost as if you anticipated needing the romantic seduction to stop her from running."

I lash out, grabbing him by the throat.

I don't know if it's his audacity or the reaffirmation of her leaving that makes me snap.

He doesn't flinch. Not even when I shove him backward, walking us down the hall, away from her listening ears. The door clicks shut seconds later.

"Watch your goddamn mouth," I snarl.

He tilts his chin higher in defiance. "You need to get rid of her."

"I'm not doing that." My voice is barely a whisper as I keep stalking us farther from the suite, my fingers digging into his neck, my aggression impatient for him to retaliate so we can take this exchange to the next level. The one where I get to dispense all my anger through a mindless pummeling of fists and decimating impact.

"Then at least tell her the truth so she can see herself out."

"She won't leave me." I release him with a shove and step back, needing space from his smug grin.

We both know I'm full of shit.

She'll leave. She'll fucking sprint.

"We need to get back to D.C." He yanks at his lapels to straighten his jacket. "I'll get the helicopter organized—"

"No." I stand tall, denying him the most logical response to a targeted shooting. Now, more than ever, I need this isolation with Layla. These hours are necessary to explain everything she's going to demand to know. To convince her to remain at my side. "I'm not changing our plans. We're staying the night."

He scoffs. "And I'm supposed to what? Sit in the hall like a guard dog?"

"We don't need protection. We won't leave the room."

His eyes harden to conniving slits. "You're losing it, you know that, right? Everything we've worked for is going straight out the fucking window because of a piece of ass."

"You're wrong. She makes me better."

"Better?" He raises a taunting brow. "Is that what you call threatening to kill Lorenzo's guards if they don't listen to you over him? If I didn't know you better, I'd say you were gearing up to take the helm."

"Fuck you." My words thrash against clenched teeth.

"Touchy subject? Have you been thinking about it, BB?"

I see red, the hint to a forbidden nickname acting like a fire poker to my rage. "Do you want to die today?"

He grins. "There he is. The villain I know and love."

"Walk away," I warn.

"I'd fucking love to. Unfortunately, your dumb ass refuses to carry a gun. So I'm stuck protecting you. Protecting *her*." He steps forward, getting in my face. "You need to tell her the truth. Tell her what she's getting herself into. Tell her all the things you've hidden just so you can keep her like a fucking pet."

I'd been trying to. I'd had the confession on the tip of my tongue. I never envisaged misleading her this long. I just didn't plan on wanting her this much when I exposed the truth.

The tiniest squeak of a door filters down the hall. I turn to see Layla inching out of our suite, her wary eyes finding mine.

I step back from Bishop and cringe at my instinct to shield things from her. She deserves transparency—honesty—even though she hasn't offered it in return.

"Go back inside." I leash the aggression in my tone. "I'll be there in a minute."

The wariness grows in her stare as she glances from me to Bishop then back again.

"It's okay, *amore mio*. I won't be long."

Her chest rises with a deep breath beneath the tempting red sundress before she silently slips back inside, the door closing with a barely heard click.

"She may have a pretty face, but don't forget she's as fucked up as you are," Bishop mutters. "We don't need that shit in our lives."

A storm rages inside me. The energy batters my veins. Sneering. Demanding.

I close my eyes, reining it in, mastering the aggression.

He chuckles, the briefest breath of sound. "Look at you, trying to battle the inevitable. This is a waste—"

I lunge, grabbing his shirt in my fist. "Shut your fucking mouth." I struggle not to lose myself to the insanity. Fight not to shove my knuckles into my best friend's throat.

He doesn't retaliate. He's the only one armed, and all he does is raise his chin as if reiterating his point.

Fuck.

I retreat, releasing his shirt. "I'll fucking tell her." I turn my back on him before I do something I'll regret, and start for the suite. "Check on Lorenzo. I don't want to see your face again until he's been looked over by his doctor."

I reach the door and grab the key card from my jacket to swipe over the lock. I stalk into the shadowed room flickering in candlelight, the fury following me.

"What's going on, Matthew?"

Layla's voice increases my struggle, her trepidation creating guilt that whirlpools with my anger.

She stands in front of the sofa, her cell in her hand, the screen lighting up her face in the darkness. "What's Lorenzo's surname?"

Shit. She's searching for him online?

I stalk to her, stepping around the coffee table, making her stiffen as I get within reach.

Jesus fucking Christ.

She's questioning me again. Judging. Fearing.

Rightly so.

"What are you doing?" I slow my approach, cautiously reaching for her hand to tilt the cell screen my way.

Lorenzo Virginia Beach is typed into the search bar with a page of irrelevant results about some specialist doctor listed below.

"I want to know what's going on." She pulls the phone back toward her and locks the screen, the snuffed glow making her face shadowed. "I tried googling him but there are too many results in Virginia Beach."

I nod, teeth clenched, limbs thrumming.

Her gaze weighs heavily on me. Every blink of her lashes acts like a physical blow. "There's a lot to explain." But the explanation doesn't come. The truth refuses to slither from the darkest depths of my soul.

And this room isn't helping.

With the closed curtains and the mass of flickering candlelight, it feels like I'm in Satan's dungeon. And I've already spent too much time there to want to return.

I march to the window and yank back the heavy drapes, the burst of sunlight searing my eyes. Yet it's not enough to assuage my darkness. Not the beach or the sun or the sand.

I lunge for the closest candles and snuff them out. One after another, after another, after another. The scent of smoke wafts in the air, the threat of the fire alarm merely adding to the shitstorm inside me.

"Matthew..."

I pause with my back to her. Straighten. Succumb.

"Please tell me."

Her plea undoes me, my knotted threads unraveling.

I turn, finding her chin raised. She already knows the impending increase of seriousness in this already fucked up situation, and she's preparing to take it head on.

I wish I could laugh at the naivety of her conviction, but there's nothing funny here. Things between us never should've gone this far. I wasn't meant to get entangled.

Bishop knew she would be my undoing. He even explained the psychology behind why I'm drawn to her. *Obsessed* with her. And yet I still can't push past the mental trickery to let her go.

"Matthew?" Her eyes beg for me to ease her suffering. To break the torturous suspense.

She's such a fucking maze, some paths leading to dead ends, others harboring threats and misdeeds. I applaud her strength. Her tenacity. Her viciousness. But the cyanide admission threw me for a loop.

I guess we've both got bigger secrets than either of us led the other to believe.

"Please, Matthew. Tell me what's going on."

I release the toxic air eating at my lungs and slump my ass onto the coffee table, letting her tower above me. Rule over me.

"Before I met Lorenzo, I was homeless."

Her lips part at my admission, her stunning eyes widening.

"Through mistakes of my own, and sabotage from others, I lost everything. I had nobody. Not a penny to my name. Only the clothes on my back and a shitload of emotional baggage."

"How old were you?"

I scoff. Too young to be without a family and too old to be a sorry son of a bitch. "A few months from my eighteenth birthday."

Pity floods her expression. "Matthew, I—"

"Don't say anything. Just let me speak." *Let me explain all the things you're going to hate about me.* "Lorenzo took me in. Gave me a home. A purpose. An income. He provided an outlet for my teenage anger. Introduced me to Bishop. And helped me get where I am today."

She shuffles closer as if drawn by my pathetic story, her sandals bumping my shoes, her eyes filled with compassion.

"Everything I have is because of him," I continue. "Without his intervention, I have no doubt I would've died on the streets."

She remains quiet, letting me bleed parts of my truth, her hands reaching out to slide through my hair in delicate strokes.

"He became my father figure and treated me like another one of his sons—harsh when I needed it, but equally supportive when necessary. He invited me into his success and I helped him achieve more." I lower my gaze, focusing on the carpet, running my palms around her waist to stop her from escaping when the truth hits. "There's nothing I wouldn't have done for him."

"He sounds like a wonderful man," she whispers.

"He is," I say with conviction. "And he isn't."

Slowly she stands taller, her spine straightening in caution.

"To me, he's a savior. A lifeline." I look up at her. "He's the reason I still have air in my lungs. But he's not what most would call a wonderful man."

Her hands stop sweeping my hair. Trepidation ebbs from her.

Quiet seeps in, curling around us with tight arms and sharp claws. Her breathing slows, long and pained. She knows where this is going. She can sense it.

"You said you're not a good person, Layla. But in my past, I've done things in the name of survival that would chill you to the core. And I've done them all for Lorenzo."

Her hands slowly withdraw from my hair to rest at her sides, the retreat emotional as well as physical.

She doesn't ask the questions I know must be eating at her. She lets the silence fester between us, its thorny spikes digging into my skin, her panicked thoughts flashing in her wild eyes.

Maybe she no longer wants clarity.

Maybe she'd prefer to remain ignorant and leave my life without the darkness of the truth haunting her.

But it's too late for that.

I refuse to let her go.

"My mentor is Lorenzo Cappelletti," I admit, taking in the stark recognition that now stares back at me. "He's Italian mafia."

25

LAYLA

I wait for the punchline. For the cruel prank to be laughed away so I can shed this second skin of shock and confusion.

But no humor gleams in his expression. There's not even the slightest sign of banter.

Instead, his expression begs for understanding. For forgiveness.

"You're in the Italian mafia?" The question is wrenched from my drying throat.

"No. I got out."

A mindless scoff escapes me before I can stop it. "You got out?"

"Yes." His shoulders slump, his handsome face losing the mask of confidence.

"I may not know a lot about the mafia," I lie. "But I'm pretty sure it's not something you can simply walk away from."

"There was nothing simple about it. I earned my freedom. Bishop did, too. We've been out for years."

That's not how it works. Is it?

Could other parts of the underworld let their members walk free? Are there ways to safeguard family secrets once someone defects? A strategy to stop competitors from targeting turncoats?

No, otherwise I would've fled long ago.

I step back, only to be kept close by the cage of Matthew's hands.

He strengthens his hold on my waist, firmly imprisoning me. "Don't walk out on me, *amore mio*. Give me time to explain."

"Stop calling me that." I push him away and stumble backward, bumping into the sofa, almost falling into the cushions before I can right myself to stagger farther.

He has no idea what he's done.

Being with him—an enemy—will singlehandedly destroy the already tattered relationship I have with my family.

They'll never forgive me for this.

"Why?" He stares at me through harsh hooded lashes, each bat of his eyes slaying me. "You *are* my love. My past doesn't change that."

"Your past changes everything," I whisper as madness overwhelms me. The questions. The stupidity. The shame.

How could I have made more mistakes? Created more complications for my brother? More and more mess that continues to compile, stealing the air from my lungs? And yet through the gasps for respite, some sickeningly, stupid part of me latches onto the tiniest glimmer of hope in his story—he got out.

He left the underworld.

He created a new life.

I walk on numb feet to the window, my gaze seeking the calm of the ocean. But the deep blue doesn't soothe me. My mind is in chaos. The sharp claws of panic shred the inside of my skull.

"I have more to tell you," he murmurs. "So much more. I want you to know everything. I want—"

"Why?" I beg, mostly of myself. "Why me? Why now? Why any of this?"

How could he make me fall in love with him when we can never be together?

How cruel can fate be?

"We're alike." He slowly rises to his feet, seeming even more handsome and commanding now that I have to walk away. "We have common enemies. We've contemplated similar crimes."

I frown.

"The cyanide," he clarifies. "Were you really going to use it?"

I snap my attention back to the ocean, wishing I hadn't made the confession. Realizing he could easily use the information against me. Against my family.

"Could you have killed someone, Layla?"

I keep my mouth shut. My lips fused.

He approaches, sidestepping the edge of the sofa in my periphery.

"Stop." I turn to face him, glaring. This is serious. I need to rewind time and remember all the things I've told him. All the clues I've given. All the insight I've shared. "Stay where you are."

His face falls. Plummets. And in the split-second of this powerful man's pained rejection, I see myself reflected in him.

I see the woman forsaken for the mistakes of her past. I see the person turned pariah due to circumstances out of their control.

"Just…" I attempt to shake my head free from the emotional onslaught. "Just give me a second."

I need to think. To understand. To do damage control.

"Layla, you're bleeding." His attention narrows on my hip, his expression transforming from devastation to concern. He strides forward, forcing me to scamper backward. "Don't fight me on this," he warns with an edge of malice. "Let me make sure you're okay. You mean so much to me. I—"

"You don't even know me."

He stops a foot away, his nostrils flaring. "*Yes*, I do."

I shake my head and glance at my dress, trying to see where the hell I'm bleeding from. "No, you don't." I twist, finding blood splotches that match the red fabric, the material nicked with tiny cuts along my side. "You have no idea."

"So everything between us was fake? Was it all for sex? For the lifestyle? For attention?"

I gape. "No, I never—"

"Then I know you. I know how I feel when I'm with you. I know how good we are together. How we fit. How we're perfectly matched. How we can hold a conversation for hours. And fuck until we're exhausted, but far from sated, because being with you means I'll never get enough." He bridges the space between us in an adamant step. "*That's* how I know you. And it's the only knowledge that matters."

His admission shakes me. Grabs me by the arms and rattles me to my bones.

I'd thought I'd known him, too.

I'd thought the knowledge I had was all that mattered. Now I'm painfully aware that's simply not true.

What he kept from me changes everything. It bends and twists the already stretched limbs I'd stepped out on to have this secret relationship in the first place. It makes the already unattainable nauseatingly impossible.

"Let me see why you're bleeding." He doesn't quit holding my gaze as he reaches out, fingering the material at my waist, bundling it in his hands.

My heart clenches, beating harder at his affection. At the weeks of deception.

"Why did you bring me here?" I blurt, unable to contain the mania.

His brows knit. "To Virginia Beach?"

"To the meeting. To the hotel. Why introduce me to Lorenzo? Why risk my life?"

"I didn't think there was any risk. Nobody has dared to target him in years. I never would've brought you otherwise." He keeps my dress bundled in his hands, his chin lifting. "I'm sick of the secrets, Layla. I wanted him to get to know you. I. want you to know who I am."

My pulse weakens, my entire body withering.

I return my attention to the ocean, unable to voice a protest when he bundles more of my dress in his grip. Unwilling to deny his cautious affection. Powerless to walk away even though I know I have to.

I thought he was my safety vest in the midst of the pummeling waves of my life. Instead, he was nothing more than a mirage. Yet I still hunger to cling to the illusion. I continue to hope he'll save me from drowning despite him being just another shark in the water.

The hem of my dress rises from my ankles to my calves, then my thighs.

I hold my breath against the exposure. I clench every muscle against the judgment of my family snipping in my ears. Their recrimination. The fury.

But Matthew hasn't lost the calming touch. He soothes me. Provides solace.

How?

How can his proximity dilute the devastation of my situation? How can he—a man now exposed as having underworld ties—comfort me?

Because despite the darkness of his admission, he's the only support I've got.

The fabric creeps higher, exposing my lace panties, my bra. He keeps pulling the dress farther until it's over my shoulders and head, then lets the clothing fall into a pool of crimson on the carpet.

I close my eyes as he steps around me, his fingertips gently gliding from my shoulder to the ribs at my back, every inch of nurtured skin awakening in a blanket of goose bumps until his touch stops at my waist.

"You're covered in scratches," he murmurs. "None deep enough to require stitches, but too many for me to escape more guilt over bringing you here."

I battle inner turmoil as his fingertips trail intricate circles along the sensitive flesh at the small of my back, the beauty of his soothing contact tearing me to shreds.

"Forgive me." He closes in behind me, one hand still learning my injuries, the other arm taking liberties to skim around my waist to my stomach, holding me to him. "I've made mistakes." He speaks against my shoulder, his breath sending a shiver down my spine. "I'm not that person anymore."

A whimper tightens my throat.

I'm not the person I used to be either.

"Start a new life with me, Layla," he whispers my wishes into existence. My dreams. My hopes. "Be with me for who I am now. Not where I came from."

"Where you came from just had us ducking for cover." I turn to face him, finally able to ignore all the parts of me that want to disappear into the shelter of his arms. "You haven't moved on, Matthew. That life is still a part of you."

"No. I walked away from their—"

"How can you say that when Lorenzo was asking you to take over right in front of me? He was begging you to come back."

His jaw ticks with tension. "I'm next in line because his sons declined the offer. He's growing desperate. But I'll never go back."

"It seems to me that you're going back every time you meet with him."

"I've been out for years," he enunciates with slow adamance. "Bishop and I—"

"Yes, tell me about Bishop." I've never trusted that asshole. "If you wanted distance from your old life, why keep him with you?"

For a moment he's silent, perhaps biding his time.

"Matthew?" I raise a brow and snatch my dress from the floor, huddling it against my chest.

"He's with me out of misguided obligation. He thinks he owes me for getting him out."

"And how did you do that?"

"I did whatever I had to. I wasn't leaving without him."

His words say nothing, but I understand regardless. I know the sins. The darkness. The bloodshed.

The duties of underworld men aren't unfamiliar to me. I'm aware of the atrocities my brother inflicts on our enemies. Hunter, Decker, and Luca, too. And all the underlings that follow.

I was raised to believe an eye for an eye is for the nine-to-five crowd.

My family is different. If someone betrays the Torian name, the cost is high and lifelong. Not merely an eye, but the breaking of one's spirit. The shredding of their soul.

I don't want to see Matthew like that. I can't picture blood on his hands and hate in his heart.

I wrap my arms around my waist, unable to deny it any longer. "You've killed people."

His jaw ticks again. "I can admit I'm not without sin. Can you?"

"Excuse me?"

"What were you planning on doing with the Costas, Layla? Why were you carrying poison?"

"This isn't about me. We're—"

"Why not?" He cocks a brow. "We're one and the same. You might not want to tell me who you are, but the fact you haven't run a million times already says we're from similar worlds. We understand each other. We can make this work."

"Our similarities are what I'm trying to get away from."

"Me too." He runs a hand through his hair. "Me fucking too."

I hate this side of him. The frustration and suffering. It awakens a weakness in me I never knew existed.

"I wish we were different people." I drag my dress back over my head. "I wish for so many things, Matthew. A lot of them involving you. But—"

"Then stop right there." He decimates the space between us to grab my wrists, the red fabric falling to huddle at my hips as he tugs me into his chest. "We'll start fresh together. You, me, Stella." He inches forward, and I'm not sure if it's his words or his proximity that sends me into a tailspin. "I've never—"

"No. *You* stop." I splay a hand against his sternum in warning. "Don't—"

"I care too much to let you walk out on me, Layla."

I shake my head. Over and over and over.

These reactions. This craziness. None of it can go on.

"I didn't grow up planning to take a path toward a man like Lorenzo," he continues. "But every decision and every fucking mistake led me to the night we met. Every crime. Every unforgivable action brought me to you."

My veins hum with fear and anticipation. Panic and power.

I'm torn. Severed in two.

"It doesn't matter." I have to get home. To monotony and misery. Solitude and sadness.

Another knock sounds at the door, rattling the wood against the frame. I snap rigid at the intrusion as Matthew growls a curse.

"Who is it?" he barks.

"*Me*," Bishop yells from the hall. "Who the fuck else are you expecting?"

Matthew doesn't move. Doesn't even loosen his hold. The only change is the flare of his nostrils as he glares at the entry. "I'll get rid of him."

26

LAYLA

I scramble to right my dress as Matthew stalks for the entry, the whoosh of the door soon following.

"I told you I didn't want to see you until Lorenzo was taken to the doctor," he growls.

"Relax," comes the arrogant reply. "He's on his way there now."

I hustle across the room, taking in the sight of Matthew at the door and Bishop scowling over his shoulder at me from the hall.

"Why didn't you go with him?" Matthew asks.

Bishop drags his gaze from me, his focus tight when he says, "Because I've got news."

There's a beat of silence. Of non-verbal communication.

"What news?" I interrupt. "I want to know what's going on."

The quiet continues, their silent communication lasting a muted microsecond before Matthew steps back, allowing his friend access to the suite.

My nemesis strides inside, his chin arrogantly high, his lips thin. He stops before the sofa and turns away from me to take off his suit jacket, exposing the gun buried in the back of his pants before he throws the item of clothing over the armrest.

It's a show. A deliberately theatrical intimidation.

I'm not buying tickets.

When he pivots to face me, I want to roll my eyes. To roll them so far in the back of my head I gag, but he doesn't need to know men like him are a dime a dozen where I'm from.

He descends to the sofa, spreading his arms along the headrest, crossing an ankle over his knee. He's attempting to appear superior and relaxed while I'm expected to cower and hide.

Not going to happen.

I want answers.

157

Matthew follows after him, his presence both comforting and daunting depending on whether I listen to my heart or my head.

"So…" Bishop drawls. "What's going on?"

"I told her." Matthew makes his way to the kitchenette, distancing himself as he scoots his ass onto the counter. He sits there, frustrated and remorseful, entirely focused on me while he leans forward in his immaculate suit, his elbows on his knees.

"Told her what exactly?" Bishop remains imperious as he watches me. Both of them attempting to slither their way under my skin for different reasons.

"That you're in the mafia." I cross my arms over my chest.

His eyes narrow. "We *were*," he growls. "That shit is ancient history."

Relief sparks a tiny flickering flame inside me. "You *were* in the mafia," I correct. "You earned your way out of that life somehow, but decided to stay together afterward. Why?"

"You didn't tell her the reason I stick around?" Bishop glances over his shoulder to the kitchen, but my lover's daunting attention doesn't leave me for a second.

"No, he didn't," I answer. Not really.

Bishop scoffs a laugh. "It's because Matty boy wants to receive his very own martyrdom status. I need to stay close so he doesn't obtain his title."

I frown, glancing from Bishop's smug expression to Matthew's cold one. "What does that mean?"

Are we talking about suicide?

"That's enough dramatics," Matthew mutters. "He's here for protection."

Bishop clears his throat louder than necessary. "If you were concerned about protection, you'd carry a gun."

"I said, that's enough."

The questions in my head multiply. There are so many more now than the millions I had before.

"Quit the look of defeat, darlin'." Bishop uncrosses his legs to kick his shoes onto the coffee table. "Your bad boy fix isn't going to end anytime soon. Not unless you finally start listening to my warnings. You should've walked when I pushed."

What? Had his aggression been for my benefit? To scare me away from all this?

"I didn't plan on dragging you into my life, *amore mio*." Matthew pinches the bridge of his nose. "You're the last thing I expected to find in Denver."

"I can attest to that," Bishop agrees. "Which brings us to the topic of the Costas and your association with them."

I cinch my arms tighter around my middle. "I think we have more pressing things to discuss, don't you? Like being shot at?"

"If you'd prefer to discuss blatant dangers first instead of those that are far more sinister in their subtlety, then that's fine with me." He shrugs. "Lorenzo sends his apologies. He understands the complications he must have caused between you and Matthew, and begs forgiveness."

"So he knew the attack was coming?" Matthew asks.

"No. He underestimated how hungry the local biker gangs are for power. There's a turf war over distribution, and Lorenzo refused to get involved. He wanted them to sort it out amongst themselves. Now he assumes this morning was a little nudge to let him know they'd prefer his involvement."

He relays the information as if it's week-old news. As if we hadn't just been in a life-threatening situation moments ago due to the drug trade.

I see through the tough-guy act, though. He'd been the first to shove to his feet when the threat arrived. He'd feared for Lorenzo and Matthew's lives, if not his own.

"He wanted you to know he's taken care of the police." He talks over his shoulder. "He spoke to them while I was downstairs and promised he was leaving to go see his doctor."

"Bullshit," Matthew mutters. "You know he won't."

"You might be right, but I'm not going to cup his balls while he takes a piss. If he goes, he goes. If he doesn't, that's not my fault. He's not our responsibility anymore."

Matthew takes the remark like a blow, his face momentarily sharpening as our eyes meet.

He's not *out*, no matter what he says. Maybe physically, but not emotionally.

"I still care for his well-being, Layla." He holds my gaze as he answers my unspoken thoughts. "That will never change."

"My boy has daddy issues." Bishop winks at me. "But who doesn't, right?"

My heart thuds a painful beat at how right he is. At how Matthew and I continue to have more things in common.

"Are you done?" Matthew pushes from the counter. "As much as I'm enjoying this provoking mood, if you've got no more information, it's time to fuck off."

"Touchy much?" Bishop shoves from the sofa to pull on his jacket. "Am I calling in the helicopter?"

"No. We're staying."

"Are we?" I scowl, making it obvious I don't appreciate the dictatorship.

"We're staying," he repeats. "You still have questions and we're not going anywhere until they're answered. If you want to walk out on me, you're going to do it with crystal clarity."

"I'm surprised she hasn't walked already." Bishop fixes his lapels and smirks at me. "Slow learner."

"Go to hell," I snap.

He snickers, breathing in my anger like a fine wine. Consuming it. "You're far too lippy for a woman who's just found herself in the middle of a gangland drug war." He starts for the hall, his gaze turning to Matthew. "Make sure you ask some questions of your own. If she's learning my secrets, I sure as hell want hers in return."

I fight against the need to stiffen as he continues for the door, leaving the suite without another word.

I should follow. Escape. Cut ties with the thin threads of hopeful possibility that have me pondering whether I could start over, fresh and renewed.

Matthew won't want me when he finds out who I really am.

Despite the instinctive connection between us, an enemy is still an enemy.

"Ask, Layla." Matthew approaches. "Whatever's on your mind, let it out."

"Whatever's on my mind?" I counter his steps, keeping the coffee table between us. "I can barely think straight."

He stops behind the sofa, clenching the headrest in both hands. "You've gotta start somewhere."

No, I don't. I shouldn't start at all.

I should walk. He knows it. I know it.

Lord knows my family would know it if they were privy to my latest phase of stupidity.

But curiosity and yearning tag team inside my chest, demanding answers.

I have to find out how far Matthew has distanced himself from his past. How he could've escaped the inescapable. And if he's truly sincere about a future between us.

If he's asking me not to judge, then maybe he won't judge in return.

He might not despise me for who I am and what I've done.

Then there's Lorenzo. If I'm going to return to Cole with my tail between my legs, the best option is to go back with information. Insight on the Italian mafia might soften my latest blow of shitty decisions.

The Cappellettis are a force.

Holy fucking shit.

The *Cappellettis.*

"What is it?" Matthew frowns. "What's wrong?"

All the blood drains from my face.

"Layla," he demands. "Fucking ask. Talk to me."

"Your mentor is Emmanuel Costa's brother-in-law." My voice is barely audible as a tremor takes over my limbs. How could I forget? How could he not have told me? After all this time, he kept his connection to the Costas a secret. "Is this a setup? Have you been playing me since the moment we met?"

"Stop. *No.*" His upper lip sneers. "My mentor is Emmanuel's enemy. They despise each other. Lorenzo can't stand the man his sister married. None of his brothers can."

I shake my head. This is too much.

Too many secrets.

Too heavy a reliance on trust that I never should've given.

Warning bells and calls for calm poison my blood, the warring toxicity increasing. I'd been happy with him. At home. I'd been empowered and invigorated and blissed.

And all this time, we'd both been lying. To ourselves. To each other.

He has no idea who he's introduced to his infamous mentor.

"I'm leaving." The words are a pained whisper over the bile at the back of my throat.

"Not like this you're not." He stalks toward the entry, preempting my escape. "Once I've answered all your questions and you have the information to make an informed—"

"This isn't merely about making an informed decision. No matter what you tell me, it won't change the fact I have secrets of my own. Secrets that make this situation worse than the hell it already is."

His face loses the tense edge. "I know you, Layla."

"You keep saying that, but you have no clue."

"You're wrong." His voice lowers, the edge of hostility replaced with a tone I can't describe. Pity? Regret? "I know who you are."

There's something different in his conviction this time. Something more pointed in his confidence over my character. Something capable of twisting mercilessly at my stomach.

My pulse increases. My panic, too.

I shake my head, ignoring his faith. Needing to brush it off.

"I know your name," he continues. "Your family. Your legacy."

I hold my breath.

He's bluffing. He has to be.

Only nothing but fortitude stares back at me.

A spike of panicked nausea rolls through me. "No."

If he knew, he never would've brought me here. Never would've introduced me to Lorenzo. Never would've said all those dreamy, optimistic things.

"Yes." He gives a somber smile. "You showed your ID to one of my bouncers. That was after Bishop had instructed them to take notes if someone matching your name and description showed up."

No. I keep shaking my head, denying my secrets have been his for what… days? Weeks? He knew all this time and didn't say anything?

"You're Layla Hart," he continues. "Sister to Cole Torian. Daughter to the infamous Luther Torian. And part of the notorious crime family that rules over Portland."

My shoulders hunch with the verbal blows that punch like a physical assault, but this time, it's not shock that overwhelms me. It's shame.

I didn't want him to find out about the sinister shadow cloaking me.

Bile sears the back of my throat, scarring, choking.

He'd known this whole time. During the lovemaking. Through the conversations and seduction.

"How could you?" The contents of my stomach surge for attention.

I stagger around the coffee table, dashing for the far hall, needing the bathroom. I shove open the closest door finding more candlelight in a room of darkness, the flames dancing from tea lights along a vanity and reflecting in the wall-to-wall mirror.

I scamper toward the faint hint of the toilet in the corner, falling to my knees beside the shower as coffee and croissants desert my body in rolling waves of dread.

I submit to the devastation. The loss of hope. The failure.

Each purge claws at me, scratching away parts of the fairy tale I never should've believed in but couldn't stop myself from falling for.

How could I have been so oblivious to the truth?

I continue purging until nothing but acid escapes. That's when I hear him entering the room, his footsteps approaching before he clatters something to the vanity beside me.

I want to scream for privacy. To yell at him to leave me to my destruction. But he moves closer, his hands finding my hair with gentle authority, pulling the errant strands away from my cheeks as more bile floods my lips.

"We'll work this out." He speaks with confidence.

I spit, clearing the dredge from my mouth. "Get out."

"I'm not going anywhere, *amore mio*. You're stuck with me."

His vow makes this worse. The caring hands. The affectionate determination.

I shrink away from him and reach over my head to flush the toilet. First shame, now humiliation. Add to that the stupidity and danger. The naivety and gullibility.

I've created a Molotov cocktail of mistakes. All I need now is to strike a match and let the flames take hold.

I pull myself to my feet, appreciating how he keeps his distance as I approach the sink that now holds company with my toiletry bag. I close my eyes briefly, thankful for his thoughtfulness and desperately despising the sensation at the same time.

How could he do this to me? How could he keep both secrets—his and mine—when alone they're problematic, but together they're catastrophic?

I retrieve my toothbrush without a word, cleansing my mouth of the humiliation while his gaze taunts the back of my neck.

I rinse and spit, rinse and spit, scrubbing the enamel from my teeth as if I were dislodging my mistakes. But no matter how hard I scour, he doesn't disappear, and neither does the romantic flickering firelight.

He remains quiet behind me until I turn to face him, broken, hollow, and defeated.

"How?" I croak. "How could you keep this from me?"

"It was no secret to either of us that we had things to hide. You wanted your privacy and I needed to keep mine until I figured out who you were."

"But you figured it out," I accuse. "You learned who I was days ago and never breathed a word of it. You never even acted differently."

He stares into my eyes, hard and strong and powerful. "I never acted differently because where you come from doesn't matter to me. It doesn't change a thing."

I scoff.

"And I didn't say anything," he continues, "because I held out hope you'd tell me yourself. I wanted you to trust me."

"Yet you knew exactly why I couldn't. There's a reason you never gave me your truth either. I'm only learning it now because you were forced to confess."

"I wasn't forced to do anything. You don't think I could've convinced you your original assumption was right? That you were the target of the shooting? That the Costas were behind this?" He lowers to sit on the edge of the bathtub, his penetrating eyes all the more commanding in the candlelight. "I could've hidden for a lot longer. I could've hidden forever if I wanted. But I brought you here because I was done with the secrecy. Shooting or not, I would've told you who Lorenzo is before we returned to D.C."

Pain radiates beneath my sternum.

Burning, branding pain.

"Did you do it for information?" The question sears my throat. "To get insight on my family?"

"Fuck your family," he spits. "I said I was out, Layla. And despite knowing how much you love to question me, it's the fucking truth."

I want to deny him. To deny all of this.

I sink against the vanity, then slide to the floor, my ass planting on the cold tile.

"We both had our reasons to keep quiet, *amore mio*. There's nothing wrong with that. It doesn't mean what we have isn't real. I fell for you long before I found out who you are."

I swallow over the mint taste dominating my tongue, wishing I was somewhere else. *Anywhere* else… Yet somehow I still want to be here with him. To remain where attraction rules and affection flows.

"Well…" I lick the dryness from my lower lip, committing the sight of him to memory. "It was fun while it lasted, I guess."

He presses his mouth closed, the tilt of his chin swift as he narrows his stare.

"My family can't find out about this. I need you to let me walk out of here and pretend we never met." My heart squeezes with every word, hating their necessity.

"They can and they will. And I'll be right by your side when they do."

I whisper a pained laugh.

He continues to believe we have a future, and my heart wants to believe it, too. If only it were possible.

"No." I shake my head. "I'm begging you. You have no idea how my brother will treat me if he learns I've been sleeping with someone who worked for the Cappellettis."

"Lorenzo and Cole aren't enemies." He slides from the edge of the tub to sit on the tiled floor opposite me, bolstering my naivety with statements that simply aren't true. "As far as I know, they've never had anything to do with one another."

"Doesn't matter. Competition is competition. And stupidity is still stupidity."

"You say that as if either one of us had any control over this." He stretches one suit-covered leg toward me. I'm sure it's to test how jittery I am at the proximity. "Do you think I'd be here if I had the ability to walk away?"

"We're not star-crossed lovers, Matthew."

"Aren't we?" He raises a brow.

I'm not sure if he's being derisive or insane.

I glance away, hating how he makes me feel warm through the icy chill of reality. We're not star-crossed anything. No matter how much I crave the opposite.

"You're mine." He leans over, grabbing my ankles to slide me forward between his open legs, my dress bunching beneath me. "I'm yours."

"Don't." I plaster my hands to the tile. His thighs cage me. His chest is within reach. "I'm not doing this with you."

"You have no choice. You walk, I follow. We won't be apart."

I glare. "How predatory."

"It would be if you didn't crave me, too, Layla. If you didn't want this, I'd let you leave. But you do. And I won't allow you to give up on something we both want just because of what your brother may say or do."

"My brother may say or do something that puts you six feet under. Do you understand that?"

"I have no issue with Cole and he has no need to have one with me. If he wants his sister to be happy, he'll give us his blessing."

I scoff. "It's not that simple."

"It can be."

"No. I let down my guard when I shouldn't have. He doesn't even know I was in Denver. That I was watching the Costas. He'll think you're trying to get information through me. That you could be—"

"I could be doing a lot of things, but I'm not." He cups my cheeks in his heated palms, demanding I believe him with an expression that bleeds sincerity. "I don't want to be anywhere near that lifestyle anymore. I don't need money. The only thing I want from your family is you."

No. This isn't how it works.

I make mistakes and I pay for them. I don't win prizes. I don't come out in front. I bleed and burn and ache. I suffer and agonize and endure.

This misplaced longing and hope has no right to be inside my chest.

"I didn't want to become distracted by you." His thumb strokes my cheek. "I didn't want any of this. But I'll be damned if I give it up."

I wince, believing him with every ragged beat in my chest. Succumbing. Yet I still know so little. I need more information. "How long had you been homeless?"

His face falls. In a blink, he's defensive and inching away to rest back against the tub, his palms falling from my face. "Not long. A few months. Maybe more."

"You don't remember?

"I remember enough… It's—" He huffs a sigh. "Give me a minute."

He shoves to his feet and stalks for the hall, his loud footsteps echoing into the living room momentarily before returning. This time, he enters the bathroom with the contents of the hotel minibar in his hands. "This conversation requires alcohol."

He reclaims his position a breath in front of me, dumping the liquor bottles to then grab my waist and deposit me on his lap.

"Matthew." My protest is weak as I clutch his shoulder. If I had any chance of leaving it was before proximity set in. It needed to be prior to the chemistry shift and the attraction deluge.

"What?" He taunts me with a raised brow and snatches the tiny scotch bottle from the tile, unscrews the lid then takes a gulp. "In answer to your question—" He takes another mouthful. "—I'm not sure exactly how long I was homeless because I try my best to forget."

I steel myself against the empathy. Against agony.

"I spent frozen nights under bridges and inside dumpsters. Then I started breaking into cars to have somewhere clean to sleep. It didn't take long to start cashing them in for drugs and booze, which is how Lorenzo found me." He finishes the remainder of the scotch and drops the bottle, the plastic bouncing against the tile. "Apparently, I'd built a name for myself for being the sorry son of a bitch who was smart enough to hot-wire a car, but too self-destructive to find himself a safe place to stay."

My muscles tense, every inch. "Are you still using?"

"Hell no. Back then I was a stupid teenage kid, and I was suffering." He holds my gaze, his face tense. "Prior to losing everything, I had a girlfriend, Layla. A beautiful, happy, and motivated girl who made my shitty family life livable. We had plans to skip town together. To start fresh."

Dread creeps into my veins, the horrible sense of foreboding suffusing me.

"But she…" He pauses, scrunching his nose in anger, his brows slicing in vicious strokes. "She died."

My heart creeps into my throat, the tightness cutting off air. "I'm sorry."

He grabs for another liquor bottle and cracks the lid. "It was a long time ago. But in the moment, she was all I had. I adored everything about her. Her smile. Her laugh. Her light… then that light was gone and my grief became rage."

I have no words. And I've suffered through enough unwanted placations and anecdotes about loss since Benji's death to know silence is a far kinder response. All I can do is blink at him through burning eyes and hope he understands my support.

"So Lorenzo's generosity wasn't only a home for the homeless," he continues. "It was a distraction for the crazed. Not to mention stability and power for someone obsessed with revenge."

"Revenge?"

His lips flatten in a tight line, his free hand tangling in the material of my dress. "Grace was murdered."

I close my eyes, his pained journey hitting too close to home.

I always knew we were one and the same. Two people from different parts of the country living such similar lives it hurt. Now it's so much more than that.

We've traveled an identical path. Climbed equivalent mountains. Battled the same enemies.

His indoctrination into the mafia seems understandable now. Acceptable. And the fact he got out… I shake my head, overwhelmed with admiration. Burning from it. Blistering with the need to whisper my support.

I reach for the liquor bottle. His strong fingers let go of the prize to allow me to take a gulp. The burn of vodka hits my tongue, my throat, then sears its way into my empty stomach.

I want to tell him I understand. That I *know* how he must have felt. But instead, a question seeks supremacy, bubbling from my lips. "Do you know who killed her?"

"I do." He nods. Succinct. "I'll give you one guess."

27

LAYLA

"Emmanuel killed her?" The question tears up my throat.

Matthew nods.

His revelation only makes our paths more entwined. It's him and me. There's not a soul in the world who could understand what we've both been through. Only us.

"Does Lorenzo know?" I ask.

"Yes. My hatred wasn't something I could hide."

"But you've never…" I let the sentence fall short.

He's been in the same room with his girlfriend's murderer. He watches him. Stalks him. How can he not react?

"There isn't a day when I don't think about ending his life," he confesses. "But as you know, there are rules. Lorenzo might despise his brother-in-law, but the man is still his sister's husband. He's not to be touched."

"So you keep an eye on him instead."

"I snoop to find things I can sabotage." He reclaims the vodka and finishes the bottle. "Being unable to physically hurt him doesn't mean I don't do it financially."

I lower my gaze to his chest, attempting to relive every moment we've had together in the hopes of understanding. Not only the implication, but what this all means for me and my plans.

"What are you thinking?" The alcohol on his breath brushes my lips, filling my lungs, intoxicating me. "What did I say this time?"

Is it wrong to still be here? To still want to make this work despite the strangling complications?

God.

My head screams with indecision. My heart yearns to salvage the unsalvageable.

"Layla?" He drops the second bottle to the tiles, his fingers finding the sensitive skin below my chin to gently lift my face to his. "Talk."

"Explain how this all started," I whisper. "How we met. What was going through your head. Were you trying to manage the threat I posed toward the Costas? Have you kept me close because I can achieve the things you can't? Or because you've needed to distract me from my plans?"

Because I've been distracted.

Entirely.

Completely.

I inch back, needing space, only to be fastened in place against his lap by strong hands clutching my waist. "Are you with me for a purpose?"

"Would you consider greed a purpose? Indulgence? I'm with you for no other reason than my own selfish desire." He stares at me, unblinking. "You intrigued me from the first night we met. You became *my* distraction. Then an obsession. And even after I found out you were a complication, and a potential threat, I still wanted more."

He leans closer, the heat of his mouth breaching my own as he reclaims my cheeks with his palms. "I haven't fallen for anyone since Grace, Layla. I've fucked, but never fallen. Not even close, until you."

His spiel sinks under my skin, the tendrils of hunger and longing infusing me with more delicious hope.

"I want you," he murmurs, harsh and low. "I need you."

He speaks to my weaknesses. My insecurities.

I've never been wanted. Not by lovers. Not even my late husband.

Being needed is just as foreign. My daughter doesn't require her mother anymore. She moved on effortlessly, already growing independent at such a young age.

There's only Matthew.

Only the man I shouldn't desire, but do with a level of force that's beyond my control.

"I had to agree Emmanuel would remain untouched if I wanted to leave my previous life behind. The same goes for his wife and children." He adds pressure to my waist, slowly dragging me closer into him. "Those rules will always remain in place, hanging like a noose if I break them."

"What happens if you defy the rules?"

"Then I'd owe Lorenzo a debt. I'd be his again. With no way out this time."

"And if I break the rules while we're together?" I whisper.

"I don't know." He holds my gaze, unblinking. "It's a grey area. Especially when I don't understand your connection to the Costas."

I'm not willing to give him that insight.

Not yet.

"You should've left me alone, Matthew. I would've done your dirty work for you. We both could've got what we wanted."

"I have what I want," he growls. "Don't you?"

He can't ask me that.

He can't possibly understand what it would mean to choose him, not only forsaking revenge, but my family, too.

I lower my attention to his shirt buttons, itching to unfasten them and press my skin to his. I've grown tired of words. I need more. Something to tether this wildness inside me. Something to dissolve the doubt.

"Do you really want them dead?" he murmurs. "Was that the plan?"

I don't know anymore. I don't know anything.

The loss of Grace should cement my bloodlust. Instead, I'm fearful of the cost my actions might inflict upon the man I'm growing to admire.

A sinner with the control of a saint.

"Which one of them hurt you?" He runs his thumbs along my hips, gently coaxing. "What did they do?"

"You didn't dig that deep into my life?"

"Bishop tried. He couldn't find a connection."

He uncovered my name. My reputation. My family's sins, but not the circumstances surrounding my husband's death or my child's abduction. *Good.* That means Cole's cover-up is tight. Not that I ever had any doubts.

I slide a fingertip over his top button, my gaze trekking the movement. "I'm not ready to share."

But I have to make a choice.

I've reached the peak of this mountain. There are only two courses of action to take. I can return to the protection of where I came from, living a life where I'm judged and loathed. Or I can take the last step off the cliff, plunging myself into an abyss of recklessness and potential bliss.

Safety and sadness.

Or risk and the possibility of emotional reward.

"I need to think first." My heart thunders a frantic beat.

I have to decide if I'm going to choose Matthew over my family.

To pick him instead of revenge. Can I choose this gloriously secretive man, with his adamance and determination, in place of everything I've ever known and relied on? Can I step toward something that scares the absolute hell out of me?

I glance up at him, desperate to read his thoughts as those dark eyes hold mine.

He drags me closer, forcing my knees to spread around his waist, the material of my dress hitching to the top of my thighs. "We need to discuss it, *amore mio.*"

"I know."

"Soon."

I nod. "But not now."

His palms add pressure, pressing my crotch into the hard length hidden beneath his zipper. I gasp at the contact, hypersensitive and hungry.

Things are different now. Cautious. Intense.

Yet the underlying energy between us is stronger. The attraction more fierce.

Every inch of me vibrates for him. It hurts to breathe. To refrain from all the luscious thoughts that shouldn't fester at a time like this.

It's as if one spark against the kindling of our magnetism will ignite an inferno I'll never control. A passionate explosion of lips and hands and spirit.

Flames flicker in his eyes, the hellish severity enough to cause arrhythmia.

"You'll learn to trust me, Layla." He grinds into me, the friction grazing my clit. "Give it time." He leans closer, his stubble brushing my cheek as he speaks near my ear. "Until then, let me atone for the secrecy." A hand slides to my thigh, his calloused palm delving beneath the pool of material at my crotch. "Let me show you how much I need you."

There he goes again with the need.

The want.

The necessity.

I may willingly succumb to him, but his yearning for me makes me soar. Fly. Free fall.

He slides his fingers beneath the elastic of my panties, skimming my clit before moving farther to part my folds.

"I won't lose you," he grates into my hair. "Not over issues that are out of our control." His lips find my neck. "There are too many things I want to do to you."

"Then do them."

"My pleasure." In a jerk of movement, his hand leaves my flesh. He shoves off the tiles, holding me in his arms to take me with him.

I clutch his shoulders, my legs tight around his waist as he takes three steps and plants my back against the freezing tiled wall. Our lips meet. Our teeth. Our tongues.

He turns rabid, devouring me. His hands on my body. His breath in my lungs.

I gasp. Cling. Claw.

I fight to unfasten his buttons only to be stopped when he hefts my dress over my shoulders. He throws the material to the floor, his hips strong and adamant against mine, his lips finding my neck.

He licks. Sucks. Bites.

One hand circles my nape. The other finds my hip. Both dig deep into flesh, possessing, demanding, while his cock teases my clit through my panties.

"We've got more to discuss." His voice vibrates against my skin. "It won't be easy."

I nod.

I know.

From his life *and* mine.

But the world can wait.

I need respite from the revelations. To have him against me, on top of me, inside me. Each moment is a reminder of why I took this risk in the first place. "For now, all I need to know is that this is real."

"It's fucking real." He digs his fingers harder into my skin. Pleasure and pain. Animal and man. "It always has been."

I ignore Cole's disagreement whispering through my mind.

Keira's denials, too.

The voices have to stop.

"Fuck me." I grind into him, whimpering as clit meets cock. "Hurry."

He pulls back, his eyes narrow, as if noting my first significant instance of sexual confidence.

I shove the jacket from his shoulders and rip at his shirt. Rabid. Starved for more.

He keeps watching, keeps stalking me with his gaze.

"What?" My cheeks heat under his scrutiny. "Why did you stop?"

"Because hearing those words is beyond a fucking turn-on," he growls. "Keep going, *amore mio*. Tell me exactly what you want."

Heat blazes down my neck. "Jesus Christ." I fist the hair at his nape and yank his face to mine. "Just fuck me."

He grins. "Don't worry. I will." He licks my lower lip, following it with a bite of teeth. "Within an inch of your life."

My pussy flutters, tingling and tight.

He smothers his mouth against mine and undoes his zipper while leveraging me against the cold tiles.

He doesn't take off his pants. Doesn't remove my underwear.

One minute, he's consuming me with kisses—the next, he's ripping the lace apart at my crotch and shoving his dick home.

I cry out as I'm filled, the walls of my pussy exquisitely stretching to accommodate his girth.

Fuck.

He's brilliant.

Perfect.

He pulls back, pressing our foreheads together as he thrusts into me. "You're mine."

"I'm yours."

He growls in approval, the vibration thrumming into my chest. "I'll never lose you."

My heart pangs.

I can't reciprocate. Not this time. Not without lying.

"Say it." He keeps plunging his cock into me. Harder. Faster. More punishing. "Tell me I'll never lose you."

"Matthew…"

"Tell me," he demands.

I'm on the cliff's ledge, arms hesitantly open, heart painfully fragile.

I can't leap. Can I?

"All that I have is yours, *amore mio*. The money. The assets." He steals my lips, punishing me with a rough kiss. "But you're mine. I won't lose you."

I cup his cheeks, my closed eyes burning as I nod.

I don't have a chance to contemplate the severity of my capitulation before he drags me from the wall with strong hands on my hips, his dick remaining inside me as he walks us to the bedroom across the hall.

The space is bathed in darkness, the only light coming from more candles on the nightstands.

He places me on the bed, decimating our connection when he descends to his knees, grabs my ankles, and drags me in one rough slide to the edge of the mattress.

I struggle to catch my breath as those forceful hands yank at the waistband of my shredded panties, dragging the elastic to fall to the floor. My legs are plastered wide, my sex on full display when he swoops in to plant his mouth directly over my pussy.

I jolt with the contact, the sudden rush of lips and tongue not merely kissing, but utterly ravaging.

His fingers dig into my thighs, the appreciative rumble from his throat vibrating deep in my core.

I grasp the bed coverings, wiggling my ass for more. "Matthew…"

I want to tell him how I feel. How I hurt and yearn and crave for this to be real. *Truly* real.

For the possibility of living without recrimination to be something other than a fairy tale. For this paradise to be more than an illusion.

"I need you, too," I admit. "I need you too much."

His growl turns to an animalistic snarl, his mouth rising to latch on to my clit. He sucks, flicking the sensitive nerves with his tongue while two fingers plunge inside me, curling into my G-spot.

I struggle for breath, my core snapping tight around his digits, the pleasure infusing me all the way to my toes.

But he's too far away.

I need skin to skin. To touch instead of being touched. To give pleasure instead of merely receiving it.

"I want you inside me." I strangle the bed coverings, my legs squeezing around him.

"I'm not even close to being done here."

"Matthew." His name is panted from my drying lips. "Don't deny me."

He pauses, edging backward, his stubble scratching my inner thighs. "I'd never fucking deny you." He rises to his feet, roughly shucks his pants, then crawls on top of me. "My mouth not good enough for you, *amore mio?*"

"Your mouth is divine." I grab him around the nape and drag him closer, licking his lips in a quick tease, tasting my own arousal. "But I want to be close. I don't want space between us."

He grinds his hips as his nostrils flare, the tip of his cock edging into me. "No space. No lies. No secrets."

I nod, not knowing what I'm agreeing to as my teeth dig into my lower lip.

All I understand is hunger. Desire. Demand.

He nudges farther, sinking deeper. My core clamps around him as soon as he's fully seated inside me. I'm already so close. The heat in his eyes undoes me.

I could come.

From his gaze alone, I could splinter.

"You're ready." He grins, backing out gradually, before sinking in equally slowly. "*Amore mio* wants to come."

I mewl, raising my hips to meet his, silently pleading for him to move faster.

"Tell me what you want."

"You," I pant.

He clucks his tongue. "You know that's not what I meant."

I whimper, my cheeks regaining the heat of unease. "Fuck me."

He increases his pace a fraction. "How?"

"Hard," I beg, kicking off my sandals. "Fuck me hard… Please… Hurry."

"All you had to do is ask." He slams into me, jolting me farther along the bed. "I'll fuck you as hard as you want." He thrusts into me, over and over. Stronger and more ruthless. "I'll fuck you until you can't see straight and neither of us can walk."

Again and again he plunges, each slam pushing me closer to the edge of no return.

"And I'll still want more," he pledges. "I'll never get enough."

I come undone, every inch of me pulsing, the waves of my orgasm consuming me.

I sink my nails into his shoulders, command his mouth to mine.

We kiss as the pleasure sets my chest on fire and gives my heart wings. Over and over he bucks into me, our legs knocking, my pussy throbbing.

I don't breathe until the tide recedes. Don't acknowledge consciousness until he stops moving and leans up on one arm to stare down at me with cocky arrogance.

"Are we done?" I tease.

He raises a brow. "I thought I made it clear we'll never be done." His free hand slides around my neck, holding me in a possessive grip. "Not today or tomorrow. You're stuck with me."

I want to be stuck.

Unequivocally. Emphatically.

His hips retreat, moving back until only the head of his cock breaches me. "This tight little pussy is mine." He slams home, harsh and unyielding, sinking to the hilt.

My back arches with renewed pleasure, my chest rising to brush against his.

"These tits..." He pays my breasts homage. Rough, ferocious kisses. Harsh, punishing sucks. "All mine."

He plunges harder. Unrelenting.

More.

And more.

And so much *more*.

"That's not all." His hand releases my neck, his palm sliding down my body and around my hip. "This fucking ass is mine, too."

I shudder with the words. Pulse with the deep dig of his fingers into my meaty flesh.

I wrap my legs around his waist. Lick my lips. Fight against the burn in my nipples.

"I'm going to fuck you there, *amore mio*," he promises, carnal and severe. "I'm going to stretch that perfect little ass and make it hurt so damn good."

Oh... My... God.

I come undone again. My imagination succumbs to his filth. My pussy enjoys the ever-loving fuck out of it.

I moan with bliss. Close my eyes. Clamp my core.

"*Fuck.*" He pistons inside me, following me into mindlessness. "Fuck this perfect little cunt."

I whimper. Exhausted. Tired. And entirely helpless against the shudders still wracking me.

He pumps harder, his fingers digging.

The pain is intense. The pleasure is incredible.

"Goddamn you, Layla," he roars.

Those hips buck once. Twice. His seed fills me until finally, he crashes down upon me, deftly dragging me to my side so his weight rests into the mattress.

We stare, breathing each other's liquor-tainted air, our bodies joined, the candlelight dancing over our skin.

I wait for morality to nip at my heels. To bite and punish and scar.

Nothing comes.

I remain shrouded in bliss, my gaze entranced by the man who owns my heart, my head free from criticism—at least for now.

I run my fingertips along the scratch marks I left on his chest. "When did you organize the candles and food?"

"This morning, while you were in the shower." His lips curve. "But I wasn't entirely responsible."

I raise a questioning brow.

"I texted Bishop. He called the hotel to make arrangements."

"Bishop?" His name leaves my mouth with incredulity.

"Yeah, Bishop." He grabs my wrist with a gentle hand and raises my knuckles to his lips. "He's cooperative when he wants to be."

"And a bastard the rest of the time," I mutter.

"Not always. He actually likes you."

I scoff. "We're both good at lying, Matthew, but you didn't come close to pulling that one off."

"No more lies, *amore mio*. I promise his caustic exterior is just for show. He didn't want you getting messed up in our world. Then, when he found out you were already in the thick of it, he tried to convince me to cut you loose to save you from complications."

"I'm still not buying it." I inch closer, snuggling into his side, sliding my thigh between his. "But I don't need to. I'm here for you, not him."

"Just as long as you know he's no threat." He places a kiss to my forehead. "He's all talk when it comes to you."

I stew on his words, unsure what they mean yet unwilling to ask.

We lie there for long moments, his arm sliding around my shoulders to keep me close, my fingers drawing invisible pictures on the muscles of his chest.

My mind drifts to our earlier conversation, the revelations slowly creeping back in. "Why don't you carry a gun?"

He stiffens. It's only slight—the mere tweak of corded sinew. "I've got my reasons."

Matty boy wants to earn his very own martyrdom status.

"Tell me one," I urge.

Just one. Any one. Even the briefest glimpse of the unknown will tide me over until we're both comfortable enough to discuss this further.

"Normal people don't carry guns," he mutters.

"But normal people don't have a past they need to be protected from."

He doesn't respond. There's only thickening silence between us.

"Didn't people come after you?" I pull back and raise onto my elbow, needing to see his face. "I assume you would've been a target for anyone wanting intel on the Cappellettis."

"Nobody came after me." He rolls onto his back to stare at the ceiling, shutting me out.

"Nobody? Not even one person? Not an enemy or a competitor? Not even someone who felt you abandoned your position?"

His eyes harden, his nose wrinkling at my heartlessness.

"I'm sorry," I whisper. "I didn't mean to say—"

"No, you're right." He sits, my hand falling from his chest, his back turning so I can no longer read his face. "I did abandon Lorenzo. But just like Emmanuel, I'm off-limits. Nobody would dare to touch me unless they wanted a fast-track ticket to death's door."

I grab at the bed coverings, dragging them to my chest in a makeshift shield against his sterility. "People always dare. Aren't you worried about the one in a million who's willing to cross the line?"

"No. I don't like guns and I don't need one. I don't know what else to tell you."

I cling to the covers.

The floodgates on information are going to be harder to open than I'd thought. "What about the suicide comment from Bishop? What did he mean?"

He huffs a sigh. "He was being a dick."

"I don't think so. He said it for a reason."

"He's jealous." He pushes from the bed, gloriously naked, his ass perfectly defined. "We worked hard to build a new life. One without violence. And then you came along."

"And I brought violence?" I follow him to my feet, standing tall at the edge of the bed. "I thought we weren't lying to each other anymore?"

His nostrils flare. Fingers twitch.

"Matthew?"

"Jesus Christ." He shoves a hand through his hair. "He's pissed, okay? Pissed at me. Not you."

"Why?"

Muscles flicker under his stubbled jaw.

"Why?" I demand.

"Because he knows I'd give my life to make sure you don't end up like Grace."

I straighten. Stiffen.

"He knows I would die for you." His eyes harden with the admission. "Either by Emmanuel's actions or by going back to work for Lorenzo, and he fucking hates it. But if that's the price I have to pay, so be it. I won't lose you."

28

———

LAYLA

"Did you grow up in D.C?" I stare at Matthew sitting behind the wheel of our luxurious rental, his sunglasses hiding his eyes.

"No. I moved there to start over."

"Once you stopped working for Lorenzo?"

He nods, keeping his gaze on the road.

Yesterday came and went in a blur of emotional overload. After the shooting, then the sex, we spent the rest of the day in a weird state of hesitant conversation.

Although the embargo on information has been trampled, it's clear we both find it hard to open up. I'd share a tidbit about my life, something insignificant and trivial, then he'd do the same.

He told me he had good grades in school. Lost his virginity to Grace. Played football. And planned to buy another club next month in Philadelphia. But I still don't really *know* his past, and the same has to be said for him with me.

I haven't told him why I hate the Costas. He hasn't divulged the work he did for Lorenzo. Secrets still linger between us. The only thing we successfully achieved was a strengthened physical bond.

We laid in bed for hours, naked and sweaty, doing with our bodies what we couldn't with our minds.

He touched me everywhere, learning every curve, committing all my sensitive spots to memory. And I did the same with him. We showered and ate, then repeated the loop all over again, adding glimpses of insight when quiet sank in, and contemplating the future when the truth became too hard.

Full disclosure will take time. And until that happens, there's chemistry to rely on.

I can't even look at him without tingling between my thighs.

That mouth has tasted every part of me. Those strong fingers have delved into parts I never knew existed.

175

This morning, we left the hotel without police intervention.

As Lorenzo promised, nobody questioned us about the shooting. Hotel staff didn't mention the events, either. The only telltale sign that anything happened were the contractors working on the damage.

It was Matthew's idea to arrange the rental car and drive to D.C. without Bishop as a third wheel. And I've spent the long hours on the road staring at my lover's profile, our fingers entwined on the gearstick, my heart fully owned by a man I know wholeheartedly and don't have the slightest understanding of at the same time.

"You're always checking your phone," he murmurs. "Have you spoken to your brother about us yet?"

I slide the cell under my leg and glance out the windscreen. "You know I haven't."

"Will you tell me before you do? I'd like to know when I should be pulling the Kevlar from the dresser."

I whisper a laugh, but pain stabs through me.

Cole won't understand what I have with Matthew. Not even when he fell for someone equally problematic.

"I'll call him tomorrow and feed him whatever information necessary to keep him off my back. But I won't be telling him about us for a while."

He squeezes my fingers, giving me support in the most subtle of ways.

"I want to keep you to myself for a little longer." I drag our entwined hands into my lap. "Is that okay?"

"It's not only okay, it's a preference. We should figure ourselves out before anyone else gets involved."

Figuring ourselves out means full disclosure.

That could take days. Maybe weeks.

I'm not sure I can ignore my brother that long. I'll try though.

As it is, Cole calls three times on the journey back to D.C. and texts twice. But the only person I reply to is Stella. I check in to make sure she's doing her homework and eating properly. Then I ask about her nightmares and the latest visit with her counselor, because here I am, living wild and free, while she continues to suffer for my mistakes.

When we arrive at the penthouse, Matthew drags our suitcase into his bedroom, discarding it at the door to his walk-in robe before pulling me against his chest. "You're quiet."

"I'm contemplative." I paste on a smile. "There's a lot to think about."

"And we still need to talk." He guides an errant strand of hair behind my ear. "We should've done it in the car, but you've been so damn quiet. One word from me and I expect you to run."

"I don't have my running shoes on."

He flashes a grin at my lame humor, the expression quickly fading. "When are we going to do this, *amore mio*?"

I don't know.

I don't want to start counting down the minutes before he starts to look at me with judgment for my role in the Costas' actions instead of the constant admiration I'm used to.

He knows what our world demands of us. He, more than normal people, will understand how low I stooped to help my father.

"Tonight?" I hedge.

His brows pull tight. "I have to work. There are loose ends from the shooting that I have to chase up."

"What loose ends?"

"I haven't heard from Lorenzo. I need to make sure everything is under control."

"You can't do that here?" I don't want to be alone tonight. Tomorrow, maybe. But not now.

"This isn't like you." His eyes narrow. "What's going on?"

"Nothing." I step back, pasting on a smile. "I just assumed you'd be home, that's all. We can talk tomorrow."

I ignore the hollowness growing beneath my sternum.

I already understand the types of things Matthew would've done for Lorenzo. The intimidation. The threats. The violence. We both have a past that's unkind. But will my sins outweigh his? What I did was personal. In comparison, his brutality would've been sterile and strategic. A necessity instead of self-fulfilling.

"You're worried." His attention doesn't soften. He stares, reading me, his intense observation sinking under my skin.

"I'm tired."

"Whose fault is that?" He grabs my wrist and drags me back into his chest. "You do nothing to discourage my hunger. But you're also lying because you still don't want to talk, do you?"

I contemplate another lie.

"What part of it is the problem?" He holds me close. "You don't want to discuss your family or your connection to the Costas?"

I don't want to discuss any of it. Not one single part of my existence before he entered my life.

I keep my mouth shut, unsure how to respond when his cell vibrates in his jacket.

"Shit." He releases me and pulls out the device. "It's Lorenzo. I need to take this."

A hard kiss is plastered to my lips before he strides across the room, answering the call as he shoves open the balcony door to step outside. He greets his mentor in pristine Italian, the words turning to murmurs once he closes the door behind him.

I watch him pace, the late afternoon sun gleaming in his dark hair, the glow kissing his tanned skin while I unpack the suitcase. Every minute of conversation adds a new notch to his stiffened posture. An increased hike to the confident set of his chin.

When he walks back inside, the placating smile he gives me is pitiful. "I need to get to Trend earlier than anticipated."

"Is something wrong?"

"Just loose ends."

"I thought you didn't work for him anymore."

"I don't," he grates. "Lorenzo heard there was footage of the shooting. Someone uploaded it to social media. It's already been taken down, but I want to make sure there isn't a trace left behind."

My pulse kicks. "What kind of footage?"

"A blurry twenty-second snapshot. It isn't a big deal."

"You're pacifying me." I can see it in his eyes. He isn't giving me the full story.

"No, I'm not. It's been taken down. It didn't gain traction and wasn't picked up by journalists."

"But we were in it, weren't we? You can see our faces." There's evidence I was with my family's competition when a shooting happened. "I need to call Cole."

"What you need to do is be rational. Involving him will only cause complications." He walks up to me, gliding an arm around my waist. "Let me handle it. If things escalate, which they won't, then you can call him."

"If word gets back to him—"

"Word won't get back. Lorenzo handled the cops. He's had the video taken down. People don't care about another drive-by shooting, especially when nobody got hurt. It's not big news." He leans in, his lips close to mine. "I just want to make sure it remains that way. Okay? It's only a precaution."

I close my eyes, letting his mouth ease my concerns as he kisses me possessively.

"I'll be home late. I'll try not to wake you." He walks from the room, leaving me in a silent penthouse that grows more desolate by the hour.

I order takeout for an early dinner. Shower. Stalk my phone.

When night falls, I help myself to Matthew's liquor cabinet to ease the constant simmer of apprehension.

I text him for an update before I go to bed. He placates me immediately, pretending everything is peachy when I'm certain nothing could be further from the truth.

But when he arrives home after midnight, his naked body finding mine under the covers, the reconnection of our bodies makes the worries disappear.

We make love in the dark. Slow. Silent. Sensual. There's only heated eye contact through the shadows and possessive touches beneath the sheets.

I don't question the new depth of our passion, or how it feels like we're both clinging to something destined to end.

I fall back asleep with his body spooned behind mine like a perfect puzzle piece, his lips on my shoulder, his arm around my waist.

The mattress doesn't jostle again until the morning sun beams around the edge of the drapes.

"Matthew?" I roll toward his side of the bed, finding him already dressed in another impeccable suit as he kneels to tie his shoes near the door.

"I didn't mean to wake you." His focus remains on his laces. "I'm going to walk to the cafe on the corner and get breakfast."

"I'll come." I fling back the sheet.

"No." He stands with a frown, still not meeting my gaze as he fixes his lapels. "I've got calls to make. Stay here until I get back."

There's no offer of clarification. No apology. Just dictatorship that doesn't have the same appeal as it does when spoken sexually.

"Is everything all right?" I cling to the sheets, wanting to give him space while instinct demands I pry. "Has something happened?"

"We'll talk when I get back." His gaze finally meets mine. "It's time we laid everything on the table."

He doesn't glance at me with admiration. Doesn't rake his attention over my body with his usual predatory hunger. He barely registers me at all before he pulls his cell from his jacket pocket to concentrate on the device. "I won't be long."

"Wait." I push to my feet, dragging the sheet along with me. "Tell me what's going on."

"I'm paranoid," he grates. "Word has spread about the shooting, and I want the two of us to be straight with each other before the world starts firing complications our way."

"The world or my brother?"

"Either. Both. It doesn't matter." His jaw ticks. "Yesterday we said no lies and no secrets. We need to start living up to that promise."

There's more to his change in demeanor. Something that sits heavy on my chest. Has he already figured out what the Costas have done to me? To Stella?

"Okay." I nod, my throat drying. "We'll talk."

"Good." He strides for the hall with no kiss in farewell, no heated promises. "Bishop will be here soon. You might want to get dressed before he arrives."

"Why is he coming?" I ask the empty doorway.

"I'll explain when I get back."

His footsteps don't pause along the hall. They grow distant, the front door slapping closed moments later.

I'm tempted to spy on him from the balcony. Just for the slightest hint of understanding at his temperamental mood. But I shower instead, quickly scrubbing the remnants of last night's eroticism from my body while wondering if I'm doing it for the last time.

It can't be more than ten minutes later, when I'm drying myself in front of the wall-to-wall mirror, that a knock sounds at the front door. My stomach twists.

I don't want Bishop here. Not for this.

I refuse to discuss my daughter's abduction in front of his smug face.

"Hold on a sec." I pad into Matthew's bedroom and steal his robe from the chair in the corner, shoving my arms through the silk as I continue down the hall. *"I'm coming."*

The knock sounds again when I reach the living room, my feet slapping against the cold tiles. "Have a little patience."

I reach the entry and check the peephole, holding out hope it's Matthew with arms full of food. Only the shoulder of the shadowed suit I glimpse isn't his. The size and shape are too damn familiar to Bishop's frame.

"I'm here." I fight with the dead bolt, then twist the handle.

When I fling the heavy wood wide, it's not Bishop who swings around to face me.

The man standing in the dimly lit hall turns my way in a tailored suit, dark thick stubble hugging a tight jawline, his posture holding an air of bulletproof confidence.

He says something. *Asks* something. Yet the words don't register. Nothing sinks past the panic rendering me speechless.

It's *Remy Costa*—Emmanuel's youngest son.

My heart sprints, my veins flooding with adrenaline.

They *did* find the cyanide. They found me, too.

Is that why Matthew was on edge?

"Did you hear me, sugar?" He smirks, his gaze raking up and down my body.

Our first meeting wasn't meant to be like this. It was supposed to be planned. Strategic. Powerful. Being a few sharp breaths away from hyperventilating wasn't in the manifesto.

I white-knuckle the handle to slam the door closed only for the momentum to stop as he lunges forward to shove his hands against the wood.

"Whoa, there. I didn't expect a welcome party, but this is a bit dramatic, don't you think?" He shoves harder against the barrier between us, overpowering me. "Where is he?"

"Where is who?" I shake my head, my voice hoarse.

He stalks forward, nudging me out of the way to continue into the living room. "Nice try. But he sent me a colorful text a few minutes ago, so I know he's awake."

My pulse stutters, ricocheting through my chest with the force of jagged shrapnel. "You're in contact with Matthew?"

He stops in the middle of the open area and swings around to face me, continuing to walk backward into the penthouse. "Look, there's no need to freak out. I'll do you a solid and make sure he doesn't blame you for letting me in. Okay?"

I drag in a ragged breath, realizing the extent of what I've done. Not only am I face-to-face with my enemy while completely unprepared, I've also let the son of the man who murdered Grace into Matthew's home.

"Get out." Venom enters my voice. "Get *the fuck* out."

"Not going to happen." He swings toward the hall leading to the bedrooms. "Dante, where are you?"

The name snaps me rigid, every ounce of blood in my body siphoning to my feet.

The asshole shoots a glance over his shoulder, levelling me with a demeaning smirk. "Sorry, you referred to him as someone else, didn't you? What name is my brother going by these days?"

I turn cold. Blood. Heart. Breath. "You've got the wrong apartment."

This has to be a mistake.

A coincidence.

Dante Costa must live in this building. Matthew has to be watching him, too.

I inch toward the kitchen, destined for the knife block calling to me from the middle of the counter.

"*Dante*," he raises his voice. "Get out here."

"Leave." My tone sounds like a beg as I reach the marble counter, my ears thunderous with my frantic pulse. "Before I call the police."

I'm ignored. Entirely dismissed as he strolls toward the dining table, picking up last week's mail. "Matthew Langston." The name rolls off his tongue with heavy criticism. "I guess it's no surprise he chose a variant of his middle name. He never liked Mateo." He swings back to face me. "So where…"

His question falls short as I slide the knife from the wooden block, his gaze narrowing on the sharp blade. "Planning on stabbing me, sugar?"

"I plan on doing whatever necessary to get you out of here." I cinch the robe tighter around my middle with my free hand, my nakedness beneath the silk making me feel far too vulnerable.

"How long has he been playing you?" His expression turns into mock sympathy.

Black dots assail my vision.

Matthew isn't playing me. He can't be. Not for weeks. Not after *he* demanded *my* honesty.

I would've sensed the treachery. Felt the deceit.

Wouldn't I?

"Get out." I thrust the knife toward the entry. *"Now."*

"Damn." His brows rise. "He's been doing this for a while, hasn't he? You poor, sweet thing."

His derision undoes me, unraveling the binds of loyalty that tie me to the man I'd fallen for.

"Dante," he calls toward the hall. *"Get the fuck out here."*

"He's not here," I scream. "It's just me. And if you dare to do anything to me, I swear my family will return the favor tenfold."

"Dare to do to you?" He frowns. "Why the fuck would I want to do anything to you?" He looks me up and down again, the frown deepening. "For starters, you're out of my usual age bracket. No offence. And I'd never lower myself to stick my dick where my brother has already been. Especially if that brother is Dante."

He doesn't know who I am?

I cling tighter to the knife, my palm beginning to sweat.

This son of a bitch doesn't recognize me? He dared abduct my daughter. Was vicious enough to participate in the death of my husband. But didn't bother to learn the faces of the lives he'd torn apart?

Fuck him.

"Look, I'm sorry he's been playing games." He crosses his arms over his chest with a look of chagrin. "But I need to speak to him about the shooting. I assume you were the one with him."

No.

I shake my head, refusing to understand the reality taking shape around me.

"I get that you're pissed." He ignores the knife as if it doesn't exist. "But don't women usually snoop for shit like this? Aren't those tactics in your DNA?"

My DNA is currently made up of rage and ruin. Devastation and destruction.

And I *had* snooped.

I'd checked the mail minutes after first walking into the penthouse. I spoke to people Matthew works with. People he knows. Not a single soul addressed him as anything other than the name he gave me. Not helicopter pilots. Not waitresses. Not one single motherfucker on the face of the Earth.

I'd also done a thorough check on his clubs. All are owned by Matthew Langston. All of them legitimately structured without shell companies or dodgy dealings.

There'd been no indication. No inkling I'd been played the entire time my heart and soul had succumbed.

"Obviously his bills aren't anything to go by." Remy shrugs. "But surely you would've thought to go through his wallet. Or his drawers. He'd have something lying around."

He's right.

If Matthew isn't who he says he is, there has to be evidence.

I drop the knife, the metal clinking against the marble as violence floods my veins. I reach for the nearest drawer, scavenging for anything to ease the sickness in my stomach.

I go through cupboards, below the marble counter and above. I search for anything with a name on it. With a hint. With a clue. And come up empty.

"Maybe try the bedroom," Remy drawls. "Go on. I'll wait."

I glare and snatch for the knife.

Admissions bubble in my chest. The confessions of where I plan to drive my blade and why, all begging to be heard.

I could kill him and claim self-defense. But the pain of possible betrayal by a man I love punishes me far more than my need to decimate Remy Costa.

I trek his every move while I stalk across the room. Then keep one eye on my back as I enter the hall.

When I reach the bedroom, where pleasure and bliss had been awakened after years of drought, I pause, hating myself with or without evidence.

If Remy's claims are true, I'll never recover.

There's no going back from this type of mistake. Not after the ones I've already made.

God, please don't let it be true.

I step inside, slam the door behind me, throw the knife to the bed, and fall to my knees at the closest bedside table.

I yank the top drawer from its holding and dump the contents on the carpet.

There are coins and buttons. Receipts and innocuous tidbits, too.

Normal things. *Innocent* things.

I pull out the second and the third drawer. Socks and underwear fall to the floor. Stupid typical items that deny me the proof of Remy's claims.

I scan under the bed. Nothing.

I scramble to the adjoining bathroom, checking the cupboards and drawers to no avail.

I run for his wardrobe, shoving aside hanging shirts. Kicking away shoes. Throwing and heaving sweaters. I move from one row of shelves to the next, yanking everything from its neatly folded place. The jeans. The gym tanks.

Row after row.

Shelf after shelf.

I don't stop until a pile of clothes lay strewn on the floor. Then I climb, reaching for the stack of blankets lying dormant on the top ledge. They sail through the air behind me, one after another until my fingers no longer feel material and instead skim cardboard.

I stretch higher, struggling on the tips of my toes, my robe gaping, my sanity failing.

My fingertips brush the corner of a box and I hold my breath as I strain to inch it into sight. Shift by incremental shift, I edge it toward me, my arms straining over my head, my body aching from the uncomfortable pull of muscle.

Once it's close enough, I wiggle it, the light weight sliding onto my palm. I descend, dragging it with me until one foot slips its perch on the shelf and I jostle to remain upright.

I lose my hold on the shoe box, the lid slipping free before the items inside topple to the pile of clothes on the floor.

"Shit." I jump down, determined to find what I'm looking for when my gaze catches hold of the contents scattered before me.

My pulse thunders in my ears. My throat. My stomach.

I feel it everywhere, the booming beat pounding through every inch of me.

But it's not evidence of Remy's accusation that litters the carpet around me.

It's worse.

My ID.

My credit cards.

My lipstick and pens and hair ties.

All the things that had been in my purse when I'd been mugged in Denver. Even the small vial of cyanide.

29

—————

MATTHEW

I juggle to hold the tray of takeaway coffee cups and the oversized bag of food as I shove into the penthouse. "I'm back."

I should've stayed outside longer. Should've taken more time to chill the fuck out and strategize my next move. But Layla had already been suspicious when I left, her eyes reading the mood I couldn't hide.

I kick the door closed behind me and start for the kitchen, stopping dead in my tracks at the sight of the asshole sitting on my sofa, one leg crossed over his knee in relaxation, his arms spread along the headrest.

Fuck.

I scan the room, looking for her, praying she fell back asleep while he somehow broke inside.

"Where is she?" I force calm as I continue to the counter, dumping my haul from the cafe.

He raises a brow, smug. "You mean the woman you've been playing?" He jerks his head back toward the hall. "I assume it's your bedroom she escaped into, *Matthew.*"

I snarl, my worst fears realized, but it's his choice of words that give me pause.

He doesn't use her name. Doesn't address her as if they have history.

Why?

"I sincerely apologize for ruining the fun." His voice drips with sarcasm. "If I'd known you were pretending to be someone else I wouldn't have used your real name."

"Matthew *is* my real name." I stalk across the room, needing to get eyes on her.

"Matthew is who you wish you were. Unfortunately, you'll never be anyone other than Dante to those who know you best."

Anger stabs through my skull, blinding in its efficiency.

I stop my progression to the hall, unable to escape the rage fighting for control.

"What is it, brother?" Remy drawls. "Does the truth hurt?"

One second, I'm determined to find Layla. The next, I'm cocking my fist as I reach the sofa and launch my knuckles at his face.

My punch connects with his chin, the impact screaming through my bones.

I launch again and again, pounding, pummeling. Seeing blood and tasting fraudulent victory.

But he's already won. I know he's ruined everything as he uses both feet to kick me backward, sending me tumbling over the coffee table, my head hitting the tiles.

"That was a fucking cheap shot." He shoves to his feet to tower above me, that smug expression now wiped from his face. "You may be older than me, but I'm no longer a kid you can push around."

I shove to my elbows, then rise to stand in front of him. "I bet you're still your daddy's little snitch, though, riding his dirty coattails all the way to the bank."

His eyes flare. Nostrils, too.

I tense for retaliation and don't have to wait long for his fist to swing for my face.

I block the strike with my forearm. It's the swift kick to my ankle I don't expect. I stumble sideways, grabbing his shoulders in the process, then punch him in the gut.

We grapple and shove. Swing and charge.

I ram him into the sofa. He pummels my head with his knuckles.

The little fucker is right. He isn't easily pushed around anymore. It takes a good two minutes to pin him beneath me before I grab him in a choke hold.

"I told you not to come here." I spit blood to the tiles.

"And I told you we needed to talk." He bares his teeth, the vicious smile covered in crimson.

"It's been fifteen years." I add pressure to his throat, clamping down on his carotid. "There's nothing we could possibly discuss."

"You were fucking shot at. Excuse me for caring."

Caring?

My hold loosens without my consent, my intuition searching for the real reason he's entered my life after more than a decade apart.

The swoosh of an opening door steals my attention. Footsteps patter toward us.

I raise my gaze to the hall, finding Layla standing there in my thin silk robe, knife in hand, face pale, eyes wild.

I release Remy and scramble to my feet. "Let me explain."

She storms toward me, blade raised in threat, while her other hand reaches into the robe pocket. "Explain this." She throws something at me, the small projectile hitting my chest before ricocheting to the floor. "And this." She grabs something else, throwing that, too.

I drag my gaze from the pain I created, the anger I deserve, and take in the items she continues to launch at me.

Lipstick.

Concealer.

A packet of tissues.

"Explain, you fucking son of a bitch." She holds up her ID. "How did you get this?"

I close my eyes, stealing the briefest second of respite from her suffering before I return my gaze to hers. "It's not what you think. I didn't—"

"You didn't what?" Her eyes spark like the devil. "You didn't play me from the moment we met, *Dante*?"

I clench my fists, wanting to slaughter Remy for what he's caused.

"Oh, shit." The fucker snickers. "The cat's really out of the bag."

"Listen to me." I step closer, needing her to understand. To think clearly. "This is what I wanted to discuss." I grab her wrist, hoping touch will help her remember our connection.

"Let me go." She fights my hold. Twisting. Tugging.

Fuck.

I loosen my grip.

She yanks to free herself, her hand sliding through mine. The ID gets caught as she tussles, falling to the floor.

"Goddamnit." She stabs the knife toward my face with a glare and bends to pick it up.

Remy's closer. He rolls onto his stomach and snatches at the flimsy plastic.

"No," she warns. "*Don't.*"

I step between them, ignoring her weapon, willing to endure a stab wound if it means keeping that prick away from her.

"Stop." She barges into me.

"Layla Hart… Portland, Oregon," he murmurs to himself. "Why do I feel like I should recognize that name?"

I'd like to know, too.

"*Give it back*," she screams. "*Now.*"

For weeks, Bishop has attempted to discover the connection between them, every turn coming up empty. There was no lead toward a romantic relationship with either of my brothers. No evidence of business ties, either.

"Layla Hart," Remy repeats, his scrutinizing gaze rising to her as he lumbers to his feet. "Layla from Portland, Oregon."

She stiffens. Swallows.

"Jesus Christ. You're a Torian." He stalks forward, his shoulders straightening in menace. "You fucking bitch."

"I'm a fucking bitch?" She lunges forward with the knife. "How dare you?"

I turn my back toward her blade, certain she wants to embed it between my ribs, and shove at Remy's shoulders. "Get the fuck away from her."

He glowers at me, then her, his fury finally settling on my face. "How could you be with her after what she's done?"

"What I've done?" she screeches. "What *I've* done?"

"Tell me what this is about." I shove him again. "How do you two know each other?"

"It's none of your business." Layla attempts to move around me, the knife slicing the air.

"As if you don't know." Remy's eyes narrow, then he scoffs a laugh. "Or do you really not know?"

"Know what, asshole?"

"Don't," Layla snaps.

"You're fucking her." Remy laughs with spite. "And you have no clue?"

Pressure bears down on my chest, punishing me.

"Stop it." This time her request is a plea.

"Looks like she wasn't the only one being played." His eyes gleam. "This bitch is using you to get to us."

"She isn't using me. I've known of her hatred all along. I just haven't known why."

"Well, brother, let me provide you with the insight—"

Layla charges around me, slashing the knife toward him. "I'll kill you."

Shit.

I grab her around the waist, hauling her off the ground, the robe gaping, the knife slicing.

"Will you kill me like we killed your husband?" Remy smirks.

Fuck. Me.

I hold her tighter, feeling the second his words make an impact. She stops fighting, her inhales vicious as she pants, the slightest whimper accompanying each breath.

"We abducted her daughter, too." He meets my gaze. "It was two years ago, but as you can see, our family made a lasting impression."

She screams, reinvigorating her fight, kicking, thrashing.

"Stop it," I snarl in her ear, ready to kill him myself. "Calm the fuck down."

She doesn't listen. Doesn't settle. She's all rage and pain and frenzy.

"Nice tits," he adds, focusing on the space where the robe gapes across her chest.

"Shut your fucking mouth." I swing her toward the hall, dumping her on her feet at the start of the carpet. "Get back in the bedroom," I demand of her, seconds away from reverting to the man I promised myself was dead and buried.

The past reignites in my veins.

The dark savagery begs to be freed.

"Go to hell." She stumbles away, then turns on me, her knife held at the ready.

"Now, Layla," I warn. "I need to speak to him alone."

"Listen to him, bitch," Remy sneers. "Because if I get my hands on you before he does, it's going to take more than a knife to save your life."

I fight against the animalistic need to defend her. To lash out and strike him down for daring to even glare in her direction.

"*Go,*" I grate through clenched teeth. "I'll be there in a minute."

"Fuck you." She straightens to her full height, her chin regally high, her shoulders broad. "You'll pay for this." She backtracks toward the bedroom. "You'll wish we'd never met."

I've already had many of those moments. Too many times to count where I regretted getting involved—for her sake, not mine.

"*Go.*" I stare her down.

She sucks in a strangled breath, belying her strength, and it fucking kills me.

If only we'd cleared the air sooner.

She retreats into the bedroom, slamming the door in her wake, the deafening vibration crashing through the entire penthouse as I stand staring into the darkened hall.

"That's a pretty impressive mess you've made for yourself, brother. I guess the grass ain't greener after all."

I curl my lip, determined not to be distracted by violence. "Why are you really here? Why contact me after so long?"

"Because of her. Because of *them*. I came when I heard you were shot at because I thought you deserved to know her fucking family have been shooting at us, too. But evidently, I got it wrong if that bitch was with you yesterday."

It's hard to decipher what he says. Hard to hear anything other than him cutting her down.

"You've betrayed the family by sleeping with that whore, Dante. Uncle Lorenzo is going to be pissed when he finds out."

"He already knows." I stalk toward him, menacing and ready to slaughter, jabbing a finger at his chest. "And if you call her that again, or refer to me by that name, I'll make you see stars. You hear me?"

He glowers, his lips pressed tight.

"Do you fucking hear me?" I repeat.

"Yeah, I fucking hear you." He slaps my hand away. "But does he know you kept quiet, not telling us they were going to declare war after two years of radio silence?"

"I don't know what you're talking about."

"No?" He raises a defiant brow. "I call bullshit."

"You can call whatever the fuck you want. But up until a few seconds ago, I had no clue about your connection to her. Let alone the depth of how low you could stoop by abducting a fucking child."

"Wasn't my decision, asshole. The point is—they shot Dad."

I don't respond.

There's nothing more than a flinch at the memory of a man I despise.

"How can you have no loyalty?" He starts to pace, his face stark apart from the hatred in his eyes. "You're sleeping with the enemy."

"She's no enemy of mine." I grind my teeth, refusing to take the bait, refusing to care one iota about Emmanuel's health just because my youngest brother demands it of me. "And I'm surprised you think your actions don't justify their response."

For the love of God. Abduction? They involved a child?

And to think Layla would've suffered every time I asked about her connection to the Costas. Each and every moment I attempted to find out if she was in a relationship with Remy or Salvatore.

Not once did she expose her past.

That beautiful, fucking unfathomably strong woman faked her way through continuous bluffs.

But he's right. Lorenzo will be pissed if Emmanuel was shot and her family were to blame. I'll need to prove I wasn't involved, and do whatever possible to make it seem like she wasn't either.

"That was two goddamn years in the past," he argues. "The situation was dead and buried. Yet, they shot Dad three weeks ago."

"It's my turn to call bullshit. He was in Italy three weeks ago."

"Was he? Or were those the rumors we had to start to hide our weakened position?" He mocks. "He's currently in a makeshift hospital room at home, struggling to ditch a chest infection that stemmed from the bullet wound in his shoulder."

"What a shame." I pull my cell from my pocket and open a new text to Bishop. "I guess you learned the hard way that the only thing that gets dead and buried in the lifestyle you've chosen are the bodies. The need for revenge lives longer than any of us."

"You're judging me?" He raises a brow. "Your sins are far greater than mine."

I type *Get here now* before pressing send. "I never abducted a child."

"If the whispers are true, it's the only thing you haven't done."

I huff a derisive laugh. "I guess you'll never know, because I'm not explaining shit to you. Now get the fuck out."

"I can't believe you." He starts for the hall, walking away from me. "We were brothers once. But you're right on one thing—revenge lives longer than any of us. And I'm sure Dad will agree once I tell him she's fucking you to get back at us."

"You're threatening her?" I shove my cell into my pocket and stalk after him. "You'd tell him?" I grab his shoulder and haul him around to face me.

"I'd take pleasure in it. Why wouldn't I when you abandoned us? You fucking walked and left us with him. Now look where we are." He throws his arms wide. "You caused this. You caused *all* of it—that kid's abduction, her husband's death. If you hadn't left, he wouldn't have spiraled."

The accusations are sharply embedded into my chest, stabbing me with guilt. With truth. "I couldn't stay—"

"Because you were humiliated that Grace left you?" he asks with incredulity. "I don't know how you became the man you did, because the brother I knew was a fucking pussy. I overheard your plans to ditch town with her. But she didn't wait for you, did she? She didn't want to stick around to finish senior year because her dad was an abusive drunk and her mom was a junkie, so she took off, not giving a shit that you weren't—"

I launch, striking my forearm into his throat, slamming him backward against the door. Not seeing. Only feeling.

I press harder, ignoring his rasped breath, not flinching as he claws at my arm. "She didn't go missing, you pathetic piece of shit." I lean close, sinking all my weight against his neck, so there's nothing between us. Nothing apart from my ignorant baby brother and the facts. "*He* killed her. He slit her from throat to gut and showed me the pictures to make sure it sank in."

Remy's eyes bug as he continues to fight me off, his breath wheezing.

"He murdered her because he knew I'd made plans to move out," I seethe in his face. "He slaughtered the girl I cared about, someone who was still a fucking child, because I wasn't dedicated to becoming his perfect little minion like you were."

Remy's mouth works like a fish as I press and press. Open. Closed. Open.

"He took the one thing that was mine and made sure it no longer existed, because he wanted my attention all to himself." I watch the panic build in his eyes, enjoying the victory through the devastation. "So yes, I fucking left. I ran away from money and prestige. I hitchhiked across this godforsaken country to put as much distance between us as I could." Spittle bubbles from my lips, my fury uncontainable. "I lived on the streets. I stole to survive. And you have the fucking audacity to think you know what went down?"

I glare.

I glare so hard I sense an impending aneurism.

"Fuck you, Remy." I pull my arm away, not giving a shit that his grown ass crumples to the floor before me. "You always were a naive little prick."

I kick his shoes and step over him, pulling the door wide to find Bishop poised with his key in the air.

"Perfect timing?" He takes me in with caution, no doubt seeing the monster I've become—the clenched fists, the heaving chest. "What the hell is going on?"

"Get him out of here." I turn for the living room. "Before I fucking kill him."

30

———

LAYLA

I close myself in the bedroom, snatch my hair into a vicious ponytail, then dress in jeans, Chucks, and a white blouse. Everything else is shoved into my suitcase and zipped tight.

I spend minutes poised at the door, overhearing muffled shouts and heavy thuds.

They're fighting again, and I don't know who I'd prefer to suffer more pain—Remy or Matthew.

No, not Matthew. *Dante.*

A goddamn Costa.

I will the sickening disgust to the back of my mind, trying not to acknowledge how I fell for a man who shares the same DNA as my daughter's abductors. My husband's murderers.

There'll be enough time to hate myself for it later.

Right now, there's too much adrenaline to think, the hormone acting like venom in my veins.

I want to hurt him. To drag the vial of cyanide hidden in my jeans pocket and throw the powder in his face. But whenever I picture his death, the only sensation to consume me is regret. *Suffering.*

I'd loved him.

I'd adored and admired every part of that man and now every memory is tainted and twisted by lies.

I open the door a crack as another one slams on the other side of the penthouse.

More shouting follows, but this time the voices aren't raised in anger. Matthew's tone holds frustration. Panic. And it's Bishop's responding aggression that brushes my ears as I inch the door wider.

"That little asshole is running back to Emmanuel as we speak," Matthew yells. "They're going to come after her."

I take the news with a sharp breath.

191

I need to get out of here. To grab my cell from the coffee table and leave.

"What did you expect?" Bishop mutters. "And isn't that why you got involved? You couldn't let her be a target on her own, you had to pin a bull's-eye on our backs, too."

Matthew growls a reply too low to understand. A threat? A warning?

I pull the door wide enough to slip into the hall, cautiously wheeling my suitcase in delicately slow increments along the carpet behind me, the knife in my free hand.

I hold my breath with each step toward the conversation, the growing thunder of my pulse in my ears making it harder to hear.

Lorenzo's name is spoken. Others', too. Men I'm not familiar with.

"What are the options?" Bishop asks. "How confident are you of an outcome?"

"My only confidence comes from knowing Emmanuel won't let this slide. He'll do to her what he did to Grace. And not just Layla, but Stella, too."

I gasp.

"Layla?" Matthew calls out.

Shit. Shit. *Shit.*

"Layla."

This time my name is a command. An impatient warning.

I straighten my shoulders and raise my chin as I continue into view.

The two men stand at the dining table. Tall. Commanding. Aggressive.

Matthew has the sense to look somewhat apologetic beneath the frustration tightening his features. But Bishop, like always, isn't welcoming.

He gives me a dismissive glance before returning his attention to the man who deceived me. "What are we going to do?"

Matthew ignores him and starts toward me. "Good, you're dressed. We've got a big day ahead." He speaks as if things between us are normal. As if he hasn't pummeled the walls of our relationship and left the bricks to fall upon me.

"Don't," I warn. "Don't you dare come near me."

He complies, rooting his feet in place and raising his chin while I stride toward my cell on the coffee table.

"Your breakfast is on the counter. You need to eat."

I maneuver the suitcase around the sofa, bumping into the armrest, and release the handle to snatch for my phone.

One call and Cole will make this right. Him, Hunter, Decker and Luca. They'll fix this mess with blood and broken bones… and hate me more while doing it.

I shove the device in my pocket, the knife still at the ready, and wheel my suitcase out from where I came to make for the entry hall.

"You can't leave." Matthew's gaze haunts me from my periphery.

I keep walking, striding out the distance to freedom.

"Layla, stop."

My body wants to obey. There's no rhyme or reason, but every muscle tenses at his command, including my heart.

"Let me explain what's going on."

He continues toward me, the dwindling space between us causing me to panic. Not from fear of physical pain, but from that of pure emotional torture.

I can't be near him. Can't let him get within reach.

I run, my black Converse Chucks squeaking against the tiles, my suitcase wheels clicking.

He gives chase, his heavy footfalls thunderous behind me as I reach the door and drop the knife to wrench at the dead bolt.

The metal clatters at my feet while I snatch at the handle. Twist. Pull.

The crack of freedom brings hope, the euphoria snatched away when his heavy palm slaps against the wood, slamming the door closed, his body caging me from behind.

"Let me leave." I cling to the handle, twisting and tugging.

"I'm not that person," he growls near my ear. "I'm not one of them."

The words whisper over my neck, poking infected wounds. Memories of him speaking against my neck in better times haunt me, crawling under my skin like torturous bugs.

"You're a monster." I pull and yank and thrash at the handle, willing it to open.

He doesn't move. Doesn't lift his splayed hand from against the wood.

"I'll explain everything later," he vows. "Once it's just the two of us."

"Later?" I swing around to face him only to jerk back at the stifling proximity.

He's there. Right there. Dark eyes manic. Stubble harsh. Face severe.

"You want to talk to me *later*?" I seethe. "Because it's easier for you to lie when we're alone?"

"I haven't lied."

"Not once have you told the whole truth," I shriek.

We stare each other down, my chest rising and falling from a body demanding punishment, his warm breath taunting my lips.

He doesn't move. Doesn't free me from the cage of his arms. All he does is look at me as if he'll tear the world to shreds if I escape. Like he'll lose his mind if I walk from his life, never to return.

It hurts.

His confusing suffering. His unsettling battle.

I want to soothe him and stab him all at once.

"Leave the suitcase." He straightens, his order blanketed with a subtle level of control. "Go eat breakfast."

I rage, wanting to yell at the top of my lungs. To claw at the severity in his eyes. To steal the oxygen from the air to dispel his intoxicating aftershave while suffocating us both.

"I'm not staying." I swing back to the door and snatch at the handle, turning the metal toward freedom, erupting with relief when it opens.

He steps into me, the wall of pressure smothering my spine as he slams the wood shut with a chest-rattling snarl.

"I'll scream," I warn.

"You don't want to do that." He presses into me, his hard body grazing my ass.

The threat is clear in his voice. The pure conviction. But my blood doesn't react in fear.

It warms.

My pulse throbs.

My body still reacts to our chemistry. Succumbing. Yearning.

"You're threatening me?" I turn again, this time concentrating on my hatred when I look him in the eye.

He's even closer now, our noses almost brushing as he intimidates me in the cage of his arms.

"I'll do whatever it takes," he purrs. "We're not done, Layla."

So be it.

I force a smile. Bat my lashes. Pray to God I'm not making another mistake. Then launch my knee at his groin, making direct impact.

Shock splashes his face. Eyes wide. Mouth, too.

He grunts.

Crumples.

My regret hits just as fast, the remorse heavy enough to suffocate.

I don't let it consume me. I scramble for the door, swinging it wide, leaving the suitcase behind. I'm one step over the threshold when I'm viciously yanked backward by a painful grip on my upper arm, then dragged into an entirely different body.

"My turn," Bishop seethes. "And let me warn you, I'm far less patient."

31

______

LAYLA

I'm shoved onto the sofa, my suitcase left at the door, my cell confiscated.

Bishop scowls at me from a few feet away, the minutes passing in silence until Matthew limps into the living room. His shoulders hunch as he makes his way to the kitchen to lean heavily into the island counter.

"I knew we had secrets, but I underestimated just how many." His voice is graveled as he clings to the marble, his face now a paler shade of sun-kissed beauty. "You should've told me your grievance with the Costas had nothing to do with dating Remy or Salvatore."

I remain quiet, my hands in my lap, my eyes glaring in rage.

"What reason did you have to keep the details of your daughter's abduction and husband's murder from me?"

I flinch at the ease with which he relays my nightmares. The simplicity. The lack of emotion.

"Why didn't you tell me?"

I scoff, finding him sickeningly self-righteous for asking about my skeletons when his pile far higher.

"Why pretend you'd had a love affair?" he continues. "Why allude to being a past lover?"

"I didn't allude to anything. You assumed."

His eyes narrow with impatience. "I could've done something. I could've—"

"You couldn't even tell me your real name."

"Matthew *is* my real name." He straightens, wincing with the movement. "They're not my family."

"No?" I raise a brow. "I think your DNA would argue."

"My DNA doesn't make them family."

"That's exactly what it does."

His jaw ticks as Bishop takes one retreating step after another until he's leaning against the far wall, arms crossed over his chest, watching us like a soap opera.

"I was born a Costa." Matthew hobbles to the fridge, pulling out a bag of vegetables from the freezer drawer to hold against his crotch. "I didn't stay one."

"That doesn't change a thing."

"No?" He raises a brow as he settles back against the counter. "So you loved your father? You loved a man rumored to traffic sex slaves?"

I press my lips tight, refusing to answer.

"Families aren't so clear cut are they, *amore mio*?"

I grind my teeth, scowl my fury, my jaw aching from the tension.

He's undaunted by my hatred, not batting an eye while he repositions the makeshift ice pack against his crotch. "You could've at least told me your family had Emmanuel shot. Especially when I told you yesterday what would happen if I was associated with him being hurt."

My mouth opens in protest. My heart races.

Is that what Cole had been hiding the last time I was home? Had he instigated war without warning me?

Jesus.

I force my chin high. "Turns out we both had secrets that could hurt the other."

His gaze assaults me, scrutinizing, a cruel smile curving his lips. "You didn't know." He scoffs a laugh. "Your fucking brother didn't have the sense to tell you."

"Jesus Christ," Bishop mutters. "She's clueless."

My fingers twist in my lap, my loathing skyrocketing.

Matthew stands taller. "That settles it then. You're staying with me until this is sorted."

"That settles it?" I dig my nails into my palms. "How does *that* settle anything?"

"You still want to run home to a brother who put you in danger?"

Cole's frantic texts make more sense now. How he wouldn't quit demanding to know my whereabouts and who I was with. If only he'd told me what was going on.

"You hate your brother," Matthew states.

"No, I don't."

I despise him at times. Am sickened and beside myself with fury occasionally. But I've never hated him. Instead, it will be Cole who detests me for the complications I've created.

"No? He treats you like shit. Are you really in a hurry to get back to that?"

"As if you've treated me any bett—"

"I've treated you like a queen. Like *my* queen. Cole's actions are the reason you found it so fucking easy to move in with a stranger."

My stomach twists, the pain spreading.

"You don't want to return to Portland, Layla." He gentles his tone. "Once we sort out our differences, you'll want to stay here."

"Of course," I drawl. "I'd much prefer to remain with someone who makes it their job to hide the truth. You even had the balls to introduce Lorenzo as your mentor."

"He is my mentor."

"He's your *uncle*."

He inclines his head. "He's that, too."

I growl in frustration, my nails embedded in my palms. I need to hurt him like he's hurting me, but shooting or stabbing would never be enough. I have to reach inside his chest and wring the life from his beating heart, just like he's done to mine.

I cut my gaze away, unable to withstand those deep, dark eyes anymore, and whisper, "My brother will kill you."

"In that case, I better make the most of our time together." He places the ice pack on the marble and rounds the counter. "Bishop, can you give us a minute?"

"Need me to do anything?" Bishop pushes from the wall, his arms falling to his sides.

"Call the charter. Have a jet placed on standby."

"Destination?"

"To be determined."

I keep my face cast in the opposite direction as Bishop strides for the entry, the front door closing seconds later.

The tension increases tenfold. My suffering, too.

I wish I still had the knife. Death by cyanide won't be gruesome enough.

"Layla, listen to me." Matthew hobbles closer. "Everything between us is real—I promise you that. But I understand I hurt you." He reaches the sofa and continues to hesitantly sit on the coffee table before me. Knee to knee. "If it's any solace, I can assure you my balls ache like a motherfucker."

I keep my mouth shut, not finding solace at all.

The quiet stretches, his gaze haunting my periphery, his body entirely too close.

"The silent treatment isn't an option either, *amore mio*. You're going to have to find a way to push your animosity aside. Remy may have already told Emmanuel about us."

I snap my head around to glare at him, wordlessly letting him know there is no *us*.

"Do you understand what's happening?" His gaze leisurely rakes mine. Unfazed. In command. "Your brother's shooting would be considered retaliation. An attempt at murder in response to your husband's death. But this?" He waves a lazy hand between us. "This is personal. Depending on what information Remy shares, you might be held accountable for taking things further. For you, *personally*, levelling up the war all on your own."

My throat turns dry.

"I don't know if they have men in D.C.," he continues, "or if Emmanuel is capable of arranging retaliation from his hospital bed. But do you want to risk leaving here and finding out how quickly they can strike a helpless woman on her own?"

"I'm not helpless," I snarl.

"No?" He sinks to his knees before me, the show of submission in conflict with the sickening severity in his eyes. "Do you really think you can protect yourself?" He places his hands on my knees, the heat of his palms seeping through my jeans. "That you'd stand a chance?"

"Don't touch me." My voice shakes with the demand. With the disgusting thrill his contact provides.

He slides his fingers farther along my thighs and leans against my shins. "You're in danger, Layla."

I know. And not only from Emmanuel.

The man before me is my biggest threat.

His touch is impending doom. His gaze promises suffering of the most wicked kind.

"Get. Your hands. Off me." I enunciate the words slowly. Violently.

"Admit it," he murmurs. "You still want to fuck me."

I raise a hand to slap him only to have my wrist captured in a vise grip. I try with the other and he steals that, too, dragging me forward by my forearms until we're face-to-face, our breath mingling.

"What we have is real whether you like it or not," he snarls against my lips. "I can see it in your eyes. You're still hungry for me."

"I'm hungry for blood." I struggle to free my wrists, wriggling, tugging, hating not only the hold he has on my arms, but the one he has on my heart. "You're going to regret what you've done."

"No, I won't. Because what I did brought us together."

His confidence sparks insanity. I thrash, scream, attempt to kick at his thighs.

"*Enough.*" He stands, dragging my arms above my head. "Want me to prove how much you want me?" He swings me sideways, stretching me across the sofa.

I buck and twist and struggle, fighting and fighting while he climbs on top of me.

"*No,*" I scream. "Don't you fucking dare."

I stop breathing, stop moving as the heavy weight of him sinks against my hips, my hands trapped above my head, his eyes never leaving mine.

I hate this.

I hate *him*.

But he's right. I want him, too.

I need him. Crave him. Can't stop my nerves tingling from the lust-drunk memories of what it means for our bodies to be joined.

And his dick—*oh, God*—is erect, hard and adamant against my pubic bone, sending me into a world of tingles.

I despise him. I love him. I loathe him. I'm lost.

He leans in, attempting to kiss me, my mouth watering in response.

"Don't." I turn my face away, not willing to capitulate. I'm stronger than this.

"*Amore mio,*" he murmurs against my cheek. "You're all that matters to me."

I squeeze my eyes shut, forcing down the pained cry that demands to be heard.

He nuzzles my jaw, my neck, his lips leaving gentle kisses along my carotid. "I will earn your trust."

"Impossible," I whisper. "I'll never believe a word you say."

The kisses stop. The nuzzling, too.

"We will see." He rests his forehead against my shoulder, a defeated sigh brushing my ear. "But for now, you need to stay with me."

"No."

"Think of Stella. Think of what they'll do to her."

My fragile pulse becomes frantic. "She's safe."

Nobody knows where she is. Who she is. Stella was enrolled in boarding school under a different surname, her tuition paid from an account that has no correlation to my family.

"Are you willing to stake her life on that? Because I'm not." He shifts on top of me, pulling back until I meet his gaze. "You don't know enough about my past. Or what I mean to Emmanuel. I may be estranged, but that bastard will always consider me his successor. I'm his golden child. Your presence in my life won't be ignored."

"Which means I should get as far away from you as possible."

"Distance won't matter. He'll find you. He won't stop looking—not when his hatred for you will be more than what he holds for your brother. You infiltrated his family. You targeted a son who wasn't involved."

Goddamnit.

What have I done?

What has *he* done?

"This is your fault." I wiggle beneath him, only endeavoring to tease my pussy against his shaft. "*You* did this."

"So let me fix it."

"How?"

The front door opens with a whoosh of air, footsteps following straight after.

I scramble, reigniting my fight to get this bastard off me. Unwilling to be seen as a victim. Especially a sexual one.

"Get off." I buck. "*Now.*"

Matthew growls and releases my wrists, removing his weight from my body. "Have breakfast, *amore mio*. We leave for Denver in ten minutes."

32

MATTHEW

Her eyes flash in fear at the mention of Denver. But she doesn't protest. Instead, she sits up, straightening to her full height to accept her fate.

She doesn't argue about leaving her suitcase in the penthouse.

Doesn't fight getting on the jet.

She comes of her own volition, taking the lone seat on the far side of the aisle while I sit across the polished compact table from Bishop, scrutinizing her.

"I don't have a good feeling about this." He taps his fingers against the arm of his chair. "I'm assuming you have a plan."

"I do."

He raises a brow, waiting for clarification while I attempt to figure out why Layla came so willingly. Why didn't I have to drag her alongside me, kicking and screaming?

"Well?" Bishop asks. "Do you mind telling me what it is, seeing as though I'm following you into the lion's den?"

"Emmanuel is no lion." I return my attention to the only friend I've had in ten years. The only man I've trusted apart from my uncle. "He's a fucking hyena. An opportunistic scavenger and a coward. But the strategy is simple. I'm going to talk to him and get him to leave Layla and her daughter out of the war with her brother."

He raises a brow. "*Talk* to him?"

"Yes. *Talk.*" I grind my teeth, hating the vow that keeps Emmanuel alive. "I won't betray Lorenzo."

"Do you plan on taking her with you?"

"Yes." I can't do this any other way. The man who spawned me won't have her killed if I'm standing in the line of fire.

At least, he never would've in the past.

Emmanuel Costa has, and probably always will, see me as the one rightfully meant to take over the family business even though I walked away.

There's a reason that fucker hasn't retired despite the money piled in his bank, and I'm sure it has everything to do with him still wanting me at the helm.

Problem is, it's risky to assume he hasn't changed.

I don't know him anymore.

Before today, I'd tried to kid myself about the lengths he would go to for success. For *power*. I'd prayed for the sake of my siblings that the rumors of blood on their hands hadn't been true. But today, Remy alerted me to a callousness I'd been oblivious to. One Layla had painstakingly survived and her family kept hidden.

Emmanuel is more inhuman than I wanted to believe. More sick and twisted.

That's where I get it from.

But as long as I stand between her and his vengeance, she'll survive.

She has to.

Bishop clears his throat, subtly regaining my attention. "You're going to take her right to your father's door?"

The description punctures my chest, wielding a vicious blow.

I slam my fist against the table and glare. "He's not my father."

Layla startles in my periphery, her fear punching me with guilt.

"Biology disagrees," she snips under her breath, settling back into her haughty posture of hostility, bratty even in the face of what's to come.

"My apologies." Bishop lowers his voice, the deep rumble of the jet giving us a modicum of privacy from her prying ears. "Are you sure you want to drag her into the heart of this? You're not worried they'll slit her throat in front of you?"

"Remy and Salvatore wouldn't dare. And Emmanuel is supposed to be laid flat from complications of a bullet wound."

"That part could be a trap. Nobody has heard a word about his injury."

"Nobody heard a word about him abducting Cole fucking Torian's niece and killing his brother-in-law either," I snarl.

"True. But still…"

He's right. This could be a setup. Emmanuel might have concocted the entire plan —a fake instigation of war, a pretend vulnerability.

Layla knew nothing about Emmanuel being targeted. Lorenzo hasn't said a word about his brother-in-law being shot.

The fucker might have even paid the Virginia Beach gangbangers to do the hotel drive-by so Remy had an excuse to find me after all these years and claim to give a shit about my well-being.

"If they attempt to harm her in any way, I'll break the vow to my uncle without a thought." It's a pledge. A fucking promise. "And if you're forced to do the same, I'll pay the price. I'll take the blame."

"Neither one of us are going back to that life. Not now. Not when—"

"I'll deal with it," I grate. "I just need to know you'll protect her if I can't." I hold his gaze, conveying the importance of what I'm about to say with a hard look. "I have no right to ask you to guard her with your life, but—"

"Consider it done." His face tightens, obligation and loyalty staring back at me.

"You know you don't owe me. You don't need to be here. Whatever happened in the past has been repaid over the years—"

"I haven't paid for shit. My debt is still owed. And even if it wasn't, I'd be here. I have your back. I'll protect her." He drags his gaze away to stare out the window.

If I wasn't a selfish prick, I'd force him to walk. To get the fuck away from all of this.

Too bad I'm the most self-centered bastard he's ever met.

I can't risk losing her.

Not to a family I despise or because of the deceit I spun.

She's mine. Has been from the night we met.

I show my appreciation with a nod, and retrieve folded pieces of paper from my jacket pocket. "These are the house plans for the property. I need you to commit them to memory."

I slide the pages across the table and wait in silence as he scans the mansion, his concentration heavy as he frowns his way along the multitude of halls and rooms on the multi-level building.

"It's fucking big."

"I've heard that a time or two," I drawl. "But it could potentially be bigger. These plans are what I had drawn up after I left Denver. God knows what renovations have been done since."

He swipes a hand over his mouth as he continues to scan the pages, his focus gradually tracking from one side to the other, over and over until finally, he slides the architectural drawings back toward me. "How many men should we expect to be guarding the property?"

"I don't know." The admission annoys me. Weakens. "Emmanuel used to be protective of his solitude, so best-case scenario—none. Worst? God only knows."

"And you don't want to bring some of our own?"

"I've already made the arrangements. De Marco and two of his team will be waiting. But this isn't a show of force. It's a negotiation. A conversation."

He relaxes back into his seat, unconvinced. "Should I be worried about you reverting to your old ways while holding said conversation?"

The question stings. "I don't know."

He nods, unfazed by the complication. "I've got one last question, then I'm done." I brace for impact as he turns his attention to Layla, his eyes callously narrowing. "We protect her with our lives—that much is clear. But who the fuck protects them from her? She's out for blood just as much as they are."

"You don't." She tilts her head to face us. "You stay out of my way, because I'm more than happy to take you down at the same time."

Normally, I'd admire her strength. But now, instead of pride, I'm agitated by her tenacity. If she's here for a misguided chance at revenge, she could get us all killed.

"See?" Bishop drawls. "She's fucking crazy."

"She wouldn't be stupid enough to make a move." I hold her gaze. "Would you, *amore mio?*"

Her eyes harden.

"This isn't a game, Layla. We can't risk messing this up."

She rolls her eyes and returns her focus out the jet window, her arms clamping over her chest. But there's something else I see in her expression before she hides her face from me. Something I hope isn't pained resignation.

She can't be willing to give her life to end those of the Costas. Can she?

Fuck.

The rest of the flight is spent relaying tactics for different scenarios, none of which are likely to come true. We land in Denver below a clear blue sky, the fall breeze rushing into the cabin with an icy edge of warning as soon as the door opens.

Bishop is the first to make for the aisle with Layla following

"Wait." I push from my seat.

She doesn't listen.

"Layla, I said wait." I start after her, lunging forward to grab her arm. "We have to talk. As much as I understand your enthusiasm for destruction, you need to be on your best behavior."

She swings around to face me, yanking her arm from my grip. "No, I need to do what's best for my family."

Her brattiness chafes. The resolute conviction, too.

I'd love to splay her over my knees and belt her ass. "You're letting your anger at me cloud your judgment. You know full well you'll get yourself killed if you start shit today."

She makes an exaggerated attempt to bat her lashes and pout her bottom lip. "But you said you'd protect me."

"I can only do so much," I growl.

"Well, you should've thought about that before you brought me here." She turns for the door.

"So you're happy to make your daughter an orphan?"

She swings back around so violently, I stiffen on instinct. "I'm going to *save* my daughter. I'm going to take advantage of this opportunity and do whatever it takes to make sure your family doesn't get anywhere near her. Now *and* in the future."

"Layla—"

"Don't *Layla* me." She holds my gaze, her big blue eyes cutting to my ashen heart. "Don't look at me in pity or reprimand. You have no right to do that anymore. You wanted me here, so I'm here—"

"I wanted you here because by my side is the safest place to be."

"No, you did it to control me. To confine me. And I didn't protest because it works in my favor. If I don't end this, at least I'll gain information."

"You won't end it, *amore mio.*"

"Oh ye of little faith."

I itch to shake some sense into her. To kiss it. *Fuck* it.

"Let me call my brother." There's more demand in her voice than request. "Give me the chance to explain what's going on. To warn him, for Stella's sake."

"Soon."

She squares her shoulders, her throat working over a swallow. "*Please.*" Her forehead creases as if the taste of surrender is vile on her tongue. "I waited until we arrived to ask so you'd know there was nothing he could do to interfere. But if this is…" Her brows pinch, her eyes gaining a gleam of vulnerability.

"If this is what?"

"The end." She regains her composure, the words snapped with a retreating step. "If I don't make it home, I need to have spoken to my family first."

She undoes me. Fucking kills me.

"You'll speak to them again, my love. I can promise you that."

She smiles, vindictive and cruel, yet still so fucking inviting. "Thanks for the vote of confidence, *Dante*. However, despite your extremely comforting reassurance, I want that phone call. Now."

My hackles rise at the name. But I understand the reason for the barb.

Amore mio, she can reluctantly stomach. *My love*, she can't.

"One phone call right now." She crosses her arms over her chest, plumping her breasts beneath the thin blouse. "You owe me that much."

I owe her everything. I'll give it to her, too. Just not yet.

I step toward her, my predatory side enjoying her continued retreat a little more than I care to admit as we make our way down the slim aisle, neither one of us stopping until her back bumps into the cockpit door.

She steels herself as I close in. Squares her shoulders. Clenches her teeth.

My limbs thrum with the desire to connect. To command. To fist her fucking hair and drag her forward until our lips mash and tongues tangle.

She wants it, too. I can tell by the way her gaze darts to my mouth, heated and hungry, her chest rising and falling with shallow breaths.

I inch closer, walking into her, my thigh parting hers.

Then, nothing.

I simply stand there, letting the chemistry between us do its thing. Allowing her to see without words or action that there's no end to the attraction we've created.

We're meant to be together. We won't be separated.

She blinks back at me, stunned yet steadfast. Panicked and panting.

I ignore the pulse of my dick and lean closer, a bare few inches from those captivating lips. "This isn't the time or place."

Her eyes flare. "There will *never* be a time and place. Never again. Do you hear me?"

I smirk. "I was talking about the phone call."

She thumps my chest, pushes and pummels, her cheeks turning red. "You're a bastard. Of course I assumed wrong when you're all over me."

"I *am* a bastard." I sober in agreement, remaining in her space as her attack dwindles. "But I'll give you everything you need, Layla. I promise. I just can't risk a phone call right now. Not with what I've learned of your brother's reputation."

She snarls and shoves past me to escape toward the stairs, mumbling, "Well, I can't wait to learn the truth about yours."

33

────────

MATTHEW

"It's only a few miles up the road." I sit behind the wheel of a rental Lincoln Navigator, driving through the outer reaches of Denver.

I've come to this hellhole of a city too many times over the past ten years and not once have I returned to the home I fled as a teenager.

We pass farming houses and million-dollar estates with masses of cropped land in between. But everything is different now. The trees lining the streets tower higher. More homes scatter the countryside. The road has been widened and marked.

"De Marco is leaving it until the last minute to show," Bishop mutters. "Where is he?"

I slow as I reach the last intersection before Emmanuel's property, making sure there are no cars in sight when I veer onto the gravel at the side of the road. "We should see him any second now."

I bring the vehicle to a stop, scrutinizing the nearby trees and bushes along the fence line, searching for the guys I've worked with on multiple sabotage tasks in the past.

"There are men running around the corner." Layla shifts in the back seat. "I hope they're yours."

I check the rearview, recognizing De Marco's bald head, Goodin's neck tattoo, and the intimidatingly wide build of Whitby jogging toward us, all of them in long-sleeve camo shirts and pants.

"Yeah, they're ours." I press a button on the key fob, opening the door to the cargo area, the back row of seats already folded in preparation to stow the men inside.

Layla bristles when they climb in, their labored breathing filling the air as I press the button to close them into their cramped hiding place.

"I was beginning to think you weren't going to show." De Marco wipes the sweat from his brow. "How's things, Langston?"

"They've been better." I hold his gaze in the mirror. "Are you guys ready?"

"Always." Whitby settles his back against the side of the interior. "We're locked and loaded."

"But this is only a conversation," Bishop mutters.

"It *is* only a conversation," I reiterate. "Do you all understand what we're doing here?"

"You've sent more than enough messages to make it clear." De Marco mimics Whitby's seated position on the opposite side of the cargo area, Goodin doing the same at his side. "We keep our mouths shut. Back you up if necessary. And get the woman out if shit happens."

I nod, my gaze flicking to Layla who stares at me through the mirror. "You can trust them."

She scoffs. "Just like I can trust you?"

I'm not fighting with her again. The last thing I need is to battle my dick when her bratty attitude takes hold.

"We scoped the place while we were waiting," Goodin adds. "Caught sight of two armed guards outside, but nothing else. There might be more in the house."

"Doubtful." I shake my head. "Emmanuel likes privacy."

"Then it's safe to assume there's two." Goodin shrugs. "But there could be fifty on standby at a moment's notice just in case you're thinking of getting cocky."

"Nobody is getting cocky. If bullets start flying the battle won't end until both parties are dead, and I have no intention of dying today." I shoot a glance to Bishop. "You good now?"

"I'll be good once it's over." He focuses out the windscreen, resting his arm on the window ledge. "Let's get this done."

I pull onto the road, increasing the pace to eat up the distance between us and imminent hostility.

"There's to be no complications. Are we all clear?" Bishop reiterates louder than necessary. "This is a conversation. Nothing more."

I don't reaffirm it. He's been given enough assurances on how this has to play out. His issue is that he knows me too well. Knows the *old* me and what that animal is capable of when cornered.

"This is it." I jerk my chin toward the upcoming property with its head-high brick-wall perimeter stretching more than a quarter mile in the distance. Large decorative spikes line the top ledge, the glossy metal maybe intended as a decorative feature, but also offering intimidation and security. "You guys in the back need to get down. Stay out of sight until we're through the gates."

They do as instructed, slinking from view as I drive by the first security camera affixed to the boundary wall. The round black devices are positioned every ten yards leading up to the thick barred gates that never existed in my childhood.

"Nothing gets said or done without my say so." I stop in front of the barrier separating me from assholes I despise, the intercom a foot outside my closed window, and shoot a glance to Layla through the rearview. "No comments. No actions. Nothing. You hear me?"

She smiles, batting her lashes in an innocent taunt.

"Don't test me, Layla."

"Don't worry," Bishop snarls. "If she fucks this up, they won't be the only ones preparing to kill her."

Her smile remains in place. "I'd like to see you try."

"Enough," I grate. "We're on the same side."

"You sure about that?" Goodin mumbles in the back. "You guys aren't giving off a fuzzy sense of comradery."

"We'll be fine," I force the misguided optimism into existence. "We're only here for a fucking conversation."

Layla rolls her eyes, crossing her arms over her chest. "We'll see."

"Yeah, we'll fucking see," Bishop mutters.

"*Enough*," I repeat. "None of us are stupid enough to fuck this up, right? So show some goddamn restraint." I lower my window and reach for the intercom to press the call button.

The inside of the car falls silent. There's nothing but the rumble from the engine and the rustle of wind as we wait.

I'm sure our presence is already known. Either Emmanuel, my siblings, or a battalion-sized security team are hiding in the wings watching. Waiting.

"Hello?" A fragile female voice breaks the quiet, the fake innocence nudging my agitation.

Adena—the woman who birthed me.

I clench my teeth against my disdain. "I need to see Emmanuel."

"I'm sorry but he's currently in Italy. If you'd like to leave your name and number I can arrange for him to get in contact on his return."

They don't know it's me. They weren't expecting a visit. Why?

"Maybe Remy didn't say anything," Bishop whispers. "You might have been wrong about him."

Bullshit. That fucker was beyond hostile. He would've told someone.

"I know he's inside." I speak to the intercom. "He's going to want to see me."

There's a pause, the briefest blip in time where I picture her squinting at the live feed from the security camera pointing my way.

"Who is this?" she asks.

My anger rises at having to use the only name she's familiar with. "It's Dante. Now open the damn gate."

The silence returns, creating a cavernous void where Layla's loathing grows. I can feel her judgment from the back seat even though those five fucking letters were put behind me when I disowned this godforsaken family.

"*Dante*?" Adena's voice fractures. "Is that really you?"

I glare at the security camera, reliving the last conversation we had and hating her more for it as the seconds pass. How she denied what Emmanuel had done to Grace. How she took his side over that of her innocent teenage son.

The gates rattle, the intimidating metal bouncing a moment before they begin to part.

I don't answer her question. Don't acknowledge her offensive excitement. I wait until the gate opening is wide enough, then drive into the heart of hell, pebbles crunching under my tires, disgust settling in my gut.

The gardens are different. The shrubs and flowers once littered in the front yard no longer exist. It's now all perfectly manicured grass. Nothing but unobstructed view to ensure intruders are seen.

"Fucking big house," Bishop murmurs. "More than enough room to confine our dumb asses for the rest of our lives."

I ignore him and stalk my gaze along the two-story mansion as we approach, checking for signs of life behind the sheer curtains, both upstairs and below.

The balcony is empty. No potted plants to block the view. No siblings to welcome me home from the wrought-iron railing.

The only sign of life comes from the two guards Whitby spoke of, both of them wearing dark uniforms as they stand at the front steps of the mansion, each of them with a hand at the ready near their holstered sidepiece.

"De Marco, it's time for you guys to shine." I pull to a stop a few yards from the front of the house and cut the engine. "Everyone else, stay in the car. Let me get a read on things first." I unfasten my belt and climb out, slamming the door behind me before Bishop can protest.

The cargo area opens as I walk to the hood, Whitby, Goodin, and De Marco all piling out to take different positions around the vehicle.

Emmanuel's guards don't show surprise. They don't talk or scowl or move. They're prepared. On alert. Adena might not have anticipated my arrival, but someone did.

I stalk toward them, jaw stiff, lips snarled, and poised to demand a meeting with Emmanuel when Salvatore opens the front door.

"Brother," he sneers in greeting. "You shouldn't be here."

"Believe me, I wish I wasn't."

"Then leave." He approaches, passing his two guards to eye the Lincoln. "Is that *her*? You brought her here?" His hard eyes cut to mine. "Are you fucking insane?"

"Are you?" I counter. "Stealing a kid? Killing a major player in the Portland underworld? Who the fuck have you become?"

"Someone loyal to my family. Which is more than I can say for you."

I smile, all teeth and anger. "I want to see him. So either wheel him out here if he's in as bad shape as Remy claims, or we're going in."

"You don't want to do that."

"I agree. But I'm still going to." It's been a lifetime since we were face-to-face. Now, there's a mere few feet of space between me and my closest sibling, who stands at the top of the three stairs leading to damnation. But the prankster kid I grew up with is nowhere in sight. The man who stares back at me is cold and calculating. "I won't let Remy twist the situation and make her more of a target."

"He hasn't twisted anything." Salvatore keeps his tone level, exuding a calm I can't reciprocate. "Nobody knows. Neither me or Remy want to continue this war with her psychotic family. So the last thing we're going to do is tell Dad you've hooked up with the enemy."

"That's not the impression he gave earlier today." I slide my hands into my pants pockets, hiding the way my fingers twitch for a gun I no longer own. "Remy made it clear he wanted her dead."

He scoffs a laugh and descends the stairs, the guards following a few steps behind him. He doesn't stop until he's squared up with me, shoulders broad and proud, chin arrogantly high.

As a teen, I towered over him, my growth spurt coming well before his, but now we're equally matched in physical appearance as well as disdain.

"He's always been more of a slave to his emotions than either of us," he drawls. "So it's only natural he reacted to yet another layer of your betrayal when he was the one who took the longest to understand why the fuck you would abandon us in the first place."

I bristle.

I hadn't wanted to leave them behind. I'd been a kid when I made those plans with Grace. I'd been young and dumb and stupid. I'd thought things would change once I was gone. That Emmanuel would wake up to himself instead of doubling down on criminal decisions.

"Don't resent me for getting out. You could've done the same a hundred times over."

He laughs with derision. "Ignorance is bliss, brother. You have no idea what our lives are like."

"Spare me the multimillion-dollar sob story. I'm not here to reminisce. Either bring him out here or tell your dogs to stand down so we can go inside."

"Do you really want to make that mistake?" He steps closer, getting in my face, the shuffle of feet closing in behind me, Salvatore's guards following suit. "Remy may have been driven by emotion if he spoke of killing her, but our father will be entirely collected when he gives the order for her death. You're shortening her already precarious lifespan."

"I'll shorten yours if you don't get out of my way."

We stare each other down, neither one of us budging until the front door opens, the slight creak of a well-worn hinge dragging my attention to Adena paused in the entry.

"Dante?" She scrutinizes me with a cautious approach. "Is that really my boy?"

Salvatore steps back, his face bitter as she breaks into a run.

Fuck.

I brace for impact as she descends the stairs and throws her arms wide, barreling into me for a hug that snaps my muscles rigid.

I don't remove my hands from my pockets. Don't reciprocate.

Guilt is a punishing motherfucker as I imagine Layla's thoughts as her enemy embraces me like the long-lost child I am.

"My son." Adena's face snuggles into my neck, the affection pathetic. "I've missed you more than you could imagine. I always knew you'd come back."

"I haven't." I retreat, breaking the connection. "Once I speak to your husband, I'm gone."

She blinks, her face falling as Salvatore comes to stand at her side. "Why? What is this about?"

"Business," my brother answers. "It's not a reunion."

Another body enters the doorway, the feminine greeting of, "Hi, brother," brushing my ears before I turn my attention to Abri.

She's in perfect costume, accentuated makeup, figure-hugging clothes, immaculately styled hair. It's the smile curving her lips that places a fault in the facade, the jubilation not matching the sadness she can't hide in her eyes.

"Abri," I grate.

I remember her as the heart and happiness of this family when I was growing up. Too pure and sweet to survive Emmanuel. Too young and innocent to be taken with me when I left.

I was wrong, though. From what I've heard, she's adapted to the changing environment, transforming into a snake who seduces wealthy married men only to blackmail them with their transgressions.

"What's going on?" She glides her attention over De Marco and his men, then focuses on the car before stiffening. "What is she doing here?"

"We're here to see Emmanuel. Who's going to—" My words fall short as the front gates rattle open behind me.

I glance over my shoulder, watching the heavy metal move as Bishop disobeys instruction and climbs from the car, his large frame moving to stand in front of Layla's window, protecting her from the view of the approaching Maserati.

"Good," Salvatore murmurs. "Remy's here to join the fun."

The vehicle accelerates, kicking up pebbles and dust to abruptly skid to a stop next to the Lincoln. In seconds, my youngest brother is shoving from the sports car, the engine still purring as he storms toward Layla's door.

"You brought that bitch here?" he accuses. "Didn't I warn you?"

"Back off." Bishop braces for attack, arms tense, knuckles locked.

De Marco does the same, closing in at his side.

I remain in place, my demons screaming for action even though I know it would be a sign of weakness. "I'll kill you myself, Remy. You know I will."

They need to see I'm in control. That I'm not mindless in my need to protect her, even though that's far from the truth.

I'd slaughter for her.

And I'd do it too damn easily.

Remy stops a few feet in front of Bishop. "Get her out of here."

"I will as soon as I see Emmanuel. Until then, keep your thoughts about her to yourself or risk becoming a folktale."

His eyes cut to mine. "She won't make it out of here alive."

The hair at my nape prickles. "You kill her, I kill you, Salvo kills me, Bishop kills him. The list goes on until a generation is slaughtered. Not to mention the aftermath from Lorenzo if anyone survives. Is that what you want?" I glare. "Because I didn't come here for violence."

Nobody answers.

"I *will* kill for her." I meet everyone's gaze in turn—Salvo, Remy, Abri, Adena, then their guards. "Without pause or guilt. So if anyone has that on their mind, start preparing to meet your maker."

"You're such a piece of shit," Remy mutters. "Lorenzo really did a number on you."

"And look what your father did to you. Clearly, you're not the pinnacle of virtue."

"He's your father, too," Adena corrects.

"No." I look at her in earnest. "Both of you gave up parental rights when you had Grace killed."

"What?" Abri stiffens, her mask of perfection slipping as her lips part in shock. "Is that true? Is that why he left?"

"No. He's stirring up lies from the past." Adena crosses her arms over her chest, every wrinkle on her tired face growing deeper as she scowls at me. "Why are you being like this? You've become just like her family." She turns her daggered stare toward Layla in the back seat. "Breaking the peace after years of silence."

"Peace?" I smirk. "You abduct a child of the Portland underworld and expect peace?"

"Two children," Abri murmurs. "There were two."

"For fuck's sake," Bishop mutters.

I shake my head, scowling at Salvatore. How the hell could he let that happen?

"Don't judge me." His jaw ticks. "You don't know me."

"Evidently… and murder?" I raise a brow. "And still, you expected there to be peace?"

"Nobody else was meant to be there," he growls. "Everything ran smoothly until that asshole spooked us."

"Everything ran smoothly?" Abri's hand tentatively climbs to her throat. "I disagree."

Salvo ignores her. Everyone does as silence falls, the hum of the Maserati the only sound.

I knew they never had the picture-perfect relationship they projected on social media. The overheard conversations at Perfezione are proof of that. But seeing them like this shows the cuts run deeper.

None of them are proud of their lives. They're miserable here.

Yet they still don't leave.

"I'm not here to recap your mistakes." I pull my hands from my pockets, raising my palms to show I'm not here to fight. "I only came to make sure Emmanuel doesn't repeat them in the future. So are you escorting me inside or am I entering by force?"

Remy sneers. Their guards grip the handle of their holstered weapons.

"Fine. Be my guest." Salvatore smirks and turns to the house, swinging an arm toward the front door. "But it's her funeral."

34

———————

MATTHEW

I open Layla's door, offering a hand to help her climb out only to fight frustration when she pushes away my hospitality.

I make sure she stays at my side as we're led into the house, Salvatore climbing the curved entry staircase, a guard marching close at his back when he enters the upper-level hall.

We become a long line of temperamental fuckery as we stride into a wing of the mansion that didn't exist when I was a child. Bishop and De Marco remain in my shadow, followed by Adena, Remy, Abri and their second guard, then Goodin and Whitby at the rear.

"You sure you want to do this?" Salvo stops at a closed door at the end of the hall, his hand poised on the handle. "Times may change, Dante, but he hasn't learned to listen."

I glower. "Open the fucking door."

He shrugs and does as requested, pushing the painted wood wide to continue inside, the guard on his tail. He exposes a sunlit room full of medical equipment, Emmanuel seated in the middle on an inclined hospital bed. The grey-haired bastard's legs are covered by sheets and a knitted blanket, his torso draped in an oversized grey shirt with heart monitor cables snaking out from one of the short sleeves and neck hole.

He's lost weight since the last time I saw him at Perfezione, his cheeks now gaunt, his skin a pale shade of grey.

"Son." He greets me without surprise, the Italian accent lingering in his voice while he repositions himself to sit taller. "I was beginning to wonder when you would come inside. It's good to see you again."

"Stay behind me," I mutter to Layla and continue forward, looking down my nose at him with blatant scorn as the peanut gallery enter behind me to suffocate the space. "I heard you were shot. Too bad they didn't have better aim."

Emmanuel chuckles, the sound morphing into a wheezing hack of a cough. "It was merely a scratch to the shoulder." The hacking continues, his struggle growing. "Unfortunately, complications came with the recovery. Sepsis hasn't been kind."

"What a shame," Layla mutters.

Emmanuel's eyes narrow on her as he reaches to the side of the bed, retrieving an oxygen mask to place over his mouth. "Ahh, yes. The woman I saw on the security feed. Let her come closer so I can take a better look."

"She's fine where she is." I raise an arm at my side, making sure Layla isn't tempted to oblige. "I'm sure you recognize her."

"I do." He nods into the mask, dragging in breaths. "And I appreciate you bringing me such a gift."

I straighten to my full height, fuming at the taunt.

Bishop clears his throat, hard, as if warning me to keep my rage under control.

I struggle to comply. I fucking battle not to reach for his mask and wrap the rubber cord around his neck until the smug superiority vanishes from his face.

"She's no gift," I snarl. "I suggest you treat her with respect if you don't plan on giving more strength to your enemies."

"You'll never be an enemy, son." He waves me away, lowering the mask. "But I know you've been sleeping with her. That you lied about your name and withheld your legacy to win her over. The news actually brought a proud tear to my eye."

Layla mutters a curse.

"And how do you know?" I turn my attention to Salvo, the asshole who promised Remy hadn't spilled.

"I didn't say a damn thing." He glances to his father. "We were going to tell you once Remy returned."

"Of course you were, son. But I have faster ways to gain information."

Faster?

Emmanuel could only have learned the news from Remy. Bishop wouldn't betray me. And Layla hasn't left my sight.

Unless… "You have someone listening in on their calls." I grin at Salvatore. "I bet that's comforting."

The muscles in his jaw tic.

"I watch my children more than most." Emmanuel drags in a deep breath and lowers the mask. "You're never too old to need guidance."

"I bet. But the guidance you offered two years ago has placed your ass in a hospital bed with the Grim Reaper stalking your shadow. So maybe your leadership skills need a tweak or two. Don't you think?"

"I'm not scared of Cole Torian. Enemies are the price you pay for power and money. And he's merely a pup. Nowhere near the type of cutthroat businessman his father was."

"My father was a sex trafficker," Layla snaps. "Cole would never aspire to be anything like him."

"And that's why he's weak. Are you as pathetic, my sweet?"

"I'll show you how pathetic I can be." She storms closer, but I block her path.

"Don't let him provoke you," I growl under my breath. "You're smarter than that."

"How smart can she be?" Emmanuel wheezes another chuckle. "She didn't even know your real identity until this morning."

I grab her wrist as she takes another thunderous step, willing her to ignore him with my strong grip.

"I can promise you, your daughter showed far more tenacity in the face of adversity than you are," he continues.

"*Dad*," Abri warns.

"She was a real little spitfire when we first got hold of her. We had a great time, though. In fact, I'd really love to see her again. I should—"

Layla screams, yanking her arm from my grip to barge past me like wildfire. She charges for Emmanuel, her face turning red, her hand shoving into her jeans pocket in search of something.

Shit. The fucking cyanide.

I lunge for her, grabbing her upper arms from behind as guns are drawn by the guards, Salvo, and Remy. My men follow suit in opposition.

"I'll kill you, you fucking prick." Layla thrashes and bucks against my hold. "I'll kill every single one of you."

"I'd like to see you try." Remy levels his barrel on her.

"Come on now." Bishop holds up a hand in placation, his weapon pointed at Emmanuel. "Nobody wants to lose blood over this."

She continues to thrash and scramble, rampant and manic. "Let me go, you bastard."

"Stop it." I smother her against my chest. "Calm down."

I stalk her from the room, Bishop hot on my trail as he walks backward to cover his ass. My anger is barely bottled as I guide her into the far wall, pressing her chest into the plaster before closing in behind her.

"What the fuck were you thinking?" I clamp both her wrists in one hand and use the other to delve into her pocket, retrieving the vial of fucking cyanide. "What was the plan?" I growl in her ear. "You'd sprinkle some magic fairy dust and try to kill us all?"

"Yes." She bucks. "At least then this would have been over."

"You would've been dead before you unscrewed the lid." I release my hold, allowing her to swing around to face me, her eyes stark, her cheeks flushed.

"You said it yourself—if they kill me, you kill them, and so on and so forth. At the very least, some of them would die."

I lean closer, glaring as our noses almost brush. "And you would've been the first."

"So be it." Moisture wells in her eyes, the liquid born of rage. "He needs to pay for what he's done."

"What about Stella? Do you think she deserves to lose another parent?"

She recoils, her gaze shooting daggers, each blink sending a scathing wave of hatred my way. "Did you hear him? He's going to go after her. I know he is."

I remain in her face, her mouth a breath away. "I'll fucking kill him before I let anything happen to either of you. Do you understand? Love me or hate me, Layla, I'll still keep you safe."

She bares her teeth, vicious and pained as footsteps approach from Emmanuel's room.

"Dante?" Abri murmurs.

I flinch at the name and glare over my shoulder to see her blocked from the hall by Bishop's large frame.

"It might be best for her to wait in the room across the hall." She glowers at the man guarding me as she pushes past. "You can keep the doors open. You'll be able to see her at any time."

"No." Layla rasps. "I want to hear every word that motherfucker has to say."

"And I want to get us all out of here alive," I murmur under my breath, leaning into her, taking liberties with her personal space. "Get yourself under control, *amore mio*. Or I'll do it for you."

She squares her shoulders, her rage smoldering.

"That's right. Keep that anger directed at me. Not him." I press my hips into hers, our cheeks brushing as I guide my mouth to her ear. "Hate *me*. Loathe *me*. Curse my fucking name for playing you the way I did, because I will never hurt you, Layla. But he will."

I'm so fucking tempted to kiss her. To steal a gasp and make her moan, just in case this is the last chance I get.

"Now move your ass into the other room." I force myself to pull back, my restraint threadbare, my gaze brooking no argument as our eyes meet. "And make sure you stay there."

She continues to glower, the only sign of fragility coming from her heavy swallow.

"I'd die for you, *amore mio*." I retreat and turn for Emmanuel's room. "But for the love of God, I'd prefer not to do it today."

35

———

LAYLA

I remain propped against the wall, humiliated at being barred from a conversation I deserve to be in.

"Stay with her," Matthew instructs Bishop, then returns to Emmanuel's room, leaving me to fight against crumpling to the floor.

I should've tried harder.

Should've stolen a gun and pulled the trigger without a second thought.

Maybe I would've died. Who's to say I won't anyway?

Emmanuel has it out for me. I could see it in his eyes.

He'll go after Stella. He'll destroy my family.

"Come on." Abri gives me a sad smile and opens the door to the adjacent room, allowing more light to spill into the hall. "Let them talk. It's clear you're a weakness where my brother is concerned, and that's the last thing he needs when facing off with our father."

I don't understand her sympathy.

I don't appreciate it either.

She saunters inside, walking out of view.

"That was a dick move." Bishop closes in, intimidating me into following her with his evil glare. "Now he doesn't have me in there to watch his back."

I reject the twinge of guilt sparking in my chest.

"Get moving." The aggression in his voice is next level. "I swear to God, if he does something he'll regret, I'll hold you responsible."

I clench my teeth, refusing to let Bishop daunt me and walk into the unfamiliar room to stop a few feet inside. I keep my lips fused as I take in the cherry-stained wooden bed in the middle of the expansive area, a matching dresser along the closest wall, and sheer curtains covering French doors leading to what I assume is the balcony.

I remain still as I search for weapon potential—the lamp on the nightstand, the ceramic female figurine on the dresser, the chair in the corner—while Abri watches my inspection from the open doorway of the adjoining private bathroom.

"Are you okay?" She frowns at me as Bishop comes to lean against the closest bedpost, the conversation reigniting across the hall, the words skirting the edges of my consciousness. "You don't seem to be here by choice."

"I've never had a choice when it comes to your family. I didn't when you stole my daughter. And I had just as much when you killed my husband."

Her eyes soften. "I'm sorry for your loss. I didn't—"

"Save it." I continue toward the French doors and inch the curtain aside, wishing I was anywhere but here.

Time passes with the rise and fall of voices. Matthew makes threats. Emmanuel chuckles. His bitch of a mother chastises every now and again.

"Can I speak to her for a moment?" Abri asks Bishop. "In private. There's a few things I have—"

"No way in hell, darlin'. I'm not letting her out of my sight."

"Beside the fact I'm not interested," I add, "I've got nothing to say to you."

"Please." Her brows pull tight. "It's important."

The vulnerability is an act. The politeness, too.

But I'm curious to know why.

She's not armed. Not with a gun at least. Her clothes are too tight to conceal a firearm. There's potential for a knife, though.

"We can talk on the balcony." She starts toward me. "We'll remain in sight at all times."

Bishop frowns, his gaze trekking her with agitation.

"*Please*. It will only take a minute." Her arm brushes mine as she opens the French doors, her long blonde hair dancing in the breeze. "I wouldn't beg if it wasn't important."

"I never knew Costas could beg," Bishop mutters.

She glares at him, then gives a brittle smile when her attention returns to mine. "He's right. We don't usually stoop this low. But like I said, it's important."

I have no idea what she's up to.

Is she going to haul me over the railing? Does a weapon lie in wait outside the door?

"You'll be fine." Bishop pushes from the bed to stand tall. "I'll be watching."

I nod and follow her past the threshold, stopping two feet outside as she stands out of view of the room.

"*Listen to me,*" she mouths. "*I can help you.*"

I frown and glance back at Bishop in confusion.

"Don't look at him," she whispers. "Do you want to get out of here or not?"

I balk. "Excuse me?"

"Do you want to leave?" Her voice is barely heard over the breeze, her pretty face pinched in apprehension.

My heart kicks up a gear, my pulse increasing. "What are you trying to do?"

She inches closer, her voice dropping further. "Despite the estrangement, I love

Dante. But I don't think you want to be here..." She pauses, waiting for me to fill the silence.

"So you'd help me escape?"

"Normally, no." There's no apology in her tone. "But I owe your brother, and I want the debt off my shoulders."

"Why would you owe him?"

"You don't need specifics."

"If there's any way I'm going to trust your help, I'm going to need them."

She sucks in a tired breath. "He showed me kindness the night your husband died. He could've hurt me, but he didn't."

"You're lying." Cole wouldn't have shown anything other than hostility toward the people who stole my daughter.

"Believe what you want. I'm not here to convince you. The question is whether or not you want to get away from Dante."

I disregard the name she uses while my stomach sinks.

Do I want to get away from him? Do I want to distance myself from heartbreak and betrayal at the cost of vulnerability?

"How?" I whisper.

"There's a window in the bathroom. The screen can be removed. If you climb through, there's an old trellis that will get you to the ground."

She's serious.

Holy shit.

"To what end?" I frown, keeping my voice low. "How am I meant to outrun nine grown men when stuck behind towering walls that are miles from civilization?"

"Once you reach the lawn, move around the back of the house to the garage. The roller doors should already be open. My car is the Bentley. The keys are in the center console along with the remote for the gate."

I stare at her, trying to find a hint of deception. "Why are you doing this?"

"I already told you. I owe Cole. This is me repaying the debt." She reaches for my arm, her fingers cautiously touching my wrist. "I'm not your enemy, Layla. I never have been. What happened with your husband was a horrible tragedy. And your daughter..." She winces. "Me and my brothers had no idea what was going on until we were in the middle of a war. It never should've—"

"Are you two finished out there?" Bishop growls, his footsteps approaching.

Abri retreats to stand at her full height, her face transforming into a mask of innocence.

Are we finished?

It seems like she's merely scratched the surface of withheld information. And none of it makes sense.

Cole showed her kindness? My husband's death was a tragedy?

"What's going on?" Bishop comes to stand at the threshold.

"Nothing." I clear my throat and swallow to alleviate the dryness. "I was just about to come inside."

I maneuver past him, hiding my face from his scrutiny as I reenter the room.

Indecision claws its way into my skull, awakening a thousand questions, stirring up more trouble. It's too much to think through. I can't concentrate to make a plan.

My instincts boil down to Matthew and whether I should trust his offer of safety or flee to find my own. The thought of escaping his manipulative protection fills me with dread. And my damn heart still clings to the hope of him making amends.

But he can't. How could he?

He lied. Had me mugged. Made me fall for him under false pretenses.

He duped me better than my father ever did, the resulting emotional scars capable of outweighing those already in existence.

I'd loved him.

Wholeheartedly.

With optimism and passion.

He made me believe in a future without darkness. A life without recrimination. He had me planning a fresh start, one that I never deserved.

My gaze treks to his across the hall, our eyes briefly locking for a pained moment while he addresses someone in the other room.

There's possession in his stare. Hunger even in the depth of this darkness.

The sight of it breaks me. Cuts me down at the knees in humiliation. In sorrow.

I'd wanted an entwined future. I'd never craved anything more.

Now our time together boils down to one question—do I stay or do I go?

I hold onto the sight of him as Abri closes the French doors. I take in the parts of him that inflicted betrayal—the hands that brought me pleasure, the lips that lied to me, and eyes that deceived.

I breathe it all in, dragging the pain deep into my lungs, and release the last lingering threads of hope with the exhale. Then I turn to Bishop, hating him for the role he played as I announce, "I need to use the bathroom."

36

———————

MATTHEW

"YOU'RE CAUGHT IN A TEMPERAMENTAL POSITION, SON." EMMANUEL HOLDS MY GAZE, HIS eyes gleaming with superiority. "Yet again you've fallen for someone who weakens you. Someone who has you begging."

I glance across the hall, watching Layla walk out of sight, a door closing shortly after.

Where the fuck is she going?

"Bathroom," Bishop mouths, reading my mind as he gestures to his dick.

Good. At least she can't cause trouble in there.

"You've got me wrong, old man." I turn back to Emmanuel and prowl closer to his bed. "I'm not begging. I'm telling you to leave her out of this. Her *and* her daughter. Otherwise I'll make good on all the things I've wanted to do to you in the last fifteen years."

He smiles. "All the things you wanted to do but were too loyal to instigate…"

"I'm loyal, yes. But not to you. Lorenzo is the only reason you still have air in your lungs."

"Dante," Adena snaps. "Don't say such things."

"It's okay, my sweet." Emmanuel doesn't break our stare. "What our son doesn't realize is that his threats are a blessing. Every decision I made in his childhood was to shape the brilliant man standing before me. My actions placed fire in his belly and strength in his soul."

Venom in my veins.

Hate in my heart.

"You're exactly what I aspired to create." He grins. "I couldn't be more proud."

My nostrils flare.

"We need to endure to evolve, my son. You never could understand that. But what I did in your teenage years was a favor. A gift."

Grace's murder was a gift?

220

Slicing her open was a fucking favor?

I laugh, otherwise I'd roar.

I picture ripping out his throat. Watching him suffer. Hearing his cries for mercy.

"That girl from your senior year was beneath you, anyway." He continues digging his grave. "Can you believe she offered to spread her legs if I promised to get her out of town?"

My body detonates. Rage and hatred collide.

I lunge for him. Two steps is all it takes to have my hand around his throat, my eyes venomous as they will death upon him. "Your actions didn't make me strong." I seethe, spittle coating my lips. "They turned me into a monster"

My mother screams. He doesn't look at me in fear. Only in satisfaction. "I'm honored," he wheezes.

Motherfucker.

I gave him what he wanted. I turned into the man he'd wished for. Someone callous and cruel. Vicious and brutal.

Goddamnit.

Cold metal presses into my temple, the barrel of a gun hard and unyielding against my skin as Emmanuel rasps for breath.

"Let him go," Salvatore demands. "Get your hands off him."

I can't.

I want to end this. To squeeze the breath from the asshole's lungs. To watch the life drain from his eyes.

I've pictured it a million times. Felt the euphoria. Tasted the victory.

"*Langston,*" Bishop shouts across the hall. "We're not here for this."

But I want to be.

I need it.

The brutality calls to me. Fucking sings.

Every wheeze invigorates me. Each stuttered breath appeases.

"He dies, we all die," De Marco mutters behind me. "Come on, man. This isn't the plan."

Fuck.

I can justify my own death, but not those who followed me here. Not my siblings, either. Not yet, anyway.

And not Layla.

Never Layla.

"Fuck you." I shove Emmanuel into the bed before releasing him. "You *will* stay away from her. You *will* leave her the fuck alone." I backtrack from the gun and glare at Salvatore, then Remy. "Fuck over whoever else you like. Ruin lives. Start wars. But she stays out of it."

"I applaud the vicious show," Remy drawls, "however, I'm deducting points for the fear in your eyes. I can see right through you."

"I don't fear you." I march to him, not stopping until we're toe-to-toe. "And I don't fear death. I fucking welcome it, because staying alive means I'll spend every waking moment wasting my time thinking of ways to torture you if you dare to touch her."

"*Stop.*" Adena rushes to Emmanuel's side, helping to place the oxygen mask to his face as he barks and chokes. "Please just stop. Don't you see how much we love you? We always have. We just want you home."

"He never left," Emmanuel rasps. "He's always remained close, still wanting to be a part of what he left behind."

"I haven't been anywhere near this house since I left years ago. This is—"

"You come back to Denver," he corrects, his voice weak beneath the mask but the intent strong. "You come back and watch us share our family meal almost every month. You listen to our conversations from afar. Soak in the nostalgia."

He's known.

All this time.

"Spying, big brother?" Salvatore lowers the gun to his side. "That's a little pitiful, don't you think?"

"It's fucking pathetic," Remy seethes. "Why weren't we told?"

"Because he's a piece of shit." I throw my arms wide with a maniacal laugh. "If he's known, that means he's let me sabotage your warehouse shipments and rat out your distributions channels. Every problem you've had in the last ten years has been my doing, and he knew the whole time."

"It's the price I paid to keep you close."

No. He did it because he's insane.

Fucking psychotic.

"Enough of this back-and-forth bullshit." I run a rough hand over my mouth, pulling myself in check. "I want your word you'll leave her alone."

"Agree to return home and I'll give you whatever you want," he counters.

I smile, all teeth, no charm. "How about this?" I step closer and Salvatore follows, his gun raising again. "I promise the next time I come back, I'll burn this place to the ground. With or without you in it."

"Dante," my mother sobs. "*Please.*"

I don't drag my attention from Emmanuel. Don't blink. Don't breathe.

I stare into those godforsaken eyes and let him know I'm not bluffing. I make it clear I'd love to watch him burn. And that damn twinkle in his eye tells me he's only growing more proud.

Jesus. Fuck.

"It's time to go," I address my team, still staring at my maker, waiting for him to say something I can't ignore.

A knock from the adjacent room breeches my ears, the subtle sound rising above the hiss of oxygen and whir of strangled breath.

"Layla." Bishop's voice travels from across the hall. "Hurry up."

I tense at her name. At the vision it provides. At the fucking yearning. But I don't move. Don't quit staring even though everything in my soul wants to focus on what's happening across the hall.

"Just like Grace, she distracts you." Emmanuel removes the oxygen mask. "How can you not see that?"

"Because a distraction from what you created is exactly what I need." I backtrack toward the door, passing Goodin, De Marco, and Whitby. "I'll do anything to protect her. Remember that if you're stupid enough to test me."

"I'm definitely going to test you, son. It's what makes you stronger."

I smirk, pretending I'm calling his bluff when I know he speaks the truth. I'm going to have to find a way to kill him without getting pinned for the blame.

I'll pay someone. Bribe. Threaten.

I'll do whatever it takes.

"Those are adamant fighting words coming from someone in a hospital bed." I turn on my heel and stride for the threshold, telling De Marco to, "Block the door," as I pass and continue into the adjoining bedroom where Bishop faces off with Abri who stands before a closed door.

"We're getting out of here." I stalk toward them. "Where's Layla?"

"Still in the bathroom." Bishop flings a hand in Abri's direction. "She's been in there for over ten minutes with no flushed toilet or running faucet. And no goddamn response when I call her fucking name."

I shoulder my sister out of the way and slam my fist against the door. "Layla. Open up. We're leaving."

There's no reply.

No sound. No shift of movement from inside.

I glare at my sister. "What have you done?"

She raises her chin, defiant.

Fuck. What the hell has she done?

I step back, panic consuming me, rage inspiring me. "Layla, move away from the door." I plant my heel next to the handle, sending the door flying and wood splintering from around the jamb.

I don't have to step inside to know she's not there.

The window is open, the white lace curtain dancing in the breeze.

I race forward, my hands sweating as I grip the ledge and shove my head outside.

A screen frame lays dormant on the grass below in an otherwise still garden.

There's no sign of her.

"Where is she?" I swing around and charge for Abri. Her eyes widen. "What the fuck did you do?'

She braces her feet apart and squares her shoulders. "Nothing."

The crunch of pebbles carries from outside. Loud and urgent. Bishop shoots me a glance, then makes for the French doors.

I'm right behind him.

"What's going on?" Salvatore yells from the other room.

Bishop and I step onto the balcony to see a Bentley fishtail around the drive, the brake lights glaring as the gates begin to open.

"It's her." Bishop shoves his hands through his hair. "*Jesus goddamn Christ.*"

I fight the compulsion to jump the balcony and chase after her the fastest way possible, knowing I'll break my fucking legs in the process.

"What are we doing, Langston?" Bishop turns to me. "What the fuck do we do?"

How could she leave?

Does she hate me that much? Enough to risk running without protection?

"Wake the fuck up, bitch." Bishop thumps my chest, the blow hard enough to jar bone. "What's the plan?"

"Is something wrong?" Emmanuel calls from the adjacent room, his derision sparking insanity.

He'll give an order for her to be chased.

He'll command my brothers. Their guards.

I've got no chance of finding her first.

"Hey." Bishop grabs my shoulders. "I know that look in your eye, asshole." He gets in my face, friend to friend, monster to monster. "We didn't come here for this. No bloodshed, remember? Just a fucking conversation."

"I can't do it." I shake my head. "I can't let him go after her."

"He's bedridden, for fuck's sake. He's not going anywhere."

"And what about Salvo and Remy? One order from him and they're out the door."

He leans closer, grabbing me behind the back of the neck. "They're pussies. They—"

"They won't hurt her," Abri whispers from the balcony threshold. "I promise, Dante. They'd never do that."

"See?" Bishop digs his fingers into my neck. "Pussies. Emmanuel's the only one heartless enough to kill in cold blood and he's too decrepit to do it."

"No." I shove him away. "They'll find her and bring her back here."

"If that happens, we'll have De Marco and the guys waiting."

"Abri, what's going on in there?" Salvo snarls with impatience. "If this guard dog doesn't move, he's not going to appreciate my lack of warning shot."

I claw my fingers into my palm, unsure which path to take as De Marco mutters something in reply.

"We'll be there in a minute." Abri cuddles her waist, the picture of sophistication and class now marred by eyes filled with regret. "I'm sorry," she whispers.

"For what? Betraying me or putting her in more danger?"

She cringes and casts a cautious glance toward the hall. "I was *helping* her."

"Why?" Bishop grates.

"She didn't want to be here. You were forcing her—"

I step up to my sister. "I was *protecting* her."

"I know what forced proximity with a man looks like." Her response is barely heard. "I know what it feels like, too."

"We don't have time for this," Bishop warns.

I fucking know we don't. But Abri's unchecked show of emotion raises my hackles. "What does that mean? Are you looking to get out of here?"

She straightens, her lips parting a crack, her eyes widening. She surprises me by not shooting down the offer. By hesitating for long seconds.

"Abri?" Emmanuel yells. "What's going on? Where's Torian's sister?"

"We don't have seconds to spare." Bishop glares at me.

"Abri?" I warn. "What's—"

"Go." She steps back from the threshold. "We'll talk later."

I keep looking at her, keep trying to read what she's withholding while my pulse beats for Layla's safety. "Let's get out of here."

"About fucking time." Bishop storms for the hall.

I follow, De Marco stepping aside as I continue into Emmanuel's room, fists clenched, pulse rocketing.

"Problems, son?" Emmanuel wheezes, clasping his oxygen mask as he smirks. "Did your pretty little thing run?"

I can't bite.

I won't.

A future with Layla can't exist if I return to the Cappellettis. I won't drag her into that. I need to find her before Emmanuel does.

I focus on Adena, glaring my hatred. "You betrayed me when I was a boy. You let him run loose, destroying the only happiness I had. You won't go unpunished if you allow it to happen again."

She stands taller, frowning.

"He's your husband to control," I sneer. "Your problem to solve. From now on, any action he takes will also be yours to absolve, and I don't punish in halves."

Emmanuel chuckles, the humming, wheezing noise growing.

I turn to my brothers, the muscles in my jaw aching from tension, my head pounding as I fight to ignore their father. "My hatred has always been for him. *Never* either of you. But so help me God, if you do anything to put her in harm's way I'll start a war you won't survive."

They don't react.

Neither in spite or understanding.

Their faces remain emotionless. Impassive and detached.

"Let the race begin." Emmanuel chokes as he laughs. "I'm sure we'll see each other again as soon as we catch her."

37

―――

LAYLA

I force myself not to think of how Matthew will retaliate as I monkey climb down the trellis, my feet getting stuck in the thick vine weaving its way through the wooden slats.

I pretend he doesn't exist as I run around the house to find the garage. And I focus on how the inside information on the Costas' home will help my family as I scramble into the Bentley and drive my ass out of there.

I don't think about how I'll get home.

How I'll survive.

I don't contemplate anything more than the broad strokes of my escape plan until now when the desolate road is stretched before me, and I have nowhere to go.

I should've thought about how the hell I was going to get to Portland without a cell, money, and identification.

I should've focused on the issues that would arise if I attempted to escape in a car that had less than half a tank of gas.

"*Shit.*" I press my foot harder against the accelerator, eyeballing the rearview mirror, waiting for the first sign that someone is giving chase.

I need to find a phone. More importantly, I need to figure out how I'm going to tell Cole what I've done.

He'll disown me. They all will.

I take deserted back road after deserted back road, using the car's GPS to navigate an indirect route around the city.

I circle the outskirts of Denver, not knowing exactly where I am once farm road turns into suburban streets. All I can see are dilapidated homes with junk in the yard and old vehicles that make my current ride look like a carjacker's dream come true.

I keep off the main thoroughfares, searching for a sign of life, finally slowing when I see three teenage girls walking along the street footpath, one of them scrolling on her cell.

I pull to the curb, slowing as I come up beside them, and lower the passenger window.

"Excuse me." I raise my voice. "I need your help."

The girls glance at me in unison, each of the teenagers sporting raised brows and expressions of disdain toward the Bentley.

"How could we possibly help you?" the closest asks, glancing from my face to the car and back again.

"There are men chasing me, and I have no phone or money. Can I borrow your cell to make a call?"

The one on the far end snorts, flicking her bleached hair behind her shoulder while she continues to walk ahead.

"*Please.*" I crawl the vehicle along beside them. "It's only one phone call."

"Get fucked, bitch." The closest curls her lip, then turns to her friends, all of them breaking into laughter.

Goddamn teenagers.

I pull away from the curb and plant my foot, speeding farther along the street. I need to ditch the car, and fast, but I need security first.

I zigzag my way through the suburb, eventually coming to a four-lane street with heavy traffic, fast-food outlets on either side, and a hotel sign looming ahead that sparks hope.

I keep one eye on the road, the other getting a brief glimpse of the dark tan four-level building as I drive past, then take the next turn in the opposite direction. I continue down another street, then turn and accelerate along another, not pulling to a stop until I'm at least a few blocks from where I want to be. Then I ditch the car and start running.

I take shady back alleys and cut across house yards. I don't stop looking over my shoulder or scrutinizing every car that passes, but none come close to the extravagance I found in the Costa family garage.

I make my way back to the main road, then continue into the hotel parking lot, my stomach bottoming at the full-frontal view.

What my split-second, drive-by glance didn't ascertain is that this place is something out of a horror movie.

Windows are cracked with grey electrical tape holding them together. The cheap blinds inside are broken and disheveled. The balconies to the three upper levels are nothing more than a red metal fire escape, the staircase exposed to the elements and rusted in parts.

But it's the man eagle-eying me from the third-floor railing, his wifebeater dirty and boxers loose that concerns me the most.

I recognize that opportunistic expression, and I have no intention of being a part of it.

I glower, letting him know I'm not in the mood to be fucked with, and keep jogging to reception, my skin prickling the closer I get to the chipped paint of the front door.

Inside is worse.

The scent of stale beer and urine hits my nose as I walk into the small room to find a middle-aged man sitting behind a counter, the sound of porn coming from his computer, his scuffed buttoned shirt crinkled, his hair thinning and skin pale.

He looks up at me, his blue eyes narrowing. "Lost?"

I contemplate retreat, but I have nowhere else to go.

"Can I use your phone?" I keep my voice strong. "It's an emergency."

He sighs and turns his attention back to the computer. "Five bucks."

"I don't have any money." I raise my empty hands. "Not on me, anyway. But if you let me make a call I promise I'll be able to repay you with more than spare change."

"Promises come easily around here, Gucci belt." He relaxes back into his chair, his gaze remaining on the screen. "Find someone else to buy your bullshit."

"*Please.*" I cringe through the plea. "It's one phone call. It won't take long."

"It's always just one phone call. One extra pillow. One more towel." He shoots me a two-second glare. "So unless you've got money, I'm busy."

I bite the inside of my cheek, holding in aggression.

"Well? Get goin'." He jerks his chin to the door. "If you hang around I'm going to assume you want to participate in the finale." His eyes meet mine as his mouth curves. "That'll get you a free phone call."

Fuck him. And every other motherfucker in this godforsaken city.

I start for the door, majorly pissed and equally helpless, until my palms press against the wood. "What about a Bentley?" I glance at him over my shoulder. "There's one parked a few blocks from here."

"And?"

"And you can have it."

"A Bentley?" He looks at me as if I'm deranged. "You're offering a car for a phone call?"

"I'm offering someone else's car for a phone call."

He raises a brow. "Stolen?"

"Borrowed."

He crosses his arms over his chest, scrutinizing me. "And the person you borrowed it from?"

"Can afford to replace it without batting an eye." I pull the car fob from my pocket and lob it toward him. "Just don't get caught."

He seizes the projectile with a grin and reaches beneath the counter to place a cell on the scuffed laminate. "I guess we have a deal."

I wish I could slump with relief, but as necessary as a phone is, the resulting call with Cole isn't something I'm looking forward to. If only I had the luxury to put it off.

I walk for the counter, about to reach for the cell when the man stands and recaptures the device.

"Hold up, Gucci belt. Where is this borrowed Bentley of yours?"

"A few blocks from here. Maybe a ten-minute walk. I can draw you a map."

He flashes a mouth full of yellow teeth. "You can walk along with me."

"That's not going to happen. Just give me the goddamn phone."

"Why would I? I already have the car key."

"You also have a death wish if you plan to fuck me over. Up until this point I've been more than civil. I promise that won't continue if you don't hand over the cell."

"They're big words from a teeny, tiny woman."

"A teeny, tiny woman who has family in some pretty dark places." I smile, hoping the curve of my lips exudes equal threat and confidence. "Have you ever pissed off the underworld before, little man?"

His eyes narrow, the squint deepening before he finally pushes to his feet. "Fine. A Bentley for a phone call."

"A Bentley for a phone call *and* a room to stay in for a few hours."

He scoffs. "She comes in here a panting, skittish mouse, and now thinks she's a ball-busting hustler."

"Deal or no deal?"

He reaches beneath the counter, the clink of metal sounding before he slaps a key with a large wooden keychain on the laminate. "Take room 102. Ground floor. Two doors down. But if I walk away from here and there's no Bentley—"

"There's a Bentley. Now give me a pen and paper so I can draw the damn map."

He complies, hovering close as I sketch the streets from memory. Once I'm done he snatches the scribbled paper and skirts the counter to stride across the small reception.

"One phone call," he warns, pulling the front door open. "And there better not be no international charges on my account when I get back."

I don't wait for the door to close behind him. I grab the device and dial Cole's most recent burner number, hoping I've remembered the digits correctly. My heart beats a rampant staccato as the chirping rings in my ear. Once. Twice. Three times. Then the message service kicks in.

Shit.

"It's me," I start as soon as the beep sounds. "I'm in trouble… I need you to call me back."

Fuck. What if this cell number isn't visible?

"Hold on a sec." I scramble for a brochure. A business card. Anything that might have the contact number of this hellhole.

Goddamnit. What's the name of this place?

"I'll have to call you back in a minute. *Please* answer when I do." I keep clinging to the cell, keep wishing for some spark of brilliance to blindside me until I concede defeat. "Please, Cole. I need you."

I disconnect the call and pace through the panic, my Chucks trekking over threadbare carpet.

I don't know if I've waited five minutes or mere seconds when I redial, but the line connects straight away. "Cole?"

"Yes," his response is gruff.

I close my eyes, the regret and gratitude hitting instantly. "I'm sorry."

"What have you done?"

I want to laugh. To scoff. To arrogantly inform him of his misconception that I'm responsible for anything. Only I can't.

"The guy I met… he wasn't who he said he was." I wait for a reply that doesn't come. "I need help getting home, and I need it in a hurry. I've got no money. No cell. No ID. I'm stuck here."

"Where?" he growls.

I drag in a long breath and square my shoulders. "Denver."

"Give me two seconds."

There's a rustle over the line, then muffled words. I hear biting anger. Snapped responses. Then the rustling clears.

"The jet is being arranged. Tell me your exact location."

"A hotel. Some seedy, rundown place on the outskirts of the city. I don't think I'm far from the airport." I maneuver around the reception desk and crouch to look beneath the counter. There are crumpled magazines, discarded rubbish, and a filthy bong.

"I need a name, Layla."

"I'm trying. Hold on." I open a drawer finding tissues, a half-used bottle of lube, and condoms. "Jesus Christ. I'm going to have to take a look outside."

"Is that a problem? Tell me what's going on." The annoyed edge remains in his voice, but this time concern lingers. "You said you're in trouble. Are you in danger?"

I wince, my stomach twisting in knots. "Yes." I move out from behind the desk and stride for the door.

"Explain. *Everything.*"

"I don't know how much time I have." I pull the handle and poke my head outside, making sure there are no fancy cars or men in suits nearby. "This isn't my phone."

"Fucking tell me. I need to know who to bring with me."

My stomach bottoms.

Normally he travels with his wife, Anissa. Unless there's a threat. Then there's Decker or Luca who can provide a show of muscle when necessary.

But there's one man who accompanies him when blood needs to be spilled.

"Bring Hunter." The request burns my throat.

"If I'm dragging him out of state and away from Sarah you better tell me why."

I jog a few steps into the parking lot to stare across the street at the motel sign. "I'm at the Flamingo Inn."

There's a pause of silence. A beat that I'm sure is filled with animosity, not frantic notation.

"*Tell. Me,*" he growls.

"*Okay.*" I run back to the security of the reception area, closing the door behind me. "I met a guy here months ago. We hit it off, and I've been staying with him in his D.C. penthouse for the last few weeks—"

"I don't give a shit about how you met, Layla. Tell me what I need to know."

My palms sweat. My stomach twists. "He told me his name was Matthew Langston. He owns nightclubs. Popular ones. I checked them out and they're legit. Successful. By the book—"

"*Layla,*" he warns. "I'm not going to ask again."

This is it. This is where he vows to disown me.

"He said his name was Matthew," I repeat, needing tc ease my way into the admission. "But that's not his real name." I swallow, not allowing the emotion to take hold. "Cole, I'm so sorry, but the man I've been with is Dante Costa, and him and his family are currently searching Denver to find me."

38

———————

MATTHEW

I RUN FROM THE HOUSE, NOT STOPPING UNTIL I'M AT THE DRIVER'S DOOR OF THE LINCOLN, unwilling to give Bishop control of setting the pace on our search.

He climbs into shotgun. I slide behind the wheel while De Marco, Goodin, and Whitby sprint for the gates, already instructed to hide at the front of the property and use any force necessary if someone arrives with Layla.

"I was certain you were going to kill him." Bishop snatches for his belt as I start the engine and hammer the car into drive.

"I should've." I accelerate hard, kicking up pebbles and dirt to escape through the gates Layla left open.

I jet down the road, the farmhouses and tall trees passing in a blur, any chance of levelheaded thought left behind.

"Where are we going?" Bishop grasps the hand rail above his head.

"I don't know."

"But you know we have to get there like a bat out of hell?"

I clench the steering wheel tighter. "This isn't the time to goad me, motherfucker." I ease my foot off the pedal. Breathe. Try to think. "You realize they'd be able to track the Bentley, right?"

"Yeah. But she's smart. She wouldn't stick with a stolen car for long. I'm sure she's already ditched it by now."

"But they'll still know her last location and we won't. How far can she get without money or a fucking cell?"

"She doesn't need to get far. She just has to hide. And she's good at that, seeing as though she hid the shit with Emmanuel for so fucking long."

I rerun his argument, focusing on the logic. The reliability. "She'd hide and wait for someone to get her." I shoot him a glance. "We need to get in contact with her brother."

He judges me harshly with a raised brow. "You're going to call Cole Torian?"

232

"Just find the fucking number. Reach out to one of his restaurants."

I press my foot back down on the accelerator and head toward the highway, creating a mental list of all the places Layla might turn to—airports, hotels—while Bishop raises his cell to his ear, the subdued ringtone trilling before a woman answers.

"Hey Alesha, I'm trying to get a hold of Cole Torian but I've lost his number."

He pauses, the responding chatter mumbling through the line. "Yeah, I understand. But it's urgent. There's been a serious complication with a contact we share. I need to speak to him straight away."

The response is short and sharp.

"It's a business matter," he clarifies. "I can't give specifics. But I will warn you someone will be held accountable if the message arrives late. I'd hate for that to be you."

I take the ramp onto the multi-lane highway, one eye on Bishop, the other on the road.

"Okay. Fine," he mutters. "Pass on the message that the situation in Denver is critical. If he doesn't call Matthew Langston straight away it will be too late."

I scowl, knowing Cole will interpret the information as a threat.

"Thanks, Alesha. I appreciate the help." Bishop disconnects and lowers the phone. "Now we wait."

"We wait?" I contemplate reaching over and slamming his head against the window. "Did you have to be so fucking dramatic? You could've paved the way for a more amiable introduction. This asshole doesn't know me."

"It was a call to action." He shrugs. "I bet he reaches out in minutes."

I bet he does, too.

I bet he dials my number with rage in his veins and death on his mind.

Bishop scans the cars around us. "Where are we headed?"

"Centennial Airport. Her brother won't get a jet near the international tarmac." I coast us down the inside lane, gliding in and out of traffic.

No call comes through though.

Not in five minutes. Or ten.

I take the turn to Centennial with increasing pessimism, haunted by the last picture I saw of Grace and wondering if it's already too late to save Layla when my cell vibrates in my jacket. The incoming call connects to the car's Bluetooth, *Private Number* flashing across the dash display screen.

"Here goes nothin'." Bishop sits taller.

I answer the call. "This is Matthew."

"Is it though?" A superior drawl carries through the speakers. I don't need to confirm it's Cole. "I've heard you go by another name."

"Not anymore I don't. But that's a conversation for a time when your sister's life isn't on the line." I pull over to concentrate, letting the car idle on a random curb while I fight the need to rub at the pressure building beneath my temples. "I need you to help me find Layla."

He scoffs a laugh. "You made the wrong choice, getting involved with her."

"I didn't know who she was when we first met."

"But you stuck around to fuck with her once you did."

I don't answer. I bite my fucking tongue until I taste blood.

"What was the aim, *Matthew Langston*?" he asks with censure. "Did you want to get to me through her? To finish what your father started?"

"He hasn't been my father for a long time, asshole. I want nothing to do with Emmanuel. Or you, for that matter. I don't know what Layla told you, but I only want to protect her."

"And are you usually this incompetent at the things you set out to achieve?"

"I'm incompetent?" I seethe. "I'm not the son of a bitch who shot a motherfucking psychopath after two years radio silence, then didn't tell my goddamn sister about it to ensure her safety. None of this would've fucking happened if—"

The line disconnects, the barely heard hum of the radio kicking back in.

What the *fuck* did I just do? What the absolute fuck?

"Well… that could've gone better," Bishop mutters. "I'm sure he'll call back."

I slam my palm against the steering wheel. Over and over. Harder and harder.

That heartless prick *won't* call back.

I sure as hell wouldn't.

He doesn't know me. Need me. Trust me.

Layla, where the fuck are you?

"Calm your shit, Langston. We'll figure this out." Bishop thumps my chest. "Either we find her and everything is apples. Or your brothers do, then De Marco will retrieve her before she gets to Emmanuel. Or fucking Torian will get his ass here and pick her up."

Maybe.

Or maybe my brothers aren't the men Abri thinks they are.

Maybe they'll kill her on sight. Or hand her off to someone who will do it for them.

"Come on." Bishop taps the dash. "Let's get to the airport and check the parking lot for the Bentley."

"And if it's not there?"

"We hustle and figure out another fucking plan. You can call your snake of a sister and figure out a way to convince her to relay the last known location of her car." He bangs his fist against the dash this time. "We've got options, Langston. But for now you need to fucking move."

"Since when have you cared so much about Layla?" I pull back into traffic, breaking the speed limit with my acceleration.

"I don't. Abri made a fool out of me back there. It's pride I'm fighting for."

Sure it is.

He gives a shit about Layla. At the very least, he gives a shit about *me* giving a shit about her.

"Message our pilot." I focus on the cars ahead. "Make sure we're refueled and able to take flight at a moment's notice."

If Layla's at Centennial, I'll make sure we're in the air within minutes. Willingly or not.

He does as requested, swiping at his device while mine begins to shudder against my chest, the incoming call reconnecting to Bluetooth.

Bishop glances my way. "Want me to talk this time?"

"If you open your mouth, I'll fucking kill you." I answer the call. "It took you long enough to wake up to yourself, Torian."

"I suggest you check the tone and the attitude, you arrogant piece of shit."

Not Torian.

Not a man at all.

The voice is female. Confident. Merciless.

"Forgive my assumption." I frown at Bishop. "Who am I speaking to?"

"Keira. Layla's sister. And I don't have the patience to deal with self-serving motherfuckers right now, so shut up and listen."

I raise a brow, grated by the attitude, yet fucking grateful for the contact.

"My sister told me she loved you," she states simply.

The blindside hits me like a bus, the tension in my ribs exploding.

"She texted me," she continues. "It was a few simple words, but she's never sent me anything like that before. Not in reference to her husband. Not when she was dating in high school. Unless she's talking about her daughter, those words haven't existed in her vocabulary until a few days ago. So why did I just overhear my brother say you were playing her?"

"I didn't play her." My chest takes the onslaught of her accusations, the L-word knocking me down more pegs than I can stand to fall.

"So you didn't hide your identity? You didn't pretend to be someone she could trust instead of someone she would despise?"

The car falls silent, my ears ringing with my mistakes.

"I'm waiting," she snips. "Explain what the hell you were thinking in targeting my sister."

"I wasn't," I admit. "I was spying on Emmanuel the night we met. She was, too. And I wanted to know why. There was no malice or ill intent. I only wanted answers."

"And?"

"And once I got them, I needed more."

The line falls quiet, the silence making me focus on the dash display to see if she's hung up.

"Do you love her?" Her voice softens.

"I've told her as much since the day we met."

It's a cop-out. My endearments have never been spoken in anything but playful banter. But *do I love her*?

I'd kill for her.

Die for her.

Keira sighs. "I don't believe you."

"Then believe this—the last time I saw her she'd stolen my sister's car. One that's sophisticated enough to have GPS tracking. She has no money. No phone. No identification. And your brother doesn't seem to give a shit."

"He gives a shit, you ignorant prick. We all do. Cole walked out of here as soon as he knew the jet was ready. He's already on his way to Denver."

"Has he brought a body bag? Or is he stupid enough to expect her to still be alive in a few hours?"

"Fuck," Bishop mutters under his breath. "Bees and honey, champ. Bees and fucking honey."

I close my eyes. Breathe deep. Force a patient swallow. "Look, I'm beside myself trying to get to her before they do, but I've got no clue where to start looking. Do you know where she is or not?"

The quiet returns.

I'm forced to stalk the display screen again. "Keira?"

"A hotel." She sighs. "I don't know which one or where exactly. Cole told Hunter it's on the outskirts of the city. She was advised to stay there until he arrives."

"Can you get me a name?"

"No. I already stole your number and am blindly trusting that my sister saw something in you that was real... At least, real enough to save her life. You're going to have to do the rest on your own."

"*We'll find the hotel*," Bishop mouths.

"Okay. Fine." I wipe a hand down my face. "I'll figure it out."

"Good," Keira responds. "Because if you don't, I'm sure you know what will happen."

39

LAYLA

I PACE THE CARPET OF THE DIRTY HOTEL ROOM FOR HOURS, ONLY TAKING SHORT intermission breaks to inch the cheap plastic blinds apart to see what's going on outside.

Cars come and go on the busy street, the frantic traffic driving by like a thousand and one potential threats.

I'm hungry.

Tired.

And although it's hard to admit, I'm scared, too.

Fear didn't eat me like this when I was under Emmanuel's roof. I'd felt protected. Stupidly immune because Matthew was by my side.

Now he's not here, and I'm unsure what will happen if the Costas find me.

"Hey. Open up." The reception guy knocks on my door. "I found that car of yours."

I remain quiet, my heart trembling, my feet cautiously creeping me toward the entry.

"I said, I found that stolen car of yours," he says louder. "Are you going to open up or not?"

"Keep your voice down." I double check the security chain and open the door a crack, finding him an inch away, his acrid breath turning my stomach. "What do you want?"

He eyes me from face to feet and back again. "I hope you're not bringing trouble my way."

"I'm not." I try to close the door only to have him lean his hip and shoulder into it.

"Well, you might like to know someone was calling about a woman fitting your description earlier. Said it was important they got in contact with you."

My pulse skips a beat. "Who was it? What did you say?"

"They didn't give a name." He runs his tongue over a rotting front tooth. "And I told 'em nothin', but that payment of yours is only going to go so far if I'm getting caught up in something that's not my business."

"You won't." I pull the door a smidge wider to chance a peek outside, then begin to close it again. "I'll be gone soon."

He thumps the wood with his hip. "How soon?"

"Any goddamn minute. Okay?"

I'm hoping Cole is already in Denver. If not, he has to be close.

"All right, Gucci belt. But just so you know, if I get another phone call, I might be tempted to sing like a little canary." He runs a hand down his chest to his stomach. My gaze isn't tempted to follow the path farther as he jerks his hips. "If you want we can come to an agreement on a cash-free transaction that will ensure my silence. What do you say?"

"Go to hell." I shove the door shut and secure the flimsy handle lock.

I return to pacing, my fluctuating adrenaline having me hyped one minute and heartbeats from being comatose the next. I'm starving, scared, and nauseated. Helpless, hopeless, and horrified at what's to come.

But it's the familiar tone calling out, "Hey" ten minutes later that has every hair on my body standing on end.

I tiptoe to the window to peek through the plastic blinds, finding a black Mercedes pulled into a nearby parking space with Salvatore standing at the open door.

"I said, hey." He focuses to the left of my room. Remy is nowhere in sight.

"What do you want?" the creep from reception calls back. "I'm busy."

Oh, shit.

I slowly glide the blind back into place and sidestep to the door, holding my ear close to the frame.

"Have you seen a girl?" Salvatore asks. "Dark hair. Jeans. Blouse."

"Pretty face?" the creep replies.

I backtrack toward the dilapidated kitchenette, my limbs heavy as I open the top drawer to find two plastic forks and a metal butter knife. There's nothing else. No potential weapon. No cause for hope.

I'm going to have to escape through the bathroom window into the alley. Then what? Run for my life? Hide around the corner until Cole comes face-to-face with a man responsible for his brother-in-law's murder?

They'll kill each other.

"I guess," Salvatore replies. "So, you've seen her?"

"No, but I'd like to." The creep snickers. "If you find her, do you think you can give her my number?"

I don't buy the act. Paranoia has me picturing the sleazy asshole blatantly pointing Salvatore toward my door.

"You sure you haven't seen her?" This time it's Remy's voice, closer than his brother's. "She isn't hiding in one of your rooms, is she?"

A car door slams. A shadow passes my window.

I blindly trek backward toward the bathroom, my limbs growing heavy. I'm about to step into the tiled area when a skitter of sound carries from the alley, the subtle rattle of my bathroom window following.

My throat burns. The pounding beat of my heart threatens to crack my fragile ribs.

Did Salvatore run to the back of the building?

Now there's nowhere to go.

I lunge toward the wall beside the open bathroom door, my back to the plaster covered in fingerprints, the butter knife clutched in my hand.

My head fills with visions of Stella, my eyes burning at the thought of never seeing her again.

I wipe my tingling nose with the back of my hand, measure my breathing, and raise the knife, preparing to strike. I won't go down without a fight. Butter knife or not, I'll cause injury.

Remy's voice continues to carry from the parking lot at the scrape of the window opening. A light footstep against the tiles follows.

Salvatore is inside. He's right there.

The ring of static grows in my ears.

I hold my breath, my raised arm throbbing, my heart frantic.

As soon as the suit-covered frame hits my periphery I lunge only to have the knife blocked, my wrist snatched, and my arm twisted behind my back before a rough hand clamps over my mouth.

"Quiet, *amore mio*." Matthew holds me against his chest. "Save your screams for later."

I hyperventilate, my breaths short and sharp as relief pummels me.

I hate him. But I hate even more that I love that he's here.

"If they find you, you're done," he whispers in my ear. "Do you understand?"

I nod, grateful and angry. Panicked and indebted. Hurting and so goddamn confused.

"Good." His palm falls from my mouth. "We need to get you out of here."

I turn to face him, retreating a step. "Cole's coming to get me."

"He's not here now, though, and my brothers are right outside your door." He grabs my wrist and drags me toward the bathroom. "Come on. The car's in the alley."

I attempt to pull my arm free, but he tightens his hold.

"Don't test me, *amore mio*." The endearment is growled. "My patience is dead."

"Please give me your phone." I implore him, no longer capable of fighting. "Let me call and see where he is."

"In the car."

I pause, barely recognizing him through the aggression. Sweat beads along his brow. His eyes are wild. And that hold of his is restrictive—tight and confounding, like he refuses to release the tether holding us together.

I shake my head, wishing I could depend on him but knowing I can't.

"You'd prefer to take your chances wasting time in here than trust me to save you?" He inches closer, his brows furrowing. "Do you hate me that much?"

My heart says no.

My head disagrees.

"Let me call him. It won't take long."

"I'll throw you over my shoulder, Layla. You know I will. Stop using my mistakes as an excuse to risk your life. You're smarter than that." He releases me, his chin rising at the loss of contact. "I'll make sure you see Cole, okay? I've already spoken to him once today. Your sister, too."

I flinch in confusion. "How? Why?"

"I knew you had no way of getting home."

I swallow, hating how useless and predictable I've become. "He knows what you did," I whisper. "And who you are."

"He told me as much."

"He'll kill you," I add, gaining face the only way I know how.

"Yeah, he made that clear, too."

"Can we get the fuck out of here?" Bishop mutters from the alley. "Save the fore-play for later."

I scowl at the interruption. At the bullshit Bishop always provides.

"Look." Matthew raises his hands in surrender. "I understand your hatred."

"No, you don't." He couldn't comprehend how my father did the exact same thing to me. How I was led to believe I was adored when I wasn't. That I was appreciated when instead I'd only been used.

"If I'd known about your connection with Emmanuel, I never would've—"

"Deceived me for every minute we were together?" I accuse. "You knew I deserved to be told they were your family."

"And you would've run."

"Exactly." I rub my wrist where his hand had just been, soothing the tingling skin. "If I'd been aware, I never would've been with you."

"What about the things I should've been aware of?" He grates through clenched teeth. "You didn't do me the courtesy of telling me I was fucking my way back into the underworld. I had to find out—"

A pounding knock sounds at a nearby room.

I freeze. Matthew straightens.

"Housekeeping," Remy shouts.

"They're going door to door," Bishop snarls. "Yet again, we don't have fucking time for this."

Where the hell is Cole?

He should've been here by now.

"I'll fight to the death to stop them from taking you." Matthew leans closer, his commanding face an inch from mine. "But I'm unarmed and Bishop's outnumbered. Do you despise me enough to risk them taking you back to Emmanuel?"

I wish I knew.

"Come on, *amore mio*." He reaches out. "Be smart about this. Do what's best for Stella."

I hate how he wields my daughter like a weapon even though his argument is valid.

"You'll take me to Cole?" I ask.

"You'll see him as soon as he arrives. I promise."

He holds out a hand as another booming knock sounds, this time closer.

I'm running out of time. Out of options, too.

"Okay." I ignore his offering and nod. "I'll go with you, but once I find Cole, I never want to see you again."

40

MATTHEW

I help Layla into the back of the Lincoln then climb into shotgun while Bishop takes the wheel.

She's safe for now. At least from herself. She can't escape again with the child lock on both doors. But my threat toward her is a different matter.

I want to throttle her. To shake and scold until she understands exactly how stupid it was to run from me.

"Ready?" Bishop shifts into drive. "I don't think we're going to leave the alley without being seen."

I know, and I have no clue what Salvo will do about it. Give chase? Give up? Who fucking knows with that asshole.

"Slam your foot down and don't stop until you lose him." I glance to Layla in the back seat. "Put your seatbelt on."

She does as instructed, her frantic eyes meeting mine. "What about the phone call?"

"Later."

"Later? That wasn't the deal."

"We're kinda busy here, *amore mio*." I turn my attention to the side mirror as Bishop inches forward, my focus on the closed window we climbed out of more than a few yards back. "If we're lucky, Salvatore and Remy will be searching one of the hotel rooms when we pass."

They know she's around here somewhere. In this suburb. Abri told me as much after the city search failed and I was forced to bribe my own damn sister.

"Evidently, we're shit out of luck." Bishop rolls the Lincoln to a stop.

"Why?" I raise my gaze to the alley, my pulse kicking at the sleek town car slowly approaching to block our exit.

"Want me to blow this pop stand in reverse?"

"That's Cole." Layla releases her belt and tugs at the door handle only to have it deny her freedom. "Let me out."

"I need to speak with him first." I shoot Bishop a hard look and shove from the car. "Keep her inside until I return and make sure you watch the back of those hotel rooms."

"No, take me with you," she demands. "He'll kill you."

I ignore her, unsure if her intent is to intimidate or warn, and close the door behind me to stride ahead. She shouts for me to stop, the muted calls trapped behind closed windows and smothered by heavy traffic, but her suffering punishes me all the same.

I'm sure I've got nothing to worry about, though.

Cole is smart enough to pause his trigger finger when his sister is still trapped in my car. I'm banking my fucking life on it as I continue forward, the two men seated in the car before me glowering, the driver lacking subtlety when he casually rests his gun on top of the steering wheel.

I stop a few yards from the hood, watching them talk, the conversation seeming relaxed as fuck.

I'd do the same—fake self-assurance in the face of my enemy. But from what I've learned about the infamous Cole Torian, we're different in almost every other aspect.

To me, death is a transaction—clinical and cold.

He sees it as a game—thrilling and ego-boosting.

I have confidence he won't shoot me before he has the chance to taunt me first.

He climbs from the passenger seat and strolls casually toward me, his equally well-known enforcer stepping out from the driver's side to remain behind the open door, his weapon coming to rest on the roof.

Cole doesn't speak as he approaches, his dark grey suit wrinkle-free, the slightly imperious set of his brows confirming he'll at least toy with me before I'm dead.

"I'm unarmed." I raise my hands at my sides before letting them fall.

"That's a mistake." He grins, the flash of teeth cocky. "You've got my sister."

"I do. She's safe and unharmed."

"But still being held against her will, otherwise she would've run to me by now."

I don't deny the obvious. There's no point.

"Let her go," he drawls. "And I'll let you live… for now."

I should scoff. Or at least mimic his arrogance, only this isn't about ego.

It's about *her*.

Layla.

Nothing more, nothing less.

"I can't do that. She doesn't want to return to Portland."

He raises a sardonic brow. "You can hear her yelling, right?"

"I can." And it fucking kills me. "But are those shouts for her freedom or my life?"

He pauses, contemplating me for long moments.

"She's been happy with me for weeks," I add. "She *loves* me—just ask Keira."

"Proof of her love wouldn't mean shit. You're not the first scam she's fallen for." He steps closer, losing the mask of delight. Now he glares. Hard eyes. Curled upper lip. "You're her MO. This is what she does—falls prey to predators. She's the walking, talking definition of gullibility."

My hackles rise. "And that right there is why I can't let her leave with you. She's told me all about her position in the family. How you make her feel worthless."

"Her *actions* make her feel worthless. She's her harshest critic."

"Are you sure about that?"

He scoffs a silent laugh. "That's some set of balls you've got, Costa."

"Don't call me that." I clench my jaw. "It's not my name."

"Sorry. I forgot Layla told me about the label change. But tell me, *Matthew,* have you informed her of your moniker yet? Has the man who wants to rescue her like a fucking hero told her what he's best known for?"

I clench my teeth harder, refusing to react.

"You didn't tell her that, either, did you?" His eyes narrow. "You're delusional if you think she could love someone with your reputation."

"Reputations are usually built on gossip and exaggeration. You and Hunter should know that better than most."

"I think we're both man enough to admit the worst of us is kept secret from the world because those who witness it die at the scene."

I fall quiet. Unresponsive.

He's right.

"I'm told you were once a monster, Matthew Langston," he drawls the name with censure. "And yet you expect me to what? Let you leave with my sister?"

"I *am* leaving with her. The only decision left to make is if it will be done with force."

"You're threatening me now?" He steps closer, less than a foot between us when he clenches a fist.

"I'm preparing you."

I don't attempt to block his punch. I take the blow to the gut as punishment and hunch with the impact, Layla's muted screams surpass the thunderous pulse in my ears.

He strikes again and again. My chin. My cheek. Each impact hitting without defense.

"That's enough," I warn.

Another blow hits my jaw. My temple. The pain rings through my skull.

"I said, that's enough." I charge, ramming my shoulder into his ribs, sending him backward in a grappling bear hug. Impatience consumes me as I hold him close and shove a hand beneath his jacket, snatching for his holster to unclasp his weapon.

The soothing familiarity of the gun is in my hand in seconds. The urge to pull the trigger calls to me.

"I deserve a few hits for the secrets I've kept from her." I place the barrel against his sternum. "But now you're done."

Rage flashes across his face. "We're done when I say we are."

"Give the order," Hunter growls beside their car. "One word and he's dead."

"If he's dead, she's dead, too," Bishop calls from behind me. "I don't have a fondness for the bitch like he does."

I smile, tasting blood. But it's Layla's silence that unsettles me.

There are no shouts.

No screams.

Bishop can threaten on my behalf all he likes, but if he's got her at gunpoint there's going to be trouble.

I glance over my shoulder, finding him behind the wheel, his upper body half out the window, while Layla's frantic eyes stare at me from the back of the Lincoln, her hands gripping the front seats.

"Interesting that you chose to threaten instead of negotiate or beg." Torian reclaims my attention. "I would've thought you'd be smarter than that."

"You wouldn't respect me if I did. And I wouldn't be a strong enough man for Layla either. I'd go to war for her. What I won't do is wither on my knees."

"So you choose death?"

"No." I shove him away and raise the gun, making a show of letting it fall limp in my fingers. "I'm the one who came unarmed, remember? I don't want you as an enemy." I lower the weapon to the asphalt and kick it aside. "Nobody needs to die today."

"Just be taken hostage?"

I expel a heavy sigh. "She's only a hostage to her own anger. We had a fight. She's pissed. But she still wants to be with me. And from what I'm told, you'd appreciate not having to deal with her anymore."

"Is that what she told you?" He frowns.

"That she's the outcast? The black sheep? Yeah. She hates her life in Portland, and loved the time she spent with me. Let me take her off your hands. I'll protect her. Provide for her. She'll never be left wanting."

"Except for the truth, right?"

My jaw ticks. "We don't have time for this. Salvatore and Remy are inside that shitty hotel looking for her. They're not going to unfurl the welcome mat if they find you here."

"I already placed a call to the owner. If he knows what's good for him, he would've gotten rid of them."

I fall silent.

Cole does, too. Both of us scrutinize each other through our animosity.

"So you think you're going to convince her you're a good guy?" He focuses on the car over my shoulder. "I say you're kidding yourself. Hunter has a sinister reputation, but even he's disgusted by some of the tales of your glory days."

"I'm not a good guy. But I'm not that man anymore either. I did everything I could to get out of the lifestyle and start over. You, of all people, should understand the dedication that required."

He continues dissecting me beneath his gaze, his thoughts loud but undecipherable. "She'll hate you before she ever attempts to love you again."

"I can live with that. But I won't live without her. I promise you I'll rain hell down on everyone until I get a chance to redeem myself. And I'm a man of my word, Torian."

"I'm beginning to see that." He grabs his lapels to straighten his jacket. "I'm assuming you love her back?"

I stiffen, every muscle, every limb.

I'm getting somewhere here. I'm winning him over. I'm not going to lie, though.

"No," I answer simply. "What I feel for her doesn't represent the whimsical bull-shit people brag about."

"Then why the fuck would I—"

"Because she fucking consumes me," I snarl through clenched teeth. "She destroys me. Rips me apart and leaves me weak. Every thought I have is savaged by her. Every breath is tainted with her scent. What I feel for her is more than the bull-shit of love. It's something you wouldn't understand and couldn't comprehend."

He raises a brow, mocking me. "Nice speech."

My anger spikes. I glance for the gun, itching to sweep it off the ground.

"I suggest you leave it where it is. Especially when I'm finally starting to not want you dead." He waves a lazy hand toward my face. "You're lucky I recognize the pussy-whipped expression. You're also fortunate I have plans for your family and no patience to babysit her while they unfold."

"With all due respect, don't you think it's a little late for babysitting? You should've told her before you made a move."

His left eye twitches, the seconds passing in reignited hostility before he states simply, "I was yet to make a move, *Langston*. Do I look like the type who would repay what Emmanuel has done with a friendly bullet wound?"

"Then who—"

"Who's to say he didn't do it to himself? It got us all here, didn't it? It gave him the attention I've learned he craves. It also fuels your siblings' hatred and makes them more inclined to follow Emmanuel's lead."

"Maybe you're right. But what does that mean for Layla?"

"It means I'll give you what you want. At least partially, anyway. You've got thirty days."

I pause, waiting for a catch.

The bait and switch.

"An entire month where you can do your best to win her back, because *yes*, I agree she deserves happiness, and it's been clear for a while that she won't find it with us in Portland." He steps threateningly close, causing Layla's screams to reignite. "But if you hurt her. If you fail to keep her safe—"

"I won't."

"Good." He strides for his gun and bends to pick it up before shoving the weapon inside his jacket. "Because no words can describe the fun things I'll do to you if you don't."

"What happens after thirty days?"

He shrugs. "If you win her over, she's yours. I won't get in the way. She'll be your responsibility and you'll get no trouble from me."

"And if I don't?"

"For your sake, I wouldn't let that be an option." He strolls back toward me, giving me a demeaning clap on the chest. "Make her happy, otherwise it'll be the last thing you fail at achieving. Hear me?"

I raise my chin. "I hear you."

He passes me, continuing toward the Lincoln. "Now, I think it's time you two were formally introduced, don't you? It's only fair that she learns she's going to be spending her days with the Butcher Boys of Baltimore."

REDEMPTION

Ruthless

EDEN SUMMERS

1

LAYLA

I slap my palms against the inside of the car window as a scream sears my throat.

My brother is outside, a few yards down the alley, pummeling his fists into Matthew's chest. His face. Smashing. Beating.

"*Stop*." My shriek reverberates through the Lincoln's interior while I fight harder against the glass, then wrench at the door handle. "*Cole. Stop.*"

I'm locked in here. Trapped by the order of the man my brother's attempting to beat to death right in front of my eyes.

"Shut up," Bishop snarls from the driver's seat. "I can't fucking think with your wailing."

No. I won't.

I don't want Matthew to die today. Not like this, anyway. If he's going to leave this world it will be by my hands.

I bang harder. Scream louder.

Matthew charges, shocking me into silence, ramming his shoulder into Cole's chest. He grapples my brother backward in a bear hug, gaining control as Hunter watches them from a few feet away, his gun aimed in their direction.

Then they stop.

From devastation to inaction in the space of seconds, and I can't understand why.

"Shit," Bishop mutters under his breath.

"What?" I shove forward in the back seat. "What's happening?"

"Langston pulled a gun on your brother."

My heart nosedives to the pit of my gut. "Do something." I shove at Bishop's shoulder. "Let me out. Let me stop this."

"Shut the fuck up so I can listen." He lowers his window and hoists his head outside.

I can't hear the exchange. Even if my pulse wasn't a thunderous staccato, I'm not sure I'd be able to comprehend the words. There's nothing but my panted breath and the *thump, thump, thump* of my frantic heartbeats.

"If he's dead, she's dead, too," Bishop yells. "I don't have a fondness for the bitch like he does."

I don't fear for my life. What frightens me is Bishop's ignorance as he attempts to intimidate my brother. Nobody threatens Cole. At least, not if they plan to live.

Matthew glances over his shoulder to us. Our eyes meet in a clash of emotion. I see his determination. His power. And beneath the already swelling cheekbone and blood on his lip, I glimpse a man with regrets, too.

Good. I hope he chokes on remorse.

He's made every moment we spent together an agonizing memory. Each blink of remembrance is a knife through my chest.

At the time, I'd been stupid enough to think we were falling in love. That our connection was driven by fate. The reality was, the only thing molding us together were his lies. His manipulation.

I despise how easily I succumbed to feeling wanted.

Matthew returns his attention to Cole and retreats a step, raising the gun in the air. He makes a show of surrender as he lets the weapon fall limp in his fingers. They're talking. Maybe arguing. I can't tell. And with each mouthed word, my stomach twists a little more.

I don't want him informing my brother of the mistakes I've made.

I need to get out of here.

I have to go home.

I slide back in my seat and clench a fist to bang it against the side window. I pound hard enough for the bones in my hand to ache. I don't stop when Bishop threatens me. I keep pummeling as the showdown continues, my brother's expression morphing from a glare to a taunting grin.

What the hell are they talking about?

I bang and thump and hit until he starts toward the Lincoln, sparking delirious relief inside my burning veins.

I've made a plethora of bad decisions that Cole will forever hold against me. But the epitome of my nightmare is about to be over. I can return to my dismal existence —home, the place that once seemed like hell, yet now resembles a refuge when pitted against my current situation. I'll slink into isolation to lick my wounds. I'll become a goddamn hermit.

Cole stops on my side of the car, parallel with the driver's seat, and glances at Bishop. "Lower her window."

I straighten. Pause. *Panic.*

I don't need the window lowered. I want the door opened. There's no time for temporary measures when our enemies are near. The men who played a role in killing my husband are in the hotel beside the alley, looking for me. The men who I now know are Matthew's brothers.

My window descends an inch, allowing a breath of the outside world to sweep in.

"Layla," Cole greets in a condemning tone. "This is quite a mess you've made."

"I know." I give another pointless tug of the door handle. "I'm sorry. I'll explain on the way home."

"I don't need an explanation."

There's something in his statement that chills me. Something callous and cruel.

"You don't?" I glance at Matthew standing a few feet away, my gaze connecting with eyes devoid of emotion. He's not enraged that I'm about to leave him. Not annoyed. Or bitter. Or heartbroken. He's a blank slate, only marred by the damage my brother inflicted on his face.

"Please let me out." I return my attention to Cole. "Salvatore and Remy are—"

"You're not getting out, Layla."

I stiffen.

Everything slows—my concept of time, my thoughts, the world around me. Everything except my pulse, which does the opposite, its frantic beats threatening to cause heart failure.

"What do you mean?" I grip the edge of the window. My fingers claw as I fail to lower the barrier. "What's going on?"

"Do you remember what we discussed the day of Benji's funeral?" His voice hardens as he steps closer.

I ignore the question, tugging violently on the glass. "Open the door." I don't want to talk about the funeral. Or my late husband. I don't want to do anything other than get out of this car.

"You begged me for peace," he continues. "You pleaded for me to leave the Costas alone for the sake of Stella and Tobias. And I complied. I delayed honor and retribution for you. For your recovery, as well as the children's. But I also told you there would be a price."

My blood turns from red-hot to stone-cold, the icy dread splintering painfully through my limbs. "Open the door, Cole." My fingers ache from my aggressive grip on the glass. "Don't do this."

"I made it clear there would be a price to pay for such a sizeable favor."

"No." I raise my voice. Shake my head. "Please."

"It's time to pay up, sister."

"*No.*" I rattle the window. Kick the door. "Let me out."

"I'm not always going to be around to fix your mistakes. You need to learn to clean up the mess you create."

My mind continues the screams my parched throat can no longer achieve.

I tug and pull and thrash against the door. I thump and punch and shove.

My brother ignores my plight. Everyone does.

Cole stares down at me, devoid of empathy. Bishop remains silent in the front seat. And Matthew—the man who stole my heart through deception and fraud— watches with his traitorous lips set in a thin line.

I clench my teeth as I glare through my heartache.

I want him to suffer. But more than anything, I want to wake from the nightmare of the last twenty-four hours and not be the victim of his lies.

"Listen to me." Cole leans closer to my window. "You need to understand the situation you're in—"

"*I understand,*" I plead. "I know the mistakes I've made."

"Like always, you have no clue. The men you've spent your time with—"

"*The men you're threatening to leave me with,*" I shriek.

His nostrils flare. "It's not a threat, Layla. This is happening. You're pulling yourself out of this on your own. What you need to be aware of is who will be by your side while you do it."

"I already know who they are." My eyes burn from the overwhelming frustration. "I'm well aware Matthew and Bishop used to be Italian mafia. I've met Lorenzo Cappelletti."

Cole gives a placating smile. "Then I'll assume you know the role they played in increasing Lorenzo's empire and the lengths they went in an effort to achieve success. And I'll guess that you're also aware these men are the reason Baltimore is now under the control of the Italians."

The chill digs deeper, sinking into my bones, freezing my marrow.

No, I wasn't aware. This insight is yet another notch to add to the tally of things Matthew kept from me.

"If you think I'm a monster," Cole murmurs, "then you'll find yourself in good company, because the atrocities instigated by the Butcher Boys of Baltimore far outweigh my own."

The moniker rips through me. Shreds.

"No." I shake my head, my stomach revolting.

I've heard tales. Myths. None of those horror-filled stories could be about the man I've fallen for.

"Yes, Layla." Cole straightens and steps back. "You found your way into the devil's bed. Now it's up to you to get yourself out of it."

2

MATTHEW

My jaw aches. My cheek, too. But nothing hurts more than having to witness the devastation tightening her beautiful features.

I'd warned her I wasn't a good man. I never claimed to have a soul.

Her mistake was thinking my crimes would be comparable to those of her people. That the wrongdoings of a small underworld crime family in Portland would be somehow similar to the monstrosities I committed to gain Lorenzo unfathomable power.

The shock in her eyes lets me know she now understands.

"Cole." Her voice is pure fragility. "Please don't do this. Even if you don't want to take me home, just let me out. Don't leave me a prisoner."

"You're a prisoner of your own making. One that will no longer be funded by family money." Her brother takes another retreating step. "You can pay for your mistakes from now on."

I clench my teeth, almost regretting the deal we made.

Almost.

"*Please.*" Tears glisten in her eyes, but not a drop spills free. "You can't do this to me."

Movement shifts in my periphery. The shadow of a body enters the open hotel window Layla and I had previously climbed out of.

"Salvatore," I state in warning to those around me, finding my brother's gun already aimed in our direction. "*Get down.*" I haul Cole across my body, using myself as his shield.

Shots reverberate through the alley. Bullets whiz past.

Layla screams. Cole ducks.

Hunter returns fire from behind us.

The noise is deafening as I lunge for the passenger door and yank it open. "Get around the other side of the car. We'll cover you."

Cole complies as I climb into the Lincoln and Bishop hits the gas. We cruise forward, Layla's brother doing a crouching run beside us to where his vehicle waits at the mouth of the alley.

"Let me go with him," she begs through the window. "Let me out."

Never.

"It isn't safe." I don't trust her with a brother who could easily give her up. She's mine to protect now.

We nose up to Cole's vehicle and he climbs inside, Hunter doing the same, before they both slam their doors. The town car violently reverses, clearing our path to escape as bullets ping off the back of the Lincoln, smashing a tail light.

"Hold on." Bishop clings to the steering wheel. Our tires screech with rapid acceleration. "Am I heading for the airport?"

"Yes." I grab my cell from inside my jacket and dial the pilot's number, my ass sliding from side to side on the seat as we speed through the parking lot and onto the main road. He answers on the second ring. "Get the jet ready. We'll be there in fifteen. I don't want any delays."

"I'll need to schedule it with traffic—"

"Get it done." I disconnect, return the device to my pocket, then lower my sun visor. I use the makeup mirror to gain a glimpse of Layla in the back seat, her bowed head and slumped posture threatening to reawaken emotions long since hibernated. "Are you okay?"

She raises her gaze, meeting my reflection with a scowl. There are no words. No actions. Just hard eyes that scream of loathing.

"We'll get you out of Denver," I vow. "You'll be looked after."

"I don't want your help. Leave me at the airport. I'll find my own way home."

"That's not an option." I can't win her back when she's not by my side. "We can discuss the future once we're settled at a safe house."

Her lip curls, her vehemence increasing, but she doesn't argue. Instead, she drags her gaze out the window while we continue weaving through traffic, Bishop slamming the horn like it's an arcade button.

We reach the airport without a sign of Cole or Salvatore. Thankfully, there are no cops on our tail, either.

Bishop takes us to the gates leading onto the private runway, escorting us inside as soon as they're opened by airport staff.

We stop by a hangar in front of the jet already waiting on the tarmac. The ignition is cut. Silence descends. Nobody moves.

It isn't until a guy pauses at the driver's door, waiting to take the Lincoln off our hands, that Bishop looks at me in recrimination. "Are you sure this is the right move?"

I don't need specifics to understand he's talking about Layla.

He wants me to leave her behind. To dump and run.

"It's the only move." I shove from the car and open her door for her to get out.

She doesn't.

She remains seated, staring straight ahead. She doesn't even look at me.

I'm not sure if I should be livid or impressed that rejection is high on her priorities even though her life is in danger.

"We need to get out of here." I pull the door wider.

She crosses her arms over her chest, refusing to acknowledge me. She's all defiance and spite. Hostility and fury.

I'd be fucking turned on if I wasn't concerned for her safety.

"Believe me, you'll have more than enough time to make your resentment known once we reach our destination," I mutter under my breath. "But if you don't move your ass, I *will* carry you."

Her chin rises, her mega-watt scowl turning to hit me head on. "Touch me and I promise you won't live to regret it."

A thrill skitters through my veins. If she isn't careful, she'll learn the hard way that defiance isn't the best strategy against me. "Then get out of the fucking car, *amore mio*. We need to disappear."

Her jaw tightens as she continues to stare me down. Seconds pass. My pulse increases.

I want an excuse to grab her. Touch her. Force her to me and make her see sense.

"Where are we going?" Finally, she scoots from the back seat and moves to stand before me, her shoulders straight with authority.

"Somewhere safe." I slam the door behind her while Bishop climbs from the other side of the vehicle.

I stalk beside her toward the jet whirring on the tarmac, the stairs lowered, the pilot already waiting in the cockpit.

I pause at the first step and indicate with a wave of a hand for her to proceed before me.

She plants her feet. "I'll follow."

No, she'll run, and I'm more than tempted to let her just for the opportunity to give chase.

She has no idea of the dangerous response she's spurring to life inside me. If she knew, her expression would be less defiant and more fearful.

"Move." I hold her gaze, daring her to defy me.

She's undaunted, maintaining my stare for numerous heartbeats. "You're such an asshole." She reaches for the hand rail and climbs the slim staircase to disappear inside.

"Asshole?" Bishop murmurs as he stands by my side. "I don't think she fully grasps the description her brother gave."

"Don't cause shit for me." I keep my focus on the top of the stairs.

"Cause shit for *you*?" He gives a derisive huff and takes the first step. "My bad. Here I was thinking you were the one fucking me over with your drama."

The slumberous itch of remorse attempts to niggle its way into my chest.

We fought hard to get away from this lifestyle. To distance ourselves from the devil's to-do list.

Now it looks like I've dragged us back in.

But this is temporary.

I follow him into the jet and jerk my chin in greeting at the copilot who waits at the entrance to the cockpit. "Get us in the air, Malcolm. The sooner, the better."

"Will do, sir." He drags the staircase inside and shuts the door behind me, enclosing us in a volatile capsule of aggression and hatred.

Bishop starts down the aisle. "I'll reach out to Irene and make sure the house is stocked and cleaned before we arrive."

"Ask her to provide any necessities for our guest."

He nods, passing Layla who sits on a window seat in the middle of the cabin.

The coastal safe house has everything Bishop and I will need—clothes, toiletries, weapons. But I don't want Layla left wanting. I'm impatient for her forgiveness. And the looming deadline to regain her love is already a tightening noose around my neck.

I've got thirty days. Yet I want to believe I can achieve it in one.

I take the seat beside her, ignoring her stubborn silence as the jet begins to move. I plan my defense while we remain in a holding pattern near the runway and indulge the quiet she obviously craves as we leave the ground.

She needs time for her adrenaline to weaken, and I give it to her, allowing her turmoil a chance to settle while we ascend and turn toward the East Coast. I watch her, though. From the corner of my eye, I note the ragged rise and fall of her chest. Her hands rest in her lap, the position seeming like a deliberate show of calm if it weren't for her constant picking at her fingernails.

"Have you eaten?" I ask.

She keeps her gaze straight ahead, unflinching. Mute.

"We've got a lot to discuss, *amore mio*. I know you're—"

"You know nothing," she grates. "You don't know what you've done. And you sure as shit seem ignorant to how I hold you accountable, otherwise you'd quit pretending we're not enemies."

"I'm well aware of the role I've played. I'm only asking for an opportunity to explain."

"I'm all out of opportunities. You can go to hell as far as I'm concerned."

I'm already there. "I didn't—"

"Don't. Talk. To. Me." She enunciates the demand slowly. Vehemently.

I clench my molars. *Fine.* I'll give her more time.

We spend the rest of the flight in silence, her tense posture unfaltering until we land at a small private airport in South Carolina.

As soon as the copilot opens the door and lowers the stairs, Layla climbs over me like a caged animal finally gaining freedom and exits the jet before I can release my belt.

By the time I step into the sunlight at the top of the staircase, she's already seated in the waiting Lincoln on the tarmac. There were no protests. No acts of aggression. Only a one-track mind to get as far away from me as possible.

I slide into the back seat with her, the quiet continuing from all parties as Bishop drives us toward the beach, the unfettered sunshine and slight warmth in the air doing nothing to soothe the animosity Layla exudes.

She wants me dead.

Rightly so.

I lied. Deceived. Manipulated. But she did, too.

The wreckage of our relationship lays at both our feet.

"Irene has cleaned the house and stocked the kitchen." Bishop meets my gaze in the rearview mirror. "Do you want me to stop to pick up anything else before we arrive?"

"No." I'm sure there are a million things I need to organize but my priority is getting Layla alone. The longer her malevolence festers, the more impatient I become.

I stare out the window, never more thankful for the partial isolation of my coastal property than I am right now. The closest neighbors are half a mile down the road. Layla can let loose and rail on me all she likes without fear of being overheard.

And she *will* let loose.

I can already feel her building detonation.

"Home sweet home." Bishop pulls onto a cement drive, pausing before the property gate to tap in the security code, and then we proceed inside.

We stop before the two-story waterfront house with its sleek architectural lines and L-shaped staircase leading to the upstairs veranda. The property hasn't changed since we last escaped here two years ago. There are no cobwebs or remnants of autumn leaves. Irene has kept the place immaculate with all the curtains now drawn from the massive panes of unfettered glass, ready for us to arrive.

Layla doesn't react to the multimillion-dollar property.

It isn't until the car stops and the ignition is cut that she drags in a long breath, releasing it in a heave.

"I have a question." She gives me a sideways glare. "Only one. And that's all I want from you."

"Ask." I tense, anticipating her interest in the negotiation I had with her brother. I won't lie to her again. But distancing her from that truth will work in my favor.

"How did you get my things?" She holds my gaze, her eyes narrowed slits. "The items from my purse after I was mugged. How did you get them? *When* did you get them?"

Shit.

She's gone straight for the jugular of my deception.

Bishop clears his throat. "I paid someone—"

"No." There's aggression in my voice as I interrupt. A harshness born from frustration over my biggest mistake. I appreciate his willingness to take the blame, but her fury is my punishment to bear. "I can handle this. Layla and I will meet you inside."

Bishop stares at me through the rearview mirror, silently warning me of the hostile situation that's about to erupt.

I'm fully aware of my fate, asshole.

"Go." I jerk my chin. "We won't be long."

He sighs and climbs from the car, shutting the door behind him.

Layla straightens, as if steeling herself against being alone with me when this used to be her fucking preference.

"He paid someone?" Her tone is flat, lifeless, along with her expression. "Paid them for what? To find my purse? To retrieve it from a dumpster?"

"He didn't pay anyone." I unclasp my belt, preparing to chase after her. "I did. And it wasn't a search or retrieval mission."

Her brow furrows. She may have been born into a vicious family but apparently, her upbringing wasn't harsh enough for her to assume how low I would stoop for information.

"I paid someone to steal your purse, *amore mio*. I arranged for you to be mugged."

She remains rigid.

The detonation I anticipate waits in a holding pattern while she blinks.

Once.

Twice.

Then the shock wears off with the thinning of her beautiful lips and a fast swallow. She keeps her devastation tempered, the buffered reaction punishing me more than her rage ever could.

"You wouldn't tell me who you were." It's a fucking lame excuse. "You used a burner phone. The name you gave the restaurant was fake. I had nothing to—"

She snaps her gaze from mine, flings her door wide, then slides outside, smacking the door shut behind her. She doesn't run. Doesn't flee in a whirlwind of emotion. Instead, she holds her head high and strides for the house, climbing the staircase with grace and dignity.

I shove from the car. "Layla, wait."

She doesn't.

"*Layla*." I stride after her.

She needs to understand my reasoning. The necessity.

She reaches the veranda and yanks open the front door, then slams it in her wake.

Fuck. I clench a fist, preparing to punch my knuckles through the car window. I anticipate the contact. Already hear the shatter of glass. Feel the distracting pain. It's a whirlwind of relief just waiting on the edges of my consciousness.

But I can't break. I won't succumb to the easy option.

I've worked hard to overcome my impulses. I'm better than that now. At least, I'm meant to act like I am.

Problem is, I'd fucking planned to tell her. I had every goddamn intention of laying my cards on the table. Then Remy sent me a text about the shooting and I'd realized too late that my time was up.

I would've explained where I came from. Who my family was—the ones who raised me only to destroy me. I intended to outline all the underhanded tactics I'd used to keep her close. To win her over. To make her mine.

Then my brother fucked me.

I climb the stairs and stalk my ass inside.

The tiled entry sparkles. The scent of lemon cleaning chemicals taints the air. I prowl my way along the cobweb-free hall and into the pristine open living area, every single pane of the floor-to-ceiling glass scuff free.

The perfection mocks me. It fucking pokes at my inferiority, screaming how unworthy I am.

Bishop stands in the kitchen, his ass leaning against the island counter as he takes a bite of a half-eaten apple.

"Where is she?" I ask.

He jerks his head toward the far hall leading to the bedrooms. "I told her to take the room next to yours."

I divert my path in search of her. We're going to talk this shit through. I'll justify my actions or die trying.

I pass my bedroom, then continue to hers and stop before the closed door. I raise my hand to knock, the gentle fall of the shower pattering in the distance. There's something else, too. A sniffle. The faintest whimper?

Fuck. Is she crying?

Her pain is an arrow through my chest.

"I told you this would happen." Bishop comes to stand at the start of the hall. "I warned you."

I brace my clenched knuckles against her door and hang my head, not daring to look at him for fear of lighting the fuse to my temper.

"I said she would bring drama." He approaches. "That she'd be a fucking complication. Now look where we're at—in the middle of a war that's not ours with loot that will get us killed."

"She's not loot." Anger mixes with my self-loathing, the potent concoction warming my veins. I fight to hold myself in check, to calm the devil within.

"Then what is she? What the fuck have you dragged us into?" Bishop keeps approaching. Keeps taunting. If he's not careful, he'll bear the brunt of the madness waging war inside me.

"What have *I* dragged us into?" I push from the door and swing around to face him. "None of this would've happened if you'd done your job in the first place."

"You're blaming this on me?"

"Why wouldn't I? All you had to do was find out why she was spying on Emmanuel at that fucking restaurant. You had one goddamn job."

He raises a brow, his lips slowly curling in a threatening smile. "Why don't we take this outside? I'll give you the fight you're itching for."

My chest hums, my soul empowered by the offer of violence.

Pain is exactly what I want. The crunch of bone. The thrill of carnage.

"I'm not fighting you," I snarl.

"Why? You worried I'll kick your ass?"

If I thought he could overpower me in my current state, I'd welcome the threat. I'd accept the hospitality of his beating and hope he knocked me out cold. But the opposite will happen.

"No." I dig my fingers into my palms, wishing the need for brutality would lessen. All it does is build. Morph. Punish. "I'm more concerned I won't stop until I kill you."

He straightens. Sobers.

He knows I'm not exaggerating.

He squares his shoulders, tightens his jaw. "If that's the case, you shouldn't be anywhere near her."

The caution pokes my self-loathing higher, making it dance with my rage.

I'd never hurt her… not physically… at least, not by my own hand.

Fuck.

All I've done is hurt her.

Emotionally. Physically. I arranged to have her mugged, which left her injured. I've destroyed the ties that bind her to her family. I've devastated her confidence and shattered her trust.

Have I ruined her just like Emmanuel ruined me?

"Take a walk." Bishop's expression tightens. "Clear your head. I don't know what the fuck you said to Torian to have him handing over his sister, but we'll discuss it later. Right now, you need to pull yourself together before this situation gets more out of hand. Scaring her isn't going to work in your favor."

"She isn't scared of me." I've caused frustration, hatred, loathing, disgust. But never her fear.

"No, but she should be."

Another muted sniffle comes from her room, stabbing more jagged arrows through my chest.

She has to understand my motives.

She needs to fucking listen.

"Walk, Langston. I'll keep an eye on her until you return."

3

MATTHEW

I walked.

I gave her time.

Three fucking days to be exact. I played the role of personal chef, supplying every meal to her bedroom only to be forced to leave it on a tray in the hall because she wouldn't unlock the door.

She won't talk to me. Acknowledge me.

I left her a new toothbrush, shampoo, and soap, yet I get nothing in return. Not even a grunt or a curse.

I'm sure she knows it's driving me insane.

During the day, I spend hours sitting on the floor in my room, my back to our adjoining wall, listening to her occasional footsteps as I drink scotch from the bottle.

The nights are worse. That's when I sit in the darkness of the deck, my attention firmly affixed on her silhouette through the sheer curtains behind the French doors leading to her room.

I'm starved for the sight of her. I need to see those emotive eyes. Hear that haunting voice. Every minute that ticks by is another wasted moment creeping toward my deadline to win her back.

She can't stay in that room forever.

Bishop's footsteps approach down the hall, his unimpressed glower at my bedroom door seconds later. He eyes the liquor bottle beside me as I sit on the floor, my head resting back against the wall.

He sighs, long and judgmental. "How long do you plan on moping?"

Moping? Seems this asshole is still looking for a fight. "If I'm not mistaken, you're the one who told me to give her time."

"So you heard me?" He crosses his arms over his chest and leans a bicep against the doorframe. "For the last two days I've been wondering if the message got lost in translation and you actually thought I told you to act like a punk-ass bitch."

He's definitely itching to get pummeled.

"We've got employees wondering why the hell you disappeared. They've got questions I can't answer, motherfucker. You need to start returning calls."

I clench my teeth, glare, and grab for a bottle I already know is drained.

"I'll ask again," he mutters. "How long do you plan on moping?"

"How long do you expect to keep breathing if you continue to test me?" I drag myself to my feet, the liquor bottle dangling in my hand.

He snickers. "There he is. The son of a bitch we all know and love."

I stalk toward him, shoving past to enter the hall and continue to the open living area.

He follows, joining me in the kitchen as I dump the bottle in the trash. "I think it's time we had a chat about why she's here. Don't you?"

And have him judge me more than he already has? No thanks. "I've got things to do." I make for the hall again only to have him block my path.

"What things?" He narrows his gaze. "You've got that look in your eye."

"This look means I'm done waiting. She can't ignore me any longer."

"If that's the case, do you want me to go out to stockpile first aid supplies? Because you're going to need them if you go in there half cut with the devil on your shoulder."

The devil has never been on my shoulder. That fucker resides in my soul.

"I'm sure she's put her isolation to good use," he adds. "Her claws will be sharp."

The thought of those claws isn't a deterrent. If anything, her touch, blood-drawing or not, has the opposite effect. I'd let her hurt me. I'd encourage it if it meant she'd acknowledge my existence.

"Look." He raises his hands in surrender. "Why don't I start dinner? We both know I'm a one-trick pony, so we're stuck with spaghetti, but at least that way you can take a cold shower, sober up, and figure out what the fuck you're going to say to stop her from stabbing you."

"She's not going to stab me. And I'm not drunk." The liquor was merely medicinal, each sip taking the edge off days of building frustration. "By now she should've realized I'm the only one who can help her. She just needs to listen—"

"Help her do what?" He backtracks around the island counter and pulls a saucepan from a cupboard. "Fix the mess you created?"

He's right. However, that doesn't mean I'm wrong.

I'm all she's got, and the fact she hasn't run by now means she's fully aware of it.

The neighbors might not be close, but they're within walking distance. She could've fled there for help. My bet is that she knows the only things the outside world can give her are temporary measures—a phone call, a short supply of cash.

"Yes," I admit. "I'm the only one who can fix the mess I created."

Bishop moves to the fridge, making a mass of noise as he claims ingredients, then dumps them on the counter. Something else enters the mix. A far-off sound coming from the hall leading to the bedrooms.

I cock my head, hearing it again. A muffled whir.

Did she flee her hiding place?

I stalk for the hall, hungry to see her, to speak to her, only to find her bedroom door closed as usual.

"Layla, are you in there?" I speak to the painted wood.

Her response is a squeak of mattress springs as the whir repeats down the hall. The washing machine? She snuck out to wash her clothes?

If only she'd fucking asked. I would've bought her every item under the sun. Shirts. Dresses. Underwear. She doesn't have a fully stocked wardrobe like I do, but it was only a matter of voicing a fucking request.

"Layla." I pause, willing the devil inside me to calm. "You've had enough time on your own. Tonight, you eat with me."

There's another squeak of mattress springs. I picture her shoving from the bed to stand tall, her chin high with defiance, her face unbelievably mesmerizing as it tightens in anger.

"Layla?" I test the handle and taste victory when the lever lowers. Did she forget to lock the door? "I'm coming in."

"Don't," she warns. "I'm not eating with you."

I grin, sinking in to the sound of her voice, loving her strength even though her tone is one hundred percent vehement.

"You've had three days." I continue to plunge the handle, then inch the door open a crack. Anticipation is a motherfucking drug as I creep the barrier between us wider and wider, seeking her out, my vision eagerly scanning past the disheveled four-poster bed to find her standing tall and proud on the other side.

My pulse increases, the dull throb turning into a heavy beat at the sight of her in nothing but a towel.

She's a vision, the peach glow of sunset streaming in through the sheer curtains, the light kissing her perfect skin. I thought maybe she'd look drawn or tired after what I've put her through, but it's the opposite. A warrior glares back at me, ready for a battle I would much prefer to have while we're both horizontal. Legs entwined. Mouths frantic.

"Get out," she seethes.

"You've had three days. Neither of us can afford any more. We need to make plans."

Her chin hikes. There's no protest. She knows I'm right and hates me for it.

"Not tonight," she grates. "I have no clothes."

"I can see that." I rake my gaze from her indignant stare to her beautifully bare shoulders, all the way over her towel-covered curves that stop where the bed blocks the remainder of my view. Then I leisurely trek back up again, appreciating everything I've been denied for the last seventy-two hours.

"Where are your clothes?" I feign ignorance to fill the silence.

"In the washing machine. You may not have realized, but I've been left in here without any luggage. Not even fresh underwear."

"You only had to ask. I've never left you wanting in the past."

Her scowl deepens at my innuendo. "I won't eat with you. You can bring the food to my door like usual and leave me alone."

"Don't get me wrong—I'm a slave to your affections, but I won't be to your demands. Tonight, you either eat with me or don't eat at all."

She scoffs an irate laugh. "Well, I'm afraid your company would only slaughter my appetite. So if you're forcing me to make a choice, I'd rather starve in isolation than in your presence."

My blood boils, only this time it's no longer from frustration alone.

Her defiance is an aphrodisiac. Her lies are like heroin.

She still wants me. I refuse to believe otherwise.

"Then let me raise the stakes by pointing out that the person you can't stand the sight of is also the one who stands between you and the only clothes you have." I smile, smug. "A little civility will go a long way."

Her eyes flash with rage.

"I'll leave you to your solitude, *amore mio*. When you change your mind and want to discuss borrowing my cell to call your daughter, just let me know."

Her face crumples. It's a split second of vulnerability before the warrior expression returns. "You're a manipulative prick."

Yes, I am. But I'm also the victor in this scrimmage.

"And you're still the most beautiful woman I've ever seen." I step back into the hall. "I'll call you once dinner is ready."

4

———————

MATTHEW

I return to the living room, breathing in the scent of garlic and basil, then exhale exhilaration and victory.

I should've forced her hand days ago. If only I'd known taunting her was the way to encourage communication.

"He returns without a scratch." Bishop shoots me a two-second glance as he opens a packet of pasta. "Color me surprised."

I divert my path to the cutlery drawer to begin setting the table. "She's eating with us tonight."

"That's going to be a hard pass from me, brother. I won't be hanging around to ingest your dramatics. You two can duke this out on your own."

Even better. I don't want an audience.

He doesn't understand my infatuation. How could he? He never plunged to the level of darkness I did. He doesn't need a lifeline like I do.

The things we did for Lorenzo didn't affect him the way they did me.

He took the brutality in his stride while each murder chipped away at my humanity until I was hollow. The more sterile I became on the inside, the more my outward facade morphed. I could schmooze and seduce without flaw. Lie and manipulate without hesitation.

Killing was no different.

With every criminal act, I learned to dissociate from the kid I once was. To despise the world and everything in it.

Until her.

She made me feel again. Lust returned. Longing surfaced.

"When are we going to discuss why she's still with us?" Bishop adds salt to the bolognese sauce, then stirs the pasta.

"Later." One hurdle at a time.

I need to retrieve the knives I stabbed into the backs of those I trust one by one. I can't have everyone despise me at once.

"Stalling isn't a good look for you." He turns and grabs bowls from a cupboard. "Whatever you've done, you're only compounding the issue by not telling me."

"I'm not stalling." I stalk for the table to lay two place settings. "There's nothing to worry about." Just as long as I win her back.

"For once, you're not a good liar, Langston. You're losing your touch."

I return to the kitchen, disregarding his attempt to goad me into a confession. "How long until dinner, asshole?"

"A few minutes."

I grab a bottle of wine from the fridge and pour Layla a glass. It isn't until I place her drink on the table that I realize liquor is a necessity to curb my rampant tongue, and return to the kitchen to retrieve the bottle and another glass.

"You're on edge." Bishop strains the pasta without looking at me. "What is it about her that messes with you? Is it the sex? Or the thrill of her family legacy? Because I can understand how exceptional fucking can drive a man to his knees, but this—"

"Nothing about her messes with me." It's another lie. One hundred percent fiction.

Absolutely everything about her tinkers with the cogs of my soul.

He slams the strainer into the sink, his forehead etched with a severe frown. "Lie to me one more time, motherfucker. See where it gets you."

He's right. He deserves better. "Let me get through tonight and I'll explain everything."

His eyes narrow. "Are you lying to me again?"

"Tomorrow, we'll talk." I place the wine bottle and glass on the table, then head to the island counter, ignoring his scrutiny. "And I'll return all my missed calls."

I'll right this derailing train. Just as soon as Layla is back on my side. In my arms.

His only response is to snatch one of the bowls from in front of me to start serving the spaghetti. "You might want to call your woman. Dinner's ready."

My woman.

The title strokes my ego. If only it were true.

"*Layla.*" I raise my voice. "*Dinner.*" I keep my back to the hall, my ears alert for the first sign of her submission, my blood simmering.

Three bowls are filled with pasta, and still, I don't hear a shift of movement.

"You sure she's coming?" Bishop rinses the pot and places it in the dishwasher before moving to the stove with his wooden spoon.

"She's coming." She'll join me, even if I have to drag her to the table by that damned towel. I won't go another day with my actions hanging over my head. I'll make her understand.

The faintest click sounds from the hall, then the soft pad of bare feet on tile leisurely approaching.

I grin, keeping my back to her arrival. "See?"

Bishop glances at me, his gaze then diverting over my shoulder. "*Jesus fucking*

Christ." He drops the spoon to the counter, the spaghetti sauce splattering over the marble as his jaw snaps shut.

She's done something. Instigated some sort of defiance to temper her battered ego.

I'm so fucking tempted to look.

Instead, I keep my attention on Bishop, trying to determine what sort of threat she poses.

I don't care if she found a makeshift weapon. She can threaten me all she likes. I'd actually enjoy a sparring match.

"A little help here," he mutters, reclaiming the wooden spoon to shove it into the spaghetti sauce. "I'm over this shit."

I succumb, hating how it takes such little encouragement to turn and look at her.

To look at absolutely *all* of her.

She saunters toward the dining table, entirely naked, her hair loose around her shoulders, her arms comfortably at her sides.

Not one stitch of clothing covers her delectable flesh. She's bare to me. To Bishop. To *anyone* who might happen to walk along the beach and glance up at the wall of glass she currently walks before.

"Which seat is mine?" She stops before the table, her expression haughty, her tits perky.

At one time, I would've enjoyed this performance. When she was mine, I reveled in the hunger she awakened in other men. I fucking thrummed every time someone glanced in appreciation at the enviable prize on my arm.

Now she's just another thing I've lost, and the blatant display acts like a knife between my ribs.

It's the perfect power play.

"*Leave,*" I snarl at Bishop.

"If you think for one second that I'm not trying to get my ass out of here as fast as fucking possible, you're an ignorant piece of shit." He slaps a spoon full of bolognaise onto his pasta, then snatches a fork. "Enjoy your fucking meal."

Layla blinks back at me, composed and confident as Bishop storms from the room. She's so fucking beautiful, her chin high with poise, her lips curved in spite.

It's a facade. One I fall victim to regardless.

She's always been hesitant when it comes to exposing her sexuality. Weeks ago, she'd been a skittish kitten when a member of the hotel staff walked in on us in the bath.

This is all an act. A well-planned strategy to push me off-balance.

I finish serving our meals and grab the bowls. I pretend I'm not approaching pure temptation and sidle up beside her, deliberately getting close enough for my suit jacket to brush her arm as I place her meal down in front of her.

"I feel overdressed." I keep my voice in check, no lust or frustration evident as I pull out her chair. "You should've warned me. I could've followed the dress code."

"It's not too late," she drawls. "And it's not like your appearance can disgust me any more than it already does."

I fake a snicker. "I don't think now is an appropriate time to remind you of how hard you make me." I walk back around her, pausing on her other side to lean close to her ear. "And besides, I prefer this dynamic. Having you exposed and vulnerable while I'm fully dressed is a fantasy I never knew I had."

"That's where you're wrong. You're no longer in a position to make me vulnerable." She sidesteps to take her seat. If it weren't for the way she quickly grabs for the glass of wine, I'd almost believe her confidence.

"And why is that?" I place my bowl on the opposite table setting and slide into my chair.

"Because my vulnerability has only ever been exposed by people I care about, and you're no longer on that list."

This time, my chuckle isn't only fake—it's forced. "You've switched from love to loathing in such a short space of time, *amore mio*. Are you doing okay with the whiplash?"

She gives me a viperous smile and takes another sip of wine. "Thank you for your concern, but I'm doing just fine."

This isn't the conversation I planned to have. The mood and tone are all wrong. Yet I can't stop lapping up her venom. Each taste brings exhilaration.

My desire for her is already mutinous. Barely manageable. My palms sweat with the need to touch. I have to taste her. Breathe her in. Even with her vicious energy.

I incline my head and grab my fork. "Well, I appreciate you joining me."

"Are you under the misconception I had a choice?" Her tone is friendly even though the question drips with resentment.

"There's always a choice."

She bats her lashes. "As much as I'm enjoying this display of truly deplorable acting, we both know you took away my power to decline your offer when you mentioned my ability to call Stella."

I raise my brows and nod thoughtfully, spinning the tines of my fork into the spaghetti. "So I guess what you're saying is that you *are* still vulnerable to me."

Her facade falters with the brief flare of her nostrils.

She concedes a pawn in this provoking game of chess.

I raise my fork and take a bite, filling my mouth to lessen my victory grin as our gazes remain locked.

She doesn't eat though. She merely sits there, more than likely tweaking her mental strategy as she remains silent.

"I appreciate the eye contact, *amore mio*." I grab my wine glass and take a sip. "I'm not sure how I could remain a gentleman with such an exquisite temptation seated before me if it weren't for those hypnotic eyes."

"Let's not continue the sham that you've ever been a gentleman, Matthew. We both know you're nothing but a monster." She cocks her head and frowns. "Or should I say *butcher*?"

I take another sip—slow, drawn, smooth.

I won't hand over one of my chess pieces so easily. "Both are fitting. Although, I will argue that I've always been a gentleman to you."

"No, you've always been a liar."

"We both lied, Layla. We're even in that regard."

She scoffs and settles back into her chair, crossing her arms beneath her breasts, plumping them, attempting to use temptation to her advantage.

I don't look. Not directly. I let those luscious mounds taunt my periphery, the tease of nipples making my mouth salivate as I fork another mouthful of food.

I chew and swallow. Chew and swallow. I allow the silence to wrap her in a false sense of security while she remains poised on her mantle of superiority.

She's getting to me, though. With each poisonous retort, I fall victim to the brain fog of lust. I crave her capitulation. I need her to admit that she feels more for me than the animosity she's portraying.

What we had can't be extinguished by a few mistruths. Especially not when we were both duplicitous.

"I hope you're not getting cold." I fork more food and make a strategic surrender, lowering my gaze from those fathomless eyes to leisurely trek downward. I skate my attention from her lips to her collarbone, then farther to those perfectly ample breasts.

I can still taste the salt of her skin. Can still remember the deliriously soft texture.

She would moan whenever I sucked her nipples. She'd shudder.

Now, though, her breathing is calm. Measured. The only sign I'm having any effect on her is the wash of goose bumps that awaken under my gaze.

"I'm fine." Her civility wavers, her tone gaining a hint of annoyance.

"Are you sure?" I gradually return my attention to hers with a slight lick of my lower lip. I don't need to pretend I'm attracted to her. *Tempted* by her. That part of our relationship never held a hint of deception. "I could give you something to wear."

She grows an inch with my offering.

Are you handing over another pawn, amore mio?

She lowers her focus to my jacket and gives a subtle clearing of her throat before returning her gaze to my face with the Stepford act falling back into place. "That would be appreciated."

I lock my jaw, determined not to cluck my tongue as I steal her rook.

She came out here ready to instigate war and backtracked before swords clashed.

"Like I mentioned earlier, you only had to ask." I place down my fork, then slide a hand over my tie to slowly loosen it from around my neck.

She watches with interest, eyeing my shirt, no doubt anticipating the rich fabric resting against her shoulders. Would she appreciate my scent against her skin, too?

She remains still, her brows furrowing as I raise the tie over my head and slide it toward her.

"You're welcome," I purr.

I witness the moment my intent sinks in. When she realizes the only clothing I'll afford her is a thin slip of fabric.

Her tightly restrained anger is a work of art.

A masterpiece.

Her cheeks hollow. Her lips lose their color. She reaches for her fork, her fingers white with the tightness of her grip.

Go on, amore mio. *Bite. Sink those teeth into me. Let me have your rage.*

"I don't understand the hesitation?" I drawl. "You wanted something to wear, so put it on."

Her glare is gradual. From picture-perfect princess to viperous hellion in long, stretching heartbeats. She raises her feral stare, nailing me with undiluted fury. "I changed my mind."

"Put it on, Layla." I add an edge of malice to my tone. I'm more than happy to do this her way. We can fight, then fuck, then put this bump in the road behind us. *"Now."*

She doesn't move. The only action she takes is to narrow her eyes, intensifying her hatred.

"Interesting." I reach into my suit jacket, pull my cell from the inside pocket, and place the device on the table. "After sauntering out here in your current state, I thought you were willing to do whatever it took to speak to your daughter."

"You're a fucking bastard."

I shrug. "And you're a tempting goddess. We use what we have." I slide my fork into the pasta and twist. "Now put on the tie."

Her evil eyes attempt to burn me to the ground as she glares and glares and glares some fucking more. I'm sure she's about to grab her bowl and lob it at my head when she snatches the slip of fabric from the table and tugs it over her head, muttering a string of unintelligible delight under her breath.

She's gorgeous when outraged. Turbulent and unpredictable.

She might not realize it, but I've never cared for her more than I do right now. I'd protect this spitfire with my life. I'd carve her name into my skin to let the world know she owns every inch of me.

The tie settles between her breasts as she gathers her hair out from beneath the material and resettles the strands behind her back, her glower pinning me the entire time.

"It looks good on you." I grin. "Now eat."

"No, thank you," she grates.

"Would you prefer if I fed you? Because I will." My pulse spikes with possibility. I'd sit at her side, her hair in my fist, a fork in the other. I'd feed her gently. Patiently. And with every insolent remark she made, I'd whisper in her ear all the punishments I had planned once her belly was full.

"I already told you I'd lose my appetite if I had to share a meal with you."

"Don't tell me I misjudged your intelligence." I raise a brow. "I thought you were smarter than this."

"Meaning?"

"Denying what your body needs hurts nobody but yourself. You'll lose strength and focus. Malnourishment will only make it harder for you to find a way out of your situation. What you should actually be doing is taking every possible action to increase your chance of success… That is, if you want to get out of your predicament. But maybe remaining with me is what you truly want." I fork another mouthful.

"Monstrous and delusional." She scoffs a barely audible breath. "God, I'd love to know what lies you told my brother to add to his reasons for disowning me."

"Maybe he didn't disown you. Maybe he understands what you need more than you do and left you here to find happiness." *There.* She has the truth. I can't be held accountable for leading her astray.

"Happiness?" Her laughter increases, her breasts jolting with faux mirth. "You're a punishment, Matthew. A sickening, loathsome form of torture."

"You told your sister you were falling in love with me."

The briefest glimpse of pain pinches her features before anger reclaims supremacy. "I fell in love with a man who doesn't exist."

"He could exist, *amore mio*. I can be that man for you. I can be whatever you need." I want nothing more than to be the embodiment of the man she gave her heart to. To be trustworthy. Honorable. A successful businessman instead of a proficient murderer.

All it would take is a little more time to chip away at the brutal default settings that have been cemented in place.

"The only man you know how to be is a pathological liar."

"Pathological is a stretch. I assure you I had a motive for each and every instance of deception." I force another mouthful of spaghetti.

"I'm sure you had a whole string of motives, but none of them would make your actions excusable."

"Without those actions, we never would've existed."

"And the world would've been a far better place."

She doesn't mean that. Her anger is a front for her pain. Her temper is a vain attempt to hide how much she still wants me. And she *does* want me. I can see it in her eyes. The heat remains there, flickering and wild.

"All you need is a reason to forgive me and I can give that to you, too." I place the napkin back on the table and hold her stare. "My actions were a direct result of my infatuation. I would've done anything to keep you close, and I still will, because you're everything to me. I'm lost to you, Layla. Life without you isn't something I'm willing to concede to."

5

——————

LAYLA

I steal myself against his admission.

Thought by thought, brick by brick, I frantically build my walls higher against his seduction. I remind myself of what he's done. I relive the hypocrisy. The malignance.

But it's hard.

Even now, with hatred swimming in my veins, I can't switch myself off to his charm.

That's why I stayed in my room for three days. I needed the time to assemble my defenses. It's also why I came out here in my current state of undress.

I'd hoped to distract him from the wicked way he weaves me around his little finger. That my body would leave him tongue-tied and disheveled. That for once, I could be the reigning force. The superior. A victor.

Instead, I've achieved the opposite.

He's far more confident and cunning now. Each retort seems perfectly constructed, as if spoken from a playbook, while I struggle to keep a grip on my hectic emotions.

The conversation I hoped we would never have is now tormenting my ears, his words of adoration stripping layers from my shield.

I'd treasured him. With all my heart, I'd *loved* him.

"You've owned me from the first night we met." He holds my stare, those dark eyes exuding sincerity I refuse to believe. "I knew it wasn't a coincidence that this beautiful woman walked into Perfezione not once, but twice, to spy on the same man I despise."

"Your *father*," I correct.

"Bishop approached you at my request." He ignores my strike with ease. "I needed to know what you were up to. Who you were. Where the hell you came from. But you looked at him in fear, and the sight sickened me."

"It mustn't sicken you now, because you certainly haven't lost your appetite."

"You don't fear me. A scared woman would never choose to walk out here the way you did. Instead, I'd place a substantial wager that you've enjoyed triggering my desire. And then there's that sharp tongue of yours." He rakes his teeth over his lower lip as his gaze devours me. "I don't like that I've earned your spite, but I'll be honest in admitting how fucking hard it makes me."

"If you ever talk to me about being hard again, I'll make sure your body can no longer facilitate the function." I struggle to regain my synthetic smile. To pretend I'm unfazed. Dauntless.

He grins, calling my bluff. His composure spits in the face of my tumultuous pulse. "If the task involves placing your hands around my dick, it might just be worth it."

I increase the brittle curve of my lips and grab my fork in a clenched fist. "Then get it out, big guy. Let me take a stab."

He takes a sip of wine. "I don't think your viciousness is having the effect you want it to."

I know it's not, and it's fucking killing me. He needs to take me seriously. To be scared of me.

"Give it time, *amore mio*. I'm certain I'll earn your forgiveness."

"And I'm certain I'd prefer to see you dead."

His brows pinch. "You don't mean that."

I know. But I wish I did.

I'd give anything to be able to treat him with the same callous disregard he gave me while I was falling for him.

"You had me mugged." I speak through clenched teeth. "Tell me, Matthew, what would've happened if I didn't give up my purse? Would you have had me beaten instead of shoved into a wall? Did my attacker have permission to rape as well as ransack?"

He raises his chin, his eyes hardening. "He was never meant to lay a hand on you."

"But he did. My face was bruised—"

"And he paid for his mistake. I know that doesn't improve the situation, but the lengths he went to were neither planned nor excused."

Curiosity twists my stomach. I shouldn't ask, yet the words escape my lips without consent. "What did you do to him?"

He doesn't look away. Doesn't flinch or waver under the question. "What do you think a man like me would do?"

A chill sinks under my skin.

"A man who was already irrevocably obsessed with you, Layla. *Enslaved* by you."

I swallow over my drying throat, hating the idiotic thrill that sweeps through me at the stupid thought of him taking vengeance against a man he contracted in the first place. "Forget it. I don't want to know."

"Are you sure? I thought you'd want the truth. *Honesty*. To learn the *real* me." He leans back in his chair. "I made him understand your worth. Your significance. I used the knives and blades that had once been my calling card to ensure—"

"That's enough." I drop my fork, the silverware clattering to the table.

"I disagree. You need clarity for us to get back to where we once were."

"When have I given you the impression there was even the slightest possibility of going back?"

"We *will* get back to where we were, *amore mio*." His voice becomes a threatening growl. "I won't accept any other outcome."

The chill escapes me, the coldness eviscerated by white-hot rage. I shove to my feet, the chair scraping loudly behind me, the stupid fucking tie acting like a pendulum between my breasts. "I'm done with your delusions."

I'm about to storm for the bedroom when he reaches for his cell, subtly tapping the device with his pointer finger

"Are you sure?" He looks up at me. No smirk. No anger. Just pure confidence in those chocolate eyes.

Fuck him.

He knows it's been days since I spoke to Stella. I have no idea what Cole has told her. I don't know where she is. Or if she's protected. I've had to rely on the assumption that my brother continues to cherish her safety even though he's discarded mine so easily.

"There's no going back from what you've done." I stand tall, trying hard to remain confident with my nudity while his tie begins to feel like a noose. "You arranged for me to be mugged. Then had the audacity to sleep with me. And that was just the tip of your duplicity."

"You're wrong." He sits straighter. "I didn't sleep with you that day. I deliberately kept sex off the table even though, if memory serves, you begged for me to fuck you. Instead, I gave pleasure and tortured myself in return."

After everything he's done, he still has the nerve to claim *he* was the one being tortured?

I want to hurt him. *Kill* him.

"Every moment we spent together was a well concocted fallacy." I push the words through clenched teeth. "You acted surprised when I told you about the cyanide—"

"I *was* surprised. Not that you had it. But that you owned up—"

"You lied and pretended and conned," I speak over him. "You deceived and distorted. You were sly and cunning and cruel."

"Because I adore you," he states simply. "And you began to feel the same about me. I gave us a chance at being together and had every intention of telling you the truth. In my own way. In my own time. If it weren't for Remy—"

I slam my fists on the table, rattling the bowls and cutlery. "Remy's appearance changed nothing. His *existence* was the problem. His *genetics*. The fact he's your *goddamn brother* and was involved in my husband's murder." I scream at him, my face hot, my blood boiling. "You made me worship a fictional character. I loved a man that was make believe."

He pushes from his seat, poised and confident. "And I'll make sure you feel the same about the real me."

My heart skips a beat. I'm not sure if it's in fear or frustration. Rage or resentment. But the tempo in my chest pauses a moment only to kick back at a manic pace.

I suck in a slow breath, begging my pulse to calm, my lunacy to ease. "It doesn't matter what personality you present. I won't stop hating you. And once I finally figure out my next move—after you did such a fantastic job of ruining my life—I hope to God I never see you again. Do you understand me?"

His lips thin. His shoulders stiffen. Everything about his expression is tight, especially the skin over the faint swelling on his cheek from my brother's attack.

Could I have finally gotten to him?

"Now I expect you to make good on your promise and let me call my daughter."

He's silent, the quiet palpable until he reclaims his seat with equal poise and confidence as when he left it. He grabs his wine glass, takes a lazy, taunting sip, then raises his condescending gaze to mine. "If you expect me to make good on my promise, you need to make good on yours. The deal was that we would eat together. You've barely lifted your fork."

Fucking bastard.

I'll lift my damn fork. I'll stab it right through his motherfucking jugular.

He doesn't care if I eat. All he wants is power. *Control.*

"I'm not hungry." I enunciate each word in a slow, drawn out growl.

"And I don't give a shit." He matches my tone, his mood shifting to menace. "Sit. Eat. Or you don't get a fucking phone call." He leans forward, roughly discarding his jacket to throw the heavy material across the table at me. "And the next time you think it's a good idea to parade around naked, be aware I won't restrain myself. I *will* fuck you, *amore mio*. And you *will* enjoy it."

6

LAYLA

I force myself to eat, taking dainty bite after dainty bite until most of my meal is gone.

I don't speak a word. I don't make eye contact.

I scoop and swallow, keeping my composure in check, playing the game.

"You will forgive me." His declaration is barely audible and still has the ability to raise the hair on the back of my neck. "I won't stop until you do."

I shiver, the warmth of his coat doing nothing to shield me from the chilling effects of his commitment.

Why did he have to be the devil? Why couldn't I find a normal man to fall for?

"I've upheld my part of the deal." I place my fork down. "Now can I get my phone call?"

I meet his gaze, being hit hard with emotionless eyes. Even sterile and impassive, he's handsome. So goddamn handsome it makes the contents of my stomach churn. It doesn't help that I'm cloaked in his scent, the deliciously woodsy aftershave sinking into my lungs with every breath.

"One phone call." He slides the cell toward me. "While in this room."

I scoff. "You think I'm capable of calling reinforcements? Who could I possibly rely on that hasn't turned against me?"

"Stay in this room, Layla."

I wait until his hand retreats, then grab the device and push to my feet. I don't waste time dialing Stella's number as I walk alongside the wall of glass, Matthew's jacket dwarfing me.

Each trilling ring makes my heart swell with anticipation. My throat burns with the need to hear her voice. But I can't let her know I'm broken. I won't put her through more heartache. Despite Matthew being a voyeur to the upcoming conversation as he begins to clear the table, I have to pretend my life is peachy. That I'm loving my beach escape with a crazed butcher.

"Hello?" Stella says in greeting. "Who is this?"

Emotion clogs my throat. "Hey, little fish." I force a chipper tone, my bravado painfully flawless. "How are you?"

"Mom? Whose phone number is this? I've been trying to call you. Uncle Cole said you went on a last-minute vacation and might not have cell service. But I call bullshit. You wouldn't go away without telling me. You didn't even send a text."

"Don't curse, sweetheart." I close my eyes against the anxiety in her voice. I've failed her for the millionth time. "Uncle Cole was right. I made a snap decision to go to the beach but I lost my phone at the airport and the cell service here is terrible. I haven't been able to call until now. Is everything all right?"

"Everything is fine. It's just not like you to go radio silent for days. I was worried."

I scrunch my nose against the building tingle. "Forgive me. I've been having such a great time that I didn't realize how many days had passed."

It's been four. I could determine the last time we spoke right down to the hour. But she needs to think I'm happy and healthy. Not humiliated and vengeful.

"Who did you go away with?" she asks. "Last time I came home from boarding school, Tobias overheard Uncle Cole talking about a man you met. Are you dating?"

Pain stabs between my ribs, savage and cruel. "No, we're just friends."

"Are you sure? Because I don't mind." She pauses, the silence heavy between us. "It's been years since Dad passed."

I clamp the cell tighter. "I know. But that's not what this is. I've been going stir crazy at home and just needed a change of scenery. Has anything exciting happened at school this week?" *Deflect, deflect, deflect.* "Are you keeping on top of your homework?"

"Nothing has changed here. Some of my friends were actually about to watch a movie together in the hall... so I've kinda gotta go."

My misery increases with every shallow breath. "Already?"

The clatter of bowls and cutlery carries from the kitchen behind me. Pots and pans follow. It's scripted, as if Matthew wants me to believe he's distracted and not devouring every morsel of my anguish.

"I don't want to miss the start, Mom. Can we chat tomorrow?"

The clog in my throat becomes a jagged rock, threatening to take over my stable tone. "I'll try. But like I mentioned, cell service isn't great here. I'm not sure when I'll be able to speak to you again." I don't know when *he'll* let me.

"That's fine. As long as I know you're okay and having fun, I don't mind. Call whenever you can."

"Okay. Enjoy yourself. And say hello to Tobias for me." I hang my head and pinch the bridge of my nose.

"I will. I promise."

"I love you, little fish." My voice breaks. It's only slight. The start of an avalanche that threatens to buckle me.

"I love you, too. Night."

The line disconnects. My heart wrenches.

But she's all right. Cole weaved fiction for me. I need to be grateful for that. He's still doing everything in his power to shield her from my poor decisions.

I delete the call log from the cell, then let my arms fall limp at my sides as I focus on the moonlight reflecting against the inky-black ocean. I have to figure out what the hell I'm doing. How to redeem myself in the eyes of my family.

Cole said I need to fix my mistakes.

How do I do that? Where do I even start?

"Is she okay?" Matthew approaches.

I wrap his jacket tight around me, needing another barrier against him. "Don't."

"Don't what?" He stops a few feet away, his commanding frame stalking my periphery. "Don't ask? Don't care? Don't speak?"

"All of the above." I hold out his cell.

He takes the device but those calloused fingers linger on mine. "You need someone to talk to. To vent to."

"Are you serious?" I release a low murmur of a chuckle as I drop my arm back to my side, my laughter increasing as he looks at me in pity. "*You're* the reason I need to vent. You get that, right? *You're* the reason I'm in need of everything right now—clothes, money, safety, shelter. I have nothing. Not a dime to my name or a shred of dignity. All because of you."

"You're safe here. And like I've already said, I can give you whatever you need. All you have to do is ask."

I shouldn't have to beg for the things he took from me.

"Ask, Layla," he murmurs.

No. I was willing to demean myself and jump through hoops to speak to Stella, but I'd rather live in the same clothes for the rest of my life than ask him for help.

"I can take care of you." He steps into my personal space, awakening all my nerve endings.

I smile, scoff, then finally sink into a deep sigh. "Do you not understand your role? Why are you acting like a misunderstood victim when you're the villain? You're vile, Matthew." Handsome and brilliant, yet so incredibly vile. "You're depraved, immoral, and goddamn evil."

The pity slowly seeps from his narrowing eyes, his gaze turning predatory.

I fight against another shiver.

He's looked at me like that before. In the bedroom. Between satin sheets. With his fingers gripping my skin and his teeth scraping my heated flesh.

I hate him for stoking those memories to life. I hate even more that my body welcomes it.

I clamp my mouth shut and glare, hoping the action will stop my tongue tingling.

"I'm depraved?" He inches closer, until we're almost chest to chest. "Immoral? Evil?" He quirks a brow. He's so close I can feel the heat emanating off him, can breathe his essence into my lungs. "Tell me, *amore mio,* what part of that description turns you on the most?"

He's right. I am turned on.

Despite the hatred and fury, he still makes me burn. But that's muscle memory. A miscommunication between mind and body. It won't last long.

"The devil comes in an enticing package," I purr. "That doesn't mean I'm willing to see past all the pretty ribbon now that your true colors have been exposed."

He leans in, those brown irises unfathomably dark as he peers down his nose at me. "But this enticing package knows how to make you feel good."

He does. Oh, *God*, how he does.

The flashbacks play on a loop in my mind. The pleasure he's given. The ecstasy he's produced. Problem is, he also knows how to shatter me beyond recognition. Heartache has never been more potent. Shame consumes my every breath.

"Get away from me," I seethe, my chin high.

"I can't." He reaches out, gliding a lone finger along the jacket lapel.

I stiffen, my head hating the contact, my tingling limbs exhibiting the opposite reaction, and my heart... *Jesus Christ*, the weak, pathetic organ falters.

It's all a game. He wants me to cave. To submit. What I don't understand is why? To prove he's the almighty conqueror? To cement his victory and my pathetic existence?

Fuck him.

Whatever the reason, I can't lose this time.

I straighten my shoulders, allowing the jacket to gape. I won't let him know I'm daunted by a simple touch. By mere proximity. "I said, get away from me."

His gaze lowers to take in my exposure, the slightest rumble of appreciation emanating from his chest. "I'll never be able to walk away from you, *amore mio*." His finger moves to the edge of the lapel, his skin making contact with mine along the inner curve of my breast.

I clench my teeth against the hardening of my nipples. I swallow over the explosion of rage.

I hate him for this. For the pleasure and the pain.

I despise the lust in his eyes. I loathe the confidence in his touch.

This is how he entrapped me the first time. He made me capitulate to adoration. To being wanted. Desired.

"I'll make sure you don't merely walk," I promise. "You'll run."

His mouth lifts at one side, the grin making me see red. "Do I need to remind you your savagery has the opposite effect to your intentions?" His fingertip brushes my stomach, the touch sparking flames in my belly.

Fuck him.

Fuck everything about him—his enviable looks, his commanding presence, his sinful eroticism.

I never understood ecstasy until he entered my life. I hadn't known what one person could stoke within another from mere words or brief glances. But when we were together—actually connected, body to body—the sensation was unlike anything I shared through years of marriage.

Only now, the zing Matthew provides is coated with a dark undercurrent of violence. A sinister, wicked intent, and I'm ashamed to admit it's all the more alluring.

"Forgive me," he murmurs, his hand trailing lower to my abdomen, then my mons.

I remain still, holding eye contact while he attempts to win me over. *Screw* me over.

I keep myself in check. Levelled breathing. Stiffened stance. I don't show a flicker of the flames he's stoking inside me.

I disassociate from my rampant pulse and aching breasts.

He sweeps his touch farther, his fingers parting to tease along the outer edges of my sex. "Forgive me, *amore mio.*"

My denial comes in the form of silence, the rejection loud between us.

"How can I redeem myself?" His breath brushes my lips, the scent of sweet alcohol teasing my senses. "What do I have to do?"

I fight a shudder, my pussy throbbing. I'm wet, my slickness dampening my inner thighs. "Your death is the only way to gain absolution."

He doesn't react. Not a flinch or a smirk in sight. He continues teasing those fingertips around the outside of my sex, increasing my need for oxygen.

He inches closer, his chest brushing mine as his mouth approaches my ear. "I would willingly die for you, *amore mio.*" The delicate sweep of his breath awakens a shiver along my neck. "But not without your forgiveness."

"Then we're at an impasse."

"I guess so." His arms swoop around my waist, lifting me off the floor. I gasp, not only at the abrupt movement but the vacuum of pleasure, as he carries me like a rag doll, backtracking me across the room.

I don't protest. Don't speak. Don't fight.

I take another strategy, letting him think he's in control while I eagerly plan my victory.

He places me down on the table, the wall of glass behind him reflecting what a voyeur might consider a loving moment but instead is a power play.

"Spread your legs," he demands.

"Spread my legs?" I ask slowly, taking my time, splaying my hands on the polished wood behind me, the coat gaping to expose my middle, my breasts on display.

He bites his lower lip, the hunger increasing in his eyes. He's starved for me. Ravenous. "Spread those beautiful fucking legs, Layla. Or I'll spread them for you."

"No, you won't."

He's not in charge here. Neither am I. But he doesn't need to know that.

His nostrils flare. He won't force me. Won't hurt me. Not physically. He prefers to do it mentally, *emotionally,* or he'd get someone else to do his dirty work.

He braces his hands on either side of my hips, looming close. "Do you want me to beg? Is that it? Do you need to hear how much I want to make this up to you?"

It's too late for that.

What I want is his agony. His torture.

Slowly, I spread my legs, giving him more room between my thighs. He acknowledges the feigned acquiescence with the slightest clench of his jaw. He thinks he's winning. Maybe he is.

"Allevia la mia sofferenza, amore mio, perché non posso stare senza di te."

"More lies?" I ask. "Speaking in another language doesn't make your words less deceptive."

"There's no more lies. I can promise you that."

I ignore the clench of my heart, the weak organ demanding my submission.

He places his hands on my knees, gradually sliding his palms higher and higher, making my core throb with the promise of pleasure.

He's so close, those hard eyes mere inches from mine. But he doesn't kiss me. Doesn't attempt to make the connection affectionate. He's smart enough to know I'd never allow that tenderness.

I hold my breath as his touch climbs higher, approaching my sex for a second round of temptation.

He doesn't quit staring at me while those fingers skim the sensitive skin at the apex of my thighs. He doesn't even blink when his thumbs reach my folds to part my flesh.

I bite the inside of my lip, refusing to show appreciation for the burst of tingles. But there's definitely a burst. After three days of unwavering heartache, the suffering keeping me bedridden, this indulgent thrill is an undeniable counterpart.

"I'll spend the rest of my life making this up to you," he promises.

I deflect the agony of his vow with a sinister smile. "Then I guess I need to ensure you don't have much longer to live."

He grins, eyes blazing, a dimple teasing.

God, I wish he wasn't so damn gorgeous.

"You underestimate my dedication." He circles his thumb at my entrance. The slightest movement. The harshest tease. "My devotion would only increase in the afterlife. What else would my spirit want to do other than adore you?"

My pulse falters.

I clench my teeth and remind myself how I got here. That the pleasure is only intense due to the preceding pain.

Focus. Focus. Focus.

He gently glides his thumb inside me. I can't stop my pussy from eagerly clamping around the intrusion. I can't quit staring at the gaze that calls to me like home. He's attempting to infiltrate my heart all over again, to decimate what little strength I have left.

"I can read your thoughts, *amore mio*." He curls his thumb inside me, hooking the digit, circling to find the perfect spot that makes me buzz. "You want this."

He's right.

The pulse in my core thunders. My abdomen heats. And my breasts. Dear Lord, how they throb.

It takes all my restraint not to plead for him to make me come.

"You want *me*." He increases his rhythm, stroking with that hooked thumb, delving it deeper inside.

I don't answer with anything other than a gasped breath. I can't hold it in. My pulse is too rampant. My desire too strong.

I claw my fingers against the table, scratching my nails into the gloss.

It's useless to deny what he stokes inside me. I'm not naive enough to even try.

Instead, I continue staring into those fathomless eyes as I roll my hips, grinding into his hand. His breathing increases to match mine, each exhale a muted growl of approval.

He doesn't attempt to deepen the connection. There are no kisses. No lingering touches. He's waiting for permission. For me to cave.

I arch my back, the jacket parting farther to barely cover my shoulders as I thrust my breasts toward him.

His gaze treks the temptation. His tongue swipes out to lick his lower lip. He wants to take this further. Wants to grasp and suck and bite. His restraint only makes me hotter.

I cherish his suffering. Devour it.

"Tell me you forgive me," he growls. "Tell me we can move on."

"Never." I grind harder, faster.

With every roll of my hips, I delight in my progress toward the finish line, knowing he won't reach the same pinnacle with me ever again. I use him, cheapening every heated moment we've shared as my pussy clenches around his fingers, the slickness of my arousal coating the inside of my thighs.

His exhales become animalistic. The heavy rise and fall of his chest simulates a beast in battle. I can sense the stiffness of his cock. Can practically feel how hard he must be throbbing because every ounce of blood in my veins does the same.

"Forgive me." He pulses his thumb, wilder, sharper, demanding submission I will never give. "For the love of God, forgive me, *amore mio*."

I let my head fall back, blocking out his sickening pleas, the mistruths, and allow my eyes to roll with the approaching orgasm.

I relax into the wave of gluttonous pleasure that overwhelms me, and come with a breathy whimper. Over and over, my core contracts, the thrill consuming my limbs. My heart. My mind.

For the briefest seconds, there's nothing but bliss.

Pure. Effortless. Freeing.

The peace I previously found in him returns as if it never left. The world corrects itself for a few brief moments.

I'm at home. Happy. Alive.

Then with each ebbing pulse of euphoria, reality seeps in.

I blink back to the here and now, where the sponsorship deal for my life is still owned by misery, and sit up straight.

He removes his touch from my body, his eyes intense with potent hunger as he raises a hand to his mouth. He swipes his thumb over his lower lip, coating the darkened flesh with my glistening arousal before deftly licking it away with his tongue.

My breath catches as his eyes close briefly and a low rumble of appreciation hums from his chest. I could come again from the visual alone. Not only his enjoyment of my taste, but the adamant bulge against his pants zipper.

I've always been hypnotized by his want for me. It's a weakness I can no longer afford to indulge, but it's perfect to exploit.

"You were right." I sit straighter, placing a hand on his chest to push him out of my personal space. "I'll concede that much."

His brow raises in question. "How so?"

"You told me not to deny my body's needs. And using you for gratification has me feeling invincible." I pause, waiting for the twinge in his expression that exposes his blindsiding failure.

It doesn't eventuate.

Instead, he regains the devil's look, his mouth tweaking in a sly grin. "You think I didn't know you were attempting to use me?" I stiffen as his gaze rakes over my breasts and lower, his focus stopping at my exposed sex with a breathy snicker. "Believe me, I was well aware this was a third-base hate fuck."

Bullshit.

He didn't know. He had no clue.

"The thing is, *amore mio…*" Slowly his attention raises to mine, his smirk increasing. "You can't use someone when their only goal is to achieve what you've just willingly given. Being able to pleasure you—*taste you*—is a blessing. A goddamn gift. So although you consider yourself the victor, I can assure you my gratification far outweighed your own."

My cheeks flame, the heat seeping down my neck, the defeat burning my throat.

"Aww, you're so sweet." I paste on a smile, not willing to surrender. "But for the sake of this awkward post-coital conversation, I think I'll take my needs to Bishop next time."

He snickers, menacing and low. The pinch of his eyes that tells me I've hit a sore spot. "You'd be giving him a death sentence."

"Are you trying to discourage or entice?" I inch forward until our noses almost meet. "Because I assure you, you've done the latter. Two birds with one stone and all that."

His nostrils flare.

Good.

I'm crawling under his skin.

Goddamn perfect.

We stay there. Breath mingling. Gazes locked.

Dopamine floods my system as rage glazes his eyes. My pulse flutters with the win.

"We're done here." He shoves back from the table, his shoulders tight, his jaw clenched. "Sleep well, *amore mio.*"

"I appreciate the well wishes. But in contrast, I'd suggest you rest with one eye open." I scoot from the table. "You never know who might attempt to slit your throat during the early morning hours."

He repeats the sinister snicker, the sound sending a chill down my spine. "As long as you're making plans to climb into my bed, Layla, I don't care what the fuck you do while you're there."

7

———

LAYLA

I wake to the cold morning air seeping into my skin. Matthew's jacket gapes over my naked chest, the soft sheets tangled around my legs.

Cigarette smoke teases my senses, the scent faint yet enough to wake me.

It's dark. No sunlight carries from the yard, but birds chirp, signaling the approaching sunrise.

I fling back the covers and slide from the bed to pad to the glass door leading outside.

Bishop stands a few yards away, facing the ocean, his forearms resting against the deck railing. A lit cigarette hangs from his hand, the tendrils of smoke bleeding into the fading night. He's already dressed, his suit pants and buttoned shirt immaculate as usual. Or maybe he didn't change from yesterday. Maybe he's like me, and this unwanted situation is making it hard for him to sleep.

A gun sticks out of the back of his waistband, the weapon sparking dark ideas that are becoming all the more common since being disowned by my family.

I unlock the door, slide it open, then walk out onto the wooden deck, the chill biting into my toes. "I didn't know you smoked," I murmur in greeting, cinching Matthew's jacket tight around my chest, the hem falling to midthigh.

He keeps his stare on the horizon, the cigarette still dangling from his loose fingers. "Only when the situation demands it." He raises the cancer stick to his mouth to breathe deep, the resulting smoke exhaled in a smooth glide from shadowed lips.

I stop a few feet from his side and mimic his position. "And what situation demands it?"

He shoots me a sideways glance, letting me know I'm the situation. "It's nice to see you've ditched the minimalist fashion sense. I assume dinner went well if you're in his jacket."

"You assume wrong. I have very few options when it comes to clothes." My only outfit remains in the dryer, ready and waiting for me to wear for yet another day.

He returns his attention to the ocean and takes another drag. "When you fuck up your life, I guess you're not one to do it in style." He flicks the half-used cigarette to the lawn, then straightens and walks away.

There's no farewell.

He descends the stairs, disappearing from view, his footsteps receding before I hear the whoosh of a sliding door.

"It's always a pleasure, Bishop," I mutter.

I don't know why I bothered talking to him. I've despised that man from the moment we met. But in hindsight, I didn't understand what his warnings to stay away from Matthew meant.

I thought it was for my betrayer's benefit. Not mine.

I stare at the growing sunrise, begging the breaking dawn to bring answers to where I need to go from here. I have to make a move. To find money, clothes, and a more effective way to communicate with Stella.

You need to learn to clean up the mess you create.

Yeah, there's that, too. I just wish I understood what mess Cole was referring to. I've created a junk yard full of trash and don't know which pile he needs actioned.

Do I have to level the playing field with Matthew, repaying him for the humiliation he caused me and my family? Or was it the discovery of my attempted revenge plot against the Costas that caused my brother to disown me? Do I need to make good on my plan to kill Emmanuel?

I'll happily do both. I just have to figure out how to do it without any money.

Another whoosh of the sliding door sounds from the ground level. Bishop's footsteps follow. He comes into view on the stairs, his scowl hard in the dim light as he holds some sort of material in his hands.

"Here." He continues toward me, then flings the clothing at my chest.

I catch two separate pieces from the air. "What's this?"

"Shirts for you to sleep in." He reclaims his position against the railing, his forearms against the metal, his gun teasing my line of sight. "Don't let Langston see you in them. I'm not taking a bullet to the brain for you."

I nod, understanding his gruffness for what it truly is—a peace offering.

"Thank you." I stare down at the soft cotton, running the material through my fingers. "I appreciate it."

He grunts. "At this point, you're welcome to my entire wardrobe if it means I never have to see you naked again."

My cheeks burn, the heat travelling down my neck. "Don't worry; you won't."

"Good. He's not usually the jealous type, but last night..." He shakes his head. "You shouldn't taunt him like that."

"Why? Do you think he'll hurt me?"

"No. He already hates himself for lying to you."

"He didn't just lie. It was—"

"I don't give a shit about the technicalities—that's for you two to argue. What you need to realize is that when he gives his loyalty, he gives it all. It's not half-assed or temporary. He moves mountains, which is exactly what happened with Lorenzo. He became obsessed with allegiance, doing whatever his uncle asked without a second thought, and he'll do the same to get you back."

My stomach hollows. My chest, too.

I breathe a soft chuckle to dislodge the yearning. "He can't win me back."

"Then prepare to watch the world burn to the ground while he spends the rest of his life failing. He won't give up, Layla."

"If that's the case, maybe I should ask him to start burying bodies. He can do my dirty work for me."

"With Lorenzo, there were too many to bury," he states simply.

My hollowness increases.

I've spent days trying to recall what I once thought were inconsequential headlines about the Butcher Boys of Baltimore. They were a threat on the other side of the country. A part of the underworld too far away to take notice of. Now I wish I'd paid more attention.

"Why are you telling me this?" I straighten. "Do you want me to be scared of him?"

"With your lack of self-preservation, I didn't think you were capable of fear. But you're not in danger, Layla. What I was attempting to inspire was concern for those around you. Now and in the future."

I frown as the building sunrise glows across his face. "What does that mean?"

"He's a ticking time bomb." He shoves a hand into his pocket and pulls out a cigarette packet. "Anyone who gets in the way of what he has planned for you won't survive."

"And what does he have planned for me?"

He shrugs. "God only knows. I'm not even sure what he said to get your brother to walk away."

I'm not certain either. All I know is that it wouldn't have been kind.

It's true Cole and I weren't on the best of terms. But leaving me with Matthew like this had to have taken an unwarranted amount of bad-mouthing from my betrayer.

"I won't be here long." I stand tall with the admission. I'm going to leave. To escape this cage without bars. I just need to figure out a plan.

He scoffs. "Sure you are."

I ignore the dismissal and focus on the birds chirping in nearby trees as the sun breaches the horizon. I should go inside and get dressed, but it's peaceful out here. Almost normal, if only I could force my reasons for being in this place to the back of my mind and simply pretend I'm on vacation.

The sun brings warmth. There's no breeze. Only crystal-clear skies filled with a kaleidoscope of orange, red, and yellow.

Behind us, the scrape of tugged curtains skitters along a track, raising the hair on the back of my neck.

I glance over my shoulder to see Matthew standing at the glass door of his room wearing nothing but boxers, his face an expressionless mask as he glances from Bishop to me.

Bishop doesn't move from the railing. He doesn't react to the threat like I do with my straightening posture, my arms crossing over my chest.

My heart shifts pace, too, the once lazy beat transitioning into a staccato.

Matthew pulls the door open, his hair mussed from sleep, his bare torso a masterpiece of temptingly smooth muscles.

"You two are up early." He keeps his focus on me. "Did you sleep in my jacket, *amore mio*?"

"It's not yours anymore."

He chuckles, his satanic smile making my stomach churn. "Have breakfast with me and you'll earn the use of my credit card to order new clothes."

I'll earn it?

I'll. Fucking. Earn. It?

I clench my teeth. "You told me last night you'd give me everything I need."

"I didn't say it wouldn't come without strings."

I switch my attention to glare at Bishop's profile, waiting for him to give Matthew the lecture on taunting just like he gave me. But the jerk doesn't acknowledge either of us, making that gun in the back of his waistband seem so goddamn inviting as he continues to stare at the sunrise.

"What's wrong, *amore mio*? Can't find the words to ask for what you need?"

"Nothing's wrong." I smile and raise the shirts Bishop gave me. "I've got all I need right here. It doesn't get much better than being able to wear an attractive man's clothes."

Matthew continues to grin, only now it's brittle. Forced.

"I'm going to get dressed." I wink at him. "I'm looking forward to smelling like your best friend all day."

8
____

MATTHEW

She saunters into her room, my jacket dwarfing her frame as she shuts the door behind her, then yanks the curtain closed.

It takes all my control to remain in place. To not stalk after her. To stop myself from killing Bishop.

"Jesus Christ." He lights a cigarette and takes a drag. "It didn't take her long to throw me under the fucking bus."

"Why did you give her your clothes?" I keep my voice level, not allowing a hint of jealousy to spill free.

"I thought that was the better alternative to seeing her tits again." He keeps his back to me as he takes another long drag, his attention on the horizon. "Was I wrong?"

I clench my teeth, picturing her in his shirt, the smell of his aftershave on her skin. Yes, it's a better alternative, but *my* clothes would've been preferred. *My* scent.

I move to his side, resting my ass against the railing, my gaze remaining on her door. "You're smoking again."

"Desperate times," he mutters.

I cringe. I haven't seen him succumb in years. Not since we were in the trenches with Lorenzo. "Has a set of tits got you running scared? I would've thought you weren't so easy to spook."

He scoffs. "It's not the tits. It's the motherfucker who owns them."

I don't own them. Or her. Maybe I had at one point, but nothing of hers is mine now, and I'm not sure if it ever will be again.

Her hatred is impenetrable. I hadn't wanted to believe it, especially last night while her pussy had clamped around my thumb, her arousal dripping to coat my hand. I'd thought I was winning her over. That desire would be the toppling point for her anger. But she'd walked from the living room with just as much vehement superiority as she'd had when she entered.

"Why are you taunting her?" He pushes from the railing to turn to me. "I just told her to quit doing the same thing, then you waltz out here to start shit again."

I don't know.

There's no strategy. I'm riding the waves here. Up one minute. Free-falling the next.

"Answer me," he grates. "Tell me why we're here. Why *she's* here." He glances toward Layla's room and lowers his voice. "What did you say to her brother? Why did he agree to let you abduct his goddamn sister? Did you threaten him? Are we at war?"

"There's no war." Not yet, anyway. Only time will tell.

"Then what's happening? Why am I playing house with homicidal Adam and psycho Eve?"

"Because I won't let her go."

He rolls his eyes. "That much is obvious. But why did he?"

I don't know. Maybe her brother felt sorry for my pathetic ass. Or maybe he knew only death would stop me from leaving without her. "She loves me."

"She *loved* you. Past tense." He points a menacing finger toward her door. "That right there is contempt."

"I'll change her mind." I pivot to the sunrise and bridge the space between me and the railing, grabbing the cold metal in tight fists. "She was somewhat receptive to me last night."

"If you're talking about your hand all up in her cookie jar, then I'm well aware. I had the misfortune of coming upstairs to return my dinner bowl and got yet another front-row seat to you two going at it." His eyes harden. "Tell me something, Langston, do I look like someone who wanted to be signed up to your OnlyFans?"

The bitter taste of jealousy assails me again.

I've never felt this before. Never come close to wanting to poke out the eyes of my closest confidant just for seeing my obsession naked.

"The correct response is no," he answers for me. "And while we're on the topic of your unhinged mating rituals, can you please clarify why you're fucking baiting her into homicide? Why can't you just give her space?"

"I've decided I prefer carnage to apathy." The former is where I'm at home. In my element. It's a fucking default. "I'm not wasting any more time. I won't let her go."

"And Torian is aware of your barbarian mindset?"

I clench the railing tighter, the brightening sunlight making me squint.

"Langston?" His scowl stalks my periphery. "What did you say to convince him to cut ties?"

"He hasn't cut them." I keep my voice low, ensuring Layla doesn't overhear.

"Are you sure about that? She's under the impression her brother disowned her."

"That's not the case. He's given me thirty days."

There's a beat of silence. A pause of building anger where the call of birds echo from the trees.

"Thirty days for what?"

I stand tall, anticipating his reaction before I voice the admission. "To win her back."

There's more silence. More increasing aggression.

"And if you don't?" he grates.

"Failing isn't an option."

"Well, winning won't be either if you continue baiting her, you stupid fuck. What happens after the goddamn thirty days?"

"Lower your voice," I warn. "He didn't say and I didn't ask."

He steps closer, getting in my face, the cigarette smoke hovering between us. "He didn't say? You didn't fucking ask? Am I just meant to—"

"It's an open-ended deal. If I fail, he gets whatever he wants from *me*. I'll be his to own. Not you. Not her. Just *me*."

He glares. Tight-lipped. Nostrils flared. Then he shoves his free hand into his hair and steps away, turning his back. "You've lost your goddamn mind."

"My life is with her," I state simply.

"She doesn't want you." He swings around to face me, livid, muscles tense. "You burned that bridge and pissed on the ashes. How can you not see that?"

"She'll forgive me." She fucking has to.

He shakes his head, incredulous.

He doesn't understand her value. How priceless it is to have someone who can quieten my demons. Without her, the darkness is clawing its way back in. My restraint toward the outside world is nonexistent.

"You can walk," I offer. "I've said it before, and nothing has changed—leave if you need to. I won't hold it against you. You'll always be my brother."

"Walk?" He grows inches taller with the straightening of his posture. "I can fucking walk, can I? With half your fucking gene pool on the attack and assholes already watching us from the shadows, I can just fucking walk?"

I tense. "Someone's watching us?"

"Yeah." He reaches into his pocket and pulls out a business card. It's pure black. Expensive stock. With one word embossed in the middle in rich font—Hunter. "You're lucky I didn't kill them."

"*Them*? How many?"

"Two. A man and a woman, if the smaller set of shoe prints are anything to go by."

I bite back a curse. "Why wasn't I told earlier? Where are they?"

"I only made the discovery during the early hours of the morning when I went outside for a smoke. They were smart enough to set up camp on the beach outside the boundary fence, just out of range of the security camera. They left the card in their hollowed-out bunker and shoe prints in the sand. There was no threat or attack. At the moment, I assume they only want us to know they're watching."

Shit.

I've failed in hiding her. "How the hell did they find us?"

"The same way we would've found them. Bribe airport staff for flight records, then scour the arrival location. They've probably spent the last three days searching every inch of coastline."

Fucking Cole.

"I'll call Torian." I should've known better than to think he would fade into the shadows while our deal was in play. "I'll get them to disappear." Either by threat or violence.

"Yeah, you do that. And while you're at it, maybe ask your new best friend what will happen after the thirty days are up and Layla still wants you dead."

He's pissed, and I get it. I've complicated his life with no benefit.

But he's also worried. For me. For himself. And given the way he handed over his clothes to Layla, it goes without saying he's worried about her, too.

"I'm going to finally get some fucking sleep." He backtracks toward the stairs. "You two are on your own for a few hours. Try not to kill each other in the meantime."

"I'll pay attention to the security system and wake you if something happens."

"Don't bother. I'll keep my notifications on." He turns and descends the first step. "At this point, I don't trust you to pay attention to anything other than your dick."

I scowl at his back, hating his lack of faith. But I still can't regret the choices I've made in bringing Layla here.

Letting her go wasn't an option. It never will be. He'll understand that in time.

I crumple Hunter's business card in my fist and march into my bedroom to snatch my cell from the bedside table.

I dial the only Torian number I have. The call's answered on the second ring.

"Is she okay?" Keira demands without pause.

My anger stumbles over the concern in her voice. Layla thinks her family hates her, that they disowned her, and I'm the sick motherfucker who hasn't assuaged the misconception. "She's fine."

"Then why are you calling?" A bitter edge creeps into her tone.

"I need to speak to your brother. What's his number?"

"Why?"

I clench the phone tighter, my patience thin. "Because his men are watching us, and I want him to have a clear understanding of what will happen once I get my hands on them."

There's no response. No bite of my meaty threat.

"I'll take your silence as a lack of concern," I grate, "and retaliate accordingly."

"No, you won't… Hold on a second."

There's a rustle of noise, the murmur of undecipherable conversation, then, "Calling to renegotiate terms so soon, Costa? Layla's always been a handful, but I thought you would've lasted longer than three days."

I close my eyes, holding my screaming demons at bay. "I've warned you about calling me that."

"My apologies." He snickers. "What can I do for you? Is my sister's fury more than you can handle?"

"I can handle her just fine, along with the men you sent to spy on us. I just wanted to give you prior warning that I don't treat trespassers kindly."

"There's been no trespassing." His superiority is potent. Sickeningly tart. "They've remained outside your property. Out of view. Layla won't see them."

"They left a fucking business card."

"Out of respect."

"Bullshit." I keep my voice low. "It's out of insecurity. Your men are here because you're second-guessing our agreement."

"My people are there because I'm not hanging my sister out to dry." The correction is multilayered, not only reaffirming his commitment to his sister, but confirming it's not only *men* that are here.

Bishop was right. There's a woman.

"And don't worry," he adds. "They're skilled enough to remain safe despite any threat you might pose."

"This wasn't part of our agreement. Tell them to back off."

"Confining my sister to a bedroom wasn't part of the agreement either."

I wipe a hand over my mouth and pace in front of the bed. This asshole is inching me closer toward the edge of rage. Or maybe it's just my compiling failure. Layla's opened me up to vulnerabilities because I can't function until I win her back. "Your sister is free to do what she likes."

"But she prefers to stay away from you for the most part?"

"I'm giving her space because she *prefers* to tend her wounded pride in private, seeing as though her brother cut her off."

"Listen here, you disillusioned Grim Reaper wannabe. I told her she was cut off for *your* benefit. This wouldn't be a fair fight otherwise, and I intend to *own you* fairly."

He's deliberately provoking me, and I have a hunch the timing is deliberate. All of this—the taunts, the blatant proximity from his people—it's because they were watching last night.

Does he think I'm winning her over?

I fucking wish.

"The only ownership will be mine over your sister. I won't fail, Torian. I can promise you that. I'm sure you've already been informed I made substantial headway at dinner." They wouldn't have known Layla sat at the table naked out of spite. They would've seen her fucking my hand and thought I was on the home stretch. "That's why your spies left a business card. You want to throw me off my game."

"All's fair in love and war."

The line disconnects, turning my blood to lava. I won't let those assholes ruin this for me. The threat alone is enough to send me manic.

Cole has no idea how close I am to breaking point.

I stalk to the hall, then straight to Layla's closed door to yank at the handle.

It's fucking locked.

My frustration detonates with my foot launching at the barrier before I can rein it in.

The doorjamb breaks, the door flings wide, and there she is, lazing on the queen-sized bed, hands behind her head, ankles crossed as her face turns to mine with a raised brow.

She's back in her jeans, but it's Bishop's grey T-shirt resting against the curves of her breasts that acts as a starting siren for another skirmish. She fakes calm, rolling her eyes before shifting her attention to the ceiling, pretending I don't fucking exist.

"It's time for breakfast." I glare. Lock my jaw.

"I'll eat later."

Like hell she will.

I storm inside and stop at the end of the bed, her bare feet within reach. I'm tempted to grab her ankles and force them around my neck. To bury my face between her thighs and feast until she admits defeat. "You can have your meal whenever you like, *amore mio*, but you will sit with me while I eat mine."

She meets my gaze, the narrowed slits of her eyes harsh yet so damn inviting. Her venom is invigorating. Exquisite.

I'd love to fuck her like this. To have her hate me and want me in the same breath. To experience the vicious push and pull. The euphoric pain and pleasure.

"And if I refuse?"

I paste on a smile. "Try it and see. I'd love the opportunity to force compliance."

She mimics my expression and reaches under the pillow beside her to retrieve a steak knife. "And I'd love the opportunity to create a puncture wound."

My dick hardens. *Sick fuck.*

The thought of her with a blade to my chest… at my throat… under my skin.

God, help her.

I grab for her ankle, prepared to drag her down the bed, wanting her violent vengeance. But she snaps her feet toward her ass, scrambling backward on the mattress until she's seated, staring and smirking. "Touch me and pay the price, asshole."

"I touched you last night, *amore mio*." I stalk around to her side of the bed. She counters by scurrying to the opposite side. "My fingers were buried inside you. You came with very little effort."

"I came because I was fantasizing about your death."

I raise a brow. "A woman with a sadistic kink. We're better suited than I thought. Maybe we should exchange notes on preferred foreplay, because wielding that knife of yours is driving me wild."

She growls and raises her weapon, flinging it toward me.

It's a good throw. Strong. On target. But she didn't aim for body mass, so a simple sidestep has it sailing past me to thunk against the wall before thudding to the carpet.

"Nice try. Next time aim for my heart." I place a hand over the thumping organ. "It shouldn't be hard to find. You own it after all."

She laughs. "You're such a contradiction. You claim you have a heart when you don't even have a soul. Tell me, Matthew. How many people did you slice open to become the Butcher?"

"More than you can imagine."

"Delightful," she drawls. "And how many did you kill?"

I stand tall against my sins. "Enough to wipe out a small village."

"So proud. So psychotic."

"I'm not proud." I won't deny the mental assessment though. "You asked a question and I didn't hesitate in giving an answer. I owe you the truth and that's what you'll get."

"And you expect me to fall for a murderer?"

"You already did." I reach for her across the mattress. "Now walk your ass to the dining table or I'll get you there by whatever means necessary. And trust me, I'll far prefer the second option."

She huffs. Glares. Then slides off the opposite side of the bed to stand facing me. "Fine. But first—do you like my new threads?" She grabs the hem of her shirt, her smile seductive as she raises the material to breathe deep against it. "It smells like Bishop. It feels like he's all over my skin."

Her blow hits its target, creating an eruption of envy beneath my sternum.

I grin through the torture. Clench my molars at the pain. "You're going to smell a whole lot like me if you don't get out of this room."

Her eyes sparkle. She delights in her victory as she takes another deep inhale of Bishop's shirt, taunting me.

If the Butcher is what she wants, I'm obliged to give him to her.

I lunge, jumping onto the bed, obliterating the space across the mattress.

Her delight vanishes. Her eyes bug.

She turns. Lunges. But I'm on her in a heartbeat, my hands snatching her wrists behind her back before she can flee.

"Is this what you want?" I drag her hips flush against my crotch, her heat seeping into my hardening dick. "Don't play pretend and tell me you weren't goading me into this."

"Why am I not surprised you think standing up for myself means I'm begging for assault? I should've known forcing women would make you hot."

"Not other women." I walk her forward, each step marked by her resistance until she's pressed against the wall. "Just you."

History repeats itself. I had her up against my front door in D.C. But back then, her anger was mindless. A tart storm to this fine wine of protest. "When are you going to give in to me, Layla? When will you forgive me?"

"Never." She bucks, her ass rubbing against my erection.

"Do it again," I growl in her ear. "I dare you."

"Get your fucking hands off me," she grates. "I swear to God, Matthew, I'll end you."

"Then end me." I release her wrists, placing my hands on the wall on either side of her head. "Because I'm not going to quit attempting to earn redemption until I no longer see hunger in your eyes."

"There is no hunger." She turns to face me with a scowl. But I still see it. It's right there. The flames of her desire warm every inch of me. "And for all the sane people in the room, can you please explain exactly how you're earning redemption?"

"Ruthlessly, *amore mio*. Just the way you like it."

She raises her chin, denying the truth, pretending she isn't tangled up in the heat of this moment just as much as I am. It's fucking clear she still wants me. *Needs* me. But it's also evident she has to see me suffer for my mistakes.

If only she understood how brutal my demons have punished me for the pain I've put her through.

"Do you want me to knee you in the balls?" she threatens. "I've done it before. I can do it again."

"If you want me to bow before you, you only have to ask. There's no need to attack your favorite asset."

She scoffs.

"I'm not kidding. I'd kneel. I'd bow. I'd kiss your feet." I lean closer, making her inch back into the wall. "Want to know what I did last night after you fucked my fingers?"

"No." She crosses her arms over her chest.

"I resorted to fucking my own hand because I couldn't pacify my desire for you." I'm so close I can taste the toothpaste on her breath, can feel the lust mingling between us. "You've reduced me to adolescence, Layla. You're all I think about. You consume me."

"Such sweet lies." Her smile returns, slow and sinister. "How long did it take your father to teach you how to manipulate women?"

"I must be wearing you down if you're resorting to the lowest of blows." There's a growl in my voice. A resentment I can't hide. "Let me guess—next you'll start calling me by my birth name."

"Is that what it will take to get you out of my face?" She inches from the wall, her cheek grazing the stubble of my jaw as she whispers in my ear, "*Dante.*"

I close my eyes against the violence inside me. "Say it again."

"*Dante.*" There's laughter in her voice.

She's playing a dangerous game. Poking a monster.

I should leave. Back away. Flee.

My hands itch to grab her. Sweat slicks my brow.

And my dick—*fuck*—it throbs for relief. For *her*.

"The Butcher," she whispers. "Dante *fucking* Costa."

Each utterance is a spear through my chest. A savage reminder of what I've lost. What I've endured. What I've fucked up.

"I suggest you stop." I raise a hand, grabbing her throat, my grip firm but gentle. I push her back into the wall, her gasp a gift and a punishment in equal measure.

She's rigid. Stiff as a board. But that hunger is still there. Still right fucking there, energetic and erotic in her eyes.

"Don't keep taunting me, *amore mio*." I lean in, a breath from her lips, our noses almost touching. "You won't like the man I become."

"I don't like the man you already are."

I squeeze gently, her carotid fluttering beneath my fingertips. "Then I shouldn't have to repeat myself again, should I?"

I'd bet my life she's wet. That those pretty panties of hers are seconds from being soaked.

Fucking her right now would be a masterpiece. A callously beautiful disaster. I wouldn't be able to think straight through my need to please her.

"Insults and name calling won't change the way I feel about you," I murmur close to her lips. "You're mine, Layla. So get used to it."

Her throat works over a heavy swallow beneath my palm. Her tongue sneaks out to quickly lick her lower lip.

I could come like this. Her throat in my hand, her eyes on mine, my dick rubbing against her abdomen. It's goddamn pathetic, but my desire for her is that rich. That cloying. Her temper stokes my lust. Fucking douses it in gasoline.

"Now, I suggest you take your sassy little mouth to the dining table," I warn. "Otherwise, you'll be the one on your knees."

9

———

LAYLA

He releases my neck and marches from the room.

I wait a beat before I buckle against the wall, my pulse wild in my chest, my limbs trembling.

I thrum.

Everywhere.

I can't tell if it's from fear, adrenaline, or a third option I don't want to face even though my nipples are hard and my abdomen throbs.

I need to hate him. With every fiber of my being, I want to look into those dark eyes and see my enemy, but whenever he's in front of me my insides turn to mush. My heart flutters. My stomach free-falls.

I can't wring out the love that still clings to me. It's burrowed deep. Tattooed in my veins.

I remain in place as I curse my stupidity, my breathing remaining rampant, my self-loathing thickening. He messes around in his adjoining bedroom, the subtle squeak of door hinges and bed springs spurring my imagination into avenues I despise.

Then his footsteps trek down the hall, the clap of shoes giving me the slightest relief that he must now be fully dressed.

I hang my head, the tide of failure suffocating me.

I have to get out of here, but I want what he promised me first. I need Emmanuel gone. *Dead*. I just can't keep myself calm enough to demand what I'm owed.

Pans clatter in the kitchen. Cutlery, too.

"Now, Layla," he yells. "Don't make me wait."

I glare and shove from the wall. He's such a fucking asshole.

I stalk from the room, going over the mental checklist of things he's done to me in an effort to regain my fortitude. I relive all the lies. The betrayal. I let the memories

299

strengthen me as I enter the living room to find him standing before the cooktop, his immaculately-tailored charcoal suit doing nothing to decrease his physical appeal.

"Take a seat at the table." He grabs a chopping board from a nearby cupboard. "This won't take long."

I bite my tongue and comply, reclaiming the same seat as last night while he confidently makes the kitchen his bitch. Bacon sizzles in a frying pan. Eggs are cracked and scrambled before being poured into another pan. He slices tomatoes, mushrooms, and spinach, the meal becoming a masterpiece I fast begin to regret rejecting.

His performance is deliberate. He's trying to prove he can provide for me. Nurture.

I don't need the reminder.

But when he walks over with a mug of steaming coffee and places it before me, I succumb to the bribe. I take the offering in both hands while he strolls back to the kitchen, not waiting for praise.

"Will Bishop be joining us?" I ask in a weak attempt to show I'm not daunted by him.

"No." He places two plates on the counter and begins to serve the bacon. "You've risked his life enough for one morning."

"Where is he?"

He doesn't pause in serving our meals, dishing up the scrambled eggs alongside the cooked mushrooms, tomato, and spinach. "Keeping his distance for the sake of self-preservation."

I roll my eyes. "You'd never hurt him."

"Your faith in me is misplaced." He dumps the frying pans into the sink, then grabs the plates and walks toward the table. "I'd hurt anyone who dared to come between us."

I tense, clamping down my body's desire to shiver. I'm not going to swoon over his obsessive bullshit. I refuse.

He places my breakfast down in front of me, a meal fit for a queen, and then takes the opposite seat. "You're welcome."

"Excuse me for not being thankful for your dictatorship."

"You're excused." He cuts into his bacon and takes a bite. "Now, I suggest you eat."

I grab my knife, clutching it like a weapon.

His lips kick up at one side. "You're a slow learner, *amore mio.* You're well aware your threats of violence turn me on, yet you persist with them."

My body is a slow learner, too. The heat between my legs sparks to life all over again.

I lower my gaze to the food and force myself to eat. I fork one tiny piece and then another before succumbing to the deliciousness awakening my taste buds.

Neither one of us breaks the lengthening silence.

I use the passing minutes to pull my shit together, stitching the holes in my restraint thread by unraveled thread.

I should ask for what I want. *Demand* his assistance with Emmanuel. But every time I raise my gaze and meet his waiting stare, my courage vanishes.

I need to work with Matthew to obtain my objective, and that's not achievable at the moment. Not when the pain of my emotional wounds are still raw.

He finishes his meal before I do and stands to clear his plate.

I watch from the corner of my eye as he loads the dishwasher, then retrieves something from the pantry and carries it toward me. A laptop he places within my reach.

I stare at the temptation as he slaps a credit card on top of it.

It's a trick. A trap.

"Consider it a peace offering." He returns to his seat. "Buy whatever you like—clothes, shoes, toiletries. I don't care. But I want your civility in return."

"No deal. I'm not going to be here long enough for an order to arrive."

"Is that so?" He raises a lone brow. "And where do you plan on going?"

Nowhere. *Anywhere.*

"Denver." I hold his dark gaze. "I'm going to finish what I started."

"You won't go anywhere near there without me."

"Then when do we leave?"

The muscles in his jaw tic. His eyes narrow. He's trying to think of something to placate me. To tide me over so he can continue playing these stupid games.

"When?" I demand.

He slides his chair back a few inches and leisurely crosses his arms over his chest, a picture of sophisticated relaxation. "Things have changed. We need a new strategy."

"I'm all ears." I finish the last of my bacon, then place the cutlery on my plate. "Tell me what I need to do to speed this up."

"Be patient."

"That's not possible in my current captivity."

"I'm yet to determine if it's best to approach Lorenzo or if we should do this under the radar."

"And I no longer care about the repercussions to your life if you break your uncle's rules." It's a lie. I *do* care. I *hate* how much. "You promised you would help me. Or was that just another betrayal?"

His nostrils flare. "Fine. We'll discuss this tonight over dinner. For now, purchase the things you need because it's going to take more than a few days to work on a plan that doesn't get us killed."

He's stalling, and he'll continue to do so for as long as I allow it.

"Tonight," I confirm, pushing to my feet to grab the laptop. "No excuses."

"I wouldn't think of it."

My smile is brittle, the edges of my lips tight with malice as I start for the hall.

"Stay where I can see you, *amore mio.*"

I pause. A cry of potent irritation builds in my throat.

"Take a seat on the sofa." His chair scrapes behind me "I'm sick of being kept from that pretty face of yours."

He doesn't trust me not to create havoc while on his laptop. I don't blame him. If I had the know-how, I'd get on the dark web and arrange to have him killed. Maimed at the very least.

I divert my path to the other side of the room and sink onto the leather three-seater.

I start my shopping spree on the bare necessities, just in case I'm unfortunate enough to still be stuck here in a few days. I order underwear and casual clothes while Matthew clears the table and stacks the dishwasher.

I'm on my third website by the time he walks onto the deck to make a call. He talks loud enough for me to hear, approving stock purchases and chatting shop with whom I assume are his staff.

Whenever I glance over my shoulder, it doesn't take long for his eyes to meet mine. His subtle smirk always follows.

I want to slap the arrogance off his face. Instead, I divert my internet browsing into more conniving territory. I splurge on a pair of Gucci sneakers. I one-click designer clothes, red-bottom shoes, and expensive makeup.

Every time our gazes clash, I add another over-priced luxury to my cart.

I'm well aware I won't get the opportunity to wear the four hundred-dollar Guerlain limited edition satin-red lipstick he just bought me. My body won't be adorned in the thousand-dollar La Perla black silk camisole with macramé frastaglio. And the La Prairie White Caviar Creme will never kiss my skin. But every purchase coats my tongue with the sweet taste of revenge.

I luxuriate in the shopping spree, drinking coffee with my legs stretched along the sofa while Matthew prowls the deck like a panther.

By brunch, I've spent five figures.

By midday, I'm inching closer to ten.

I invest in limited edition books from authors I haven't heard of. Signed memorabilia gets added to the list from major sporting clubs I didn't know existed. And the pièce de résistance is how I've memorized his credit card details, the digits firmly secured in my mental bank for safe keeping.

"What are you up to?"

I jolt, snapping my gaze toward the sound of Bishop's voice to find him approaching from the hall.

He glowers. "Did I scare you?"

"Not in the slightest."

He continues into the living room, his disapproval raking over the shirt I'm wearing before turning toward Matthew on the deck. "I'm going for a drive. Do you want me to get you something to eat?"

My stomach squeezes. I'm unsure if it's from hunger or trepidation. "Can I come with you?"

He looks at me as if I'm scum on the bottom of his shoe. "You're kidding, right?"

No, not kidding at all. "I don't want to be left here with him."

"Well, you probably should've thought about that before you decided to wear my fucking clothes in front of him after I told you not to."

"He doesn't care." I click the final order button on my most substantial purchase and close the laptop. "He knows I only put it on to annoy him."

"Is that what he said?" He scoffs. "Come on, Layla, you're not that naive. His temper would be soaring beneath the surface."

I follow his gaze to where Matthew watches us from his position near the railing, his cell still plastered to his ear. There's no hint of any temper as he stares inside. There's no hint of any emotion at all with his smirk no longer in place.

"I assure you," Bishop continues, "every second my clothes are on your skin, he's imagining how to rip them off."

Matthew strolls forward, headed for the door.

"See?" Bishop glares at me. "He can't even stand us being alone in the same room. Don't say I didn't warn you."

The door is flung open, Mr. Calm and Casual walking inside. "Yes. I'm keeping an eye on it," he speaks into his cell. "I'm not concerned, but let me know if we approach the limit."

My stomach fills with unwanted butterflies as he disconnects the call and places the device in his inner jacket pocket, his attention fixed on Bishop.

"You're awake."

Bishop juts his chin. "I am. I was about to go for a drive and find something different to eat."

"And I'm going with him." I place the laptop on the seat beside me and stand.

Matthew's lips thin. "No, you're not."

"You're not my keeper."

"Aren't I?" His brow raises, the haughty expression hacking into my restraint. "When you've got no money or support outside these four walls, I wouldn't test that theory. You might not like the outcome."

"I'm leaving." Bishop turns for the entry. "For the love of God, could you two sort your shit before I return? I'm fucking sick of the ping-pong match."

He disappears into the far hall, Matthew's presence becoming all the more suffocating the closer we creep toward being truly alone.

"I'm going to my room." I leave the laptop and credit card on the sofa to flee.

He doesn't answer. Doesn't follow.

Thank God.

I count down the minutes until dinner in my room, lazing on the bed, my back against the headboard, a pillow clutched to my chest while new phone conversations murmur from the living room. I can't even close the door properly to give myself privacy because the super villain broke a piece of the latch with his entrance earlier.

The longer I spend here, the worse it gets.

The increased suffering. The prolonged pain.

But after tonight I'll have a blueprint for freedom. Once plans are in motion for Emmanuel, I can figure out the rest. I'll get home using Matthew's credit card details, and from there I have my own cash stashed in a safe. At least enough to tide me over until I determine how to make amends with my brother.

This is the homestretch.

"*Amore mio,*" Matthew calls in a chastising tone. "I need you to come out here."

"I'm busy."

"Would you prefer if I came to your room and we picked up where we left off?"

I sigh and fling the pillow to the other side of the bed, then storm for the hall and enter the living room with a huffed, *"What?"*

He glances at me from his position near the dining table, his eyes playful as they settle on mine. That's all it takes to rile me up again. My blood turns scorching. My heartbeats are frantic.

"You look tired," he drawls. "Your shopping spree must have been exhausting."

"Not at all." I place my hands on my hips, my fingers clawing into my jeans. "Spending your money came naturally."

His grin is subtle, the softest curve of the most enticing lips. "So I've discovered."

"Checking up on me already? Where's the trust? Where's the love?"

He chuckles, the sound almost friendly as he prowls toward me. Predatory and sleek. I stiffen, my pulse increasing, the closing proximity making my throat dry.

"I wasn't checking up on you. The bank called for a second time, wanting to confirm if your last purchase was legitimate before they approved the transaction."

"It's legitimate." I don't falter even though I've been caught red-handed.

"I didn't take you for a Tesla kind of woman."

"Well, you also thought I was someone who would forgive and forget, so your analysis of me has never been accurate." I hold his gaze, those confident eyes consuming me.

He doesn't flinch. He holds himself in that arrogant state of command while I'm forced to look away, turning my attention to the waves, willing the ocean to consume me.

I despise the exquisite aftershave that penetrates thick and rich in my lungs, the erotic scent of sandalwood reawakening unwanted memories.

I stand frozen as he reaches out, his fingertips the most delicate brush against my skin as he guides a stray strand of hair behind my ear. "How long are you going to keep punishing me?"

The question cuts deep. The vulnerability in his tone. The plea in his words.

"Forever," I whisper.

He takes liberties with more of my hair, brushing additional strands from my cheeks. Excruciatingly slow. With brutal gentleness.

I want to scream for him to stop, to leave me alone, but I can't even back away. His touch is a vise I can't deny.

"Why can't you accept my apology?" he murmurs.

Because it hurts too much. Because his betrayal cut far deeper than any other.

I'd let down all my guards for him. For *us*. I'd handed him my vulnerability in a ribbon-covered package and he'd set the threads to flame.

"I'd kill kings for you, *amore mio*. I'd betray gods." His words are poetry, articulated with reverence, evoking weakness. "I'd slit my wrists if it would make you happy."

I raise my chin and meet his gaze, his regret-filled eyes slicing right to my marrow. "It would."

He holds my stare, reading me, scrutinizing, his hand falling to his side. "Then so be it." He turns and walks for the kitchen, shucking his jacket along the way to throw it onto the island counter.

He pulls open a drawer, the clink of cutlery harsh as he snatches a paring knife and places it on the counter. "You want a physical wound to make up for your emotional pain?" He faces me, his hand aggressively yanking at the button on his shirt cuff. "Then will you forgive me?"

"Stop being dramatic."

"All I'm doing is clearing up any misconception that there are limitations to my apology." He aggressively folds his sleeve to his elbow, then reclaims the knife. "You want my suffering, so I'm offering it to you. Would you like to do the honors?"

I keep my mouth shut. He won't go through with it.

"Layla?" My name is a warning. "You or me? Tell me how to do this right to get you to forgive me."

My heart clenches, the tormented organ threatening to wither and die.

I want him in agony. In anguish. I want him withering with the misery that his lies have created. But I also can't stand to see him in pain. I'm too weak. Too fucking pathetic.

"Don't falter now. If this is what you need, take it. Slice me. Stab me. Cut me into a thousand pieces."

I cross my arms over my chest. "I know you're bluffing."

"Like hell I am. I'm standing here, willing to give you whatever the fuck you need to forgive my sins. And you've seen me naked enough times to know nobody else has gotten close enough to leave a scar. You'll be the first. The only. Then I'll have the privilege of having a physical injury to match my internal misery because even though you don't want to believe it, *amore mio*, I'm fucking suffering just like you."

I glare, unwilling to fall victim to the sincerity in his tone.

He's lying. Manipulating. He's taunting me with the offer of violence because he knows I could never follow through.

"Then do it yourself," I grate.

"As you wish." He swivels the three-inch blade toward his arm and buries it in his flesh.

Bile screams up my throat. Panic takes over my pulse. And all he does is stare at me. Questioning. Silently asking if the steel embedded in his forearm is enough.

"Want more?" He retrieves the knife, sending a trail of blood over his wrist to spill to the tile.

"No." I tremble. Shake.

I'm livid and sickened and weak.

"I can make a lengthy gash this time." He looks down at his injury. "Straight down the vein instead of a flesh wound. Blood loss might be your best friend. There's no hospital within forty miles."

"Stop it." My heart screams for me to go to him, to check the damage and quit this stupidity. It's my head that keeps me in place. My pride. My self-preservation.

"This is what you asked for." He starts toward me, crimson streaming down his arm and along his hands, leaving a spotted trail behind him. "It's what you want." He holds the knife for me to take, the hilt coated in blood.

He knows I won't grab it. He knows I'm a coward.

I hate myself for it. The disgust eats at me. Gnaws.

"Take what you need, Layla."

Tension forms beneath my sternum. "Nothing will fill the gaping hole you creat-ed." My voice fractures. "No stab wound. No amount of bloodshed."

His jaw hardens, but his eyes are pained. Pleading.

I wish his vulnerability repulsed me. Instead, his suffering makes mine greater. "I trusted you."

"I know."

My palms itch to slap the undeserving sorrow from his face. "I *loved* you."

His chin raises before he nods.

He's doing it again. Manipulating me. Molding reality.

"*Stop it,*" I snap. "Stop acting. Stop pretending like you give a fuck."

"I'm not. I'd do anything for you."

Agony screams inside me, bursting to break free. The pressure intensifies. The insanity builds.

I snatch for the knife. He doesn't protest. The handle slides into my palm slippery and wet. I raise the blade to his neck, his eyes on mine as I hold the threat bare millimeters from his skin.

I could end this with a nick of his carotid. I could kill Emmanuel's golden child. His firstborn. I could do what Cole asked of me and make up for the mistake of trusting a stranger. A *butcher*.

"Do it, Layla." Matthew slides his hand over mine, strengthening my threat against his neck. "If this is what it takes to heal you. If my death is what you need, take it."

My skin awakens with goose bumps, every inch of me shivering despite the mindless adrenaline.

He adds pressure to the knife, digging the blade into his skin.

"Don't." I try to pull it back, but he denies me, his hold adamant and far stronger than my own.

Blood wells along the steel, the tiniest rivulet of red making me hyperventilate.

"I lied to buy more time with you," he admits. "I knew once you found out about Emmanuel, you'd leave, and I couldn't stand it. I hid who I was to quieten my fear of losing you. I hurt you because I can't live without you."

He slowly moves our hands, dragging the blade across his throat. It's only light. The barest slice of skin, but it's enough to carve flesh.

"Stop," I warn.

He holds my gaze, the knife continuing its path of destruction.

"*Stop.*"

Blood seeps down his neck to his pristine shirt, the pure white tainted with deep red.

"You need this." His eyes slay me. Slaughter.

"No. *You* do," I accuse. "You're trying to buy your way out of guilt and that's not how this works. My pain will still be here once your cuts heal."

"At least you acknowledge that I feel guilt." His voice is a whisper. "I guess that's a start."

"I acknowledge that you're doing this to take the easy way out. You want a quick fix."

"Or maybe I'm giving *you* the easy way out. Because as long as I'm breathing, I won't let you go, Layla." He wraps his free hand around the back of my neck, his fingers gripping me tight. "End me or forgive me, *amore mio*. Put us out of our misery."

I shake my head. Glaring. Faltering.

He leans in, his lips approaching mine. For a moment, I'm tempted to let him make everything disappear with the brush of his mouth, the taste of his tongue. But at the last second, I tilt my face away.

He growls, the deep rumble vibrating in his chest. "*End me.*" He grabs my chin and forces my gaze back to his. "*Or fucking forgive me.*"

"No. You can suffer."

His eyes harden, his lip curling. "Then we suffer together." He smashes his mouth to mine, the kiss harsh and punishing.

I scramble, frantically pulling my hand away from the knife, the weapon clattering to the floor. I fight, shoving, scratching.

He doesn't quit. He keeps attacking me with his affection, slaughtering my defenses with his returned grip on my neck, cutting me down at the knees with the swipe of his tongue against my lips.

It's too much. The passion. The worship.

My mouth tingles. My heart gallops.

I quit fighting his war strategy and attack with my own. I kiss him back with increased ferocity. Our mouths spar. Harsh movements. Vicious lashes of tongue. I shove my hands into his hair. Pull the strands. Claw his skull.

His growling continues, the animalistic rumble living inside my chest as he grabs my hips and turns to walk me back to the island counter. He dumps my ass against the cold marble, then tugs me forward, forcing my legs to part around his waist.

I burn. In my heart. My limbs. No place more fiercely than between my thighs.

It's agony. Potent and tart. It's what I deserve for being so pathetic. So weak.

He yanks Bishop's shirt over my head and possessively reclaims my chin to slam his lips back on mine.

His other hand is everywhere, cupping my breast, my ribs, my ass. He leaves a trail of blood all over me, marking my skin, painting me in his possession.

I don't want this. Not the passion nor the lust.

But I don't want anything other than this either.

I grasp his waistband while our mouths tussle. I blindly undo his belt. Tug his zipper. He does the same with my jeans, yanking the material down my legs along with my underwear.

Everything is a mass of wildfire and licking flames until his cock drives into me, the intrusion making me break away with a pleasured gasp.

We stare at each other, frozen, panting, hating, while his wrist drips with blood. The ruby-red stains the counter. My arms. Thighs. Cleavage. But all I know is the hardness of him inside me. The contact that sends me all the way back to love, affection, and thoughts of forever.

"Don't stop now," I snarl. "Fuck me."

I need this mistake to be over. For the pleasure to come and go so I can start regretting my actions. Because right now, all I want is *more*.

He's slow to comply with a roll of controlled lethargy. It's a meticulous thrill.

I arch my back, thrusting my breasts toward him, my nipples hard through my lace bra. He watches the movement, his gaze devouring every inch of me with ownership I yearn to submit to.

"Harder," I demand.

I can't withstand lazy and loving.

This needs to be a punishment.

Harsh. Fast. Cruel.

I focus on the blood oozing from his neck, the liquid seeping into his collar.

I tug and rip at his buttons, hungry to see more of him. I don't stop until his shirt hangs open, his muscled pecs on display, the beautiful canvas blood free but not for long.

I run my palm over the crimson on his throat, then trail my touch over his chest. I leave a path of carnage, increasing the gore, letting his punishment soothe mine.

"You like to watch me bleed." His stare tracks me with something akin to fascination.

"I like to watch you suffer." I reinforce the lie with a glare.

"*Arrenditi a me.*"

I scoff. "That dreamy Italian has become a crutch, Butcher."

"Really?" He claims my neck in his hand and grins. "You think I need foreign words to make you come?" His hold tightens. Restricts.

The confinement is riveting. Disturbingly delicious. It makes my pussy pulse around his cock.

"You don't understand how perfect you are." He strikes at my heart, each word a punishment I won't allow myself to believe.

"And you don't understand that I'm only using you again," I counter.

"Use me all you like." He smashes another kiss to my lips, speaking into my mouth. "Use me for the rest of my life."

Emotion tears me apart as his thrusts deepen. Quicken.

I could cry from the relief of it. The *pain* of it.

I yearn and despise. Love and loathe. And still, he brings me pleasure, his cock gliding in and out, his adoration seeming to increase with each undulation.

He cups my cheeks. Kisses me tenderly, then ferociously. He digs his fingers into my thighs. Palms a fistful of my hair.

It's chaotic. Wild. At least until a foreign sound breaches my ears. A chink of metal. A thud.

I stiffen. Freeze.

The front door opens in the distance with a squeak.

Shit. Bishop.

I shove at Matthew's chest, jostling and scooting to get out from under him. He stands solid, not budging an inch, his cock remaining buried inside me.

"He'll leave," he grates. "This isn't over."

"Yes, it is. We're done. *Move.*"

He grips my chin, his eyes vicious as he gets in my face. "I'm not letting you go. I won't lose you now."

"You never had me to begin with." I push at his chest only to have his hands lock tight around my wrists.

"That's a lie," he growls.

Bishop's footsteps approach, the rhythmic thud stopping as soon as he comes into view in my periphery. "Jesus fucking Christ, is that blood?"

I twist my arms free, then grab for the T-shirt on the counter, pulling it over my head while Matthew remains plastered between my thighs.

"What the fuck is wrong with you two?" Bishop's steps trek toward the bedroom hall. "One of you better be dying, otherwise I'll be fucking disappointed." He continues out of view, his stomped steps fading down the stairs.

Matthew doesn't acknowledge the anger. Neither do I.

I'm too busy bathing in shame, the carnage soaking me inside and out.

"Stay with me," Matthew demands. "Don't backtrack now."

It's too late. Regret has its hooks in me, the barbs buried deep.

"Don't say it," he warns. "Don't fucking say it, *amore mio.*"

"This was a mistake." I shove at him, using all my force to make him take a retreating step. I scoot from the counter and onto my feet, sweeping my jeans and underwear from the floor. "I can't do this anymore. I won't be baited." I meet his gaze, my chin high, my shoulders strong despite the weakness chipping away at my limbs. "I want what you promised me. Then I never want to see you again."

10

———

MATTHEW

I CLENCH MY TEETH AS SHE WALKS AWAY, THE CUT ON MY NECK STINGING, THE PUNCTURE wound on my arm throbbing.

The closer I get to her physically, the farther she pushes me away afterward.

It's a ratio I don't understand and can't fucking balance.

I right my pants as her door slams down the hall, then lean my hands against the blood-smeared counter while silence takes over the house.

She's goddamn stubborn. But so am I.

Footsteps echo from downstairs, the noise getting closer until Bishop stalks into the room to throw a brown paper bag at me. "Here's your lunch, you perverted prick."

I snatch the projectile from the air, the soft food inside scrunching on impact.

He stalks to the opposite side of the island counter to glare at me. "I hope you choke."

"Duly noted."

"What the fuck is with the blood?"

I glance down at my torso. Her handprints are plastered over my chest, the crimson beginning to harden and flake. "What can I say? We discovered new kinks."

"That arm is going to need stitches."

"I'll handle it."

He scoffs. "So she's forgiven you?"

"Hardly." I open the bag to find numerous paper-wrapped sandwiches. "We need to get back on track with Emmanuel. I promised her we'd make plans over dinner tonight."

"Then go back on your promise. We both know he's a complication we don't need."

"He's a loose end we need to tie." I dump the bag on the counter and trek to the pantry to grab the first aid kit.

"What about your promise to me? You said we weren't going to live like this anymore. We gave up the bloodshed, remember? Now you're having sex in it."

I remember.

All too well.

"Admit you miss the thrill," he demands.

"I don't." I dump the kit on the counter and go in search of alcohol. The only thrill is Layla. She's the one who brings the adrenaline. There's no darkness involved. Only the warmth that accompanies the thought of making her happy.

It's not my fault her happiness revolves around death.

"Bullshit."

"I'm not in the mood, Bishop." I wrench open the liquor cabinet and snatch the last bottle of Macallan. "Take the food to her. Make sure she's okay."

"Hell no. I'm not stepping foot near that woman while you're like this."

I hang my head, the weight in my hands falling limp at my sides. I'm at my wit's end here, and the ache from my compounding blue balls isn't making my impatience to win her back any easier. "She needs to eat."

"And I need to live."

I swing around to scowl at him. He glares right back.

"This shit with her needs to end," he warns. "You're reaching the edge."

"Then don't push me any further." I shove the paper bag toward him, then start for the hall with the first aid and alcohol. "Take the fucking food to her. She doesn't deserve to starve."

BY NIGHTFALL, my blood is tinged with the faintest hint of scotch, the liquor doing nothing to quieten my demons as I sit on the deck in the dark.

The slight scratch on my neck has hardened. The wound on my forearm has been stitched by my own shitty craftsmanship. I took my time dragging the needle through my skin in the hopes it would distract me.

It didn't.

Every time I close my eyes, Layla's there. There's no escaping the storm we've created.

The sliding door opens behind me.

I already know it's not her. She won't come in search of me.

"She offered to cook dinner." Bishop takes the seat beside me. "Don't worry. I confiscated anything poisonous from under the sink. If she's going to kill us, it won't be through something ingestible."

I glance over my shoulder to the kitchen, finding her at the counter chopping vegetables. "Why would she offer?"

"Maybe because she's sick of staring at the same four walls."

Or maybe she's been snooping and found the sleeping pills in my bathroom.

"You realize those fuckers are probably out here watching us, right?" he asks.

"I don't give a shit." I take another mouthful from the liquor bottle. As long as Hunter stays in the shadows, the blade in my pocket will remain hidden.

"And when we start talking about Emmanuel?" He snatches the scotch from my hand and throws back a gulp. "What then?"

"They won't hear us from the beach." I can barely hear myself think over the waves and sea breeze.

He doesn't respond. He doesn't need to. His judgmental thoughts are loud and clear while the clatter of pans echoes from inside.

He wants to tell me how much I've messed up. To run through the list of my mistakes. And how much I've changed. How much I've risked.

"Hurry up and say it," I mutter. "I've known you long enough to understand you can't hold back from rubbing in my failures."

He settles into the deck chair, the scotch returning to his lips momentarily. "Who's to say you failed? I'm pretty sure that blood ritual of yours was successful. I'm just waiting for the demonic creature you summoned to show."

The reminder of the violent sex has my mind racing back there. To her fingers splayed on my chest, her skin covered in crimson.

"I spoke to her when I took in the food..." He hesitates, as if waiting for me to attack.

"And?"

"And I'm no connoisseur of the female psyche, but you only seem to be pissing her off more. Have you ever thought about doing the opposite of what your instincts suggest?"

"Don't start being a smart-ass." I attempt to snatch the bottle back only to have him yank it out of reach. "I'm on the precipice here."

"I know. That's why you're cut off until further notice. No more alcohol for you tonight. We're making plans for Emmanuel, remember? And you sure as shit won't be doing it with a gut full of liquor."

"I'm not drunk." Not even buzzed.

He raises the scotch along with a brow. "There's barely any left."

"I used it as antiseptic, asshole." I'm well aware I need to be on my game for the dinner conversation. I can't fuck up the only reason Layla's remained here.

"Good." He takes another chug as the outdoor lights turn on, blinding me. "*Jesus.* What the fuck?"

The door opens behind us while I blink. Layla's gentle footsteps head toward the outdoor dining setting. I squint as she brings a stacked tray to the table, then removes placemats, cloth napkins, and cutlery.

There's something different about her.

I scrutinize her as my eyes adjust, taking in the paler shade of her skin, the slightly rounded shoulders. She's lost the rigidity in her posture. The defiance.

She places the salt and pepper shakers down, then turns back toward the house to make for the door. "We're having warm chicken salad for dinner. It should be ready in fifteen minutes."

There's no strength in her voice. Only layers of exhaustion that intensify my guilt.

"Did she say *salad*?" Bishop asks as she closes the door behind her. "She knows we're men, right?"

"She knows *I* am." I return my attention to the inky ocean. "I'm not sure about you."

"Okay. This has gone too far. I took the perverted sex in my stride. I haven't complained about living on a lick of sleep. But salad? Come on, man. Nothing is worth putting up with *salad*."

"Then go discuss it with her."

"I risked it once, but I'm not going anywhere near your girl on my own again. That shit is suicide territory when you're like this."

"Then quit complaining." I grab for the scotch, only to have him swipe it out of reach for a second time.

"I will *never* quit complaining about salad. What am I, a fucking gopher?"

I slide my hand into my pocket, discreetly removing the plastic cover from the knife. I need something to take the edge off.

I creep my fingers along the steel as Bishop continues to mutter nonsense. I tilt the blade, digging it into the material against my thigh, then deeper into my flesh.

The first pinch of pain is cathartic. Sharp and serene.

I drag in a slow breath, leaning into the relief. The clarity.

The tension wanes. The guilt eases.

I close my eyes and dig the blade deeper, more than a scratch, the tip of the knife slicing through skin.

"Are you listening?" Bishop's voice hardens. "I said, are we going to talk about Emmanuel before she gets out here?"

I meditate on the burn in my thigh. The twinge of discomfort soothes. "No."

He falls quiet, the silence condemning me, stealing my tiny glimpse of peace.

"All you need to know is that the dinner conversation has to run smoothly." I release the knife and give him a warning stare. "Don't cause trouble."

"*Me?*" His face scrunches. "I'm not the one who's been—"

"I mean it. Whatever she wants, she gets, okay? Even if it's Emmanuel's head stuffed and mounted on her wall. As far as I'm concerned, whatever she asks, we deliver."

He holds my gaze, his disgust increasing as he raises the scotch to drain the remaining liquid.

"Whatever she wants," I repeat.

He dumps the bottle beside his chair, refusing to respond. He won't dare to defy me. Not when I'm so fucking volatile.

I return to my meditation. Eyes closed. A hand on the knife. The blade digging into flesh.

I pull myself together. Focus on the end game. On what will happen once I succeed.

I'll take Layla away from here. Out of reach of family. Hers and mine. And we won't return until her feelings for me are stronger than they were before.

We'll make plans.

A future.

"Dinner is ready," she calls from the kitchen.

"Fucking salad," Bishop mutters pushing from his chair.

She returns outside, using her foot to slide the door closed behind her. This time her tray is filled with dinner bowls and sparkling glasses already filled with white wine, along with the remainder of the opened bottle.

I approach as she places one of the salad concoctions at the head of the table. "This is mine." She puts another down to her left. "And yours, Bishop." She shoots me a cursory glance while putting my bowl to her right. "And yours..."

Our gazes barely meet, but there's something different in her eyes. Something that causes tension beneath my sternum.

"And the wine?" Bishop's tone holds blatant skepticism. "Are those already designated?"

She reaches for the lone glass in the corner of the tray. "This one is."

He clears his throat and glowers at me, sending a message that's far from silent.

Specified meals. Stipulated drinks.

If she's striving to drug us, it's far too blatant. But am I careless enough to throw caution to the wind in a vain attempt to show my trust? Maybe.

I take my seat.

Layla does the same.

Bishop continues to glower.

If she wants us dead, I can't fulfil my obligation to kill Emmanuel. But we discussed my commitment before our last fight. Before the sex and violence and blood.

We fall mute. Nobody eats. Nobody drinks.

The meal becomes a game of chicken. A standoff. I don't want to risk being incapacitated if her intention is to run.

"Fine." She scoffs. "You don't trust me?" She grabs her fork and leans toward me, stealing a piece of chicken from the top of my meal to stick it in her mouth. "Satisfied?" She speaks as she chews, then does the same with Bishop's dinner. "That's why you're both not eating, right?"

He nudges his glass of wine toward her. "This, too, kink queen."

She stiffens slightly. "I want Emmanuel dead." She grabs Bishop's glass and takes a sip, immediately following with mine. "And I know I can't do it on my own. What would be the point in spiking your food?"

"You forget that I walked in on your demonic sex ritual," Bishop drawls. "At this point, I think you'd poison me for shits and giggles."

I barely acknowledge their conversation, my interest no longer on the food or wine.

My instincts are tuned in to her. Searching. Scavenging for clues.

She's different. There's no fight in her eyes. No frustration in her posture.

All I see is resignation.

"I'll take care of Emmanuel, Layla." I grab my fork and dig into my meal, the taste of oyster sauce and soy coating my tongue. "Consider it handled."

"That's not what I want." She places my wine down in front of me. "I need his blood on *my* hands. I want to be the one who ends his life."

Icy dread skitters down my spine, my hand itching to reach for the relief that would come from palming the blade in my pocket. "It's too dangerous."

"I'm not asking for permission. I need to do this for myself. For Stella. I won't risk being fooled by your promises again." Her words lack hostility. It's an admission of humiliation, not a taunt.

"In that case, the plan will take longer to organize." I stab a piece of chicken. "I'll want a million contingencies in place for your safety before we step foot in Colorado."

"I don't need a million. You should consider this like any other assassination. I'm sure you know how to be efficient but cautious. No strategy will be foolproof."

But this isn't any other assassination. This is about *her*.

"It's nonnegotiable, Layla. I'll give you what you're owed as long as you're patient while I create a plan that ensures your protection."

She lowers her gaze, remaining poised. "How much time are we talking about?"

A lifetime. Forever. I can't imagine putting her in more danger.

What I've dragged her through already has been bad enough.

"A long fucking while," Bishop cuts in. "Lorenzo is never going to give you permission."

"Forget Lorenzo," I mutter. "I'll deal with the repercussions later."

Her shoulders straighten.

In appreciation? Or merely shock?

"You're going to defy him?" Bishop grates. "Don't be fucking stupid."

"He won't find out. We'll cover our tracks."

"Fucking perfect." He punctures a piece of lettuce, his gaze narrowed on the leafy green as if it's the root of all evil. "Can you explain how we're going to do that when we won't be able to get back inside the Costa property? We've already burned that bridge. And with Emmanuel sick, he might never leave the house."

"I'm sure he'd have doctors' appointments in the city." Layla shrugs. "Rehab at the very least."

"But that's an assumption we need to confirm." Bishop grabs the lettuce from his fork and hikes it over his shoulder to the lawn below. "He may have arranged home visits. So recon is essential."

She doesn't respond. Instead, she takes dainty bites of chicken and salad, then a sip of wine.

The silence stretches. The awkwardness, too.

"How long?" This time her question is a faint murmur as her gaze meets mine, her suffering hitting me head on. "A few days? A week?"

What have I done to you? How do I fix this?

"Let me make some calls." I'm well aware I'm on a tightrope. If I give her a timeline that's too short, I'll risk not winning her back. If it's too long, she'll see it as a deliberate delay. "I'll get a team together. They can watch the house and give us an idea of what we're working with."

"Don't you have someone who could hack their security feed?" She takes another sip of wine. "They could skim over the recordings of the last few days to see when people have entered or left the property. Decker has done stuff like that before."

"Well, unfortunately I'm not Decker, and Langston is far from a tech guru."

Bishop punctures another piece of lettuce to hike it over the railing. "Since when have you been impatient to end your life?"

"I'm not." Her eyes narrow, the fiery goddess flickering to life before being quickly snuffed when she lowers her gaze to her meal. "I'm just well aware *someone* is trying to keep me here as long as possible, and it's a waste of all our time. I won't be staying once Emmanuel is dealt with."

I pick at the chicken. Chew on a piece of carrot. Savor the wine.

Our rendezvous on the kitchen counter unsteadied her. But I'm unsure if it was in a bad way. Is she close to succumbing to me? Is her lack of fight the first sign of surrender?

She's definitely shaken. Unsteady. But is she susceptible?

"What about Remy and Salvatore?" she asks after Bishop has thrown half his vegetables over the railing.

Foreboding skitters down my spine. "What about them?"

"They want me dead."

"*Emmanuel* wants you dead," Bishop corrects. "So we kill the king and the empire will crumple."

"And what if we kill the king and his bastard sons want revenge?"

I keep my mouth shut, wondering if she's heading down this path in an attempt to punish me. *Spite* me.

"I don't want to spend the rest of my life looking over my shoulder." She grabs her napkin and dabs at the corners of her mouth. "And I won't allow that for Stella either."

"I'll assure your safety." I keep my tone in check. No instability. No aggression. Just a simple vow.

"You can't do that when I'll be living on the opposite side of the country."

If only she knew what lingered underneath all this pretense. If I don't win her back, her brother will have me in Portland doing his dirty work. Right under her nose.

"We're not getting rid of his brothers." Bishop stabs at his meal. "Those fuckers aren't worth the time it would take to dispose of the bodies."

"They killed my husband." She raises her chin.

"Doubtful." He shoves the forkful into his mouth, chewing as he speaks. "They're not built for violence."

"They had no problem playing a role in the abduction of children. And they were there when Benji was shot."

"So was Abri," Bishop adds. "Yet she was the one who fucked me over by helping you flee Emmanuel's house. I'm telling you, they don't have the balls to kill anyone."

"They were literally shooting at us a few days ago." Her voice raises with brittle emotion.

"No, they weren't," he adds. "The bullet holes on the car weren't above thigh height. They weren't aiming to cause injury. They didn't hit anywhere near the back seat windows. They barely broke a taillight."

She frowns, her attention turning to me. "Is that true?"

She doesn't want the truth. She wants ammunition. Condemnation. But I can't give that to her.

I incline my head. "I assumed they were warning shots."

Disbelief enters her eyes. "Why?"

"Maybe that's something you should find out before planning their cremation." Bishop pushes his bowl away and grabs his wine glass. "Just a thought."

She holds my gaze, attempting to read me. "Why, Matthew?"

I've wondered the same thing myself. They were sent to retrieve Layla yet made no real attempt to do so. Salvatore had a clear shot at Cole. He could've hit Bishop and didn't try. Maybe he was aiming for our tires, but even then, he didn't come close. Which means he's either a pathetically shitty shot or he bailed on Emmanuel's orders for a reason.

"I don't know." My phone vibrates in my jacket. "It's been a long time since I've been able to predict their motives." I retrieve the cell and excuse myself from the table as I answer the call. "Hello?"

"Brother," Abri says in greeting.

I slow my trek across the deck. We haven't spoken since Denver. Since the awkward goodbye at Emmanuel's house.

"I know this is unexpected," she says into the growing silence. "But I thought I should tell you father's men are out hunting for you."

"His men or Remy and Salvatore?"

"Both. I don't think they've got a clue where you are at the moment, but they won't quit. Father won't let them." Certainty strengthens her voice. "They'll find you."

"Well, you can tell him his minions won't return if they do." The admission twists my gut. I don't want my brothers dead, but I'll kill anyone in an effort to keep Layla safe.

"I'd prefer not to tell him anything seeing as though he's unaware I'm making this call. And before you ask, yes, I'm using a burner."

"Why call at all?" I turn toward the house and stare at my reflection in the floor-to-ceiling glass. "Is this to help Layla again?"

"No, it's to help *you*... and *me*. I hate what's become of us. I need you back in my life."

Paranoia and skepticism claw at the back of my thoughts.

I want to believe her, but it's not that simple. She chose the life she's in, just like I chose mine. She accepted her father's behavior. She encouraged it by staying at his side. "Get rid of Emmanuel and I'll see if I can make that work."

"It's not that easy."

I glance to the table, my attention latching onto Layla staring back at me. "Then I'll do it myself."

"You can't kill him," Abri whispers. "I understand it's what he deserves, but please don't be reckless enough to try."

I keep staring at the woman who owns me. The one whose pleas I need to value more than any other. My siblings made a choice. They could've walked away like I did. They may not have known about Grace's murder, but they were well aware of Emmanuel's dark side.

"Look, I've gotta go," she says in a rush. "I don't want to get caught talking to you. But please be careful."

I frown. "What's this really about?"

"We'll speak later."

She disconnects before I can stop her, leaving me to speculate about her intentions.

"Who was it?" Bishop asks.

I slide the device back into my pocket and return to my seat at the table. "Abri."

His eyes narrow. "What did the viper want?"

"To help, apparently. She said Emmanuel's men are looking for us."

"How is that helpful? It's common fucking sense. My guess is that she traced the call."

I reclaim my cutlery, hoping for Abri's sake that she isn't trying to make me an enemy.

"Unless she's still working with you somehow." Bishop pins Layla with a stare. "I never got an explanation as to why she helped you escape Emmanuel's house."

"She was helping herself. Not me." She shakes her head. "She told me she owed Cole a favor. It was something about him showing her kindness the night Benji died."

"And why would he show her kindness?" Bishop asks.

Good question. I don't like the thought of that fucker anywhere near my sister even if she is trying to set me up.

"I don't know." She shrugs. "Maybe if I hadn't been disowned I'd be able to get an answer. Instead, I'm here—potentially being surrounded by my enemies. With no one to trust. Am I even safe? We're out in the open. Everything is—"

"You're safe," I cut in. "There's camera surveillance. And a panic room inside if necessary. I'm also tracking inbound flights from the private airport." At least I have been since Hunter made himself known. "We'll have enough notice to get out of here if anyone arrives."

"And when all else fails—" Bishop finishes the last of his wine and grabs for the bottle. "—we have a reputation for a reason."

She raises a condescending brow. "Is your butcher status meant to be comforting?" It's yet another emotionless question. No heat. No taunt. Just words strung together by apathy.

"It should be," he counters.

I clear my throat. Shoot him a warning glance. Shake my head slightly.

She's been through enough today without his input.

He rolls his eyes and guzzles another glass of wine.

"Well, if there's nothing more to discuss regarding Emmanuel, I'm going to my room." Layla pushes back in her chair and grabs her bowl. "Is it too much to ask to be kept informed? That you'll let me know what your surveillance team finds?" Her gaze meets mine and for a moment, a glimpse of fortitude flickers in her eyes, but it fizzles. With one blink, her confidence vanishes and she dips her attention to her hands.

"It's not too much to ask." I silently beg her to look at me. Talk to me. Give in to me. "Whenever you want an update, all you need to do is ask."

Her expression flinches. "Good." She walks away, opening the door without dramatics and closing it without a heavy slam.

I don't like it.

This whole subdued, peaceful interaction twists my fucking balls.

"I don't know what type of seesaw relationship fuckery you two have going on..." Bishop grabs for the wine for a third time, pouring the remainder into his glass. "But the transition from bloodlust to dreary lethargy has me confused. Did I miss something?"

If he did, so did I, and I need to figure out what that is.

I push from my seat to follow her.

"Come on, man. Leave her the fuck alone." He leans back in his chair and kicks a boot onto the table, crossing his feet at the ankles. "Remember what I said about instincts? Do the opposite. Stay out of her way instead of trying to get into her panties."

I grab my bowl and glass. "I'll be back to clear the table."

"You'll only push her further away."

He could be right, but she might also be on the precipice of being shoved toward submission.

I stalk inside, dump my bowl in the sink, and continue down the hall.

Her body craves mine. The carnality between us with every interaction is more than enough evidence of that. All that's left to win over is her head and her heart, and maybe now's the time.

I stop at her door, and for a second I think she left it open because she wanted me to follow, until I see the splinters of wood on the carpet from when I broke the latch.

I've terrorized her today.

"Layla—"

"I need to see my daughter." She cuts me off as she peers up at me from her position on the closest corner of the bed. "If this plan with Emmanuel isn't a trick, and we're legitimately going to take action, I want to see her first."

"I can arrange that." I can do anything. Whatever she needs. Whatever she wants. "I'm not tricking you."

"Okay, then when we leave for Denver, can you organize a detour to Chicago first?"

"That's where Stella goes to boarding school?"

She rakes her teeth over her lower lip as she dips her head once in a quick affirmation.

I'm caught off guard by the vulnerability she's just exposed. Completely blindsided with optimism.

"I'll make sure you see her." I step into her room, hungry for more of her trust. "I'll do whatever—"

"Don't." She raises a hand. "That's all I want. Nothing else has changed."

I stop. Stiffen. It's not her words that turn my feet to stone—it's her eyes. The ocean blue fills with desolation. Bleakness takes over her expression.

The woman once alive with aggression and sass is a brittle shell.

"Layla, what we did earlier today—"

"I already told you." She pushes to her feet. "It was a mistake."

"I agree."

Her brows narrow.

"I'm being honest." The pain. The trauma. The fucking blood. It was all a mistake. I pushed her too far. Toyed with her too much. We both craved the violence but I know now that she's too pure to revel in that toxicity. "Everything I've done since we arrived here has been a mistake."

She turns rigid.

"Except maybe giving you space when you first arrived," I amend. "I should've allowed you more time to think over what happened. I regret taunting you into fighting with me."

Her chin raises an inch.

"How do I make you understand the obsession you've created?" I chance another inch toward her.

"Please stop." She lowers her attention to the carpet and shakes her head. "I'm tired."

"Me too."

Me. Fucking. Too.

Her plea only makes it worse.

"I'm tired of not being heard," I admit. "And you're tired of fighting me, *amore mio*. Tired of denying how you feel."

She keeps her focus on the floor, her face the most beautiful inscrutable mask. "Is an admission what you need for this to be over?" she asks. "Is that what it will take? Your ego needs to hear that I still love you?"

Not my ego—my soul.

"Fine," she whispers. "I still love you, Matthew."

My entire body becomes motionless under the weight of her admission.

"But I despise myself for it." She raises her gaze to mine, the misery in her eyes slaughtering my ability to breathe. "I *hate* myself. I can't even look in the mirror without wanting to claw at my skin. And it took having sex with you, while covered in blood, to realize that I can't hold you accountable. At least, not entirely."

"Layla—"

"No, you were right when you said we were both at fault. I kept things from you that put you in danger," she states simply. "And I agree that it's part of the lifestyle we're in. Our secrets and safety are paramount. We do what needs to be done to cover our tracks."

My chest pounds with her sorrow. With her brutal fucking anguish.

"But the difference between our two betrayals is that I never knew your identity. I wasn't aware until Remy told me. Yet you understood Emmanuel was my enemy, and you went right ahead with seducing me into sleeping with his son. The offspring of my daughter's abductor. The same flesh and blood as my husband's killer."

I grind my teeth against the guilt.

"You knew I was in a temperamental position with my family, and still, you ruined what little integrity I had left. You didn't stop the games. You continued to drag me into an emotional entanglement that had no future. You created a world I needed. You gave me all I ever wanted even though you had to have known our lives couldn't coexist the way they were."

"They can coexist—"

"Stop," she warns. "There's no way I can be with you while continuing to respect myself *and* my daughter. You had to have known that. So why were you so cruel in giving me all I ever needed? Why did you make me fall in love with you when it was going to cost me *everything*?"

Because I'm a fucking monster.

"All I've ever wanted was someone to care for me the way you did." Her face crumples.

"The way I *do*," I correct. "You're everything—"

"My mother died when I was young, Matthew. My father pretended I didn't exist unless he wanted something. And my husband..." She winces and looks away. "I think I've already told you it was practically an arranged marriage. I fell pregnant from a one-night stand, and there's no way anyone in my family would've allowed Benji to live if he'd abandoned his responsibilities."

No, she didn't fucking tell me, and the insight is a bitch.

"But that's what I was." She meets my gaze again, the beautiful blue of her eyes swimming in emotion. "A responsibility. A chore. He never loved me. I've only ever been a hindrance. And the worst thing is that I thought you were different. You made me feel welcomed. *Cherished*." Her voice breaks, the fissures splintering into me like knives. "You spun the most beautiful lies and I believed every one of them. In your presence, I was smart, and brave, and empowered. I had hope, and meaning, and hunger for a better future."

Every word is a punishment for my lies.

Every admission a torturous truth.

"You were so incredibly good at deceiving me that I find it hard not to applaud you for it." She laughs to herself, half-hearted and pained. "You've won, Matthew. I still don't know what you set out to achieve, but I keep losing. I lost in Denver. I lost last night at the dinner table. And again this morning, when I tried to buy a Tesla and ended up sleeping with you instead. But I need to stop losing now. I can't keep doing this."

"I'd never diminish your suffering, but you've got this all wrong."

"Suffering is such an easy word for what I feel." She holds me in place with her hollow gaze. "Do you want to know what I wanted to do once the thrill wore off last night? Once I did the walk of shame from the dining room and came in here to be alone?"

"You wanted to kill me."

"No." She shakes her head, her tongue snaking out to lick her drying lips. "I wanted to kill *me*."

My stomach hollows. Fucking bottoms.

"For a split second, I wanted out of this mess. Permanently." Her face scrunches as she struggles to keep her voice steady. "I wanted to make everyone's life easier by taking my own."

I clench my fists.

I did this.

I did something far worse than Emmanuel ever did to me.

"So, I'm begging you, please stop." She straightens her shoulders. "Quit fighting me, give me what you've promised, then let me go."

11

LAYLA

"As you wish, *amore mio*."

That's all he says before turning on his heel to leave the room.

I expected him to put up a fight. Or flirt. Or beg for forgiveness.

Instead, he let two days pass with nothing more than murmured greetings or well-mannered questions when we happened to cross paths, which isn't often.

He's kept his distance, allowing me to recover the slightest semblance of pride after spewing my truth at him. He's spent the time on his phone, pacing the deck, his conversations easily overheard from my bedroom as he talks strategy about Emmanuel.

I assume it's for my benefit that he's remained out of reach yet within listening range.

He's assembled a team in Denver. I think it's the same men who helped us get onto the Costa family property last week, but I'm not willing to start a conversation to confirm.

It's best to remain alone.

Whenever Matthew's in the kitchen, I escape to my bedroom. While he's in the living room, I waste hours on the deck.

My packages started to arrive yesterday, giving me something to do while isolated. I've received a mass of cosmetics, books, and lingerie. But no clothes have shown up, which means I've been forced to wear Bishop's T-shirts to bed and the same worn jeans and blouse during the day.

"Your drinking hours are getting longer." Bishop climbs the deck stairs with a judgmental glower.

I glance at my wine glass, the liquid glistening in the beaming sun as I laze on the outdoor lounge chair.

"Should I be worried?" he asks. "Is this yet another attribute I didn't know about like the knife-and-blood kink?"

"Go to hell."

Unlike Matthew, Bishop hasn't given me a wide berth. He's done the opposite, always checking to make sure I've eaten, his annoying face constantly poking into my room to see if I'm still alive.

I take another sip of chardonnay, focusing my annoyance at the ocean. "I don't have kinks." And it's midafternoon, for Christ's sake. It's a socially acceptable time to drink.

"Sorry, am I using the wrong term?" He stops a few feet away and leans his hip against the railing. "Kink... Fetish... Perversion... They all mean the same thing to me."

"What do you want?" I glare.

"I just thought I'd let you know Langston left thirty minutes ago."

My heart skips a beat. "He left? Why?"

"He should be back in twenty. So you might want to ditch the wine and maybe do your hair."

I frown, confused.

"Or you could continue to look like a cheap drunk while on your hundred and fifth day of wearing the same clothes." He shrugs. "It's up to you, but you'll regret it once our visitors arrive."

"Someone is coming here?" I push to my feet. "Who?"

He pulls out his cell, ignoring me.

"*Bishop?*"

"Sorry. I can't hear you." He flicks a finger over his cell screen. "I'm too busy buying my ticket to hell."

Asshole.

"Can you at least tell me if I need to be worried? Did he go back on his word? Has he changed plans for Emmanuel without telling me?"

Who would Matthew trust enough to bring here? Lorenzo? Another mafia connection?

"You've got nothing to worry about." He keeps flicking his cell screen. "Unless you don't brush your teeth. Your booze breath might be a red flag for our guests."

"You want to see a red flag?" I step closer, throwing back the last of my wine. "Keep provoking me and I'll wave one in your bad-boy-wannabe face."

He grins. Snickers.

I stalk to the French doors leading into my room and lock them behind me. I comb my hair. Brush my teeth. Then finish with a touch of mascara, eyeliner, and a thin layer of BB cream in the hopes of hiding my exhaustion.

When I return to the deck Bishop is still in the same spot, his attention fixated on his cell.

"This better?" I ask, heavy with sarcasm.

He flicks me a two-second stare. "You've still got clothes on—that's always a bonus. I guess that means your exhibitionist kink hasn't been initiated today."

My aggression spikes as I reclaim my seat. "I'm not an exhibitionist."

"Tell that to my therapist."

I know he's only having fun. But these cat-fight conversations make me feel more alone. I haven't had a supportive ear in weeks. The diet of ridicule is draining.

"Can I borrow your phone?" My throat aches with the plea. "Just for a few minutes."

He looks up at me with a scowl. "Why?"

"I haven't spoken to my daughter in days."

"Have you asked Langston?"

My fingers twitch in my lap. "No. I think you're well aware I've been trying to stay as far away from him as possible."

"And let me tell you, it's been a blessing not to walk in on another porn act."

My cheeks heat, the flames equal parts rage and humiliation. "Can I have your phone or not?"

"Sorry, kink queen, you're going to have to wait until your guy gets back."

I fight not to give him the bird while the sea breeze whispers past my ears, the ebb and flow of the ocean doing nothing to soothe me.

Once Matthew returns, I'll have to risk speaking to him about our plans in Denver. I won't let him drag this on any longer. Two days has been enough.

"He's here." Bishop pushes from the railing and returns the cell to his jacket.

I stiffen at the faint rumble of a car carrying from the front of the house. A door slams, increasing my anticipation.

Then another.

And another.

And another.

I sit taller. "How many guests are there?"

"Why?" Bishop waggles his brows. "Are you getting excited that it might be a gang bang?"

Fuck you.

"What's going on?" I demand.

"Wait five seconds and you'll find out."

Footsteps carry around the side of the house. Fast. Light. Someone is running.

I shove to my feet and rush to the railing to peer into the yard. A young girl runs onto the lawn, her long dark hair flowing behind her back.

My heart stops. Breath evacuates my lungs. "Stella?"

"Mom?" She glances around the backyard.

"Up here, little fish." I tremble, my hands shaking, my throat drying as she swings around, her face tilted skyward.

She beams a smile at me, then runs for the stairs. All I can do is stare while my knees threaten to buckle.

I glance to Bishop in question. In confusion.

He smirks. "Aren't you glad you brushed your teeth?"

"You're such an asshole." A sob clogs in my throat.

He starts for the living room, sliding the door closed behind him as Stella reaches the top step.

Her pace increases. She flings her arms wide while I rush to meet her halfway. *"Surprise."*

I close my eyes, hugging her tight, nestling my face in her hair. "What are you doing here?"

"Aunt Keira took me out of school. She said I deserve a few days off."

My heart skips another beat. "Aunt Keira?" I pull back to read her expression.

"Yeah." She leans toward the railing to stare into the yard below. "I think she misses you."

My stomach bottoms as I follow her gaze, finding my sister on the lawn. Longing isn't what stares back at me though. It's indifference. Sterility. From her and Decker at her side.

I don't bother glancing toward Hunter and Sarah, who close in a few feet behind them. I'm not wearing enough clothes to withstand their arctic chill.

The only one who looks at me with any civility is Matthew, who prowls around the mini crowd toward the stairs. Watching. Supervising.

I'm not sure if he's trying to determine if I'm okay or if I'm about to run off with my child. Because I could. Skipping town is an option now that Stella is here. But only if I had the intention of letting her live on the streets.

"Well, it's a lovely surprise." I swallow the foreboding threatening to suffocate me and return my attention to the most beautiful girl in the world. "God, I've missed you. How did you get here?"

"The jet. Then *Matthew* picked the three of us up from the airport." She says his name with an exaggerated teasing lilt.

"The three of you?"

There are five new arrivals. Not three.

"Yeah. Hunter and Sarah were already waiting with *Matthew*." She does that teasing, playful tone again, but it doesn't stop the pit of my stomach becoming a cesspool.

"How were they already here? When did they arrive?"

"I don't know." She shrugs. "Please tell me I can stay longer than one night. Aunt Keira said you'd kill her if I missed more school, but it's not a big deal." She bats her lashes. "A few days won't make a difference—"

"You've been here two seconds and you're already blinking those puppy-dog eyes at me?" I kiss her forehead as my firing squad makes its way up the stairs. "I hate to admit you're your mother's daughter."

"Is that a yes?"

"That's a hard no." For starters, I don't know why she's here. I asked to see her in Chicago. A quick reunion before our task with Emmanuel got underway. I don't want her in the thick of this—surrounded by men she would hate if she knew their lineage.

I clear my throat. "School is important."

"School is painful."

"I thought you liked being in Chicago." I hold her gaze as Matthew enters my periphery over her right shoulder. "Has something happened?"

"No. It's just school, Mom. Nobody likes it."

The deck fills with an audience, each approaching footstep chipping away at my confidence.

The majority of people in the vicinity have given up on me. Discarded. Abandoned. And I'm meant to smile and pretend it hasn't happened.

"Hey, sis." Keira gives me a subdued finger wave, playing the amicable role. "I hope our arrival isn't too much of a shock. Matthew said he didn't tell you we were coming."

I turn my gaze to the man in question. "No, he didn't."

"I wasn't sure we could pull it off." He shrugs. "I didn't want to get your hopes up."

My stomach does a sweeping drop. What is this? Has he teamed up with my family to reinvigorate my torture? Has he brought my daughter here to prove he's still calling the shots?

"Well, you definitely succeeded in surprising me." I keep my tone level, my distress hidden. "I had no idea."

Keira beams a smile at Stella. "I'm just doing my best to maintain my status as the favorite aunt."

"You're my *only* aunt." Stella rolls her eyes.

"It's still a tough mantle to maintain, kiddo. And it's also not entirely true. Anissa is your aunt now, too."

"Not by blood."

There's a pause of silence, the awkward atmosphere settling in like a building storm.

I don't have the resilience to play pretend. At least not convincingly. Not when Sarah stares at the house so she doesn't have to meet my gaze, while Hunter and Decker do the same toward the ocean.

"Why don't I get you set up inside, little fish?" I glide a hand around Stella's shoulders. "We haven't spoken much lately. You need to fill me in on all the gossip."

"Sure."

Keira straightens, as if understanding my desire to get as far away from her as fast as possible. Did she expect me to fall to my knees and beg forgiveness? Am I meant to grovel? She'd only despise me more for the show of weakness. Earning my family's respect has only ever been achieved through strength, and that's not something I possess right now.

"Good idea." Keira nods. "We'll get our things from the car and meet you in the house."

Hunter, Sarah, and Decker remain silent. They don't even glance my way.

I wish the rejection didn't hurt, but it does. It festers inside me, weakening limbs and organs.

The three of them have done far worse than I ever have. They've betrayed us all in their own way. But apparently, their sins are forgivable because they've also killed to protect us.

Matthew leads the way toward the living room. I'm loathe to follow as he pulls the sliding door wide and waits for us.

It's Stella who makes the first move, striding toward him with a smile of admiration. "Thank you."

If only she knew his family killed her father.

"You're more than welcome, *principessa*."

I give him a reprimanding scowl, silently warning him not to manipulate her with his dreamy Italian like he does with me. But he doesn't meet my gaze. He's too focused on my daughter, his expression kind, his posture nonthreatening.

"Did you bring your swim suit?" he asks.

"Why?" She balks. "It's too cold."

"You can't come to the ocean and not take advantage of the surf. I've got boards in the garage that haven't seen the light of day in over a year. We can't leave them draped in cobwebs."

"Are you serious?" She glances to me with excitement. "Surfing?"

"She doesn't know how to surf." My friendly expression is fake. My kind tone, too. "It's best to leave it for another—"

"Please, Mom." She clasps her hands in prayer as she hovers at the threshold. "I want to learn."

I hold the dark eyes of the man who has already worked my daughter around his little finger, trying to let him know he's crossing multiple lines.

"Forgive me." He raises his hands in surrender. "If you don't have a bathing suit, it's better to surf some other time."

I keep staring, glaring, because unlike his ignorant ass, I know it's already too late to backtrack.

"I can wear shorts and a T-shirt," Stella counters. "Or we could buy something. Are there shops around here? *Please*, Mom."

I don't know how he does it. Is it the easy smile? The confident posture? The deep, chocolate eyes?

He's won my daughter over faster than he did me. But he doesn't stare back in victory. There's no demoralizing grin or smug smirk. His eyes are questioning. Cautious. Does he actually care that he's betraying me again?

"We'll see." I shoo her forward with a wave of my hand, then follow her inside. "You're not going to be here long, remember? You might find something more exciting to do."

"Like what?"

Good question.

I take the lead toward the hall, leaving Matthew in our wake. "I'm sure there are a million things."

She sighs as I step into my bedroom with the mess of half-opened packages strewn across the floor. I tidy the rubbish, grabbing crumpled paper and plastic as she belly flops on the bed, her body bouncing on impact.

"Time to spill the details." She turns onto her back, her long hair covering her face. "So, Matthew is the guy you've been spending all your time with? I thought you were just friends."

"We are."

"Mom, he's clearly simping over you."

"Simping?" I turn away, hiding from her scrutiny. "Do I want to know what that means?"

"He likes you." The bedsprings squeak with her movement. "He couldn't stop talking about you in the car, which means he really, *really* likes you."

The words shouldn't hurt, but they do. They lash with the force of a knotted rope.

I'd thought the same thing. I'd *wanted* it, too.

"Where did you meet? What's his last name? What does he do for work?" She peppers me with questions that seem more like accusations, each one harder than the last. "You said you two were working together, right?"

"Calm down, little fish. We've got all the time in the world to talk about me. I want you to tell me about school first."

"Forget school. Something is definitely going on with you two." She grins. "I've been here five seconds and it's already obvious he thinks you're the goat."

"The goat?" I squeeze a tissue paper tighter in my grip, compacting it into an aggression-filled ball to throw into an empty box in the corner. "Where are you getting all these words?"

"You're so old. It means the Greatest Of All Time."

I shouldn't have asked.

"How long have you known each other? Have you met his family? Have you kissed?"

"Stella, please." I turn back to her, my eyes pleading. "I told you, it's not like that."

I don't want to lie to her. Not about this. I also can't stomach telling her even the slightest snippet of truth. Problem is, she's old enough to remember all the things I might lie about if the reality is eventually revealed.

I need to lay low. Glide under the radar.

Distract. Divert. Redirect.

"Do you want to sleep in here tonight?" I force energy into my voice. "There's plenty of room in my bed. We could stay up late and watch the stars like we used to."

Her nose scrunches as she breaks eye contact. "Are there any other rooms?"

"There are plenty of rooms. I just thought…" I don't know… I guess it doesn't seem so long ago that she was crawling under my covers in the middle of the night, her face soaked from tears, her mind a mess from nightmares of her father's murder. She spent months cuddled into me. Almost a year. Now she doesn't even want to spend a night. "Where would you like to sleep?"

"It's just that I kinda like my own space now. And I wouldn't want to wake you if I get up during the night and check my phone. I get good cell reception here, by the way. I don't know what carrier Matthew uses for his phone, but he needs to change."

I smile despite her revealing my first lie. "Well, you better hurry before Aunt Keira takes the best room."

"Are you sure?" She scrambles from the bed. "You don't mind?"

"Not at all." It's more dishonesty. "Go. Claim the comfiest bed."

"Okay." She dashes for the hall, her eager footsteps clapping into the distance.

I don't move. Don't even twitch.

I remain weighed in place while sorrow consumes me.

I thought being with her would strengthen me. That all I needed was to see the one person who loves me unconditionally. But pretending I'm not dying inside has only increased my suffering.

The worst part is that I hate acknowledging I have no fear for her safety under this roof.

Yes, Matthew might worm his way into my daughter's heart, or Bishop could say something highly inappropriate in an attempt to make her laugh. But I don't doubt for a second that the men who have ruined my life will never hurt her.

It's just me that the world wants to bring to its knees.

I force myself to move. To keep busy tidying the remainder of the mess as doors open and close through the house.

Voices murmur from the living room, a low grumble from Decker, a soft reply from my sister, then a sarcastic drawl from Bishop. They should be killing each other. Why aren't they?

Footsteps approach along the hall, the heavy thuds coming from a man.

I pause in the middle of crumpling tissue paper in my hands, hoping it's someone walking to a nearby room. Luck isn't on my side.

The shuffle of movement stops at my door. The heat of attention tickles the back of my neck.

"Your sister brought this for you," Matthew murmurs.

I turn to him standing in the doorway, a small duffle in his hand. "What is it?"

He places the luggage at his feet. "Clothes, I assume."

"How did she know I needed them?"

He shrugs, the collar of his crisp white shirt rubbing over the cut I left on his neck. "I may have mentioned it."

I don't know what hurts more—the fact he's on speaking terms with my family or that they disrespected me enough to let him make plans for my daughter. They couldn't have known I'd trust Matthew around Stella. That the goddamn Butcher Boys of Baltimore could provide a safe space for a child.

"Where is she?" he asks.

I walk for the sheer curtains covering the French doors, needing the peace of the ocean instead of the struggle that comes with staring at his face. "She went to find her own room. Apparently, she no longer wants to share my bed."

"If it makes you feel any better, I know someone who would eagerly take the offer."

I sigh. "I thought we weren't doing this anymore."

"You asked me not to fight with you, and I haven't. Nothing else has changed. I still see hunger when you look at me, Layla. I'm not giving up."

"You're mistaken."

"I assure you, I'm not."

The hot rush of anger adds to my sorrow. I force myself to focus on the gentle waves. *Breathe in. Breathe out.* "You shouldn't have brought her here. I asked to see her in Chicago."

"I didn't want to risk someone following us to her school."

"So you called my family?" I murmur.

"Is that a problem?"

Everything is a problem. Every thought. Every action. Every inhale.

Then there's the paranoia that has me questioning who he spoke to and what was said. Does Cole still hate me? Will my brother ever forgive me? Is he happy that Matthew is now my caretaker so I'm no longer a burden to my siblings? And why the hell were Hunter and Sarah already here?

"I didn't know you were on speaking terms." I pull back the see-through curtain as I glance at him over my shoulder, my fingers clutching the material for support.

"Neither did I, but for you, I asked."

My pulse pounds with the need to know the intricacies of his conversation, but with every second Matthew looks at me with pitiful longing, he chips away at the meager morsels of strength I have left.

"You should speak to your sister." He inches farther into the room, his hands sliding into the pockets of his suit pants. "She might be able to clarify any questions you have."

"No, thank you." I turn to face him. "And you can stay right where you are."

He complies, somehow unbelievably predatory even in his stillness.

"Does Stella's arrival mean you've made headway with Emmanuel?" I ask. "Can we finally get this over and done with?"

"Soon. He's left the property while under surveillance, which is a start."

"It's more than a start. It's enough to warrant going there and watching for ourselves. Any time he leaves the property—"

"I won't budge when it comes to your safety. So don't bother trying."

I turn back to the French doors. "You're stalling, and as soon as Stella is gone, I'll be putting a stop to it."

"Enjoy the time with your daughter, Layla." The soft pad of his steps retreats toward the hall. "Let me know if you need anything."

I swallow over the lump in my throat, his kindness causing more volatility than his aggression ever did.

Everything he does kills me. Every facet of his personality is a direct hit to my heart. I want it all. The possession. The compassion. But there can never be a future with a man who can warp my reality.

I wait until his presence is a brief brush of sound in the distance, then go in search of Stella, finding her in the farthest room down the hall. The bed is perfectly made. The curtains are pulled wide. Sunshine beams in on the beauty of her as she stands at the large bay window overlooking the garden, her finger frantically tapping against her cell. She has to have grown an inch in the past few weeks.

"Like the view?" I walk to her side, wishing she was still at the age where cuddles were all she ever wanted.

She looks up at me with a smile as she pockets the device. "It's so nice here. Why do we never come to the coast?"

Because Uncle Cole prefers the safety of isolation, not the risk of open space. "I guess our family have always been city people. My parents rarely took me anywhere like this either."

"Can we go for a walk on the sand?"

"Of course."

I lead her outside via my bedroom so I don't have to come face to face with my sister.

We don't walk far, maybe half a mile, before we sit on the dry sand. I listen as she quickly chatters about the new boy in class who used to tug her hair whenever he passed until Tobias punched him in the stomach. She tells me how hard her advanced math class has become. And how her grades are improving. Then she diverts the conversation back to Matthew, as if the prior information was a strategic info dump to appease me before she could get onto the only topic she's excited to talk about.

I'm forced to fudge my way through tricky answers.

No, I haven't met his family.

Yes, I know what he does for a living.

He's a nightclub owner. He lives in D.C. He's a good man.

"Do you still think of Dad?" Her tone remains energetic, but it doesn't hide the vulnerability of her question as she digs her toes into the sand.

"All the time, little fish." I slide my hand around her shoulders and pull her closer. "I promise I'll never stop."

"I don't think about him as much as I used to." She digs her feet deeper, breaking my heart with her admission.

"How come?"

"It hurts."

I kiss her temple, buying myself time to respond without breaking. "Do you want to come back home? Would it be easier to return to school in Portland?"

"No. I like the friends I have now. And I can't leave Tobias. Who would keep him out of trouble?"

I scoff. "Tobias shouldn't be getting in trouble."

"Somehow I don't think that's an option." She chuckles, half-hearted as she glances over my shoulder toward the house. "Who's that guy watching us?"

I follow her gaze to the suit-clad monstrosity standing over ten yards away. "His name is Bishop. He's Matthew's best friend."

She makes a noise. A high-pitched questioning humph.

"Before you even ask, I'm not his goat either." I nudge her shoulder. "There's no goat business at all."

She laughs. "What's he like?"

I chance another glance at the man leaning against the white picket fence of a neighboring yard, his arms crossed over his chest. "He's..." I frown, attempting to come up with a way to describe him. "I guess he's a lot like the men you've grown up with."

"Overprotective, grumpy, and always thinks he's right?"

"That's an apt description." I turn back to her with a smile.

"And Matthew?" she asks. "What's he like?"

I look away, wincing at the first word that comes to mind—*perfect.*

Perfect for me. Perfect for my insecurities. Perfect for my soul. If only the things I adored weren't perfectly fictional.

"He's the same."

I sense her eyes narrowing in my periphery, her scrutiny potent. "Why can't you admit you like him?"

Because his family killed your father.

"He's just not the right man for me. We're too different." Or maybe the problem is that we're exactly the same. Either way, there's no escaping the red flags that accompany us being together.

"Different is good, isn't it?"

"It can be. But there's a lot more to it. You know we're not like most people. We need to be careful with who we align ourselves."

"And he's not someone you should be aligning with?" She glances toward Bishop again, giving me the briefest reprieve.

I can't keep distracting her from the truth. I don't want to feed her more white lies. But... *Goddamnit.* I hate this. "He's familiar with some of our enemies."

"Familiar how?"

I turn to her. "It's nothing for you to worry about, I promise. And his familiarity was only part of the issue. The real problem was that he hid it from me. He lied."

She frowns. "Why would he do that?"

I don't know... Because he's cruel. Deceptive. A born liar. "It's complicated."

"Why do you always say that when you don't want to give me the real answer? It's so annoying. You treat me like I'm too young to be told stuff, but I'm not. I know a lot more than you think."

"It's usually a nicer way of saying I don't want to talk about it, little fish."

"Well I *do* want to talk about it. If he's a liar and familiar with our enemies, why am I here? Isn't it dangerous?"

"No, not at all. You're safe. *He's* safe." I brush a hand through her hair. "I'm still working with him. I'm just no longer wanting to be in love with him."

"So you *were* in love?"

Goddamnit. "Stella, please."

She grins. "I want you to be happy, Mom."

"And I want you to stop asking questions, my sweet little pumpkin seed."

She laughs. "I'm just trying to understand because you being in love is huge."

"I don't feel that way anymore," I lie. "So can we please drop it?"

"But if you're still working with him even though he knows our enemies, then your problem must be about him lying... and you lie to me all the time. If I can forgive and forget, why can't you?"

"What have I lied about?"

She lowers her gaze to her toes popping up from beneath the sand. "Everything. You hide things from me, too. I always find out, though, and it's ten times harder to hear it from someone else."

I ignore the icy chill working through my limbs. "Stella, I'm sorry. But sometimes I keep quiet on issues so you don't worry unnecessarily. We have a lot of things that make people envious—"

"I'm not talking about that. It's the things I deserve to know that make me mad."

My pulse increases with apprehension. I don't want to ask.

"You should've told me about Granddad," she murmurs. "I had to find out from Tobias."

All the blood rushes from my face. "What did he tell you?"

"That his dad liked to humiliate women." Her throat works over a heavy swallow. "That he hurt them. *Raped* them. Probably even killed them."

Oh, God. "Stella…"

I don't know what to say.

"He was my family," she continues. "I deserved to know."

I grab her hand, encasing it in mine. "No, you deserved to be free from those horrible thoughts. I didn't want you to feel the way I felt after finding out."

She meets my gaze. "And how did you feel?"

Guilty. Dirty. Vile.

I swallow over the tightness building in my chest. "I was ashamed."

"Of what?" Her nose scrunches. "What he did wasn't your fault."

I wish that were true, but who knows what that monster accomplished due to the secrets I fed him. "He was the man who created me. Whose blood flows through my veins. His soul made mine."

Her face crumples. "Mom…"

"Please forgive me." I squeeze her hand. "I never meant to hurt you."

"I *do* forgive you. I always will. I just wish you understood that I can handle the truth."

No, she can't. Not the real truth. Not the darkest deceptions.

Even I can't handle those, and I'm the one who committed them.

"I'll try to do better in the future." I nestle close against her side, both of us turning our attention to the setting sun. The day creeps toward night in varying shades of orange, pink, and purple, the waves gently gliding across the sand as the breeze dances in our hair.

"Could it be possible that Matthew lied to you for the same reasons you lie to me?" she asks softly.

I lean in to kiss her temple, closing my eyes with the light brush. "It's getting close to dinner. We should head back to the house."

"*Mom,*" she begs. "I want to talk about this."

"You've made that clear, sweetheart. But can you understand that it hurts?" I push to my feet and hold out a hand to help her do the same. "I don't want to think about it anymore."

"But you were in love." She wipes the sand from her butt. "Surely if I can forgive you for the things you lie about, you should be able to forgive him."

I start along the beach, wishing I'd put more thought into a plan before I opened my big mouth. "Forgiveness is hard."

"Believe me, I know."

"Well, it's even harder when you're an adult."

She hustles to keep pace at my side. "But not impossible, right? Surely if you both love each other you can work things out."

Vultures take over my insides, picking me apart, scavenging for the mere morsels of strength left behind.

"He doesn't love me, Stella." He never confessed the emotion. That was all on me. *My* assumption. *My* mistake. *My* stupidity. "Now can we please drop it?"

12

LAYLA

Matthew is on the deck when we return, his gaze on mine the moment we walk into the yard.

"I've never seen a man look at you the way he does. Not even Dad." Stella releases my hand. "It sure seems like love to me."

She doesn't give me the opportunity to respond as she takes off across the lawn. "I'm going to freshen up for dinner." She bounds up the stairs two at a time, stealing Matthew's attention once she reaches the deck to share murmured words.

I walk faster, tempted to break into a run to hear what they're saying, but she's already inside by the time I reach the upper level. "What did you say to her?"

He turns to me, raising a lone brow at my tempered aggression.

"And what did you say to her before she arrived?" I hiss. "She has certain misconceptions about us that I don't appreciate."

He scowls, his concern fake. "What sort of misconceptions, *amore mio*?"

He's tempting me to fight with him again. Poking. Prodding.

I want to get in his face. To demand he quit calling me that stupid endearment. To stop being a manipulative prick and toying with my emotions.

"You know exactly what I'm talking about." I chance a cautious glance inside, finding an audience of Stella, Keira, and Decker in the living room. *Shit*. I force a smile and relax my shoulders, not wanting my daughter to realize I'm a prisoner of circumstance. "She's becoming more convinced that I'm here for romantic reasons."

"I think you are, too." He steps toward me, entering my personal space.

I huff a laugh and turn my back to the house so I have the freedom to glare. "Don't push me, Langston. When it comes to Stella, I attack first and ask questions later."

"Langston?" he muses. "I don't think I like you calling me that."

"Then back the hell off," I growl.

He inclines his head. Subtle. Submissive. "I assure you, apart from answering her questions about you on the way from the airport, I've barely talked to her. I deliberately didn't want to step on your toes. And I'm not trying to lay blame, but I'd assume your sister is the one who's given the little *principessa* the wrong idea. You really should speak to her."

I'm almost tempted to believe him if it weren't for his second suggestion—to confront Keira. He knows I won't go there. My pride is too brittle to go crawling to her when I'm yet to make up for my mistakes.

"Stay away from my daughter." I stand taller. Straighter. Attempting to see right through the charm he's laying thicker than glue. "I told her you're a liar. She knows you're not to be trusted."

His face falls. It's a split second of confounded shock before his eyes narrow. "Whatever you say, *amore mio*."

"And don't call me that in front of her. She already thinks you're obsessed with me. I don't need you making things worse."

"Knows," he clarifies. "She already *knows* I'm obsessed."

My hands itch to grasp the fight he's offering. To dive headfirst into it in one rapid release of endorphins. But he'll win. He'll wrap my ovaries around his little finger like always and then I'll be a slave to shame all over again—this time in front of a daughter who will hold me accountable.

"I'm not doing this with you." I start for the French doors of my bedroom.

"I like seeing you like this," he says to my back. "Your protective side is captivating."

I snatch at the door handle and pull it wide. "You act like everything about me is captivating."

"It's not an act, *la mia piccola sporcacciona*."

I stop myself from slamming the door behind me and continue to the bathroom to douse my face in cold water.

I hold my breath as I splash and splash, attempting to wash away his attention, but I'm already warmed by it. *Heated.* His affects sink under my skin. Delve into my lungs.

He promised to quit antagonizing me only to revert to yet another effective strategy—seduction.

Bastard.

I slump onto the lowered toilet seat, water dripping from my face onto my clothes while the scent of spices filters into the bathroom.

Cutlery clatters from the kitchen. Stella's laughter echoes down the hall. The world keeps spinning while I slowly unravel on a goddamn toilet in a town I don't even know the name of.

"*Mom?*" Stella calls out. "Are you coming for dinner? Hunter bought Chinese."

"Yep." I drag myself to my feet, pat my face with a towel, and suck in a deep breath.

"*Mom?*"

"I'm coming." I meet Stella in the hall, her attention far too scrutinizing as we walk toward the living room.

"You okay?" she asks. "You look tired."

"It's nothing an early night won't fix." I craft a subdued smile while everyone takes a seat at the dining table and begins eating.

I don't make eye contact with anyone.

Not Matthew, who sits to my left, or Keira, who's in front of me on the other side of the table.

I focus on the takeout containers. I fork food onto my plate that I don't have the stomach to consume. I stare at the wine glass someone left at my place setting and wonder how many seconds it would take to drain it clean.

The conversation is smooth around me. Keira, Sarah, and Decker talk to Bishop and Matthew as if they're friends. They discuss the weather. The stock market. The damn NFL, for Christ's sake. Hunter retains his usual air of ice-cold indifference.

To the untrained eye, everything is normal. There's no hitch in conversation or pause of discomfort for Stella to latch onto. Not one hint to trigger her suspicion that the family surrounding her have disowned her mother.

They all play nice—the loved ones who divorced me and the man who betrayed me.

I should be grateful, but the agony builds beneath my sternum with every nibble of chow mein.

"Can we come back to this place sometime?" Stella asks. "I love it here, and I haven't had a chance to look around."

"You're always welcome." Matthew drapes his arm over the back of my chair. "In fact, we can make plans before you leave." His eyes meet mine, taunting in their hunger. "What do you think, *la mia piccola sporcacciona*?"

Bishop clears his throat, the slightest laugh shaking through.

"She can't miss any more school." I hold Matthew's gaze, ignoring the warmth in my belly, the flood of adrenaline in my veins.

"Then summer vacation sounds perfect. You can stay however long you like." He stares me down, waiting for a rejection.

Nobody else speaks. All eyes are on us.

"Our work will be done by then." I grab my napkin and dab at my mouth as I wink at my daughter. "But don't worry, little fish. I'll find us a sugar daddy with a bigger beach house."

Stella snorts and rolls her eyes. "Gross, Mom."

Matthew inches closer, making me tense as his lips brush the sensitive skin below my ear. "You know I can give you all the sugar you need."

I ignore him. The words. The proximity. The contact.

I shut everything out and slowly reach for my glass of wine.

"Well, that's a visual I never knew I didn't need." Bishop grabs for the container of rice. "Did anyone want any more of this before I eat it all?"

The conversation diverts away from me. Away from *us*. But Matthew doesn't move.

He keeps his arm around my chair, his body nestled close as Stella laughs at her aunt's recollection of a childhood vacation at Salt Lake City.

My wine goes down too easily. I punctuate every bite of shame and twinge of regret with a sip of Chardonnay which requires my glass to be filled repeatedly until everyone is finished eating.

"Can I go to my room to check my phone?" Stella places her cutlery on her empty plate and bats her lashes at me. "I'm waiting to hear from Tobias?"

"Sure." I force a smile. "I think we're all finished here, aren't we?"

"I believe we are, *principessa*." Matthew nods at her, and Keira agrees.

Stella hustles for the hall, taking every ounce of fraudulent conversation with her. The table falls silent. Discomfort suffocates the room.

My skin crawls.

I suck in a deep breath and push back in my chair. "I need fresh air." I don't wait for a reply before I stand and walk for the door.

I leave the fake civility behind, not stopping my escape until my hands clutch the deck railing, my fingers aching from the tight grip.

I barely have a chance to lower my pulse before the door slides open behind me and heavy footsteps approach.

"Everything okay?" Matthew stops a few feet away, awakening the hair on the back of my neck.

I don't want his concern or his questions. I don't even want his attention. But my body continues to respond as if it needs him, warming despite the cool breeze.

"You've done a great job raising your daughter." He moves to stand beside me, his attention on the moonlight beaming a path across the ocean. "I've never known someone her age to settle into adult conversation the way she does."

"She had to grow up a lot earlier than most." I want to inch away, to get out of the intimacy zone where his aftershave plays havoc with my senses. But he'd know exactly why I'd needed to move and I don't want to give him that ammunition. "That growth only increased when your family killed her father."

He sighs and turns toward the house, his arms leisurely crossing over his chest as he leans back against the railing.

He doesn't defend my attack. Doesn't match me taunt for taunt. Instead, he remains quiet, letting me suffocate from guilt.

"I shouldn't have said that." As much as I don't want to be near him right now, I'd despise anyone who used my father's actions against me. "I'm sorry."

"You're forgiven, *la mia piccola sporcacciona*."

I slump at his quick pivot toward seduction. "What does that even mean?"

"Do you really want to know?" The grin lifting his cheeks tells me my answer should be a hard no. "It roughly translates to 'my dirty little girl.'"

"And you said that in front of my daughter?" I gape. "You're such a jerk."

"I am. But you lied when you said you told Stella I'm not trustworthy, so I guess we're as bad as each other."

"I *did* tell her. She knows you broke my heart by lying to me."

His brows raise. "Interesting."

I want to claim otherwise. That it's not interesting at all. That nothing about my daughter's feelings toward him are even vaguely intriguing.

"She still likes me, Layla. Why is that?"

I don't respond.

"She smiled when I put my arm over the back of your chair," he continues. "She blushed when I spoke to you in Italian. Every time I glance at her, it's as if she's silently giving me permission to keep trying to win you back. Why do you think that is?"

Son of a bitch.

He wasn't testing *me* with his actions at dinner. He was testing *her*.

"Stop manipulating my daughter," I seethe under my breath.

"I wasn't. All I did was investigate the boundaries on what she wants for her mother, and clearly, she wants you to be happy with me."

I glare. "Do I look happy to you?"

He takes the time to rake his gaze over my features—my nose, cheeks, chin. His attention lingers longer than necessary on my mouth before returning to my eyes. "You look like you're still fighting your love for me, and I hate watching you struggle."

He pushes from the railing and closes in behind me, caging me in place.

I stiffen, every part of him awakening every inch of me. I stand taller, shifting my hips away, but all he does is lean closer, pressing his crotch harder against my ass.

"*Matthew.*"

"Yes, *la mia piccola sporcacciona*?" he whispers against the back of my neck.

I swallow over the dryness decimating my throat. "What do you want from me?"

"Everything." His lips burn my skin, sending wildfire over my shoulders. "I want the love you've held hostage. I want the future we deserve. I want your passion without the malice."

I shudder, the low cadence of his words horrifically hypnotizing. "Why? We both know this is a passing phase."

"Is that what it feels like to you?" His question is barely audible. "Is the fire in your lungs burning out? Has your attraction begun to fade?"

I dig my nails into the railing.

"Mine either, *amore mio*. I still want your pants around your ankles every time I see you. Your bite marks on my skin. Your claw marks over my chest." His voice grows deeper, richer with lust. "I want to do things to you that would make a sinner blush. Then afterward, I want to hold you. *Care* for you. *Protect* you."

"You're the only thing I've needed protection from." I turn in his arms, realizing the mistake of my actions as soon as those dark eyes slay me with their proximity.

He stares at me with hunger. With pure infatuation. The potency sizzles through every place our bodies connect. Into limbs. Through organs.

I swallow. "Let me go or I'll—"

"I beg you to say something violent." He leans his waist harder into mine, the length of his cock aligning with my mons. "Your brutality does things to me that keep me up at night. Extremely dirty things."

He smirks and raises his hand to glide a thumb over the cut on his neck. "This is a constant turn on, *amore mio*. A perpetual thrill." He inches closer, his breath brushing my lips. "I can't wait to have my blood back on your beautiful skin."

"*Move.*"

"Like this?" He grinds his hips into me, the friction electric.

I burn. Heart to hands. Throat to thighs.

"Quit fighting this." His tongue snakes out to deftly swipe his lower lip. Devilish. Sinful. "If your own daughter approves of me, why can't you?"

"I. Won't. Quit." I enunciate the words slowly as movement enters my periphery. I glance over his shoulder, finding my daughter returning to the living room, her attention fixed on me and Matthew as she strolls toward the sofa. "Stella is watching."

"Good." He weaves a hand around my waist.

"Stop it."

He's betting all his chips that I won't lash out. He knows I won't fight him in front of her.

"I won't give up what's mine," he repeats.

The need to scream builds, the tension forming a choking mass in my throat. He has to stop. I can't keep doing this.

"Have you ever wondered why Cole disowned me so easily?" I grate. "Did it ever cross your fucking mind to question how such a notorious family could discard one of their own in the blink of an eye?"

"I don't need to know."

"Yes, you do." I press my forearms to his chest, attempting to leverage a breath of space. "My brother would've been relieved that your ignorance has taken me off his hands. He probably laughed at the stupid asshole who didn't understand he was claiming a traitor. A pariah. Someone who ratted her own brother out to a monster all for a little money."

His eyes narrow. "Nothing you say will change the way I feel about you, if that's what you're attempting to achieve. Your family still care for you, Layla."

"My family despise me, but they'd do anything for my daughter," I correct. "You have no clue who I really am. You've never met the real me. The liability. I'm a threat to whoever remains close to me. Why do you think I'd allow the one thing I treasure most to be sent to a boarding school on the other side of the country?"

"You think I don't know you're a liability?" He stares at me, eyes intense, breathing heavy. He raises a hand, killing me softly as he glides a stray hair behind my ear. "Anything that weakens me is a threat to my existence. And nothing weakens me more than you."

"Are you deliberately ignoring what I just said? I'm not trustworthy. I'm not a good person. I sold out Cole for years. My own flesh and blood. My father wanted information and I willingly gave it. I told him my brother's strategies. His secrets. His plans."

"I'm not ignoring it. But I'm well aware there are parts of your story that would excuse your actions. Why did you give up the information, *amore mio*? Were you blackmailed? Threatened?"

"No."

"Then why?"

Because I wanted affection. Attention. I wanted someone to be proud of me. To love me.

The same way I thought you had.

"You won't answer me because deep down, you know I'm right." He strokes my cheek with his thumb, leisurely back and forth with savage tenderness. "You paint a horrible picture of yourself, Layla. But I see you. The *real* you."

"You see what I want you to see."

"You're many things but a good actress isn't one of them." His gaze holds unflinching confidence. "You can't push me away."

"You're not listening. I betrayed those I love. I did it over and over—"

"You made mistakes. We all do. If it weren't for mine, Grace would still be alive."

"Stop it." I thump my fist against his chest. "You're making excuses for something you know nothing about."

"That's because I don't give a shit." His mouth is almost on mine. So close. A breath apart. "I will never give up on you."

God. But I need him to.

"Well, I've already given up on you." I raise my chin through the lie. "And I'll tell you exactly why—my father manipulated me into stealing Cole's secrets. He used my desperation for love against me. He fed off my need for affection just like you did."

His lips press tight. His nostrils flare.

"I can't be with a man who has that much power over me. I won't risk doing that to my family again no matter how much they hate me."

"I'm not your father," he growls.

"You're right. You're nowhere near as proficient as he was because you were stupid enough to get caught in your lies. You're a poor man's version of Luther Torian. Now get the fuck out of my face."

He scowls. Sneers. Retreats. "Don't for one second think that I don't know exactly what you're doing."

I stride for the living room door, my heart in my throat, my restraint in tatters.

"I'm well aware you push me to the brink to distract yourself from how you feel," he mutters. "But the time will come when you can't keep kidding yourself. And I'll still be here. Waiting. It's inevitable, *amore mio.*"

13

MATTHEW

I wait outside, dragging the cold night into my lungs, wishing that shit would dull the lust coursing through my veins.

She keeps pushing me away.

There's always a new excuse. Another reason. A different story.

None of it fucking matters. I'm not going anywhere.

I want *her*—mistakes, lies, and all.

I watch her in the living room as she approaches her daughter. She says something that has the young girl moving to her feet, then the two of them head for the hall.

Once they're out of sight, all eyes turn to me—Decker, Hunter, Sarah, and Keira.

I have no idea where the fuck Bishop is, but the family descends on me in a pack, the four of them walking outside with varying degrees of annoyance.

"What was that all about?" Decker asks.

I raise a brow. "You're going to have to be more specific."

"Layla came inside, clearly flustered," Keira says. "What's going on with you two?"

"That's none of your business."

Hunter chuckles, low and menacing. "I assure you, it is."

Bishop enters the living room, his long strides eating up the space to the door that he yanks open, his expression set in stone. "I leave the room for five seconds to take a piss and the scavengers descend."

He's ignored. All scrutinous eyes remain on me.

"Can you at least tell me if she's okay?" Keira asks. "She's barely spoken a word to me."

"And why do you think that is?"

She winces, wrapping her arms around her middle.

"Are you making headway?" Hunter moves to the outdoor setting, cocking his hip against the corner of the table. "Or do we start making plans for you to join us in Portland?"

"He's still got weeks, asshole," Bishop snarls. "Don't get your hopes up."

"I can't help it." Hunter's grin is subtle. "I can't wait to start riding his ass into the ground."

"You sure your bitch won't get jealous?" I jerk my chin at Decker. "He seems like the possessive type."

"I'm possessive as fuck, sweetie." Decker takes a threatening step forward. "But don't worry. I'll get a turn riding your ass, too."

"Stop it." Keira moves in front of him. "We're not here to cause trouble."

Decker glares at me over her shoulder.

"Listen to your boss." Bishop maneuvers around behind them, his attention on my hand as I slide it into my pocket to palm my blade. "You don't want to start a fight you won't win."

I dig the metal into my thigh, deeper, harder, distracting myself from the call of violence.

"We're not fighting," Keira says. "All of you need to go inside so I can speak to Matthew alone."

Nobody moves.

Nobody quits staring at me.

Keira swings around. Not to her man, or the enforcer, but to Sarah. "Get them out of here."

I smirk. It must chafe their balls to be commanded by a woman. Then again, I'd let Layla do far worse to my pride.

"Him, too." She glares at Bishop. "I want to speak to Langston alone."

Bishop leisurely meets my gaze, as if waiting for approval.

"Go." I nod.

His attention lowers to my pocket, his eyes narrowing.

"*Go.*"

He complies, leading the charge inside with Torian's cronies following.

Once the door closes, Keira strolls to the railing, her focus on the inky ocean. "Please tell me she's okay."

I wish I could, but I'm not going to lie to make this bitch feel better about her family's actions. So instead, I keep my mouth shut.

"Can you at least tell me what you've told her about the situation?" she asks.

"Nothing." I keep my voice low, knowing Layla could be right up against the French doors trying to overhear every word.

"So you're still lying to her?"

"No," I mutter. "She hasn't asked questions and I haven't offered information."

"Does she know about your agreement with Co—"

"I've told her nothing," I snarl. "Not a fucking thing. Now lower your goddamn voice before she hears you."

She shoots me a sideways glance—a glare—then slumps her shoulders with a sigh. "She's hurting. But it's obvious she still has feelings for you."

It's true. One hundred percent on both counts.

"I can see it in her eyes," she adds. "She truly believes we've disowned her. That we think less of her. And she already battled with a misconception about our commitment to her before you two met."

"Her self-worth isn't her strongest attribute."

She nods. "This situation is only making it worse. I'm worried this is causing trauma that she might never recover from."

What's her angle? Her game plan? Is she trying to trip me up?

"I'm not lying." She reads my mind. "I can't stomach what damage this is potentially creating. She was already too fragile."

"She told me she ratted out your brother. Is that true?"

"It was years ago, and I wouldn't describe it like that. She was manipulated into thinking she was helping the family. But all she did was strengthen a monster." Her voice lowers to a whisper. "She's never forgiven herself so I'm surprised she told you."

"She's trying her best to push me away."

"Is it working?"

It's strengthening my concerns about the damage I'm creating. That this situation has the potential to break Layla forever. That's why I tried to encourage her to talk to Keira this afternoon.

I drag in a deep breath. "You should tell her."

Keira straightens. "Tell her what?"

"All of it. Everything. She deserves to know the truth."

"She's always deserved to know. What's changed?"

Me. I was too fucking naive to understand how hard it would be to watch her suffer through a false perception. I was an asshole for thinking I could win her back without tearing her apart. "Just fucking tell her, Keira. Do it in the morning."

Her eyes narrow. "Is this a ploy to get out of your arrangement? That if I spill the details it'll somehow nullify the deal you made with Cole?"

"Nothing will nullify the deal. I made a commitment and I'll stick to it. But Layla should know the truth."

"Then *you* tell her."

"I can't. She doesn't trust me. She'll think I'm trying to mess with her somehow."

"Well, neither can I. My brother will kill me."

"Bullshit. We both know her insight will only work in his favor." If Layla knows she has a safe haven back home, she'll leave, and I'll be forced to follow. "She doesn't know how you all feel and that's the only thing keeping her here."

Keira's nose crinkles. "I'm confused. If you know she'll leave, why tell her?"

Because even though Layla loves me, I want her to love herself even more. I can't watch her wallow in self-loathing. I can't put her through more shit.

"Langston?" Keira cocks her head. "Talk."

"All you need to know is that she's suffering from what your brother made her believe. So get it done."

"Do you understand what will—"

"Get it fucking done." I stalk for the door, pull it wide, and ignore every single motherfucker along the way to my bedroom.

I'm shooting myself in the foot. Sabotaging my own goddamn future.

But there's no way around it.

Layla's misery has to end.

I take a shower, letting the water's spray wash the bloodied cuts along my thigh. Then I drag on my boxers, cut the lights, and climb into bed to stare at the fucking ceiling for hours after everyone else has gone to sleep.

Layla will walk. No doubt about it. And when I follow, I won't have access to her on my terms. She could lock herself at home. Or worse, in her brother's house.

Cole won't grant me any more concessions. He's given me enough already. So sinking back into my old lifestyle, this time under Torian's reign, is inevitable.

Given the circumstances, I guess I never left.

A normal man wouldn't spy on his woman. He wouldn't pay to have her mugged. Wouldn't manipulate or mistreat her.

A squeak of noise catches my attention. The sound is faint. Those fuckers are planting bugs while the house is quiet.

I slide from bed, grab my blade from under my pillow, and creep to the door to gently glide it open.

Everything is dark—the hall, the living room, the staircase leading to the lower level. But someone is there. I can make out a frozen silhouette near Layla's door.

"Did I wake you?" Stella whispers.

Shit. I inch the knife behind me, slipping it beneath the waistband of my boxers, the blade digging into my tailbone. "No. What are you doing up so late, *principessa*?"

"I couldn't sleep. So I thought I'd crawl into bed with Mom… But when I got here, I started to wonder if maybe you were already in there… ya know… with her."

She's fishing. Attempting to broach a subject I won't touch with a ten-foot pole.

"Not at all. Enjoy your time with your mother." I backtrack into my room.

Her shadowed silhouette approaches, her footfalls short and sharp. "You don't want to go in there instead of me?"

"I think she'd much prefer your company, Stella. Now go get some sleep." I grab the door handle.

"Wait." She places her hand on the wood. "She said something to me today that I'm hoping you might be able to get out of my head."

Warning sirens fill my ears. Loud. Deafening. "Ask me in the morning."

"Please. I'm obsessing over it. She said you were familiar with our enemies. *Our,*" she repeats. "Meaning mine and hers, not my Uncle Cole's. Which got me thinking, because as far as I know, I only have one enemy, and that's the family who abducted me and killed my father."

Jesus Christ.

"So, I'd like to know how familiar you are with them. Because she meant the Costas, right?"

Jesus fucking Christ.

"Stella, this isn't something we can discuss. Any questions you have need to be directed at your mother."

"Why?" Her shadowed face peers up at me, her features unreadable through the darkness. "Because I'm too young? Because I won't understand?"

"Because I don't want you to be scared of me," I answer truthfully.

She falls quiet, the thickening silence wrapping its hands around my throat.

"Go to bed, *principessa*."

"How familiar are you with them?" she whispers. "Are you, like, friends or something?"

I keep my mouth shut, my hand tightening on the door handle.

"Do you work for them? Do you help them? Are you the reason I was taken?"

"Jesus. Fuck. No." *Motherfucker.* This kid is treating my paternal heart strings like a fucking jungle gym, and I never even knew I had any. "I despise the Costas," I seethe. "I hate them just as much as you do."

"Then why would I be scared of you?" She steps closer, her foot nudging my door wider, the proximity exposing the glint of something metallic in her hand.

A knife?

"You looking to stab me, *principessa*?"

"All I'm looking for is the truth, and as much as I love my mom, I know she'll never give it to me."

I could disarm her. With a strike of a hand or the kick of my foot, she would cease to be a threat. But I refuse to upset her.

"It's funny. My mom thinks I'm this innocent little kid, but I've never been that way. I've never been a kid at all. And Tobias hasn't either." She steps closer again, forcing my retreat. "So after we were abducted, and kept in the dark about what happened, we decided to figure it out on our own. We spent a year learning all there was to know about the Costa family. We tracked school records for Abri, Remy, and Salvatore. We got copies of birth records. We hired someone to search newspaper archives. And even discovered an older son of Emmanuel's that nobody mentions on social media. But do you know who did mention him?" She cocks her head. "A girl called Grace in his senior yearbook."

"*Stella*," I warn.

"I knew who you were the moment I got off the jet. I know all about you. What I don't understand is why you now call yourself Matthew and what you're doing with my mom. Does she know who you are?"

"Yes." I clench my jaw.

"Why are you two working together? Why did you change your name? Why aren't you part of the Costa family anymore?" She lobs questions at me without accusation or emotion. "And what have you been doing since you left them? As far as the internet is concerned, you disappeared after you finished school."

"I'm going to wake your mom." I move to step around her, but she counters to block my path, the knife raising.

"No. Don't. Obviously she knows the truth, if you're willing to wake her. But she said you were working together. Doing what?"

"I'm losing patience, *principessa*. I won't betray your mother by discussing this with you."

"Then tell me I don't have to worry about her while she's with you. Tell me you hate them for what they did to me. Tell me you love her."

"I wish Emmanuel dead for what he did to you."

She sucks in a ragged breath. "What about my mom? Do you regret hurting her? Why did you lie?"

The questions from a barely-known child punish me harder than I could've imagined. I want to protect her. Help her.

"There were a lot of reasons. Safety was one of them. Preservation of what we had was another. I care about your mother, Stella. I never wanted to upset her."

"I figured as much from the way you stare at her."

"You're perceptive." I maneuver around her and approach my bedroom door, waiting for her to follow. "Are you done or am I waking her?"

"I'm not done. I want to know why you changed your name. Why did you disappear?"

I start into the hall, prepared to wake Layla and cause World War III.

"Wait. Fine. I'll stop." She shuffles around me and guides me back to my door with an adamant finger pointed at my chest. "Just answer one more question—what's your new surname?"

I shut the door on the kid's face, her heavy sigh carrying from the other side.

"Night, Matthew," she whispers.

I slink back to bed, blindsided.

I continue staring at the ceiling, contemplating where the fuck I go from here.

Stella is going to get herself in trouble. All she needs to do is dig into the wrong person's past and she'll be snuffed. Which means I still have to tell Layla what her daughter has been up to.

Great.

That conversation will be less enjoyable than a prostate exam. And how the fuck do I broach it? Subtle or sledgehammer?

I spend hours trying to figure out the best course of action as sleep evades me. Then as soon as I pass out, a shuffle of noise wakes me again.

I sit, the bed coverings falling to my waist, the faint hint of early morning sunshine highlighting a silhouette at the end of my bed. "*Amore mio?*"

"It's Stella."

Are you fucking kidding me? "Is something wrong? Is your mom okay?"

"She's fine. Still sleeping. I just thought, seeing as though I was awake and it's really early, that we might be able to go surfing before she gets up."

She's joking, right?

"Where's that knife of yours?" I scrub a hand down my face.

"Back in the kitchen. I was hoping I could make up for last night by getting to know you better."

I blink her into focus—the innocent shadowed features, the goddamn shorts and shirt I assume she's already wearing in place of a swim suit. "I don't think that's a good idea, *principessa*. Your mom already said no to surfing."

"Because she said we wouldn't have time. But I got up early specifically for this."

"I think you're smart enough to know that wasn't the only reason." I slump back onto the pillows and drag my arm over my eyes. "Go back to sleep. We'll surf next time."

"There won't be a next time. Not unless you figure out how to win her back." Her footsteps carry closer to my side. "Come on. Aunt Keira said I could."

"Your aunt Keira said you had permission to go surfing with me?" I ask slowly, as if everyone under this roof is insane. "I find that hard to believe."

"Then ask her yourself. She's already up making coffee."

I'm fucking tempted to do exactly that. To put this meddling little schemer in her place. If only I didn't appreciate her tenacity.

"I'm doing you a favor." Her tone gains an edge of superiority. "This is your chance to get the inside scoop on all things Layla Hart. I could teach you how to win her back. How to gain her forgiveness. Isn't that what you want?"

"I want your mom to forgive me, not kill me."

She giggles, feigning innocence I now know doesn't exist. "Come on, Matthew." She grabs my wrist, dragging it away from my face. "I know you can make her happy. I just need to teach you how to convince her of the same thing."

I growl and sit up as she tugs my arm. I can't deny her any more than I can deny her mother. "Meet me downstairs. The boards are in the garage."

She makes a soft squealing noise—a sound of pure delight as she hustles for the door.

I fling back the covers. "And, *principessa*…"

"Yeah?" She stops at the threshold.

"If your mom wakes up and doesn't approve, I'm throwing you under the bus as hard and fast as possible. Understood?"

She chuckles. "Understood."

I stalk for my walk-in closet and wait until she leaves before changing into swim trunks. When I get downstairs, she stands in the fluorescent light of the garage, her hair pulled back in a ponytail.

"I don't have a wetsuit in your size." I grab the first board from the rack, then open the roller door. "We're going to have to brave the cold."

"If you can do it, so can I."

"Homicidal and an optimist. The world better beware." I jerk my chin for her to walk ahead.

"I think my mom would describe me as more of a harmless people pleaser."

"Which one of us is correct?"

She shrugs. "Both."

We walk around the side of the house where the breaking sunrise greets us, then into the backyard. Hunter glares down from the deck, silently warning.

I wait for him to make a threat. But he doesn't say a word, just watches with narrowed eyes as I lead Stella to the back gate and hold it open for her to walk onto the beach.

"Don't worry about him." She stops a few feet onto the sand to wait for me. "He's always like that."

"An arrogant prick?" I grate before common sense kicks in.

She chokes out a laugh. "Yeah. It's his job. He used to be meaner before Sarah came along."

"Well, I'm glad I didn't meet him back then." I close the gate behind us and continue toward the surf where the breeze is more savage. "You sure you still want to do this?"

Goose bumps cover her arms as she bundles them close at her sides. "Of course. Like you said, I can't come to the beach without surfing. And we haven't even talked yet. I've got a whole heap of questions, like what happened to your arm?"

I glance down at the square bandage covering the stab wound. "There was an incident in the kitchen."

"And the scratch on your neck?"

"Same thing."

She raises a brow. "You're either a really bad cook or you haven't learned your lesson on lying."

"Believe me, I learned that lesson well."

She sweeps the stray strands of hair away from her face and shoots me a sideways glance. "Will you tell me about your father? What did he do to you?"

I stiffen. "I don't refer to him that way."

"As your father?"

"Yes."

She stops. I do the same, hitching the board higher under my arm.

"He hurt you more than he did me, didn't he?" Her eyes turn somber, but I'm not sure if the emotional display is real. She's a perfect little actress.

"Nothing hurts more than losing your dad, *principessa*."

"But he hurt you, right? What did he do?"

"He killed someone I cared deeply about. Just like he did with you."

"I'm sorry." She gives me an awkward look. Half cringe. Part wince. Then starts walking again. "Was it a long time ago?"

"Sometimes it feels that way. At others, it's as if it were yesterday." I take the lead, wanting to be in front of her before she steps into the ocean in case there are jellyfish.

The first trickle of water is like liquid ice. The second is more punishing.

"That's what it's like with my dad, too." She follows me into the shallows, her mouth gaping as a gasp escapes. "Holy crap. It's freezing."

"I did warn you."

"I know, but…" She bounces on her toes. "It's so cold my feet are stinging."

"Does this mean we're not surfing, *principessa*?"

She drops her bottom lip. Slinks her shoulders.

"Okay, let's get you back inside." I smirk. "Your mom won't forgive me if you get sick."

"Can't we sit on the beach for a while? I haven't told you how to win her back yet." She looks at me with Bambi eyes, making me question whether she came out here to surf at all.

"You sure are manipulative, aren't you?"

"I take pride in my work." She bounds out of the water, her arms wrapping around her middle as she plops down onto dry sand, completely ignoring Hunter and Decker who stand at the edge of the house yard like guard dogs on patrol.

I'm almost inclined to give them a reason to attack just so I don't have to dodge questions from the miniature detective.

"So who did he kill?" she asks as I dump the board out of the way and sit beside her.

"It was the woman who mentioned me in the yearbook. It happened when I was a teenager."

"And you stopped calling him your dad after that?"

"The very same day."

"My mom doesn't like her dad either. You two have a lot in common… in a bad way. And you're kinda like Romeo and Juliet with the whole family rivalry kinda thing."

What a delightful fucking omen of what's to come.

"Family can be a blessing and a curse," I mutter. "We don't get to choose which."

She nods. "Why won't you admit you love my mom? She says you don't but I know she's lying."

I clench my teeth. Glare at the horizon. "It's complicated."

"You sound just like her."

I keep my mouth shut, hoping she'll quit this line of questioning before I have to demand we go back inside.

"You know, my dad never looked at her the way you do."

I clench harder. Glare with more ferocity.

"I don't think he loved her like she deserved," she continues, compiling my anger. "I didn't notice until a few years back when Aunt Keira and Uncle Cole met Sebastian and Anissa. I hadn't really been around other couples before that. But seeing them together made me realize my dad didn't treat Mom the same."

Commenting on her father is a trap. One I don't plan to fall into. Not now. Not ever.

She sniffs, as if emotion is getting the better of her or maybe just the impending Emmy nomination. "Tobias said he heard my dad had cheated on her."

I lean forward, elbows on knees, hiding my fisted hands in my lap.

"Would you ever do that to her?" she asks.

"Never. And I'll take that vow to the grave."

"Why do I believe you?"

God only knows. I don't even understand why she wants to be near me. "Is it time to go back yet?"

A throat clears behind us, the tone feminine.

Yep. Definitely time.

I don't bother glancing over my shoulder. I can already feel Layla's laser focus burning through the back of my head. But Stella turns, her sigh quickly following.

"She's awake," she murmurs. "And it looks like she got out of the wrong side of the bed."

"So much for helping me win her back, *principessa*. You didn't give me any pointers."

"I didn't need to." She pushes to her feet. "You win her back by winning me over. And you did that with flying colors."

14

LAYLA

I STARE DOWN AT THE MAN WHO DEFIED MY ORDERS AND MY DAUGHTER WHO SITS CLOSE beside him, their conversation unheard over the ocean.

They're talking though. The two of them converse as if they're best buddies.

Resentment eats through me, the cold breeze nothing in comparison to the chill in my veins.

I cross my arms over my chest, restricting my billowing pajama top, and clear my throat.

Stella straightens as she turns to look at me, her eyes softening with apology. She knows she's done the wrong thing. She predicted my disappointment and came down here anyway. All because of him.

She says something else to Matthew, then stands, wipes the sand from her butt, and starts toward me.

"Morning, Mom." Her arms are covered in goose bumps, her smile wide. "Don't worry. We didn't go in the water."

"I'm glad to hear it." I tug her in for a hug, easing the panic I felt when I woke and found her gone. "Breakfast is ready. I'll see you inside."

"Okay. But before I go…" She glances over her shoulder at Matthew who still hasn't turned to face my wrath and lowers her voice. "Can I tell you how much I think he's perfect for you?"

"Not now, Stella." I kiss her temple and drop my arms from her shoulders.

"But he really is. You two have so much in common and he really adores—"

"*Not now, Stella.*" I add a warning to my tone. An annoyance that I don't want to inflict when she's one meal away from returning to Chicago.

She sighs. "Mom, he made a mistake. Give him a second chance."

"If you don't hurry, Bishop will have eaten all the bacon."

She looks at me with disappointment that smarts.

Matthew gets compassion while I get frustration. It isn't fair.

"I'll be there in a minute." I swivel toward the house where Hunter and Decker remain waiting at the yard gate. "Tell the guys to go eat, too."

I already told them as I passed but obviously they want to watch the fireworks.

She gives another sigh and starts toward them, shoulders slumped. I wait until she's at the gate before I move closer to Matthew, stopping a foot away to watch him stare at the ocean.

He doesn't acknowledge me. Doesn't even spare me a glance.

I want to hate him for it. For everything. And I guess I do. But the negative feelings only dilute the furthest edges of my longing.

"We need to talk," he mutters to the ocean.

"You're goddamn right we do. What the hell were you thinking bringing her out here when I told you not to?"

"That's the least of our problems." He stands like a shirtless Greek god in the early daylight, his dark hair falling around his eyes. "Stella knows who I am."

I freeze. Blink.

My mind doesn't compute.

"My thoughts exactly." He bends over to pick up his surfboard.

"You told her?" I can barely hear my own voice through the static in my ears. "How could you?"

"I didn't do shit, Layla. She knew who I was from the moment she got here. Apparently, her and Tobias have spent a substantial amount of time digging into the Costa family behind your back."

"No." I shake my head. "She's just a girl."

"She's a fucking crafty genius with balls bigger than mine. And she needs a leash. She's going to get herself killed if you don't pull her into line."

He's lying.

He told her the truth to mess with me. Now he's blaming it on her.

"How dare you?" I can't think through the anger.

"Excuse me? What the fuck have I done apart from stay up all night, pandering to her interrogation?"

"Her *what*?" My legs weaken. My pulse trembles.

"Interrogation," he repeats. "She came at me with a million questions all while wielding a goddamn fucking knife, *amore mio*. She said she has copies of birth records and school yearbooks. She knows the family I was born into, and exactly why you're angry with me... Well, part of it, anyway." He stares at me in concern. In *fear*. His features tight, his lips thin.

Oh, God. He's not lying.

I raise a shaky hand to my mouth, my head suddenly light, my limbs heavy.

"*Hey.*" He drops the board and grabs my upper arms. "*Shit...* don't pass out on me."

I sway, unable to blink away the encroaching darkness.

"*Amore mio*, it's okay. I'm sure it's just normal crazy kid stuff. I bet they all do it."

He's willing to bet all kids instigate a dangerous search on the people who abducted them?

No, this is insane.

I can't breathe. I can't get enough air.

"Forgive me." He smashes his cold mouth to mine. Harsh lips. Dominating hands.

He consumes me in an instant, the sizzle jolting through me like lightning to snap me out of my daze.

"Get off me." I shove at his chest.

"You're welcome." He steps back, smug. "Color is already returning to your cheeks."

I bet it is. The heat of unwanted lust races through me in a rush of wildfire.

"You're a son of a bitch." I swipe the tingling remnants of his kiss from my lips with a rough hand.

"I know, but sometimes it's nice to get a second opinion."

He's distracting me. Attempting to divert my attention from Stella's complete and utter lunacy. What the hell was she thinking snooping on the Costas? What if they caught her? What would they have done?

Matthew clears his throat, regaining my attention. "You should get someone to track what she does on her cell. Or any other device, for that matter. Tobias, too. Keeping an eye on what they're searching online and who they're contacting might be enough to keep them safe."

And if it's not? What then?

I pinch the bridge of my nose, trying to stem the forming headache. This can't be happening. I sent her away in the hopes she'd be better protected. But space didn't help. I still failed by sheltering her so much that she went in search of her own truth.

"Do you want me to organize it for you?" Matthew asks. "I can make a few calls—"

"Was she scared of you?" I drop my hand to my side. "Is that why she had the knife?"

"The knife wasn't for protection, *amore mio*. Personally, I think it was because she's a bad-ass like her mom."

"Are you trying to be funny?" I snip.

"No. I'm trying to be honest. Like I said, she knew who I was from the moment she arrived and not once has she acted in fear. Even in front of you—am I right? I think she sees me as an ally against Emmanuel."

I shake my head. "It's not like her to act this way, though. It's so far out of left field, I'm struggling to believe it."

"Kids do stupid shit. I'm sure it's only natural."

"Coming at you with a knife isn't natural, Matthew. As hard as it might be to believe, I never brought her up to be violent."

"And she wasn't. She was confident. Determined. Some might say a chip off the old block."

I glower. *Glare.* "I have to speak to her." I start toward the house.

"Don't." He grabs my wrist. "Not while you're worked up. Stay out here a while. Breathe. Don't go to her until you know what you're going to say because I'd place good odds on her already having a watertight defense prepared for her actions."

"Oh, God." My shoulders slump. "This is ridiculous."

"I haven't even told you the best part yet." He releases me and bends over to grab his surfboard. "For the sake of being entirely transparent, she woke me early this morning because she wanted to give me pointers on how to win you back. Isn't that cute? She approves of me despite the family I was born into."

"I bet a history lesson on the Butcher Boys of Baltimore would change that," I mutter.

"But what if it only made me more of an idol in the eyes of your knife-threatening offspring?" He starts for the house. "It's a crazy world, *amore mio*. Who would've known your daughter would be my biggest support?"

I bite back the need to scream. To shove. To slap.

But I've done all that before without relief. I've snapped. I've fought. I've fucked.

All the things I hope will ease my suffering never do. The mindlessness only continues to build. And I sure as hell won't give Hunter front-row tickets to my breakdown while he remains on his own at the gate. Watching. Judging.

Matthew passes him, then continues through the yard while the breeze whispers through my hair, the pain of my failures building to new heights.

I force my chin high and follow, ignoring Hunter's narrowed gaze as I approach.

"Everything okay, Lay?" he taunts. "It seems like you two have problems."

"You're the only one who's going to have a problem if you don't get out of my face." I stop to stare him down, but his superior expression doesn't falter. "You're not welcome here."

"It's my job to keep an eye on you."

"No. Not anymore. Not after Cole disowned me." I keep my voice strong, my shoulders stiff. "When the jet takes off this morning, I want you on it. I already know you were here before Stella arrived, but you're not sticking around once she leaves."

His jaw ticks. "I'll need to call Torian to—"

"I don't care what you have to do. But you'll take off with everyone else." I push through the gate, stalk onto the deck, and hustle inside before my tough exterior evaporates.

I lock myself in my private bathroom and slump against the counter as I hyperventilate.

I need to talk to Cole, but I don't have a phone.

I have to arrange closer surveillance of Stella and Tobias, but I don't have any money.

Shit.

I pull on jeans and a woolen sweater while laughter and conversation echo down the hall. I chastise myself for not keeping a closer eye on my daughter while the clink of cutlery signals the family meal being eaten without me. And I fight the desire to continue hiding while I put on a bare hint of makeup and a spritz of my new expensive perfume.

Maybe I shouldn't address Stella's actions just yet. Maybe I should let her think she's gotten away scot-free while I do some snooping of my own.

"*Fuck.*" I grip the counter and scowl at my reflection in the mirror. The eyes of a traitorous failure don't spark any bright ideas on how to handle this.

I'm clueless. And running out of time.

I force myself to leave the bedroom, hoping enlightenment will strike me with each passing breath. I paste on the flimsiest fake smile before entering the open living area where everyone is seated at the dining table.

Everyone except Matthew, who is nowhere in sight.

"I saved you some bacon." Stella pulls out the vacant seat beside her. The one that also happens to be next to my sister. "But you're right. Bishop did try to eat it all."

"I'm a growing boy." He shoots her a grin from across the table.

"You can never trust men to be chivalrous when it comes to food," Sarah mutters. "Believe me, I know."

I take the offered seat and ignore Keira as she stalks my periphery.

"Want some eggs?" She leans forward to grab the serving spoon, placing a heap of scrambled mush on my plate before I can respond.

"What's wrong?" Stella leans into me, bumping my shoulder. "You're not angry with Matthew for taking me to the beach, are you? We didn't go surfing, I promise. I barely put my foot in the water."

"I'm not angry." No more than usual, at least.

"Good." She scoops the remaining scraps of her breakfast onto her fork. "I'd hate to think I got him in trouble."

"He does that well enough on his own." Bishop snickers to himself.

I pick at the mushed eggs, unable to stomach food, despising yet another charade. "On second thought, I'm not that hungry." I push from my chair and claim my plate. "I'm going to make coffee."

"I'll help."

I hide a cringe as Keira follows me to the kitchen where I discard my food in the bin.

"Sorry about the whole surfing thing." She grabs the juice and milk from the counter to place them in the fridge. "I didn't realize she wasn't allowed."

I pause in front of the coffee machine. "Given the circumstances, I would've thought it was obvious."

She straightens. Nods. "I guess she twisted my arm like she always does."

"She asked you for permission?" I thought Matthew was the one who'd trampled over my rules.

"Yeah, she said you only denied her because there wasn't enough time. So she deliberately got up earlier to make it work."

Stella is turning into someone who enjoys manipulating authority and the thought of those skills increasing through her teenage years makes me shudder.

"You need to consult me first." I place a coffee pod in the machine and a mug under the nozzle. "I wasn't even told she was being brought here."

"I know." She inches closer, entering my personal space. "I'm sorry about that, too."

But not sorry for disowning me?

"Can we go somewhere and talk?" she asks. "We need to leave soon, and the two of us really have to hash out a few things before we go."

"No, thank you."

I have no intention of *hashing out* my mistakes.

Or letting her *hash out* a hundred I-told-you-sos.

I press the start button on the coffee machine. "I'd prefer if you left without causing drama."

"Layla—"

"I said no." I meet her gaze. "I'm not perfect, Keira. I've made shitty choices. But I'm not going to relive them with you. I plan to make up for what I've done and prove my worth, exactly like Cole expects. But I don't owe you any more than that."

"That's not what I want. If we could just—"

"It's time to get moving." Decker pushes from the table, the legs of his chair scraping along the tile. "I just got a text that the jet is prepped and waiting."

"I can't." I lower my tone, hiding my words from the rest of the room beneath the gurgle of the coffee machine. "Stella will get curious, and that girl already knows too much. Just let me get on with the ramifications without drawing more attention to how I got here. That's all I ask of you."

Her face falls, her eyes pleading with mine. "I have to speak to you. If not now, then soon."

"Soon. Later. Just not now." I grab my filled mug and turn toward the island counter as Matthew strolls into the room.

He's dressed in one of his pristine suits, his hair freshly washed, his aftershave infiltrating the air. He glances from me to Keira, his questioning gaze lingering longer on her than me. *Why?*

"They're leaving." I raise the mug to take a sip. "Will we all fit in the Lincoln if I come to the airport? I want to be able to say goodbye to Stella."

"Yeah." Matthew pats his suit pockets as if searching for a key. "How many are leaving?"

I pivot to the group, my attention on Hunter to see if he'll dare to defy me.

He glowers, lips pressed, one brow raised in rebellion.

"We all are," Sarah answers for him. "It's time to head home."

"I'll get our bags." Hunter's expression doesn't change as he pushes from the table. Decker follows. Both of them dump their plates and cutlery in the dishwasher as they pass.

"Can somebody grab mine?" Stella asks around a mouthful of juice. "It's already on my bed. I just need to get my phone and charger."

"I can get it." Keira brushes a hand over my arm. "But we really need to talk."

"Later." *Never.*

Matthew stalks for the coffee maker as my sister leaves the room. I watch him watching her. His attention isn't casual. It's cautionary. Questioning.

They're up to something.

"I need to have a quick shower." Sarah takes the remaining plates from the table while Stella begins clearing the condiments.

They flitter around, tidying up while I sip my coffee, remaining silent until they both disappear down the hall.

"Did you say something to her?" Matthew asks.

"No. And I don't think I will. She needs to think she still has freedom while I put added security measures in place."

"Are you sure that's the right move?"

No. I have no clue. "It's all I've got right now."

He raises his brows. "Then in that case, be careful, *amore mio*. I lost the woman I adore by using the same tactics."

I fight against a wince as Bishop pushes from the table.

"What are we talking about?" He throws a bite of crispy bacon in his mouth and walks toward us. "I heard something about tactics."

Matthew turns to him. "You need to sweep the house while we're gone. I want every inch of this place searched."

"Why?" The reply drips with sarcasm. "You don't trust our guests?"

"Just get it done." Matthew dumps his remaining coffee in the sink, then starts for the entry, his gaze brushing mine. "I'll be waiting at the car."

"Did I miss something?" Bishop narrows his attention on me. "The tension between you two is different."

"I don't know what you're talking about." I place my empty mug in the dishwasher and go in search of Stella, even more unsure what to say to her after Matthew poked at my plan with brutal logic.

She's in her room, on the bed, her focus riveted on her cell.

Who are you spying on now, little fish?

"Reading something exciting?" I ask.

"Nope." She pockets the device and smiles up at me. "Just messaging Tobias to let him know we're leaving soon… unless you've changed your mind about letting me stay for one more night."

"Maybe next time." I open my arms, wordlessly beckoning her forward. "But nice try."

She walks to me, nestling her head against my shoulder, her arms around my waist.

She's not a little girl anymore. She's not a child, despite her age.

My heart hurts over the playful years she was denied. I ache for all the innocent years she's missed.

"He told you, didn't he," she murmurs into my neck. "I knew he would. He learned his lesson about keeping things from you."

I close my eyes and squeeze her tighter. "Stella, it's dangerous to dig into the lives of powerful people."

"I know. But it's also wrong for those same people to get away with murder."

My pulse falters. What is this beautiful girl planning?

"That's true." I swallow over the dryness taking over my throat. I need to appease her. To temper her thirst for revenge. "But I would never let that happen."

She pulls back, her eyes questioning as they meet mine. "It's been years, Mom. Nothing has happened to them."

"It will."

Her gaze narrows. Her head cocks to one side. "Is that why you and Matthew are working together?"

I give a somber smile. "I need you to trust that we've got this under control."

"What are you—"

I shake my head. "I'm not discussing this with you, little fish. I'm your mother. I was Benji's wife. It's my duty to take care of them, and I will. But you need to be aware you're risking your life and mine by snooping. If you're caught—"

"I'll stop," she vows. "We won't do it anymore. I promise."

I want to believe her. I wish I could. But as I stare down at her, I struggle to recognize my little girl in the woman she's growing into. She's far more independent than I've ever been. A lot more cunning, too.

"Good." I lean in to kiss her forehead. "Because I'd hate to have to drag you back to Portland to keep a closer eye on you."

"You won't. I'll speak to Tobias. I'll tell him you're handling it."

Her statement strikes through me, her words making it clear they had plans of their own.

"Stella, do you realize what could've happened if you were caught? If Emmanuel—"

"We weren't going to get caught. Tobias has a whole heap of money in his savings account from Uncle Cole, so we've been paying someone to do the digging for us."

"You can always get caught. If they found the person you paid, they could find you. Everything is traceable."

"It's just information, Mom. It's not—"

"Listen to me." I cup her cheek with my palm, calm yet determined as I force her to hold my gaze. "If something ever happened to you, I wouldn't be able to live through it. Losing you would kill me. So I need you to be safe for the both of us, okay?"

Her face falls. "I know. And I already promised. I won't do it again."

"Tobias either."

She nods. "Tobias either."

"*It's time to go,*" Decker shouts down the hall.

I ignore him, my palm still cupping her cheek, my eyes holding hers.

"I wish I could stay," she whispers. "At least until you and Matthew make up. I really like him."

You wouldn't if you'd been snooping more in his direction.

"No more matchmaking, little fish." I kiss the tip of her nose and step back. "Go say goodbye to Bishop. You heard Decker. It's time to leave."

15

———

LAYLA

I keep my attention on Stella as I endure the long drive to the airport, the two of us squished into the very back seats while Hunter rides up the front with Matthew, and Sarah, Decker, and Keira take the middle row.

Stella's hyped, the energy in her voice making me realize how incredibly tired I am as she conspiratorially whispers all the things that would make Matthew and I a great couple.

"You have the same lifestyles… He has an awesome beach house… He thinks you're the goat… I bet he'd treat you like a queen, too. Just look at the way he's staring at you in the rearview mirror.

I don't look. I don't dare.

But I'm sure everyone else does because even though she's whispering, her voice is frustratingly loud through the silent car.

"Do you have any assignments due this week?" I ask.

"Mom, don't try and change the subject."

"I'm not."

Sarah clears her throat as if punctuating my lie.

"How much longer until we get to the airport?" I direct the question toward the front of the Lincoln, still not daring to glance toward the rearview mirror.

"Five minutes," Hunter mutters.

Damn it. Stella will have our wedding vows written and the rest of our married lives planned before her departure.

"Our time is almost up, little fish. I'm going to miss you so much. Don't forget to start thinking about what you want for Christmas. I'll need you to write me a list soon."

"Christmas?" she drawls. "Really? Do you want me to change the topic that badly?"

Like you wouldn't believe.

359

"It's not that far away. You know how fast time flies." I keep her busy with innocuous conversation while praying that I'm financially back on my feet by December. "We should plan a surprise escape. Maybe even take a trip to somewhere on the coast."

She rolls her eyes but reluctantly plays along, naming potential holiday destinations until Matthew pulls into the small private airport and stops at the gate leading to the tarmac. A jet is already waiting, the whir of the engines humming through the vehicle.

The ignition is cut. Hunter and Matthew climb out to get the bags. Sarah, Keira, and Decker follow, and once the side middle seat is lowered, Stella and I do, too.

"Do you need anything at school?" I cling to her free hand as she closes the car door. "Socks? Underwear? New uniforms?"

"I'm all good, Mom."

I'm not sure what I would've done if she'd said otherwise. I don't have the funds to help her.

"Don't get all emotional." She turns to face me, wrapping her arms around my waist. "You know I hate when you do that."

"I don't get *all emotional*, thank you very much." I squeeze her tight, breathing in the scent of her hair. It's always jasmine. Sweet and pure.

"Yeah, you do. I can already sense the waterworks about to take hold."

I mimic her laughter, doing my best to lighten a situation that tears me apart. The encroaching isolation. The torturous defeat. "I love you so much. You know that, right?"

She pulls back to look at me. "Even after last night?"

"Of course. You're everything to me, Stella. You always will be."

She nods, solemn with her half-hearted smile. "I wish you'd give Matthew another chance. With me living on the other side of the country, you need someone else to love. And to love you back." She glances to the front of the Lincoln where the man in question waits, his ass pressed against the hood, his arms crossed over his chest as he stares at the jet. "I like him."

"You've made that abundantly clear."

She engages those puppy-dog eyes of hers. "Let him love you. You deserve it."

"Be good at school." I guide stray strands of hair behind her ear, fervently ignoring her. "Make sure Tobias behaves."

"I will."

I kiss her forehead and close my eyes. "I miss you already."

"I miss you, too." She retreats, each step squeezing more air from my lungs.

"Be safe." I raise my voice over the jet engines. "Be sensible. Don't kiss any boys."

Her beautiful smile beams before she pivots away, her stride leading her to Matthew's side. I hold my breath as she engulfs him in a hug—one that's reciprocated. He's so good with her. How does he do it?

"I'll be on the jet." Hunter grabs the suitcases at his feet and starts toward the aircraft.

I don't acknowledge him. Or Decker and Sarah, who follow his lead with the remaining bags as Stella pulls back to say something to Matthew.

I can't hear what she says, but I witness her adoration. It kills me. She's naive and dauntless.

It's a dangerous combination around a man like him.

With an infectious smile, she swivels toward the aircraft and jogs to catch up with the group. The only one left behind is Keira who remains within reach, watching them from beside me, her silence increasing the awkwardness.

"Can we talk now?" she asks. "I need to say I'm sorry."

She wants to apologize?

"I let you down." She speaks softly over the roaring engines. "You told me you were in love and instead of showing support, I judged you."

"You didn't just judge me, Keira—you *disowned* me. And I get it. If anyone else made the mistakes I did, I'd hold them accountable, too. But right now, I don't need another reminder."

"That's not what this is." Her eyes plead with me as Matthew climbs back into the Lincoln. "I never disowned you. Nobody did."

"Tell that to our brother." I walk for the car only to be stopped by her hand around my wrist.

"Our brother is a fool. All men are. You know that." She hustles in front of me, blocking my path. "We *haven't* disowned you. Okay? We still love you. Nothing has changed."

"Everything has changed. I'm *stuck* here. I was running for my life in Denver and Cole refused to help. I had no phone. No money. He *made* me leave with Matthew."

She winces, her gaze cutting to the man behind the wheel. "Has he treated you well?"

My stomach lurches as my mind does a painful recap of his so-called treatment—the encounter on the dining room table, the blood-smeared kitchen bench, the seductive words, the heated arguments.

"Layla? How has he treated you?"

I can't answer.

I won't lie and say he's treated me well. I've been engaged in a constant battle against the heart-wrenching tactics he's used in an attempt to win me back. But he hasn't treated me horribly either.

"Listen." Keira sighs. "I understand that you don't want to talk to me, but you need to know you haven't been disowned. Matthew made a deal with Cole."

My blood turns cold. "Excuse me?"

"He convinced Cole to give him thirty days to win you back. That's why you're here. That's why Cole let you leave with him in Denver."

"He didn't *let* me leave. I was *forced* to go. Cole cut me off financially, then took delight in informing me I would be reliant on the Butcher Boys of Baltimore while ignoring all my pleas to return home. He stood by while the man who lied and betrayed me was left to be my only support."

"He stood by while the man you loved was allowed a second chance to win you back," she counters.

My pulse becomes erratic.

"I'm sorry. I should've said something sooner, but…" She reaches for me, her fingers gently gliding over my wrist. "You two seemed like you were getting along when we first arrived. Maybe not perfectly. But it looked to me like you were trying to make things work. You were close on the balcony last night, and Hunter had already said you'd hooked up on a more—" She bites her lip. "—explicit level."

I raise a hand to my mouth as disgust burns the back of my throat. "I can't believe this."

"All any of us want is for you to be happy. And you *were* happy with him, right?"

"I was happy when all I knew were lies. I didn't know who he was back then."

"But you didn't fall in love with his name. You fell in love with the man."

I glare. "Well, I sure as hell would've thought twice if I'd known who he really was."

"I understand. And I should've spoken to you as soon as I arrived. I just..." She shrugs. "I didn't want to get in the middle of the deal they made. But you can come home. There's nothing stopping you from flying out of here with us."

My stomach hollows. My chest, too.

I turn my attention to the aircraft, trying to determine if that's what I want—a way out, an escape.

"I realize leaving would mean Matthew lost the deal and would have to face the consequences," she continues. "But if you're not—"

My gaze snaps to hers. "What consequences?"

"Well, obviously Cole didn't go into the agreement without a potential reward. You know him as well as I do. He isn't someone who would let an asset like Matthew slip through his fingers."

Matthew sold his soul?

I glare at him. Glare so hard my temples ache. But he stares straight ahead, not paying me attention as his hands hold the steering wheel in a white-knuckled grip.

"You still love him," she murmurs.

"No." My denial is instantaneous. "I was a fool—"

"You weren't a fool, Layla. You were in love. With a man who clearly adores you."

I turn my glare to my sister, my pulse thunderous. "He lied to me."

"No man is perfect."

"When I wouldn't disclose my full name, he had me mugged in a successful attempt to steal my identification."

She cringes. "While I'm not condoning his tactics, I will admit Sebastian did far worse to me before we hooked up."

She doesn't understand. What she went through with Decker isn't the same. "Matthew's family abducted Stella and Tobias. They killed Benji."

"His *family*," she reiterates. "Not him. He showed the goodness in his character by disowning them years before the Costas crossed our path."

"The goodness in his character? Keira, he became the Butcher of Baltimore."

"Then abandoned his role," she argues. "How many men do you know who have been dragged into our world, then fought to get out? How many men do you know who would be *allowed* to walk away? I might be on my own with this opinion, but I think what he achieved shows a level of integrity well beyond anything we're accustomed to."

I rake a hand through my hair, tugging tight on the strands.

"Leave with us," she repeats. "It's what he expects."

"He knows you're telling me?"

"He asked me to. He said you'd suffered enough, thinking we no longer loved you."

"Then why not tell me himself?"

"Because he thought you'd assume it was a trick. That you wouldn't believe him. He said I was the one who needed to break the news."

Is that why he told me to speak to Keira? Was he trying to push me toward the truth?

"I'm sorry." She gives a sad smile. "I wish I wasn't making this more difficult for you."

"You're not. I just don't understand. He has to have motives I don't know about."

Her forehead creases, her pity hitting me with force. I step back, needing space. Needing answers. Needing... *God*, what the hell do I need to stop this train wreck?

"*Keira*," Decker shouts from the jet. "*How long are you going to be?*"

She doesn't move, just keeps staring at me. "Are you coming with us?"

I should.

If I'm not truly disowned... If I don't have to fix my mistakes... If all of this was an opportunity for Matthew to win me back, I should just board the aircraft and put what he did behind me.

But...

I glance at him sitting in the driver's seat, his intense eyes now on mine, his expression tight.

He knows I'm no longer clueless.

The thinly veiled panic in his gaze says he's waiting for me to flee.

"I can't." Even if I don't have to earn my family's forgiveness, I still need to deal with Emmanuel for my own sake. For Stella's. I turn back to Keira. "There's something I have to do first."

"That's what I thought you'd say." Her lips lift in a teasing grin as she steps forward, engulfing me in a hug. "I love you, sister. Have faith you're making the right decision."

I haven't made a decision. All I'm doing is sticking to my original plan. "Before you go, I need to ask a favor."

"Anything." She pulls back.

"I found out this morning that Stella and Tobias have been doing some digging on the Costas. From what she told Matthew, they've obtained birth certificates and school information. But who knows what else they've come up with?"

Her eyes flare. "Those sneaky little shits."

"Exactly. They're lucky they didn't get caught. So I need you to stay a while in Chicago and arrange to have some sort of cloning and tracking software put on their devices. Even though she promised to stop, I don't want to risk her doing anything else behind my back."

"Of course. I'll get it organized as soon as we land."

"Make sure they don't find out."

She nods. "No problem. Consider it done. Is there anything else?"

"No, that's it." Even though she claims I haven't been disowned, I still don't deserve to be asking for blessings I haven't earned. There's a lot of drama to make up for.

"If something else comes up, call me." She treks backward toward the jet. "No matter what it is."

"I can't. I don't have a cell."

She grins, then swirls toward the jet, shouting over her shoulder, "Then maybe you should've checked the duffle I brought here for you."

16

MATTHEW

Layla climbs into the car. Without a word. Without acknowledging me.

For once, I don't have the balls to break the silence.

Instead, we remain locked in the calm before the storm as the aircraft approaches the runway, then finally takes off into the overcast sky.

I don't need to ask if she knows. The shock, anger, and wince of betrayal were written all over her face as she spoke to her sister. What I don't understand, though, is why she's still here.

I placed all my bets on her boarding the jet to leave me behind.

I even messaged Bishop to tell him I might not make it back to the house because I planned to follow her, but that fucker is ignoring my theatrics.

I start the ignition, giving her more time to perfect the verbal barrage she's about to assail me with, and drive from the parking lot.

She keeps her gaze on the sky, her hands in her lap, her shoulders stiff.

Each second of silence eats away at me. Gnaws.

Until she finally says, "Why didn't you tell me?"

"And have you convince me I was wasting my time, *amore mio*?" I indicate onto the quiet road leading back toward the beach. "No, thanks."

"You make no sense to me, Matthew. You tell me how you don't want to return to your old lifestyle, but what exactly do you think will happen when you're not successful?"

"I have no intention of failing."

She shakes her head. Slow and steady. "I won't be guilted into changing my mind, if that's what you're thinking. I only stayed because you promised me Emmanuel's death."

"I don't need guilt when you still love me."

She stiffens. Huffs.

"Have I not proven my loyalty?" I ask. "Have I not shown sincerity? Can't you see I'd give up everything for you, even a future with freedom, all for the sake of calling you mine?"

"You've told me conflicting stories. If you were me, you wouldn't believe any of it."

"I've shown you every side of me. The good, the bad, the vulgar. The facets are conflicting because that's who I am." I clench the steering wheel tighter, my palms sweating. "I'm a cold-blooded killer, Layla. Yet knowing I hurt you has filled me with more guilt than a thousand deaths. I can't fucking think straight through my want for you."

"Yet you still get angry at me."

"I get angry at my obsession with you. At my mindlessness. At my mania." I press harder against the accelerator, needing to get home to speak to her face to face. "I don't know how to win you back and it's destroying me."

She sucks in a long breath, the exhale shaky.

"Layla, what do I have to do to—"

"Pull over."

The demand cuts through me, her aggression a bad fucking sign. "I'm not trying to make a scene out of this. I just—"

"I said *pull over*." She reaches for the door handle.

Shit. I slap my foot against the brake, not willing to let her risk her life just to spite me.

As soon as the car stops, she shoves the door wide and escapes.

"What the hell are you doing?" I shout.

She slams the door in response.

For fuck's sake. I unclasp my belt and follow.

"Layla." I storm after her, fists clenched, pulse thunderous. "Stop."

She doesn't. The woman born of fire and brimstone continues striding away like she's on a marathon mission.

"*Fucking stop*." I lunge, grasping her upper arm to haul her back to face me.

The moment her glassy eyes meet mine, I'm done for.

Winded.

Broken.

Her tear-stained cheeks punch right through me.

She doesn't fight my hold. Doesn't yell or wail. She merely stands there, skin pale, lips trembling.

"Talk to me," I demand. "*Scream* at me." Because I can't stand her silent suffering a moment longer.

"I don't get you." She shakes her head. "For the life of me, I can't work you out. And the worst part is that the more I try, the more I blame myself for this mess."

"It's not your fault."

"It definitely is. My father *always* told me he loved me. It was the prelude to every manipulation. He used the emotion like a weapon. He knew it was all I needed to do his dirty work. All I wanted was his love. His pride. And that's originally how I thought you manipulated me, too. But you know what, Matthew? You never said those words to me. Not once. Not when I confessed my feelings to you. You didn't even attempt to use love against me during this shitshow when you've apparently been trying to win me back."

She throws her hands in the air and scoffs. "You've said you're obsessed. But you've never whispered a hint of that one enslaving word apart from that stupid fucking endearment. So I must be here for another reason. Something important enough to have you throwing away your future, because Cole will make your life a goddamn misery."

"My life is with you, whether I'm free or under your brother's control."

"Bullshit." She blinks up at me. Stark. Vulnerable. Another tear spills free, the trail racing to her chin to be quickly swiped away. "What do you want from me? Why can't you let me go?"

I don't know how to tell her. The thought of fucking this up one more time suffocates me.

"Forget it." She wiggles her arm from my grip and turns to continue along the roadside, the black tar to our right, the dense shrubs to the left. "Like I said, I blame myself. You never loved me. I created this mess all on my own."

"Layla…" I follow. "Give me a second to figure out how to explain this in a way that—"

"In a way that what—lets me down gently?" She raises her voice. "Why start now?"

"Jesus Christ, would you fucking stop?"

"No. Just give me some space to figure this out. I need to think."

"You need to fucking listen." I grab her again, latching onto her elbow. "You didn't create anything. You know how strongly I feel for you. That was never a lie."

She raises her chin. "But you don't love me."

I wince. I can't help it. That word pisses me off.

Emmanuel *loves* me. My uncle *loves* me. Yet one killed the first girlfriend I ever knew, and the other had me killing men as if they were flies.

I would never do that to her.

I would never place my feelings for her in the same category as the affections those men inflicted upon me.

I open my mouth to tell her why I can't say what she needs to hear, but she raises a hand in warning.

"Don't play pretend. I can see it in your eyes." She pastes on a smile so fake, it's painful to watch. "I hate those words anyway. I despise what they've made me into. The weakness they induce. I never want to hear them again."

"Good." I tighten my grip. "Because I'll never fucking say them."

She sucks in a breath, heartbreakingly fragile despite the show of strength.

"I don't love you, Layla. I never will."

She attempts to yank free from my hold. Once. Twice. Each tug is more vicious than the last. "Let me go."

"I'm not finished." I drag her closer so we're foot to foot. "I need you to hear me out."

"I don't want to." She twists her arm from my grip, then runs.

I chase, catching her in two steps to haul her off the ground. "You're going to fucking listen."

"Let me go." She wiggles in my hold. Thrashes. "*Stop.*" She screams as I carry her back to the car, fighting me, pummeling my chest.

I dump her on her feet beside the Lincoln, caging her against the metal with my body. "You're going to hear me out, because we both know this moment is either sink or swim for us." I grab her chin, forcing her face to mine. "And I'm going to need you to look me in the fucking eye while I talk to you, because if I mess up my words, at least you'll be able to see my goddamn sincerity."

She refuses.

I tilt my head into her line of sight, smothering her harder against the car's exterior. "I don't love you, Layla. What I feel for you isn't close to what other people describe. I say I'm obsessed because I am. I'm consumed by you. I'm infatuated and intrigued. I'm fucking captivated and enslaved. I can't think past you. You're all there is. All I have. And that's not love. There's no way it could be, because the fucking world couldn't function if everyone felt the way I do." I pause, catching my fucking breath, imploring her with my goddamn eyes. "Do you understand me?"

She doesn't respond. All I get are more tears and a deeper tremble to her lips.

"I'll never tell you I love you, Layla. That's a vow. From now on, I won't even call you *amore mio*. Because you're *la mia ossessione. La mia vita. La mia anima. Il mio santuario*." I cup her cheeks, wiping away her tears with my thumbs. "My obsession. My life. My soul. My sanctuary. I'll spend every day making sure you know your value is worth so much more than three fucking words."

I lean close, my mouth a breath from hers. "Every time I look at you, you'll know you're valued above any other. That you're cherished and adored. If you fall asleep at night thinking you're anything less than perfect, then I've failed you, and I expect you to hold me accountable. Because that's what you are to me. It's all you've ever been."

She swallows, her eyes remaining pooled in moisture as she licks her lips.

"Talk to me," I beg. "Tell me you understand."

Her nose scrunches, bringing a new trail of tears down her cheeks.

"Tell me what you're feeling. What you're thinking."

She drags in a shuddering breath. "I'm thinking that I want to hate you."

I wince, taking the hit to the chest. "I know. I want to hate me, too."

"So why don't I?" she whimpers. "Why am I so weak?"

"Weak?" I swipe those fucking tears away. "How can you be weak when you're the only one capable of bringing the Butcher to his knees?"

She shakes her head.

"It's true. You destroy me, *la mia stella polare*. You tear me apart. Don't you understand how powerful that makes you?"

"You have all the power. You always have."

"That's not true." I brush my nose over hers, my chest heating with the contact, my dick hardening. I can already taste her, her heated breath filling my lungs. "You rule over me. You always will."

"I don't want to." She sniffs. "I don't want any of this."

"Yes, you do. Your problem is that you think succumbing to me makes you vulnerable. But it's the opposite, Layla. Nothing is stronger than the two of us together. I promise you that."

She closes her eyes, a trail of tears escaping her closed lashes.

"Kiss me, *mia dea*. Tell me you're mine."

She drags in a shaky breath, her hands moving to grip my arms.

"Kiss me." I wait for her to push me away. To destroy me with her rejection.

Her inhales become ragged. Fractured. Broken.

I don't know what else to do. What to say. So I repeat what she means to me, whispering her value against those fragile lips. "*La mia ossessione. La mia vita. La mia anima.*" I close my eyes, resting my forehead against hers. "*Il mio santuario. La mia stella polare. Mia dea.*"

She sobs, killing me with her suffering.

"Forgive me," I demand. "Absolve my sins. Let me spend the rest of my life making this up to you."

She shakes her head, denying me.

"Layla," I beg. "You're killing me."

"No, you're killing *me*." She opens her eyes, the bloodshot depths drowning in sadness. "I can't take it anymore." She wraps a hand around my neck and smashes her mouth to mine.

Euphoria hits me like a motherfucker, blinking the world from existence.

I devour her, tasting her tears, surrendering my soul.

She clings to me, her nails in my skin. Our tongues dance, parry, attack.

I've never felt more overwhelmed with relief.

"I need you," she pants into my mouth.

I'll give her what she wants, just not on the side of the road against a dusty car. Not after waiting this long. "Let's get back to the house."

The next time I pleasure her, she'll be in a comfortable bed where I can give her the attention she deserves.

"No. Now. Here," she pants.

"I want to fuck every inch of you. But I'm doing this right." My dick thrums in protest. I succumb to temptation, grinding my cock against her abdomen. "You need to get in the car."

She moans, reclaiming my mouth.

We kiss as if we're starved. Desperate. Our bodies grind. Our breath gasps.

"This isn't something you're going to walk away from again, is it?" I pull back to stare at her, trying to see sense through the lust. "You're mine now, Layla." It sounds like a statement but it's not. It's a question. A fucking pathetic plea.

"I'm yours." She nods, her brows pinching as if she's in pain.

She's mine, but she's torn. She's succumbed to fate but hasn't been convinced of her decision.

"I'll make it up to you." I palm her throat, using pressure to guide her head to the side to expose her delicate neck. "I'll make this right."

She mewls, her eyes fluttering shut as I lean in to kiss the sensitive skin below her ear.

I lick and bite and suck. I taste and savor and consume.

I'm so fucking hard for her. My dick throbs against my zipper. My chest pounds like thunder.

I want to be inside her. To be all over her.

"Matthew." Her back arches, her phenomenal breasts brushing my chest. "We need this."

I hold her tighter. Kiss her harder. *"Sei perfetta. Così fottutamente perfetta."*

She whimpers.

My dick takes note of every sound. Every movement.

I don't understand the hold she has on me. The consumption. The mindlessness. We're dry humping on the side of the fucking road, like teenagers, and I can't drag myself away.

I'd kill for her.

I'd die. I've never been more certain.

"La mia ossessione," I whisper. *"La mia vita. La mia anima. Il mio santuario."*

Her throat works over a heavy swallow beneath my palm, her chest rising and falling under ragged breaths.

She releases my arms, her neck craning away so she can meet my gaze. "Remind me what that means."

"My obsession. My life. My soul. My sanctuary."

Her gaze regains the sheen of moisture as her nose crinkles. Then she quickly glances away.

I've upset her again. "Tell me what's wrong?"

She shakes her head.

"Tell me." I palm her chin, brushing my mouth over hers. *"Trust* me."

"I can't." Her shoulders slump. Her entire body weakens. "I want to. I *need* to. I just don't think I can."

I stiffen, taking the punishment I deserve.

She winces, understanding my suffering. My guilt. "Matthew, I need you to promise me this is real. That it always will be. That you'll never lie again. But as much as I need those promises, I won't believe you. I *need* those words, but I don't know how to accept them."

"Then it's my job to convince you." I kiss her gently. Reverently. "Nothing has ever been more real, Layla. And I plan on spending the rest of my life proving that to you."

17

MATTHEW

I keep my waist pressed into hers, our gazes tangled for long silent heartbeats while she contemplates me with sorrow.

I've got a lot of work ahead of me. I have to prove myself without force.

But I will.

I'll make her believe.

"Let's go." I check my watch, annoyed that Bishop hasn't responded to my last text. "We'll finish this at the house. Then we need to pack."

"We're going to Denver?"

"Not yet. I still need a few more days. But I don't want to risk your safety by staying here." I retreat, mourning the loss of her heat.

"Why would it risk my safety?"

"Because I didn't give our address to your family. They found us on their own."

"But I thought you arranged for Stella to come here."

"I did." I pull her door open and help her climb inside. "Problem is, Hunter and Sarah were here before that, meaning someone at the Denver Airport needs to be taught a lesson on manners."

She frowns as I close her door, then trek around the hood to climb in the driver's side.

"What were they doing here?" she asks as I start the ignition.

"Checking on you. Making sure you were safe."

"Oh." Her mouth forms the subtlest circle. An almost shy expression of surprise.

"Your brother always cared about you. He never stopped."

She rests back into her seat, shifting her attention out her side window to the wild shrubs bordering the side of the road. "He's always had a funny way of showing it."

I reach for her hand as I pull onto the road and drag her knuckles to my lips. "I want you to know I didn't ask him to act as if you were disowned. I didn't know he was going to go down that path until it was too late."

"And you couldn't tell me afterward because I would've run straight home." She keeps her gaze diverted. "I get it."

"But do you forgive me?" I turn her arm to kiss the inside of her wrist.

She doesn't respond. I'm asking too much.

"Ignore me." I focus on the road. "I know it's too soon to ask."

She sucks in a breath, letting it out gradually. "I need to take this slow. I know I'm probably giving you mixed signals, but I'm still hurting."

"There are no mixed signals, *la mia stella polare*. And you don't need to explain. I understand completely."

She squeezes my hand. "I like the sound of that endearment more than *amore mio*. What does it mean?" She shoots me a glance. "Or don't I want to know."

I grin, unable to stop myself from kissing her again, this time in the middle of her palm. "It means 'my northern star.'"

She sits taller. Her chin higher. "I definitely like that one better."

"*Sei la mia stella polare. L'unico posto che chiamerò mai casa.*"

"Not fair," she drawls. "You're trying to seduce me all over again, aren't you?"

"I wouldn't dream of it."

She smiles, subtle, slow, and so fucking stunning.

"*Così fottutamente bella.*" I smirk at her. "*Non vedo l'ora di averti sotto di me.*"

She grins right back, raising her brows in challenge.

"Do you want more, *mia dea*?"

"What does that one mean?" She turns her body, giving me her full attention.

"My goddess. But from memory, I think your favorite is *la mia piccola sporcacciona.*"

Her eyes narrow in a faux glower. "I remember that one, Matthew, and I assure you, it's not."

I keep smirking. Keep holding her hand. Keep thanking my lucky fucking stars as I drive us toward the place where I plan to spend hours cherishing her.

"Tell me more about the terms you agreed to with Cole." She leans her cheek against the edge of the seat. "What did he ask of you?"

"Does it matter?"

"I guess not. But I'd like to know exactly what you were willing to risk."

"And if the terms weren't generous enough? What then?"

"Somehow, I don't think that was the case." Her gaze narrows, her appraisal gentle. "What was it? What were the exact terms?"

"We didn't have any. As far as I was concerned, it was all or nothing."

Her brow furrows, her confusion potent. "And there's really nothing else you want from me? No insider knowledge or Torian family secrets?"

"There's only ever been you. I don't need anything else in my life."

"But you wouldn't have had a life if Cole got his way. How could you risk your future like that?"

I focus on the road, slowly kissing her knuckles, her wrist, her palm. "Because you are my future, Layla. I hope I can prove that to you one day."

She releases a heavy breath as I kiss her again and again. Lazy, lethargic worship. Quiet and content affection.

"And nothing has changed with our agreement on Emmanuel?" she asks. "We're still on the same page?"

"Always. The particulars haven't changed. Your safety remains my priority, with his death being the goal."

"I don't think I can wait much longer. I've been striving for this outcome for two years, and I'm more tired than I've ever been. I need it to be over."

"Then let me do it on my own." I meet her gaze. "I can leave this afternoon. He'll be dead by morning."

She swallows. Bites her lip.

I can't tell if her hesitation is because she still doesn't trust me, or because she's battling with her desire to concede.

"You'd never have to worry about him again." I turn my attention back to the road. "And I wouldn't have to risk your safety."

"But you'd risk my sanity." She drags her arm away but latches her hand around mine to take it with her. She mimics my affection, kissing my knuckles, my wrist, my palm. "I'd go insane worrying about you. I need to be there to make sure you're okay."

"Then we do it together. We just need to do it right." I turn onto the road leading to the beach house. "Two more days should be enough. In the meantime, I want you to rest. Relax. And *eat*. Don't think it hasn't skipped my attention that you haven't been looking after yourself."

"Heartbreak doesn't make for a healthy appetite."

I stifle a wince. "Well, there's no more heartbreak now. I promise to keep you fed and rested. In fact, I don't think I'll let you leave the bed."

Her chuckle is breathy. "How selfless of you."

"I can be extremely generous."

"And single-minded," she adds.

"Always. There's only you, *mia dea*. That's all there is."

Her smile turns solemn as she diverts her attention back to the road. She's still not all in, and that's okay. I can't expect her to get to my level of obsession within minutes of reconciling.

But she'll get there.

I'll make sure of it.

She keeps hold of my hand as we reach the property. She doesn't let go as I enter the pin into the panel at the gate. And our palms remain united while I shift into park and kill the ignition.

She doesn't move to get out. Doesn't release her belt.

"You okay?" I ask.

She nods, her expression a gentle statement of peace as she looks back at me. "I just want a few more seconds of this before I have to deal with Bishop."

"Don't worry about him. I'll keep him occupied."

"Promise?"

God, she's beautiful. With playful eyes and a slight tweak to her lips, I could die a happy man with her as my final image.

"Cross my heart." I strike a finger across my chest.

She snickers, her attention diverting over my left shoulder.

Her posture stiffens. Her humor evaporates. Her hold on my hand tightens.

She's scared.

Panicked.

Someone's in the yard.

"There's a gun in the glove compartment." I lower my voice. "Can you grab it?"

She shakes her head. Swallows. "He's right there."

A silhouette enters my periphery, making my blood surge.

"Who?" I slowly release my belt. No sudden movements. No risking her safety. But the question becomes redundant when Remy creeps into view on her side of the car.

He meets my gaze, his navy suit and matching tie boasting professionalism while the Glock in his grip awakens my demons.

"Salvo's behind me?" I ask.

She nods. "What do I do?"

"Nothing. Stay still. It's going to be okay. I won't let anything happen to you."

Her attention returns to mine, her eyes silently screaming for help. "They want me dead."

"They won't succeed." I squeeze her fingers. "They're not going to hurt you."

She continues to nod, the action short and sharp. She's in shock. A breath from fight or flight.

"Don't make any sudden movements, okay, *mia dea*?" I release her hand, gradually lowering my fingers to my thigh. Then my pocket.

"Get out." Remy taps the barrel of his weapon against her window, only pausing a moment before he yanks her door open.

Salvo does the same on my side, his gun entering my line of vision.

"Proceed with caution," I warn. "If you touch her, there will be hell to pay."

"We don't want trouble." Remy places his barrel at the back of her skull. "We just need you to get out of the car."

She could be gone in a blink. Without hesitation or remorse.

"Move the gun away from her." I can barely hear through the roar of blood in my ears. "If you hurt her, I swear to God it'll be the last thing you do."

"Get out of the fucking car," he repeats, nudging the weapon into her head.

She whimpers. Flinches.

I grind my teeth. Clench my fist around the blade.

"Get your hand out of your pocket." Salvo steps closer, thrusting his gun toward the side of my face. "Start moving."

I can't be separated from her. But I also can't start a gunfight in the fucking Lincoln when all I have is a blade.

"Why don't you help me, asshole?" I stare at her. I don't take my eyes off hers as Salvo creeps closer.

"You want me to drag you out, brother? Because I will." He grabs my suit sleeve with his free hand and tugs.

I lunge, twisting my body toward the gun, forgoing my blade for his barrel. I grip the metal. Shove it downward.

He recoils. Panics. Pulls the trigger.

Layla screams, her limbs flailing as Remy drags her from the vehicle.

I elbow Salvo in the face. Capture and twist his wrist hard. Then charge while he's reeling from the impact, throwing myself out of the car to shove him off-balance.

He stumbles backward, the gun loosening in his grip.

We fall. The weapon does, too. All three of us clatter to the pebbled drive.

My body slams onto his. My forearm finds his throat. My hand finds my blade.

"You're dead." I stab the metal into his upper arm and his roar explodes in my ringing ears as I retrieve it. "But not before you suffer."

I scramble to my feet, dragging him with me by the front of his suit, needing to get eyes on Layla.

"*Fuck.*" Salvo clasps his shoulder as I lever him backward into my chest, my blade at his throat. "You stabbed me."

"You're lucky I haven't blown your fucking brains out." The gun is right there. A few feet away. He'd be dead if he hadn't dropped it.

I would've killed my own brother.

Without thought.

Without hesitation.

That's why I don't fucking carry.

"Let her go." I drag Salvo to the hood until Layla is in full sight on the other side of the Lincoln.

Remy copies my stance, his arm around her neck, but his gun is trained on me.

Big mistake. I'd risk a bullet for her. I'd chance death.

"Let her go." I drag Salvo farther, making him stumble to the other side of the car, getting as close as I can to Layla whose chest heaves with rapid breaths as her fingers cling to my brother's arm for stability.

"Matthew," she begs.

"It's okay." *It's not fucking okay.* "You're going to be fine." *He's going to kill her.*

"Stay where you are." Remy drags her backward, his hold tightening on her neck. His forehead beads with sweat. He's fucking scared.

I'm petrified. "*Let. Her. Go.*"

His eyes widen as if I'm insane. "Do you really think I'm going to do that when you've got a knife to his throat?"

"We just wanted to fucking talk," Salvo grates through clenched teeth. "Jesus. Dante. You fucking *stabbed* me."

"I'm going to do far worse if he doesn't let her go."

"Listen," Remy snarls. "If you calm down, we can explain."

Where the fuck is Bishop? I glance to the house, searching for a sign of life.

"Your man can't help." Salvo stumbles along with me, one hand clutching his shoulder as I continue to stalk after Layla. "But he's fine. He isn't injured."

"Then where is he?"

"In the house."

"Just chillin', watching TV?" I drag him farther. Harder.

"He's taped to a fucking chair in one of the bedrooms." He groans. "God, can you stop for a minute?"

"No." I can't stand the sight of Layla's fear. She's tearing me apart one frantic blink at a time. "If you want to talk, then talk. But for your sake, you might want to hope baby brother doesn't make one wrong move, because if he does, you're both dead."

Salvo mutters a string of profanities, then raises a hand in surrender. "Let her go."

"Are you fucking serious?" Remy's face is wild with disgust.

Layla remains quiet, her attention never leaving me, her hands clutching at my brother's arm as he continues to lever her backward.

"Do it," Salvo demands. "Now."

"*Fuck.*" My youngest brother licks his lips. Swallows. Then finally, he loosens his hold around her neck.

"Run for the house, Layla." I keep hold of Salvo, my blade remaining at his throat. "Get inside."

She's hesitant, slowly inching away from her attacker as her gaze darts between my brothers.

"Now, *la mia stella polare*. Find Bishop." I point the blade at Remy. "Remove the magazine. Then kick the Glock away."

He shakes his head. "Not until you release him."

"Fucking do it," Salvo snarls. "Before I bleed out."

"You're not going to bleed out, you goddamn pussy." I keep leading him forward. Shoving. Pushing.

"Excuse me for not having firsthand knowledge of stab wounds," he snips. "Not all of us have extensive experience like you."

"You've got more experience being stabbed than I do, asshole. I've never been careless enough to be wounded."

"Maybe not, but you've inflicted more than your fair share."

"Then maybe you should be fucking thankful you're still breathing. It would've been easier to plunge my blade into your throat."

Remy releases the magazine, then drops the weapon.

"Throw the bullets." I get closer as he complies. Five feet. Four. "Then kick the gun away." I chance a glance at Layla over my shoulder, finding her at the bottom step. "Keep moving, *mia dea*. Don't stop." I bridge more space. Three feet. Two. "I said kick the fucking gun."

I don't wait for him to follow orders. As soon as I'm in lunging distance, I cold-cock Salvo with a closed fist. He topples to the grass, senseless, as I throw the blade at Remy. Hard. "I warned you." I aim low, hitting him in the thigh.

He yells as I charge, launching my fist at his cheek. The impact knocks him backward. He falls. I follow.

I straddle his chest, my hand gripping his neck, the other grabbing the knife from his leg to raise it to his throat. "I told you not to touch her."

He inches his chin away from the blade, his breathing ragged.

"I fucking warned you." I press the tip of the knife into his skin, my vision red, my mind violent.

"You're the one who attacked," he snaps. "We didn't come here to fight."

"Instead, you started a war." I dig the metal deeper, drawing blood.

"*You* started it, you trigger-happy motherfucker." He glares at me, eyes stark, skin flushed. "This is on *you*. *Your* actions. *Your* knee-jerk impulse. So what are you going to do? Murder me? Is that what we've come to?"

"Maybe," I snarl. "It's what you deserve."

It's what he's earned for scaring her. *Threatening* her.

"Matthew." Layla's plea whispers through my rage, her light footsteps approaching.

I keep staring at Remy, devouring his suffering, feeding off his fear.

"Don't kill him." Her gentle hand comes to rest on my shoulder. "Use him instead. He can give us information on Emmanuel."

She's such a treasure. A fucking godsend in a moment of madness.

"Did you hear that?" I sneer. "My woman just saved your life."

"Probably because your woman has more fucking brains than you." His nostrils flare as he remains rigid.

Salvatore groans from a few feet away, regaining consciousness.

"Get behind me." I shoot Layla a glance and wait until she complies before I push to my feet. I drag her close, one hand on her waist as she stands at my back, the other holding a tight grip on the blade at my side.

Both brothers remain on the ground. Remy clings to his injured thigh. Salvo clutches his head. Both of them sit with knees bent and shoulders slumped. Defeated but far from punished.

"Are you here to take me back to Emmanuel?" Layla asks. "Or just to kill me?"

They don't acknowledge her. Don't even wrench their gazes from me to pay her the respect she deserves.

"Answer her," I demand.

"We've already explained why we're here." Salvo raises his chin, his eyes hard. "We told you we came to fucking talk."

"You came with raised guns," she counters.

"For self-fucking-preservation." Remy looks to her, finally, with resentment. "After what we've done to you in the past, we didn't think a gift basket would've been a sufficient peace offering."

Peace offering? "What the fuck are you two playing at?" I keep my hand on her, not letting her away from my touch. Not trusting them for a second.

"It's a long story." Salvo labors to his feet.

"Find a way to make it short."

"As if we fucking wouldn't if we could." Remy removes his belt and wraps it around his thigh. "A lot has happened since we were kids."

I tense, not understanding why they need to delve that far in history. "Who's this about. Me? Or Layla?"

"It's about all of us, you psychotic fuck." Remy struggles to stand, the blood on his leg soaking into his suit pants. "We wanted to get away from Emmanuel and thought our long-lost brother might help. I just didn't anticipate it being in a fucking body bag."

18

LAYLA

I keep the shock bottled inside my chest.

Matthew became someone else while I was under threat. Sterile. Calculated. Cold. He was the Butcher, and I'm ashamed to admit I'm as drawn to his dark side as I have been to his seduction.

The way he fought for me was exquisite. His severity profound.

"You ambush us, dare to hold Layla hostage, then have the balls to ask for help?" He's a predator ready to pounce, his anger tightly corded into every muscle.

"It wasn't meant to be an ambush." Salvo continues clinging to his injured shoulder. "We just wanted to get you in a position where you'd listen without us being slaughtered."

"You had a gun to her head."

"I fucking panicked." Remy clings to the belt strap around his thigh. "You're a scary son of a bitch when under threat."

"Then you'd better hope Bishop is okay, because you're going to see some next-level shit if he isn't."

"He is. Go check for yourself." Salvo jerks his head toward the house. "He's in one of the downstairs bedrooms."

"Is he hurt?" I ask.

"Barely. I swear to God, we never wanted any of this shit. Not the guns, or the violence, or the threats."

"Tell that to my dead husband." The bitterness spills from my lips before I can rein it in.

Salvatore cringes. Remy quits playing with his belt and straightens.

That's all I'm given for my loss. For my daughter's nightmares.

I should be ending their lives. Repaying what they did to Benji. Instead, my mind is stuck thinking about Matthew's hesitation when I spoke to him days ago about killing his brothers.

He'd been stricken. He may have hidden it well, but I'd known.

He still feels loyal to them. No matter what they've done to me.

At least, he did before today.

"I swear it wasn't us." Remy meets my gaze. "That night was out of control, but we were firing air shots for cover. We didn't kill anyone. It was Emmanuel's guards."

The hatred I've let fester for two years doesn't budge. It's bone deep. Embedded.

"You shot at us in Denver," I counter.

"And I could've hit your brother without even trying. But didn't." Salvatore shucks his suit jacket, exposing a white button-down with a sleeve stained in blood. "Or at a bare minimum, your car tires. Those shots were warnings to get you to hurry up and skip town."

Matthew doesn't deny their claims.

He doesn't say anything at all.

I slide a hand over his. Questioning. Searching for insight.

He squeezes my fingers and drags me to his side. He doesn't look at me. Doesn't dare to take his attention off his brothers, but I see his struggle.

He wants to believe them.

"Why?" I ask Salvatore. "Why didn't you aim at my husband? Or at us in the alley? Why pretend? Why play games?"

"It's not a game."

"Not a fucking fun one, anyway," Remy drawls. "This shit has gotten old real fucking quick."

I don't understand.

"They weren't willing participants, *mia dea*," Matthew mutters. It's not a question or speculation. There's confidence in his voice. Certainty in his expression.

"Meaning?" I ask.

"Emmanuel forced them to participate in the abduction of your daughter." He meets my gaze. "And they never wanted to be a part of your husband's death."

I frown. Shake my head. "How do you know?"

"I didn't. I only had suspicions until now."

"Suspicions since when?" I can't hold the accusation from my tone.

"Denver. When you took off in Abri's car." His eyes seek my understanding, his hand loosening around mine. "If she was loyal to Emmanuel, she never would've aided your escape. Then she spoke to me as if she wanted help but seemed too scared to ask. I didn't know why. I thought her fear may have been over your brother's possible retaliation. But I always wondered if it was because she hated her father's actions as much as I did."

"You should've told me," I whisper.

"You wouldn't have listened." He cups my cheek, rubbing his thumb over my lower lip.

He's right. I would've denied any leniency toward his siblings. I still want to now.

"Give us a chance to explain." Remy limps forward. "We'll tell you everything."

I don't stop looking at Matthew. Don't stop trying to read his thoughts.

"It's up to you, *la mia stella polare*." There's no inflection in his tone. He doesn't beg for them. Doesn't show weakness or attempt to sway me with guilt. But I feel it regardless. I sense the yearning for understanding over a family he lost. "They hurt you. Threatened you. It's your choice how we proceed."

No, it's not.

He's already made the decision for me.

"Please, Layla." Remy stands tall. "Give us a chance to explain that we're not your enemy."

"But are you an ally?" I raise a brow. "If we hear you out, will you willingly give information to help us kill your father?"

The brothers exchange a look. A tense visual standoff.

"It's not a trick question," Matthew growls. "There shouldn't be any hesitation if what you're claiming isn't a setup."

"There's no setup, but there's also no easy way to answer." Remy rakes a hand through his hair, inching forward. "If you're willing to talk this through, we can explain."

"Stay where you are." Matthew slides in front of me. "Don't get any closer."

Remy sighs. "I'm not going to hurt her. I think we've unintentionally done enough of that over the years. I just want her to see my sincerity. We never wanted to be a part of your darkest days, Layla."

They weren't merely a part of it. They were the creators. The instigators.

"One conversation," I concede, "that can be ended at any time."

Matthew looks at me over his shoulder. "Are you sure this is what you want?"

No. But it's what *he* wants. What he *needs*. And I'm willing to give it to him. "I'm listening. That's all. I'm not offering forgiveness."

He frowns. "Layla—"

"It's okay. I promise." I paste on a half-hearted smile. "I trust that you'll allow me to end the ceasefire at a moment's notice if I change my mind."

His shoulders straighten. Stiffen.

I know he's thinking about the most important word in my statement—*trust*.

He's earned it, at least a little, after almost killing his brothers to protect me.

"You heard her." He leans in, planting a smacking kiss to my lips, before swinging back to my enemies. "You've got one chance. So make it good."

Salvatore relaxes. "Where do you want to do this?"

"Inside." Matthew points his knife toward the stairs. "Lead the way."

Salvatore starts for the house, his injured shoulder hanging low while Remy limps a few feet behind.

I wait until they're halfway to the front door before I step away from my human shield to grab the Glock from the ground, then the magazine. I load the gun as Matthew watches, then shove it into the back of my jeans.

"Are you sure you're okay with this?" he asks. "You've already been through enough."

"We both have. But if what they're insinuating is true, I want all the details. Who knows? Maybe they're innocent."

"It's been years, Layla." His brows furrow. "If they weren't willingly complicit with Emmanuel's actions, then they were weak for far too long."

"You're right. But I know what that weakness feels like, because I was someone who did horrible things in the hopes of my father's love, not realizing the cost until it was too late."

His eyes harden. "You're not like them."

"That's beside the point." I grab his hand and entwine our fingers. "We need to hear them out."

"They don't deserve your kindness, *la mia stella polare*."

"Maybe not. But you do." I bring his knuckles to my lips. "The truth will set us free, right?"

He falls quiet, his thoughts loud behind his piercing stare.

I hear his affection through the silence. His adoration. His concern.

"Come on." I tug him toward the house. "I'll find Bishop while you organize first aid supplies."

"First aid supplies?" He scoffs, following along beside me. "Now you're just being soft. They're fine. I stayed away from arteries and the blade is small." He holds it up in front of me. "Barely big enough to require a Band-Aid."

I chuckle at his immunity to carnage. "Humor me. I don't want to be left cleaning up a blood trail. And besides, we can't get their side of the story if they bleed out."

He pauses before the bottom step, his brothers already poised at the front door.

"Whatever you say, *mia dea*." He kisses me softly. Warm lips and gentle affection from such a brutal man. "But just so you know, they're probably going to need a lot more than a first aid kit once Bishop gets hold of them."

We continue inside and part ways in the living room.

His brothers approach the kitchen sink. Matthew heads for the bathroom. I hustle downstairs to pause on the bottom step.

The silence is eerie. Unsettling. "Bishop?"

A smothered yell carries from a nearby room. Then a clatter of furniture.

"I'm coming." I jog toward the sound and stop in the doorway to a darkened bedroom, the curtains closed and bathing the room in shadow.

I flick on the light, illuminating Bishop, bound to a wooden chair by thick, grey electrical tape.

He's mummified, ankles to torso, his suit barely visible beneath his bindings, with a lone strip over his mouth. I'd almost feel sorry for him if it weren't for the glare aimed my way, his eyes tiny slits of rebellion.

He's livid. Bloodthirsty.

He yells beneath the tape gag. It's aggressive. Clearly insulting or threatening.

"I don't like your tone." I scan the room for something sharp. A knife. A pen.

He scoots the chair forward an inch, reclaiming my attention, and jerks his chin at the bedside table.

"There's something in there?" I stalk for the drawers, pulling the top one open to claim the pocket knife inside. I flick the blade open, walk to him, then remove the tape over his mouth with a quick rip.

"*Motherfucker*." His lips are red. His eyes furious. "Did you stop to contemplate, even for the slightest second, that you could've removed the tape from my mouth the moment you walked through the fucking door?"

I crouch at his side and start cutting the bindings at his wrist. "Did you stop to contemplate how much your silence is preferable to your attitude?"

"*Funny*," he snaps. "Where the fuck is Langston?"

"Upstairs." I saw through the heavy tape from his hand to his elbow, not caring if I'm destroying his suit.

"And those fucking pussies?"

He yanks his arm free and begins clawing at the tape on his chest as I work on his other wrist.

"They're up there with him."

We work in silence, the shredding of stitching and tearing of bindings filling the room before he finally asks, "Did they hurt you?"

I pause, not sure why he'd care. "No."

He pulls his second arm free. "Did they touch you?"

Apprehension trickles through my veins. His concern is unsettling.

"Layla?" he growls. "Did they touch you?"

"No. Why?" I kneel before him, turning my attention to the tape at his ankles. "Have you grown a heart all of a sudden?"

He yanks harder at his bindings, wobbling the chair. "What I've grown is fucking attached to a stellar reputation that I have no intention of losing."

Of course. Silly me.

I slice harder at the tape, dragging the blade between his legs, moving past his knees, then toward his upper thighs.

"I appreciate the help." He snatches the blade from my grip. "But the last thing I need is you with something sharp near my dick."

"Are you sure?" I lean back on my haunches. "I could teach you some manners."

"If that's what you call the shit you've been doing with Langston, then it's a hard pass from me. All I need right now is revenge."

I stand as he stabs the tape to shreds. "How did they get you down?"

"From my lack of memory and one hell of a fucking headache, I'm assuming those sons of bitches sucker punched me when I was doing a perimeter check." He throws the last of his bindings to the floor and shoves to his feet, his suit in tatters. "You might want to stay down here a while."

That's not going to happen.

I follow as he stalks for the hall. He pounces up the stairs three at a time, arms swinging, posture rigid.

He storms into the open living area and straight toward Matthew's brothers at the island counter, who are tending to their wounds.

Salvatore is shirtless, the muscles on his chest smeared with diluted blood as Remy sits on the counter, one leg of his suit pants cut open as he affixes a bandage to his thigh.

My gaze turns to Matthew in panic, already anticipating the carnage that's about to ensue. But he doesn't move from his settled position against the far counter. He doesn't even change his lazy stance, his arms and ankles crossed.

"*Fuck.*" Remy scoots from the counter.

Salvatore pivots toward the threat.

Bishop storms forward, shoulders broad, face menacing, and launches a fist at Salvatore's cheek.

The blow isn't defended. My enemy takes the hit, his head flinging to the side as he stumbles into the counter.

Bishop strikes Salvatore's chin. Mouth. Jaw. Each punch is fast and precise before he pivots to Remy, grabbing the younger man by the shirt to drag him forward. Chest to chest.

"Your turn, cockroach." His knuckles pound Remy's nose. Eye. Cheek.

Matthew barely blinks as my pulse thunders, his thoughts almost perfectly hidden if it weren't for the way he unfolds his arms to clutch the counter behind him. He white-knuckles the marble. His chin hitches higher.

"That's enough," I warn Bishop.

He doesn't stop. He swings again and again as Remy ducks into the blows.

"I said, *that's enough.*" I raise my voice. "We need them in a position to talk, and they can't do that without teeth."

Bishop hesitates, his back stiffening as he pants, chest heaving, nostrils flared, his grip still tight on Remy's shirt.

"Let him go." I walk to his side, tilting my head into his line of vision. "Now, Bishop."

Remy doesn't move. Doesn't speak.

He stands there, fearless in the face of another deserving blow as Bishop snarls, then finally shoves him away.

"Are we good now?" Remy limps, his blotched face pinched while he struggles to regain footing on his injured leg.

"Not even close, you fucking bitch." Bishop swipes rough hands down the front of his shirt, smoothing the crinkles. "I'll never be *good* with someone who throws cheap shots."

"Cut us a break." Salvatore licks the cut on his bottom lip, then prods at the swelling flesh with a gentle finger. "We waited until the kid was gone. We didn't want trouble. We just needed you out of the way."

Stella. They were watching while she was here?

"You waited until you weren't outnumbered," he corrects. "You knew Torian's men would've killed you without hesitation."

Salvatore glowers, denying the obvious.

This could've turned out so much worse. They could've approached while my daughter was around. Could've petrified her like they have before.

"Hey." Matthew draws my attention, his palm patting the counter at his side. "Come here."

I drag my feet toward him, thankful for the support while Bishop marches to the fridge, muttering under his breath. He yanks the freezer drawer open and grabs a handful of ice.

Matthew drapes a protective arm over my shoulder, nestling me into his side. "Is he okay?" he murmurs in my ear.

"I think so." I assume, aside from a headache, the only thing wounded is his pride.

He kisses my temple, then sucks in a long breath. "Okay, motherfuckers, now that the welcoming party is over, you two need to start talking."

"Can't we do this without your guard dog?" Salvatore keeps his death stare on Bishop as he grabs his blood-stained shirt from the counter to pull it back on. "It's a family matter."

"He *is* family. *My* family. And you wouldn't be in any position to talk if it weren't for his leniency. So I suggest you quit asking for more favors."

"Hear that, boys?" Bishop's expression turns smug as he holds the ice on his knuckles and leans over the sink. "My beating was lenient. Next time I'll have far more fun."

Remy rolls his eyes, grabs his belt from the island counter, and begins threading it through his pants. "Like we said outside—we want to get out."

"Out of what exactly?" I ask.

"The family." He looks to Matthew. "We want to walk away from Emmanuel like you did."

Bishop scoffs. "Like he did? So you're prepared to become homeless, form a drug addiction, then earn your living by slaughtering strangers?"

Salvatore gives Remy a pointed look. "I told you this was a bad idea."

"You're damn fucking right about that." Bishop's jaw tenses. "You should've listened to your brother."

"I thought you'd understand." Remy keeps staring at Matthew, undaunted by the judgment. "That you'd have sympathy."

"Sympathy for what?" Matthew drawls. "Your wealth? Your career? What part is my heart meant to bleed for?"

"We don't have wealth." Salvatore shakes his head. "Not a fucking penny. None that we can access anyway. It all goes into a trust that we can't touch." He turns his attention to me. "Maybe you'll understand our position better than anyone. I'm told our father learned his tactics from yours."

A chill skitters down my spine. "Meaning?"

"Emmanuel has always said Luther Torian used his children like pawns."

I try not to flinch, but I'm not strong enough. His arrow makes a direct hit to my pride, the shame exploding through my chest.

"Like *weapons*," Remy clarifies. "And that's exactly how Emmanuel treats us. We never wanted to be a part of this mayhem. We were manipulated into it, and the fucking humiliating part is that we should've seen it coming"

"Pathetic is another accurate description," Bishop mutters.

I have a million questions, each one locked behind a cage of trauma and pain.

I don't want to believe them. I don't want to be sympathetic or obliging or lenient. But I can't help wondering if our lives could possibly be carbon copies. If they're dealing with emotional wounds like mine.

Salvatore returns his attention to the man at my side. "After you left, Dad lost his fucking mind knowing he could no longer control you."

Matthew's jaw twitches. "It was lost well before that. Otherwise Grace would still be alive."

"Well, it avalanched from there. He began to script every part of our lives. From the classes we attended, to after-school activities. And every time we fought back against his control, he used your disappearance to justify his actions. He said he wouldn't allow us to ruin our lives the way you did."

"That's it?" Bishop asks with incredulity. "Dear ol' Daddy picked economics instead of trigonometry so now you're throwing a tantrum?"

Remy's expression tightens. "The classes were an example, asshole."

"Well, it wasn't a fucking good one, was it?"

"How's this for a better example?" Salvatore bristles. "For Rem's fifteenth birthday, he was forced to go to a strip club where a woman was paid to take his virginity."

"That's not your fucking story to share," Remy snarls.

Matthew turns rigid. "Is it true?"

My stomach hollows as Remy's nostrils flare. His fists clench.

"Is it true?" Matthew demands.

"Yeah, it's true." Remy pins us with a judgmental stare. "But don't look at me like that. I was a fucking teenager with a twenty-four-seven hard-on. It wasn't like I didn't get my kicks."

Breath escapes my lips in a rapid vacuum. He's excusing the abuse. Rationalizing rape.

"What else?" Matthew pushes from the counter to pace in front of me. "Tell me every-fucking-thing he's done."

"You name it, he's done it. We've been threatened and manipulated. We've been part of a multimillion-dollar fashion label for years without seeing a penny of income."

"How?" I drag my gaze down his tailored suit, all the way to what look to be polished Dior shoes, then back up to his designer watch and styled haircut.

"You think this means something?" He indicates his appearance with a wave of a hand. "Everything we earn goes into a trust that's guarded by legal loopholes we don't have the money to defend. We survive through the accounts Emmanuel has opened at a long list of businesses. We can spend whatever we want as long as it's within the parameters of his control. He knows what we're buying and when we're buying it. There's no freedom. We can't do anything without his knowledge."

"That Cartier watch would cost more than my housekeeper's yearly salary." Bishop drawls. "Ever heard of a pawn shop?"

"Ever contemplated that Emmanuel has spies everywhere?" Salvatore sneers.

"You know what? I'm getting really sick and fucking tired of your attitude." Remy straightens to his full height. "Do you think we want to ask for help? Do you think we'd be here if we weren't scraping the bottom of the—"

"Did all your friends turn you away, pretty boy?" Bishop matches his posture, taking a threatening step forward. "You can't even crash on someone's sofa while you pull your shitty life together? Or better yet, go public with your father's manipulation and let cancel culture take the wheel? Social media will dismantle his empire quicker than any of us can."

They stand toe to toe. All madness and malice.

"There are no friends," Salvatore mutters. "The only people who have permanent access to our lives are those that Emmanuel allows. And going public isn't an option either because every illegal action we've been forced into has been documented. He's kept the fucking receipts. So when we say he's gained control over everything, we mean it. He *knows* everything. Influences *everything*."

"If that's the case, then he knows you're here." Matthew plants his feet. "And you've placed Layla in more danger."

"No." Remy shakes his head. "We were strategic. We fed him information to stay off our tail. We told him we bribed an airport official for details on your flight out of Denver. We said you landed in Charleston, and that's where we flew into, then hired a car so we weren't pinned in your actual vicinity. But it's only a matter of time. If we don't give him results soon, he'll send more men."

"I'm not fucking convinced." Bishop throws the ice into the sink and stalks for the floor-to-ceiling windows. "All this smells like bullshit to me."

The room falls silent.

I don't know what to say. Or think. Yet there's a part of me that leans toward belief. I hear truth in their words. I see it in their pained expressions.

I hate it, but it's there.

Matthew rubs a rough hand down his face.

Bishop stares at the ocean.

Remy braces his hands against the island counter and hangs his head.

Salvatore sighs.

None of us want this. And all of us know something needs to change.

"Tell me about your role in my daughter's abduction." I swallow over the weakness in my voice. "Was it planned? Did you know our children were going to be taken?"

"We didn't know a damn thing until after Emmanuel had us board a jet to Sacramento and those kids were on our doorstep." Remy looks up at me through hooded lashes, his dark eyes intense.

"Until after your brother was in that penthouse," Salvatore corrects. "Even after the kids arrived, I thought we were just looking after them until Torian came to pick them up. But Emmanuel blindsided us again with the blackmail."

"And the guy your brother killed…" Remy cringes. "It was the first fucking time we'd had to dispose of a dead body."

"It was the first time I'd *seen* a dead body," Salvatore mutters.

Matthew walks to my side, gently maneuvering me away from the counter to stand behind me, hands on my hips. "Was it your last?"

"No." Remy shakes his head. "Dear ol' Dad has put his dirty fingers into some pretty fucked-up pies of late—extortion, guns, drugs. We've had to learn how to cover our tracks better so he couldn't get as much ammunition against us as he did that day. We made so many fucking mistakes back then. He has security footage of us handling the body and buying the chemicals to clean the crime scene."

"Because every penny you use is through his accounts." Matthew lets out the faintest huff of a laugh. "He's smarter than I gave him credit for."

"But those smarts only work to his advantage while he's breathing," I murmur. "So why is he still alive?"

Remy gives a bitter smile. "I don't appreciate having to state this word for word. But seeing as though you haven't already realized, he's fucking smarter than us."

"He already has a system in place that ensures we'll never gain access to the family trust if he dies of anything other than natural causes." Salvatore presses on the swelling at his cheek. "That's hundreds of millions of dollars, all down the drain. And as much as I want him dead, I want a fucking future more."

Are they saying they want to take murder off the table?

I wrap my arms around my middle, my unease building as Matthew tightens his hold on my hips.

I won't live in a world where Emmanuel isn't punished for what he's done to me. What he's done to my daughter. Stella deserves to be free.

"What about Abri?" Matthew asks. "Is she treated the same?"

Remy nods. "If not worse. The money and control is no different. But he's got something over her that she won't discuss. Or even admit."

"Then how do you know it exists?" Bishop swings back to face the group.

"Because she's always been the most defiant out of the three of us until a few years ago when she disappeared off the face of the earth. He took her somewhere. For months. One minute, they were fighting over family dinner—the next, she was gone. He left her God knows where. And when she returned, she wasn't the same. She was fucking compliant."

This isn't happening.

I'm not caving to the plight of my enemies. I can't be.

It's anger that claws at my throat. Rage that burns my eyes.

I walk toward the sofas, needing space, craving hope. I stare at the black television screen, attempting to visualize a future that isn't a continuation of this nightmare. But their situation is changing everything.

"So let me get this straight." Bishop stalks back toward the island counter. "You're here for Matthew's money, right? You want him to pay for the mistakes you were too pathetic to escape from and bankroll your future."

I drag in a breath, despising that image.

Their future is reliant upon Matthew. Meaning, if I stay with the man who owns my heart, I'll become a part of their picture, too.

"We don't know what we want." Remy's voice is hostile. "We just know we need to get out."

19

MATTHEW

I rub the back of my neck, every muscle tense as Layla stares at the blank television.

She's suffering again. We both are.

I don't know how to help my siblings without hurting her.

Hell, I'm still not sure if I fucking believe them. But I want to.

I want them back in my life—if only it wasn't at the expense of her happiness.

"Honestly, Dante." Salvo's voice weakens. "We wouldn't be here if we weren't—"

"That's not his name," she warns. "That's not who he is anymore. If you're here begging for help, the least you can do is offer him the respect he deserves."

I raise my brows, not expecting her passion. Her defense.

"I meant no disrespect." Salvatore clears his throat. "It's habit."

I keep looking at her. In pride. In gratitude. "Everyone, out. I need to speak to Layla alone."

"You don't have to tell me twice." Bishop stalks for the hall. "I'm tired of this shit show. I'll be downstairs."

Salvatore and Remy exchange a troubled glance.

"I guess we'll go for a walk on the beach." Salvatore heads toward the deck door.

"Walking is going to be a hard pass for me." Remy limps after him. "I'm going to find somewhere to sit."

They leave without protest, their murmured words filtering into the quiet of the house until they slowly descend the outside stairs and head out of sight.

Layla watches them leave, her arms wrapped around her middle, her shoulders rigid.

I want to go to her. I'm fucking drawn to her side. But the anguish woven into her posture is enough to give me pause.

Anguish *I* caused.

If only I'd killed Emmanuel when he took Grace from me. If only I'd had the balls to give him what he deserved all those years ago, nobody else would've had to suffer.

"How do you want to proceed, *la mia stella polare*?"

"You can't ask me that." Her voice is frail. "This isn't my decision."

"Yes, it is. You're in control here."

She shakes her head slowly. Solemnly. "No, Matthew." She turns to face me. "I need to leave."

"Like hell you do." I stride for her, not stopping until we're foot to foot, my hands claiming her waist. "I just got you back. If you walk out on me now, I'll tear the world apart to find you again."

"We both know you have to help them. And I can't be around when you do."

"Why not?"

She lowers her gaze to my chest. "You know why."

Because of Stella. Because of her husband. Because history is cruel and understanding doesn't equate to forgiveness.

"I'm sending them away." I start for the deck.

"Stop it." She grabs my jacket, clenching her fingers in the material. "They're your family."

"They *were*. A long fucking time ago."

"Matthew…" Her big blue eyes blink at me in sorrow. "You've spent a few days trying to win me back. But I bet you've spent years trying to gain closure over walking away from your siblings."

Her accuracy is pinpoint. An arrow straight through the heart.

"See?" She winces. "You can't leave them again. You can't give up this opportunity to bring them back into your life, especially if they've been manipulated this whole time. Think about Abri. Think about what her future might be like without your help."

I clench my jaw, denying the imagery that fights to be seen.

"You understand where Emmanuel could've taken her, right?" she whispers. "If he's anything like my father, he could've sent her to a human-trafficking hub. She might have been forced to spend time with sex slaves. And what if he has that hanging over her head if she defies him again?"

I clench harder.

"Even I can't live with that." She gives me a sad smile, her hand raising to graze the stubble along my jaw. "And I hate your family more than anyone. So there's no way I'll let you deal with that guilt."

"But you'll allow me to suffer through losing you again?" I capture her wrist, lowering it to her side. "You underestimate what I'm willing to live with if it means keeping you."

"I'm not yours to keep." She makes another direct strike with her gentle honesty. "And I know you're not that callous. You've told me before that you have no one. There's only Lorenzo and Bishop—"

"I have you."

"I don't even have *me,* Matthew. I'm not someone anyone can rely on. I've made too many mistakes. I've hurt everyone I know. Basing your future on me isn't good for either of us. You need to choose your family."

"I choose both."

She shakes her head. "You can't."

"Like hell," I growl. *"I. Choose. Both.* And I get what I fucking want, *la mia stella polare.* So don't think I can't figure this out, because I will. You're not walking away. I'm not letting you go. I know this is a hard fucking crossroad, but we'll find an outcome that works for us. Trust me."

She glances away.

I drag her close and press my lips to her temple. "Trust me. Okay?"

She sighs and nods as she nestles into me, her palms resting against my waist, her hips leaning into mine.

I hug her to my chest, resenting the fact that she's trying to emotionally slip away while still in my arms. She's giving up too easily when I'm sure I can figure this out.

My resources are unlimited. My contacts extensive. My determination lethal.

"Our agreement hasn't changed, *mia dea,*" I murmur into her hair. "Emmanuel will die and we'll be the cause."

Her exhale is long. Ragged. "I need to lie down for a while. I'm getting a headache and I can't think straight."

If she's lying, it doesn't matter. We both need space to contemplate our next move. Just as long as that move is together, I don't give a shit where she draws her conclusion.

"I'll make sure the house remains quiet." I kiss her temple and drop my arms to my sides, fucking despising Emmanuel more than ever as she walks away without a backward glance.

I return to the kitchen, grab a glass of water, and Tylenol from the first aid kit sitting on the counter, then follow her.

She's in the bathroom when I enter her room, the door closed, the faucet running.

I place my offering on the bedside table and continue downstairs to Bishop's room, stopping at the threshold.

He stands with his arms crossed over his chest, glaring at the wooden chair at the end of his bed, electrical tape littering the floor around it.

"It's a good thing we quit working for Lorenzo when we did." I lean against the doorjamb, despising how far we've fallen. "We became complacent too damn quick."

His lips thin. "Then why does it feel like you're worming your way back in?"

"It's temporary."

"Is it, though?" He raises a brow. "First, there's your agreement with Cole. Then the promise to kill Emmanuel. Now, you're contemplating playing Mr. Fix-It with your brothers' lives, or have you already committed to helping them?"

"I haven't decided."

He scoffs, his smile vindictive. "Like hell you haven't. You just don't want to admit it because you know it's a fucking mistake."

"You need to find a new catch phrase. The 'mistake' lecture is getting old."

"I guess that means you're right on cue to tell me I can walk whenever I feel like it." He turns to me. "But I swear to God, if you say that one more time, I'll kill you myself. I'm sick of being insulted, especially since I'm the only one who's ever had your back."

"What part of this pisses you off?" I stroll toward him. "Is it Layla gaining all my attention? Do you resent her?"

"Your attention is the last thing I need, asshole, so why would I fucking resent her?"

"If it's not resentment, then what is it?"

"How I feel about her doesn't matter when she's going to be dead soon. There's no way she'll outlive Emmanuel. He's fucking smarter than we thought, and we've already been found. *Twice.*" He points a hand toward the outside wall. "Who's to say he didn't follow those roaches here? He could be a mile down the road, waiting for us to fall asleep, and your dumb ass still won't carry a gun."

"If I carried, my brothers would've been dead the moment they pulled Layla out of the car."

"Now that's a conclusion I can get behind." His arm falls to his side. "I'd much prefer to be disposing of their bodies than helping fix their fucking lives."

I don't buy it.

We've spent years spying on my family. Not once has he shown enough investment to react this emotionally toward them. They've always been a job. A task.

Not only that, but he's never shied away from an adrenaline fix. Bishop loves anything with a hint of danger. I'm the one who had to convince him to leave Lorenzo, even though he's always craved a return to the darkness.

"What's up with you?" I scrutinize him, taking in the tightness of his expression, the way he keeps working his fingers as if he's overrun with energy. "Why are you pissed off about this?"

"Because you're making a mistake."

"By helping them?"

"By getting more involved. You're going to get her killed."

He's said that twice now.

This is about Layla. Her safety. Her life.

"This is you being protective," I muse. "You're worried about her."

"Like I give a fuck about the bitch you're banging."

"That's it, isn't it?" I grin, letting the slur slide because I now understand the glimmer in his eyes is fear. "You care about her. You want her to be safe."

"Like I said," he snarls, "I don't give a fuck about the bi—"

I launch my palm at his throat, my fingers digging into his jugular. "I let you insult her once. We both know I won't let it happen again. You're deliberately goading me into a fight and I'm not in the mood."

"Fuck you." He shoves my arm away. "Her death is a complication I don't need. You're obsessed with her. So what happens when she no longer exists? Where does that leave us? Where the fuck does it leave our investments and staff?"

It's a cop-out.

He can't admit he's worried about her because he's never been inclined to feel

that way about a woman before. All he's ever known are the escorts he's paid to
share his bed.

"If she dies, I die with her," I state simply. "Then everything is yours."

"There you go, insulting me again." He gets in my face. "If I wanted your money,
I would've slit your throat a long time ago, *stronzo*."

And there's no way my body would've been found.

"So what's the plan?" he asks. "What should I expect in this next episode of How
Much Can Langston Complicate My Fucking Life?"

"She wants to leave," I admit with a shrug. "She thinks I should help my brothers,
but she doesn't want to hang around while I do it."

"Can you blame her?"

"No." I step back and rake my hands through my hair. "But I think I can figure
out a strategy that works for all of us."

"Since when did your lizard-sized brain grow big enough to do that sort of shit?"

"Since when did you stop reading me well enough to determine when I'm ready
to choke you out?" I start for the door.

"Where the fuck are you going? We're in the middle of a conversation."

"No, you're in the middle of a tantrum and I need to speak to my brothers. Are
you coming to lay the ground rules?"

"Do I have to play nice?" he growls.

"Not at all."

He follows with a huffed breath. "In that case, I'm in."

We walk through the laundry and into the backyard. Remy sits perched near the
top of the deck staircase, his injured leg outstretched, the hole in his pants gaping
while Salvo stands close to the bottom.

They eye us as we approach, their pinched expressions more focused on Bishop
than me.

"I'm going to make one thing emphatically clear." I stop before them, Bishop
doing the same at my side. "I'll help but only while Layla's happiness is at the forefront of everyone's thoughts. Her life won't be complicated by this. You will consider
everything you've put her through before you make the slightest decision, and if
your assessment concludes that your intentions will give her even the tiniest discomfort or heartache, you will stop whatever the fuck you were planning and thank the
heavens that she's allowed you to live long enough to make any plans at all."

Salvatore stands taller.

"You will treat her with respect," I continue, "and acknowledge that she is your
ticket out of this. Not me. Your future is in her hands. Not mine. Is that understood?"

Remy jerks his chin. Salvo inclines his head. Their expressions remain pensive.

"Is it understood?" I repeat, my tone lethal.

Salvatore raises his hands in surrender. "Yeah, it's understood."

"Loud and clear," Remy adds.

"Good. Because we already have plans for Emmanuel, and those aren't going to
change. So get used to the idea of starting over."

"Starting over? Meaning we'll lose access to the family trust?"

"He's going to die. That's nonnegotiable."

Salvo scrubs a hand over his face, muttering something unintelligible as he breaks eye contact.

They want him alive. Or they're not willing to risk their money for their freedom. Either way, the hesitancy to kill the man enslaving them doesn't sit well with me.

"Layla must mean a lot to you." Remy struggles to his feet, the skin on his left cheek already turning purple as he stares at me. "How long have you two been together?"

"Five seconds."

I ignore Bishop's snappy retort and incline my head. "She means everything. The first of those five seconds was enough to determine she'd be mine till the day I die."

"But what about D.C.? She didn't know who you—"

"Bringing up D.C., where you royally screwed me over with her, isn't the best move. What you need to concentrate on is your complete and utter respect for her moving forward."

"What about Abri?" Salvo asks. "Where does she stand in all this?"

"We'll help her, too, as long as she agrees to the terms."

Remy hangs his head and nods. "I don't think we should tell her. Like we said before, she changed after she was sent away. She won't approve of an attack on our father."

"Then she gets kept in the dark." Bishop claps me on the shoulder. "But what I'm concerned about, which my man here seems to be ignoring, is that this could all be a setup. Who's to say you two aren't buying time until Emmanuel gets here?"

Remy looks up with hard eyes. "Call the house. As of this morning when we spoke to Abri, he was still there with his men. He's barely back on his feet. The fucker can't walk more than ten yards without hyperventilating."

"It's no secret he taps your phones."

"That's why we got new ones." Salvatore reaches into his pocket and pulls out a cell. "It's turned off but feel free to check it. Only Abri has the number. The phones our father knows about are waiting back at a hotel in Charleston."

Bishop ignores the device. "And you trust Abri not to rat on you? You admitted she's got secrets. Who's to say she won't stick with Emmanuel when this all blows up?"

"There's nothing to rat on. She doesn't know where we are or what we set out to achieve. And we haven't called her within twenty miles of this place." Salvo's tone hardens. "She's not the threat here. What you need to worry about is Dad growing tired of waiting for you to be found. He'll send more men. And that snitch on the Denver runway will lead them right here."

"I've got eyes on the local airport. We'll know if anyone flies in. But we'll leave in the morning." I glance at them in turn, waiting for a protest. "I suggest you strap in for a bumpy ride because your lives are about to get hectic."

"Where are we going?" Remy grabs the railing, shuffling on his good leg.

"You'll find out once we get there. For now, sit tight and stay out of Layla's way." I start for the laundry, Bishop following a step behind.

"Wait," Salvo calls out. "Can't you at least tell us how this is going to work? Is this a long-term reunion kind of thing? Or merely transactional, where you give us money and we part ways once we're on our feet?"

I tense. Stop.

I don't have a clue about the family situation. A lot of our future depends on Layla. But one thing's for sure. "I'm not giving you a damn cent. I started from the bottom without a dime to my name, and you can do the same. But I'm working on a plan that might get you places faster than I ever did."

20

MATTHEW

The house is quiet when I return through the lower level

"Tell me about this plan." Bishop stays on my six.

"Give me a chance to speak to Layla first. I'll find you once I'm done."

"I'm relegated to second-string already?" he mutters.

"What can I say? She's got better tits than you." I make a beeline for the stairs. "I'll find you once I'm done."

"I guess I'll be in the kitchen eating all the leftovers then."

"Have at it. But organize the jet while you're there. Have it ready midmorning for Virginia Beach."

"I'll get it done."

"Just keep it quiet. If Layla's asleep, I don't want to wake her."

We part ways at the top of the staircase, my steps slowing as I approach her ajar bedroom door. I anticipate the relief of seeing her resting, snuggled on her side like she always slept in my D.C. apartment.

But she's not there.

The bed is made. The covers flat and crisp. The curtains open.

I don't have to move any farther to determine the atmosphere in the room is hollow. Her floral scent doesn't linger. I can't feel her presence.

I drag my feet inside, finding the glass of water and Tylenol untouched on the bedside table. "Layla?"

There's no response. Nothing other than the rabid beat in my chest.

I continue to her private bathroom, my blood heating in rage.

It's empty. Her toothbrush is gone from the counter. Her makeup and deodorant, too.

Fuck.

I pivot, swinging back to the bedroom, scanning it from top to bottom.

The duffle her sister brought is gone. The clothes. The shoes. All that remains is a box in the corner with the trash from her packages compacted inside.

She ran.

She fucking left me.

"Jesus goddamn Christ."

She's risking her life out there on her own.

I palm the knife in my pocket, digging it into my skin as I storm for the hall. I have to find her before anyone else does. Before I lose my goddamn mind.

I trek for the living room, passing my bedroom, my steps skittering to a halt.

Did I close my door?

I backtrack, my temples pulsing, my palms sweating as I reach for the handle. I'm holding my fucking breath for a miracle as a faint brush of noise carries from inside.

"Layla?" Adrenaline has me by the balls as I open the door, gut clenched, chest tight.

She sits on the far edge of the bed, staring toward the ocean, her back to me, her duffle on the floor near the dresser, Remy's gun on the bedside table.

"Gesù dannato Cristo." My pulse takes off, wild and unrhythmic. *"La mia stella polare,* you scared me half to death. I thought you left me."

She glances at me over her shoulder, her smile forlorn. "Sorry. I didn't feel comfortable in my room with the door lock broken. Not while they're here."

I decimate the distance between us, falling to my knees in front of her, clasping her hands in her lap. "I'll speak to them. We'll find them somewhere else to spend the night."

"No. It's okay. I want this for you."

I want this for you. Despite her fear. Despite her enemies being under the same roof. *She wants this for me.*

She wants my happiness. My closure.

"Mi dispiace che tu ti sia guadagnata l'ergastolo con me."

"What does that mean?" she asks.

"It means you're mine." I drag her toward me, taking her mouth with my own. Hard. Fast. Frantic. "That you're stuck with me. That I'm never letting you go."

Her reciprocation is meek. A gentle palm presses on my sternum.

I lean back, seeing the torment she doesn't try to hide. "I can't live through another betrayal, Matthew. If you hurt me for a second time, I'll…"

"You'll kill me," I answer for her. "You'll realize that none of this was your fault and that I'm a pathetic son of a bitch who deserves to die, and you'll fucking kill me. Is that understood?"

Her nose scrunches, the scars of my past transgressions still raw as she lowers her attention to my chest.

"But it won't happen." I grip her chin, tilting her head upward, reclaiming her attention. "I swear it to you. I make mistakes, Layla. But I never repeat them." I drag my thumb over her lower lip. "I promise your heart is safe with mine. We'll make this work."

"How?"

I move to sit beside her, sliding an arm around her waist to pull her close. "We'll leave in the morning." I follow her gaze to the waves sweeping the shore, my lungs filling with the scent of her shampoo.

"I already know that part."

"We're no longer going back to D.C."

She turns her gaze to mine, her eyes questioning.

"We're going to Virginia Beach."

"To see Lorenzo?" She pivots toward me, reading me. For long moments she stops and stares, quiet in her appraisal. "You're going to ask for his permission to kill Emmanuel instead of hiding our plan."

"Of sorts."

"But if he says no—"

"He won't."

She gives me a wary look. "But you said he has for over ten years now. And besides that, your brothers expect to lose millions if their father is murdered."

"I have an idea that will ensure they bounce back quickly. Trust fund or not. They'll have their own income and influence. They'll slide straight into a position of power far greater than Emmanuel ever had."

Her face slackens. "Matthew…" She's figuring it out. Putting the puzzle pieces in place. "You can't be serious."

My lips kick with pride. She's smart. Or maybe she has the ability to read me like a book. Either way, she's fucking perfect. "It's a win-win for all of us."

"You want them to take over from Lorenzo so he can retire?" She pushes to her feet. "Don't tell me they agreed to do that. It's crazy. Their father's schemes are one thing, but this is…" She shakes her head. "This is insane."

"They don't have a choice."

"So they *did* agree? Or they *didn't*?"

"We haven't discussed it yet."

Her eyes bug. "You haven't told them? Matthew, this isn't the type of situation you spring on someone. Their lives will be changed forever."

"For the better." I reach for her, sliding my fingers around her wrist to pull her between my legs.

"How can you say that when you worked so hard to get out? You hated that lifestyle."

"I hated being alone," I counter. "I went from having a girlfriend and a family to being an orphaned, drug-addicted teenager who killed for a living. I had nothing. But they'll have everything."

"They'll be in danger."

"They already are. They've dabbled in the drug and gun trade for years. They've abducted kids and disposed of bodies. God only knows what else they've been involved in." I slide my hands around her hips. "Yes, there will be teething problems. But it's the perfect fit. They're getting exactly what they want. Protection. Money. Security. A career—"

"Taking on a criminal empire isn't exactly a career."

"*Mia dea*, they're already in this lifestyle whether they like it or not. And the only two options they have are to start from scratch with no money and prospects or slide straight to the top of the food chain. Because either way, Emmanuel is going to die, and they're not going to see a cent of what they're owed."

She peers down at me, her brow furrowed, her teeth digging into her bottom lip.

I hate seeing her like this. I fucking wish we could go back to when she didn't know who I was. When she was all smiles and shy seduction.

I'd do everything differently.

"It won't work," she whispers. "You're going to set this up with Lorenzo and then your brothers will back out, leaving our plan with Emmanuel exposed."

"It will work."

"If you're so confident, then what's worrying you?" She cocks her head. "There's something you're not telling me."

"I'm not worried."

"Don't lie to me," she warns. "I can see it."

"It's not concern for the plan. I'm convinced all parties will understand the favorable opportunity this provides."

"Then what?" She narrows her gaze. "There's something—"

"It's guilt, Layla."

She balks, pulling back. But all too soon her shoulders slump, her tension easing. "You blame yourself."

"Wouldn't you? I left my siblings to be extorted and abused. I walked out on them, and Remy was sexually fucking assaulted."

"No." She shakes her head. "You couldn't have known what Emmanuel was going to do."

I scoff. "But I knew what he did to Grace. I knew what he was capable of and left them anyway. If I'd stepped up and done the right thing when she was murdered, nobody would've suffered. My family would've been without a patriarch, but it would've been better for it. Stella wouldn't have been abducted. Your husband would still be alive."

"Matthew…" She beseeches me with pleading eyes.

"At the very least, I should've gone back for them." I tug her onto my lap. "Once I had a stable life with Lorenzo, it was my duty to save them."

"When did you ever have a stable life? When you were the Butcher? When your days were spent catering to Lorenzo's demands?" She places her hands behind my neck, her mouth close, her breath teasing my lips. "You told me you wanted nothing more than to get out. So why are you blaming yourself for not dragging them into hell with you?"

"It wasn't hell—"

"But it wasn't a life you wanted either. You can't take responsibility for this." Her voice becomes a whisper. "This isn't on you. It's on him. *Everything* is on Emmanuel. Both your hardships and mine."

I cup her jaw. "You don't believe that either. I know you still blame yourself, too."

She lowers her arms to her sides, her attention falling to the bedcoverings.

"*Mia dea*, how can you lecture me on blame but not listen to your own advice?" I rub a thumb along her cheek. "You wanted your father to love you. There's no shame in that."

"There is if I wanted that love despite the cost." She tilts her face away from my palm. "I hurt so many people."

"We all do. It's part of life."

She turns her back to me, straddling my thigh to return her attention to the ocean. "Well, I don't like it."

"Me neither." I press my face into her hair, breathing her in.

We stay like that while Bishop tinkers in the kitchen. After Remy and Salvatore return inside. For long minutes and quiet moments of nothing but contemplation.

She nestles into my chest, returning to the woman who was comfortable in my presence, not protesting when I wrap a slow, possessive arm around her waist.

I try to forget the guilt. To ignore it and focus on gratitude.

I've reclaimed my woman.

She's all I need in this world.

"Once the dust settles…" I graze my lips down the side of her neck, "How do I make you happy?"

She doesn't respond, not in words. There's only a weary inhale.

"*La mia stella polare?*" I nuzzle her ear. "Tell me what your perfect future looks like for us."

"I'm not sure I understand what happiness is anymore, let alone being able to imagine it."

Her sadness stabs through me. She wasn't like this before I betrayed her. She still had hope.

"What if I tell you mine?"

She sighs and sinks farther into me. "I'm listening."

I circle her waist, my hands resting on her stomach. "We live together in D.C. Just you, me, and Stella when she's home from school."

"What about Bishop?" she murmurs. "Your boy will be devastated."

"He can visit on weekends." I snicker against her hair. "We'll holiday in Italy. I'll take you to fashion shows in Milan and spoil you in Florence."

"And will you call me your dirty little whore like you did in front of my daughter?" she drawls over her shoulder.

"You were never my whore." I kiss her jaw. Her cheek. "You were *la mia piccola sporcacciona*—my dirty little girl."

Her lips tweak before she turns back to face the ocean. "Apparently, not all Italian words turn me on."

"Are you sure?" I grin against her neck. "We'll make love under the Sorrento moon and I'll remind you why *gli Italiani* have such a great reputation in the bedroom." I slide my hands over her abdomen to the apex of her thighs.

"You've already shown me more than enough of your bedroom skills to have formed an unshakable reputation."

"But there's still so much to learn about the intricacies of your body, *mia dea.*" I rub a thumb over her jeans zipper, my dick hardening at how she inches up to meet the friction. "We have years of discovery ahead of us."

"Not if Emmanuel gets his way."

"He won't. We'll bury him. We'll bathe in his blood if you like."

She cranes her neck, giving me better access to the sensitive skin below her ear. "I just want to be free."

"Then we'll find freedom together." I scrape my teeth along her carotid. Release the button on her jeans. "We'll find everything your heart desires."

She swallows as I lower her zipper. "We shouldn't. Your brothers are here."

I cock my ear toward the hall, listening. "I don't hear much of anything. Do you?"

There's only her shaky breathing.

She slowly shifts against my thigh, nudging her ass against my cock. "What about Bishop?"

I kiss the base of her neck, the skin awash with goose bumps. "What about him?"

"Is he still in the house?"

"I don't know." I turn my face toward the door. *"Bishop, are you still here?"*

"Yeah?" His shout carries from the living room, his footsteps following as I slide a hand beneath the waistband of her silken panties.

"What are you doing?" She grabs my wrist.

"What we've always done."

Bishop enters the doorway, meeting my gaze with a roll of his eyes. "You couldn't have waited for a more appropriate time to summon me?"

"Where are my brothers?"

He strolls into the room, his hands casually sliding into his pockets as he approaches. "They said they had a car nearby and needed to borrow the Lincoln to retrieve it. I respectfully declined their request, so the gimp and his sidekick are now walking to get it. Hopefully never to return."

"See? You have nothing to worry about." I nuzzle Layla's neck. "We're all alone."

Her nails dig into my wrist in warning.

Bishop rounds the bed to stop before us, his attention pinned to Layla who turns rigid under his appraisal. "I suspect we have differing interpretations of 'alone.'"

"We have differing interpretations on a lot of things." I delve my hand lower. "But I think, when it comes to the woman in my arms, we have similar views, too."

"Meaning?" she pants.

"Meaning the heartless son of a bitch standing before us was worried about you earlier. In fact, he was downright territorial and aggressively protective." I graze my touch over her clit, earning a jolt in response.

She gasps. "I find that hard to believe."

"It's true. You've won him over. So having him here is a great opportunity to ease his concerns." I part her folds, her slickness coating my fingertips. "Tell him you're okay, *mia dea*. Tell him he no longer has anything to worry about between us. That we've reconciled and all plans for our future will be made together. As one."

She whimpers, staring Bishop down as I glide two fingers into her heat, the eroticism hidden from view beneath her tight jeans.

"I'm all right," she pants.

He raises a brow.

"I don't think he believes you." I slide those fingers deeper, curling them in a slow rhythm as my other hand snakes under her blouse toward her breast.

He inches closer, right up to her, his expression tight, his gaze transfixed. "She isn't very convincing."

"I'm fine." She cranes her neck to maintain eye contact, her head falling back to rest against my shoulder as I play with her.

"You're more than fine, Layla." He reaches out, cupping her jaw. "But my concern is for your wellbeing. Do you understand your life is at greater risk if Langston helps his brothers?"

She nods. "He has no choice."

"Yes, he does. He could steer you toward a future with less danger. One that doesn't include their bullshit."

"I wouldn't want that future. Not when he would be left to wonder what could've been. He deserves his family, if that's what they really are."

His thumb strokes her lower lip, his attention fiercely trekking the movement. "You don't want them to suffer?"

"If what they're saying is true, then they already have." She slowly grinds into me, rocking her ass against my dick as she blinks up at him. "Or do you disagree?"

"I'm undecided." His thumb delves into her mouth, her lips tightening around it, her cheeks hollowing as she sucks.

Jesus.

I could come just grinding against her.

"Lei è perfetta. Vero?"

He makes a noise. A grunt. Neither a confirmation nor denial of her perfection.

"Ora capisci la mia ossessione." I curl my fingers faster inside her, rubbing the heel of my palm against her clit.

He drags his thumb back to her bottom lip, not taking his gaze off her as her breathing increases. *"Sì. Sei un uomo fortunato."*

"Tell me what you're saying." She whimpers.

"We were merely discussing how fortunate I am." I bite her neck, then suck to soothe the sting. *"Chiudi la porta mentre esci."*

"And now?" she whispers.

I taste her skin, graze it with my teeth, my fingers twisting and pulsing inside her. "And now, he's going to close the door on his way out."

She shudders, rapturous and exquisite.

Bishop drags his thumb over her lower lip. Slow. Rough.

He's hard for her. He *wants* her. And if she was interested in experiencing sex with more than one man, I would be happy for him to oblige. But today is about rekindling what we lost. It's about strengthening her position at my side.

"Enjoy yourselves." He steps back, his gaze lingering on her before he turns on his heel and strides for the hall.

Layla pants. Grinds. Her tempting pussy squeezes my fingers so fucking tight. And once the door closes behind him, she scrambles off me in a flourish, stumbling to her feet. She turns to me and climbs straight back onto my lap chest to chest, her cheeks and lips flushed.

Her hands cup my jaw. Her mouth smashes into mine.

She devours me. Savage. Starving. Then frantically tussles with the top buttons of her blouse, swipes the material over her head and throws it to the floor.

"Slow, *mia dea.*" I grab her waist. "I want to savor you."

"And I want to fuck you." She slams her lips back on mine. Crazed. Mindless.

I'm a slave to her demands.

I let her fumble with my belt, releasing the clasp as I casually loosen my tie.

"Why do you do that?" She unfastens the button on my pants.

"Do what?" I pull the slip of material over my head, keeping hold of it while I palm her ass.

She moans, her eyes rolling. "Publicize our sex life."

I grin. "Because, *mia dea,* it's a sin to hide a beauty like yours, and I've already earned enough tickets into hell."

"So sharing me with the world is your penance?"

It's more than that. It's my validation. My proof of worth.

Without her, I'm nothing.

"Sharing you is my salvation."

She looks at me as if I've told her the secret to life. Amazed and captivated. "You say such pretty things."

She lowers my zipper. Delves beneath my waistband. As soon as her touch grazes my cock, I tense, every inch of me already prepared to explode.

"I said, slow, *la mia piccola sporcacciona.*" I snatch her hands, making her gasp. "Don't make me restrain you."

21

———

LAYLA

"WE CAN SAVOR LATER." I NUZZLE HIS NOSE, SNAKING MY HAND INSIDE HIS BOXER BRIEFS to palm his shaft.

He's so incredibly hard. Thick.

I need him inside me.

"Not this time." He grabs my wrists, clamping them together. "We're taking it slow."

"Please." I sweep my hips against his.

"*Slow*, Layla." He uses his tie to bind my wrists, the silk tight against my skin as he weaves the material in, out, and around.

"But I need you." I attempt to distract him with my mouth on his neck. His stubbled jaw. I work my way up to his ear and whisper, "I want you fucking me so damn hard."

A hint of a growl emanates from his throat. Feral and fierce.

He stands, making me squeal as I'm hefted upward, his arm cradling my ass when he turns to place me on the mattress.

"You'll get that soon enough." He crouches, removing my shoes with leisurely care, giving my cravings time to smolder.

Next, it's my socks. Then those talented hands are gripping my waistband, tugging me close to the edge of the bed to wrangle my jeans. He strips me, dragging the restricting material down my thighs as I flop backward and wiggle to speed things up.

My jeans are thrown to the floor while his gaze fixates on the apex of my thighs.

He devours the sight of my sheer white underwear. The material hides nothing. My peaked nipples are on display. I bet there's a damp patch between my legs, too. A blatant show of how hot he makes me.

"You're so fucking exquisite, Layla." He stands, peering down at me as he shucks his jacket, then starts on the buttons of his shirt.

403

I fight to free my bound wrists, needing to touch. To taste.

"If that tie comes loose, I'll make sure your next bindings don't. And it won't just be your hands, *la mia stella polare*. I'll have your ankles strapped to the corners of the bed with your pretty little ass stuck in the air." He throws his shirt to the floor. "Now be patient."

I groan, eager to get my fingers on all the sculpted muscles displayed before me.

He's suave. Flawless. And I don't even get to touch.

He lowers back to his knees, spreading my thighs with forceful hands. "I've been denied this for too damn long."

"You were denied because you were undeserving." We both were. We made so many mistakes.

He pauses. "And now, *mia dea*? Have I earned your taste on my tongue or would you prefer to be fucked hard and fast so you can pretend this is still lust and nothing deeper?"

That's why he wants to go slow?

I know it's deeper. I feel it in my bones. I always have.

He leans in, placing a kiss on my inner thigh. "Let me worship you." He moves to my other leg, placing another kiss, then another. He creeps higher and higher with the affection, inching closer to the part of me that burns. "Let this be the beginning of my penance."

I divert my gaze to the ceiling, my bound wrists itching to break free as they rest on my stomach while his lips ascend. "I know this is more than lust. I'm just…"

"Scared." His mouth hovers near my pussy. "Don't worry. I am, too. I'm fearful of your hold on me." He places another kiss near the elastic around my left leg. "Of how you control me." Then my right. "How you can destroy me."

"I don't want to destroy you."

"I never wanted to destroy you either, *mia dea*."

He grazes his teeth across the inside of my thigh. So damn close to my pussy.

"God, you smell good." He places his mouth over the crotch of my panties and sucks on the material. "You're so fucking wet."

He slips his fingers beneath the waistband, slowly dragging, torturously sliding them lower and lower until they flutter past my ankles to the floor.

Those palms grip my knees, spreading me wider, leaving me entirely on display. I tingle under his gaze. Burn.

He repeats the trail of kisses up my thighs, killing me with his listless affection.

Each press of lips makes it harder to breathe. Each inch he creeps toward my heat results in an excruciating struggle to think straight.

"Matthew," I plead, raising my hips off the bed.

He uses the leverage to slide his hands under my ass, digging his fingers into my flesh. I clench as he creeps closer, manipulating my legs wider, until he's poised at my entrance.

He kisses each side of my slit. Then my mound.

It's torture. Pure and decadent. "God, *please*. I need you."

"I'm the opposite of God, *la mia stella polare*. You know this." That mouth clamps over my pussy, his tongue delving deep. He licks me from top to bottom, thoroughly tasting. "If it were legal, I'd tie you to my bed and never let you leave."

"Since when have you obeyed the law?"

He snickers. Licks. Laps.

His stubbled jaw grazes the inside of my thighs, providing the most delicious friction.

"You taste like home, Layla." He releases my ass, sliding a thumb to my entrance while his lips finally move to my clit. "You taste like you were made for me."

And his mouth feels like it was created with the sole purpose of bringing me pleasure. I whimper at his mastery while he concentrates on that tiny bundle of nerves, flicking and sucking as I roll my hips with his penetration.

I'm greedy. Senseless.

I reach for his hair, sliding my hands through the strands, pulling tight. He's exactly where I need him. His thumb right on that spot.

Over and over he hypes the perfection, building it higher and higher.

I burn for him. Blaze. And not once does he deviate from what he's doing. He *knows* how good this is. He listens even though I don't speak.

I'm already so close. Too close.

I pulse my hips against his thumb. I pull his hair with each delicious suck.

I'm going to come.

"Not yet." He pulls back, reading my mind, kissing my inner thigh, taking away his heat.

I mewl. "*No.* Please. I was right there."

He grins, kissing a trail to my abdomen, then over my stomach toward my breasts. They ache for his attention. All of me does. Every single inch of my body wants his lips. His hands. His gaze.

That smile tweaks higher. He's devouring my torture.

"You're enjoying this," I muse. "You like watching me suffer."

"I like watching you want me." He mouths my breast above the sheer bra, his tongue flicking my nipple, nibbling it against the fabric.

"It's more than want," I pant. "It's urgency. Necessity. I have to have you, Matthew."

"And you will." He grabs my bound wrists as he moves higher, dragging my arms over my head while his face meets mine. "You'll *always* have me."

He plasters our lips together, his free hand delving back between my thighs, his fingers sliding to my pussy, straight to my core.

I buck as we kiss, frantic and breathless.

He savors me like a treasure, like a gift, his hard cock adamant through his pants.

I can't take anymore. My veins thrum. My head screams.

"*Please*," I whimper. "*Please.*"

"*God*, that sound," he murmurs against my lips. "You have no idea how much I hate denying you, but I fucking *love* that you need me."

"I do." I nod, our noses nuzzling. "I need you. Inside me. *Now.*"

He slides off me in a sweeping vacuum of pleasure and stands. With intense eyes and rough movements, he shucks his pants, then his boxer briefs.

He towers before me, a man carved in muscle and held together by volatility. A beast scarred by trauma and built with strength.

I drag my gaze over every inch of magnificence—the light sheen of hair across his chest, the chiseled stomach. My exploration stops at the top of his right thigh.

"What happened?" A multitude of cuts mar his skin. Small. Savage. Deep.

He leans down to crawl back over me, taking one of my legs with him, hooking it over his shoulder to expose my sex as he bends me like a pretzel.

"Matthew? What happened to your thigh?"

"*I* happened."

I push my bound wrists against his chest, demanding his attention. "What does that mean?"

"They're reminders, *mia dea.*"

"Of what?"

"That I don't deserve you. That I'm too weak to walk away."

I stare at him. Shake my head. I don't understand. "You deliberately hurt yourself?"

"I was hurting you more."

Another piece of me becomes reclaimed by him. Imprisoned. My heart forgives him a thousand times over.

His hand returns to my mound, his lips to my neck. I close my eyes, drowning in longing, my chest burning with hope. We're going to make this work or die trying. I vow it.

His fingers slide through my slickness as he nuzzles my jaw. "*Sono fottutamente duro per te,* Layla," he murmurs against my skin. "*Non ci sarà mai nessun altra. Solo tu.*"

I mewl with every word. Whimper. Gasp.

He works me into a frenzy of pants and moans, my limbs heavy with anticipation. My heart full from his worship.

"Please fuck me," I beg. "I want you more than anything."

"Have I earned my place inside your sweet cunt?" His thumb rubs my clit. His fingers twist with the same rhythm.

"You know you have."

He licks my neck. "I need to make sure, because there's no regretting this, *mia dea.* Once I'm inside you, that's all there ever is."

I nod. It's all I'll ever want.

"Are you sure?" He slides higher, aligning the head of his cock with my pussy, the hard length teasing my entrance.

"Positive."

"To forever then, *la mia stella polare.*" He plunges inside me, effortlessly. Sinking. Stretching.

I moan, my hands seizing the coverings, my back arching off the bed. He gives me what I asked for. Hard and so incredibly fast.

He keeps my leg pinned over his shoulder as he plunders, our eyes locked, his expression fierce.

His reverence roars at me without sound. His devotion is felt through every harsh thrust. His worship consumes me through the slap of flesh and build of pleasure.

The organs he severed with his lies regenerate. The limbs he broke become renewed. He builds me back stronger. More determined.

"Matthew." His name is a gasp. A plea. A prayer.

I can't hold on much longer.

He groans, driving me to the precipice. To the point of no return. *"Mia dea."*

"I'm close...So close..." I grasp tighter to the coverings. "Whatever you do, don't stop."

He guides a hand between us, reclaiming my clit. *"Non mi fermerò mai."* He adds pressure, sending me over the edge, making me cry out as I come. *"Non quando sei mia ora."*

22

LAYLA

I RAKE A HAND THROUGH HIS HAIR, OUR LEGS TANGLED, OUR NAKED BODIES SPLAYED ON the bed as I stare into his eyes.

We've been like this for almost half an hour.

Quiet. Relaxed. No words. Just touch.

But bliss can't last forever.

I suck in a deep breath, letting it out on a long exhale. "What about my family?"

"Hmm?" He raises a brow, his fingers continuing their lazy circles along my hip. "What about them?"

"You painted a picture of our future earlier, but only Stella was involved. What about the rest of my family?"

"I didn't mention the rest of your family because I don't want to play a role in dictating that part of your life. It's yours to decide."

I push onto one elbow. "And if I decide I want to live in Portland?"

"Then we figure out how to live in Portland."

"Is that possible? Can you be civil with Cole after everything that's happened?"

"Sure." He smirks. "As long as I'm heavily medicated for the duration. But I'm more worried about how you're going to get along with him."

Me too.

I'm going to have to call him. And soon.

"Don't worry. I can be civil for you." He grabs my hand, dragging it to his lips to kiss my fingertips. My palm. "I can be civil because although I don't respect most of the decisions he's recently made on your behalf, we wouldn't be here without them."

I rest back into the pillows and snuggle into him. "He hurt me."

"I know. I'm sure he regrets it as much as I do."

I become lost in contemplation, our lazy silence stretching until his brothers return, their voices carrying from the living room.

"I need to check on them." Matthew pushes from the bed to tug on his clothes. "I'll bring you something to eat."

"It's okay. I'll follow you after I take a shower."

I make an effort not to hide in the bedroom for the rest of the day. I lounge on the sofa, my gaze affixed to the news broadcast on the television while my ears stay attuned to Remy and Salvatore's conversation at the dinner table.

They haven't discussed anything to trigger my paranoia. They speak loud enough to be heard, but always on topics that reaffirm their story.

They contemplate their future. They worry about the fallout. They fret about Abri.

The more I listen, the more I buy in to their situation, despite hating every step I take toward belief.

Matthew makes a million calls, his excursions out to the deck for privacy always bringing him back to me where he murmurs intel to validate their claims.

He finds supporting evidence of a substantial family trust. His bank contacts verify none of the Costa siblings have access to cash accounts. And someone Matthew knew in high school confirms there were once rumors that Remy lost his virginity in his early teens at a strip club.

Their story checks out. For the most part. But I still try to pick it apart all afternoon.

By the time night falls, I'm neck-deep in brain fog, my mind entirely exhausted when the doorbell rings.

"Who's here?" I push from the sofa, the gun in the back of my jeans digging into my spine.

"It's not who, but what." Matthew starts for the front door. "Dinner has arrived."

He disappears down the entry hall, returning moments later with both arms carrying cooking trays covered in foil.

"Who delivered this?" I walk with him to the island counter, salivating over the scent of meat and herbs.

"I bribed the housekeeper." Matthew winks at me. "That woman knows how to cook."

His brothers join us in the kitchen, pulling plates from cupboards and cutlery from drawers. The three of them work in a conga line of food service like they've been doing it for years. Like nothing ever came between them.

Matthew cuts the meat. Remy plates it while Salvatore does the same with the baked vegetables. It's nice to see Matthew at home with someone other than Bishop. But it hurts too. These are the men who devastated my life.

"Can I get you a glass of wine, Layla?" Remy wipes his hands on a new pair of pants he must've had in his rental and walks to the fridge for a bottle of red.

I meet his gaze, sensing his optimism. The alcohol is a peace offering. One I'm not ready to accept.

"No." I clear my throat, reluctantly adding, "Thanks."

His expression slackens. It's only a flicker of change, but his disappointment is clear as the room remains quiet.

We all know I subtly snapped the olive branch he offered. Forgiveness will take time.

"You can pour me one, little gimp." Bishop pushes from the sofa, his smile dripping with venom. "I'm always happy to have your bitch ass waiting on me."

"My bitch ass will spit in your drink."

"Do that and I'll skull fuck your sister."

"*Hey,*" Matthew warns. "That went from banter to crossing the line too fucking fast. Abri is off-limits."

I hide my grin as I grab a glass from the cupboard and fill it with water from the faucet.

"Everyone grab a plate. I'm starving." Matthew slides his from the counter and claims a seat at the head of the table.

I wait until everyone has taken theirs before I grab mine and head toward the sliding door with my water. "I'm going to eat on the deck. I need to clear my head."

Matthew pushes to his feet. "I'll come with you."

"No, please don't. You have catching up to do." I'm just not in a place where I can listen.

He remains standing, his expression forlorn.

"It's okay." My smile is honest. "Don't worry about me."

He inclines his head in appreciation as I walk outside, not returning to his seat until I close the door behind me.

I eat alone, the bitter fall breeze my only companion through delicious bites of crisp potato and juicy mouthfuls of meat. Then the door slides open, and I glance over my shoulder to find Bishop approaching.

"Mind if I join you?"

I turn back to my meal. "Is that a rhetorical question? Because I doubt you'll listen if I decline your generous offer."

"Look at you proving how well you already know me." He takes the seat opposite me, placing down his meal and a glass of red wine. "Are you doing okay?"

My cheeks heat at the memory of the last time he asked. "Yeah. I want them to figure this out. I just can't be a part of it. Not yet anyway."

"And in the future?"

I stab a roasted carrot and take a bite. "I don't know. I've hated them for a long time. Stella has, too. I can't begin to imagine how I'd explain this to her."

"She's a smart kid. I'm sure she'll understand whatever view you take on this."

"Whatever view?" I raise a brow. "There's more than one?"

He shrugs. "I'm not convinced they have good intentions."

"You think they're trying to set us up?"

"Maybe. And usually, Langston would tend to agree. But his judgment has been clouded lately." He gives me a pointed look. "He's not listening to me."

"Did he listen to you when plans were made to have me mugged?"

He scoffs. "None of this mess would've happened if he'd taken my advice and smoked you the first night we met."

I blink. Blink again.

"I'm joking." He rolls his eyes. "I didn't tell him to snuff you until you turned up in D.C."

"It's always a delight to speak to you, Bishop." I stand, preparing to eat elsewhere.

He pushes to his feet and reaches across the table to grab my wrist as I pick up my plate. "Sit down," he grates. "It was a joke."

"You expect me to giggle about how shitty you've treated me?"

"The only thing I expect from you, little exhibitionist, is a promise you'll start fucking behind closed doors. I'm getting damn tired of seeing private parts best kept hidden."

I stare him down. "Anyone would think Matthew does it on purpose to make you jealous."

"It takes more than a willing victim and a firm rack to trigger that response, princess. I prefer my women less lippy."

"And I prefer my men with more than a two-inch dick. So I'm glad we both agree your earlier involvement in the bedroom has been confirmed as a one-time event."

He chuckles, his grip loosening on my wrist. "Yeah, nothing but a one-time event." His touch becomes gentle, the sweep of his thumb seductive. "But fun all the same."

He reclaims his seat. "I didn't mean to insult you, Layla. You already know I was hard for you. Any sane man would've been. But fucking you isn't something I think about unless it's shoved in my face."

"It's never been my intention to shove—"

"I know. He likes to show you off. I can understand that."

"I'm glad you do, because he still confuses me. A few days ago, I couldn't talk to you without him being jealous. Now he's…"

"Now you're back together, his confidence has been restored." He jerks his chin toward the house. "Look. He doesn't feel threatened because he trusts you."

I glance over my shoulder, meeting Matthew's gaze.

Heat stares back at me. Hunger.

"He might have earned a savage reputation, but Langston will worship you till the day you die."

I sit, lowering my attention to my meal, shuffling vegetables around with my fork while I contemplate the bliss of that type of future.

"You realize you're stuck with him for life, right?"

My heart falters.

I think I knew the length of my commitment this morning at the airport. Maybe even the night he drew me a bath in Denver—the day he had me mugged. Or right at the very start, when his dark eyes met mine in Perfezione and he offered to help me take down my enemies.

"Yes," I admit. "I'm well aware."

"An exhibitionist and a sadist." He scoffs as he stabs a cut of meat. "You two are going to have a colorful future."

"Wait. Which one am I?"

His brows pull tight in fake contemplation. "Which category does stabbing someone then fucking in their blood fall into?"

"He stabbed himself."

He gives me a quizzical look. "I'm not sure that makes the situation any better."

"Could it make it any worse?" I place my cutlery on the middle of my plate, my appetite lost to the explicit topic.

"I guess not." He snickers. "But it seems our conversation has had a negative effect on your hunger, so I'm going to leave you to clear your head in peace. I do want to clarify one thing first, though." He pushes to his feet. "I might not want to fuck you, Lay, but I will protect you. I'll do my best to make sure you're always safe."

I lower my gaze, awkwardly humbled. "Thank you."

"In return, all I ask is that you keep your private parts out of my line of vision."

I press my chin to my chest, hiding a grin. "I'll do my best."

"For the love of God, please do." He takes his plate and wine glass, then returns inside, leaving me to chuckle into the sea breeze.

After dinner, I stack the dishwasher while Matthew and his brothers reminisce about childhood memories. I shower. Dress. Then climb into bed to contemplate the danger that will arise tomorrow.

It isn't long before Matthew comes in to kiss me goodnight. A long, suggestive kiss that has me panting by the time he pulls away.

"As much as I want to spend the night with you, I won't be in here long. Bishop and I will take turns staying awake to make sure my brothers aren't up to something."

"And if they are?"

The muscles in his jaw tense. "Then the problem will be resolved before you wake in the morning."

Those words leave me unsettled for hours.

I toss and turn, wondering if I should call Cole for guidance. For security.

I fall asleep alone.

Sometimes I wake cold and isolated. At others, I have a possessive arm wrapped around me, with Matthew sleeping peacefully at my back. He isn't restless. He's calm in the face of what lies ahead.

I need to trust that he knows what he's doing. That he can predict how Lorenzo and his brothers will react to his suggestion.

When I wake in the morning Matthew is spooned behind me, his gentle breathing brushing my shoulder.

I haven't lost the urge to reach out to Cole. If anything, the compulsion has increased. I'm anxious over what's to come. And fearful of the possibilities.

I want Cole to know he lost the deal with Matthew. That the Butcher won my heart and no action can be taken against him.

And I also need a reminder that no matter what my future holds, my family will take care of Stella. That she will be looked after and cherished if anything were to happen to me.

I inch out of bed, careful not to wake Matthew, and tiptoe to the duffle to silently feel around the interior for the cell Keira stowed.

I take the device outside, sneaking through the French doors to turn it on and scroll through the two numbers already stored in the contacts. The first is *K*. The second is a devil emoji.

It isn't hard to pick which one is my brother. The tiny little graphic should be enough of an omen to make me second-guess my actions. But I don't allow myself time to pause.

I dial his number, my bare feet freezing to the wooden slats of the deck as the ringtone carries through the device. Then it stops, along with my pulse.

"Good morning, sister," Cole says in greeting. "I didn't expect you'd want to speak to me for quite some time."

"Keira told you she gave me a phone?"

"Who do you think told her to plant it?"

"Why?" Why offer support when all your other actions are cruel?

"Because I want you to be safe."

"Yet you're the one who trapped me here with the son of my husband's murderer." My words are barely audible. It's the pounding pulse in my chest that's loud.

"Did I make a mistake?"

For the sake of my pride, I wish I could lie.

For once, it would be nice if Cole was wrong and I wasn't the one always messing up.

"No. But did you do it for my sake or yours?" This isn't the conversation I planned to have. I don't want to fight again—especially since I'll be walking back into the heart of the Italian mafia within hours. But now that we're here, I need answers.

"I did what I thought was best for you."

"So it wasn't to gain power over a man who has skills you could exploit?" I ask. "You didn't want him for yourself? To use the blood on his hands to your advantage?"

"I'll admit, the strategy had benefits no matter the outcome. But my intent was your happiness."

"You had no idea how I felt about him, Cole. All you knew was that he was Emmanuel's son. That he'd lied to me. That he was the Butcher. How could you—"

"That's not true," he cuts me off. "I knew that when you came home with a bruised face while being with him, you lied for his protection. You *lied*, sister, even though you'd come close to being ostracized for the same actions in the past. I *knew* that you were risking the very little forgiveness we'd given for your mistakes. And after all the shit you've been through in your life, I fucking *knew* it wouldn't have been easy for you to trust any man, let alone a lover."

I clench my stomach to counteract the tightness consuming my chest.

"You fell for him, Layla. And once I spoke to him, I knew he'd done the same for you. There aren't many men who would threaten to start a bloodbath for a woman, but he's one of them."

A bleak smile pulls at my lips, my sorrow and gratitude circling like vultures.

"Did I make the wrong choice?" he asks.

I should say yes. I should make him suffer for the days I went to hell and back wondering where my future might lead. I should give him a taste of the medicine I had to swallow while being stuck under the roof of a man I had to hate while still being neck-deep in love. "No."

"Good."

The conversation pauses, the waves of the ocean filling the thickening silence.

He clears his throat. "Is that all you called for? To set the record straight?"

"There's more." There's so much more I struggle to formulate the right words. "I just… I guess with all that's gone on, I'm struggling with my mortality and want to make sure you'll always be there for Stella. No matter what happens in the future."

"Why?" Sharp curiosity enters his voice. "What's going to happen?"

"Nothing… Then again, who knows when it comes to my track record on shitty choices, right?" I fake a chuckle. "I guess my parental instincts are feeling a little frazzled now that I've made the decision to be with someone who has a past as checkered as ours."

"*Layla*," he warns. "Tell me what's really going on."

"I just did." The lie stings, the bitter taste coating the back of my throat. But I won't risk him getting involved in our plans for Emmanuel. I'm sick of delays and roadblocks. "I'm emotional, that's all."

"Then come home. Bring Langston. We can sit down and discuss arrangements for your future."

"My future isn't up for discussion." And besides, after Matthew cast a vivid picture yesterday, I've found it hard to imagine my life if I return to Portland. I want D.C. I want fashion shows in Milan and seduction in Florence.

"Then come home and properly introduce your man and his punk-ass sidekick."

I snort. "Bishop is far from a punk. A thug maybe. But he can be a good guy, too. He reminds me of you sometimes. They both do."

"Are you trying to flatter or insult? Because I assure you, you've done the latter."

"If you knew them you'd think differently. You'd approve of the brutality of their protection and the underhanded calculation. They have no fear, just like you."

"I have fear, sister. And right now, the biggest part of it revolves around Langston dragging you into something that could risk your life."

"He'd never drag me into anything I didn't want to be a part of. I've always made my own decisions. Even the horribly bad ones. They were all my doing. And that won't change. Whatever happens in the future is mine to own. Never blame Matthew, okay?"

"*Layla*." My name is a more ominous warning this time. "What the fuck is going on? You're talking as if—"

"I'm talking as if I'm at a crossroads, and I'm sure you can understand that given my situation. I want to be with Matthew and that's going to mean a lot of disruption to my life. But before I take the first step, I'd appreciate your forgiveness for all I've done in the past. I never meant to betray you, Cole."

There's a pause. A temperamental build of silence.

"Come home," he demands. "I'll send a jet. You can—"

"No. Please don't." The gentle whoosh of a door opens behind me. *Matthew*. "I shouldn't have called. I'm sorry for confusing you. But I promise I'm fine."

"Layla, get that fucker to call me. I want to know—"

"He's not going to call you." I speak over the top of him. "I'm not your problem to deal with anymore. Okay? We'll speak again soon." I disconnect as Matthew settles in behind me, his arms circling my waist.

"I hope you didn't end the call on my account," he murmurs against my neck, placing one gentle kiss after another.

"Not at all." I turn, my breath hitching in my throat at the sight of him shirtless and stunning. "You don't seem surprised I have a cell."

"I'd be more surprised if you didn't. Your family are cunning."

I grin. "When they want to be."

Something vibrates. Short and sharp.

Matthew glances at his watch, the display alighting with an incoming call from a private number.

"I assume that's my brother." I wrap a hand around his neck, holding him close. "Please don't answer it."

"I didn't plan on it." His hands glide over my ass, dragging me closer.

I wait for his interrogation. For him to question if I've betrayed our plans.

But he doesn't ask. Instead, he stares at me like I'm his next meal, one side of his mouth lifting in a predatory grin.

"I wanted to set things straight." I run my nails along his nape. "He knows where I stand with you now."

"You don't have to explain. Your family is important. What you discuss with them is none of my business."

"But I want it to be your business." I inch back. "I don't want there to be any secrets between us."

"In that case, I'm all ears, *mia dea*." He leans back in, nuzzling my cheek, kissing my jaw. "Tell me all the details."

I shudder as his stubble tickles my skin. "You're in a good mood today."

"Why wouldn't I be? You're in my arms and were in my bed. And by nightfall, Emmanuel will be dead."

"What?" I push against his chest, needing space to understand. "That soon?"

"That soon." He stands tall. "Isn't that what you want?"

"Yes…" I just didn't think things would happen so quickly. "I thought we were leaving for Virginia Beach."

"We are. We'll meet with my uncle straight away, and once all parties agree with my plan, we'll take the jet to Denver."

Apprehension and anticipation swirl inside me. There's nervousness, excitement, hope, and terror, too. "So you trust them?"

"I'm trying to. I did a lot of digging overnight and I can't find anything to discredit their story. Remy even asked for his gun back and I'm contemplating whether permitting it would be a good test of his loyalty."

"You're not worried they'll kill us?"

"They could've yesterday. But today, Salvo can barely raise his arm and Remy couldn't run to save his life. And he'd need to if he ever contemplated betraying me, Layla. He knows I'd flay him alive."

I know it, too.

"Are you okay if I hand their guns back?" He glides my loose hair behind my ears. "It isn't a problem if you don't want to."

I definitely don't want to.

Remy's Glock remained on my bedside table all night. Protecting me. Comforting me. "Can you take the bullets out? Maybe make them carry them separately?"

"Of course. I can keep hold of the magazines until you're ready. That isn't a problem."

It isn't really testing or trusting them. But it's all I can allow right now. I'm not willing to trial their sincerity as much as he is.

"Do it." I swallow over the unease. "As long as you handle the magazines."

"Okay, *mia dea*." He places a kiss to my temple and entwines our fingers. "You better start getting ready. We leave in less than an hour and there's a lot to do before we go."

"Like what?"

He smirks as he leads me toward the bedroom. "I'll give you one guess."

23

MATTHEW

We're in the air within ninety minutes, the flight smooth as we coast toward Virginia.

My brothers have barely spoken a word. There have been no concerns, objections, or speculations. Their level of trust is unnerving.

They should be asking questions. Demanding answers.

"Do they know yet?" Layla murmurs over the rumble of jet engines.

"No. It's best kept quiet."

"What about Bishop? What did he say?"

"I haven't told him either."

She glances over her shoulder at him farther back in the cabin, then returns her gaze to mine. "Why?"

"He wouldn't approve. He doesn't trust them." I slide my hand over hers, bringing her knuckles to my lips. "I also didn't want to risk him feeling obligated to give Lorenzo any prior warning. I'm keeping my cards close to my chest until we get there."

"But he knows where we're going, doesn't he?"

"He would've assumed, yes, and probably speculated that we're going there to use my brothers' stories to gain permission to kill Emmanuel."

"You could do that?" she asks.

"We could. But putting my brothers in power would mean I don't need his permission at all. It takes away the risk of being denied."

She lowers her gaze, her brows knitted.

"It's going to be okay. I'll keep that card up my sleeve if Lorenzo decides they're not the right candidates to take over." I squeeze her fingers as the jet starts to descend. "Once we're on the ground, I'll give him a call and let him know we're on our way. Don't worry. It's all under control."

She nods, her nervousness hidden behind her confident posture as she sits back in her seat. It's her eyes that betray her. She's anxious, and our upcoming meeting is merely the prelude to our venture.

The danger begins in Denver.

"I believe you." She turns her attention to the window, the ground creeping closer beneath us.

As soon as the wheels hit the tarmac, I pull out my cell and dial Lorenzo's number.

"*Figlio,*" he greets in thick Italian.

"We've just arrived in town. I need to see you."

There's a pause. A sigh. "I assume the late notice means it's not a casual visit."

"No. This is important."

"In that case, come to the house after lunch."

A faint vibration carries from somewhere in the cabin. Somewhere along the sofa-style seat to my right where my brothers are.

I glare. Then shoot a glance at Bishop, who's already doing the same.

They said their phones were off. That there was no way for them to be tracked.

"This can't wait," I tell Lorenzo. "I'll be there in half an hour."

"Now isn't a good time, Matthew."

My anger increases as Salvatore nudges Remy in the ribs, the incriminating cell still vibrating.

"Make it a good time, *zio.* We're already on our way." I disconnect the call, pocket the device, and pin my youngest brother with a scowl. "I thought your phones were turned off."

"They are. But—"

"But what, asshole?" Bishop stands, the jet bobbing as it taxis through the airport. "You've risked our safety."

They've risked *her* safety, and the potential threat to Layla's life is inexcusable.

"Answer it," I snarl. "Put it on speaker."

"Only Abri has this number." Remy retrieves the device from inside his suit jacket. "Nobody else knows it exists."

"Answer it," I repeat.

"Okay. Fine. No problem." He taps the screen. "Hey, Abri. What's up?"

"Where are you?" she asks.

"Still in Charleston. Why?"

"You have to come home. The gala is on this afternoon and I don't trust the men Dad has arranged for my security. I'm freaking out." She's rambling, her words building in pace. "I don't think I can do this again. I'm so sick of his goddamn shit, Remy."

Do what? I frown at Salvatore in question.

His only response is the tic in his jaw.

"It's going to be all right." Remy wipes a rough hand down his face. "I'll call Phillip and get him to tag along."

"Phillip isn't answering his cell. None of them are. I think Dad already gave up on you finding Matthew and sent them your way. The entire team is gone."

"Do you know where he sent them exactly?"

"No idea. I booked into the Four Seasons yesterday. I can't stay at the house with him any longer."

Layla's hand slides over mine.

"It's okay." I squeeze her fingers, my eyes remaining on Remy. "We got out in time. We'll be safe here."

"Please come back," Abri begs. "I don't think I can get through today without you."

"We can't right now, Bri. But we're working on a way out. You just need to hold on for a few more days."

"A way out of what?" she asks. "What do you mean?"

"I mean—he can't keep controlling us. We're going to set up a new life. He won't be able to use us anymore."

She doesn't respond. There's silence. Thick and foreboding.

"It's going to be okay," Remy repeats. "Just get through the gala and—"

"No. Whatever the hell you're doing, you need to stop." She's angry now. A fucking kaleidoscope of emotion. "I can't believe you haven't discussed this with me first. And where the hell is Salvo?"

"I'm right here," Salvatore answers. "We've got everything under control. Tell me about the gala. What's he got you doing that requires more security?"

"You know what the hell he's got me doing, you selfish fucking asshole. But forget that shit. You've successfully switched my panic to whatever the hell you two have planned. Why was I kept in the dark?"

"You weren't. We haven't done anything."

"No?" She raises her voice. "That's not what you said a few seconds ago. You told me you were working on something to get us out. Something I haven't been informed about, *Salvatore*."

Both brothers look at me. For guidance. For permission.

They want to tell her what we're doing but that's not a fucking option.

"Not over the phone," I warn. "If you want to tell her, it gets done in person."

"Who was that?" she asks. "Someone else is with you?"

They keep staring at me. Glaring.

I unclasp my belt and lean forward to snatch the cell. "Abri?"

"*Dante?*" she asks.

I ignore the offense. "Is this a safe connection?"

"What are you doing with Remy and Salvo? Where are you?"

"I need to know if this connection is secure first."

"Yes. The phone is new. Salvo gave it to me the day you showed up with Torian's sister. As far as I'm aware, Dad doesn't know I have it."

Salvatore inclines his head in confirmation.

"Tell me what's going on at the gala," I mutter. "What's the event? What is Emmanuel making you do?"

The line goes silent, the quiet stretching as the jet pulls to a stop.

"Abri?"

"Put Remy back on the phone." Sterility enters her voice.

"In a minute. Right now I need to know what's going on with you. Are you alone? Are you—"

"*Put Remy back on the phone,*" she demands. "*Now.*"

My youngest brother holds out his hand and nods.

She's not going to talk to me. She doesn't trust me. I concede, handing him the device.

"Sis, you need to have faith in us." Remy pinches the bridge of his nose. "Can you hold out for tonight and then we can—"

"Come home." Her tone is vehement. "You have no right to make plans without me."

"They're only plans. We haven't taken action."

"I don't care."

"I'm done living under his dictatorship." Salvatore leans closer to speak into the cell. "We all are. We can't go on like this."

"*Please.*" The aggression leaves her voice, the layers of anger stripped back to expose her fear. "We need to talk about this. We can't just 'get out.' It's not that easy."

"Why?" I ask. "Give me details."

"Get me off speaker," she snaps.

I shake my head, warning my brothers not to comply.

"Listen." Remy keeps pinching his nose, the skin beside his fingers turning pink. "We'll get home as soon as we can. I promise. But we can't leave right now."

"You *can*. Or I'll never forgive you."

My brothers exchange a glance. A pained, regretful stare.

They're going to bail. They're going to fucking walk.

The pilot leaves the cockpit to open the cabin door, allowing a gush of cold air to glide in as he lowers the staircase. "Was it a smooth enough flight, Mr. Langston?"

I ignore him, keeping my attention on the paused conversation.

Remy stares at me. Stares right through me. "Abri, give me a second to call you back, okay? We've gotta work a few things out."

There's no response.

"Abri?" he asks louder as a chime sounds, announcing the disconnected line. "*Fuck.* She ended the call." His hand falls from his nose. "We need to return to Denver."

Layla's hand slides away from mine. It's the only sign of heartbreak over a plan that was meant to bring her happiness.

"It's okay." I squeeze her thigh. "This changes nothing."

"It changes everything," she whispers. "Without them—"

"We're not doing anything without them. They gave their word." I return my attention to my brothers. "Do you hear me? If you leave, you're breaking a vow that won't be forgiven. You won't be allowed a second chance to fuck us over."

The pilot slinks back into the cockpit, silently closing the door behind him.

"And what about Abri?" Remy accuses. "She doesn't get upset for no reason." He switches his attention to Salvo. "We can't abandon her."

"I know. But what if this is the only opportunity we get? Are you willing to risk it?"

"You're one conversation away from a new life," I warn. "Choose wisely."

"And that conversation could mean our sister is left to suffer alone through a fucking nightmare. We don't know what he's got her doing at this gala, but it's obviously something more fucked-up than usual."

"What's the usual?" Bishop asks. "What does Emmanuel get her to do?"

My brothers fall silent.

"What the fuck does he get her to do?" I demand.

"Whatever the hell he likes. Entrapment. Blackmail. Extortion," Remy barks. "He uses her like a goddamn whore on retainer." He heaves the phone across the cabin, the device splitting as it hits the wall, then splinters to the floor.

Layla gasps.

Bishop mutters a curse.

Everyone functions around me while I'm stuck on pause, barely able to think through the rage tightening my skull.

"Let them go back to Denver," Layla whispers. "We'll figure out another way."

I can't fucking allow it. If they leave it means more delays. More torture. More punishment for Layla, who needs closure.

My brothers are the gatekeepers to an easy slaughter.

But my sister…

"Let them go," she repeats, her calm expression forced. "We'll figure it out."

My lungs tighten with the failure. My temples fucking throb.

"I'll go," Bishop mutters. "You don't need me here, right? I'll fly to Denver and get Abri to calm her tits. You guys can meet me there by nightfall."

Nobody speaks.

Is his suggestion mindlessly reckless or the perfect alternative? He'll be on his own in Emmanuel's territory. But on the other hand, he isn't needed for the conversation with Lorenzo.

"She won't talk to you." Remy stands and faces my right-hand man. "You won't get anywhere near her."

"Let me worry about that while you concentrate on remembering the terms you agreed to yesterday and how you gave your fucking word. I don't take kindly to liars."

"We didn't—"

Bishop's lip curls. "Get off the fucking jet and let me deal with your sister."

They glare at each other. Two grown-ass men trying to win a testosterone building competition as they stand hunched in the cabin.

"He's right." Salvo pushes from his seat to move between them. "We gave our word. We need to see this through."

"And what about Abri?"

Salvo sighs. "We're going to have to trust that he'll take care of her."

"He will," I vow. They might not trust Bishop, but they're here because they trust me. "He'll handle her until we can get there."

"And *how* will we get there?" Remy looks at me with hostility. "You're making snap changes to a plan we don't even know about and expecting us to sit here without complaint."

"I never asked you to remain silent. You could've asked questions."

He points at me in accusation. "You made it clear yesterday that you weren't going to tell us what the fuck was going on. And when it's my fucking future on the line, forgive me for not daring to push."

I release my belt and raise a placating hand. "Everyone needs to calm down. We've got this under control. Bishop can take care of Abri. We're going to speak to Lorenzo, and we'll catch his jet to Denver as soon as we're done."

"Can you tell us what we're going there to talk about?" Salvo asks.

"You'll find out in twenty minutes if you don't hightail it out of here." I'm not ready to give them full transparency. They need more time to calm down before the storm. "But it will mean a future where Abri can have freedom and nobody will be able to use her again."

Remy glances away, his jaw clenched, his eyes narrow slits.

"I don't think we have a fucking choice." Salvatore rakes a hand through his hair. "Running back to Abri is a temporary solution to an escalating problem. We can't keep letting Emmanuel win."

"Well, you all better pray this fucker can look after her." Remy stalks toward the staircase. "Because if he doesn't, I'll hack his fucking face off with a crowbar." He disappears outside as the jet engines whir to a stop.

"I'm a little disappointed nobody scolded him for stepping over the line," Bishop drawls. "Surely that threat was worse than me promising to skull fuck his sister."

I glare.

"What?" He screws up his face. "I'm just sayin' what Layla's thinkin'."

She clears her throat beside me. "I assure you, you're not."

"I better go after him." Salvo holds my gaze. "Can I call Abri back?"

"Yeah. Just don't tell her where we're going." I push to my feet. "The driver should already be out there waiting. We'll follow in a minute."

Layla moves to stand behind me as he walks hunched through the cabin, her hands resting on my hips while I turn to Bishop. "Are you sure you're willing to go on your own?"

He shrugs. No fucks given. "I was willing to do whatever it took to get those two fuckers to stop whining. That shit drives me insane."

Layla snickers under her breath.

"You need to be careful." I clasp his shoulder. "Keep a low profile. Don't do anything reckless."

"I don't appreciate a lecture from an asshole who doesn't carry a gun."

"*Touché*," Layla murmurs.

I pat the blade in my pocket. "I have all I need. It's never failed me before. But you need to keep your head on straight," I warn Bishop. "Don't mess around. Emmanuel will have men everywhere."

"You heard Abri. His posse are out looking for you. If anyone is in danger here, it's not me."

"Don't make assumptions." I drop my hold on his shoulder and start for the stairs. "And stay on your toes with my sister. If memory serves, she's feisty when blindsided."

He scoffs. "I have a feeling she's feisty regardless."

24

MATTHEW

Layla is rigid beside me as we drive toward Lorenzo's Keeling Cove property. Salvatore sits up front with my usual driver while Remy meets my gaze with trepidation whenever I look to him in the row of seats behind us.

Abri hasn't answered her cell despite the calls we've made, and all Layla can do is stare at hers.

"What is it?" I peer down at her phone, only to have her lock the screen.

"Nothing." She shakes her head.

"It's something." I drag my attention back out the window. "Whether or not you want to discuss it with me is a different matter."

"I've made my brother worry. That's all." She places her hand on my thigh, a gentle, reassuring gesture. "He keeps calling. I think he has a sixth sense that something is going on. I'll need to speak to him once we're finished here."

"Are you asking permission?" It sounds like she is. "You know that's not necessary."

"No, I'm not. I just wasn't sure what I should tell him."

I place my hand on top of hers, impatient for Emmanuel's death so I can have her to myself. "He won't stop our plans regardless of what he knows if that's what you're worried about."

She gives me a skeptical look.

"*La mia stella polare*, your brother is a man with a city." I lean close to whisper in her ear. "And I'm a monster who decimated a state. I promise he won't get in our way."

She shudders. In fear or pleasure, I'm not sure. But it makes me fucking hard.

I'm still hungry for her. Always ravenous. Even after the half-hour session in the shower, my tongue in her slit, her hands in my hair.

I'm not sure I'll ever be sated. Or if I want to be. The constant craving is an addiction I'm eager to remain bound to.

"You got the code, sir?" My driver pulls up at the wrought-iron gates blocking us from Lorenzo's estate.

"Yes. And you already know I'm not willing to share." I climb out and round the hood to the security panel, entering the digits to allow us entry.

The gates groan, bounce, then slowly slide aside as I circle back and climb into my seat.

"This is where Lorenzo lives?" Salvatore inches forward in the front seat as we continue down the curving drive. "I always imagined he'd live in a dark, high-rise penthouse for some reason."

"He's got one of those, too." This place is more of a sanctuary. His hideaway.

"It's beautiful," Layla whispers.

I struggle to see it through her eyes.

To me, this place is a fortress.

The tall trees providing a canopy over the yard act as a shield from the outside world. The creeper vines twisted around the trunks hide the mass of mounted security cameras. And once we get outside, the air will be alive with the call of tropical birds from the massive aviary—nature's own alarm system to back up its state-of-the-art counterpart.

The car stops in front of the sprawling house and the middle-aged Italian guard at the front door approaches the vehicle.

"What do I do?" Salvo lowers his sun visor and stares at me through the mirror. "Is there a certain protocol I need to follow? A secret handshake?"

"I'll handle it." I get out before the guard reaches the car. "Hey, Aldo. It's been a long time."

He inclines his head. "The boss wasn't expecting you until later."

"This couldn't wait." I reach toward Layla, helping her to slide across the seat. "Where is he?"

"In the backyard last time I checked. You can wait in the house until he's ready."

"Thanks." I help Layla to her feet, keeping her close with a protective arm around her waist as Remy and Salvatore climb out.

"Is the car going to stay here?" she asks as the driver lowers his window.

"No. I might be the only one with Lorenzo's gate code, but that doesn't mean he favors me enough to allow my driver to loiter." I jerk my head for the chauffeur to leave. "I'll call you to get us once we're done."

He nods and shifts the car into reverse while my brothers stare at the grey brick mansion, their expressions masked, their shoulders taut.

"My hands are sweating," Layla whispers.

"There's nothing to be nervous about. It's only a conversation."

"One that could cause major problems." She starts toward the house, following Aldo up the three steps leading to the front doors. "What if your brothers don't appreciate your plan?" she whispers. "Or Lorenzo shoots us down in flames? What then?"

I glide my hand under the hem of her top, brushing my thumb against warm, soft skin. "After living through Emmanuel's reign, my brothers should be used to doing what they're told, and Lorenzo needs a successor. I don't expect any of them to be enthusiastic, but they'll know it's a strategic way forward."

"I understand that part... I just..." She huffs a pained breath. "Something doesn't feel right."

I feel it, too. "It's because Bishop isn't here." I kiss her temple. "Once you get used to his bullshit, it becomes a crutch."

She huffs a chuckle. "Maybe that's it."

We reach the front doors, one side of the thick, glass-paneled wood opening with Lorenzo's housekeeper filling the open space.

"*Matthew.*" The older woman opens her arms wide as she marches forward, descending the steps to clasp my cheeks, planting air kisses on both sides of my face. "It's been too long."

"Forgive me, Maria. I've been busy convincing the most beautiful woman in the world to be mine." I indicate Layla with a wave of my hand. "I'd like you to meet Layla Hart."

"Oh, *mio dio.*" The housekeeper places a hand to her heart. "You have outdone yourself."

Layla blushes. "It's lovely to meet you."

The women exchange a casual hug where Maria murmurs something I can't hear. Whatever it is makes Layla laugh.

"He's a perfect gentleman." She shoots me a grin. "*Most* of the time."

"Only most?" Maria clucks her tongue, backtracking toward the house. "Come, come." She directs us inside the lavish entry and waits at the door for my brothers to follow. "I hope you're hungry. I've made enough food to feed a small village."

"I could always eat." Remy cranes his neck up at the glistening chandelier beneath the overhead skylight.

The five of us walk down the long hall, passing the study, then the library, to the open entertaining area. Sunlight streams in from the wall of windows overlooking the backyard, the lawn perfectly cut, the pool pristine blue.

"Help yourself to a drink from the fridge." Maria continues across the room. "It's so nice to have you all here. The house hasn't seen this many guests in a long time."

"This many?" I meet her gaze. "Lorenzo used to have more than the four of us over all the time."

"Oh, no. Everyone else is on the pool house deck." She stops at the door leading to the yard and pulls it open. "Isn't that why you're here?"

I pause, tightening my hold around Layla's waist. I don't want her exposed to any of my uncle's acquaintances. Remy and Salvo follow my lead, stopping a few feet behind.

"I didn't realize Lorenzo had visitors." I inch forward, exposing my gaze to more of the yard, narrowing my attention on the people under the cover of the deck on the far side of the pool.

Layla snaps taut. A gasp escapes her lips.

A mass of volcanic emotions erupt in my chest as I take in what's scared her.

Lorenzo sits across the outdoor setting from Emmanuel and Adena. Two guards from each party stand a few feet behind them, positioned like corners on a protective square.

My mentor and my nemesis are face to face for the first time in more than a decade, with Emmanuel in a wheelchair, an oxygen mask over his mouth, his posture still holding the fortitude of an ox.

The call to violence suffuses me. Every thought. Every heartbeat.

Rage becomes a mindless demon inside my chest, the demand to take action roaring inside my skull.

The world will burn for this.

My brothers will die.

"What do we do?" she whispers.

I turn, guiding her behind me as I face the betrayers at my back. "You set us up."

Salvatore remains mute.

"I've gotta hand it to you. This took some balls." Smarts, too. They came at me crying for help, anticipating I'd go to Lorenzo in return. But their effortless ability to manipulate Bishop into leaving for Denver so I didn't have backup was a tactic even I would've struggled to pull off.

"What are you talking about?" Remy stalks around me, taking in the backyard.

"Is everything all right?" Maria asks from the door.

"What's the play?" I ask. "Is this where you plan to hand her over, because no matter what shit he spins out there, Lorenzo will always be on my side?"

"Jesus fucking Christ." Remy's eyes widen as he backtracks, grabbing Salvatore by the arm. "Emmanuel's here. We need to leave."

Salvo yanks free from his hold, storming forward to check for himself. "*Fuck.*" He rakes rough hands through his hair. "What do we do?"

He turns to me, his face full of fear, his eyes cold as ice. Is it a bluff? More sabotage?

"Come on." Remy strides for the hall. "*Move.* We've gotta get out of here."

"I don't know what's going on." Layla's hands cling to my waist. Her shuddered breath tortures my ears. "Did they know?"

I don't know. The aggression coursing through my veins is turning everyone into an enemy. I'll kill them all. Emmanuel, Adena, Salvo, Remy. I'll kill Abri, too, if her phone call was part of the scheme. Fuck Lorenzo's rules.

"Are you going to pretend you didn't set this up?" I snarl.

"I told you that son of a bitch is always one step ahead." Salvo's face turns pale as he starts backtracking with his brother. "He *always* fucking knows."

"*How*? How would he fucking know anything if you covered your tracks like you said you did?"

"You tell me." Remy raises his voice. "You think I'd dare to betray you after you fucking stabbed us both?"

I palm the knife in my pocket, the devil on my shoulder screaming for a repeat of history.

"Call the driver." Layla tugs on my jacket. "We need to run."

We can't.

We're safest under this roof. Under Lorenzo's protection.

If we leave, we're on our own to outrun any men Emmanuel might have circling the property.

"We didn't do this." Salvo holds my stare. "And we're in just as much danger as you are now that we've shown our faces with you."

"We're fucked," Remy seethes. "What do we do now?"

Maria clears her throat. "I'll get Lorenzo." She hustles from the open doorway as my brothers look to me for guidance.

Jesus Christ. Unless they've mastered flawless poker faces since we were kids, they didn't fucking know.

"Why would he be here if they weren't involved?" Layla whispers. "What would he want with Lorenzo?"

I dig the blade deeper into my thigh, the steel edge bringing temporary relief to the mindlessness. "He must know his days are numbered and the only thing keeping him safe from me is our uncle."

"Will Lorenzo support him?" Salvo asks. "How the hell do we get out of this?"

"I need a gun." I won't have Emmanuel around Layla while I'm unarmed. I don't care how easy it is to pull the trigger.

Neither of my brothers acknowledge my request.

"Give me a fucking gun." I lunge for Remy, grabbing his shirt. I shove my hand beneath his jacket, find his holster, and take the weapon.

Lorenzo strides across the yard and storms inside, his displeasure at my arrival adamant in his condemning eyes. "I told you this wasn't a good time."

"And it seems, for once, I should've listened." I load the magazine from my pocket into the Glock. "Why is he here?"

"He hasn't made that clear… but I assume it has something to do with the three of you reuniting, no?" His attention lowers to the weapon. "That gun is to remain unused, *figlio.* Are we understood?"

He knows I can't commit to that promise. I won't.

"Matthew," he warns. "Don't forget my rules."

"Your rules are why I'm here."

His jaw clenches, the wrinkles of an ageing man growing deeper with his annoyance. "We will discuss this later." He treks his gaze to Layla and pastes on a welcoming smile. "It's a pleasure to see you again." He steps forward to take her hands, kissing both knuckles.

"I wish I felt the same." Her eyes shimmer with unease. "But it seems we've been blindsided by your guests."

"Consider this Switzerland, *bella.* There is nothing to fear." He releases her, turning his attention to Remy and Salvatore. *"I miei nipoti,* it's been a lifetime. You were young boys the last time I laid eyes on you. Now you're strong men."

Remy doesn't respond as Lorenzo approaches, grabbing him by the shoulders to drag him close, planting a kiss on both his cheeks.

"I wish it were under better circumstances," Salvatore grates.

Lorenzo waves him away and gives him the same affectionate greeting. "We will discuss circumstances later. For now, we will join your parents in the garden."

"No." I shake my head. "That's not—"

"You have already defied me once by your unscheduled visit." He raises his voice. "Don't do it again."

I grind my teeth, my blood searing through my veins.

"You *will* join us, *figlio*. And you *will* mind your manners."

"That's not an option. Layla's not safe around them."

"You dare to insult me?" His expression fills with contempt. "While on my property, she is under my protection. Since when have you questioned me?"

Since her safety became more valuable than the air I breathe.

"There's nothing to fear, *bella*," he reiterates. "I will look after you."

Her smile is fragile. "It's not me I'm worried about."

He raises a brow, giving a faint chuckle. "Don't worry about Matthew. He's stubborn. But he also understands the etiquette we live by." He starts for the door. "Now come join us. Maybe we can put past differences behind us."

"I'm sorry, Lorenzo." She remains in place by my side. "I understand the etiquette, and none of us are here to be disrespectful. It's the opposite actually. We wanted to offer you a solution to your problem. We only need a few moments of your time."

He pauses, shifts, then rakes us all with a narrowed stare, his attention finally coming to rest on me. "And what problem do I have, *figlio*?"

He's annoyed. Disappointed. He thinks I've fallen into old habits with my hatred for Emmanuel, but he'll understand once he learns the truth. "We're here about your retirement."

His brows raise. "You've decided to take over?"

"No." I clutch tighter to the gun, prepared to fight this with words but extremely tempted to use bullets. "But I've found someone who will."

25

LAYLA

Lorenzo falls silent, the stretching bleakness making my stomach churn. He needs to say something. Anything. This quiet is torture.

"My sons," Emmanuel's rasped call carries from the yard. "Don't be rude. Come outside and say hello to your father."

Salvatore curses under his breath.

Remy stands rigid as if one wrong move will end his life.

"We will discuss this later." Lorenzo sucks in a long breath and sighs. "For now, I need to return to my other unexpected guests."

Matthew's fingers tighten around mine. "*Zio*, this is important."

"All the more reason to discuss it later when we won't be interrupted." He continues toward the door. "Come. Be civil. I'm sure we're all familiar with biting our tongue in front of our adversaries." He casts one last look at the weapon in Matthew's hand, then continues outside. "Get rid of it."

Adrenaline suffuses me, intoxicating every nerve. "What do we do?"

"For starters, you can clarify who the hell you have pegged to take over for our uncle," Salvatore demands. "Because I've a sinking fucking feeling I'm the lamb being brought to the slaughter."

Matthew shoves the gun into the back of his pants, hiding it beneath his jacket.

"Well?" Salvatore ping-pongs an aggressive look between us. "Talk."

Matthew squares his shoulders. "It's true."

"Fucking Christ. You can't be serious."

"That's why we're here?" Remy's voice drips with venom. "*That's* your plan?"

I lick my painfully dry lips and start praying.

"It's the best option," Matthew states simply.

Salvatore balks. "For who? Because it sure as shit isn't me."

"Do you really think you still have the option to start fresh?" Matthew slides a protective arm around my hips. "What do you think this is? Disneyland? You don't buy a one-day ticket then kiss this lifestyle goodbye. You've committed crimes. Disposed of bodies. You've made enemies—ones like her family." He clings tighter to me. "You don't get to walk away from that. Taking over from Lorenzo is the only path that gives you some semblance of freedom."

Salvatore's nostrils flare. He's livid, his brow breaking out in a sweat.

"Matthew's trying to protect you," I say softly. "You'll be safer with Lorenzo's name and reputation behind you. And at least this way, you'll be in control."

"And what do you both get out of this?" His vehement eyes turn to me. "Apart from ruining any hopes for my future."

"We get Emmanuel's death," Matthew answers. "Lorenzo has forbidden family blood to be spilled, but if he's not in charge, he doesn't make the rules. So you vow to take over and I convince our uncle there's no point delaying the inevitable."

Salvatore's laughter is cruel. "Great. Not only am I meant to become some illustrious mafioso, but my first act of notoriety is to kill my father? That's fucking perfect."

"*I'm* killing him. You only need to be in the position to give the order."

"Is that meant to be comforting?" Remy asks. "Because I can assure you it doesn't dull the edges of this fucking nightmare. We don't know the first thing about this side of the family."

"You'll work it out. It won't be easy, but at least you'll be free."

"*Free*?" Salvatore asks. "We'll be in prison before the year is out."

"*Remy. Salvo.*" Emmanuel calls again. "*Outside. Now.*"

My pulse wavers with the fluctuating beat of my heart. I hate his voice. I despise his existence.

"What's it going to be?" Matthew asks.

Remy shoves a hand behind his neck, clawing at his muscles with tense fingers. "Abri will fucking kill us."

"She won't." I shake my head. "She'll be protected here. Nobody will dare to touch her."

The brothers exchange a glance, troubled and bitter.

"I know it's a shock." Matthew reaches into his jacket pocket, retrieving the second magazine. "But I'll trust you with our lives if you trust me with this decision."

I hold my breath, the oxygen festering in my lungs as Salvatore focuses on the offering.

We all stare at him. Watching. Waiting.

"I can't believe this," he mutters to himself. "I don't know the first thing about Lorenzo's business."

"You won't need to." Matthew inches the magazine closer. "You'll be taught what to do. You both will."

My heart pounds painful beats as Salvatore falls quiet. Contemplative.

We can't just stand here. We need to do something.

"Let's fucking do this." Remy steps forward and snatches the magazine. "But there's no point giving this to him. His shoulder is wrecked." He holds out a hand to

Salvatore, wordlessly demanding the gun. "I guess it's my job now to guard the future director of all things underhanded and illegal, right?"

Salvatore mutters a curse. "This isn't happening."

"It is." Matthew releases my hip, taking my hand instead. "But not right now. First we need to confirm everything with Lorenzo, then we get to hunt Emmanuel down."

Remy shoves the weapon into the holster beneath his jacket. "Well, time's ticking, and we still need to get back to Abri, so let's get this shit done." He starts for the yard, his shoulders strong, his head high in the face of fear.

"You won't regret it, Salvo." Matthew reaches out to squeeze his arm. "It's the right choice."

"I find that hard to believe."

"Give it time." He leads me toward the door, but I'm slow to follow.

I can't walk out there like this.

"What's wrong?" Matthew turns to me.

"I can't hold your hand out there." I wince. "I don't want to look weak in front of him. I need to stand on my own. To walk without you."

He straightens in offense. "We're not weak together, Layla."

"He doesn't know that. And I don't want him interpreting my affection as vulnerability."

"Okay." He waves a hand toward the door. "Whatever you need. Just remember, your safety is my priority, Layla. And if, for one second, I think Emmanuel is becoming an imminent threat, I won't just be holding your hand, I'll be using my body as a shield. Agreed?"

I don't answer. I don't want him putting his life on the line when we both decided to weather this storm.

"*Agreed.*" This time, his tone isn't questioning. It's a statement. A demand.

"Yes. Okay." I walk for the door, reaching out to drag a hand across Matthew's stomach when I pass. I need one last touch. One lingering contact before I'm on my own.

"I'll go first." Salvatore strides around me to lead the way—a move of dominance or protection, I'm not sure.

I follow, Matthew close at my back, practically walking in my shoes.

A water fountain trickles somewhere in the distance. Birds squawk an occasional song. My thundering pulse drowns it all out.

The scene we approach is picturesque, the outdoor table adorned with food fit for a high tea with ceramic three-tier cake stands littered with assorted baked goods. There's coffee and juice. A water jug with crystal tumblers. Bread plates are covered in half eaten treats. Exquisite bowls are piled with jam and cream.

Then there's the devil who sits on the far side, his eyes sparkling as he lowers his oxygen mask to leer at me. His placid wife sits to his left, a portrait of excessive prestige. Two of their guards stand at attention a foot behind them.

Lorenzo has already reclaimed the seat opposite his brother-in-law, his profile stony to match the security duo flanking him.

"Father," Remy snarls as he stops a few yards from the table. "Mother."

Salvatore claims the space to his brother's left. I stop on the right, with Matthew close at my side. We're a wall of defiance. Of pure hatred.

"You brought her to me," Emmanuel addresses Salvatore with a grin. "I'm proud of you, son."

"Don't be. I think we both know what this really is," Salvatore says.

Emmanuel feigns a look of ignorance, but I swear, he already knows. Behind the confused blink of his eyes, he hides his volatile anger. "What do you mean? Didn't you follow me here to hand over your pretty bounty?"

"Make one more comment about her, old man, and it'll be your last," Matthew warns.

"Enough." Lorenzo claps a hand on the table, rattling plates and cutlery. "I don't want to ask anyone to leave, but I will if you don't behave. You are all well aware she is my guest."

"You made that perfectly clear." Emmanuel inclines his head. "My apologies."

Rage heats my cheeks.

He doesn't care about Lorenzo's rules. He doesn't even care about his own children.

"I do have one concern though." Emmanuel raises his oxygen mask, takes a long inhale as we all wait, then lowers it again. "Should we hide the knives, boy?" His attention shifts to Matthew. "We've all heard you're quite adept at using them, and it sounds like your restraint is a little shaky."

"I'm more than happy to give you a demonstration." The words are grated beside me, every syllable hostile.

"Emmanuel. *Figlio*," Lorenzo growls. "We're family. Treat each other accordingly."

"Unfortunately, *Zio*, not all of us have the same standards of treatment," Matthew stretches his neck from side to side as if preparing for battle. "Isn't that right, Emmanuel?"

There's no response, only the quiet hiss of his oxygen mask and the slight narrowing of Adena's eyes.

"Explain." Lorenzo reaches for a tea cake, leisurely placing the delicacy on the plate in front of him.

"I've recently found out my siblings have lived for years in a lifestyle more accustomed to slavery."

"That's a lie," Adena sputters. "You're always lying, Dante, and I can't understand why. We gave you every—"

"You gave me nothing but pain. But you've treated my brothers with far more contempt. You've held them hostage from their own finances."

Emmanuel rolls his eyes. "Do they look destitute to you?"

"You've tapped their phones," Matthew continues. "Blackmailed them with crimes you forced them to commit. You've enslaved your own children because we all know they would've left you long ago if you didn't."

"Is that true?" Lorenzo asks.

Nobody answers.

"Is it true?" he growls, his focus turning to Salvatore.

"Yes." Remy winces. "We've been without freedom for years."

Emmanuel sighs and pulls out his phone to tap nonchalantly at his screen. It's a subtle snub at the accusations. He doesn't care. He's not ashamed.

"We handle their finances." Adena dabs at the corners of her mouth with a cloth napkin. "We contracted the best financial planner in the state to help them invest in their future. The money is in a trust. They all know that."

"Their money is used as a weapon," Matthew snarls. "Isn't it, Emmanuel?"

The old man chuckles into his oxygen mask, still preoccupied with his phone.

"You're not going to address the allegations?" Lorenzo places his cake down on his plate.

"I have a feeling he knows his hours are numbered." Matthew inches forward and edges toward me, becoming a partial shield. "Isn't that right?"

"My hours aren't the concern." Emmanuel lowers the mask. "It's your whore who will be dead before nightfall."

I open my mouth but my snappy retort is lost to an erupting melee.

Lorenzo shoves to his feet. Matthew drags me behind him, then lunges for the table. I stumble, Salvatore's hand reaching out to stabilize me as the man of my heart grabs a butter knife and flings it in a blinding flash of silver toward the guard over Emmanuel's right shoulder.

A scream lodges in my throat as the blade skewers the guard's eye, sending his head backward, his body following in slow motion.

He hits the deck with a nauseating thwack. Emotionless. Dead.

Adena scrambles to her feet with a wail as guns are drawn from every angle—Emmanuel's remaining guard, Remy, Matthew, Lorenzo's security—all of them in a mass standoff while my heart becomes a jackhammer.

"No more bloodshed," Lorenzo roars over the deafening squawk of birds. *"Lower your weapons."*

I'm jostled from all angles as Matthew shields the front of me, Remy and Salvatore closing in on my sides.

"The time for peace is over, *Zio*." Matthew keeps his barrel trained on Emmanuel. "He no longer deserves your protection. Either support me or become my enemy."

My stomach nosedives. "Matthew," I whisper.

He doesn't want this. Making an adversary of his uncle wasn't the plan.

"What you need is time to air your grievances without an audience." Lorenzo holds a hand out to me through the protective shield of men, his gaze kind. *"Bella,* I think it's best if we wait in the house. Let the family vent their injustice in private."

I wait for Matthew to protest. For him to demand I stay by his side. But he doesn't say a word. He keeps his back to me, his body stiff.

"Matthew?" I whisper, unsure what to do.

A man lays dead on the deck. The remaining guard has his aim pointed right at me through Salvatore's shoulder. And those birds, *my God*, they scream for the tension to stop.

I have no weapons. Nothing to protect myself with apart from the masculine wall surrounding me, most of whom were my enemies only yesterday.

"I will stay with her, *figlio*." Lorenzo reaches around Remy for my hand. "She will be far safer in the house. She won't trigger you in there. Or be a temptation for others."

A trigger? A temptation?

I don't want to be either of those. But I know I am.

I'm Matthew's greatest weakness and I'm going to get him killed.

"I'll go." I squeeze his hips.

"No." He reaches behind his back, grabbing my wrist, his fingers punishingly tight as his attention remains on the threats. "You stay with me."

Emmanuel chuckles beneath the oxygen mask as he tugs Adena back to her seat. "Yes, let her stay. It's much more fun this way."

I ignore him.

I ignore *everything*. The fear. The panic. The hysteria.

All I focus on is Matthew and how to get us out of here alive.

"*Please*." I press my forehead to his back, begging him to understand. We can't risk him breaking Lorenzo's rules by murdering Emmanuel. I won't let him steer his life back toward everything he's tried to escape. "Don't let him get to you."

"What is she saying?" Emmanuel asks. "Is she pleading for you to save her? Begging for her life?"

Every second I remain here, I'm giving that monster more power.

"What are we doing?" Remy mutters under his breath. "What's the plan?"

"I'm going inside." I squeeze the hand holding my wrist. "Get whatever you need off your chest, because as soon as we have permission, this will be over." I twist my arm from Matthew's grip and maneuver between his brothers.

Lorenzo opens his arm to me, his guards protecting us with raised weapons as I'm hustled toward the pool.

My escape is narrated by the rustle of leaves from the canopy above, and the gradually dwindling caw of birds. My frantic heartbeat, too.

"*Wait*," Matthew shouts.

I pause. Turn.

He storms toward me, gun clenched at his side, eyes predatory.

But it's not Matthew anymore. The man stalking toward me is the Butcher. The savage.

Lorenzo gives us space as my face is cupped between a weapon and punishing palms, the ferocity of Matthew's manic stare bearing down at me.

"Give me permission," he demands.

My heart crawls into my throat, cutting off my ability to breathe.

I don't need to clarify what he's asking. He wants to end this now. Without our plan in place. Without Lorenzo's approval.

"No." I shake my head. "We do this the right way so you don't have to live with repercussions later."

"I'll handle the repercussions." He leans closer, his nostrils flaring as his lips hover so close to mine. "Give me permission."

"No. You don't have it. You're not going back to that life."

"I won't need to," he growls. "This is temporary. Salvatore will be in power. Let me end this now."

I want to believe him. I want to trust that he can predict what's going to happen. But I've made so many bad decisions in the past. I'm not going to do it again. If I can wait for closure, so can he.

"Talk to him," I plead. "Get whatever you need to off your chest. Because the time is coming to end him. But it isn't now."

He straightens his shoulders. Raises his chin.

"Please, Matthew." I inch into him, clutching his shirt. "You're *la mia vita. La mia anima. Il mio santuario.*" I recite the words he spoke so reverently to me yesterday, trying not to wreck the beautiful language. "I can't lose you."

The Butcher wavers, my Matthew returning for a blink of pained vulnerability before the severity slips back into place. "Then you need to take this." He grabs my hand, placing the gun in my palm.

I hesitate. "What if—"

He cuts me off with a harsh shake of his head. "If I have this, I'll kill him. I'll break my promise and do it without thought." He smashes his lips to mine, his free hand clamping tight around the back of my neck. "But don't worry—I'm handy with a knife. I just need to know you're safe."

26

LAYLA

LORENZO LOCKS THE DOOR BEHIND US, PUTTING THE KEY IN HIS INSIDE JACKET POCKET.

"Is that necessary?" I ask

He gives me a wolfish grin. "*Bella*, I'm an old man and far too tired to chase you if you decide to run back outside." He pats his jacket pocket. "This ensures those boys get the time they need with their father."

Maybe I should feel threatened. Confined.

I don't.

His smile is genuine. His eyes kind.

"Coffee?" He makes his way to the kitchen. "Juice?"

"No, thank you." I can barely stomach breathing, let alone liquids.

I remain before the wall of glass, scrutinizing the meeting outside. Lorenzo's guards followed us to the house and remain at attention outside the doors, their guns palmed at their sides, their expressions blank.

"Watching them won't make the situation resolve itself any quicker." He opens a cupboard and pulls out a mug. "Sit. Relax. Let them converse without scrutiny."

"I think we both know Matthew has more than conversation on his mind."

"I understand." He moves to the coffee machine, pressing buttons until it gurgles and splutters.

I turn to him. "You understand? Does that mean you approve?"

He has his back to me, his focus on the filling mug.

"Lorenzo?" I step closer, placing the gun on the dining table as I pass. "After all these years denying him what he wanted, are you now okay with it?"

He twists, leaning his hip against the counter as he meets my gaze. "I wasn't denying him. I was *delaying* him." His accent is thick, his words slowly articulated. "After all these years, I think he might finally be ready."

He shows no sign of the hostility he harbored when we arrived. No temperamental concern or demand to respect authority.

"You look at me in confusion, *bella*, but I assure you my intent was quite clear. I forbade Emmanuel's murder because up until now, I was certain Matthew couldn't handle the repercussions of killing his own flesh and blood. He already harbors a heavy burden of regret. I didn't want him to take action then spend the rest of his life punishing himself for it."

"You did it out of protection?"

He inclines his head. "*Si*. And I never regretted it." His lips curve in an apologetic smile. "At least, not until I met you and discovered what you mean to him. I'm sorry my decision took so much from you, *mia cara*."

I breathe through the emotion beginning to fester beneath my ribs, refusing to show weakness. "Your decision didn't take anything from me. Emmanuel did."

He nods. Solemn.

"Tell me what changed?" I take another step closer, charcing a glance over my shoulder to make sure the situation outside hasn't devolved into chaos. "Why do you think Matthew is capable of this now and not before?"

"Because a ship in a storm needs a tether. And now he has you."

"Is that what it's always been about? You've wanted someone by his side before he took action?"

"I already ensured he had someone by his side. But a brother wasn't enough. The darkness still haunted him."

I take another step. "Bishop?"

He grabs the filled mug of coffee from the machine. "Yes.'

"You *ensured* it?" I shake my head, not sure I want confirmation on the assumption whispering through my mind.

"Don't look at me like that, *bella*. Bishop has not betrayed Matthew and neither have I. He was paid to protect the fiercest soldier I ever had because I hoped Matthew would one day return to take over."

"You paid him to stay at Matthew's side?"

He sips his coffee, eying me over the rim of the mug. "Bishop never would've left otherwise. This lifestyle is in his blood, but Matthew needed a companion. A brother. So I made a compromise—he would work for me from afar and return when he was ready."

I raise a hand to my neck, the betrayal tightening my throat. "Matthew will be devastated. He won't forgive you."

"He's a smart man." He lowers the mug to the counter. "I doubt he will be surprised. But I strongly advise you to keep this to yourself. It can be our little secret."

I hear the threat. I don't see it through his kind eyes and gentle smile, but it's definitely hidden in his words. Even the birds seem to hear it, their siren call squawking louder from outside, the cacophony growing as if they sense the rising hostility.

"I take your silence as judgment, Layla, but I assure you my heart has always been in the right place where Matthew is concerned. He means more to me than my own children, and I've never shied away from that admission. What I've done for him has been out of protection and love."

"But what you did went behind his back. It was without his consent."

"And sometimes it's better to ask for forgiveness than beg for permission."

The doorbell rings, the loud chime startling me.

"More unexpected visitors?" Lorenzo frowns, his gaze trekking to the hall. "Is that Bishop?"

"It shouldn't be. He was on his way to Denver."

"Maybe he sensed the hostility and changed his mind."

Fast footsteps shuffle nearby. I assume Maria is on her way to open the door.

"Should I be worried?" My nerves are on edge.

"No. Cars can't enter without a code or approval from the guards on patrol." Lorenzo pulls his cell from his suit pocket, along with a pair of spectacles. "These damn security apps will be the death of me. Too many notifications and not enough peace." He starts for the entry. "Excuse me, *bella*. I'll be back in a moment."

I saunter back toward the wall of glass as he leaves the room, dragging my fingers over the gun on the table while I pass, needing a touch of confidence. Outside, Matthew stands tall, his shoulders tense.

I wish I knew what he was saying. How he was feeling.

Aggressive conversation carries from the front door and I cock my head to the hall to listen. Lorenzo admonishes someone in Italian, his vehemence raising the hair on the back of my neck.

The birds caw and crow over their owner's voice. The cacophony grows louder. Screeching higher.

I start toward the hall, curious to hear more clearly when a piercing scream ricochets through the house.

I freeze. Panic.

A muted blast pummels my ears. *Silenced gunfire.*

I sprint for the table, lunging for the gun.

"*Hide*, bella," Lorenzo shouts. "*Run.*"

Another muted pop echoes off the walls as I scramble for the doors leading outside, my hands slipping against the lever that won't budge.

It's locked.

I'm trapped.

I bang against the glass, desperate for Matthew's attention. My fist pounds harder and harder to be heard over the shrieking birds.

He swings to face me, his eyes stark, his hand in his pocket.

The guards near the door raise their weapons. Remy does, too.

But nobody's attention remains on me. They all shift their fixation to the side of the house. On the armed men who storm the yard.

A pop sounds. Lorenzo's guard is shot in the head. Right in front of me. His blood splatters the glass.

"Oh, God." My hand shakes around the gun. "It's an ambush."

27

MATTHEW

"Put the phone away." My tone brooks no argument.

"I'm not much of a follower, boy." Emmanuel continues to play with his cell screen.

"You weren't much of a father either." I palm the blade in my pocket as he chuckles into his oxygen mask, the sound barely heard over the squawk of birds.

"You know, at one time you were my greatest hope for the future, Dante. Now you're my biggest disappointment."

"The feeling is mutual, but at least you won't have to dwell on it for long. We all know how this ends."

He cocks his head. "Do we?"

"Cut the shit, Dad." Salvo pulls out a chair, dragging it away from the table to take a seat. "We're done. Remy. Abri. Me. We're all out."

Adena's gaze cuts to her husband, her eyes desperate. "No."

"Don't worry, my darling." Emmanuel smiles at her, all arrogant confidence. "They won't survive without us."

"We don't need your fucking money," Remy spits. "We'll make it on our own."

Emmanuel lowers the mask, his expression turning feral. "I don't mean the money, *son*. I mean pure survival. You won't outlive defying me."

Remy flinches. It's an innocent backlash of movement that makes it fucking clear he still hasn't comprehended the sickening level of his father's malice.

"Death threats don't go down nicely around these parts." I glide my pointer finger over the tip of my blade, drawing blood, seeking restraint. "Lorenzo won't stand for violence against family. His rules are the only reason you're still breathing. But I'm sure you know that."

"Then maybe I don't start with family. Maybe I start with your girl."

His confidence turns my veins glacial. "You won't get a chance to hurt her."

He flashes his teeth. "I can't wait to see the look on your face when I prove you wrong."

I glance over my shoulder, needing to see Layla after he's effortlessly triggered my paranoia.

She stands with her back to me, her focus on Lorenzo who walks for the hall. She's safe behind the bulletproof glass, the guards close by with weapons at the ready.

"Your days of toying with us are over." Salvatore crosses a leg over one knee, feigning relaxation that isn't shown in his tight posture. "And I'll make sure all the money you stole from us is reclaimed tenfold. You'll be destitute."

Lorenzo's parrots screech louder.

"I'm not toying with you." Emmanuel places the oxygen mask on the table beside his cell. "I'm defeating."

The noise grows, the panicked birds shrieking.

We need to get out of here. I'm done having patience for his shit.

"Come on." I lean forward to clap Salvatore on the shoulder. "This is pointless. We need to finalize our plan with Lorenzo."

"Wait." Emmanuel pushes to shaky feet. "I have something for you."

"Whatever it is, we don't want it," I raise my voice over the crow. The caw. The flutter of wings. But there's something else, too. Something subtle. A rhythmic thud.

Footsteps.

A faint banging carries from the house.

I swing around. Layla's fist hits the glass, her eyes screaming for help.

"*Fuck.*" Remy draws his weapon, but his attention isn't on her. It's on the men rushing around the side of the house, dressed in black, guns in hand.

A shot is fired.

Salvatore shoves to his feet.

"My gift to you." Emmanuel grins, raising his arms at his sides. "Purgatory."

"*Get to Layla,*" I yell at my brothers, lunging for the table. "*Help her.*" I snatch a butter knife and heave the projectile over Adena's shoulder at the guard raising his weapon toward me.

I hit him in the gut as Salvatore runs for the house. The guard drops his weapon, clutching at the silver protruding from his stomach.

Adena cries out and launches to her feet.

Gunshots erupt behind me, the blasts blazing in all directions.

I flip the table, needing cover, making Emmanuel and Adena skitter backward. Then I pounce at that fucking asshole, my shoulder charging into his chest, sending us both toppling toward the floor, taking the wheelchair out along the way.

Kill the king. Crumple the empire.

Once he's dead, Layla will be okay. These men won't fight without a leader. Without payment.

I climb over him as he struggles, pinning him to the deck to the soundtrack of Adena's screams, the birds wailing louder.

"I've waited a lifetime for this." I get in Emmanuel's face. Eye to eye. Man to man. "Until Layla, I wanted nothing more than your blood on my hands."

"No," he rasps. "Wait."

"Did you wait for Grace?" I snatch the blade from my pocket, my chest pounding as I sink it into his gut. "Did you listen to her beg?"

He jolts with the impact. Mouth agape. Eyes bugged.

I thought this would feel victorious. That the energy-rich adrenaline I'm accustomed to would smother me in relief. But there's only fear. Blinding. Terrifying.

I need to get to Layla.

"Did you?" I sneer. "Did you listen to her plead for her life?"

Adena surges toward me with a wail, her fingers clawing for my face. I grab her wrists and backhand her, sending her toppling to the deck floor.

Emmanuel snatches for the blade, but I reclaim it first, pressing harder into him, digging the knife deeper.

He closes his eyes, his chest jostling. Over and over.

With the discord pummeling my ears, I can't tell if he's coughing, choking, or fucking crying. But it disgusts me all the same. Right up until his lips curve, a smile breaking through to make it known I was wrong on all assumptions because he's not struggling at all. He's fucking laughing.

"Yes, I listened to her beg." He flashes his teeth now tinged with the slightest hint of blood. "And I dreamed about it for years. She was such a pretty little bitch. With a tight fucking pussy. I bet Layla will be the same once my men get hold of her."

I yank the blade free and roar as I plunge it into his neck.

I steal his humor, snatching it away with a strike so clean and hard he falls silent.

No. Adena scrambles from me, coming at me from behind as I saw the blade, cutting through his throat, coating my hands in his blood.

He gapes, clutching for his throat as weight slams into my back. Then agonizing pain. I launch from his chest, swinging into a crouch behind the table, the corner of my eye catching sight of a shard of porcelain plate embedded in my shoulder near my neck as bullets ping off the pool house.

"You fucking bitch." I snatch the blade from Emmanuel's throat, pointing it at Adena as his arms fall limp to the floor. "You realize you're as much at fault here as he is. You let him get away with everything—with using your kids, with torturing them. His death is on your hands."

Her chest rises and falls, while tears course over her cheeks. "All of you had everything you ever needed," she screeches, her gaze trekking to her lifeless husband, her face crumpling. "You're the one who deserves to die. Not him."

She's delusional.

Unhinged.

"You need to get out of here." I keep low, hunched to protect myself from the continued gunfire as Remy shoots at men who round the corner of the house.

"You're the one who deserves to die," she repeats, oblivious to the danger surrounding her.

She's going to attack. I can see it in her eyes. In her tightly coiled posture.

"Don't do it," I warn.

"I wish you were never born," she wails, running for me.

I drop the knife and brace for contact. I feel the impact a second before she hits.

Her barrage strikes me in the gut. Her fists aim for my face. I grab her arms, rolling onto my ass with her momentum, sending her sailing over my head.

She clatters into the table, the collision hard, her cry loud.

I keep rolling, gravity pulling me farther backward until my shoulders hit the deck, sinking the shard deeper into flesh. *"Fuck."*

Nausea hits.

Vertigo decimates me.

I climb onto my hands and knees as men shout and birds squawk, my shoulder pulsing like a motherfucker. But Adena doesn't make another attack. She crawls past the slayed guards near the pool house wall, rises to her feet, then runs.

"Make sure we get them all," Remy yells.

I struggle to stand, blinking through clouded vision.

"Matt, you okay?" Salvo calls across the yard.

I'm fucking peachy and entirely ripe for the field day Bishop is going to have with my injury. Who gets stabbed with a fucking plate? By their own goddamn mother?

"Matt?" Salvo shouts.

I hear him. I even raise my head to look at him. But my eyes act as if I'm high as a kite. The world blurs. Darkens into obscurity. And my gut. *Fuck.* It burns.

"Where's Layla?" I squint toward the house. Stumble from the deck. *"Shit."*

I can't even keep my legs locked. They're too heavy. Too fucking weak.

Something isn't right.

"Matthew?" Remy jogs toward me. "You okay?"

No. I'm not.

My heart beats out of my chest. And my head. *Jesus.* What the fuck is wrong with me?

I collapse to my knees. Then my hands. "Save Layla."

28

LAYLA

I scream as Matthew tackles Emmanuel to the ground.

"*Bella*," Lorenzo shouts as the front door slams. "*Hide.*"

I don't know what to do. Where to go.

I have to get outside.

My grip sweats around the Glock as I aim it toward the glass, preparing to shoot.

"Layla, *no*."

I turn toward Lorenzo's voice. He stumbles from the hall, his face grey, a gun in one hand, his cell in the other.

"Maria's dead." He pockets the phone. "But the house is safe for now. I have to get you in the panic room before that changes."

"I can't leave Matthew."

"Help is already on the way." Lorenzo beckons me with a wave of his weapon. "Come. Hurry."

A thud hits the glass behind me, making me scream.

I swing around and Salvatore is there. On the other side of the door. Peering at me through the blood splatter.

He grasps the handle, frantically working the lever.

"It's locked," I yell, then twist toward Lorenzo. "Give me the key "

He shakes his head. "I can't risk the threat getting inside. Matthew would never forgive me."

"I don't care." I run to him, prepared to claw through each of his pockets to find which one hides my freedom, but I skitter to a stop at the blood dripping from the hem of his black pants to pool beside his foot. "You're hurt."

"It's a scratch." He limps toward the hall leading away from the entry. "Follow me."

"No. Wait." *Shit.* He's bleeding too much.

"Layla," he grates.

"Please. Let me take a look. You can't help me if you die. Now sit."

He raises his chin, stubborn.

"*Sit.*" I grab his shoulders and add pressure as gunfire carries from outside. I want to cry. To scream. But I hold it in. I push it down.

"I understand why he's infatuated with you," Lorenzo murmurs.

"You won't for much longer if you don't sit."

He heaves a sigh and leans into the hallway wall, sliding down the plaster to come to a hard stop on the tile. He hisses in pain, his face scrunching into a mass of weathered wrinkles.

I place my gun on the ground and rip at the hole in his suit pants. He's been shot. I push at his leg, twisting the limb to find the exit wound. "It went straight through. In and out within a few inches."

"See? Nothing to worry about."

"You're still losing a lot of blood." I yank off my sweater, wrap it around his thigh above the injury, then knot it tight.

"*Figlio di puttana,*" he growls.

"Sorry." I meet his gaze. "You said help is on the way?"

He rests his head back against the wall. "My men and my surgeon."

I swallow and lick my drying lips. "I don't know what else to do for you until they arrive. But I can help Matthew."

"You'll only get in the way."

"Please don't argue with me." I grasp his hands, the blood on our skin making the contact slippery. "I don't want to have to hurt you to get the key, but I think you know I will. I'll do whatever it takes."

His lips press tight. Offended or stubborn I'm not sure.

"*Please*, Lorenzo."

He glares. Snarls. Then leans to one side, wincing as he reaches into his pants pocket to retrieve the blood-covered key. "Shoot first and ask questions later. At least for my sake. I have a feeling I'll be the next person on Matthew's kill list if you don't survive."

I snatch the offering along with the gun and prepare to scramble to my feet.

"Wait." He clutches my wrist, his head cocked toward the yard. "Listen."

I frown, not hearing anything but the screams of wildlife and the shout of men.

The screams of wildlife…

The shouts of men…

No gunfire.

No battle.

"It's over?" I push to stand, gripping Lorenzo's forearm to help pull him up with me.

As soon as he's stable, I run for the glass, taking in the bodies strewn across the yard.

Salvatore remains at the door, his back to me, his attention focused across the pool.

"Matt, are you okay?" He stalks away from the house.

I follow his line of sight and watch as Matthew stumbles from the deck.

He's ghostly white.

Hurt.

I fumble to put the key in the lock, my fingers trembling, my limbs shaking. I miss the hole over and over, my heart contracting like a vise. "Help me." I don't know who I'm pleading with. Myself? God? "I can't get the door open."

"Let me." Lorenzo limps forward, taking the key from my quivering palm. He inserts the metal into the lock, twists it, opens the door, then pushes it wide as Matthew collapses to his knees in front of Remy.

I run for him. Oblivious to any danger. Unconcerned about threats. "*Matthew.*"

I reach him alongside Salvatore, both his brothers guiding him to the ground, turning him to his side to expose the shard embedded in his back.

"It's okay." I kneel next to him, cupping his face. "Help is on the way."

"What help?" Salvatore asks. "This place is a bloodbath."

"Lorenzo said a doctor is coming." I keep my eyes on Matthew, drowning in the bleakness of his expression. "You're going to be fine."

He doesn't look fine.

He looks like death.

"Don't wimp out on me, brother." Remy crouches behind him to inspect the injury. "This is a far sight less than the stab wound you gave me yesterday."

"No." I shake my head. "There has to be something else." Something more. Matthew is too pale. Too quiet. Too still.

"Tell me what's wrong?" I scan his body. His jacket. His suit pants. But he remains motionless, one arm limp on the lawn, the other resting over his middle. "I can't see where you're hurt."

"Forgive me, *mia dea.*" He winces. "I failed you again…"

"No. You never failed me. You always *fought* for me." Fought to have me. Fought to cherish me. "Talk to me. Tell me where you're hurt."

His eyes roll. He's losing consciousness.

"What's wrong with him?" I scream at Salvatore. "What's happening?"

"Not… my shoulder." Matthew raises the hand resting on his abdomen, revealing the blood soaking the white shirt beneath his jacket. "I'm sorry, *la mia stella polare.* I thought we'd have more time."

No.

No.

My throat burns with the need to scream. "Everything is okay. I'm going to get you to a hospital." I shove to my feet, attempting to drag him with me. "Someone help. I need to get him to a car." I pull on his uninjured arm, trying to leverage him to his feet. "*Someone help,*" I cry.

Remy and Salvatore grab his arms.

"Layla," he groans. "I can't."

"Don't you fucking leave me. I already lost a husband. I won't lose a soul mate."

"You will never lose me." His eyes turn solemn. "Even in death, you'll be my obsession."

"Stop it." I can't get enough air. My lungs are too tight. "Do something," I demand of Salvatore. *"Help him,"* I scream at Remy. I glance around the yard, finding the remaining guard. "Help." Then Aldo stumbles around the corner, his face bloodied. "Why isn't anyone helping?"

29

LAYLA

"Bring him into the house," Lorenzo shouts from the door. "Backup has arrived."

"Help me lift him." Salvatore moves behind Matthew. "Grab his legs."

Remy complies while Lorenzo barks harsh Italian into the yard, inspiring his men to hustle toward us.

They assist in lifting Matthew as he loses consciousness, carrying him across the lawn, past the dead guard near the door, then Lorenzo, until they're inside. I follow like a rickety train wreck, my mind running a mile a minute while my body functions on autopilot.

"The surgeon is already preparing in the basement." Lorenzo squeezes my shoulder as I pass the threshold into the living area. "Everything will be okay."

I don't believe him. I don't think anyone does.

I shadow the men across the room, my attention fixated on the blood being trekked over the pristine tile. I focus on each droplet. The contrasting crystal-clean white against the deep red of death chills me to the bone.

He has to survive.

He can't leave me.

They charge for the far hall, away from the entry, taking him to a door that's kicked open by the unfamiliar guard holding Matthew's left shoulder.

I'm led down to the lower level, my feet stumbling over the stairs to an open space resembling a hospital operating theatre. An older man and a middle-aged woman wash their hands in the far sink. Both are in scrubs and surrounded by cabinets of medical supplies and monitoring equipment. There are metal trolleys. Display screens. Wires and vials and fluid.

But all I see is Matthew and the blood he *drip, drip, drips* on the floor.

"Place him on his side." The doctor stalks toward us, the woman doing the same as she rushes to pull on gloves. "Be careful of the protrusion in his back."

The men dump Matthew on the operating table beneath the huge dome of a surgical light affixed to the ceiling and step away, allowing the woman to hold him in place.

"Be careful with him." I take Matthew's limp hand, his brothers at my sides.

"What am I dealing with apart from the shoulder injury?" The doctor wields a pair of scissors and cuts at Matthew's clothes.

"We think it's a bullet wound to the stomach," Salvatore says.

"Any known allergies?"

"IV contrast." Remy's voice is weak as he rakes a hand through his hair. "He had it as a kid and blew up like a puffer fish."

"Blood type?"

Remy shakes his head. Salvatore, too.

God, I don't know either.

"Don't worry. We'll figure that out." The doctor slices at Matthew's jacket. "That's all I need. You can leave. We don't work with an audience."

Lorenzo's men start for the stairs.

I don't move. I keep clinging to Matthew's hand, wordlessly begging his eyes to open. "I'm not going anywhere."

"Then he dies." The old man stops decimating clothing to stare at me, emotionless, giving no hint that he's sworn an oath to help the sick and injured.

"I won't get in the way," I promise. "I won't say a word."

"You'll leave or he dies," he repeats. "All you're doing at the moment is stopping me from arranging the units of blood he's going to need to survive this."

"Come on." Salvatore slides a hand over my shoulder. "Let the doctor do his job."

I don't know how.

The thought of walking away… Of not being here if something happens…

"*Please.*" I peer down at Matthew, his skin ashen, his chest barely moving.

"Layla, come on." Remy grabs my hand. "We'll wait upstairs together."

"I don't want to wait upstairs." Fire burns my lungs. "He needs to know he's not alone."

"He doesn't need to know shit right now, lady." The doctor glares at me. "Get out of here. *Now.*"

Salvatore gives me an apologetic smile. "It's okay."

"*Please,*" I beg. "I—"

Remy grabs me around the waist, hauling me off the ground and over his shoulder.

"*No.*" I push against his back as I'm carried up the stairs. "Please take care of him. Don't let him die."

I beg.

I plead.

I pray.

Nobody listens.

I'm taken into the upstairs hall, the door to the basement closed behind us by a guard who shifts to block any chance of my return.

"Put me down." I wiggle against Remy's shoulder. Push. Thump.

"In a minute." He continues into the living room where Lorenzo snaps Italian at a line of people streaming in through the front door.

I'm placed on my feet as men in suits pass by carrying oversized duffles toward the yard. Women begin cleaning, the pungent scent of bleach already infiltrating the air.

"*Bella.*" Lorenzo limps toward me, my sweater still tied around his thigh. "How is he?"

I open my mouth, but nothing comes out. No words. No sound. I'm hollow. Empty.

"We don't know," Remy answers. "We were told to leave."

Lorenzo inclines his head, turning his attention to the people entering the room. "Flores prefers to work unsupervised. But I will check on him once my team is under control. I need to get everyone moving before the police arrive."

The conversation filters in, but I don't hear it. I don't care. How can I when Matthew might be dying?

I walk for the front door as Salvatore volunteers to help with the crime scene.

"Hey," Remy calls after me. "Where are you going?"

"I can't breathe in here." I follow the trail of blood to the entry, where Maria's lifeless body is being rolled onto a rug by two men. They flop her around. Without a care. With no compassion.

"Don't look." Remy hobbles to my side, grabbing my arm to lead me through the open front door, shielding me from the view of her sightless eyes. "Don't stop until you get outside."

He drags me past the threshold where a man lays dead, his gaping head wound bleeding all over the polished cement.

Remy tugs me farther, down the three steps, not letting go until we're on the drive. "You're not going to pass out on me, are you?"

I'd give anything to close my eyes and not wake up until Matthew is better. But no, I'm fully awake, my ears ringing, my brain a mess. "You can go back inside. I'll be fine."

I focus on the men storming around the front of the property, the energy out here just as bustling as it is inside. Cars line the drive. Numerous men scan the yard, combing the lawn. Another carries a pressure-wash machine and a bottle of bleach.

"Lorenzo would have the cops in his pocket, right?" Remy murmurs. "My leg isn't in the best position to make a run for freedom."

"I'm sure he has it under control." I don't give a damn though. Not about the cops. Or the bodies. Or the evidence.

All I want is Matthew.

I wait for the men to carry the rolled rug through the door, Maria and the dead intruder bundled inside, then walk for the front of the house. I slump onto the top step, legs bent, elbows on knees, my face in my hands.

I stay there as the whir of sirens approach in the distance. I don't move when men pass me, muttering about the crooked cops accepting the story of kids playing with fireworks.

I keep my head buried and relive every moment of the past hour. The gunfire. The blood. Emmanuel.

"What happened to your father?" I raise my gaze to Remy, still standing a few feet away.

"He's dead. Matthew took care of it."

I swallow, wishing I felt relief instead of desolation. "And Adena?"

"I don't know." He shrugs.

Torment dances in his eyes—a torment I'm all too familiar with. I suffered through enough of it when my own father was killed. It's a horrible sensation. The grief of losing someone you despise. The mourning for what should've been.

I'd pity Remy if I wasn't so numb.

"You should find out." I wipe my blood-stained hands on my jeans, wishing they were clean, wishing even more that I had the energy to wash them. "If she's still alive, someone needs to be looking for her."

He breaks eye contact to glance back at the house. "Are you going to be okay on your own?"

I keep staring at him, the man I once considered my enemy, the person I held partially accountable for my daughter's abduction and my husband's murder. "Yeah. I'll come inside when I can."

He staggers toward me. Up the stairs. To the threshold.

"You realize I still hate you, right?" I say over my shoulder.

He huffs a laugh. "Yeah. Nothing says hatred quite like signing someone up to run a mafia enterprise."

I wince as his footsteps fade down the hall.

I return my head to my hands while the cleanup continues around me. Each second seems like a year without word on Matthew. Every heartbeat feels like it could be his last.

My emotions sprint through different stages of grief—shock, anger, denial.

I try to think about what I'll say to him once he wakes up, but pessimism takes over and all I can picture is his lifeless body. His funeral.

I drown from the weight of it.

I curse myself for wasting the time we had. I should've forgiven him sooner. Cherished him longer. Why the hell didn't I?

"Layla?"

I snap upright, stunned by my sister's voice. "Keira?"

She sprints up the drive, Decker, Hunter, and Sarah jogging close behind her.

I struggle to breathe as I shove to my feet and scramble down the stairs to engulf her in my arms. "Why are you here?"

"Why are *you* here?" she counters, embracing me, holding me close. "What happened?"

"I don't know." I shake my head, trying to clear the white noise. "We came to speak to Lorenzo, not knowing Emmanuel was here. There was an ambush."

She pulls back, her grip tight on my arms as she scans me from head to toe. "Are you hurt?"

"No. But Matthew is. It's bad, Keira. I think he might be dying."

"Where is he?"

My throat tightens. "There's a makeshift hospital in the basement. I'm not allowed in there."

She drags me back into her arms and doesn't let go.

I want to cry. To sob. But the tears won't form. They're trapped in my chest, building like a hurricane, pummeling me from the inside out.

"Are we safe here?" Hunter asks.

I glance up at him over Keira's shoulder. "With Lorenzo's men, yes. But against another ambush? I have no idea."

He looks around the yard, taking in the cleanup operation. "Seems like these guys have shit on lock."

"Yeah." I release Keira and take a step back. "How did you get past the gate?"

"I can be persuasive." He shrugs. "And it helps when Torian called ahead to make sure we had safe passage."

I frown, my gaze switching from Hunt to Keira, then Decker and Sarah. "How did you know where..." I sigh as clarity dawns. "The cell, right? You tracked me here."

Decker gives me an apologetic smile. "Not here exactly. The software only gave an approximation, but the mass of cars outside the property helped. Cole had us in the air from Chicago first thing this morning. You scared him with that phone call."

My stomach clenches.

They rushed to help me. They *care*.

Their concern shouldn't have this effect. Keira told me yesterday that she loved me. Cole explained this morning that he feared for my safety. But seeing it... feeling it...

After I've spent so long being the black sheep of the family, their support is overwhelming.

"I'm going to do a walk around the perimeter and offer my services." Hunter closes in and grabs my wrist for a quick squeeze. It's the most sympathy he's ever given me. The most I've seen him give anyone apart from Sarah. "It looks like this shit with you and the Butcher is a permanent thing, so now's as good a time as any to pave the way with Lorenzo."

"Lorenzo's busy being stitched up," Salvatore says behind me.

I stiffen. My family does too.

Shit.

Decker and Hunter reach for their weapons.

"Wait. Stop." I rush to move in front of them. "It's okay. He isn't a threat."

"No?" Hunter sneers. "But I am to him."

"Please don't." I raise my hands in front of me. "Emmanuel tortured his sons more than us."

"They killed Benji." Decker glares.

"*Emmanuel* killed Benji. It wasn't Matthew's brothers. They wanted out. That's why we're here." I glance at Salvatore over my shoulder, waiting for him to back me up. "Tell them."

"Now isn't the time. I'm sure we'll hash this out in the future." Salvatore crosses his arms over his chest. "Until then we can be civil, right?"

Hunter doesn't answer. Decker's lip curls.

"Any expertise is appreciated, though," Salvatore adds. "We've got a lot of shit to clean." He speaks with authority. With power.

"You've spoken to Lorenzo." I turn to him, trying to read what his stony expression hides. "Have you come to an agreement?"

"We will."

He's going to take over. Maybe not today, but soon. He already exudes more confidence than when he shuffled off the jet earlier today.

"I don't like this," Keira whispers. "We shouldn't be here with him. We need to speak to Cole."

I swing back to face her, finding the other three nodding.

"We have to leave." Hunter grabs the crook of Sarah's arm. "Let's go.

Keira steps forward, her fingers sliding over mine. "Come on. We can wait at a hotel nearby. Get someone to call you when there's news on Matthew."

"There already is news," Salvatore says.

I freeze. Panic.

"I'll be waiting inside when you're ready to hear it."

30

LAYLA

"Go." I squeeze Keira's hand. "I can't abandon Matthew."

"Then I'll stay, too."

"No. I understand why you have to leave." I release her and retreat toward the house. "I'll speak to you later." I swing to the door and stride after Salvatore, my heart in my throat. "*Wait.* Tell me. Please."

He stops before the library and turns to face me. "It isn't much."

"I don't care. Whatever it is, I want to know."

"They got the bullet out. It wasn't deep, which the nurse said was good news. It means the damage was minimal. But his blood loss is an issue. They're waiting on units to arrive, and until then, his heart is under pressure while they try to stitch him up."

I drag in a deep breath, trying not to fall back into the pit of despair.

It's hard though. So goddamn hard as I stare at the dark eyes that look so much like Matthew's.

"He'll make it through." His throat works over a heavy swallow, belying his statement.

"But he might not either, right?" My voice cracks. "He could die. The trauma and blood loss could kill him."

His lips press tight. His jaw tics.

Oh, God.

He grabs my arm and drags me into his chest, one hand cradling my head, the other nestled against my back.

My enemy and my comforter.

I'm petrified, and Salvatore is right there with me.

But I still can't break. All my tears continue to compile in my chest, the pressure building like an impending explosion.

"Story of my life," Remy drawls from nearby. "I get the hatred, he gets the hugs."

Salvatore releases me, his arms drawing back to his sides as he ignores his younger brother. "You should pour yourself a stiff drink. I've already taken a shot or two."

"They still won't let me downstairs?" I ask.

"Not until they're finished." He glides a hand around my waist and leads me to the kitchen to drag a bottle of Macallan across the bench.

Someone should call Bishop. He deserves to know… But without insight on Matthew's health, making him worry isn't the right thing either.

I stay there for hours on a stool at the island counter, cradling a finger of scotch and a heart full of fear.

A shady courier with a cooler of blood comes and goes. The team of cleaners pack up and leave. The men clear out, taking the dead bodies with them.

By midafternoon it's just me, Salvatore, and Remy, with a large contingent of guards manning the property.

The house is silent, the atmosphere eerie, which makes the door opening down the hall deafening.

I push to my feet and hustle across the room as the doctor comes to stand in the archway, now dressed in a T-shirt and jeans, his surgical gear nowhere to be seen.

"I've done all I can," he offers in greeting. "Evelyn will stay overnight and keep watch. But for now, the only thing we can do is wait and see if he wants to live."

"Can I go to him?" I ask.

He nods.

My heart catches. I hustle around him, down the hall, and straight into the basement, Remy and Salvatore following. I jerk to a stop on the bottom step.

Matthew is unconscious on a portable bed in the corner of the room, his large frame dwarfing the single mattress, a white sheet resting over his abdomen while sensors connecting him to an EKG machine are plastered across his chest.

"*Bella*." Lorenzo pushes to his feet from the chair at Matthew's bedside. "Come. Take my place."

I'm not sure I can move any closer. I've waited all this time to see the man I breathe for. To get confirmation he's alive. But he still looks like he's clinging to this world by the tips of his fingers.

"It's okay." Lorenzo waves me forward. "He's stable."

The label doesn't fit. Matthew is frail. Fragile.

"Come on." Salvatore leads me forward with a hand around my wrist, his hold releasing me at the foot of the bed.

Lorenzo murmurs questions, at me or the brothers, I'm not sure.

I don't answer. I don't listen.

My attention is fixated on the beeping of Matthew's monitor while his chest slowly rises and falls.

"Why don't we give them some time alone?" Lorenzo says. "Yell out if you need us."

I nod in appreciation and move behind the chair as the men ascend the stairs.

"I'll go, too." Evelyn approaches me. "He's heavily sedated. He won't wake up for a while, and when he does, he'll be groggy. But you should talk to him." She gives my shoulder a quick squeeze. "Some say that helps recovery."

I wait until the door squeaks shut behind them before I crumple into the chair.

"Matthew," I whisper.

He lays there, eyes closed, his dark lashes resting against pale skin.

My vision blurs, my caged tears finally ready to break free. I weep as I drag a hand over his body. Across the remnants of blood. The cut I caused on his neck. The stab wound on his wrist.

Heat trails my cheeks as I lower the sheet, dragging my touch farther past his boxer briefs to the slices on his thigh. Then I finally lead my fingers to circle the surgical tape surrounding his bandage along his abdomen.

He was a blank canvas before he met me.

Now he's a man riddled with scars.

"Forgive me." I lean forward, draping an arm over his chest, resting my tear-slicked face against his bicep as I succumb to heaving sobs. "You always seem so invincible. And now that you're like this—" My throat dries "I can't live without you, Matthew."

I hear the echo of his voice in my mind, the words he said earlier coming back to haunt me. "*I'm sorry*, la mia stella polare. *I thought we'd have more time.*"

I thought we would, too.

I thought we'd have a future. That I'd finally found happiness.

"Please come back to me," I beg. "I'll do anything."

I remain nestled against him, clinging tight, my tears finally ebbing to dry against my cheeks.

I stay there when the nurse reappears to check his stats and don't move once she returns upstairs.

Remy brings me food, the sandwiches and bottle of water remaining untouched all afternoon.

I fall asleep at one point. Nightmares keep me company. I see snapshots of the shard in Matthew's back. The blood staining his shirt. But I hear him. His voice is there, so clear and tangible in my ears.

"I'd never leave you, *la mia stella polare*." His touch glides over my shoulder, the contact light. "*La mia ossessione. La mia vita. La mia anima. Il mio santuario.*"

I startle awake, my pulse alive at the sound of his voice. But when I look at him, he remains lifeless.

"He's been in and out of consciousness for the last hour," Lorenzo murmurs behind me.

"He was awake?" I shift, taking in the shadowed room, the lights dimmed.

Lorenzo leans against the surgical table, dressed in a fresh suit. "Not entirely. He's trying to get back to you, *bella*. I think the drugs are making it difficult."

I grasp Matthew's hand and bring his fingers to my lips. "I'm here." I kiss his knuckles like he's done so many times to mine. I do it over and over. Not daring to blink in case I miss a sign that he's returning to me. "I'm with you."

There's no response. Not even a flicker of consciousness.

"How do you say, 'I need you' in Italian?" I ask Lorenzo.

"Ho bisogno di te."

I groan. "Trust me to pick a difficult translation."

"I don't think he has to hear it in Italian. He'll value whatever you say no matter the language."

I nod, my eyes watering as I lean close, my cheek brushing Matthew's. "Please come back to me." I kiss his jaw. His chin. The corner of his lips. "I'm right here waiting for you."

I hold my breath, impatient for something. Anything.

"I'm begging," I whisper.

His fingers twitch against mine. The movement ricochets through me. I pull back as his brows furrow.

There's a moan.

"Matthew?" I inch closer.

"La mia stella polare," he croaks.

Relief steals my breath as those dark eyes flicker open, his lips lifting in a faint smile.

"Mia dea." I cup his face.

"That means 'my goddess' but I'll take it." He snickers, wincing. "Do you have any water?"

I grab for the bottle Remy brought and crack the lid. "Here. Take it slow." I help raise his head while he takes a sip, then slowly rest him back against the pillows.

"Now I need that mouth." He wraps a weak arm around me, dragging me close. Our kiss is delicate, fragile, before his hand falls back to the bed. "How long have I been out?"

"It feels like a lifetime. But maybe seven or eight hours." I scoot back to the chair. "It must be night by now."

"It is," Lorenzo confirms.

"Fuck." Matthew rakes a shaky hand through his hair. "Have you heard from Bishop?"

Shit. I forgot about him. And Abri. "No. I haven't heard a word." I turn my attention to Lorenzo. "But I bet you have."

"Bella," Lorenzo murmurs the endearment, his tone holding a warning.

"You haven't then?" I raise a brow. "I would've thought you'd be the next person he'd call if he couldn't get hold of Matthew."

He doesn't answer, just stares at me, his expression masked.

"What's going on?" Matthew cups my jaw, his thumb delicately brushing my cheek to draw my attention back to his. "Has something happened?"

I hold his gaze, questioning what good can come from being honest when he's bedridden. But *God,* do I feel territorial. Matthew was messed over by his real father. Lorenzo was meant to be the devoted replacement.

"Layla?" Matthew's scrutiny sharpens.

"Bishop never stopped working for Lorenzo," I say softly, patiently, allowing the information to sink in and the shock to take hold. "They've worked together since you left all those years ago."

His hand doesn't move from my jaw, but his eyes stray, their attention turning to Lorenzo for a pointed look.

I wait for persecution. For another volcano to erupt.

"I know." Matthew's gaze returns to mine, heartfelt and warm. "Bishop told me a long time ago."

"He did?" *Shit.* I outed Lorenzo for nothing. Right in front of the mafioso's face.

I straighten, cautiously shifting my focus to the older man who grins down at his polished shoes. *Grins.* As if my lack of loyalty was a comedic performance.

"I told you Matthew was a smart man." He pushes from the gurney and staggers toward me on unsteady feet.

"Then why threaten me to keep quiet?" I ask.

"You threatened her?" Matthew growls, his hand falling from my face.

Lorenzo's grin widens.

"No," Matthew murmurs to himself. "You were testing her."

"*Sì, figlio.*" He shuffles forward, making me hold my breath in caution as he approaches. "And you passed, *bella.*"

He drags me in by the arms, kissing both my cheeks. "I don't usually approve of loyalty above *la famiglia* but in this case, I couldn't be more forgiving." He releases me and slides a comforting hand across Matthew's wrist. "When the time comes, you have my blessing."

My pulse skips. Races.

"I'll let you two have privacy." Lorenzo limps to the staircase. "But I'm sure there will be eager visitors soon." He walks into the upstairs hall, closing the door behind him.

I stare at the bedsheet through lengthening silence, my heart warmed by a blessing I would've presumed was far too premature.

"I need you beside me." Matthew pats the tiny stretch of mattress next to his hip. "Let me hold you."

"I don't want to risk hurting you."

"Your denial is hurting me. Not having my hands on you is fucking torture." He reaches for me, his touch light against my arm.

I climb onto the mattress in slow increments, taking my time to make sure I don't bump him. I nestle my hip against his, my cheek to his chest, his arm cradled around my back. "This isn't hurting your stab wound?"

"I can't feel my face, let alone my back."

I smile, but those tears threaten to return.

I never thought I'd have this again—his warmth, his affection. I truly believed I'd lost my only chance at happiness. That God's plan was to make me suffer for the rest of my life.

"I didn't think I'd get to hold you again." His hand glides through my hair in the most gentle kiss of contact. "I was so fucking scared of losing you, Layla."

"It was my fault for taking your gun." For denying him Emmanuel's death. For being a distraction and a trigger. "I'm sorry."

"You have nothing to be sorry for."

Yes, I do. But I'll make it up to him. I'll spend the rest of my life chasing the happiness we both deserve.

"Are you sure I'm not hurting your back?" I reposition myself, trying not to rest too heavily on him.

"Not at all. I think the pain of that injury will always be more emotional than physical."

"Why?" I whisper. "What happened?"

"Adena."

My stomach twists. "She's the one who stabbed you?"

He nods against my head. No words are needed.

"I'm sorry." I hug him tighter. "Is she the one who shot you?"

"No. I don't know where that came from. She was running at me when it happened. All I felt was a punch to the gut. I thought I was anticipating her barreling into me, that my instincts were predicting the impact. It wasn't until I tried to stand and get to you that things went south."

He continues to play with my hair. Nurturing. Comforting. "Is everyone else okay? You weren't hurt, were you?"

"No, but Lorenzo was shot in the leg."

"Shit," he mutters. "I didn't even notice."

"I don't think he wanted to notice it himself. He wasn't entirely cooperative when I tried to tourniquet the wound."

His chest jostles with a chuckle. "That sounds like him."

"But your brothers are okay. They're waiting upstairs."

"They didn't go to Denver to help Abri?" His hand pauses in my hair.

"No. I assume they were too worried about you."

"Have they spoken to her? Is she all right? *Fuck.* I need to find my phone and call Bishop."

"I'll look for it." I push onto my elbow only to have him drag me back down.

"Give it a minute. I'm not ready to let go of you yet." He holds me, the seconds folding into minutes. The constant *beep, beep, beep* is a soundtrack to our quiet reunion.

I can't go through this again.

I lost Benji. I thought I was going to lose Stella. Now Matthew. Our lives have to change moving forward.

"Are you still awake?" I ask softly.

"Yeah."

"What are you thinking?"

"Just about what Lorenzo said earlier." He plants a kiss to my forehead. "I think it's time, *mia dea.*"

I close my eyes. *Oh, God.* My heart hammers.

"Marry me," he whispers.

I squeeze my eyes tighter, clinging to his words for precious moments before I'm forced to let them go.

"Layla?"

"You're high on pain meds." I place a gentle hand against his chest. "Ask me again once the drugs have worn off."

"*La mia stella polare*, you already know I spent some dark days jumping from one drug high to another. I might not be able to feel any pain but I'm not wasted."

"Even so, this is a conversation for another time." A vibration carries from the other side of the room, saving me with its distraction. "Do you hear that?"

"All I hear is rejection."

I climb off the bed. "I think it could be your phone."

"And I think you're dodging the subject."

I walk across the room to the sink as the vibration stops. "Forgive me for thinking it's an inappropriate time to discuss a lifelong commitment while you're so dosed you can't feel your face."

"I can feel all the body parts that matter," he drawls. "Come back here and I'll prove it."

I keep my back to him, attempting to hide a smirk as I open a metal drawer. "I'm sure that nurse of yours will return any minute to check your stats."

"Since when has an audience ever stopped us?"

A laugh escapes me. "We're not having sex. Now or in the near future. You'd die."

"A happy man," he counters, then pauses a beat before saying, "Marry me." It's not a question this time. It's an order. A possessive demand.

"Matthew, my life is with you. I don't want anyone else, and I can't see that ever changing. So my response is already determined, but it won't be given until you're back on your feet. I want to save this moment for when you're healthy enough to get down on one knee. Doesn't a future wife deserve that?"

He sighs in defeat.

I don't feel victorious.

I shove the drawer closed and lift things off the counter, moving discarded cardboard packages and plastic gauze wrappers until I find his cell.

"Look." I turn to him, holding up his device crusted in a flaky red film. "It's filthy, but it's still working. You have a heap of notifications."

"Check them for me. The pin code is five-seven-two-one."

"Give me a sec." I grab a paper towel from a dispenser near the sink, dampen it under the faucet, then begin cleaning what looks to be dried blood from the casing as I unlock the screen. "Twenty-three missed calls from Bishop and one voicemail."

"Listen to the message."

I dial into his voice mail and turn up the volume as bed springs squeak behind me.

"*Langston*," Bishop barks down the line. "Where the fuck are you? Call me. My patience with your sister is growing thin, and I fear for her safety if you don't get your fucking ass here. And I assure you, the danger isn't coming from anyone but me."

"*Shit*," Matthew mutters. "I need to get to Denver."

"You're not going anywhere for a while." I throw the damp paper to the sink as the EKG machine stops beeping and shifts into an alarm shriek.

My heart plummets with the high-pitched tone. I turn to Matthew.

He's climbing off the bed, the cords from his chest monitors clenched in a tight fist before he throws them to the floor.

"What are you doing?" I race to him. "*Stop*. You'll hurt yourself."

He collapses, falling to hands and knees with a grunt.

"*Matthew*," I cry. "We'll send your brothers. You don't need to go—"

"I'm not going anywhere."

The alarm keeps ringing. I start panicking.

I grab his shoulders, helping him upright.

"Did you really think I'd delay this once given clear instructions?" he asks. "You know me well enough to understand I wouldn't waste time making you mine."

"I'm already yours." I use all my strength to try and move him, to no avail. "Please let me get you back into bed."

He places one foot on the ground, stabilizing himself as he wavers on one knee. "Marry me."

"How can you be so careless as to risk your life over a question you already know the answer to?"

"I'd risk the world to make you mine."

The door swings open and a rush of feet clambers down the stairs. Evelyn is in the lead, then Salvatore, followed by Lorenzo and Remy both limping behind.

"*Sir*." The nurse gasps. "You need to get back in bed." She runs for him, grabbing his other arm. "Did you remove the heart monitors?"

"Of course I removed the fucking monitors," he growls at her, not taking his eyes off me. "Make that damn ringing stop."

"Sir, please. Your stitches—"

"He's fine," Lorenzo warns her from the stairs, Remy and Salvatore remaining nearby. "Give him a minute."

Matthew looks up at me, his dark eyes intense as he tugs my grip from his arm and cradles my hand.

He's so much more than fine.

He's protective and brutal. Intelligent and loyal. Devoted and courageous.

He's everything. My hopes. My dreams. My future.

"*Mia dea*," he murmurs. "Marry me."

Please consider leaving a review on your book retailer website or Goodreads

Other Titles in the Hunting Her World

Hunter

Decker

Torian

Savior

Luca

Cole

Seeking Vengeance

Ruthless Redemption

Information on Eden's other books can be found at www.edensummers.com

ABOUT THE AUTHOR

Eden Summers is a bestselling author of contemporary romance with a side of sizzle and sarcasm.

She lives in Australia with a young family who are well aware she's circling the drain of insanity.
Eden can't resist alpha dominance, dark features and sarcasm in her fictional heroes and loves a strong heroine who knows when to bite her tongue but also serves retribution with a feminine smile on her face.

If you'd like access to exclusive information and giveaways, join Eden Summers' newsletter via the link on her website.

For more information:
www.edensummers.com
eden@edensummers.com